PENGUIN TWENTIETH

THE APES

Percy Wyndham Lewis, painter, novelist and essayist, was born off the North American coast in his father's yacht in 1882. He came to England in his early childhood and was educated at several schools, the last of which was Rugby. He then studied at the Slade School of Art, where he won a scholarship, and afterwards spent some years travelling in Europe, with a period of bohemian living in Paris. By 1914 he had emerged as the leader of the 'Vorticist' group, of which some of the main figures were T. S. Eliot, Epstein and Gaudier-Brzeska, and with Ezra Pound he founded the periodical *Blast* (two issues, 1914–15) which Lewis edited.

Wyndham Lewis always regarded himself as an artist first, a writer second, and was one of the most advanced English painters of his time, influencing both his contemporaries and other young artists after the Second World War. Lewis's satirical and polemical writing was largely directed against the cultural and literary movements of the 1920s – as represented by D. H. Lawrence, James Joyce, and the Bloomsbury Group. His first novel, *Tarr* (1918), drew on his life in Paris. It was followed by *The Childermass* (1928), the first part of his great trilogy *The Human Age*; the two subsequent parts, *Monstre Gai* and *Malign Fiesta*, appeared in 1955. In 1930 he published his great ironic novel *The Apes of God*, a gargantuan demolition of the cultural life of the 1920s, of which T. S. Eliot said, 'It is so immense I have no words for it.' His other works include *The Lion and the Fox* (1927), *Time and Western Man* (1927), *Men Without Art* (1934) and two volumes of autobiography, *Blasting and Bombardiering* (1937) and *Rude Assignment* (1950). In 1949 he began to lose his sight and he became totally blind in 1953. Wyndham Lewis died in 1957.

Wyndham Lewis

THE APES OF GOD

PENGUIN BOOKS

PENGUIN BOOKS

Published by the Penguin Group
27 Wrights Lane, London W8 5TZ, England
Viking Penguin Inc., 40 West 23rd Street, New York, New York 10010, USA
Penguin Books Australia Ltd, Ringwood, Victoria, Australia
Penguin Books Canada Ltd, 2801 John Street, Markham, Ontario, Canada L3R 1B4
Penguin Books (NZ) Ltd, 182–190 Wairau Road, Auckland 10, New Zealand

Penguin Books Ltd, Registered Offices: Harmondsworth, Middlesex, England

First published by The Arthur Press 1930
Published in Penguin Books 1965
3 5 7 9 10 8 6 4 2

Reproduced, printed and bound in Great Britain by
Hazell Watson & Viney Limited
Member of BPCC Limited
Aylesbury, Bucks, England

CONTENTS

CONTENTS

The designs in this book are by Wyndham Lewis

THE APES OF GOD

BY

WYNDHAM LEWIS

LONDON
THE ARTHUR PRESS
1930

Prologue

DEATH – THE – DRUMMER

OH DEAR MABEL!

A CAT like a beadle goose-stepped with eerie convulsions out of the night cast by a cluster of statuary, from the recesses of the entrance hall. A maid with matchless decorum left a door silently, she removed a massive copper candlestick. She reintegrated the gloom that the cat had left.

The cat returned, with the state of a sacred dependant, into the gloom. Discreet sounds continually rose from the nether stair-head, a dark whisper of infernal presences. The antlers of the hall suggested that full-busted stags were embedded in its substance. A mighty canvas contained in its bronze shadows an equestrian ghost, who otherwise might have ruffled the empty majesty of the house with confusing posthumous activity.

Should a visitor, from just within the entrance, have been able to proceed at right angles to his left, overcoming septum after septum, hung as though with gigantic medals with the bulging gilt frames, he would have reached the gardener's tool-shed, and an arrangement of flagged steps – where the impeccable staff indulged in those trite exchanges, inseparable from the menial life, with the more alert of the tradesmen's messengers. There was a gap where the rhododendron hedge was just exceeded by the stalwart street-front balustrade – where between the bulbous stone the policeman could be observed at his usual occupation known as Oh-dear-Mabel!, *which consists in a repeated readjustment of the stiff melton trouser-fork, by a simultaneous flexion of both legs.*

In a room upstairs a dead domestic, sneezing behind his hand because of the chill he had received as he entered the vast apartment, placed heavy chiselled blocks of coal within the well of a grate, armoured with a transverse caging two inches thick.

THE TOILETTE OF A VETERAN GOSSIP-STAR

A grey-haired lady's maid stood with a monk-like reverence before the figure of her mistress. The veteran beauty awoke and the maid cast down her eyes. She then approached, armed for the carding of her lady's hair.

Trapezoid in profile – an indoor model of theMaya Pyramid, the building for which that structure is the blank pedestal represented by her savage head – Lady Fredigonde Follett received the combing at first with immobility.

'We will dispense with the second transformation, Bridget!'

The voice of her ladyship abruptly boomed upon the air of her colossal bed-vault and boudoir in one.

'Yes, milady!'

The response came from the tutelary penguin, clockwork answering clockwork, while it figged out the other as if it had been its big doll.

'I have not worn that cap for some time!' thundered the magister, the aristocrat, strapped up erect in her upholstered box, puncheon within puncheon, tossing with temper. The comb relaxed in its strokes until the reports had ceased bursting from the crater of her lips.

'Which cap was it your ladyship wished for?'

The comb slowed down not to rock the breath that was to expel the mistress's answer through the slack parchment tinted with lipstick.

'The one of course I got the pattern of from old Mrs Hennessey, before her death perhaps you recollect – the one old Pamela Hennessey passed on to me you understand!'

The lips of parchment whinnied 'hennessey', and shaken at the same time by the vicious plucks of the comb, the large false-teeth rattled in the horse-like skull, while she panted at this person for so long a body-servant with a patrician scorn bridled and bitted, with hissing politeness:

'Can you find it do you think – I should be so glad if you could, today for a change I fancy I might use that one, what do you think – can you put your hand on it, are you sure?'

Putting her hand in fancy upon the caps, Bridget responded –

'I think I can milady. Is it the cap that your ladyship – ?'

'It is the cap, it is the reticella,' shortwinded there was a lacuna, 'a pattern I got,' an asthmatic air-pocket, a particle slipped, 'old Mrs Hennessey.'

Huzza huzza huzza! there followed a thin peppery coughing.

'Yes milady.'

'Mrs Hennessey.'

'Your ladyship?'

'Hennessey!'

She scoffed out the winged word in a long brazen whinny.

'Will your ladyship have the clan ribbons?'

The ribbons that went with the caps, of startling buff scarlet and agate, of her clan-tartan. Also perhaps the lozenge to which as Fredigonde she was entitled (both according to the Lyon Office and the Ulster Office) chiselled upon the face of a locket, reposing upon the ribbon and fixing it to the cap, or else a Houssa brooch from Gando, a talismanic gift of Mr Zagreus. There was a pause, it was followed by a muted bellow that buffeted Bridget busy behind her.

'How can I put tartan Bridget upon reticella?' then in a harsh hushed aside – addressed to herself as if to a third party – 'Upon reticella!'

Bridget was dumb.

'Is it feasible to place tartan upon reticella, it is impossible tartan upon reticella!'

This went unanswered too – ear-trumpet in hand, to catch any whisper of contradiction that might escape the naked ear, Lady Fredigonde frothed up the silence with the spermy energy of her tongue.

'Dash it Bridget can you be so blind!' in sudden testy open temper. 'Dash it Bridget have you eyes in your head? I think not.'

The echo died away. There was a guilty hush but without so much as the ghost of a sporting peccavi. Tartan upon reticella! *The four walls swam – around the culprit in giddy charivari – splashed with the tartans of Scotch-Whisky posters. The silence hummed horridly with the nasal complaint of the pipes. Lady Fredigonde delivered a large detached sniff: as if the signal for the tart reply of the so-far tongue-tied dummy, it was answered in prompt undertone.*

'Milady has worn' Bridget was heard to object, but not loudly 'the clan-ribbon upon all her caps –'

But her voice stopped at caps. Fredigonde heavily fluffed the dialogue before her 'caps' was out.

'Since Christmas!' *in a withering assent 'since Christmas I have done that,' and her ladyship nodded to the air, curtseyed clumsily with her skull to Its Emptiness.*

'Since December your ladyship.'

Picking at a scurfy root Bridget muttered her qualification.

The pedestrian cap, of unimportant toilettes, had, day by day, lain beneath the tartan.

'Since Christmas I have done so yes' yawned her ladyship, remitting suddenly these black provocations, 'since Christmas. It was a barbarous expedient – temporary measure.'

A spasm of asthma transfixed her, faintly colouring her temples.

'It was my idea by that means to admonish a barbarity.'

'Yes milady.'

But this was too much, if Bridget was to persist, the old mule, what next!

'Please, Bridget, keep your nostrils away from my nuque, you tickle me as I've remarked before. I believe there's a beetle in my hair, will you be so good as to remove it? No there, over my ear. That's it.'

As the comb tugged at the pale green yarn, Lady Fredigonde met it with a massive libration – she was glad to rock her head. Aside from that for self expression there was nothing left her in her body. The neck had survived, that was still elastic, but it dwelt upon a plaster-bust. Her arms were of plaster – they moved, but upon either hand of a lay-torso. Too stately to maltreat – as she had been used with her person, in her hey-day, like a naughty horse – she still would exercise her headpiece sharply, upon the ruined clock-work of her trunk. In dumb-show or stationary make-believe she would sweep out and roll with it, as if it were still carried hither and thither, from apartment to apartment, or swept through the air above her hunter, strapped to a black billy-cock, as it galloped after foxes, or else, tossed in the sports of Venus in preposterous four-posters of the epoch of the middleclass Elizabeth, Victoria. Ex-Gossip-column-belle, she behaved like an independent elf that had crept into this roughly carved knap. She directed the eyes this way and that, propelled the tongue and lips with appropriate phrases, peering now and then down the dark shafts, godspeeding the offerings of milk, fruit and eggs. In this manner she had composed her differences with matter.

'I think my hair is a very surprising substance: nothing seems able to pull it out.'

'Your ladyship has beautiful hair, still. It is very strong.'

'It must be conceded that it is very strong.'

She made her head buck viciously against the comb.

Heralded with a low nasal growl that took the aspect of a 'though' asthmatically Fredigonde burst into a petulant rumination, the oldest spoilt-baby in Britain by seven summers – oldest veteran Gossip-Star.

'Though rather a disgusting colour, don't you think – why is it not a proper white? I am sufficiently old, it cannot be on the score of age that my scalp has not quit dyeing the follicles old gold or is it what I eat? It can't be the sandwiches. I must knock off chocolate.'

The distinct silence, say a quarter-minute, to establish a respectful distance twixt answer and question, was clocked out by the servant.

'If milady would allow me to order – '

'I have said once' crashed out the raging voice of the mistress, 'that you shall not order for me the trash you have often mentioned from the chemist. Am I compelled to repeat it!'

The clock struck off a good number of hefty seconds, standing, in the centre of the mantelpiece, upon its bandy bronze legs and claws.

'It is a recognized bleaching agent milady' with thrilling quietness the maid insisted in the most appropriate language to persuade – 'of great efficacy.'

As an afterthought she whispered – 'By all the medical profession.'

The irresistible formula fell flat. A nasal purr spread to her chest and with a puff Fredigonde retorted:

'Of great efficacy, what is efficacy! I have never heard of it! You use the thing yourself if you must my girl. Efficacy! as though I wanted to be decorated with spots like Lady Hortense Spankmann-Trotter that was, who sought to be white before her time – as I should be if I listened to your tips for bleaching dirty dowagers!'

The maid's hand still swept with her hand-harrow with the action of shuttles up and down the green rood. It was grained with all the sea's coastal colours. The head-growth was as heavy as seaweed, in the maid's palm.

'No milady.'

Then the hair must still be the strange green of age, not the beautiful white of eternity – in spite of the tips sub rosa of the beauty-doctor and cosmetic statistics, cut out of the Fortnightly Gentle-lady.

Fredigonde squatted plumb, approximately at the centre of a great room, her formidable image framed by a cheval-glass. The room accommodated a state-bed where it grew dark almost a decametre from the windows. A sleeveless garment hung to the floor contained by a silver morse, from which each stiffened neaf projected, occasionally touched by spasms as her temper rose. Her buccinator muscle let down a pasty shield upon either side of her face. Like two dour blinkers that had slipped, these cheeks flapped sometimes as she spoke, and her eyes flashed in the white helm of her head.

The carding was succeeded by the ritual of the construction of the bun. The bold wattlework was effected in swift-fingered in-and-out of human basket-making. The bun was completed. Twenty minutes had elapsed. Bridget now moved to the right-hand side of the vast chair, tongs in hand, in order to address herself to the manufacture of the curls.

As the curls were being laid down, beside each other, in stiffened cylinders, the eyes of her ladyship glazed. She began to pooh with a soft whistling pout. This was a nap upon which the solitary mason of this quick monument, so sharp-tongued a monolith, counted. Bridget put the finishing touches to the beldam, her mighty mistress, point by point, stepping about the passive purring skull that was her cult and old single-woman's bachelor passion.

Her ladyship awoke as the last touches ceased. She raised her head with slumberous majesty and she perceived that the curls were there. She was now at eye-practice for a spell after the glooms of sleep. At present she moved her gums, upon which the teeth hung, in and out, preparatory to a dialogue.

'I think we will have the cap, now we will have the cap.'

The first uncertain whinny after the doze was thick.

'Milady.'

'The cap. The cap.'

'Yes your ladyship the cap is here. Will your ladyship have it?'

'Have it? Certainly. The cap.'

It was the cap, modelled upon that of Mrs Hennessey, of the finest reticella.

Lady Fredigonde lifted from her knees a hand-mirror, her hand grasping it as a diver's flexible masked paw might mechanically seize some submarine object. She held it steadily before her and examined the curled but capless bust.

What a decadent emperor! Bridget crowned her with the cap. Gingerly held on high, she lowered it, breathing through her ears, down upon the crown of the head. The seagreen of the hair, the formal surf of the cap, coalesced.

'A little more over the left eye: no a thought forward and up, forward and then up, over my left eye – my left one. You're not tall enough really are you to attend to me, you are too short by half-a-foot.'

The reticulated eaves were poked up from the green margin of hair by two forked fingers with their lustreless plates of copper skin.

'Dear me, my head one would say has grown: how very odd that would be if it were the case.'

She rocked her headpiece as if it had been a pumpkin and the surface of the vegetable's mother-earth had extended just beneath her chin.

'It is not so big as I thought. An alternative to my head having grown is I suppose that the cap may have shrunk in the wash.'

'Your ladyship will pardon me, I think it is the same as it was before.'

'Which. The cap or the head?'

'The cap your ladyship.'

'I think you are mistaken, I should certainly say that it is a quarter of an inch out quite that – I am very familiar with this landscape garden.'

Indomitable, detached geologist, she cast a professional eye over her polar ice-cap.

But cap and hair had not conformed to her canon – the pattern of the cap-cum-curled-temples of fancy. She replaced the mirror upon her lap and she looked sideways at her maid. Bridget refused her face of an old sheepish scapegoat (which she had averted) to the lazy circling of the predatory eye. Fredigonde heaved a surly breath and as before took up the hand-glass.

The elements of the arrangement proposed were as follows. Three distinct zones were involved. There was that of the white arcs in perspective of the cap, there was the green region of hair, and there was the pallid copper of the skin. She snapped them together, half shutting a connoisseurish eye and expected the synthesis.

Depositing the hand-glass and the hand fixed round its handle upon her knees then, she said –

'I give it up, did you hear me Bridget – let us after all have yesterday's cap.'

The servant wearily rustled in her shadow, her dark arms rising to remove the reticella.

'Will your ladyship have the clan ribbons?'

The old lady's hands trembled and she thundered

'Yes!'

Her Yes *had that full-chested hiss of dark volumes of escaping steam, spat from a geyser, noted by travellers. It was such an absolute* Yes *in its empty force, that her hands quaked upon her lap.*

So back to the tartan!

SAINT BRIDE

That ended the toilette.

Like the lights in an Astoria after midnight one by one snapping out, until the complete pile is switched off, and in a black block, signs of animation went dead one by one in her ladyship, from curled cap-rest to uncut semi-celestial finger-tips.

Cut off from the optic or tactile connections, Fredigonde passed most of her time in her mental closet, a hermit in her own head. Sometimes she would Stein away night and morning to herself, making patterns of conversations, with odds and ends from dead disputes, and cat's-cradles of this thing and that – a veritable peasant industry, of personal chatterboxing and shortsighted nonsense. It had been at the allotted span that the great reversal had been completed, of outside into in – so all that is external was become nothing but bursts of dreaming, railed through and fought out foot to foot upon the spot.

Outside, external and restless, she could feel her servant, full of a faint pneumatic breath, never far off, poor parasite that she was, with apathy around her like a lovesick moon. Mournfully she moved up against her dully at this moment – she felt her apologetic hand, her dry breath.

Horace Zagreus is a great dear huskily she purred – she did not care what they said – much that he says is undeniably most sensible and true. Horace confessed that by the name of her attendant he was somewhat puzzled. 'It is not every day you meet it – Bridget.' To be a 'Bridget', he told them when she was there, was to combine in one the images of a monastic bog-saint with the brutish british Saint

Bride – Patron of prisons was it? Yes the Brideswell – it was prisons.

That all-the-world-over in his words was to be a Bridget.

Bridget became Budget in the mouth of Kathleen the comic Limerick parlour-maid: that he noticed and chuckled when she called to her Budget. – Brudget actually – a smudge, not a naming.

And Bognor! The perfect servants' holiday, a week of freedom – Lady's lady! She would *go down to the sea in ships she would and naturally fell in the flood. That served her right! – When she told us about her accident – 'Poor old virgin,' he had exclaimed. Poor old virgin! That is appropriate, most.*

(If Horace came she would ask him outright. She had often speculated herself but of course.)

Unless you chanced to be raised to the honours of the altar, it was a clear case of the compulsion of words.

'Come here then Bridget you still unravished Bride of quietness, that I may ask you a question' his voice had cried softly to her, and the old maid had crept smirking up to his feet, the sly old puss, and stood there like a tuppenny tin-saint in fact, meekly awaiting the gentleman's pleasure.

Well Horace Zagreus is a most attractive person really. A great dear in his way is Horace – he is attractive, with such lovely fluffy colourless albino locks and moustaches, or were the moustaches mother-of-pearl – and all that he says is most sensible and true or has something that's worth listening to at all events, which is more than can be said for most. He is a gentleman.

'Budget!' (He was a very good mimic.)

'Yes sir?'

'Are you a virgin?'

'Get along with you mister Zagreus sir!'

Is Budget a virgin? Query. Is she intacto the old virgo?

If Horace comes I will get him to ask her to her face, smirking old horror.

What's in a name? Bolts from the blue they flop on men and women from nowhere, in their cradles, on each anonymous noddle – all of us worse luck have to be a Something! Seeing how at random names fall upon the heads to be accommodated with tags, descriptive whatnots – the shower of Violets, the downpour of Jacks, Joans, Peters, Toms – what reference can there be? No but seriously.

To think of the nondescripts that answer to the names of

first-class saints – a practice, that, which emphatically should be discontinued! All against that – that everybody should be called the same blessed old thing – as if the understairs staff were to be a man Fredigondes, just as illustration!

But numbers for us all round – *that would be as bad if not worse. No – all against* numbers! *Numbers I should hate. Suppose he did not mean it really – he does one was bound to admit pose the least bit though such a lot that he says is true in its way and always quite sensible.*

About his own assumed name it was he got on to that topic. What made him call himself Zagrooce is a mystery to me, his own name was scarcely more difficult. 'Iron-rust' or 'Egg-roost' that's the sort of thing that happens. Egg-roost. Delightful!

There are tramps sport the name of Herod – french tramps he declares baptized Hannibal. But we survive by words *he says –* things *perish. He got that most likely from one of those Smart Alicks he goes about with. – In some respects he is a master of paradox.*

By words, this is it seems the idea, we are handed over to the tender mercies of the Past. That is that parasitic no-longer-with-us class of has-beens, he cleverly calls it. In other words the dead.

Horace has the most charming eyes which have always reminded me of Duncan's. Why has he not married? I could wish he went about less with those beastly boys. It lays him open – but that is his business.

To the dead he is most delightfully disrespectful! All clever men are. – I am all for that. The dead get us, as he puts it, caught at the extremity of a sentence, baited with a sweet rhyme – that is excellent. Then in lexicons we succumb at every turn, they are ambushed. 'All language whatever is a dead tongue.' How true that is! But that is how they catch us live-ones dash it, the old devils – those life-coveting dead 'uns, to live upon us All-alive-ohs *– as second-rate succubuses.*

I myself have been imposed upon by the dead all the days of my life who hasn't.

At this Fredigonde preened and shook herself heartily and heavily. She took a long and searching breath. She sniffed without nostrils a disembodied odour that was not there.

So far at least that abominable stench had kept away that was something! It was *a disadvantage there was no denying, that dis-*

gusting mouldering scent – a little bit too near corruption! No sooner had the eyes ceased to function than the nostrils announced it. Like a whiff of Pluto's pantry, on an inner wind blown against the inside of the senses, filling the brain, it was there, almost immediately.

And then as to Death's daily dancing in the street! If householders would only combine to prevent that music. A veritable death-dance it was, there must be troops of drummers. The great panes in the morning-room rattled, shook by the percussion: all day one was compelled to listen to its idiot-step – afro-american, nigger-footed: watching as one did when it was windy the wild seesawing of sunlit clusters of ashes, that tossed to the wave-length of atlantic rollers, quite out-of-time with the machine-tap of the detested rapid measures. Above all things she hated that street-music. Wind-and-percussion street-drummers, jazzing in the gutter, rattling their boxes for coppers. But the jazz is fate, *Zagreus insisted – whereas the trees roll in the hollows of the wind (which of course bloweth whither it listeth and is not fate) in a vaster dance. Everytime she heard it, at the foot of the block coming rat-tat up-hill, a grimacing Saint-Vitus chorus she would cross her fingers detecting its first drum-tap, its first soft cymbal* – crash-*crash*, crash-*crash.*

I am practically certain to go (considering with cold caution these slippery subjects she harangued her private ladyship) barring accidents – *to go to live when I die (she admitted the daylight into a filmy eye-ball, to introduce a few hasty fragments of recognized matter for luck) in – No – never THAT! What an anti-climax!*

Rank death that would be – why it was posthumous murder to ask it! to be buried undead and sentient up to your neck in the disobliging bosom of a domestic – thank you for nothing! In Bridget! What a survival!

At that identical moment hi presto! the especial effluvium of death, *like a stale peach in her nostrils, with cold sleepy wind. She experienced a most offensive ghastly chill but not of the grave but of* Bridget! *Actually the dank impact of that dismal woman! Death stung her hotly on the occiput with whirling nightstick. – Ai-ee! The soul bolted like a pip into her poor partner and silly shadow. Had the actual Brideswell – not its press-yard not even that, the complete prison – been bodily present, in that instant of time, matters could not have been worse. Embedded in Bridget! What an end! –*

(in a passion of escape she was back again with the rush of a howitzer's muzzle-velocity, her heart ticking like one-o'clock!)

To announce her evasion the great hectoring voice tolled out in a peal of panic:

'Budget! Bud-get! BUDGET!'

'Your ladyship!' Budget's voice was on the spot.

Fredigonde raised her ear-trumpet as though to wind a stentorian challenging revelly.

'When I die you understand, I forbid you Bridget I hope you follow me, ever – you hear me, ever – to think dream or excogitate of myself in any manner whatever – should you – should you as I pray you may not, survive me, you are attending? If those were my last wishes as they are not by a long shot, would they be perfectly clear or not?'

'Yes your ladyship.'

'Are you perfectly certain you have heard me, it is most important?'

'Yes milady.'

'I have never had such an experience never!' If when her soul came to take its departure (and enough's as good as a feast) it simply was to go of all places there *(the fingers of Bridget upon her head, crawling under her cap, fishing – timid family of worms, imperfectly animated – for a lost curl, caused her a frisson) and from thence into Bessie – even so – and in a fainter condition still more stodgy and dim over into the offspring of Bessie – if it was to be that, she would clear the house at once of all these walking coffins, living henceforth indeed without servants. She would seek death-the-drummer out, with his insulting strut, his hypnotic tapping: when the house was empty except for Sir James, go to the bath and bleed into it like a Roman, from an incision in an artery!*

Her eyes held fast and stern, the motif of roman suicide gave them a glyptic fortitude. Immediately she put over the big ruthless question:

What would be the last thing alive in that room?

Beyond all doubt things, *not* PERSONS. *Was not the clock yonder already a Methuselah!*

'Morbid!' thought Fredigonde. 'Merely morbid', a word, that, ever-favoured since she first learnt it as a young person of fashion – one that did its work well – upon the people who were 'morbid'.

The quilted lavender-laden envelope with the caps, ready to the hand of the busy toilette-saint, lay upon the toilette-table. Phalanges and scallops of expensive lace protruded. In terms of mortal survival, as a thing not a person, the significance of the Lace-cap was at once apparent.

The great lady went through the action of wetting her lips, with the grey cactus-welt of her rubber tongue, flourishing harshly in the drought of the desiccated head.

'Bridget!'

'Your ladyship.'

'Bridget I think I shall bequeath my collection of laces to the – some museum, that is my idea.'

'Yes your ladyship!'

'I wonder which is the best!'

There were museums and museums – the Valhalla of Things. (There was no Valhalla of Persons, it was understood.)

'I must ask Sir James when I see him, he knows best about that sort of places.'

'Yes your ladyship.'

Far calmer at last, Fredigonde again withdrew. She closed her eye-lids to relax herself. The day and night cinema that exists immediately within was encouraged to operate. The brain on its own initiative from its projector was flashing lace-caps upon the screen. All her collection was idly called forth, in startling close-ups, for her inspection.

The question seemed about ripe for solution and she was nothing averse. For survival she did not give a button. Let her by all means survive as a cap – there were worse things than that, by Jupiter!

She imagined at once the museum. – It was not the British, or Kensington, the Soames or the Wallace: outside its window might be the gravel of the Tuileries, yet it was not precisely the Louvre – she attempted to ascertain its position. She could not see out: really no indication. But there were the lines of horizontal cases. In the cases were the headdresses of course; she had often seen them.

Lady Fredigonde Follett *would be written upon the typed etiquette.*

There was a chill in the gallery, of an alpine april. The shadows of passers-by struck across to where she was sitting, a schoolgirl perhaps; they were bending over the cases, she felt cool in their tremendous shadows – these were TIME-SHADOWS *of spatial beings – they cooled her shoulders like the shadows from precipices. From what a distance they must be projected, to be so icy!*

Her name was constantly spelt out, in foreign accents, very halting, from the typed etiquettes, by sluggish baedekered visitors, frequenting the cap-cases – it was natural, it was there to commemorate a head. Cap-wearing victorian heads. There were even photographs under the glass – how the ribbons were knotted – and a bust with a cap upon it. A tone of distinct mockery she did not at all relish occasionally reached her, in some of the voices. Fredigonde! *It would appear that the name – yes there was too much chuckling and muttering frankly to be pleasant.*

Of course there was scarcely any doubt (with some difficulty she caught glimpses of this prophetic photo-play in a violet mist) that many unsuitable persons must in the nature of things examine the exhibits. That was only to be expected and that they would spit, several had spat – foreign habits, doubtless Americans. The name of Follett must be spelt out by ignorant trippers, what more natural, stopping at the cap-cases. 'Fredigonde' itself would be offensively stuttered. They approached, just perceived by her ladyship with difficulty. It was a school of children. The caps were examined by the hundred bloodshot eyes of a Red Sunday-School.

Cloudily she acquiesced in the sleepy Sabbath or Anti-Sabbath, of the museum-gallery. The robot-youth, in double-file, submitted itself to summary instruction. She attempted to estimate the numbers of the caps in the cases – all that could be said was that they were very numerous, to judge by the cases: idly she took to totting up the gob-capped polls of the members of the Red Sunday-School.

Docile periwinkle eyes blinked and squinted at the laces. Communist skull-caps of orphanage-cut flooded the fairways of the mahogany showcases. Dr Barnardo and Barney Barnato inscribed their names simultaneously in the Visitors' Book but did not appear, except on an Out-of-Work's brick-red banneret a small Scout colour-sergeant was carrying.

At a word from the spectacled Red Scout-Master (in a vermilion flannel-shirt with polished police-whistle, and blood-red Kiwi leggings, of honest yeoman calfiness) the little jumping bolsheviks smash the glasses of the show-cases. A thunder of small fists breaks out, like a crash of kettle-drums. Death-the-drummer! *With idiot-yawp, civilized and whitmanic, they distribute the expensive headwear swiftly, passing from hand to hand. Each adjusts one to its cropped noseless skull: like the spangled paper headdresses torn from a super-Christmas-cracker, the caps decorate the cropped bullet-heads.*

The Red Scout-Master, arching out his Kiwi calves and protruding his Robin-red-breast, reserves for himself the prize-cap, that of Pamela Hennessey. He tries it on. He smirks in the glass of a show-case. He is seen to be in reality an old woman, just an old woman as was to be expected – a matriarch in sheep's blood-red clothing.

Breathless, Fredigonde perceives that it is indeed her old friend Pamela Hennessey, who has become a Red Scout-Master and a dirty bolshevik. She withdraws a little, she has no desire to get mixed up in that. *She does not wish to be questioned. A quoi bon? A quoi ça sert-il?*

All commence to perform a carmagnole, heading off with a fine Red picknicking impulse down the glades of a gothic tapestry, pursued by a passionate official who has come upon the scene unperceived, in a towering passion, and who brandishes a gold-ringed watchman's fist.

Lady Freddy as-ever-was picks up her skirts to make off as well – for perhaps who can say she has no right there at all, it is possible. But, thrilling coincidence! she cannot move a muscle! This is a singular contretemps – with consequences not to be readily foreseen.

Upon glancing down casually, she notices that her feet are attached to a circular platform. More strange if anything is the sensation in her hem hem! *nether limbs, such as you get in waxen dummies, of brown beeswax. At this she begins frankly undulating her body, it is the best thing to do.*

In the manner of an abandoned Andalusian she offers, very crâne and quite sauce-box, very oh la la!, *a stunning stomacher seemingly of scarlet: to one side first, then to the other. As she does so she most archly raises* – oh peepo! – *from the trixy ankle, her brocaded pannelled frock – with a* Whoopsie! *and a* Houp-la!

The natty little high-born trotters come free with a slight report: she steps gaily down upon the tiled floor of the gallery.

'YOUR LADYSHIP!'

Ominous words to have addressed to one in that galère-ry! – in that connection, under circumstances – really! Ahha! how now! she has been observed it seems – it is only a matter of time for her to be unmasked completely!

Fredigonde a fugitive! She has a gesture to dissimulate the twinkletoes – she pushes down the stiff stubborn state-dress of a wax-work effigy's wardrobe – about to escape from the custodian, who has his eye on her *now – an absconding exhibit! It is too late! Square the keeper! That is the first thing, it is most important – she thrusts her hand into the bombasting of her farthingale, into a manly pocket in fact, to extract a fiver or if possible a pony if it is there too.*

YOUR LADYSHIP!

Ho ho! again that tell-tale address. The game is up – I am but a lost body!

That was, it is as well to remark, the voice of Bridget. What! Bridget here? a strange coincidence!

The girl can help in this emergency it may be – where there is life there is hope – it is but a step to the porch of the Wax-Work – then the streets and freedom!

'Bridget, assist me to leave this building at once!' she mutters to the figure that she cannot however remark, for she does not make herself known but only calls and remains hidden.

'Ladyship' is that Open Sesame, *the magic watchword, granted – but not there! There is a time for everything.*

The cloud lifts. Ladyship has been uttered in another connection – with heavier lips, of flesh and blood, propounding with insistence their words of brutal weight. Ponderously she passes into a sequence of solider facts. At every step she takes an avoirdupois, of a logic less startling. She is no longer in the cast of her private photo-play: she is being heavily miladied. Bridget is there at her elbow, holding out an identification disk.

'Is that Bridget?' she enquires pointedly: she is stiff – strapped down again now, it is impossible to move, but she is master of the situation.

'Put it down,' she says.

Bridget places the locket she has been holding upon the table.

THE BODY LEAVES THE CHAIR

Keeping her eyes away from the face, that is quickly restored to consciousness, not to catch its eyes of her ladyship – marking time with a halting hand – Bridget patted the cap which she had just placed upon her mistress's head. With a small fan, in the other kand, she simulated the draughts from beneath the doors or advancing from chimneys which might disturb the heavy tendrils of the hollow sculptured curls. She tests their solidity, sending gusts, as well, over the extremities of the fronds of the lace.

'I must have been asleep,' said, with the voice of an equal, this peculiar picture-fan, straight from her private cinema, 'did you notice it? I had a most eccentric experience.' The stiff fist of Fredigonde closed upon the handle of the glass. Sticking it (without looking) up into the air, she then cocked a detached pale eye, with a fatigued deliberate archness, at the maid's handiwork. The eye made its routine rounds, in matter-of-course up and down: it found it good, or not at all bad.

'Yes that's better aint it, I think that is by no means bad; that will have to do Bridget, it is not bad at all. The curls are excellent – they lie well.' More and more abstractedly. 'It is a good piece of work. Not bad, Saint Bride, not at all bad.'

Sceptical of the extinction of the critical spirit, the maid stood to attention, awaiting, at a great pitch of passive resistance, the outcome.

'By no means bad, you have wielded the tongs well!' the voice cooed and sneered. The glass rested again upon the brief broad ledge of her lap. 'That will do. Not another touch – you would undo it. It is a masterpiece.'

'If your ladyship – '

'Yes yes – do not wait for more compliments. You have acted for the best. Un petit maître, un petit maître!' she sneered and panted.

Posterity for the moment held no further interest for her – one museum was much the same as another. All of her that was museum-fähig should go whither the wind of death blew it, at her departing.

*

The old body-servant was in a distant spot, she came up with a noiseless even tread and stood resting with patience upon an alpenstock. Her ladyship perceived the alpenstock: she directed peremptory injunctions throughout her ruined establishment, to the entire vasomotor system beneath – bells rang hot-temperedly in every basement and galley.

A local briskness, of a muscular nature, was patent, in the depths of the chair. The massively-anchored person shook as if from the hidden hammering of a propeller, revolving at her stern, out of sight. A determined claw went out and grappled the alpenstock. It planted it at a forward cant to obtain the preliminary purchase.

Without fuss the two masses came apart. They were cut open into two pieces. As her body came away from the dense bolsters of its cyclopean cradle, out into space, the skimpy alpaca forearm of the priestly Bridget, a delicate splint, pressed in against the small of the four-square back. It was applied above the region where the mid-victorian wasp-waist lay buried in adipose.

The unsteady solid rose a few inches, like the levitation of a narwhal. Seconded by alpenstock and body-servant (holding her humble breath), the escaping half began to move out from the deep vent. It abstracted itself slowly. Something imperfectly animate had cast off from a portion of its self. It was departing, with a grim paralytic toddle, elsewhere. The socket of the enormous chair yawned just short of her hindparts. It was a sort of shell that had been, according to some natural law, suddenly vacated by its animal. But this occupant, who never went far, moved from trough to trough – another everywhere stood hollow and ready throughout the compartments of its elaborate animal dwelling.

They passed out at the bedchamber door in their dead-march time – the dark coadjuvant in awful step, skull bowed, with the countenance of a pallbearer. And then (black as a Spade-queen) the pall itself as it were, the dolmen, the catafalque, advanced on end, in a dreadful erectness. It struck at the furniture in its path, with the abandon of the blind, stamping with its stick, till this first portal had been reached. En bloc they passed through that, pinched for a moment by its stolid jambs. In the vistas of the stairways and passages of the solitary hotel, servants were seen, who watched their translation. That opposite door was opened at their approach by a brass-buttoned footman. They passed through the second door without a stoppage. Their funeral goose-step was timed upon the rigid pattern of the second-hand of a considerable clock – with the left-left left-left *of its difficult, heavy tick. Once well inside the fresh apartment her ladyship looked up. She discerned her chair, lighted by the sun, in the middle-distance, placed near the embrasure of a splendid bay-window, that, with its web of high-slung lace and blinds half-drawn of honey-amber, had the appearance (at the end of this drill-hall of a salon) of a lighted stage. Fredigonde proceeded – eye-fixed, her gait acquiring a slight roll, as though in liveliness – to rollick, to dance, a little, after the manner of a dying top.*

When they were near the rear of the chair, they took a course at a tangent, then tacked, passing around its left arm. They entered the spotlight shot in a shaft computed to be ninety million miles from the solar projector – so stupendously aloft, in its narrow theatre, for this human performance. She lowered her body into its appointed cavity, in the theatrical illumination, ounce by ounce – back first, grappled to Bridget, bull-dog grit all-out – at last riveted as though by suction within its elastic crater, corseted by its mattresses of silk from waist to bottom, one large feeble arm riding the stiff billows of its substantial fluted brim.

There were some moments during which she lay bolt upright, like a deadbeat Marathon competitor. Only Bridget stood idly at her side and no restoratives were offered – it seemed a toss-up if she would come-to. Her fixed eye was bloodless and without any animation, a stuffed eagle's sham optic in fact, or a glass eye in the head of a corpse – though the bellows plainly worked still, the shoulders slowly grinding on, blown up and let down with the labour of the breath. Gradually however her personality made its appearance. Fragment by fragment she got it back, in rough hand-over-hand, a bitter salvage. Her fingers could be seen groping slightly upon the chair-arm. Last of all the eyes began to strike more firmly and to register. It was apparent that a mind had moved in behind them. There was a great bustle all at once. Her head was lived in once again. A strong wheezing sigh, as the new air went in and the foul air went out, and then she realized the tones of a muted fog-horn to exclaim—

'There will come a time Bridget when I shall not be able to move about like that!'

Bridget started, she approached her quickly.

'I hope that will be a long time yet your ladyship.'

'I am persuaded that that must occur.'

'Your ladyship I hope is mistaken – not yet I hope for a long time, your ladyship.'

Between them they fastened the mournful yankee-pebbles upon the high bones of her nose and behind her ears. Each strut was covered with a green festoon of waxen hair. She directed her eyes upon the narrow opening in the curtains – where the important thoroughfare, beyond the gates of the private road, was visible. Idly she was watching the bodies of the omnibuses fit themselves into the space and slip out of it, slacking or speeding according to the pulsation of this current of machines. As if they had been shadows upon the ceiling, cast into a darkened room from a sunlit street underneath, she remarked their passage. The window before her shook with the weight of the super-traffic. The amusing skeleton of new skyscraping flats entered into novel combinations with the geometric maze of the patterned curtains.

The manufacture of olivets, the Clapham Sect, the Book of Common Prayer – Stanley and Crescenda – Valentines with their faded lenten doggerel, obventions for mortuary pomp, clematis vitalba 'the traveller's joy,' oleographs of Ophelia – Christian striding through VANITY FAIR, vademecums, lockets and church-hassocks – cockatoos, japanese lacquers, curry and Port Wine – Linley Sambourne, DROPPING THE PILOT – Douglas Jerrold and love's-old-sweet-song *– crept like an illicit wave with the rustle of her silk petticoats, up to her six and ninetieth birthday: had* just *licked the base of the GREAT WAR –* just *wafted her softly beyond it, like a large and sodden leaf.*

Part 1

DICK

THE windows trembled ever more forcibly: the sound of heavy vehicles reached Fredigonde in a faint incessant roar, caught in the funnel of her trumpet. – A more deliberate uproar however made itself heard. It shattered the air with reports and stopped. What was that? Was it the shudder of the shipwreck of a bus? She turned her head towards her maid.

'My nephew should be here soon. Do you happen to have heard any movement suggestive of his arrival?'

'I believe I did hear a motor your ladyship.'

'Find out if he is here will you Bridget. Let us get that over.'

Bridget moved towards the door. She had not reached it when the floor shook slightly: a confused disturbance occurred immediately without. Then the door rocked, there was a sound of blows, and then one loud distinct rap cut them short. Bridget stopped standing her face towards it. For a moment there was a cessation of these sounds of a disquieting irregularity. But the door slowly came ajar, it seemed to hesitate: a further fumbling occurred outside: next it flew briskly open and an enormous bronzed and flannelled figure burst in, exclaiming in deafening point-blank discharge:

'Hallo Aunt! May I come in?'

A lush vociferating optimism, hearty as it was dutiful, was brutally exploded in her direction: a six-foot two, thirty-six-summered, army-and-public-school, Winchester and Sandhurst, firework – marked 'boyish high spirits' – simply went off; but only as a preliminary demonstration, as a benefaction by-the-way to the world-at-large.

This huge ray of sunshine hung fulgurously in the doorway. All towering bright-eyed juvenility, Dick was respectfully backward in coming too rapidly forward. But at last covered by the half-veiled eyes of Bridget (who now stepped hastily aside), he started himself off. Flinging forward tremendous feet to left and to right, he got well into the place, piecemeal, in jolly sprawling fragments, and looked round with the near-sighted surprise of a rogue elephant who had perhaps burst into a parish church.

'How are you Dick?'

Fredigonde watched him approach with expressionless attention. Then, as if calling to mind something she had omitted to do, she removed her spectacles – lifting them clear off her nose and unhooking them from her ears, calmly but as quickly as possible; for she feared that he might break them when at last he reached her.

'Was that your new Bugatti that I heard Dick? You nearly shook the house down as you stopped. Ah you young space-eating spalpeens, you, I'm sure I don't know what we're coming to!'

At this there was the promptest possible burst of full-chested clucking, as the 'young spalpeen' threw six-foot-two of brown seasoned manhood heartily about: the simple giant was frankly enchanted at hearing himself called a young spalpeen – the charming old word! He focused the misty shape of his ancient relative (naturally with nerves shattered by these inventions) with an effort. Poor old Lady Freddy! – rather a dear all the same.

This spontaneous response having spent most of its force, Dick turned round upon the door. He inclined his stature towards it, his eye fixed upon its handle: with clumsy careful hand he seized it, but it swiftly ran away from him and banged.

Nonplussed Dick bucked slightly back with nearsighted alarm (as if something upsetting had been thrust impromptu rudely up under his smallish greek beak, a little snubbed, in a big face – for him to smell): then, his trousers cork-screwing, he plunged gallantly forward – he seemed in danger of falling as he dived after the escaping door-handle.

Before ushering himself into the presence of her ladyship the fact was he had entirely omitted at first to move forward as he should, out of forgetfulness. Hence the delay in the opening of the door. Once inside however he had completely overlooked the necessity of closing up the gap made by his entrance, that was it. Ever-absent-minded whimsical personality, a door for it was a puzzling obstacle.

All the dislocations in which successively he had become involved are soon recovered from (with an effort replete with a gauche grace born of large extremities and loose obstreperous limbs): hands sunk in the side-pockets of the soiled sports-bags, belted stomach protruding – a happy 'here-I-am' smile upon a bronzed beaming boyish face, he kicks his jolly way over to Lady Fredigonde. As he goes he laughs blushing happily around the roots of his prussian-blue jowl-stubble, and upon the tanned tonsure exposed in all weathers ('All handsome men are slightly sunburnt') and in the big cleft of the bull-dog chin so difficult to shave – a blush of bland embarrassment at the thought of the joke that his arrival palpably was – a 'here-I-am' joke, concerning the unquestionable oddity, so pleasing to others, of being 'Dick' – of just getting, hit or miss, from spot to spot – turning up, being present awhile, drifting, then disappearing – a welcome, a notable, a regretted apparition.

'How are you Aunt? Quite well, I hope? I am so glad – you do look most awfully well – you astonish me more everytime I see you!'

He bent down and pressed his mouth upon the firmest stretch of flesh he could find, in a quick mannish peck. While she patted his hand dutifully, he patted her in return upon the forearm, with an easy patronage. He rose from the enforced contact, with a healthy open-air man's distaste for old female flesh interfering with his smiling, with a wry illumination, as though he would have spat.

He had seen the lipstick's trail at close quarters, he had smelt the breath blowing straight out of the no man's land of death at the hollow heart of the decrepit body. His eyes rested upon her for a moment, in the process of straightening himself to his fullest height, with a spasm of disgust, in self-defence, at having been let in for a disagreeable experience.

'How are you Dick! Not alarmingly well, I hope' Fredigonde's voice followed him up, with surprising force. 'But still able to get about – that is excellent! When did you arrive?'

'Oh – I have just come!'

He turned brusquely upon the woman of the bedchamber.

'How are you Bridget?'

A still mellower patronage escaped from the gigantic glow-worm before her at every pore, as, affably inclined, he gazed down at the shrinking dependant, devouring her in one brobdingnagian gulp of bluff grinning savoir-faire.

'Quite well thank you sir' came the abashed voice in-duty-bound. 'I hope you are quite well sir.'

'Oh yes thank you Bridget, *quite well!*'

Well was not the word! – in the absence of some expression of a more crashing heartiness it must pass muster. But floods of indulgent laughter were forthcoming, to give this assurance its proper medium of a kindly banter. Bridget was rapidly devoured, all over again, with a scorching beam of overbearing good-will – cooked in the fat of her own joke – the common joke of being the maid – to wait hand and foot upon – of my great-aunt Lady Freddy – called 'Bridget' for fun. He pulled himself up to exclaim in a different key:

'Where is Sir James? I hope he's remembered Rogers is coming?'

An abrupt peevishness baaed up, in reproachful crescendos of anticipatory alarm – in near-sighted query he stared at the old lady. A querulous frown gathered, for the benefit of the responsible party.

'You had better remind him about Mr Rogers without delay!' her ladyship warned him very earnestly: 'I suppose he is sitting downstairs in his study: that's where he generally is about this time. You really had better remind him – is it important?' She did not pause but in decided accents pursued: 'I am glad to see you looking so well Dick, and if I may say so, *strong!*' She paused and there was a strong silent hush of short duration. 'Still you were never very delicate were you – I suppose we should be thankful for that.'

The young spalpeen turned on the excited naïf illumination, at once, for the eager baby eyes. The switch for all that was open, boyish and enthusiastic if anything over-functioned, and those qualities abounded in the apartment. He tossed one huge foot out, threw back his head, the dark hair streaked with grey waving bravely around the patch of tanned common – chucked a mouthful of laughs up in the welkin, at the ceiling, and exclaimed with a super-crashing heartiness:

'Yes I feel terribly fit!'

And there was a noise like the wrath of he-goats associated

with the bright bravery of healthy he-men in the first flush of nascent manhood.

'But *you*, Aunt Fredigonde – I've never seen *anyone* ever look so terribly well! How do you manage it? It's too marvellous!'

The watery beer of fourscore years with a decade and a half on top of that in her old Gossip-starring eyes spilled a little from their brims. She patted her face with a handkerchief.

His hands knotted, presented symmetrically like buffers in the pockets of the soiled mauve bags – face inclined to the ground – the bright essence, regardless-of-cost, left burning in his staring head-lights – the spacious involuntary tonsure now visible as he slightly rolled forward his head, the good Dick paced away from her, faced unstably about and returned – with the action of the refractory child being dragged along by something like its umbilical cord, while mischievously but indolently it kicks objects in its path, to obstruct high-handed Nanny's dragging.

'What lovely ribbons Aunt Fredigonde!' he exclaimed, peering with half-closed eyes, in owlish attention, at the vivid parterre of her cap. 'I've never seen *those* before have I now Aunt Fredigonde! I think they are too lovely!' Booming, arch and boisterous, he danced before her, flinging out his feet of Gogmagog.

Slowly Aunt Fredigonde rocked her head, impersonating Any-Woman-Flattered, as it were. Dick drew back damped, eyeing her with a dying growl of heartiness upon his lips. Large lumps of dental gold disappeared with the sunset of his smile.

'I'm not sure if you have seen them' Aunt Fredigonde replied. 'Haven't you surely – it is the tartan of my mother's tribe, the McAras. I put them on as it happens to annoy Sir James – to elicit some trace of better-feeling in that old stot. (Excuse me that was a harsh expression.) Such was my intention.'

'Oh really?' Dick trilled, with puzzled high-pitched patronage. 'Why does that cause annoyance to Uncle James?'

Lady Fredigonde Follett raised a hand to her lips, to remove a particle of foreign matter, to give her well-chosen words the freest access to the air.

'Your uncle has always been a man of very strong antipathies my boy, you have noticed that I expect more than once. The old man's dislike of his mother-in-law was very marked at the outset.

It gradually extended to the whole Scottish nation.' After an impressive pause she whetted her tongue upon her lips up and down, and continued.

'He became convinced that the Scottish People were aiming at a new world-hegemony, of an oppressive character that beggared description, with the noble weltstadt of Glasgow as its capital and main port, that was his persuasion, the fruit of a great deal of obscure and I fear not very creditable meditation. In every land they are to be found, he argued, in positions of the highest trust: England, he would doggedly affirm, is run by Scots – that of course was why it was going to the dogs – and he predicted freely that the day would come when all nations of the earth would eat porridge and worship in a kirk!'

A burst of applauding laughter broke out at once from the towering audience.

'How lovely! did he really believe that do you think? It sounds too fantastic even for Sir James – .'

Aunt Fredigonde waved aside all qualifying interjections with a dogmatic index-finger, at which Dick barked again, with mellow glee, and danced a hornpipe – as performed by a deep-sea diver for the camera men before entering the skiff and so below, to show he is not downhearted.

'It was in vain that I protested that half of the Scotch were now Irish' roared as best she could Aunt Fredigonde, in the highest spirits, 'owing don't you know to irish immigration, and that Glasgow was more irish than scottish – that was absolutely no use at all! He would reply that the more mixed they were the worse they became, and indeed the more *scotch!*'

'What an extraordinary idea!' boomed Dick.

'Yes, a most preposterous paradox, and perfectly mad,' bellowed the super-aunt of this super-nephew.

'I don't think he can have been really serious' protested, bashfully mellifluous, the clumsily-dancing Richard.

'My dear lad, no Scot was ever more in earnest' insisted the stationary mammoth idol before which he slightly charlestoned: 'but I had no idea that he still harboured such feelings. Then the other day I had startling proof of it. Sometimes Sir James is revolting.'

Dick charlestoning as he stood, the two knots of his fists deeply entrenched in the gnarled Oxford bags to which he now imparted a ponderous molten shiver, Gog or Magog turned a dervish, was irresponsible. He softly whistled: Aunt Fredigonde was not usually so long-winded! He hoped she would soon change the subject or he would.

'Don't you find hatred in the old, Dick, as unbecoming as love my child?' Master Richard pricked his ears up – could love *become* – was love *becoming* – ? His legs kept turning to the massed gramophoning of his slowly revolving eardrums, like the disks of records, while he answered with genial off-hand kindness, softly –

'I don't know. – Why!'

A rich round booming sudden 'whoi', sent over with a quick grin.

He stopped the impromptu ballroom practice. There was a pause of respectful uncertainty. What was expected of one whom everything became – in all modesty! A shamefacedly half-hidden smile at the odd sibylline utterances of the aged perplexed his face. Then quick and bright, with mellow respectful matter-of-factness –

'I don't think hatred becomes anybody!'

That was the proper answer, sober and trite.

'Don't you?' clamoured the image or the imposing sibyl, from Age's mighty pedestal – before which he bowed with a will: but not to be too servile he would say –

'No.'

Very respectfully decisive, *no*, with a whimsical pained smile – but guns must be stuck to, isn't that so Aunt Fredigonde? even if only an old-fashioned ordnance: and the spectacle of adolescent loyalty associated with a thoroughly effete object is highly picturesque. Was not he a pattern of duty? And was what she had just said appropriate to a pedestal? Undeniably that had not been the case – it was right to recall her to the proprieties – Bowing with respectful shame his head, he corkscrewed four times, very slowly, from left to right.

'At all events, for my part,' her ladyship retorted, 'I find all passion offensive in elderly persons – just as I look for it in the young, that is understood.'

Aunt Fredigonde looked over at him – looking genially for passion, with a flattering pointedness.

Dick bashfully responded, looked the part with expedition: he looked away, in pleasant abstraction.

'They are all the same, Sir James's family,' continued to remark the persistent old sibyl. 'Their passions have no age I am sorry to say, I am exceedingly sorry to have to say that! To treat themselves objectively – they refuse to do that altogether – it is unpleasant, you must concede that it is that.'

But this was upon ground where Dick felt strongly: he roared dogmatically at once (about the 'objective' a term he had cause to mistrust):

'Should people treat themselves objectively? After all why should they?'

The high-hearted spirit (if not exactly passion) that was to be expected, burst out, most argumentative. But the mummy, with its fixed idea, went on, as though he had not spoken with such rapid youthful cogency at all:

'There is your grandfather. He illustrates what I am advancing, he who got married again did he not at sixty-six – to a child of thirty-five odd or a mere forty; yes it was a forty, I beg your pardon, and had the unsuitable idea of going for a honeymoon to the venetian Lido. – I believe you will agree that that was offensive. The Folletts are like that I am sorry to have to say, to a man, they are prone to such peculiar lapses of taste.'

'You are very hard on the Folletts, Aunt Fredigonde!' Dick exclaimed with a violent rapture of caressing reproach – letting out a long airy chain of laughter – nasal, protesting.

He averted his eyes from the sibyl, now, however – there was much malice in fossilized 'Gossip'. He brought to an abrupt close his stationary jazz with a peevish abruptness: flinging a foot forward a yard about, he moved off heavily in the direction of Bridget (who eluded him, quickly removing herself, under the shelter of the massive chimneypiece).

'I was not including you my dear' the slightly obnoxious figure upon the pedestal screamed after him.

'Thank you so much Aunt Fredigonde! I was sure you weren't. I'm only half a one a Follett anyway!' he howled back over his shoulder towards the ear-trumpet, pointed after him:

he was full of fight and he raised his voice till even to him it sounded a shade harsh, to make sure he would be heard, though her ears were sharp enough when she wanted them to be.

'The lot of them are all only half Folletts too, of course' she agreed.

(But half a Follett – there are no Folletts really!)

'Of course' in retreat he assented very shortly now.

'Do you like them?'

Dick drove up the room, feet flying and teeth bared, while with full-throated irony he bellowed back as he advanced:

'Not terribly. I try to!'

He was always *trying* – mixing up the Folletts with the McAras. Still, patience with this old bore of a Freddy – we shall soon be losing her now, there was that much about it.

'You will succeed one day young man – *Kopf hoch, nur Mut!* – If you go on as you're going that's understood. I applaud your reserve – you perceive I see the drift of my remarks! – What Bridget is the time my child? Master Dick I know has not the time, it is useless to ask him the time.'

No, he would not go so far as to say that Aunt Fredigonde was his favourite relative, *but* – her dazzling past as Gossip-belle and ex-Chat-champion must awe Dick, so thinking almost with large physical thoughts of this renown he laughed apologetically – he took a very firm hold of himself almost in comic corps-à-corps. Responsibly frowning he drew up before her, a picture of public schoolboyish duty, gigantic and sheepish.

'It is five minutes to twelve your ladyship.' Bridget had consulted the clock.

'Five to twelve – thank you Bridget.'

'Your ladyship will not require me any further?' Bridget asked from the neighbourhood of the door.

'No thank you Bridget, not for the moment.'

As the door closed upon Bridget, Dick flung his body into a sofa (which gasped in its wheezy bowels) and then slightly eructated, with a heavy zigzag movement up his body, the back of his flat occiput becoming for a moment as stiff as a poker – from hair en brosse, flourishing straight up into the air in the same plane as his neck, and so in a sheer undeviating drop to his coccyx, against the high-backed squatting apparatus to which he had brutally committed his person. Once more a ball of wind made its way irresistibly up his neck. His trunk shook, contracted and relaxed, to assist the slight explosion.

In a brown study, Richard did not seek to dissemble these indecorous accidents, or to give a colour to them by coughing – he was well-pleased just now with the bucolic directness of his body. His feelings might be even more forcibly conveyed if it let itself go! He sat with the earnest look of schoolboy-application to the first steps in scholarship, fresh from play, come into the presence of the form-master, and grimly confronted with the instruments of learning.

For a moment his giant aunt stared over at him.

'Well here you are back in your cradle Dick' at last she sighed – 'so to speak.'

'That's the idea' the rattle of conventional applause clappered genteelly in Dick's throat, while his eye shot up into his aunt's face to catch her meaning – the luminous youthfulness damped, with a doggish eye of cross reproach he returned to her countenance silently, and looked away: a very trying old woman indeed, as she was always apt to be, though terribly *brilliant*.

'I shan't be in my cradle long this time however.'

'How is that?'

'Oh I just shan't be long here today that's all I meant – I'm going down to March by the three-forty.'

'Such a short visit?'

He got up and heaved himself over to the fireplace. He dissimulated a series of yawns, set up with promptitude by the contradiction he had experienced, in the course of the consequent fatigue. With ringing blows upon the fire-bricks of the grate he discharged the dottle from his bulldog pipe. Smartly he struck it down at the end of its stem, as in the game called Conquerors.

'How have you been getting on with your lessons?'

'How do you mean?'

'Oh the lessons with the – what is the man's name.'

'Oh do you mean with Mr Mundy?'

'What is that?'

'Quite well, I find it rather boring. – I am not having any more. I am painting by myself.'

'Indeed! Why?'

'Oh I dont know.'

'I suppose you're anxious to get through with your education now, Dick.'

'That's the idea! I'm a big boy now aren't I Aunt Fredigonde!'

'You *do* grow, I believe, you surely must have a little since we last met, haven't you?' Tremendous yawns following great fatigue broke his face in half.

'Well, I think I'll go down and see Sir James' – smothering yawn after yawn which now came crowding on him, very tired.

'You seem tired, my dear child' said Lady Fredigonde coaxing her nephew.

'I am a little. I was up rather late with Duff going over things. Well I'll go and see Sir James, Aunt Freddy!'

A stern look came into his face as he referred to duty manfully met. Small needle-like glances of pinpricking reproach were darted deftly over at the old woman, at the same time that he addressed her.

'Do, Mr Rogers will be stopping to lunch I suppose?' she said.

'I suppose so.'

Out shuffled Dick, burying his resentment rapidly in a lofty absent-mindedness. His eyes sank, a prey to gravitation, floorwards, as he moodily receded. Behind him the door stood unshut, he took no notice.

As Dick reached the stair-head a strident tearing sneeze crashed in the room he had just left. A slight smile of self-understanding, comfortable and private, came into his face. When they sneezed like that – it was not far off! Another sharp winter would do it! A second sneeze shrieked out behind him. Cocking one eye to the ceiling he stood still and in quick succession released two rasping snorts from his anus. A third sneeze screamed with a stupid violence as he relaxed from the cocking position.

At the same time he noted in his tablets – in the vernacular of the army he had left five years previously to marry, before he knew he was an artist or 'genius', 'Snotty old barstard!'

Sounding the melancholy hour of twelve, the Major's clock in

Armadale prevailed solemnly over the bell-like stillness of the house. Dick kicked the hours moodily, like footballs, in front of him as he descended the stairs. Each hollow resurrected hour as it presented itself in this concentrated form for him, preceded by the rushing of the noisy instrument, was accompanied by a foot flung out, and twelve of the imposing stairs were passed, stroke by stroke, on the downward path, to Sir James's study.

'Hallo, Sir! Goodmorning! How are you!' the rich bright growl of man-to-man buffeted the leather faces of the study. He bent down and opened a volume resting upon Sir James's knee. *The True Intellectual System of the Universe*, *Ralph Cudworth* he read, and then closed the book again as though with quiet understanding.

An irish tweed, given a tint of desiccated blood with the bodies of mexican insects, upholstered Sir James's withered trunk and arms. A clouded tiger upon a stand, stuffed and rampant, recalled early days in Borneo, before he had succeeded to the title. Sustaining the cracked scales of his aged brain – in which he had been balancing Cudworth's weighty niceties – he had wearied, and the book had subsided at the same time as his failing machine. He fixed his eyes upon the clouded tiger. He did not recall the day when with a bullet he had stopped this swift restless clockwork dead. A vivid shadow of life, he was too familiar with it to replace it mentally in its distant series.

Sir James Follett took Cudworth from his knees and placed him upon the table at his side, across the prose works of Dryden. In the gentle debate set up in his mind between Dryden and Cudworth, the latter being on the side of the imminent angels had won the day.

'Ah hallo Dick, that's you is it? When did you get here? You were expected quite early, for some reason. How are you?'

'Very well indeed!' Dick shouted to wake the dead, with grateful gusto, performing a shambling war-dance, hands in pockets, all his joints dislocating themselves in succession, his huge feet constantly flung outwards, a stomach protruding in that manner that made him appear a jerky and unwilling toy dragged forward by a ghostly umbilical cord.

'That's capital! How have you been getting on? Have you seen your aunt?'

'Yes I've just left her ladyship!' Dick threw in a slight growling laugh to keep the snobbish epithet (used in snobbish servant-mockery) company, as was expected of him. 'She was in surprising form! She sent me down here almost at once!'

He threw half-a-crown up into the air and caught it with an animal deftness, his knees stuck together, the feet pawing outwards with enormous blunt tips.

He then stamped up and down, for a little – the silver piece, grasped in his fist, back in his pocket – with the travesty of the man-with-a-game-leg, and acting the part of a person who had left the room a minute gone, say to fetch his pipe from his pocket in the hall, instead of reappearing after an absence of three months.

Sir James did not look at Dick at all but gazed ahead, holding his weak eyes wide open, with a civil smile frozen absent-mindedly upon his face.

'Her ladyship has been in almost unexampled form recently' Sir James then remarked. 'Indeed I have been somewhat uneasy, in a woman of her age it is not of the best augury.'

'What nonsense, sir! I'm quite sure she will outlive all of us! I'm quite certain, at all events, that she will outlive me!'

A rheumy sideglance struck the outsize health-advertisement like a wet ghost.

'I'm sure she'll outlive *me*' Sir James grinned in bland repose, the death's head sweetened with the faintest irony. For a moment they grinned in each other's eyes – the animal, which has suddenly caught sight of its own person in a glass, and for a moment, before it thinks it has happened on another dog, perceives itself. The presence in their thoughts of the bitter matriarch whom he had just left, and under whom Sir James had suffered for half a century, conspired to compel their minds together in what was almost a caress.

With whistling lips percussioning upon the air a sugared one-step monotone, Dick trailed his always astonished, reluctant hoofs down the apartment – his neck craned in swan-like trances, his Adam's-apple jutting out, the nose smallish and female sniffing shortsightedly six feet above the savage jazzing hoofs. *Those are pearls that were his eyes* he heard a voice muttering in the thick of the perpetual music, inconsequent cutting-in, in the accents of Haarlem: but he detected a tramping in the hallway outside.

'Oh sir!' he exclaimed recalling himself urgently from Richard Whittingdon's proverbial abstraction: 'You haven't forgotten have you sir that Mr Rogers is coming this morning – I came down to remind you.'

'No he should have been here by now. What is the time? It must be almost time he was here.'

'It's after twelve – It's about ten past. I thought I might find him here. I believe I hear him though.'

Dick's voice rose in a querulous startled howl to put in quickly a fresh question, while his eyes were directed towards the door, with angry anxiety.

'I suppose no one else is coming?'

'Not as far as I know – no, no one but Mr Rogers, unless her ladyship has anyone coming.'

'She didn't mention that she had.'

The door opened as though to swallow a room. A small man in black was first revealed holding it by the handle.

'Mr Zackroost sir, to see you.'

A tall figure eclipsed at once the body-servant of the invalid baronet, and like the shadow of that first commanding figure another tall form arrived at the same instant, out of the twilight of the hall. Crossing the threshold almost neck-and-neck, they both swept quickly forward, at unusual speed for human beings.

'How are you uncle? I hear that you are expecting your lawyer. This is Mr Boleyn of whom I have spoken to you, Mr Daniel Boleyn, sir.' His shadow came forward, and bowed to the aged invalid.

'Mr Boleyn is only nineteen' Mr Zagreus remarked, looking at Mr Boleyn.

'Is that all?' Sir James said. 'Won't you sit down.'

Mr Boleyn bowed again.

'He has a great future – Mr Daniel Boleyn has a very great future – of course as yet he is too young to have done much, but he has written one most lovely poem. I will show it to you.'

'Thank you very much' Sir James replied. 'I should like to read it very much. Is it in free verse? I suppose so.'

A look of momentary indignation appeared in the face of Horace Zagreus.

'Not at all – it is in a quite traditional metre. Absolutely the *youngest* generation, sir, do not write in free verse – they have gone back to *quite* traditional forms.'

'Have they? That is very interesting.'

'Yes quite the youngest generation! It is only, you will find, the thirties and the forties that believe in violent experiment – the *very youngest generation'* Mr Zagreus thundered, his eyes flashing 'are super-victorian now, if you like – are classical *to a man!'*

He returned with a fine frenzy of false fierceness, his arms a little raised, towards Mr Daniel Boleyn – While another person was speaking, the eyes of Mr Zagreus never left their face: when he spoke himself he moved his mouth often in violent pantomime, as if conversing in dumb-show: on occasion his lips would move, too, without any words coming to account for it.

The death's head in the chair gathered (reaching over) in the pale fields of death a voltairean flower of the most colourless irony, and smiled faintly with its lips. Whereas the three towering figures stood before it, one full of passion, and two profoundly silent – one an enigma of nineteen, the other speechless with rage.

Boleyn's expression did not change. He stood with his eyes fixed upon the baronet. But the latter was gently repelled by the future, as much as Horace Zagreus was its notorious devotee, and he looked the other way. These boys-big-with-futures turned up periodically. Always with the same futures, such as now was said to resemble, to perfection, the past. Sir James would have preferred the future as it was.

Dick however had stepped back, his expression at its crossest – as the two tall interlopers, instead of Rogers, had stormed the threshold of the study at a gallop. – Now he was watching with what was growing into a wrathful grin, what was passing; but at last, as the pause persisted, impulsively he forced his way towards Zagreus, his hand advanced.

'How are you Horace?'

'Oh how are you Dick? I didn't see you. Boleyn, this is my cousin, Mr Richard Whittingdon, Mr Daniel Boleyn.'

'How do you do!' Dick flashed a gold-toothed signal towards Mister Only-Nineteen.

Mr Boleyn, with an innocent eye spying the reverent tonsure of his patron's cousin, exclaimed demurely:

'How do you do – sir!'

They all stood looking now at the old man for a moment, hesitating: where attack this deafness and remoteness next? With resignation Sir James awaited the onslaught of their tongues. The cost of the responses they might require of him, in terms of energy, he gently computed. He kept his eyes away from the stranger, for he feared, if he did not, he might speak – or perhaps burst into song. Into 'traditional' song.

'I hope you and Mr Boleyn, Horace, will stay to lunch. Dick and I have Mr Rogers coming, oh yes they told you that didn't they: we are expecting him at any minute, he should have been here by now.'

'I'll take Boleyn up to see her ladyship. When will you be done with Rogers? Perhaps we had better not stop to lunch.'

'Oh we shan't be long' Dick replied for them. 'That is I don't think so – what do you think sir?'

The door opened.

'Mr Rogers is here sir.'

'Ask him to come in.'

Boleyn formally bowing, the lawyer passed in as Mr Zagreus and his young friend passed out with swift strides, their arms swinging and clothes flying, like a young bodyguard-recruit of the Household Brigade, and a seasoned colour-sergeant on their way to the orderly-room.

'Now we'll go up and see my aunt. She is a very interesting old lady. She is the *ancêtre*. She's the last of the family portraits, but she has never been painted – no artist could ever stick it out, it was a battle between the tongue and brush. No, this way. Tread softly because you tread on my dreams. – Mind the step.'

Mr Daniel Boleyn had stumbled slightly as they had passed, abreast and at breakneck speed, from one level of the gloomy entrance-hall to the next. The perfectly handsome features of Horace's young client expressed the deepest melancholy; as he stumbled his passionate velvet eyes of the richest black had looked up with burning reproach at his white-maned superior, for his callousness, and the look said more plainly than words that he wished he had slipped and broken his neck on the spot, or sprained his ankle: but the stern mentor, with his cavalry moustaches, did not so much as notice the least in the world the movement of passionate protest: he passed on relentlessly, an imperial votary he swept them forward to the foot of the staircase – he paused a moment, stretched out his arm to indicate their path, carpeted with his dreams, and then he charged breathlessly upward.

*

Archie Margolin examined a stupefying instrument of ugliness that was sino-british, a great screen. He was conscious of the vast unoccupied spaces of the drawing-room. The hulking chairs gaped vainly for the bottoms of the defunct, the capacious Eighteenth-Century posteriors. His was a spare one – no seats here to his measure by a yard. His slightness was delicious – he rejoiced in his neat pygmy stature. It was the child-height!

The great bluff psyche of British brawn had left its uncouth fingerprints, throughout this domestic museum. So much by mere space had it not expressed itself, in a futile extension?

So a gold-curled flat-buttocked East-end cupid, he sveltly stood, in the day-dream of his scornful vulgar elegance, surrounded by such upholstered shells of vanished cyclop beefeaters (and their dead belles, whose strapping ham-pink limbs in fancy he decorated with bulging period furbelows, window-dressed, baldly spreadeagled, for his distant appetites). Watched by substances of an alien life he was nevertheless oppressed and contemptuous: this culture was dead as mutton but its great carcass offended him – it would take a hundred years to melt. He grinned and yawned.

He might have been standing in a slow, heavily-beaming, rose-fresh georgian sunrise in a drawing-room, perhaps a hostile ghost surprised by daylight, in this silent mansion, except for the tremulous roar of distracted surf from the traffic-way, beyond the gates of the avenue.

'The space-mad, the English! – from their spacious days of their great Elizabeth to the Imperial Victoria. But – now that space, itself, has shrunk under their feet, by time contracted –

what a race of pygmies!' So the great furniture shouted to his senses the message of its empty scale.

A sparrow outside the window, hawking for crumbs, dropped towards the kitchens while he watched it.

Underneath an army of slavish snobs still! The basement was full of people, they were collected near the ovens, coal-holes, sinks, dustbins – a sewer-people his soul sang, in marxist fierceness, for these upstairs-pleasaunces, the Follett masters and mistresses! One shrilled a dismal rag about a honey-stick. The heart broke for Dixie: the voice cracked and crooned, all on account of nigger-heavens – it was funny! The lives of other idiot slaves, in cotton fields, excited it to mournful passions! (Of more musical slaves naturally.)

'Whoop-eeee!' went the mocking Archie softly, grinning beneath his golden african curliness. The footman or the chauffeur's voice was joined by the outburst of the early afternoon Savoy Hill program. It was an organ recital.

He listlessly attended to the howling of the man. The organ dragged itself up and down bellowing painfully. He smiled the weary smile of the true Hebrew, beneath the veneer – with some hip-movement he went over to a pier-glass, to plunge his image into it – a bitter little Narcissus, with strained quizzical eyebrows.

Ears cocked, he examined his face. It was smooth and almond yellow. He advanced his gold hair, of the newest Margolins, to his mind shoddy – pushed forward it got rid of that bald appearance that began with his pale unlashed eyes.

Turning again to the window, he went over to it and looked out. There stood the Bugatti, or lay, like a very large metal lizard, the mechanical toy of his patron. Again he smiled.

He returned into the centre of the room. He approached another mirror and observed his face, inclined to burst out laughing as it watched him slyly in the polished surface.

From the hall came a muffled shouting. Smiling he stepped back softly towards the spot upon which he had taken up his position. As he reached it, the door flew open and Dick's voice broke the stillness, to atoms, it made Arch's head feel as though it were vast and empty.

'That's splendid!' boomed the bright-eyed Dick circling

towards him like a cautious ring-giant. 'I'm so glad you were able to come – I thought the notice might have been too short!' At the thought of the *short notice* Archie simply grinned a broad proletarian grimace; but he almost laughed outright at the figure of the strutting Goliath.

Dick flung his feet out this way and that – he stamped up and down upon the swagger carpet of his *Rittergut* to show his East End visitor how *he*, the jew-boy from the slum, would have behaved, if he had been absolutely at home, as was Dick, and had he trodden these exclusive mansions from the cradle up.

'I'm sorry I wan't able to get away before' he exclaimed in hearty crashing accents of delighted patronage, as happy as a sandboy – with a sidelong glance at the speedy nozzle of his Bugatti, which he could just catch sight of through the window. 'The old family lawyer's here – and Mr Rogers is not the man to be hustled I'm afraid!'

Dick was radiant at the thought of the deliberate methods of Mr Rogers which was unspeakably funny; but his face relaxed into a decorous melancholy, as he found himself definitely mastered with compassion for this octogenarian attorney.

'He's an awfully nice old boy all the same – he's the old family lawyer – quite a good lawyer I believe.'

Archie looked up with the most insolent naivety.

'Have you a family lawyer?' he gazed round the huge apartment where they stood, as if he realized for the first time that he found himself in an establishment that had an old lawyer to live on it – as well as two butlers and a big Bugatti on its back.

Dick savoured with seigneurial restraint the simplicity of the jewish slums, in condescending cool haw-haws, while he flung his oil-stained Oxford bags this way and that, in buxom spasms of shyness.

'Yes we have a family-lawyer' he trilled in deep contralto. 'I sometimes wish we hadn't! The poor old man gets unspeakably fussed if he's asked to move a fraction quicker than they did in 1850.'

They both had a good laugh about 1850 especially Richard. They imagined the velocipede, exposed to the competition of the Bugatti. Archie Margolin took the opportunity of having a really good laugh at the same time on his own account – which he had felt if he did not soon give vent to he would burst his bladder.

Passing over abruptly into a rather grander manner, squinting over Archie's head at nothing in particular, Dick drawled:

'There were several things that had to be fixed up – you know I've let March Park. I had to see Mr Rogers about that, there are a lot of other things that have to be settled. He'll be here in a moment – it's a bore, he's stopping to lunch. – I hope you don't mind!'

Archie smiled nicely once and dismissed with a swift harsh gesture the family lawyer – the family seat, the castle of March, rented to rich Jews, and the rest of this nonsense, turning restlessly towards the windows.

'I thought you might have got lost' said Dick then, compelled to pursue him a little across the room: 'did you find your way – without too much difficulty?'

Archie turned to his host with a theatrical roughness and replied in a croaking voice full of gutturals, which he was at no pains to disguise, ill-assorted with the feminine gold of the crimped head and the insignificance of the body:

'Yes quite all right. I know my way about here, you know' aggressively Arch barked, while backing away from his pursuer. 'I've not been here in years' (Dick smiled at the locution *in years*) 'but I've come all round here with my elder brother Isidore, I used to help him carry his box – you know his goods. He hawked all round these areas. I came with him.'

He must be popular and in present company he had struck the popular note, of what all of his race ought to be, the Dickens-Jew of *Our Mutual Friend*, a myth he freely hated. It had a strong appeal for the historic sense of his host. For his part Arch enjoyed himself in the bitter-sweet of its comic revival – *Positively last appearance!*

'Oh really!' chuckled richly the happy dupe of this stock-figure of Old Comedy very broad-minded, socially as also intellectually. 'How absurd! Used you to sell much?'

'Not so bad' grinned Arch, with a still more thick-tongued croak, in perfect character, fixing a fierce eye upon this comic-cut of a capitalist.

'I wonder if you ever came here!'

'What *here?*'

'Yes to Number Six. That would have been most awfully strange – I suppose you don't remember!'

Arch barks, with a small short cough of half-rabid waggishness, the militant slum-Jew in excelsis.

'It's a long time. Yes I think we did.'

Amused eyes of broad-minded patronage play down upon him steadily.

'What did you sell?'

Matey, from on high, this lordly sportsman certainly gives proof of an intelligent interest in the small commerce of the gutter, which is charming and Archie chuckles, pleased to accommodate, and Dick laughs to put him at his ease.

'My brother peddled tin wrist-watches and plate, in plush cases – suitable for skivvies who well you know are making a home, for their boy.'

'No how sweet! – I'm sure Ethel had a nickel soup tureen!'

Dick's two sunburnt fists rooted for sheer sport in the innards of his bulky bags, and he hooted at the image of Ethel, the blond english villager, standing in pained discomfort before her ladyship, with her white frilled domestic comb of a she-lackey, spotlessly bibbed and belted in muslin and black alpaca, with her gentle foolish eyes: she was a standing joke second only to Birdie, but in some ways odder than Skelton the cook, from the same Wiltshire hamlet.

'Who is Ethel?' asked Archie with his cheapest mass-production grin, for the part of the Sham-Yid.

But as to a Who's-Who of the staff, Dick was not the proper quarter – .

'Oh' crashed the affable heir-apparent, 'Ethel is a housemaid.'

'Oh. *A housemaid!*' echoes Arch, slow and blank and glotzaugenisch but just short of squinting. He waits and then he says, not to be backward, 'Yes that's right, we did sell a set of posh nickel-plate to a girl – it may have been next door. It's a long time.'

'How long?'

Arch wrinkled up the dry skin of his brow and stuttered grinning:

'How long? Yes *how long!*' he suffered a minute attack of hysteria, it would have been better to stamp and scream. Then frowning heavily to adjust his mind to a topic depending on arithmetic. 'Let's see! How long was it!' he asked with a teasing beady eye, a catch-me-if-you-can confusion. 'Where are we now?' stuttered he – this needs thinking out! 'It's nineteen-twenty six, I'm twenty isn't that right, or is it twenty-two – I don't know. When was it – my blooming memory's gone – I'm young to have lost my memory!' He spluttered over the aphasia with idiot-mirth – of course *the Fool of the Gutter*. 'Three years – no four! Yes four, that's right, four. It was four.'

'I want a new wrist-watch!' after enjoying the joke that never came Lord Dick jauntily declared, looking down where the left watch-bearing paw betrayed its presence, by occasional movements, in the plastic of the mauve bags. 'Now if your brother were only on the prowl today we might do business!'

Archie laughed most heartily – he made his eyes shine obligingly, as he gazed into the foolface, with the pleased glitter expected, at the thought of gain. He shook his head. – After considering for a moment, Arch looked archly up, with a very ponderous candour, and in the most sinister growling guttural he had yet employed he repudiated his blood relation absolutely.

'I wouldn't recommend you to go to my brother!'

'Why?' the bantering contralto query sounded honest Dick's deprecation of this attitude to a blood-relation – even when a brother – and even if a pedlar, who (agreed) is perhaps not over-particular.

'He's a robber – no although he is my brother. I couldn't not honestly recommend him.'

In grating monotone the repudiation was repeated. This was taking a solemn turn – so pleasantly it had been meant, but the famous business-instinct of the Perl-and-Potash order had taken it at the foot of the letter.

Steadfastly Archie Margolin, own brother to Isidore, stared at Gentleman Dick, till that gent felt a guilty party – he shuffled before this complex scrutiny.

'I couldn't not to be fair, recommend my brother, not to you!' Arch repeated, with impressive dullness, throwing in a handful of *nots* for local slum-colour.

'I'm sorry to hear that!' objected Dick heartily, and began grinding the millstone of his outsize foot-wear in heavy Charleston practice.

'It's true' remarked Arch still more impressively to the discomforted Dick. 'It's too true Dick, he's what you'd call *awful* Dick, is my brother Isidore, he's a proper old shark!'

'A shark?'

'He sells tin watches to poor kids like Ethel, the old Skylark – I mean Shylock – that aren't worth no not sixpence, for half-a-quid. He's some lad is Isidore not half! No. *I couldn't recommend him!*' Arch wound up passionately. As though half asleep he went on repeating that *he couldn't recommend* his brother Isidore – not to his friend Richard-the-lion-hearted – no, not Isidore.

'Well I'm sorry to hear Archie you're not able to recommend your brother' said Dick yawning with stiff upper-lip stretched down over the food-hole, like a polite hand – while he Charlestoned grandly, in a steady stationary sunset-rolling, of great ships vibrating in the hearts of oceans, 'Because I might have bought a wrist-watch off him.'

Archie shook his head with idiot-sadness, from side to side.

'I couldn't recommend him not Isidore' he reaffirmed almost with an ethical passion of sober emphasis, and almost shrieking desperately: 'No really. – Here!' The smallish mongol-yellow of the Margolin was clouded with a flush and frown of prophetic buffoonery. He swelled himself up with wind in the chest and threatened in jest, with his small eyes, the gigantic gollywog before him – disintegrating beneath the tom-toms of Tennessee.

'Here!' Arch shouted again in ragtime bluster, at the grinning latterday dickensian Dick. 'Here Dick! Why dont you protect your people downstairs in the coal-hole you know the staff, against robbers like my brother. His wrist-watches never go! I would if I was you – no straight I would!'

Dick collected himself, he addressed himself to this jewish crossword-puzzle in servant-management. How make this little Jew understand! What a picture – Dick interviewing the cook and warning her against his guest's brother's spurious electroplate! – he laughed in leisurely puzzlement to himself choosing the words of the answer as he scratched the polished ink-blue stubble of his great cleft chin.

'Well Archie' said he then, in caressing tones of almost paternal moderation: 'I am afraid they wouldn't listen to me.'

'Perhaps they wouldn't' Archie admitted, dropping his prophet-mask, as he looked over impartially – not to be outdone in chivalry – at Dick. 'Perhaps you are right!'

With a flourish of generosity he gave this trick to Dick and turned half away, with the gesture of *Charlot-triste* – biting a lip.

'I am quite sure they wouldn't. So long as you don't interfere with them' Dick laid it down, condescending but emphatic, *en connaissance de cause*, for this enquiring young outcast 'they don't mind what you do! Servants are very queer people – you have to know how to take them or they resent it and will do nothing for you.'

'I suppose you do – I suppose they are' Arch followed, vaguely spouting into the air, in mock-grand-manner, wilfully a long-way-after the master Richard, to the manner born.

'Yes they are indeed' Dick vaguely drawled, imitating his guest's too witty counterfeit.

'We all are!' exclaimed Archie in his usual voice with a beaming grin.

'We all are' assented Dick with dramatic hushed sobriety.

Philosophy had passed between them.

Archie, with a swift movement of his small limbs, went to a cabinet, and, opening it, removed an old and crusted mesopotamian riderless pony, and held it in his hand.

'Rather jolly isn't it?' Dick said watching him with a lightly-drawn smile. Hush! The instincts of the race probably at work – he was *valuing!* – Dick continued to observe him with a smiling impassible attention.

Archie looked up, proposing to make some remark before replacing the object: detecting the drift of the attentive amusement, he smiled broadly, in a flash, patting comically the statuette.

'A nice little gee-gee!' he said. 'A good little gee-gee, and no mistake! What did you pay for it Dick?'

A flash of gratified astuteness lit up the honest face of that acute observer, and Dick laughed easily as he answered:

'Ah that I can't tell you Archie! The house is not mine – it was not I who bought it!'

Margolin thrust it back into the case.

A gong began to boom.

'Oh there's a gong. I wonder what that's for!' Dick cried testily, 'This house is full of gongs. It's like a Bayswater boarding house – that's for lunch I expect.'

They listened to the gong: it died away in a pale roar in some distant passage-way.

'I wonder what on earth's happened to Mr Rogers!' Dick moved crossly towards the door – the lawyer threatened to interfere between the inner man and its expectation of succulent meat-dishes.

They went into the hall and found Horace Zagreus talking in a low voice to the lawyer. Just behind him like a military servant stood Boleyn.

'That's how it stands. I will ring you up tomorrow morning' Zagreus said to the lawyer, leaving him precipitately as he saw Dick approaching.

'Horace, meet Mr Margolin!' exclaimed Dick facetiously. Archie veiled his eyes and gave a limp hand to the imposing figure. (What was a thracian god doing in this galère?) Horace Zagreus had moved rapidly away.

'Horace is a most extraordinary person!' Dick was saying crossly to Archie Margolin, as they made their way towards the luncheon. 'In his time he's done everything I should think. When he was at Oxford, I've heard, everyone thought he was going to do wonders.'

'That must have been a long time ago' said Arch.

'I suppose it was' Dick agreed loftily and abstractedly. 'He is a failure, no doubt.'

'What did he fail in?'

'Oh – just a failure: – as a matter of fact he was a surveyor by profession. He's as deaf as a post!'

Archie looked after the two quickly moving figures, who had reached the front door.

'What has made him deaf?' he asked.

'He was born so, I believe.'

'Is that your family-lawyer, Dick?'

'Who? the old boy going in – there? Yes that's Mr Rogers!' Dick laughed heartily at the bowed respectable back of the Law.

*

'What was his name – Margolin?' muttered Horace Zagreus to Daniel Boleyn as they were on the steps, looking back into the open hall.

Dan nodded his head.

They retired in impeccable time and perfect order, with the same swift tread, along the short semicircular carriage-drive.

'I rather liked him!' Horace remarked fiercely. 'I wonder where Dick collected him? I expect he has some designs on our relative's pocket – good luck to him! – most people have!'

Outside the gate stood the Bugatti. As they passed it Mr Zagreus gave it a smiling side-glance, remarking to Daniel:

'There's that old baby's latest toy!'

Daniel gave a startled look at the machine, and looked hastily away again.

'The Bugatti!'

Horace Zagreus laughed as he named it, passing his hand over his moustache, helping it to its upward flourish.

They turned into the wide thoroughfare, running beside the dirty lawns of the Park. Mr Zagreus drew a large sealed envelope out of his breast pocket. At that moment his eye fell upon an approaching figure. He quickly thrust the envelope back again. Taking Daniel's arm, he turned them into the road, his eye calculating, left – right. He headed them diagonally across the closing jaws of traffic, bearing towards the less swift of the two approaching extremities. As they mounted the opposite pavement he sighed.

'What – is the *lapis manalis* off this morning? That's the second ghost I've seen.'

He placed his hand in his breast-pocket. About to draw the sealed envelope out once more, suddenly a few yards ahead the figure he had believed they had successfully avoided stepped out of a rift in the moving mass of vehicles, on to the pavement in front of them. Sternly fixing his eyes upon the grinning face, Horace Zagreus bore down upon it, his arm through that of

Boleyn, but his body a little in advance, covering to some extent that of his protégé.

'Hallo Horace! I thought I recognized you!' and a hand stopped him as they were abreast.

Mr Zagreus released Daniel, thrusting him behind him as he did so: then facing about, his face still very stern and expressionless, stood looking down at the figure that had stopped him.

'Well and what then Francis?' he asked.

'Oh nothing,' replied Francis.

Raggedly framed eyes full of an ageing blue were stuck perfunctorily in a tanned face, of small and blunted features. It was somewhat puffed and flushed beneath the thinning tan. Francis was a man of forty or just under that, an unnecessary moustache, of withered sandy stubble, suggested a convention for which the face was unsuited. Exposed to the penetrating stare of the impeccable Zagreus (like a worm confronting its Setebos, with an insolent 'You are responsible for me!' in its eyes) the figure addressed as Francis basked in the disapproving attention he had drawn upon himself.

'How have you been getting on all these years Zagreus?'

'Much the same, thank you. How have you been getting on, Francis?'

'Not too badly, pretty well, in fact. I'm off to the West Indies again this week.'

'Doing well?'

'Not so badly.'

He signalled a stream of offensive messages from his small extinct expressive lamps, into the big face of the powerful Sphinx, which did not move a muscle. – Some of the human dirt must surely get in, and interfere with the stately brooding. (The same face! Embalmed in his beastly money! He must be sixty if a day!)

'You haven't changed!' Francis belched out from his compressed grin.

Zagreus drew in a long draught of air up his extremely handsome equine nostril, his eyes rolling wildly like a horse's for a moment, as though he were about to rush away in terror.

'Still as interested as ever in the young, I see' Francis

remarked, in a confidential undertone, glancing round the obstruction of his friend's shoulders, to where Daniel stood.

'Yes, you have observed correctly.'

'You old succubus! Let's have a look at your latest suffix!' Francis cried, raising his voice, and suddenly moving forward in the direction of Daniel. 'Your latest *suffix* I suppose!' he called out, grinning ferociously in Dan's face: 'your favourite word, do you remember?'

Horace Zagreus interposed himself quickly between them, like a hen-bird shielding her young.

'I'm in a very great hurry Francis: so I'm afraid I must leave you now. That's your direction, Francis, isn't it?' he said, taking his hand, and holding his old friend firmly before him, with the grip of a blacksmith.

'Yes. But aren't you going to ask to see me?'

'Ask to see you?'

'Yes. Don't you want to meet me?'

'What do you mean Francis?'

'You understand I think Horace. Don't you remember—?'

Throwing a depth of insulting sly sex-appeal into the strengthless eyes and shapeless pipe-sucking lips, beneath the harsh faded ginger stubble, Francis squeezed the athletic hand with his fleshy fingers.

'Well goodbye!' Horace exclaimed hastily.

'Is that all?'

As a ghostly reminder of the old days were a pair of spotless white spats.

'Run away Francis, like a good boy!' said Horace firmly as he turned away, while, strong in the emanations of the unhealthy days of long-ago, the old companion's claim to recognition for things dead and gone, thrust on him its cruel caricature.

Rejoining Boleyn, Horace Zagreus swept away at a gallop. Once he turned his head: he discerned the mean genteel figure of Francis Dallas (his legs straddled in a middle-class, a middle-aged, jauntiness, in white spats and exotic sub-tropical wide-awake, a pseudo-topee) looking after him, standing at the spot at which he had left him.

For some time he said nothing to Daniel, hurrying him forward at breakneck speed.

'That is an awful man!' at last he remarked.

He thrust his hand roughly for the third time into his breast-pocket: he drew out the sealed envelope. Daniel Boleyn, striding beside him, watched his actions with anguish. Holding the heavy yellow envelope before him he seemed to be acquainting himself with its weight, while with his wide abstracted eye he dangled, in the air, pros against cons. After that, in a very measured way, he replaced it in his pocket. Dan turned his head away, flushing angrily and biting his lips.

They had been nearing one of the principal gates of the Park. As they reached it Mr Zagreus stopped. He stood in front of Dan, in the full frowning splendour of his handsome presence, one hand, thrust under his jacket, caught stiffly on his slender hip.

'Dan, the unexpected encounter with that disgusting person has thoroughly upset me. So goodbye. I will write to you!'

Turning upon his heel, he left Daniel Boleyn at the Park gate, staring after him open-mouthed, with twitching lips.

In the remote distance two white specks were visible. They were the spats of Francis, who still was standing upon the empty pavement, where he had been said goodbye to.

For at least five minutes Daniel stood by the gate of Hyde Park at which he had been left. Horace Zagreus had long since disappeared, into one of the many openings of streets that led away from the precincts of the Park. At length he turned, and entered the gates.

It was a Saturday afternoon. A considerable number of couples, of boys with their girls, were stretched upon the grass, the faces glued together. Daniel Boleyn stepped out upon the dirty field of grass, and advanced aimlessly among these swooning pairs, who lay quite still, as though struck dead, locked in a public preliminary to hymen. Coming upon an unoccupied space, he flung himself down upon the ground, and, burying his face in an arm despairingly thrown up, he burst into tears.

'His latest suffix – his latest suffix!' he lisped and blubbed at once, without thought or meaning, with misery undisguised – all among the frankly clipped and lip-locked sonny-boys and honey-sticks.

[illegible] of the little [illegible] Daniel [illegible] with a [illegible] turned with [illegible] in the air, [illegible] against him. [illegible] replaced [illegible] This [illegible]

[illegible]

[illegible]

[illegible]

[illegible]

It was a [illegible] afternoon. A [illegible] were [illegible] Daniel [illegible] of grass, and [illegible]

[illegible]

Part 2

THE VIRGIN

MATTHEW PLUNKETT picked up the thing, that was a round pale shell. The table was strewn with stones and shells upon a sand-buff napkin of cotton. Does shell-making express a primitive mode of excretion? Or not? He swung his head up. The impressive displacement (on the pattern of the heavy uprising from the pond-foam of the skull of a seal, with Old-Bill moustache, leaden with water, as exhibited at the Zoo) released the pinch of neck-flesh which had been wedged between the stud and shirt-band. With self-possession Matthew dropped his chin deftly again into its place. He fixed a large moody eye upon the shell. It was just a rotted punctured husk. Head lazily rolled to one side he considered it – with staring swimming eyes and moist pink muzzle, pulpily extended – plum locked in plum.

The clock struck in a tower in the damp air to his north, out of sight, in a square near Euston. Sighing Matthew lowered the shell down upon the table, swung at the end of a drooped, limp, swan-wristed hand. This white-jacketed ossature, playing the crane, deposited it softly until it rested flanked by two stones and a scallop. He rubbed his eyes – that was the hour to eat. It had struck.

He sighed and stood up.

Go I must!

Tempting to continue, the idle apprentice, among the twisted relics of little life – cartonnages of molluscs, an orchestra of whispering toy-trumpets, corkscrew-curls, stars and thimbles. In sympathy with the waves – detached from the glassy Evolution – it would be pleasant to grope keenly among a handful of old natural puzzles, a few scraps of a feast of reason of Eminent Victorian giants, along with for his proper count a floating notion or two, of the dejected present. But no it is a case of *Go I must!* – go he must now where he would find his midday snack, washed down with a Pilsner (to be said with a blink, nasally as well, as though you had a cold) for companionship.

Generally Betty came just before three. But it had been sometimes earlier: return he must. He yaw-yaw-yawned with the blank bellow of the great felines, behind their bars at the scheduled feeding-hour (smelling the slaughtered meat for their consumption and sighting the figures of the keepers, moving to be their waiters, at their public table d'hôte, watched by herds of blanched apes, who had confined them) he roared – disparting and shutting his jaws, licking his lips, baying and, with his teeth, grinding, then again baying, while he stretched the elastic of his muscles elevating his arms with clenched fists, in heavy reproduction of the plastic of the Greek. Then he carried one of his exhausted hands to his head, and scratched it, between two sandy bushes, somewhat sun-bleached.

Next the dummy-beach, the shell-sprinkled buff napkin of the table, and short of his second, and third, work-benches (which bore jolly retorts, a Wimshurst Machine, contraptions that could be heirlooms inherited from Boyle, the gas-king of the history of physics, bottles and a saw) there was a space, in which he vaguely moved with hesitation for a time. The medium-sized-boy's clumsy body, of the elderly-looking student in untidy tweeds, got simply lost, in the centre of his room.

'He who hesitates is lost!' Betty's favourite words of doom rang in his ears however. He grasped together manfully his dispersed volition. He must not be late, she would not tarry, not she the wench! He pushed forward obedient to the shop-girl catch-word, towards the exit. With a heavy-weight, certainly fifteen-stone, gesture, he at once wrenched it open, reshutting it behind him with a frank angry bang.

Frowning he planted his feet with burly resolution upon the planks of the landing and the scrap of mat and stamped as he descended, tugging at the banister-rails like a muscular harpist and clearing his throat, bucolically. There was a great muscular insistence upon the *heel*, in his tread, the door passed, and the unmistakable brutal presence of shoe-irons. A live man and no mistake was upon the stairs! He trod them as a cock treads its hen-folk but more so. The down-trodden public floor-boards squeaked and clucked.

The Bloomsbury square with its museum of much-etched,

and then untidily painted, victorian trees, untidily posing, sluttish and sly, came to life (at Matthew Plunkett's emergence as he stepped boldly out) with a terrible explosion, between the wheels of a Shell-van full of petrol-tins, nosing its way round the railings. Vans simply farted and passed on he thought, as he jumped up a little, as though he were shot, and his pulse clanged in his heart, upon the second step. SHELL IS SO DIFFERENT!

He glanced up at the plaque for Hazlitt on Number Twenty-Nine – beneath which broken-hearted milkmen, with love quite dismayed, still yodelled hours before the last phantoms of the century-before-last of Enlightenment, and of Illumination, were up at all. Meanwhile a cat would make its way from the basement of the Stephen Skenes' towards the area of some Clives (even the cats were catty, in this Catfish Row of the victorian hinterland) where it considered the milk might be pushed over or, if not, tampered with by an intelligent domesticated Tom – since the Clives rose late, breakfasting generally at noon, so the deposits left by the representatives of the several trades, by appointment, to these shabby Bloomsbury potentates, were in the habit of collecting – for they were as a rule rich middle-aged sluggish students and dispensed with chars. 'Young Woodley' who lived in a small room, shared by two monogamous male ménages, came out at six in shorts and sandals to run round the Zoo, but he was an exception and not allowed to touch the milk, although he charred for both – he went back to bed, from which they liked to pull him when they rose, with a hollow spank – *Aschenkottel* that he was! – or *Va donc!* as Bulwer Bell would frenchily splutter, or *Fi donc: fainéant!* – as he approached him in his brocaded dressing-gown, with his little cane. But now the last milkman of this auroral ballet had long yodelled himself out of the square. It had struck one, in the tower at Euston. Roger Bulwer had breakfasted and taken in his victorian wig of a long haired 'great man' from the window-sill, as a signal to Bloomsbury: the circus was awake.

Coming out into the public-air, Matthew examined fiercely that physical image, heavy with calf-love, that was his favourite photograph of himself in his mental album. Before it disappeared the lovesick face grew appreciably infantile, from freudian calf-love to Songs of Innocence of Blake being but a step, and it took it before the axe fell.

Head-on Matthew collided with incomplete surprise with the railings: he might *never* learn to get round that corner – it was the curb. That was inhumanly lofty, whereas the boots used to scale it were outsize, although his feet were much smaller, in fact standard-average, so he was that is to say too small for his boots. But it was a short-cut, every advantage must be taken of the accidents of the terrain, time pressed. It would be a serious matter if Betty – in short, he must be there and not allow her – in effect!

In case the Stephen Skenes were looking, Matthew thrust his hands brutally into his trouser-pockets and assumed an expression of aggressive imbecility, half scowling tramp-comedian, half baby-boy. It was a rhythmic tramp-tramp-tramp, with every third step or so a stumble, that took him to the end of the square. As he passed beneath the windows of the Skenes he loudly smacked his lips, as he thought of course of the Pilsner, hoping it was cold. Without manufactured ice my word (now there was no real ice any longer) what a different place the world would be! Matthew turned the corner into Biddenden Street without raising his head, stumbling for form's sake. He was stopped by a tall and loitering figure, that of Dan.

*

To be always so affected by this shape of *Dante-young* – forever rising up in his path without notice like a black ghost – he recognized that his limbs had shaken like a lover's though for a twelvemonth he had got over it fortunately: but he had been quite unprepared.

With a huffy heave of the bowed studious shoulders Matthew came to rest. There was nothing for it, stop he must. He sent over a preliminary glance of disgust. That tall composure, all-too-well known, it was indecent – as though really one had nothing better to do than to be at the beck and call of Boleyn, when one must without fail get back – there must be no muddle not this time! – and probably he wanted to be taken back and talked to – it looked like it, or he was expecting Matthew to go somewhere it was quite likely – well (thinking of Betty, using her dialect) he was *unlucky!*

He turned up a hostile face to Dan.

'Hullo Dan!'

'Hullo.'

That was it: 'hullo' – that's all. Thought as much!

Daniel Boleyn looked at the pavement and blushed. Oh god, would he never stop blushing – even if he was only nineteen! Give him the slip, it was the only way – must positively be *brutal*, it was no use – make him see it was most inconvenient.

'What's brought you over here, I thought you were in Ireland,' in his manner advertising loudly that the wish was own father to the thought and he wished Old Erin that had bred him had kept him.

Dan shook his head.

Andrew gazed at the tall melting glowing young debutante, fixed in a stock-still confusion, standing suffused with a hot maidenly bloom.

Had one come up (lout that one recognized one was) and dropped a brick – come out with a hearty spanking sex-epithet as an instance, of the real said-roundly, brawny and bollocky, brew – arriving foul-mouthed in the presence of this beastly virgin – with the savage hiccup bred of a black Pilsner – then one would have understood! One would have apologized. One would have been in the wrong. One would have felt sorry. One would have blushed too!

With the manliest possible directness he squared up to the hundred-per-cent adolescent blushing sphinx, towering in front of him foot on foot. In vain: for veiled and silent it stood impassibly where it had stopped, beyond question in no hurry, to move, or to answer.

God god! (blasphemous Bloomsbury he cried) in a passion of dark prayer, as he awaited the pleasure of this obstacle in his path. He did nothing but glare over, biting his lips, at this downcast madonna-face, sensitively pained lips, blushing cheeks.

Almighty heavenly Papa *shatter* this virgin – Oh Merciful Destroyer as well as Cruel Creator! Oh for a *real* common or garden brick and no nonsense, to pick up and hurl at it, and smash it outright himself, if God hesitated to deal in that way with one of His precious creations.

Dan would never look up, he would not he knew that for certain, there was no chance at all – he would stare down forever if necessary, with his beastly blush confound him, it was hopeless!

'Will you come up for a moment?' Matthew asked in a tone of the most heavily-taxed restraint – he could see nothing for it but that, so he supposed they must after all go up, he made his voice convey, and was silent.

After a moment he spoke again.

'I am extremely sorry but I have to go somewhere, I must not be late. It is essential.'

Dan did not move.

The mystery of a huge body not yet born or thought of when he was a student of twenty drove him into a sullen frowning, counting on his fingers the stupid summers, more or less – up and down. The prestige of the 'under-twenties' was too great by half for him, he never would be able to say 'bo' to an Under-Twenty, however large his boots, he knew – not with enough conviction, or without stammering, to be noticed, his training had too strong a hold – but with the worst grace in the world he growled out:

'Well let us go back for a moment, won't you? I am sure you must have a great deal to tell me.'

There was a spell in which the two, vis-à-vis, stood both staring hard at the pavement – this was the most ticklish passage of all, where tempers are generally lost, Matthew kept a very tight hold on himself.

'I don't want to come up.'

Dan's voice was low, of course, strangled with emotion.

'No? It's just as you like.'

Vicious and cross was no longer what Matthew was – this was awful! – he was beside himself out and out. Technically a smile it was, since the teeth were visible and the eyes in a blaze of derision affected to laughter, as a dark half-cousin, with which promptly he proceeded to contemplate the blushing virgin colossus – but it was frankly hideous, like painted masks of battle.

He would not give him his eyes – not he! the contemptible little sneak – to do battle with his bucolic pair, of true fighting blue – he would hang his head till doomsday, rather than face the music of those masterful glances that would tell him soon enough the sort of figure that he cut, in one pair of eyes, at all events.

Word for word too if you please – he 'had not wanted', thank you all the same! – word for word – this precious *sainte nitouche* – it's all the young oaf had learnt to say! A year ago – then some meaning might possibly have attached. (Matthew recalled the occasion.) As dead as mutton was his love beyond recall: that would not wash today! Also (Matthew flattened the plum-lips, into the ruthless-cruel line of an old bulldog-sultan's – supplicated by a discarded odalisk, desiring to be taken back) – a year had not improved Dan's appearance!

Betty, ever-present maternal form, though so slight beside the masculine vastness beneath his eyes, bore down upon him at this point – he witnessed, in anguished fancy, her self-possessed arrival at his house-door, but he not there to receive her: he had been prevented from getting back by Dan. It would be fatal – Zulu Blades forever on the sharp look-out. The door upon the second floor opened, Zulu stood there – where he lay in wait, generally, behind it. Betty hesitated – *then she passed in!* He saw it all.

Shaking roughly the vault of his bookworm shoulders, of the studious-husky, Matthew took one heavy striding step. At the same time he remarked with great force out of his twisted mouth in profile, by way of farewell,

'I'm sorry I'm afraid I must go!'

Dan looked half-up, with a gesture of alarm or surprise.

Matthew stopped. Dan moved round a few degrees towards him.

'Well' very roughly indeed, with a surly jerk, 'would you like to come up?'

Assent was indicated very simply by Dan, in instantaneous action – by stepping namely with great promptness past Matthew, making without more ado for the corner, and turning briskly into the square.

'Unspeakable beast! This is too much!' It was the speech

of the speechless-with-indignation. Purple with elderly passion (in an impromptu imitation of his father at the height of the old monkey's extremest rage) with the salute of a fellow-flush but of rage under-hatches, he threw himself bodily about: with Dan a pace ahead, they went down the square, over the ground just laboriously covered, on the outward journey, in a rapid procession, towards his house-door. He was upon Dan's heel all the way – halting, with the bucolic inhibition cramping his style to prevent him from drawing abreast. Dan strode with the stiff gait of a bearskinned Palace sentry, went straight to his objective without looking back – the house-door namely of Matthew, with *Plunkett* on a piece of paper, fastened with two drawing-pins – where he stopped dead, drawn up rigid, heels together at the attention, presenting buttocks in good order to the street.

The little foot in Matthew's clodhopper tingled, the toes clenched with rage. They ached to drive good yeoman shoe-leather against Dan's trouser-seat. Coming up roughly upon the door-step, a key-bunch torn from a hip pocket, this robot had to be man-handled – he was pushed aside – even to get at the lock at all. Matthew let him in. Straight as a die, head high, he passed plumb into the opening.

They thundered together up the staircase – Matthew's ascent threatened every board in the building, but Dan leapt up from step to step sometimes missing one, and the romantic stairway shook. It was no good, the boards were pre-Palmerston: he would trample this Bloomsbury house down finally – really he was against it, no Bloomsbury at heart, he would break it up with his tolstoian heels – long live the simple workman!

On the third floor a person of very mixed race, and probably low and confused antecedents, came out of a room, in his Summit shirt-sleeves – he was smiling slightly. This was Zulu Blades. Silently he observed the pair of them. Dan's host-in-spite-of-himself's look of black annoyance became a grin of insane hate.

Dan went in swiftly, upon the turning of the handle. Matthew followed and flung-to the heavy panelled door, with a formidable crash. All the little shells danced to see such sport upon the napkin of cotton, as also the neglected laboratory furniture.

Now for a confrontation at least, his blood was up as never before: he turned towering with rage bluntly upon his young visitor.

'You ungrateful little beast you!' he panted up at him, very purple, in a strong vixenish shriek 'can't you see – must you always be so beastly selfish! You treat me like a paper-bag – you wanted – I won't stand for it! Find somebody else! It's not for nothing – ! If I *did* starve myself for a fortnight to buy you a great-coat you needed and a suit of pyjamas because you told me at night out of poverty you went naked in bed' (he stopped to laugh bitterly – a hard laugh). 'Pyjamas!' (He gave a sneering snort over the night-suit that was chocolate, with vivid spots of geranium). 'I'd see you damned first before I did it – I'm through with you – I suppose you think – there's nothing like having a good opinion of yourself. I don't love you a fraction of! You're nothing but a little cheap beast – there's no occasion for you to smile – I didn't ask you to come! You poison the air of this room, the sooner you hop it the better as far as I'm concerned – why did I bring you up! *I wish I hadn't now!*' (in a dashing luscious lisp he spat in hot singsong complaint). 'You've grown particularly ugly as well let me tell you in case you've overlooked it – I thought I better put you wise on that not unimportant point – as you evidently haven't remarked it yourself!' (a scoffed sneer was aimed at the whole six-foot of melting adolescence). 'Your face has appreciably coarsened – it's a puzzle to me where my eyes were, in my head, what one could ever have seen in! I fail to – really – no! It certainly can't have been your *intelligence*!' Winding up out of breath Matthew snorted. He leant upon the work-table, his shoulders doubly bowed, as if with a double burden, coughing.

Dan was before the door, not moving a muscle, he stood erect, chin-out, palms on thigh-sides, as if attending the super-prussian commando. But his eyes were in the corner of the tin-soldier head, on the opposite side to that of his fiendish friend, startled and averted.

The host's eyes turned away, affecting rapid loss of interest, as he coughed.

Then, with a gulp, back shot the head, armed to the teeth, fanged for the attack.

'I *hate* you! I detest you! I abominate you!' it spat – plump plump, plump the enraged feuilletonist, of the lowbrow-highbrow purple-passion, dropped his *hates*, bomb by bomb – spitting over his work-table at his towering ex-would-be-mistress, drawn up before his door: and the pseudo-sentry instinctively raised his hand to ward off this cowardly bombardment as best he might.

'You may laugh!' hissed Matthew fleshing him with a white eye.

'Are you mad Matthew!' Dan whispered. 'I am not laughing! Can't you see!'

'I don't care if you are!' Matthew shouted in savage devil-may-care, jauntily and as was to be expected turned on his heel.

'This is too awful!' whispered in still fainter accents Dan from the doorway, the lower of his rose-red grecian lips alone slightly moving, to compose the tremulous whisper. The sentry manifested signs distinctly of an unstarching, as the hot shafts went home (attacked on duty), though still making the most of his stature, his eyes still strictly averted, in a permanent Eyes-right. But Matthew flung himself about in a trice, teeth-bared, as he heard it.

'Awful. What? You're right, it is, *awful* it – you are – and I'm glad you know it. At last. Thank god! You disgusting little cry-baby!'

A muscular spasm was set up about a group of ribs, upon his left side, and his eyes swam with a sickly dizziness, and Matthew sat down hastily. Clutching at his heart, his eyes frowned upon the floor-boards – he sat still.

Dan the sentry went to pieces (although he had not turned his head) in sympathy with his superior. In sympathy he turned his back, looking at a print of a galaxy of Victorian boxers, surrounded by tophatted patrons of the game, pinned beyond the door. As there was no sound, after a long pause Dan continued to revolve, and was shortly with pained dreaminess facing Matthew, but not point-blank – with a respectful dreamy obliquity. He gazed half-down upon the invalid posture of his host, with a look equally compounded of surprise and compassion.

'Do you feel ill Matthew?' Dan whispered, hazarding a gentle approach, under the circumstances.

He stepped softly forward, though a little sideways, looking across the work-table at the asbestos of the gas-stove.

'Can I do anything Matthew?'

Without raising his eyes Matthew waved him away, exclaiming – the rough male struck-down but unwilling to be pitied by wifey:

'Nothing except you can take yourself off as soon as you like!'

Pain at this unkind rebuff left its mark upon the face of Dan.

A manner of expectant rigour a little electrified the limp trunk, sunk in nervous overthrow beside the table. Matthew held his breath. He rolled an expectant eye. Then with an abrupt tremor from stem to stern, he was delivered of a large dull hiccup, worthy of a better man.

Immediately he straightened himself in the chair, the face cleared, he rose briskly. He stamped over to the window, with the archaic gait of Gaffer Giles. The window was overthrown and forced down, with the utmost brutality, quivering and banging it fell. He stepped back frowning from it, as a man might who had just put a steer upon its back, in one jolly jujitsu of cattle-raising fists, red in the gills but with a brow still pallid.

The lips advanced, in a threat to flower, alluringly bud-bursting, he quitted the window. He turned about in the room, a bull in its own china-shop, passing in burly bafflement from spot to spot, questing after something mislaid (only the nature of which he had forgotten) with abrupt animal actions, of pseudo-rooting and scratching.

'*Matthew!*'

A voice fluted, low in the scale, in supplication and melted the silence – in that part of it near the instrument of the lips though elsewhere it was as though he had not spoken.

'Oh are you still there?'

A whisper, 'Yes.'

The humble beauty was still at the table-side; occasionally he wafted a glance of the most pensive casual reproach in the direction of the restlessly-moving Matthew.

'Have you anything to say by chance?' Matthew asked, turning his head towards his visitor, but sending his eyes down slantwise beneath the table, where was Dan's neat black leather extremity. Dan of course had nothing whatever to say.

'You must have come up for *something!*'

No: Dan took up a book and turned it over upon its back as gently as Matthew had thrown down the window harshly.

The clock, in the tower at Euston, struck the half-hour.

'I can stop here no longer!' Matthew exclaimed in the midst of the chime in a raging voice.

'I have something to ask you!' Dan shyly muttered, picking up the book and still more softly reversing it.

'What is it?' snapped Matthew who had passed into Old-Man Plunkett whom he took after, out of fatigue. His fingers pressed the back of a sheet of stout foolscap. His attention was aroused. Lifting it up he brought to light a miniature pencil mounted in gun-metal. It was the object that had been hiding so it was the end of the chase. At the foot of the foolscap sheet he wrote, in large infant-script:

'Back almost at once. Matthew.'

This he tore off, three square inches of paper.

'Well?'

Dan had his hand upon the bedroom door. A rather brighter look had come into his face and, in speaking, with the faintest possible smile he looked towards Matthew.

'May – I leave the room!'

The hush of the class-room, following a *Please Sir!* bracketed with some super-simplicity, fell on them in minute-long eclipse, while Dan, blushing and incontinent, fingered the door-handle.

Old Man Plunkett positively skipped with rage, as far as his junior's massive footwear permitted, in the impersonation.

'Leave the room – no you may not!' he thundered from the window, glaring across the littered tables.

The young puppy was going too far for Old Man Plunkett, what next!

'Is it out of the question?' asked Dan faintly.

Matthew glared speechless across at him for a weighty instant, taken aback, almost parting from his parent in the fever of the novel emotion.

'Yes!'

Matthew's voice was quite quiet and short, he kept a puzzled wary eye flashing up.

Dan dropped his hand off the handle, and withdrew from the neighbourhood of the bedroom-door. With head bowed, with a guilty expression, representative of a beaten hound, tail tucked between its slinking hind-quarters, he went.

'I thought you had something to ask me?'

The voice now used by Matthew was almost casual.

Dan took up his wide-brimmed hat and revolved it sun-wise turning with sheepish looks, upon his stomach, picking with his finger-nails at the hatter's stitches.

Matthew watched him beneath discoloured brows, the flush spreading from the gills upward. Two plumes of grizzled-blond whiskered his cheek-bones, in front of the ears, and, above, the sandy curliness suggested in picturesque wildness the restless scratching fingers of the student.

'Well!'

'Well' said Dan suddenly 'I know you don't care but I am *so terribly unhappy!*'

Dan's mouth began to give way, in an alarming wobble, whereas at the same time his wide-open eyes of nigger-brown took on a shade of moister velvet.

'What is it now?' Matthew demanded, in sullen tones of the male confronted with the extremities of the feminine nature.

The meat-red surfaces of the lips of the disturbing visitor continued to quake. The eyes shone with an illumination that the host recognized immediately as that of love, in a word. There was such a hush in the room as preceded the first howl of the unchained elements.

'Unhappy!' blustered Matthew. (How we men are at a disadvantage, when the fair sex get steam up with the water-cart my word!)

Dan drove his teeth into the quivering jelly of his lips.

'What is the cause, if I may ask?' Matthew sneered over at his guest.

A stormy pallor gained the whole of Dan's countenance. The howl broke from him as he flung himself upon the nearest work-bench bodily, rocking the Wimshurst Machine as he fell and sending flying a bottle of Nitrate of Soda, labelled Phosphate of Lime. The hellenic patent of nasal perfection, the flawless nose of him, flattened itself to nigger squabness, upon the boards of the work-bench, while his arm that was flattened as well went entirely about the dark curled head, a muscular belt fitting the skull. The youthful prowess-promising shoulders heaved slowly: the lips in a prolonged wail gave forth, upon the first volume of escaping wind, the sound 'Zag', and upon the second the more continuous complaint of 'rooooooce!'

'What's that, Zag-rooce!? What! you mean to tell me' Matthew screamed 'that you actually came here in order to inform me of *that*! It was for that that you have made me miss my – you have upset my plans – really! – to be your confidante – Horace Zagreus too no really – and you come here and throw yourself about my room – you have broken my bottle! can't you see what you've done! Pick it up! I'll make you pay! – This is too much! get off my work-table! Do you hear? Take your nose out of my test-tubes at once you great selfish oaf – you noisy ox – you little beast you! This is positively the last time you put your nose inside this place on any pretext. I'll give Mrs Cochrane orders to say I'm not at home – I shall be out – do you hear? I wish they'd keep you in Dublin! I shall write to Stephen!'

Stephen Boleyn his Dublin cousin should hear from him about this son of his, he would certainly write to Stephen, in Dublin, and tell him to keep his precious offspring a little more at home, or find him suitable work, or send him to a colony for a little while, to make a man of him with a little cow-punching, or tea-planting or gand-dancing – if he did not – he would warn him – there would be the devil to pay, he would say nothing more. But have him up in his rooms he would not! He might be a relation – and he did feel responsible for him while he was there: but he was not his beastly nanny. He would not tolerate such a domestic burden as this, it should not in any case be at large – if Stephen couldn't afford to keep it – and that was probably why he was here – he should be frank about it. Out of sight out of mind. Probably Stephen thought once out of Ireland it could shift for itself and whore its way round Europe for all he cared, bad luck to him – so long as *he* was left in peace! That was all very well. He should not have had children, if he was not prepared.

He would write and tell him so too. In any case he would not play the father to this waif and stray, he must go and howl himself into someone else's good graces! Perhaps old Horace would keep him, that might be the solution but have him round there at all hours of the day and night he would not – he was frankly sick of the sight.

Matthew moved crossly hither and thither, in quest of something or other, whatever it was, he did not care, ruminating the most striking phrases in the cross letter to Stephen: he found his hat, where it had fallen beneath a table. It was that. He put it on his head. Dan remained, the better half of his body shored up on the central work-bench, occasionally shattered by a sob. Matthew, hat on head, the slip of paper with the message grasped in his hand, stood over him in passing, gazing down with the robustest contempt.

'Well are you going?' he asked at last.

Dan shook all over but said nothing.

'I am going now!' said the host very roughly to the back of the dejected head of profuse black curls. 'But I shall be back in half an hour and I want this room! I shall expect you to have left it by then – I hope you hear me. And don't come back!'

At these pile-driven words of harsh dismissal the figure upon the table shook from head to foot. Matthew made his way with an unnecessary degree of noise to his door, and as Dan heard him reach it he wrenched up his head, in wild-eyed forlorn appeal.

'Matthew!' he called out, in a most moving voice of last-hour entreaty.

Putting his head again into the room, Matthew watched him for a moment, with cruellest scrutiny, as if he had been a big shell, imported for research.

'What?'

'I did not mean to offend you' Dan with difficulty remarked, brushing the tears from his cheeks, 'by mentioning Zagreus – I am sorry Matthew! Why are you all so unkind! Zagreus *hates* me – *hates* me!'

He howled out *hates me* and flung himself back even more violently than before, upon the work-bench, with a childish roar of involuntary complaint.

'I shall expect you to be out of here by the time I get back!' Matthew shouted into the room. 'Can you hear? Wipe your eyes and go home. You can have a good cry there. This is not your home, it is not the place to do that in! – Also pick up my bottle do you mind? I shall send in a bill to your father for anything you break.'

He slammed the door behind him, leaving Dan in the same position.

*

The Camden Distillery met him before he had been out long, there it was, he had been composing his letter to Stephen, frowning and slouching his way hurriedly along to the Distillery. He drew up – the great pub was across the road, apart from the baptist chapel, at the Mews corner, where its lavatories ran back under the whitewashed arch, up to the first motor lock-ups. Lightly like a gas-balloon his mind had brought him there through the clouds, and he stood smacking a wet beer-drinking lip, as he grasped the situation, come to earth, with a cough.

Standing upon the edge of the pavement, blinking over at the Distillery, the traffic did not stop. He looked up west to see how much there was to come. But there was a sharp explosion. That van again! Like a bad penny, cracking off as it went, the thing had turned up. It had rushed past him with its bomb. SHELL IS SO DIFFERENT! He grinned after it, it was a thing that was a music-hall turn, the clown-van. He and the clown-van played peep-bo in Bloomsbury, each had a distinct rôle who could doubt. The thing had recognized him immediately: it went petarding into the next street, tail up. What a van!

*

Within the Distillery he was driven sideways by the lunch-hour rush. It came in behind him – it was One. The place was, yes, *to capacity* – he would be drowned if he did not swim in the swirl of these fluid bodies. Above the herd of shoulders he looked over at his regular place. That was near the street-entrance but there was a long glass-passage. He lowered his head. With eyes averted from the nearest body, he thrust it aside and advanced. Outsize boots to the fore, his hands feeling biggish and capable, he started rush-tactics. He dealt similarly with the next body. It jumped as if in protest but melted away when firmly attacked. Beyond that with all those fixed between him and that position, at Violet's end, he fought, under cover of the stampede, as he had with number one. He bored a path.

The ground regained, along the side of the glass-passage, he entered by main force the rank of drinkers, wedged in a half-circle of perhaps fifty units about the central counter.

To get himself seen through the port-hole of cut-glass swung upon a pivot, he bent, moving the revolving shutter with his handy manly jaw. His arms were pinned to his sides. Within, the strapping staff of tapsters, trousered and skirted, but all athletic, plunged up and down. They worked at a great pitch of intense business – politely cannoning with their loaded trays: parts of each came and went as he blinked sheepishly but keenly in. Hundreds of throats competed, there were those that signalled, some broke into laughter, or chaff, on all hands. In a circle of swarming bars, from the Saloon to the Bottles and Jugs, this latter-day London beer-hall had the beefy roar of a bear-pit. A spittoon for a footstool, Matthew had one foot lifted, the other stood in black malt-wet sawdust.

Softly he called 'Violet' into the peep-hole. Violet's flying hams, the headlong stomach he spotted as hers, were visible, as she charged down the bar with a Baby Polly a Black and White and two Watneys, but followed and crossed by the elastic centres of colleagues.

He bellowed at the hole with a frowning smirk: 'Virelett!'

At his side a man started. He could feel the next body turning upon him. As part of the same system his own trunk revolved, as well, a little. A breath of Cheddar and rank Bitter fanned the chest and chin of Matthew. An eye of point-blank animal scrutiny came to life at the side of his head, with the smell of the Cheddar, looking hard at his tell-tale mutton-chops; with difficulty it ascended, in raw amazement, to his dove-grey slouch-hat. It dragged itself all over Matthew's face, backwards and forwards, the fishy slug – he felt its dampness.

There was another turn of the screw. He allowed himself to

be revolved half-left, until a magnified jaw, upon the opposite side, came into action, a half-inch from his profile. As the teeth shattered a luncheon-biscuit, a mild cerulean eye was dragged open by the rumination, into a startled cow's sidelong stare, and slid shut.

Still eyed up and down by a face nearer than was nice or at all human, where to be a man was to be distant, as is usually the case, he mused down upon the counter at a sprig of mustard and cress, and at an embossed sheet of water, the splashings of a jug. He buried a smirk from the intrusive eye to the right. It must throw a pale disk of light, no doubt, upon his neck.

At last it had enough! There was an abrupt movement, the body could be felt revolving back. He went back with it. They were as-you-were.

The publican's plastron, and gold hunter clock-cable, were featured in the cut-glass and mahogany gap.

'What's it for you sir? Is anyone attending to you?'

To get in touch better the man bent down and showed a brown jewish eye and fat eyelid.

Matthew blinked into the opening twice. The publican could see his lips. He thrust them out: he blurted faintly:

'A P-p-pilsner!' The nasal stammer, modelled upon the effects of a severe catarrh, melted in the hubbub.

'Sir?'

Matthew cleared his throat, he blinked with the deeper and more owlish ceremony of the regulation shyness. Violently in his direction the massive right-hand cog began to revolve. He stuttered faintly in panic at the publican's decorated belly, the timepiece massively anchored in its embonpoint:

'A P-p-pilsner!'

He grew red. He was being geared round by his absconding neighbour, independent of his will. But now he was threatened with complete reversal. Settling down into his trusty stogies, he seized the counter-edge with both fists. He was able to arrest the movement. In stricken emphasis of his lips' fastidious percussion, as if with a deadly cold in the head, he bellowed into the bar:

'Pilsner – a pilsner please!'

'A Lager Beer? A Lager Beer here Miss!'

A great strain was put upon his wrists. The body to the right was resolved to go, it was a serious moment, his bull-dog grit was at the breaking-point.

'Sorry old man! It ain't 'arf a tight fit. Blokes like you and me takes up a tidy bit of room, don't we mister? What, did I tread – ? *I'm* sorry old man!'

'Not at all! There's nothing like leather.'

'Ah you're right.'

The man began violently turning back.

'Are you returning?' stuttered Matthew.

'I don't seem to be able to drag myself away does I old sport, not from you!'

He seized a pipe upon the counter. He again proceeded to revolve, in the direction for departure. He placed a boot squarely upon one of Matthew's.

'Was that you again old man? *I'm* sorry.'

'Not a bit.'

'We're a couple of outsizes down below I reckon.'

'We seem to be.'

'Well cheery ho – sorry I can't stop and all that.'

'The pleasure is mine' Matthew sneered: he let go of the counter.

'Gently does it!' said the man.

That body went, a much smaller one was substituted: Matthew turned completely about, for the final evacuation.

Matthew felt forty round the chest, his neck had a pugilist's amplitude, in his heroic footwear the puny toes puffed themselves out with grown-up pride, and on the return journey the toe-cap, out of control, blundered into his neighbour. With a husky stutter he growled 'sorry,' a man amongst men, and cleared his throat with gusto, hoicking deep down with the roughest there, and shooting at the spittoon.

As the bar came round again the Lager was present, and the centre of the body of Violet appeared between the counter and the shuttered partition. Her smile came down to signal and her eyes peered out.

'Good morning. Will that be all you require?'

'Ah Violet! Thank you' he swaggered gruffly, frowning. 'No. I want *two* – I want two ham-sandwiches if you don't mind

– two. And – Violet! – I want one shrimp – one portion. Shrimp! Portion!'

'Shrimp?'

'Shrimp – yes please.'

The British bar-shrimp was brought upon its finger of damp toast, from its circular glass-case.

'It's a fine day!' said Matthew, very bluff and surprised, to the Violet.

'Yes' Violet agreed 'if it only keeps fine!'

'That's it!' said he, examining a handful of silver as though the pieces had been cowrie-shells: he became absorbed and his eyes began staring and his mouth pouting – since always in order to think he returned to the wet milky pout, the vacant stare, of the teething infant.

'I hope it will' she remarked – 'softly' as she would say, tender and arch, to evoke the personality of an important sheik, standing by, helmeted in the gutter, with his quivering pillion.

'I hope so too' he insisted.

She was hit full in the buttock by a rushing body. She drew in her muscular hinny, and over her shoulder she discharged a scented simper that was both sensitive and sweet after the rushing body. In the dispatch of their respective duties bodies must, in the intemperance of the involuntary motions, genteelly collide, that being one of the laws of nature which ladylike bodies spent their time circumventing, alas with incomplete success.

Matthew raised a half-crown from his overflowing palm, and put it down upon the counter. Violet took it sweetly smiling, and made of the return of the change an action that seemed to remove all the filth from lucre.

Brutally Matthew chopped the shrimp and the finger of toast in two with one crash of his ivory-bristling jaw. The half that fell back into his mouth he swallowed. The half that remained in his fingers he regarded with astonishment. After a moment he pushed it into his mouth, and swallowed it, too. Raising the Pilsner heartily to the same place, his tongue laid down like a drugget for its reception, and so into the Red Lane, he washed down the bisected shrimp and its severed raft of damp toast.

The hand of the pub-clock, as he watched it, suddenly gave a convulsive jump. Abandoned as he had been to a mesmeric staring, when it jumped it hit his head up, and he started violently. Four minutes had elapsed. Hastily hashing up the rest of the sandwich, in bucolic crunching bites, he wolfed it swiftly down, pursued it with Pilsner, and smacked both lips heartily twice.

The luncheon-rush was already past, the glass passage was dark with departing people. Matthew looked round him apprehensively: his eyes returned to the clock. At that moment the heavy black sword that was its minute-hand leapt again: up it went, like the sword of a robot executioner, by inches, until it should get aloft to its maximum, when it would be two o'clock, when it would be ready to fall: and he had the disquieting mental pictures associated with the name of Zulu Blades. But Matthew hurriedly left the Distillery, before the sword of the minute-hand should have cut the number twelve in two.

*

Betty had not been there: the paper slip marked 'Betty' was still pinned beside the bell. Matthew sweating freely, after his return at top-speed, tore it off, and put his hand with it into his jacket-pocket.

In the hall he removed a letter from the box upon the door, separating it from two envelopes to the address of Zulu Blades. Both these were in pale blue papers, they scented the letter-box. He frowned and sneered, as he dropped them back.

Up the stairs, one at a time, he took his lusty amazon land-girl boots, his tired little trotters as red as lobsters, in their monster cases, after the recent gallops. During the ascent he beguiled the time with topical reflections. In the main they were concerned with Zulu Blades. The man's enterprising nature gave Matthew no peace day or night – Blades was the 'black beast', an evil neighbour: what with his upstart disrespect as well for his metropolitan betters, since he had brought the hearty habit of the african out-stations into their midst, here. His skill with women was natural, it was true he roped them in like steers, he must be working off ten years' solitary confinement in the Veldt.

A fruity laugh broke apropos from a feminine throat just as Matthew passed that dangerous door upon the left – they all went in by that one, and they came out by the other. Betty's voice had not that volcanic sound, rich and stomachy, but he walked on tiptoe. A second lusher wallop of laughter – the peculiar women the fellow roped in – a third broke and stopped – no doubt she was kissed by Zulu at that minute, so that accounted. The disgusting beast had been telling her one of his fruity yarns as usual which made them so noisy – if only he would change his methods – or tickling her armpits – nothing if not primitive. Sometimes they laughed till they wetted themselves: they probably found the stories remarkably funny but he didn't. Dirty colonial – they're all the same! Orestrylians, Africanders, Kanucks – what an empire!

He passed the second-floor doors slowly, his ears pricked: as he withdrew upwards towards his garret-suite, he heard a rushing and pig-squeaking from a different quarter of Blades' flat – doubtless the sleeping apartment, he'd got her on the run and she'd gone in there: the obscene quadroon or whatever he was, was in pursuit, from room to room he was hot on the scent the great hearty short-winded sheik – the fat beast's puffing could be heard or was it the hunted doe's? – I don't know. The fellow's hands were full for the time being, that was the main thing. – He slammed his door, in a manner that should convey his annoyance, charged with contempt: and he stamped over their head for five minutes like a wild ass, hoping to put Zulu off his stroke.

After walking about noisily between his work-tables, Matthew sat gently down in the chair before the shells and began thinking of shell-making and excretion. At random he took up the shell of the pearly Nautilus. Then he surveyed the miniature landscape. He lay down on the beach, kicking his heels, it was a midsummer holiday, he was the callow schoolboy – today was a holiday. Fixing his eyes in big subaqueous Bloomsbury stare he soon was sufficiently mesmerized: they were directed upon the landscape, rather than upon the specimens.

This was a scene, for his intelligence, resembling a section of seaboard – for were there not shells and stones in considerable numbers and where are there shells except upon a coast? – a scientific landscape, for the cliffs of books upon biology massed at the extremity of the table in stratifications were reminiscent of the geologic book-plate, and the fancied sheep – in his landscapes there were always some head of sheep, for preference at lambing-time – upon their polished summits: and in his mind's eye a victorian valley, beyond but occult (though none the less actual) behind the books, as that might be, trodden by bearded Guardsmen of Ouida, but in leggings and trappings of buck-rammed gamekeepers, a shot-gun tucked up under the hirsute arm-pit, on their way to the houses of the maidens, in the parsonages. – But aloft the metropolitan sky, contemporary (but for that none the more actual) arranged in indistinct cockades– like the vertex, the tops of the panaches, of a festal procession – traversed the speckled fog of the window-dust – the Bloomsbury room as well held everywhere these romantic deposits, dust was even in his hair and of course nostrils.

But upon the pane a cloud and an insect approached each other, travelling in that gloomy transparency of glass – protagonistic, powers of the earth and air: the latter was climbing and turning, the measured rapprochement was effected with a dizzy slipping, on the part of the animal. He observed these movements, awaiting frowning the collision, gazing into the mysterious shadow of Time, dark with 'events', examining this most proximate exemplar breathlessly, and stealthily, while he held neglected the shell in idle suspense above the other specimens. Then he replaced it quickly and took up a new one, without looking at it, though he was conscious of the movement of his fingers, like the legs of a crustacean.

Stealthily without stirring he withdrew his eyes from the cliffs of Old England, the volumes of biology; a shade of cunning entered the lowered face. He directed it upon the insect and the cumulus. The event was imminent, the cumulus had made head-way, and the insect, although it always came back, seemed moving its path in the direction of the cloud.

A violent ring, in the passage outside the door, brought him to his feet with staring eyes, and with burly strides he proceeded as quickly as he could outside. It was the finger of Betty that had touched the button. He disappeared through the open door and the insect merged with the cumulus upon the Bloomsbury pane.

*

Betty very much breezed in with bow-legged, bantam strut, welcoming herself with a matter-of-fact smile. She occupied the room, peeling off prettily her great coat, tessellated black and green, as she came through the door. Matthew followed upon her heels – musing and absent-minded, smirking to himself. He was the clownish Gudgeon of Regency prints, member of the silly sex – falling for a Petticoat. He took for granted the small visitor ahead of him; his eyes ran before him on the floor-boards, like two scuttling rats in leash, drawing him along, the fairy giant of a Bloomsbury pantomime.

Betty Bligh was short and slight, to the point of being the doll-woman. This was an all-puppet cast. In her features as well as in stature Miss Bligh was the four-foot-ten adult-tot in toto, stunted at the mark of her fifteenth summer, with ears and nose of a waxen smallness. No extrovert jaw-lines or dominant eye-glint whatever, that Matthew could detect. Betty's scale was propitious – he had taken the precaution to measure her, un-heeled, against his door-post. The mark was upon it, quite low down. *She satisfied the canon of the Analyst!*

Betty Bligh was the opposite of a big masculine sweetheart, and there was nothing outwardly real or discomforting. The flow of the libido from him to her would not be disturbed or frustrated by surplus escapes of imperfectly introverted libido in her. She was the woman of the magical prescription. The scale was O.K. The insects were fairies – it was only bulk that made the human world, and he must be a Gulliver in Lilliput. Frumpfsusan had spoken.

Scale was of the essence! All else being equal – the jewish witch-doctor's face had smiled broadly, naturally who wouldn't, as he had counselled – '*No overmatching.*'

'Scale my dear boy' Dr Frumpfsusan chose his words with understanding – the idea behind the *my child* of the catholic father in this Analytical confessional was not neglected: the doctor smiled serenely into the calf-like face, of puffed and faded english boyishness – he laid the flattering hand of eld upon the sensitive forearm (anything the witch-doctor did not know about flattering where the *age-complex* of a prosperous patient was in question, was material merely for the trash-bin, it was certain) 'scale my dear boy' Dr Frumpfsusan of Zurich had announced 'is too often disregarded by us. For successful extroversion you must dominate the scene – you must contrive a Lilliput. That is the first condition. For that truly uppish self-feeling, which you will find essential for a free flow of libido through the tap, you must *choose your friends small!*'

The imposing black-bearded Analyst had extended a mighty hand full of mental power at a certain level above the carpet of the consulting-room of the clinic: and it had been, as nearly as Matthew could compute, four-feet-ten-inches that he had sketched in the atmosphere. This (as measured by Matthew at her first visit) was exactly the height of Betty Bligh.

'It is of great importance my dear lad' (the subtle physician had proceeded on the soothing lines of Mother Siegel, with a rare magnetic eye worthy of what the Roman called *Chaldean*) 'believe me, *you cannot choose your lady-friend too small*. For you Matthew the woman must be well below the average height – else – !' There was a menace in the soft withdrawal as the physician gently turned away, as if from the spectacle of some disaster – if an average-sized woman that is were mistakenly employed!

Now Matthew he told him (the third party they had met there, the two detached intellects to dissect) was *a civilized man*. He was a modern man, *von diesem Zeitalter, nicht wahr?* – was it not on that account indeed that Matthew had sought his advice in the first instance and had the intensely original idea of submitting himself to Analysis, yes? But what was the diagnostic of the truly civilized person? 'To be prepared, was it not, to discuss himself, to have himself discussed, with a freedom quite staggering to the mind of the uneducated? The modern man whether of Bloomsbury Baltimore or Berlin has vanquished vanity – he offers himself to his own inspection as the worm he turns out to be. If he is vain at all, and it must be conceded that self-love is hard to kill, it is about his *humility*. His own *Vernichtung* is his greatest pride the laying bare of the nullity, the *Nichtigkeit*, that is the 'self' at the heart of energy (which is merely the doctrine of Xt that '*he who humbleth himself shall be exalted*'! Be modest, protest you are *nobody*, a biological bagatelle and hi presto! you will get top-marks, and be given authority, that is the idea – it is the christian strategy. If taken too far it is highly unsuccessful? Of course – but we are assuming you are not a Christian for nothing my dear Matthew).

'In effect then my dear young friend' exclaimed the Analytical Uncle-of-the-children's-hour – a more oleaginous Uncle at every moment in his Zurich consulting-den, to the little latterday british Tom Thumb, come all the way from London Town to ask big Wise Man Frumpf of the Ancient East, beard and all, why funny little Matthew sucked his thumb so much and why he dreamed of snakes, the little introvert – 'you must say to yourself – *von Haus aus, verstanden?* from the outset of your *Kampf* (and all your fighting glands must be called up) that must be your *strategy* that you must be *modest* in your ambitions, because your powers are not considerable enough to warrant *at the outset*.'

Good-boy Bloomsbury listened with glee, modestest exhibitionist he felt like a pea-nut, which would do its best, do its little damnedest, and he was amused by the doctor, they laughed at Matthew easily together (he was a funny homunculus), fixing his handicap.

'There is a talmudic saying' smiled Dr Frumpfsusan frumpishly and jewishly (old style) with a wise old eye, 'as follows. In choosing a friend, ascend a step. In choosing a wife, descend a step. When Froggie-would-a-wooing-go, when Froggie is you, my dear boy, he must step *down*, as many steps as there are beneath him – even unto the last! To be frank with yourself Matthew, and that is the essence of Analysis, an animated doll is all, as things stand at present if they may be said to stand at all, you can really hope to take-on. So I say to you – it is impossible to choose your baby-girl too small."

And they had another hearty giggle together, to put this matter of absolute modesty upon the right footing. Human vanity *must* be kept under at all costs. So far they had got on capitally.

But the Psycho-analyst gave him a taste of his metal, it was time he showed this earth-worm he would not be trifled with! Enough of this giggling!

'Nungut!' growled der Herr Doktor Dingsda heartily (very altdeutsch and very up-stage): 'You will follow my programme, yes, upon your return to Blumensbury? Are we agreed upon that point, sir?'

'I swear to keep your commandments' exclaimed Matthew fervently 'as I am a child of Christ and an inheritor – '

'Enough!' the doctor cut him short and put his name in the register, as a regular patient. 'For preliminary examination (extroverting one Bloomsbury, sent me by my trusted agent Alan X., Coptic Street, w.c.) fifty guineas.'

'Thát will be one thousand and fifty Swiss marks."

The doctor flung himself back in his chair. He put his fingers, grown fat in subnormal-pulse-palping and after that complex-catching, into his black beard – put his head upon one side, and bit his principal hand-nail, while Matthew made out the cheque.

'It is worth it!' said Matthew as he handed it to him.

'It is worth it if you do what I tell you!' Dr Frumpfsusan thundered, with a furibond eye-roll, placing the cheque carefully in a drawer of his desk.

'I shall be most careful to take full advantage of all your advice' Matthew replied.

'Ausgezeichnet!' crashed the doctor, banging the drawer in, and turning the key.

After that the mollified specialist threw in a further short lecture, and his new patient was all ears.

'One of the most common and one of the least understood complexes' he sententiously remarked, 'is what I call the scale-complex. It is upon that conviction that I have been acting. What I refer to is not a matter of inches. It is a psycho-physical *Minderwertigkeitsgefühl*!' He paused to contemplate his fifty-guinea piece of complexity.

'Many men with small noses have it' he then went on. 'A sketchy body will do it. Narrow shoulders plus a pasty face – such things tend to go in pairs. Any combination of things that takes with it a sensation of physical meanness and unimportance. Glasses. Going to the Zoo and looking too long at the lions. Hairlessness. Beady eyes. Small-scale pudenda. Palpitation of the heart. Spatulate hands. Prolonged constipation. Rabbit teeth. You see what I mean?'

Matthew saw what the celebrated Analyst meant and he looked suitably guilty, and as small as possible, much smaller than could be strictly necessary but he was zealous where it was smallness that was in question.

'The best of us, my boy, have one or more of these smallnesses, hence potential scale-inferiority-complexes. We all feel small sometimes, then we go to the nearest Analyst. Ich tu's ja auch! Selbstverständlich! Ich komme eben von einem Kollegen, der, wie ich, Spezialarzt ist!' Frumpfsusan sought to appear small to his client. 'A collection of such smallnesses – it is that, however, that crystallizes the complex, that it is that sends us haggard and blubbering to the nearest clinic of the Analyst! – Many small-nosed men have large feet. Das ist also ein bedeutungsvolle Ausgleichung! It is the *combination* that – '

'Natürlich!' remarked Matthew, with his best Bloomsbury blink.

'On the other hand, small nose, small feet, *and* small pudenda – that is a fatal combination! A virulent scale-complex of psychical-inferiority is inevitable.'

'Natürlich!' assented Matthew more faintly.

'But the more closely we examine these things, the more we discover that it is not the physical so much that matters. Again: inferiority-feeling may result from an actual superiority! The handicap of genius, isn't it? you see that can make inferiority-feeling.'

'Is it able to?'

'It is a matter of common observation,' pursued the Analyst. 'The self-feeling bears no relation, amongst quite normal men and women, to physical fact. The nature of their particular physique, is not that the last thing of which they think? Look, an intensely ill-favoured woman she will frequently behave as if she were very attractive. No one is surprised – for they in their turn are they not beauties too? stunted puny men, to turn to men, do they not possess the assurance of a champion athlete? Well then, all these people have the sensations of being what they are not: whatever happens, a something more favourable than the facts isn't it! This is the rule of the normal average.'

'That is indeed so.'

'For them we have to *manufacture* inferiority, if we desire to see it!'

'I suppose that is so.'

'*What is the secret of these normal people?*'

'That I cannot guess!'

'Ah!'

'Do you know?'

'But that it is our business to find out!'

The Analyst took it easy for a moment after his orgy of exposition and contemplated Matthew full of the utmost self-satisfaction possible.

'That perfectly *normal* capacity to – well that is – to falsify nature, to one's own personal advantage, isn't it – that is what I am able to do for you. That is what, Matthew, I shall do for you!'

'You will earn my life-long gratitude!'

'I shall!'

'You certainly will.'

'It is not *their* secret, it is Nature's, that we have surprised.'

'I guessed something of the sort!'

There was another pause in which they both relished the great resources of Analysis, staring out of the window at a *Turnier* in progress organized for resident patients, on the tennis-courts beyond the bathing-brook.

This was all very well, but little Bloomsbury would have his little joke and make Big-man Analyst giggle on the other side of his chops if he could before he left him – there was no mistaking his intention, he was as mischievous as mischievous.

'But please Doctor Frumpfsusan' piped little Bloomsbury, in a little sly stammer, 'are you amongst the normal or wouldn't you say that?'

'How do you mean Matthew?'

'In your *Kampf* with nature, no minderfertigkeits-feeling has hampered – I only ask in admiration at.'

'It is natural.'

'What you say is remarkably true. But like Galvani with the cooking-frog, Newton with the falling apple, has your scale-complex discovery had an origin in – ?'

Dr Frumpfsusan allowed his lips to flower contemptuously extroverted meatily in the depths of his cryptic Analytic beard.

'I am a Jew' exclaimed the worthy doctor with considerable truculence. 'When I possess such a first-class source of "inferiority" as that, in the eyes of my fellow-men, what need have I of any other? Does it not put all and any in the shade at once? It does I think! It has secured me against all the inferiority-complexes to which flesh is heir! I am a Jew. I am immune.'

'I see! That is really very fortunate for you.'

'I think so.'

'You cannot supply me homeopathically with such a counter-complex as that, to eclipse all other complexes?'

'No.'

Matthew felt as crushed as if Moses had put one of the stones of the Decalogue, or all the Decalogue together upon him, and sat on it.

But what was perhaps quite the best money's worth of the trip in its way, an invaluable counsel he had taken to heart for keeps, without thinking about it, was connected with deportment. Body was mind's big brother really. It followed the other fellow's lead. The first-born, the biggest-waxed, the imposing elder, was Body. When a person's down in the blousiest blues of the dumps, all he has to do we all know that is to affect a jaunty demeanour, adopt an elastic step and avoid a brooding droop. The effect is electrical. Once big-fellow-Body is up, the little spirits will follow it, like Mary's little lamb – they will be *high-spirits*, in no time, once the body is cock-a-hoop. 'Upon that simple old principle however you must model your deportment my dear boy,' the fulminating Frumpfsusan had counselled, 'upon the (often I admit ridiculous) deportment of the Extrovert. Take the burliest for your model – take me if you like!'– *Study the male! Get under his skin!* If you succeed in catching his physical attitudes, my lad, you will soon find that you are doing the things he does. Also! Gib acht! – with your mate – for that purpose as I have shown she must be *petite* – be *rough!* Be tough Matthew! A foot or eighteen inches advantage will help wonderfully – you have no idea what a difference! Stick at no extrovert absurdity, in the pursuit of your object, however much you have to laugh! Sie mussen doch lachen – jawohl! das weiss ich schon, aber das macht nichts aus! Also fort! Um Göttes Willen, seien Sie doch ein bischen Ubermensch! – Then another expedient – you will find it of the greatest use. *Learn how to bully!* It is a golden rule in all these cases. *Swagger*, like a true-blue Casanova of Seingalt, you can afford it – but see you pick them *petite*' to this Doctor Frumpfsusan ever returned 'there is nothing so depressing as the sensation of having strayed into a cathedral. Overmatching would be fatal!'

Today was the day, it was to be the great experiment. Zulu Blades was to be put in the shade. So Matthew now went swaggering rockily in like a rustic torero, upon the heel of his midget-bull.

Betty was equal to the occasion. She had come in with the perfect animal assurance to be expected of a puppet, it led her to strike her feet down as if the earth were ringing steel, that sounded. Upon her bony bobbed blond head, was an old black wide-awake, copied from the Virginian Planter upon the 'Gems' packets, borrowed from a Chelsea academician in a large studio, full of old hats, suitable for planters. She had a scarlet scarf, as worn by Isopel Berners, suitable for a prosperous canal-amazon: she wore homespun suggestive of a bookworm, and carried in her hand a book.

Matthew took the book from the girl's hand, with a rough buccaneering gesture almost snatching. It was the *Hard Boiled Virgin*. He gazed – with wide eyes of vacant critical blue, quizzing and frowning, the smirk left to wrinkle wryly the twisting mouth – at the book. He poured down upon it the amused gazing of the Bloomsbury grimace and correctly lisped:

'*I-i-i-is* that a' short pause '—a *new* book?'

Betty looked suspiciously at the grinning Bloomsbury with a hard Wigan what-is-the-joke-now air about her.

'No' she said cautiously 'I don't think so. Tommy Sillmans gave it to me to read, have you read it Matthew? Why do you ask Matthew?'

She flung the black hat down upon the shells and gave her curls a vigorous doggish shake-up, sturdy and bow-legged though diminutive. Then the bold-eyed round-buttocked small-boy's body vaulted backwards slap up on a table-top that was ever so high up, in sitting posture, dangling the little plover's-egg home-spun doll-leggies brightly to and fro.

'Why do you ask Matthew?' she repeated, shaking her corn-red shock up on high.

Matthew stared down at the *Hard Boiled Virgin*, his head on one side, wryly smirking.

'I don't know' said he.

'What do you mean Matthew?' asked the straightforward doll bluntly, with more than a suspicion of Liverpool in the tones of her high-pitched drawling.

'What – hard-boiled was. Is it the egg?' The dull-thinking interval of the Bloomsbury *malin*. 'Or is it the virgin? It *can't* be a cooking egg. It *must* be the virgin!'

'Oh you are potty Matthew of course it's the virgin!'

'I thought it was.'

'It's an american word. Haven't you ever heard hard-boiled said? It's *american*.'

'Is it?'

She nodded.

'Great day!' she exclaimed 'didn't you know that Matthew?'

She imitated the american accent and chewed the gum of the U.S.A. for local music-hall colouring.

He watched her chewing. The grinding of her grenadine tinted lips was what he watched, her small painted beak was sucking the imaginary juices of transatlantic trees: he took up a burlier attitude before her, bluff sailor-fashion and a little threatening. Then he smacked his own lips slightly twice, while he watched hers closely.

'What did you say?' he asked suddenly.

'When just now do you mean Matthew?'

'Yes.'

'*Great Day* – ? That's what MacCorquodale used to say, Great Day, to me!' she squawked back at him and squealed the little weeny 'me.'

'MacCorquodale, what is that, is that american too?'

'Which Matthew?'

'MacCorquodale.'

'It's a *boy!* You're swanking Matthew you do understand!'

'I am not really Betty. I am very stupid!'

'You mean I am.'

Matthew extended a tapering hand as slowly as possible till it lay, in mid-air, off her left ear, immobile for a moment: then moving it in he began smoothing the tiny curls of his dollie. At the full distance of his stiffly extended arm he persevered in this solemn exercise, while with a portentous concentration he stared at her, daft and abstracted, as if she were a shell, or the flax that he fingered had grown elsewhere and not on the head of a person.

Up and down, in a sawing movement, the hand passed in mysterious astonished caress.

'Are you trying to send me to sleep Matthew? You are potty!' Betty shook up the flax for him, so that it would be nicer to stroke.

Matthew frowned. He did not welcome movement at such a juncture. He allowed his finger-tips to assemble upon her nuque. Then he grasped her convulsively, still held at arm's-length: he hooked her, after the manner of an apache dance-number.

'Why are you looking at me like that Matthew?' Betty asked, slightly annoyed.

'I don't know' said Matthew, frowning again, to discourage such risky interruptions.

Her nuque was as cold as tempered steel and excessively hard. Matthew breathed very deeply. He took one cart-horse stride to the front which brought him up against the table. The sham-gum-chewing lips grinned up at this funny boy. With both hands he seized her head, holding it in his palms like an orangoutang which had possessed itself of a coconut, and preparatory to breaking it, held it chest-high, to delect itself with its intact and hairy roundness, like that of an animal-head. He gazed fiercely down into her eyes. The passive baby-girl gazed back, a little inquisitive.

The constipation of his senses so far held stoutly out, as dead as mutton. In impotent steadfastness he hunted in her face for something that was not there at all it seemed: as time passed his veins swelled in his head with the effort. *There is absolutely nothing there!* – that was the painful thought. But at last he seemed to have struck something. There was a spark at least.

He felt a distinct vibration, in the recalcitrant depths of his person. Something was not quite as it formerly was or he was very much mistaken. In portentous slow-movement of gruelling close-up, his lips forced out to forestall the contact, he approached the rose-bud mouth beneath by the fatal sinking of his head down upon hers. With awful slowness the four lips met. He closed in lower down at the contact. He experienced a second spark.

Now really flushed with triumph, he introduced a hand beneath her jumper. He felt her delicate toy-spine, as cool as alabaster, as neat as the couplings of a small boy's locomotive. There was a distinct vibration throughout or in many distinct parts of his person.

The bookworm shoulders rolled above the ravishing toy-girl, like impending seas above a pygmy skiff: in hooligan hardiness he clutched the little skull, he had the sensation of great knees sticking out, giant toe-tendons clenching in the rough workman's footwear: many flattering indications of a probable event were distinctly signalled, as he thought, sluggish but sure, from the most improbable centres – there was really a palpable stir, if not in the true sense a bustle. Betty at that moment when his eyes first fell upon her a trimestre since was to be his true helpmeet something had told him: a really natural dawn of love was at hand, beyond question – the sun's red and swollen rim was visible, low down in the atmosphere, the tip of the fiery Phoebus, pushing up over the chilly horizon. Soon the entire valley would be flooded with his bounteous rays.

In every way reinforced in the conviction that the Great Day had sounded and the hour of triumph struck – with still the hieratic stiffness of limb that had characterized all his movements since Betty had first started gum-sucking, and he had surprised a change in the direction of the tide of his libido, and had noted with delight that it was turning *outward*, with an impulse that could only be described as extroverted – he drew back a half-step. His eyes measured Betty Bligh perching upon the table as a husky furniture-remover sizes up a half-ton travelling-trunk. Knotting the muscles of his shoulders and forearms, conferring upon himself the stoop of the larger apes, he stepped forward and moved to the right. He picked Betty Bligh up from the table as though she had been a half-ton feather. He staggered back a step with Betty Bligh in his arms.

'Whatever are you doing now Matthew? Oh you are potty' Betty said. In hurried strides he bore her towards the bedroom-door. He flattened her against the wall, pushing desperately against her as though he were preventing the wall from falling, while he turned the handle of the door.

'Matthew have you gone potty! You're hurting!' high up on the wall Betty protested, with what wind she had left.

The door came open, he caught his little Humpty Dumpty dexterously in a shaky armful, and he passed with her fiercely into the bedroom upon staggering legs.

Bent over his burden, his eyes almost closed, he had but one thought – that of his inner libidinous tides, of their imminent outbreaks: so he was startled out of his wits by a full-blooded scream, such as could not have issued from Betty Bligh. He came to a standstill – the sluggish metaphoric tide froze and then turned back – at the same time he raised his flushed and blinking face up at the room.

Lo there upon his bed in wild-eyed alarm, preparing to spring off it, blushing to the roots of his hair, was Daniel Boleyn.

Matthew simply dropped Betty – all that was about to be between them was over now in any case. He advanced empty-handed to the bed-side, one stiff outstretched finger denouncing its present occupant outright:

'What are you doing here!' he thundered at the intruder.

At point-blank range he pointed his whole stiff arm sharpened into one finger-tip at the bed-crasher, straight at the guilty head.

'Didn't I tell you to go!'

Dan shrank from the stiff finger, he eagerly nodded.

'What are you doing here!'

'But I had nowhere to go!' Dan muttered, edging away.

'Didn't I tell you to make yourself scarce!'

Dan gasped, and said,

'I went to sleep!'

'What right had you to use my bed. What right had you to come in here!'

'I wanted to leave the – !' – he got no farther – *that* he should not be allowed to say! – a roar from the chest of Old Man Plunkett cut him short.

As Matthew, blue to the lips with ungovernable wrath, charged down upon him, Dan slipped with the rapidity of a lizard to one side: he smartly hurdled over the foot of the bed, which possessed a small brass rail, then shot in a black mass through the open door. In the neighbouring room he vacillated a moment then vanished as he heard the bay of Matthew coming in his direction.

There was on Matthew's side a momentary argument with the pillow and bolster, Matthew struck out at both. With a snarl after that he turned and rushed over the prostrate form of Betty, who moaned upon the floor rubbing the homespun knee-cap.

At the stair-head, from which he was just able to catch sight of the black perspective of an arm below and hear the last thunder of retreat on the last flight of stairs, he drew up, shouting down, to kill his head,

'Never let me see your face again! I'll knock you down you unutterable little sneak! U-u-u-ugh!'

Zulu Blades came through his door in his shirt-sleeves, out on to the landing, hands stuck in pockets, and, looking up the staircase, contemplated Matthew with irony. The discoloured face hung over the banisters, and inverted, returned the neck-stretching scrutiny, eye for eye, and tooth for tooth.

'Is anything wrong?' asked Zulu.

Matthew withdrew, in three raging strides, the bang of his door blending with the laughter of the preposterous so-called Zulu.

*

Dan rushed out haggard and hatless into the street. He panted like a stricken doe. He gazed wild-eyed and dishevelled to right and left, he started as if pursued, he cast a look of swan-necked alarm over his shoulder – finally he drooped upon the curb-stone, staring at the gutter. A policeman, with the ominous waddle of The Force, passed him eyeing him up and down, from under the beak of his helmet. Two flat hands like a pair of limp white gloves stuck under his belt (one upon his left waist-line, the other upon his right) he proceeded on his beat – but throwing his eyes backwards, over his shoulder, at each slow rolling step. As the distance increased a slight rotation was required at the same time as a lateral roll, in order to keep his man under observation.

At length Dan started to walk away, he continued for two

miles and he came to the house on Sharratt Hill, in the neighbourhood of Chalk Farm, in which Mélanie Blackwell lived. Chains of goods' trucks rattled past the foot of the garden. As he reached the garden entrance to the studio an Express, screaming, tore the air as it rushed past, causing the dirty gully to quiver and reverberate. Mélanie was bringing her dogs out.

'Dan!' she exclaimed, naming him, as though spotted dramatically and nicknamed in a breath. He blushed deeply. They walked in the garden together.

'Bromo will not love the noisy trains' Mélanie said: 'Bromo never changes, nothing is skin-deep with him is it darling Bromo! Sweet Bromo!' She clingingly caressed the shaggy trunk. 'He can't suppress it he knows that, he has tried to hasn't he. Now he just shuts his eyes – what a wise dog you are Bromo darling – and so beautiful!'

Dan considered the hairy beauty of Bromo with a burning blush.

'Where have you been?' the quiet question was accompanied by the fine tired irony of lifted eyebrows.

Dan looked down at the animal sniffing its way from spot to spot more attentively, and did not answer her.

The dog's hair had the impeccable white curl of its breed, with the comic limbs that endeared it to *Tatler*-readers and Bronzo-lovers from Balham to the Bund. Mélanie moved away and plucked a number of twigs from a rose-bush.

'It is a difficult matter' said she in sing-song, milady in her garden, 'to prevent these roses from going wild again.' She ceased to include her four silent companions any more in her wandering discourse. The smallest of the three white dogs quickly cocked up a fluffy hind-leg and watered the rose.

'I'm sure I should go wild too if I were not interfered with' Mélanie remarked. 'But I am not a rose!' she smiled the pained-coy smile of sentiment.

Bromo growled, as he wandered, at the buffer-kissing of the goods' trucks in the ill-smelling gully at his back.

'Bromo-darling!' Mélanie complained. 'Where are you going then and all?'

Bromo was going towards the road, out of earshot of the insulting trucks.

Dan raised in a stately way a single hand, and he removed with intense difficulty one dead twig. Mélanie continued on neighbouring bushes her unhurried gardening, Dan turned away from the plant he had touched as if shutting it completely out of his mind. He waved the opposite hand lazily at the departing Bromo.

Mélanie went into the studio, Bromo, Rabs, Bluff and Dan followed at her heels.

The studio was damp. It was full of brushwood and logwood for a large open fireplace. Baskets for Bromo, Rabs and Bluff were at the sides of the chimneypiece. On the canvases appeared in different parts of the room, two upon easels, slick poster-landscapes of Riviera type, garish and geometric.

'Are you coming to Azay-le-Promis next week?'

Dan shook his head.

'Why not?'

Stealthily Dan let himself down upon a very low settee. It had wild-animal rugs and square cushions of scarlet leather. He looked hard at Bluff, the elderly bitch.

'You are a strange young man!' Mélanie said, who had lighted a cigarette. Her thin body was in an elegant pullover. 'What is there to stop here for in London for any young man? You would be better in Azay-le-Promis.'

She considered with theatrical irony the problem of 'the young man.'

'Have you made the arrangements you hoped to with Matthew Plunkett? I expected you yesterday.'

Dan shook his head. A deep blush stole over his face at the name of Matthew. What he had been called upon to witness at the last, at Matthew's, came back to him of course. The circumstances of his sudden withdrawal were all too fresh: Matthew breaking into that awful bedroom with a strange young woman in his arms, the thud of the shameful human burden upon the floor, Matthew's extraordinary unkindness – his blows, his narrow escape, driven from the bed where he had been resting – for he had been so hopelessly out of sorts and still was. But he could not rest here! Oh where should he go?

Dan buried his face in his hands. These peculiarly unsuitable events of such terribly recent occurrence were far too pictorial;

like stopping one's ears he stopped his eyes – not to see such goings on any more.

'What is the matter now Daniel?' Mélanie wailed a little, her voice becoming more egregiously irish, for she came from St Louis of an immigrant galician family who were tailors, who had taken a fancy to the name of O'Konolly – becoming bigorras. Her husband's estate had been in Tyrone (they had met in Chicago when he was attaché at Washington and he had fallen in love at first sight with the beautiful irish-american girl) and in Tyrone she had lived and hunted: but Mr Shaun Blackwell was dead some years.

'Ach! what is ut than Danieldarling!' Mélanie began miserably keening at him. 'Haven't ye been able to get the help ye had counted on at all!'

And sure he hadn't, his downcast head and bust answered as plainly as possible, while Mélanie continued to address her distressed enquiries to the eyes hiding, under the hands, shut against the brutal doings of Matthew.

'Well Danieldarling but what are ye going to do now – with no place to go to and all me poor child – go somewhere ye must. It's a fact is it ye've got no money left; poor Stephen has none to give you I know that.'

Daniel blushed in his hands at the crude mention of money. Then Mrs Mélanie Blackwell went back to the holidays.

'Out at Azay-le-Promis' said she with a slight inhalation: 'you could do as you liked: I'm out working all day.' She glanced at a dazzling landscape of Azay-le-Promis. 'You could stop there as long as it suited you – till I come back next year if you wanted. There's no one there would interfere with you. You could pass your days just as you pleased – it really is quite pleasant. You've never been to France. Why don't you do that? – Come along now Danieldarling and don't be so coy and all! You need a mother you know you're such a great baby – I declare it's not safe at all for ye to be at large in this wicked city if I heard ye'd been run over Danhoney I'd never forgive missilf an' all! Why don't you come with me next week to Azay Dan – to Azay!'

Dan remained in his corner – he was that big black oyster – he would not come open, however much the sirens fluted over celtic airs to it.

Mélanie moved to a low stool some feet nearer to Dan.

'Com-*mon* now Dan' she cried – her voice extended to a gamut of irish no longer confined to Erin – it crossed the Atlantic and back in its passion. 'Say you'll come to Azay-le-Promis Dan like a good sensible person – do now Dan Honey!'

Dan moved his feet, to show the refusal was flat – but she would not take *no*, not at least from the feet, and persisted.

'What is there against it? I can't understand. You're not afraid of *me* by any chance are you now – is that it? Why I'm sure almost old enough to be your own mother. Haven't I grey hairs and all, yes haven't you noticed? Ah yes!' she nodded very bitter-sweet and wistful indeed, though he could not see her pointing at her black straight hair, parted in the centre. She continued to move her head mournfully up and down. The thin arch of the eyebrows pathetically ascended the delicate terraces of the peculiar jutting brow – lined like an actress's from many grimaces, actually due with Mélanie to the elasticity of her daily pathos. '*They are there!* Every morning I pull out several. See – there is a large white hair Daniel! Let that be your chaperone!'

In lengthening incantation she pursued the human-tin-opening, with iron resolve – to force this shut-up gallant ajar – impossible to blush unseen any longer it must be! She watched the red ears with a runic anguish, clearing her throat.

'With me at Azay-le-Promis' she chanted 'you will be safer Danieldarling than ye will be in these parts. What did I tell Stephen that I'd take you under my wing. "Whhhhing is ut?" said he, "you'll have your work cut out!" he said – he knew what he was talking about – that I can see now!' She nodded at the obstreperous fledgeling, archly maternal.

Mélanie rose from the stool by the open fender, casting a few spirited twigs upon the fire forlornly, in a manner that made the open fireplace look more than ever like a stage-scene. She sat down again upon the sister settee to that occupied by Daniel.

'What have you after all to keep you here Dan? You have no friends except Matthew.' But at the name *Matthew* Dan crushed his face still more closely into the embraces of his hands.

He would have looked up even – but he felt Mélanie might easily be able to catch sight, in the dark mirror of his eyes, of that equivocal picture: Matthew would be seen driving him from his bed in order to – but no! his fancy *should not* be allowed to protract that offensive spectacle!

'What other friends have you, to whom you can turn?'

Dan listened, he began *turning* – turning to friends to whom he could turn. Convulsively to himself he simpered. At this Dan opened painfully his hands – his flower-like face burst out of this convex bud, cleft in the centre where the edges abutted. Or it might have been an event like suddenly disparting shutters, in the Spanish East – heavy peepholes for a secluded beauty – and there as they parted was her solemn face!

Dan looked at Mélanie with a grave enquiring blush.

'You have no one to whom you can turn.'

As the phrase recurred there was unearthly lightning in the depths of his black celtic eyes: Daniel turned away his head, snapping his fingers at Bromo. He knew that if she used it again he should laugh outright, he could not help that – the too physical idiom it was that tickled his fancy: for he had always moved everywhere with the silence of a spirit, speech now and then had this effect upon the mind of Dan.

In mock-hibernian whine, very trailing and melancholic, Mélanie's voice struck up again. In profile he sat quite still to listen.

'Horace Zagreus is in London I am told. You have not seen him Dan I suppose?'

But Dan nodded – yes he had.

'You have seen him. Horace Zagreus? I did not know that.'

Dan gulped and his distress was evident, but he had seen him.

'I did not know you had been seeing Horace' said Mélanie with offended slowness. Dan nodded, a dumb *yes yes yes!* at her. He had been seeing Horace, yes! (It was a monster lisp, if it had been spoken.)

'But if you have been seeing Horace – that is a pity!' Mélanie was annoyed with Daniel. At first she looked away from him. 'He is not a fit friend for you Daniel! Horace is all right, but as regards young men Horace is really impossible that is the trouble, he cannot help that of course. I am sorry for Horace.

I reproach myself very much for having let you meet Horace – it can do you no good to frequent Horace Zagreus. I hope you will take my advice in that and see Horace as little as possible.'

An expression replete with reproach collected in the face of the poor human dumb animal, with the speaking eyes of lustrous brown. He gazed at Mrs Mélanie Blackwell in a dense appeal, refusing to listen. If I could only *speak* (his beautiful brown eyes cried out) I could tell you how you wrong him, with your words!

'Dan honey is it possible! I suppose it is, perhaps you really don't know what I mean about Horace? I confess that had not occurred to me – of course but I should have said to myself that a great simple irish school-boy like yourself fresh from the sanctuaries, the sheltered places of the catholic mind, would not understand what it meant at all.'

Dan opened his lovely eyes to their widest extent to express the far-flung circumference of his utter ignorance.

'Dan you are so incredibly helpless! I had better tell you at once. Horace Zagreus has a very bad reputation. He is not a suitable friend for any young man, let alone one like you who does not know how to take care of himself more than a baby at the breast.'

Dan blushed deeply at this metaphor.

'You really have never heard – none of those peculiar men have ever with such a beautiful young man as you – well tried Dandarling to show you their feelings at all – is it possible?'

The black and foggy rain of average London weather commenced to strike the high pent-window, and its percussion filled the studio with a sharp rattling. It grew dark. Dan looked up at the roof in alarmed enquiry.

'It is raining' said Mélanie, glancing up too.

Upon this Dan again considered the window, in renewed astonishment – as if rain were a substance unknown in the sanctuaries of the sheltered catholic mind.

'Oh Mélanie!' Dan exclaimed suddenly, clutching at the hair of the rug upon the divan.

'What is it then Dandarling!'

Mélanie leant forward with eagerness, her eyes fixed upon the delectable boy.

'I am so unspeakably unhappy!'

His mouth commenced to wobble wildly – the word 'unhappy' never trod it but it left it quaking. He bit his lip extremely hard to secure a measure of composure.

'Tell me Dan-darling what it is!' Mrs Blackwell panted in her broken irish, as she rose to her feet in business-like preparation for suitable action. She filled her face with a smoke-screen of sentiment – her two capable eyes measured the path with unction to the delectable body of the incredibly helpless boy-in-distress (no longer luckily in the catholic sanctuaries, safe from the vampires of this earth).

'Zagreus!' Dan uttered the name and stopped, wrestling with both of his emotional lips together at once. Mélanie stood still and frowned. She fixed her eye in cold enquiry upon the disintegrating adolescent sphinx.

'He is so horribly unkind to me – oh Mélanie he does not appear to love me' (a long pause of the tautest description) '*at all!*'

Dan almost shouted this and flung himself at full length upon the settee, against whose hairy surface he pressed his face, moist with a flurry of hectic tears.

Mrs Blackwell thought she would sit down again – she went back and sat as before upon her divan: it was plain that she had met with something in the nature of a facer.

She collected herself with a cigarette.

'Oh!' she said at last. 'I did not know things had gone as far as *that*. I have made I see a small mistake!'

A muffled demonstration of distress from Dan.

'Well!' she said.

'Boo-oo-ooo' murmured Dan.

'Yes' she said 'I understand of course. It is most unfortunate. – It's my fault just the same.'

There was consolation in the guilt and that it was *through her*.

'So that's it!' she then remarked.

'Yes!' cried Dan, raising the back of his head into the air two inches 'Yes' he nodded convulsively at the settee, while his tears dropped upon it 'that's' (he gulped) '*it!*'

'Oh!' said Mélanie 'I am very sorry! Under the circumstances I don't see what I can do! I am de trop here I can see.'

She signalled to Bromo. With a grunt Bromo got up and, stretching, came over slowly to her side.

'Yes darling I said I would comb you and I had forgotten.'

Dan groaned.

Mélanie turned towards him, a sharpish turn, driving some of the cigarette smoke streaming from the nostril into her eye.

'I don't know what I am expected to say Dan – ought I to be sympathetic? I wish you'd tell me. What is a poor girl to do? I wonder what Horace has done to distress you so much. Horace is a dirty old beast anyway. I shall tell him so when I see him.'

There was a muffled wail of protest from Dan, at *dirty old beast*.

'And you're just as bad!' Mélanie exclaimed. 'Yes you! I wish you'd sit up and take notice and try and behave like a sensible being Mr Boleyn! You deserve a good spanking!'

Mr Boleyn released a howl of pain at the word *spanking* and he slightly squirmed upon the settee at the thought of a spank.

'Yes what you want is a thorough caning on that big bold bottom of yours young man and then to be put to bed like a naughty child! That is all that you are!'

Dan was silent. Dan did not like direct references to the dimensions of his body. For himself Dan was always small-boy's-size and there was an end of it.

If he caught sight of his head protruding above a crowd of people, he hurried away and hid, with an attack of inferiority-feeling. Sometimes this might last upwards of a half-hour, before he could return.

'Did you hear what I said?' – it was the voice of the martinet Mélanie. Dan thought of the secluded villa among the olives of Azay-le-Promis and he shuddered.

'Did you hear what I said young man!' Mélanie said 'young man' with such utter unction that it summoned to the palate more saliva than 'peaches,' and the young man could hear her breathing a little thick and clotted.

'You ought to be ashamed of yourself young man!'

She was working herself up! Dan rapidly calculated the distance across the front of the fireplace and the prospects of escape – his retreat to the door was cut off. He might, in feverish reflection he decided, hit her with a canvas: if he got it well down from over-head (in spite of her superiority in height, as he felt it to be) her head would no doubt go through it. Like a circus-dog stuck in a hoop with paper too thick for the trick, she would be out of action, for good, for she could not do much with one of the canvases for a collar – at any rate not *bite*, only bark.

Something appeared to have occurred to relieve the tension for she breathed less hard: she was smoking furiously.

'It is Horace is most to blame!' he heard her say. 'Why can't he leave young men alone!' *Young men* had as before upon the lips of the châtelaine of the neighbourhood of Azay-le-Promis the dangerous unction of peaches, of such verbal money-value as 'Young Men in Love,' on any play-bill or dust-cover, punctuated with the responsive chop-licking of hot-blooded spinsters – imaginary or in fact *best-buyers*.

'Horace has no right to interfere with my guests!' she called out, as if Horace were within ear-shot.

'I'll get through to the old devil and give him a piece of my mind!' she vociferated and sprang up.

Mélanie and Dan sprang up at the same moment, both as if shot, both with eyes pugnaciously shining. Mélanie directed her steps, without paying attention to the agitated form of the resurrected young-man-in-love, towards the telephone.

'*Please* Mel-an-eee!' Dan exclaimed now with clasped anguished hands, pursuing her across the studio in a series of attitudes of progressive supplication, as they both converged upon the instrument. Bromo thought it best to bark, monotonously argumentative, at their strained attitudes, commanding them to unbend.

'What is his number?'

She stood beside the installation, Dan halted behind her, his hands locked before him, his eyes slightly cast up – the perfect model for Salvator Rosa, melting beneath chocolate skies, bedewed with colossal tears of high-lit crystal.

'Oh I have it here' she said and took from a drawer an address-book.

'*Please!*' Dan called to her with all the high-pitched intensity of his high-lisping stilted grief.

'Go and sit down now Dan do!'

'Please do not telephone about me to Horace Zagreus, I shall never forgive you if you do so!'

'Do you think I'm going to allow Horace to use my house! – go and sit down Dan like a good boy, do as I tell you – I'll settle with Horace. He's gone too far – with anyone else except you I shouldn't have minded so much.'

Dan swayed for a moment, wringing his snow-white plaster fists, subtended in the modest attitude of statues, before him: then as Mélanie took down the receiver, he burst out in a melting torrent of tenor-sweet tear-swept complaint:

'Oh *why* are you so unkind! Oh why are you so *unkind!*'

Rapidly stepping across the parquet of the studio he rushed at the settee. There he awaited, the victim of this sacrifice (in posture convenient for execution) the blow that was about to fall. He might even surprise the angry accents of the god, out of the machine.

'Cremorne double O one O! Double O one O.'

It was the fatal number that he heard, he recognized it. He gave vent to his feelings in occasional desolate sounds.

'Is that Horace? This is Mel-an-ee, yes Mell-lan-eee!'

It *was* indeed – Dan writhed in silence. Oh this woman, this fiend in human shape, this preposterous busy-body!

'Horace I have a bone to pick with you!'

A staccato muttering came from the instrument. Those were the very vibrations of Zagreus!

'Yes I know all about that!' yapped Mélanie Blackwell boorishly back. Dan could have slapped her. 'No it is not that as it happens.'

She was again interrupted.

'Yes yes I am sure that is just as you say Horace but I have a bone to pick – a *bone*, you idiot! Can't you hear me? Where is your ear-trumpet? But you are not so deaf as all that!'

She was pulled up, there was the waxing of a contradictory rattle. As she listened her foot tapped out a morse tattoo upon the parquet.

'I don't want to hear about that' she suddenly barked back into the belled mouth for the message, from which she removed her hand she had used as a stopper. 'I don't – want – to – hear! – Can you hear what I say? No I have said I don't want to.

Daniel Boleyn is here. What? Daniel – Boleyn. Yes. The poor young man is in a fearful state of mind. What? Awful state of mind! What have you been doing to him, you old wretch? Yes! He is here. What have you been up to – yes I mean it!'

There was another interval, of a staccato jabber, while several times her mouth made a dart for the transmitter but withdrew again – she bit her lips.

'He may be all that' she said. 'He may be. All that.'

'Oh *please* Mélanie do tell me what he has said!' Dan exclaimed, stretched out still in an anxious coil.

'That's what I expected!' called Mélanie. 'What do you say? Hallo! Are you there? Hallo!'

She shook the instrument.

'Hallo!'

Mélanie waited.

'Hallo!'

Her body relaxed, she hung up the receiver.

'He has rung off! He's deafer than ever! It is impossible to telephone to him!' She returned to the fireplace with the gait of a tenderfooted seaside bather ascending to her tent, heavy-limbed as well after the buoyant seawater. She sat down.

Dan choked. At length he contrived to whisper, writhing a little in anticipation.

'What did he say – was I mentioned?'

She gave him a lofty quizzical look before she replied, in her best sham-irish:

'Ach he said you were the tiresomest young man that he had ever met this many a day and hoped he'd never see you again!'

She observed the blow fall, as she rattled the words out, with watchful relish – when she had finished she lay back to await the result with eyes half-closed, her lotus-eating glance skimming the slender surfaces from bust to knee – Dan visible in perspective beyond, transfixed with the shafts, unable to move.

When the howl of the stricken lover broke at last from the lips of Dan, and he rolled over out of sight, as if shot, upon his capacious divan, Mélanie sniffed unpleasantly. She sat up and lighted a cigarette without looking at the casualty. Then she stretched back again, her head burrowing in a cushion. Face roofward, she blew smoke-rings up through her nose.

There was an intermittent disturbance. When silence reigned once more, Mélanie sat up.

'Well there's another romance ended' she said harshly. 'How do you feel? Be a man Dan darling! You're only a man once!'

She rose and went over to the side of his divan. When she touched him he was quite limp.

'Get up Dan and come with me! I have something to show you.'

She shook him. He appeared quite inanimate. Next she rolled him over on his back: the entire six-foot-three of peach-fed, top-drawer, long-legged manhood gaped, a little pale, beneath her. The lips were open, the eyes were slightly rolled up as with a half-woken dog. The hair was a mass of tumbling locks, one great black tongue of hair licked the whitened cheek of the massive mask of Dante-Young.

She stood back: she blew a few rings of tobacco-smoke through her nostrils and gently inhaled, her thin shoulders drawn up square and high.

'Dan in your present condition you can't go out, you don't want to do you? You might get run over then what should we do? I will write and tell your father he had better send for you. Come into the house now. I have to go out. But you can go up and lie down. The room you had before is not occupied, you can go up there.'

There was no visible impression to denote that he had heard.

'I suppose I shall have to carry you' she said. She suited the action to the words at once.

Seizing him suddenly around the shoulders roughly, she dragged him into a sitting posture. He threatened to fall forward, but she kept him upright while she scolded:

'No! *Not* drop back! No! You must come with me. You must come with me! *Not* drop down!'

Dan suffered himself to be urged to his feet: with an arm about his waist, and a hand upon his bicep, Mélanie led him out of the studio, followed by Rabs, Bromo and Bluff.

As they approached the main entrance to the house, coming up the path connecting the street and garden, they met a small man, standing just inside the gate, his shoulders shrugged up, a ring of tobacco smoke issuing from his nose, who observed their approach with irony.

'Michael, Daniel here is not very well, I am going upstairs with him, to show him where he can lie and rest for a while. Will you take Bromo and Bluff out for a little run like a darling and come back here after that Michael? Thank you so much, you are a darling Michael! Rabs is not just himself today. Martha will take care of you darling. Oh Michael – I may be out. Wait for me. Thank you.'

Michael went in with them, he stood aside, his shoulders uplifted. This distortion went with an air of deeply and subtly inhaling some delectable fume. Ironic and silent, tobacco-smoke stealing from his nostrils, he allowed them to pass.

He took two dog-leads from the hall table, and, bending languidly down over Bromo and Bluff, attached them under their chests and over their heads.

Slowly Mélanie and Daniel went up the staircase, followed by Martha the french bonne silently in her felt slippers, who had come up from the basement after they had entered.

*

Dan still sat upon the edge of the bed in the room assigned him. His head was a chaos of hair, while his eyes looked out with a wild gravity at the blank wall before him. Books, writing-material, a sitting-room beyond: these were very comfortable quarters, for a fatigued young man. The door opened. Martha passed him with towels; she returned, without recognition of the sad immobile visitor, with her mechanical tread, and sallow mongol peasant-headpiece, and once more Daniel sat alone. He looked round with stealth in the direction in which Martha had disappeared, then turned his head back, to scrutinize the floor. The door opened. He hung his blood-red nether lip.

Mélanie entered. She was in hat and coat. She sat down upon a leather sofa, facing the bed, in front of Dan.

'I think you should lie down Dan' she said. 'Should you not lie down Dan. You have had a very trying experience my poor darling, you must be in some great need of rest I should say!'

Dan stared before him in a most stupid manner, which invited the belief that he was in need of a long and refreshing sleep.

'I think you need to rest, Dandarling' reported Mélanie in monotonous accents, that were calculated to attack with drowsiness any man already fatigued, and in need of rest. In the face of Dan the fatigue then deepened, moment by moment – it was certain that Dan required a mental détente so to speak, that only sleep could give, in a really comfortable bed, upon which at that time he sat in fact, but which he did not enter. Why?

'After a long rest Dan which you are wanting you will feel better. Why do you not lie down Daniel and forget what has happened? When you have slept that will pass off. That will pass off when you have rested a little!'

Mélanie dragged those weary drugged accents one by one out of her thin languid body, while she dragged it gently along the sofa, nearer to her haggard guest. Her keening head was stretched out in painful fellow-weariness, her lips distilled as she advanced the honey-dew or poppy-drops of her sham-Erse.

Dan sighed with bated breath, in sympathy, involuntarily. His nose began very gently to bleed. He brushed away a pale crimson smear from his lip.

'My poor Daniel' Mélanie Blackwell sighed at that. 'See! you are not yourself at all my poor honey, there is blood on your mouth my little sugarstick – let me wipe it away for you Dandarling!'

And having dragged her cat's body the length of the sofa, she launched it in a melting movement that was a running crouch, towards him, and she alighted upon the divan-bed, with a head slowly nodding above him, in a mimicry of commiseration, heavier-lidded at every instant, as she drew near to the point at which they might melt into one. With a handkerchief in her white-gloved hand she was wiping the discoloured portion of his lips. She did not remove her gloves, lest she might alarm him, but now she began to unbutton slowly his jacket, crooning hypnotically in his ear and nodding heavily and sadly with her head, her drugged senses smoothing the way, as they rocked her sluggishly, to effect this sultry capture.

'Take off your jacket Dandarling, you will be easier without your jacket, you cannot lie down in it you know honey, and you are too tired aren't you and all, to use your precious fingers just now – rest is all that you can do and you have not the strength to address yourself to ut, my poor wild black lily!'

With a dazzling white-kid-skinned hand she brushed back the savagery of his hair into ordered heaps, a coal-black sculpture, with a rhythmical motion, while he closed his eyes, he blushing deeply. She undid his waistcoat: his hand ran after hers and disputed with the other every button until they were all unfastened. The shirt too lost its stud, and there were finger-fights over its small mother-of-pearl buttons. But he was left with a shirt to his back after all though she had pulled at it too, somewhat. All the time she had been talking at him to keep him from getting too alarmed and restive, too conscious and shy.

'You're only a child Dandarling aren't you now but a big baby, I'll be your nursemaid this time honey and put you to Bye-Bye, I know how to do that – no let Mélanie do this for you, silly – don't be contrary! You must be undressed and all else you can't get to sleep you know: let me pull off this jacket it will make you more easy: and the little waisty! Oh it is a tight little waisty and all – there, it's stuck on the little shoulder-boulders! but off she comes, yes that's come nicely! That wasn't difficult was it now, come off with those big manly braces – no over the shoulder! That's right – now the other! Things that way are more simple, that's a big improvement: you can lay down your beautiful tired head on the pillow honey, it's all over.'

There was nothing to be done. Against this army of maternal fingers marching against his modesty as if it had been his chastity, one could but blush and blush and blush. Soon big baby-fellow would be as nude and naked as if this woman had just brought him into the world out of her very self and all, that was it – he was so helpless. It was the trick of the mothering that was being his undoing. Oh he was so terribly conscious of the *nude pieces!* – How she hurt him with her gloved fingers!

But now they were lying down side by side like mother and new-born infant and she held him – she had got his head down upon the pillow and her head had come there too if you please. Mélanie's mouth had certainly come up on to his mouth suddenly, in some manner, this was unpleasant but it scarcely mattered. His head rolled away, to escape these attentions. The other mouth came after him as if it had been hungry.

Beat off her hands he must – she was abusing! He did not like the warm breath of this woman – he would dress and leave this place at once! This house of ill-fame! Mélanie was going too far there were limits. To no purpose to *push* – she was as strong as a boa-constrictor the devil take her as he would for the wild woman she was! No *that* he would not allow!

'What are you doing?' he asked as he gave the woman with her eyes shut, who had covered him with her overcoat, a hard push. Mélanie did not answer, but strained her head sadly towards his, smiling with a drunken sadness.

'Is this hospitality?' he panted with a wealth of indignant reproach, in the low silver of his voice of a conscientious objector.

'Is it aisier ye are and all Dan dear, are ye feelin much better?' The panting mock-irish went on at his ear-drum. Was Mélanie mad entirely or what was it! Was she not going to leave now surely? It was his fault he should not have stopped there then this could never have happened. There was a spell of gruelling no-pleasure for anybody in this confused encounter an uphill crescendo – he fought off with baffled little *nos!* and *reallys!* the mechanical fury of kid-gloved slogging: the white kid-skinned instrument had got through all defences. Oh this woman was without mercy! The burglar of his electricity meantime got shocks from the handle of the machine and she shuddered at her mad devotions, her blind head stretched out in keening prayer.

A painful throbbing filled Dan's body at these unaccustomed contacts: shortly, there were icy needles that tore a passage. He was jumping clean out of his skin he was with alarmed sensations! Almost he shot his bolt of terror in one agony after another. 'Stop!' he insisted in rich tones of righteous anguish but Mélanie was not after stopping – she was after going right on to the bitter-sweet end of it, and it would be an explosion if she did for he would plainly burst with shame, in one big banging red blush – the virgin victim.

Off with your lips the harlot-woman! Off with the sticky and shameless mouth of you! – his disgust knew no bounds, he spat on the pillow. He heaved up the desecrated head of him out of reach of her lips, the whore of Babylon, in a grimace of disgusted protest that pleased her – the sad sensual kid-gloved harpy she was, and she smiled wanly. The small earnest face was all intent up under the lea of his quivering jaw, and sweating: he noted now at fever-pitch the veins in the lotus-eating eyelids and desired to vomit upon the whole machine, so fell and rhythmic and untiring. He was about to cat – in a moment he would be retching. And then his entire body fell down and gaped, it was sunk in a hot wallow of new shame – the thought of it! But had he, then, been sick or what, that there was this pulsing agony? It was the biggest blush of all! Dan shook her off, it was enough – he lay back with his eyes shut fast, unmolested, for she seemed to have risen – in darkness he collected his shattered senses that had given way beneath the strain. Mélanie kid-gloved as ever was stroking, it now seemed, his brow, with the hard kid-skinned fingers.

'Is it better that ye're feeling now stretched out upon your bed and all, is it not better honey!'

Dan could not trust himself to express his feelings. He was uncertain what they might be. He knew that some were at best too violent to be decently uttered. Also he was too lazy really far too heavy and absolutely sleepy – it was no use to attempt to move a muscle. Just now he would not he thought move a muscle. – But was this hospitality? It was his one thought – *Was this hospitality?*

'Dandarling now you'll be after sleeping won't you honey! Go to sleep Dannie. Go fast to sleep my little Dannie!'

Mélanie was leaving the bed, his prayer had been answered, this woman was going. But was this – but was this – but was this *Hospit* – ! Instantly almost Dan was soundly sleeping.

Part 3

THE ENCYCLICAL

DAN took out of his pocket Mélanie's five-pound-note that she had left upon the mantelpiece with a message. He handed it to the lodging-house keeper, and the lodging-house keeper went downstairs and came back with the change, that was two pounds ten. At the same time, wiping her hands upon her apron first, she held out a great sealed letter that was heavy, and must have come from a Firm.

Dan took it and compelled the powerful envelope to enter his jacket-pocket, bent in an elastic arc. It made a hollow in his clothes, on the side of him. An empty goitre of a pocket it was, as if implemented with whalebone to puff out the hip.

Pictures of unexpected fortune violently seized upon his fancy, without resistance. Clem and Pat his two first cousins had to be got rid of on the same day in a boating accident, it was a sudden squawl – his uncle Brian Macdonnell, their father, about the same time met his fate from decrepitude in County Down: he had a weak spot for Dan as was notorious. Clement and Patrick drowned in the lugger and out of the way the property was his. This letter when opened would say 'You are the heir'. He would be a landowner and go to Down and back, riches at his disposal now – instead of this poverty!

The nearest Tube station for Hampstead was there round the corner its salmon tower dominating the gardens. He started off smartly with a will: the books in the suit-case caused it to be a good load, he was not a strong boy: at the end of a few steps he slacked down at once. As he slowly carried the weight along, his arm was a tired pendulum – hurled the case along a little at each return and he got forward, but as best he could.

As he crossed the street he was bound to recollect the counsellings of Mélanie, about crossing the street. The escape from Sharratt Hill on this attractive morning, to go for his suit-case, had not taken place without his roundly being scolded in mock-irish for his absent-mindedness and all: sure and he was not safe to be let out of her sight in the streets unaccompanied, should she get Michael to go along with him to keep an eye open? No, not for the moment then: he was indeed a very careless young man, he was a young man who ought not to be allowed out by himself but it was so hard to know how for the best: a young man he was, that was a young man he was – but what was the use, her good counsels were lost on him: there were nineteen chances to one he'd get lost if he did not stick to the centres like Piccadilly, on no account must he go to Richmond or out to Pinner, he must not dream of crossing the big bridges across the rivers, there was a tide in the Estuary, the North Sea, and the Atlantic, and there were some Tubes that were worse than confusing, they led straight out into the wilderness right off the map into deserts of country – would he be sure to ask a porter? – if he met with an accident what should she say to her old friend Stephen? She did not know she was sure. But he would promise not to grow inattentive? or to dawdle too much? Never to talk to strangers! The men were worse than the women! He thought he had promised it was difficult to remember – at all events he had given her to understand. He never talked to strange men, emphatically.

If he were run over! The likelihood! There were however accidents: young men fell every day, they were found under taxis, many young men succumb to omnibuses, and young men fell to large drays, there were statistics available. So he would be picked up suffering from grave lesions and surgical shock and then dying before the ambulance came, for the policeman to find the sealed-up letter upon his person and would open it to detect the identity of the strange young man. 'This poor young man has just come into a considerable estate!' the good London Bobbie would confide to the passengers in the street and gaping loafers, gloating at accidents. 'He knew nothing about it though, poor young chap! Yet perhaps it was just as well that he should not have learnt of his good fortune sealed up in his pocket from the solicitors of the defunct, one Brian Macdonnell.'

In the Tube was where he opened the sealed envelope. He drew out a number of typewritten sheets. There was no will at all after all: what was it?

Reading at random he spelt out some phrases. They were full of mystery.

'The supreme judge is constantly absent . . . a successful partizan.'

'The finding of the supreme judge would automatically dissolve us all into limbo.'

Legal matter of some description. But his eye caught the word 'encyclical'.

As he was thinking did it come from a priest he saw it was addressed to Horace Zagreus. The strangest coincidence. A personal letter from His Holiness to Horace. But he put it away. He blushed very much for a big blond man was observing him.

*

When he was back at the house at Sharratt Hill he drew out the envelope. He was sitting in the large leather chair at the time by the window. Michael, the russian *drug-pimp* had Zagreus not said – *cocaine* – was smoking a cigarette at the gate. His shoulders were drawn up. He inhaled, supercilious seemingly, with Bromo or Bluff upon a lead. The Slave of the Dog – like the Slave of the Lamp, and a drug-pimp, a peculiar person. On his way to the Vet Michael was. Dan looked down at him and he wondered how old now Michael was – he had said he was thirty-nine. That was impossible: it was the age of his father, Stephen Boleyn, he had evidently mis-heard; thirty he might be. He had large estates from which he had to fly from his peasants. Mr Zagreus had said, '*He is a bolshevik.*' That was not possible. He was a penniless landowner, as he Daniel Boleyn hoped one day that he might be – now if that wasn't irish!

Upon the floor was a folded white sheet of paper. Dan regarded it in silence, determined not to make the first move. It had dropped from oh somewhere – there was not the energy in Dan to pick up anything just now, he looked down on it thoughtfully, thinking he might sneeze.

Now Dan turned to the encyclical, or the advertisement – he avoided the name at the top naturally. His heart was sore, it hungered for Horace, but he had to suppress such private emotions knowing his limitations. Nothing betrayed the reason for the dispatch of this official whatever-it-was, a bulletin for some vote. It was probably a public meeting. He lighted a cigarette, imitating the inhaling of the Russian Michael. His shoulders rose towards his ears and thereupon he became a russian fugitive who had had oh thousands of hair's-breadth escapes.

The high shoulders of the exiled Michael moved up the road above the walls of the villa-gardens, leading Bromo, or Bluff. Exaggerated distances in a lotus-land were what the quietism, or indolence, of Michael expressed – in which one led dogs up and down appointed paths in residential districts. Dogs were de rigueur – it was a mere convention that did not affect the mind's creature-comforts, as it moved idly, in the prearranged paths, grass or asphalt, nor did it matter when the Vet kept them for a week for treatment, there were others. Dogs were lost souls. Their leads led into one's everyday pocket.

With a straight shoulder-line risen some inches, Daniel watched Michael. He went over the bridge. He was out of sight. Dan stopped staring and dropped down his shoulders with a run. He had not noticed that they had got up it was a fact though, their descent was a surprise.

Sinking into the corner, he reached over the leather bulwark of the chair a lazily fishing arm to it and picked up the white sheet of paper from the floor. He unfolded it, but no sooner had the sheet come open than he was stunned with feelings that whirled round and round like hot Catherine Wheels in his middle.

The paper was a letter from Mr Zagreus. It was to *Dear Dan*. Horace had written! The Son of the Morning shouted for joy, this letter was manna! He was on his feet at *Dear Dan* in a bound as if it had been a word of command from High Heaven. He could not sit still with such a thing in his hand it was impossible. He gazed at it blushing with new life. He dropped back into the chair, overcome with a faintness: he had to wait for some minutes while his heart beat a tattoo, before he could look at it. Then tears burst from his eyes. They dried quickly on his red-hot cheeks. – A moment after he was able to read it.

This was a letter in duplicate. It was marked C.6307. It was dated Thursday. He read it and reread it, again and again. And it was written as follows.

Dear Dan. You must excuse me for so hurriedly leaving you today at the gate of Hyde Park. I was upset by the meeting with that very rude fellow, who accosted me. You may have remarked that I drew from my pocket, just before that, a sealed letter. It had been my intention to hand it you before we parted

The letter I had in my pocket was the enclosure that I now subjoin. It contained an invitation, the material part of which I now reproduce. This then is what I have to say.

You are nineteen and just come up to London and have not yet found your feet. 'People are in general what they are made, by education and company, from fifteen to five-and-twenty' Lord Chesterfield wrote to his son. You are approaching the meridian of that period. Things are critical. Will you place yourself in my hands? If you consent, I will acquit myself to the best of my ability of this task – to do for you what was done for me. If so late in life that system of enlightenment could be so effectively carried through on my behalf, all the more should it be able to accomplish that for you, and put you on the right track for good.

The society you are now entering you must understand or perish: I mean your mind. *I believe absolutely in your genius.* You are a child of the Moon, when I first set eyes on you I knew it, you possess the *virtus vegetandi.* I solicit the privilege of being your gardener at this crisis, oh delicate moon-flower. Have I your permission? Please give me your answer without delay, there is no time to be lost.

As to the document that accompanies this, show it to no one. Several years ago I received it, it is written by a man who is in everything my master – I am nothing, he is everything. It speaks for itself. In it he describes what he then undertook to do. He was successful I rejoice to say: I will (not as he could but to the best of my power) perform in your case a similar service.

Telephone to me as soon as you get this.

Adieu.
Horace Zagreus

Having read every word of this message a dozen times through Dan rose. He was dazed with his happiness and the joy of the letter. Slowly he rubbed his eyes. He took up with a reverential carefulness the typewritten pages that accompanied it. He read slowly the following document, from start to finish.

EXTRACT FROM ENCYCLICAL ADDRESSED TO MR ZAGREUS

In my review of this society, especially with regard to its reaction upon art, I rather insist upon than seek to slur over the fact that

I am a party. But it is from amongst the parties that the acting judge is ultimately chosen. Where else should you get him from? The supreme judge is constantly absent. What we call a judge is a successful partizan. It is on account of the superior percentage of truth in the composition of your glosses that your statement is erected into a standard. And 'Of an opinion which is no longer doubted, the evidence ceases to be examined.' The finding of the supreme judge would automatically dissolve us all into limbo. Some – who are upon the outside limit of the gaussian law of error – we instinctively admire most, not least. We feel I think that they are most alive. But you cannot "be alive" and adjudicate. – There is no universal consent upon the subjects of which I am treating. The *novelty* of any time enables people to pretend that they are existing in the state of society that in fact they have superseded. (It is an old political expedient to pretend to be what you have destroyed.) They will pretend that their abuses are old abuses and that only their reforms are new. – Things however that I have put forward as facts – not as fair comment – will be verified by you in due course. Fortunately there no one can balk the truth of my evidence.

The dreams of the economist-utopist in a sense are already realized, upon a small scale, today. In that respect the society of the future is already with us. He could study, in its full working effect, one of his favourite and most attractive theories, and upon a considerable scale: namely that of Everyman possessed of leisure and means to enjoy the delectations of Art (when Parnassus becomes a recreation ground of unlimited extent and the humblest citizen is an amateur of some or of all the arts).

The economic reformer is not himself usually an amateur of any art. 'He knows what he likes' perhaps. If you suggested that his *taste* invited improvement he would be indignant. He is an economist and at figures he is good. – He is generally a poor observer of the life around him – else he would often remark his favourite schemes in effective operation in current life (upon a miniature scale), and this in many instances would discourage him.

For example. Any art-school containing a hundred students, could demonstrate for him what happens when a hundred people *chosen for their talent*, devote *all* their time to the prosecution of *one* art. Their subsequent professional career (upon the walls of the Royal Academy or in the illustrated journals) he would be forced to conclude was not encouraging for his enthusiastic picture of a universal cultured amateurism upon the Western super-democratic pattern.

But better perhaps than that, our speculative economist could be shown to-day, in full flower, a society of people with ample means and leisure – living in full contact with art and artists – in the only modern city traditionally famous for the exploits of the intelligence. He could not ask for a better test. He could not receive a more discouraging answer!

The traditional 'Bohemia' has changed radically since the War. The reason is this. Everyone able to afford to do so has become a 'bohemian'. This is the term still employed by the more naïf of the transformed majority. But of course traditionally that person was called a 'bohemian' who could not afford to be anything else. The tramp, or the cynic *by choice*, upon a vast scale, constitutes a novel type.

Paris where there are incomparably more people living on familiar (and naturally contemptuous) terms with Art than anywhere else, is in reality a very large club for the well-to-do. The well-off find the studio-café society the only one in which they are free to live as they choose. It is unnecessary to say that these large groups of people, numbering many thousands, are not for the most part occupied in any pursuit more exacting than that of paying calls, and acting as clients to the Paris night resorts. A floating population of very young students lends the necessary air of 'bohemian' illusion and juvenility to these large idle cosmopolitan settlements. They provide constant human currents and freshets in which the more hardened old sinners can fish.

It would be unnecssary to give these 'bohemian' populations a second thought if they were merely engaged in amusing themselves to the extent that their incomes allow them, and if they exercised no influence upon the creation of art. Why a closer and less benevolent scrutiny is required, is because wherever an individual, through the ages, has had leisure and money to spare, he has relied upon the artist to supplement his wits with the resources of a more serious study than he is prepared to devote, himself, to anything. He has relied upon the artist to provide that significant apparatus of intelligence and beauty, which makes the pleasures of the wealthy less empty than they otherwise would be.

But these numerous bohemian populations, notably in Paris, are no exception to this rule. For (living in studios and cafês and in consequence identified for the uninitiated with the traditional world of the 'Vie de Bohême') although they do not for the most part paint or write or compose music themselves, yet they find the art that *is* being produced in their neighbourhood a source of stimulating tittle-tattle. And the intellectual gladiators engaged in such occupations become a sort of perpetual game-of-ninepins for the malice or conceit of their *désœuvrement*.

Painting – that art that depends more upon spatial conditions than any other art – is as might be expected heavily handicapped, to start with, by the mere fact of these hordes occupying the studios that were intended in the first place, it is to be assumed, for painters. Another difficulty is this. When fresh 'studios' are built it is usually upon such a sumptuous scale that no genuine 'struggling artist' can afford to rent them. They are built upon this scale because the landlord is quite aware that the last person likely to occupy them is *an artist*. Still another point is that the affluence of his pseudo-artist tenants is not lost upon the landlord, and studio-rents in consequence rise daily.

Again since the people of whom we are talking are always ostensibly 'poor', the small pokier studios (which might otherwise be left for a painter) are taken by them. It is so 'quaint', 'attractive', and it is such 'fun' to rough it. – Still, art it would seem is a tenacious flower. So in a few back-rooms at the top of small hotels, or in chilly ill-lit shacks just holding together, that sprawl against each other in some damp courtyard, an occasional artist succeeds in painting a picture, or modelling a piece of clay. Sometimes, in some very inconvenient corner of the town – overlooked by, or too far out for the New Bohemians – a real studio falls to the lot of a painter. For painters (although they have not got them) are always thinking and talking about *studios*. And so occasionally, owing to the persistence of this obsession, they get on the track of some derelict garage that is falling vacant – for some reason forgotten by the sleuths and agents of the wealthy Bohemian. – It is in reality still very much the squalor of Henri Murger for the real painter.

These conditions, upon a different scale, are reproduced in London and probably in other cities.

But again, if such were the only misdemeanours of our prosperous friends, we should not need to say very much about them – although they would still serve as sardonic paradigms for our speculative economist – for no opportunity is denied them of occupying their time in the most elevated pursuits as he would have them do, and yet towards which they display a most consistent shyness.

But there *is* a more active type. And it is with him that I have principally to deal. All that remains to be considered is this active minority – and how the whole of this immense and costly *aping*, by the idlest of the rich, of the artist's life has affected, and is likely to affect, the occasional apparition of genius.

Being born in a stable does not make you a horse. But living in a studio produces in some persons a feeling that they should dabble and daub a little. Again, possessing independent means (a rarer thing every day) and in your native conventional milieu life growing less and less accommodating, should you by some chance always have possessed a certain 'high-brow' proclivity – have had a taste for music, for instance – you are apt to go and live in Paris or Italy. The exchange doubles your income – the amenities of life are of a 'pre-war' character. But Paris still rings with the activities of THE ARTIST. It is still the centre of 'civilization' as much as ever. You become an amateur, in the sense that you must be able to talk about what other people are always discussing.

My information upon these subjects is quite first-hand. You may think that the picture I draw is unfair (if you like 'ferocious') or that my sources of information are interested and unfriendly. You must judge for yourself when you visit Paris, or know London better. The fact is, then, that all these masses of Gossip-mad, vulgar, pseudo-artist, *good-timers* – the very freedom and excess usually of whose life implies a considerable total of money, concentrated in the upkeep of this costly 'bohemian' life – are the last people, as every artist will tell you, from whom support for any art can be expected. They are as vulgar as any of their more simple-hearted and simply ostentatious *nouveau riche* first cousins – usually as illiterate, more insolent and vindictive where their betters are concerned, and a hundred times as damaging, in their influence, to every form of creative thought.

They are more damaging for the very reason that they are identified, in the mind of the public, with art and with intelligence. Their influence is brought to bear invariably in the propagation of the second-rate – for that does not challenge their conceit, and it fraternizes with the fundamental vulgarity with which they have not parted, in their new surroundings. Yet the indications of their favour are considered as direct tips from the stable, as oracles of inside information. They are the *friends*, the bosom friends of art. And their opinions are invested with the authority of this intimacy. Unlike most friends, however (whose malignities are often illuminating) theirs seldom bear any relation to the original. They are the *un*paying guests of the house of art: the crowd of thriving valets who adopt the livery of this noble but now decayed establishment, *pour se donner un air* – to mock, in their absence, its masters.

If you enquire how it is that these people come to play this rôle, I should say that there are two main reasons. The first is this: that in the case of a genuine 'amateur', or collector of pictures or more generally, any habitual 'supporter of the arts' – like the classical patrons of the renaissance, the great patrons of Turner and Gainsborough or the French Kings – he will have a personal interest – if it is only an economic one, or one of prestige – in the things with which his name and personality are associated. An opinion can be changed every week, but not a substantial possession, to which your judgment is pinned. And such 'amateurs' as these were the only people, formerly, who had a personal entrée to the world of art, or any personal interest in it. The legions of contemporary 'amateurs', with rare exceptions, have no such interests. For they are careful not to involve themselves economically in a thing they can get as much out of as they require without spending a penny-piece.

The second cause (and this applies to a much smaller number of such people – only indeed, to the very cream and élite of them) is that some (born with a happy or unhappy knack not possessed by their less talented fellows) produce a little art themselves – more than the inconsequent daubing and dabbing we have noticed, but less than the 'real thing'. And with this class you come to the Ape of God proper. For with these unwonted and unnecessary labours, and the *amour-propre* associated with their results, envy steps in. The complication of their malevolence that ensues is curious to watch. But it redoubles, in the natural course of things, the fervour of their caprice or ill-will to the 'professional' activities of the effective artist – that rare man born for an exacting intellectual task, and devoting his life unsparingly to it.

There I think you have the two main causes of this atmosphere of restlessness, insecurity and defamation – in which books painting or music of a serious sort is produced today. For this vast array of troublesome 'supers' that swarm all over the stage are a far more noisy and presumptuous fraternity than the gallants who insisted upon invading the Elizabethan Stage – sitting among the actors, to display in that way their personalities to the best advantage, and whose stupid and insolent chatter was such a source of irritation to the players, apart from their inconvenient presence upon the boards when a play was in progress.

It is as regards this second active category of *amateurs*, these *productive* 'apes', that I may be useful to you. I can point them out to you, and find means for you to be among them – appreciate the truth of what I have described, and draw your own conclusions. In a little artificial world of carefully fostered self-esteem I will show you a pseudo-Proust. I shall be able to introduce you, among a family of 'great poets', (each of them upon a little frail biographical family pedestal) where all the exultations of labour, a passionate experience, and probably a straitened life, issuing in works of great creative art, are thinly parodied, at great expense. The general rabble that collects under the equivocal banner of ART – the 'crowd' in as exact a sense as any other easily-swayed, brutal, readily-stampeded, collection of human beings – I will leave you to examine where you like.

I will here insert a necessary caution: namely that I am not identifying poverty with genuine artistic success, or riches with its opposite. Cézanne and Manet for example were wealthy men, as much as Van Gogh or Ingres were without fortune. Montaigne had money, Villon had not; and so on. You Zagreus have money. But that will not condemn you to futility, any more than would poverty, if only because you are an 'original' (excuse me). It is to what I have called the Apes of God that I am drawing your attention – *those prosperous mountebanks who alternately imitate and mock at and traduce those figures they at once admire and hate*. And bringing against such individuals and their productions all the artillery of the female, or bi-sexual tongue, will abuse the object of their envy one day, and imitate him the next: will attempt to identify themselves with him in people's minds, but in the same breath attempt to belittle him – to lessen if possible the disadvantage for them that this neighbourhood will reveal. I will make them parade before you in their borrowed plumes like mannequins, spouting their trite tags, and you shall judge if my account is true.

So far I have spoken principally of Paris. But the same conditions can be studied upon the spot – in Chelsea, Bloomsbury, and Mayfair. In England for a very long time this sort of *societification* of art has been in progress. It is even possible that the English were the first in the field with the *Ape* art-type. The notorious *amateurism* of the anglo-saxon mind makes this doubly likely. In *Bloomsbury* it takes the form of a select and snobbish club. Its foundation-members consisted of monied middleclass descendants of victorian literary splendour. Where they approximate to the citizens of this new cosmopolitan Bohemia is in their substitution of money for talent as a qualification for membership. Private-means is the almost invariable rule. In their discouragement of too much unconservative originality they are very strong. The tone of 'society' (of a spurious donnish social elegance) prevails among them. Where they have always *differed* has been in their *all* without exception being Apes of God. That is the first point. All are 'geniuses', before whose creations the other members of the Club in an invariable ritual, must swoon with appreciation. There is another rather curious way in which they differ – namely in their dress. For whereas the new Bohemian is generally as 'mondain' and smart, if a little fantastic, as he or she can be, this little phalanstery of *apes of god* went the length of actually dressing the part of the penniless 'genius'. In this way they presented the curious spectacle of a lot of men and women, possessed of handsome bank balances, drifting and moping about in the untidiest fashion. This rather scandalous shabbiness it was, besides a queer exaggeration of speech (bringing to one's mind the sounds associated with the spasms of a rough Channel passage) that cut them off from the outside world – also perhaps their freakish *literal* interpretation of the august aloof originals. – They yield to none, however (and in that provide an instructive analogy) in their organized hatred of *living* 'genius'. Even they have made a sort of cult of the *amateur* – the child artist – and in short any imperfectly equipped person. Naturally they exercise their influence in the interests of what is virtually their club. A certain network of not very remunerative patronage extends over outsiders who are not too important. In their headquarters in Bloomsbury it would be possible to visit them. But altogether too many Apes and wealthy 'intelligentsia' have come on the scene for them to have maintained their unique position. I think you can disregard them. *Bloomsbury* is really only what is called 'old Bloomsbury', which is very moribund – the bloom is gone.

To sum up what I have said: By adopting the life of the artist the rich have not learnt more about art, and they respect it less. With their more irresponsible 'bohemian' life they have left behind their 'responsibilities' – a little culture among the rest. Indeed they are almost as crudely ignorant as is the traditional painter. Besides – living in cafés, studios and 'artistic' flats – they are all 'artists' in a sense themselves. They have made the great discovery that every one wielding brush or pen is not a 'genius', any more than they are. But they have absorbed a good deal of the envy of those who are not 'geniuses' for those who are (having in a sense placed themselves upon the same level) – and the contempt of those who are, for those who are not. The result is that they abominate good art as much as bad artists do, *and* have as much contempt for bad art as have good artists! There is more indifference to and often hatred of every form of art in these pseudo-artistic circles – in the studios, in short, now mostly occupied by them – than in all the rest of the world put together. How does this affect the 'good' art? The *patron* having come to live more or less in the artist's studio – that has not been found to answer any better for one sort of artist than for the other.

As to the class of well-to-do people who say 'Why should I not write a book of verses or paint a picture? I could not do it worse than so and so, whose profession it is. Also I have more time than the poet so and so, or the painter so and so, to write or to paint – as they have to make money.' These people are not likely to be of very much use to the art of which they become not a supporter but an exponent. For who ever heard of one artist helping another, his competitor? Except such rare people as exist as well among the wealthy as among the poor.

When you consider that the whole of the graphic and plastic arts at least have in the past been sustained upon the structure of stable wealth and seigneurial or burgess ostentation, of those people who (such as are left) have metamorphosed themselves into a sort of ever-swelling tribe of mock-artists, then the distress of an artist who is not rich, especially whose gifts are not spectacular, is easy to understand. But there are many valuable artists in every period who are without money, and whose talent is not immediately obvious.

Without going further into this, I have laid bare for you the present predicament of art. I have given an outline of the present dispositions of its natural audience – showing how the decline in their wealth, culture and sense of responsibility has brought down with it those intellectual activities that depended upon it. Naturally individuals of finer stamp and pattern always are to be found. But the great majority not supported by any personal interior life perfectly account for the extreme disarray that you will witness.

To return to what I began by saying as to being *a party*. I am not in agreement with the current belief in a strained 'impersonality' as the secret of *artistic* success. Nor can I see the sense of pretending – as it must be a pretence, and a thin one, too – that in my account to you of what I have seen I can be impartial and omniscient. That would be in the nature of a bluff or a blasphemy. There can only be one judge, and I am not he.

I am not a judge but a party. All I can claim is that my cause is not an idle one – that I appeal less to passion than to reason. The flourishing and bombastic rôle that you may sometimes see me in, that is an effect of chance. Or it is a caricature of some constant figure in the audience, rather than what I am (in any sense) myself. Or, to make myself clearer, it is my opposite.

To be *an artist* now he had always wished thought Dan to himself, meditating about all this – he had never been able to afford a brush and he supposed the pigment and plaster casts, as they were so poor in Dublin but now Mr Zagreus had made him the offer to be an artist – he *absolutely* believed in his genius (what artists had) he had written to him. And he would take a great studio for him in the Paris Latin Quarter, Dan was simply as exultant as a swan and his throat half-burst with rapture: he sprang to his feet: he plunged out of his apartment, the letter and the manuscript flourished in his fist, and he burst headlong into Mrs Blackwell's studio in the garden.

The dogs Bromo, Bluff and Rabs sprang up and barked *intruder!* one after the other. Mélanie in an overall sat upon a high star-punctured tabouret. She was painting a bright picture, full of the Warm South, with a bright volcanic blush, parched stucco farm-shacks, plages and so on. There was a puff-puff, off-stage, and a great clock to time the light and shade, and the ellipse of the distant partridge-tent.

Dan stood panting at some distance. The tall boy swayed giddily, his expression all radiant with new-born hope and the sacred fire of the *genius* that one living creature at least believed in. – His own father had never said – it had been left to a total stranger to discover!

'Mélanie!' in ponderous lisping rapture he articulated her name to call her attention.

'Dandarling!' she exclaimed sentimentally, folding her hands in her lap with the brushes.

'Can you teach me how to paint pictures in oils oh do please say *yes!*'

'What on earth for!' Mélanie was thoroughly astonished. But she put down her brushes then she mocked the notion: 'To paint is it! But you're crazy entirely – what are you after wanting to paint for Dan-honey, tell me that now for the love of Mike – that is a most dangerous risky occupation that I could never bear to think of you pursuing without someone there with you at all events – ye'd be wiping the white lead off of the fingers into the dear great brown eyes of ye, or be jazers ye'd be after sucking your thumb that was all blue and Prussiany and poisoned entirely! No Dan-darling don't you be putting that great novel burden upon me poor weak fiminine shoulders honey – I should never have a day's peace and all!'

The transports of Daniel Boleyn fell to zero while Mélanie was speaking, and doubt succeeded to his exaltation. Perhaps, thought Dan, he would never paint in oils after all – Zagreus could not be expected to take him up unless he had first shown his mettle with the brush, his poem though traditional

'Cynthia do not spoil my hair,
Harp-tongued tigress – Cynthia'

and cetera of which Mr Zagreus was so fond and had kept a copy, would give no guarantee of genius – oil-painters and the sopranos of the Opera had it, he did not think poets were like that. He must steal some of these paints here of Mrs Blackwell's, but where oh where perform the Oil that was necessary? And without one of those sticks with a ball on the end that he had watched Mélanie holding, to rest on, sighting her brush, with erect little finger he would be lost. For he was positive his hand would never do it without a rest or be sufficiently steady to draw in oils – paint. Oh dear!

He lifted up a pearl-pale hand. He looked at it and he saw it steadily and saw it whole. It was as firm as a rock!

He dropped it sighing to his side. Ah yes, but in the heat of creation it would tremble like an aspen! He knew it only too well. His hand was not reliable and could not be depended on in the crisis, the falterer. It defeated its own ends.

Dan had become very melancholy now. He was perplexed.

'Mélanie!' he said in a sad plaintive accent.

'Yes Dan-darling' said Mélanie 'what is it?'

'What is the *Ape?*'

'The ape?'

'The *Ape of God*'

'The ape of *what?*'

'Of God, Mélanie' said Dan in a sinking voice, at the word 'God' veiling his lustrous swimming honest-to-goodness eyes of Abie's irish rose.

'Are ye mad entirely today Dan-honey? Oh what has happened!' She got quickly down now from off the great stool, extremely concerned. 'Has anything happened Dandarling to cause ye to wander in ye reason, that ye come bursting in here with such strange questions and all!'

Dan blushed and simply gazed hopelessly at the floor. Less and less did he comprehend what was expected of him or how he could become an oil-painter there was no time.

With her face for keening and her eyelids growing more caressingly heavy at every moment, Mélanie began to glide towards him, wailing miserably as she approached:

'*Strong i' th arm and weak i' the head* as they say in Liverpool Dan. That's where it comes in – the least thing upsets the dear wandering mind of ye and makes ye talk in that wild manner – it's for that Dannie that I'm so unaisy when ye go out at all child in the great public streets. For if one of those great brutes of police got hold of ye they'd not understand. Mightn't they spirit ye away to some place of confinement and we should never any of us see ye again!'

Now she stood beside him dwarfed by the great wild statue of a young man that he was. And reaching up her hand to his head, its passage over his body having the gesture of the hands of the hypnotist, over the person of an entranced medium, she brushed back the shog of unstemmed wobbling locks that had tumbled upon his forehead – at the time he rushed from his room with his news.

'And what is that honey that ye've got hold of so stiff and tight in your little fist there now? Is there something confined in it – have ye brought it to show me!'

She reached up her tough dry lips, her neck stuck out in yearning keen. She kissed him upon the chin, while her hand closed in upon his where the letter and document were.

Dan handed her the letter, and the document.

Frowning as she uncovered both, she said:

'What is this? Horace Zagreus – may ill-luck be in his road!'

Mélanie went over quickly to her usual settee and Dan to the second, the red-cushioned one, and they sat down.

'Is it he that has told you to paint, is that it then? He's only laughing at you Dannie, can't you see that darling – Horace has kissed the Blarney Stone and everything to him is a joke that is all! He's pulling your leg my poor angel!'

She started to read the manuscript.

'Have you seen him?' she said as she read.

Dan shook his head.

'I told you a lie yesterday Daniel do you know – Horace never said anything about you, I made that up. It was necessary to save you from his clutches bad luck to him. He'd ruin you if he could. I am responsible.'

Dan almost looked angry, as he frowned with pain, for she had opened the wound of yesterday. As there was no stir she quitted her reading for a moment and said:

'You must not be vexed – a white lie it was only you poor helpless baby, you should thank me for it so you should!'

She returned to the document. For five minutes she read on without remark. The smoke of her cigarette poured from her nostrils upon the paper at intervals.

'Ah Ape of God! Now I see what that was – Ape of God!' she sneered, scornful and weary. She discharged two frail nose-blasts of blue scented smoke at the offensive page. Again the attentive reading went on in silence.

'What does all this mean for mercy's sake!' she muttered. 'I've never been within a hen's race of such nonsense!'

She put down the manuscript upon the settee beside her as she finished it and looked across at Dan with a hint of a suspicious challenge. But his expression conveyed nothing but that he was conscious of being born to paint in oils and that yet he might never do so owing to circumstances over which he had no control.

'Have you read this?' she asked him.

Dan nodded sadly – certainly. It had been read by him, yes.

'Horace has gone mad!' she exclaimed. 'I do really think he is not quite in his right senses. I had heard he had become peculiar lately. Here is the proof of it.'

Almost weeping, Dan whispered,

'He says he believes in me and will take me a studio.'

'Where does he say that?'

She opened the letter. Still frowning she read it through with a quick capable eye.

'I can't see that anywhere. Where does he say that?' she repeated, looking up at him.

Dan made a helpless gesture towards the manuscript, and towards the letter.

'You must have dreamed that Dan – that is not what he says at all. He has sent you a tirade about all of us by that charlatan Pierpoint.'

Dan looked puzzled.

'You have not heard of Pierpoint? No one ever sees him now – he has shut himself up for some reason. Pierpoint is a painter turned philosopher. He says he wants a studio, but as he never paints I can't see what he wants one for. He models himself upon Whistler.'

Dan rolled his lovely eyes.

'I do so wish that I had a studio Mélanie!' he murmured wistfully and then was quiet.

Mélanie put her head out to keen and she filled her face with the drowsiness of the Twilight of the Gael.

'And what Dan should you be after wanting a studio for now Honeystick?'

There was no answer from *the-genius-without-a-studio*, except for a dumb appeal for a studio. Mélanie sighed. She looked about her, with the contempt bred of familiarity with much studios.

'I suppose Pierpoint would call me an Ape' she said. 'Yes I am an Ape of God all right, according to this.' She slightly lifted the manuscript.

Dan opened his eyes wide and examined her closely.

'Yes I am an Ape of God' she droned wearily over at him, showing her teeth, nodding her head up and down, *ah-yessing* poetically.

Dan scrutinized her still more closely.

'I have money, Pierpoint would say far more than is good for me. I do nothing with it of any service to – whatever it is he thinks. I have a studio! Though for thinking I have no great turn, I paint to amuse myself. So you see. I am afraid I am an Ape of God!'

Dan looked hard at the Ape, then looked away in embarrassment.

Mélanie sighed and smiled but cast off this burden of apehood, and then she proceeded.

'What idea has Horace been putting into your young head Dan – has he been at his blarney with you, telling you you're a grand pictor ignotus is it – do you think you would like to be an artist now because of some nonsense of Horace – it's some practical joke that he's played on you, and you've believed him to the nines. I think it's all flattery, he hopes he will get you in his power by that, ill luck be in his road! I could wring the neck of him!'

Dan nodded his head violently.

'You wish to paint do you mean?'

Dan nodded his head with greater vehemence.

'Come with me to Azay-le-Promis! I should love to teach you how to paint Dandarling! Or perhaps you would teach me.'

Immediately Dan grew distracted and sad. He was Horace Zagreus's especial genius and not the genius of Mélanie. He got up and walked swiftly to the door, eyeing her paints and brushes as he passed them. He frowned upon the studio in toto.

'Where are you going Dandarling?' Mélanie exclaimed with anxiety.

He had gone with the determined gait with which he strode beside his master – when they should go out to meet the Apes, upon their escapades.

He was going to Horace Zagreus, who believed in his *genius!*

Part 4

BE NOT TOO FINICAL

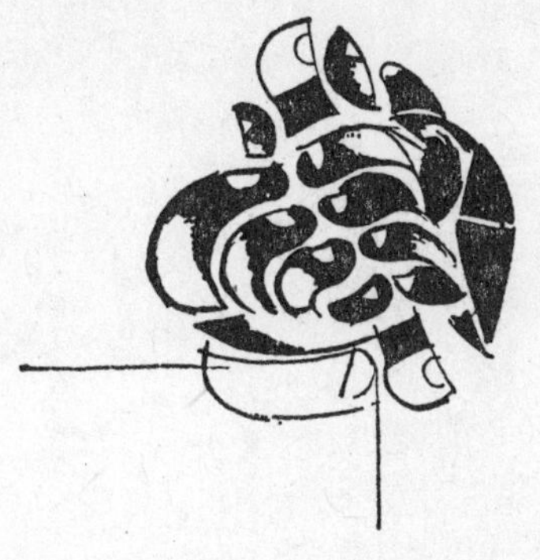

FROM Dan to Beersheba, he had not faltered. Hillman had met him at high-noon. There had been three visits before tea had come round, a dinner with Orchard Bassett and Hedges, at the Shanghai in Greek Street, and so to the Old Vic. The Merchant of Venice was a nightmare. That had been *his* pound of flesh. He withdrew to the lavatory for two long periods. The second time he had gone to sleep with his head between his hands. The last act he had spent being counted out – what had this week of plays to do with the matter?

He had met three hundred and sixty Apes since Tuesday, and since last Saturday he had only seen Horace Zagreus once and he had hardly spoken to him, except to say '*Well?*'

Well!

He had left the Old Vic in a stupor. But with the tread of a gladiator he had passed out into the Borough High Street. No one would have guessed. Bassett was with him. And then a long night-party, with fifty persons some dressed as beach-Pierrots. He had conversed with several, escaped from five determined women, two of whom were quite young – hidden in a garden latrine, crouched behind a rolled-up mattress, noted the presence of many minor Apes, and left more dead than alive at three in the morning. And even then before retiring for the night he had made up his log, in ink, by candlelight.

Two kindly Apes had escorted him home, the night before that, which was Thursday night. *The Apes are kind*, he had said in his heart, but at the door one of them had taken a liberty. He had pushed him over (for he was drunk) by accident. Three policemen had arrived and the second Ape had decamped. The one that was upon the ground and who had expectorated at him from that position, had been carried off. But he appeared to mollify the constables, for in the distance he had observed them release him. In a taxi he had seen him finally depart from the neighbourhood, and he believed he noticed one of the night-police waving a handkerchief but about that he could not be sure.

He might have been menacing his assailant, or just blowing his nose. The street-lamp was not bright enough.

This loneliness was terrible!

Dan lay and yawned upon his spartan pallet. His feet were so sore he was reluctant to rise. Three weeks of this already, he was but a wreck! He was a shadow of himself. At the prospect of the six weeks in store, he stared in despair at this ominous cell, chosen for him to banish comfort and enable the Ape-hunter to lay down his tired body merely and keep it hard and well, when not absent at the chase. There was a punch-ball beyond the table. But Mr Zagreus believed in him utterly. *You are a genius!* he had said last week as he had been showing him his log in which he had written out something like this only better: 'Met Monty Hampton. He is an Ape. He is rich. He has thirteen studios. Bronze medallist *Salon d'Automne.* Has whipped three greek boys to death.' He knew he had invented the studios in order to please Mr Zagreus but that was nothing, the greek boys were accurate as far as they went, but that was Michael Beck. The muddle was not his in the first instance. Willie Service had pointed him out as having – it was only afterwards he had found it was not Hampton but Beck. – Tooting Beck – that reminded him of – there was a rare Ape in that district. He had heard of him from Willie. He had a chicken farm and he called him the 'butter and egg merchant' – he wrote verse, and was very rich, he had persecuted eight young penniless poets one mortally, he was reputed to know more firemen than any one in the West (end, that is), and to be in hiding really, hence Tooting. He had caused three fires in Clapham. *He was rich and incendiary.* He had many houses and was of american origin. He had heard of this Ape through Willie, who was on his track. *The butter-and-egg-merchant-Ape* – it would look well in the log he felt certain. – But such were merely the idle dreams of a busy sleuth before he put his sore feet to the floor and took up the day's routine. The coffee was cold, but he could hot it up on the gas-ring in the saucepan. From one glazed eye he had seen Mrs Phillips put what looked like two letters beside his plate. He rose and had a pyjama-stalk for a match to light the gas fire and the gas-ring.

His feet were sore – and his bones ached – then he took some vaseline and rubbed it between his toes. He put on his overcoat.

The coffee-pot was next emptied into the nickel saucepan and the gas-ring began to hot up the coffee.

A book belonging to the small library supplied for his special use by Mr Zagreus was open beside his bed. It was one of the fifteen 'livres de chevet' especially recommended. He took it up and read the following lines, upon a page marked for his attention.

The rough Hippolitus was Phaedra's care;
And Venus thought the rude Adonis fair.
Be not too Finical; but yet be clean;
And wear well-fashion'd Cloaths, like other Men.
Let not your teeth be yellow, or be foul;
Nor in wide Shoes your Feet too loosely roul.
Of a black Muzzel, and long Beard beware;
And let a skilful Barber cut your Hair:
Your Nailes be pick'd from filth, and even par'd;
Nor let your nasty Nostrils bud with Beard.
Cure your unsav'ry Breath, gargle your Throat,
And free your Arm-pits from the Ram and Goat.

If he had pondered once, he had pondered a hundred times upon this enigmatical passage, or one with such a cruel ambiguity, brought to his attention by Horace Zagreus. The tears stood in his eyes as he gazed at the page, with its beastly injunctions.

Why oh why should he be treated in this way by Horace? He had had a horrid dream when he had first come upon this hideous page in which a black and white kid nestled in the left and right pits of his arms which were enormous as though they had been children of the Orc, deposited in Cyclopean bird's-nests, with a rank stink. His nostrils, which had not the suspicion of a bristle, seemed in his nightmare to be obstructed with an inky undergrowth. His fingernails were charged with a moist packing of opaque foulness, in mad mourning, at which he had picked and picked, as he had been ordered. For it was not written in that dreadful treatise that, though to avoid the Finical was quite essential, yet you at all cost must be *clean?* And in his anguished sleep he laboured to rid himself of his goats and rams – to blow his nose lest his nostrils should be called nasty – and to excavate the foul deposits of both finger and toe nail.

'Cure your unsav'ry Breath, gargle your Throat!'

As he came to this abominable line he flung the book away from him in a passion. Oh why did Horace Zagreus hate him so much! Oh why did he love Horace – and it was himself was in need of his kindness – when Horace did nothing but insult him!

Dan sat down to the table. The striated lemon-white wood was spotless, as scrubbed by Mrs Phillips the house-char.

The first letter had a foreign stamp. He stuck his finger into it, he tore at it with this hook, he removed its kernel – a wide sheet of blue folded paper, headed *Villa Saint-Genest. Azay-le-Promis. B. du R.* from Mélanie Blackwell. He read.

Dan darling. I am so anxious about you darling. Why don't you write me a word at least as you promised you would to say you are alive? Have you perhaps moved? The room here is waiting for you when you want it. I have written to Horace to say what I think of him. I know it is no use my saying anything more at the present moment. When your infatuation is over and you have found him out come out here at once. – Send me a wire. Mélanie

The coffee boiled, Dan put down the letter from Azay-le-Promis, and when he returned he took up the long typewritten envelope, that contained his instructions for the day. He ripped its head quickly up and unsheathed the familiar broadsheet, which was shorter than yesterday's. He read.

HERE ARE YOUR ORDERS FOR THE DAY

After your usual excercises please report at one sharp at the house of Ratner. He will occupy your attention till 3.30. At 3.30 tell Ratner you have an engagement. Go by tube to Kensington (ask your way very civilly of any decent-looking policeman, but check what he says by consulting a second). So you will reach Grotian Walk at approximately 4 o'clock. There you will find my relative Dick Whittingdon, to whom I have represented you as a young man very interested in painting.

Leave Dick as near five as possible. Walk smartly down Hurst Gardens and present yourself at B. flat. Valetta Mansions, Yarmouth Place. Mrs Farnham will be at home for tea. There you will find Mr Arthur Wildsmith, whom you have already met. It is a first-class monkey-house. You will enjoy yourself. – Do not stop too long at Mrs Farnham's however. Hurry due south and a Miss Stella Ansell an awfully nice girl will be waiting for you in her studio – No. 3, Lynes Studios, Piddinghoe Row. When you have examined Stella, return to your room. As it is saturday night you can make up your diary, it may be in arrears. So to bed.

N.B as to the Apes to be visited.

Julius Ratner whom you have not met is a true enlightenment. He is my favourite paradigm for a certain class of rather obscure Apes. Pierpoint used him as an illustration, when I had my course, and it was through him I met Ratner. At the time of my invitation I received a report of him from Pierpoint. I will use it for your instruction.

R.'s career opened not long before the War when he emerged from the East End, with Freud for his Talmud and amongst what the café-world of the time offered he manœuvred sexually up and down. During the War he went away. That over, like thousands more he marched out upon what was left of life, painfully anxious to make up for lost time. A promised land (purified by bloodshed and war debts) lay stretching to the horizon. Julius married a big carrotty anglish intelligentsia. Thereupon he had dough. He settled down to be a gentleman and to forget the ghetto.

They lived in married intellectualist sin in Chelsea. But one fine day this buxom heiress marched off to Rome with a lover. Julius was left in the soup. The blow was bitter. The world had, as far as R. was concerned, been purified in vain (with blood and debts) and *made safe for democracy* to no object. Thousands of R.'s who had not shot their bolts swarmed all about him. R. at thirty odd (putting the clock back to twenty-five thereabouts for the purpose) took too-late-for-success or even to stand a dog's chance to homosexual intrigue. – But he made money in the book business. He paid two old men at this time to take an interest in him. One of the old men cheated and went off with a *forte somme*. He chased him to Vienna and had the law of him. Generally these tardy efforts overstrained the psychic resources of Julius. He went to a mental hospital. These events he inclined to discuss with all comers, with his own glosses. He paraded a hundred simultaneous complexes and was happy after a fashion, weaving an ingenious web of cheap glamour – with a spider that was Eros, and himself the little gilded fly. Women he would approach with deferential circumspection, his head on one side, and, with the profit derived from his trading in second-hand books, he set himself up *tant bien que mal*. But Ratner had lost the land flowing with milk and honey: he knew it would never spontaneously drip. He was sad for good, but in a drab practical, indeed rather lousy manner.

Pedagogue of his own complexes Ratner's knowingness is of a good old fashioned garrulous order. Of the type he represents he is *ancien régime*. He should give you a good lunch, he pays everybody unobtrusively to let him unburden himself to them, and explain the unpleasant mysteries of his sex-life. Do not omit to feel some compassion – such as you would experience, it may be, if you met a dung-beetle and it had just had what it believed to be the last ball of excrement in the world taken away from it. He is a valuable specimen of the Ape of God.

Dick Whittingdon (do not confuse him with the Lord Mayor of London) is another thing altogether – he is the authentic Ape, the world's prize Ape, I am ashamed to say. (I have to show him to you – I apologize for this member of my family.) Where Ratner is intelligent in a sort of misbegotten way Dick is a mere fool. There are one or two points of contact. He is parted from a wife; a considerable property he inherited shortly after the War, March Park, opened to him superficially, from the other extremity of the social scale, the land of milk and honey of *Shiebertum*. But he was not only too old as he regretfully decided but far too clumsy and not very clever (as well as bald and rheumatic) to become an Oxford-voice *fairy-prince*. So Dick Whittingdon cast around for some recognized vice that might compensate for this social handicap. The pornographic literature of the camp and barracks (and for Dick the horizon of Letters was more or less that) suggested a solution. So he is a noted amateur *flagellant*. Whip in hand, Dick Whittingdon faces the world. It is the birch-rod of the decrepit gallant, in the old love-books, that gives the poor man a face, and enables him to hold up his head in a universe of dogmatic perversion.

Do not forget to ask to see his *whips!*

Next week I will accompany you myself to several choice places.

Adieu.

Horace Zagreus

After the signature came a few further instructions, scribbled in pencil.

Of all this Dan retained nothing at all as he ended, except the concluding sentence – 'Next week I will accompany you myself'

– made him feel quite giddy with joy. He stood up, swayed, and sat down, his eyes were swimming with ecstasy.

The door knocked, there were two knocks, Willie Service entered slowly. He was dressed in a hairy lounge suit of silver-blond, and pale suède brogues and felt hat to match. He was extremely attractive with a slight dark moustache. He went over to Dan and attempted to salute him goodmorning facetiously upon the cheek. Dan furiously blushing repulsed him and left the table, with precipitation, a piece of toast in his hand. He unobtrusively drew his overcoat closely about him to dissimulate the erotic splendours of his night-suit.

In a sleek falsetto Willie began in the heavy Berlin lisp:

'Also es war niemand da? – No sign of the newt?'

Dan showed it was in the negative, while he stuck the toast into his blushing head, and avoided by means of a graceful series of retreating and compensating forward steps, a clot of marmalade, which pitched down from his raft of toast.

'I thought as much' said Willie.

Dan smiled sheepishly, in heavy clownish mastication revolving the round O of the sheepish smile, a greedy boy.

Willie Service gave the punching ball a smart cuff and the ball darted at him through the air. But he side-stepped, puffing a laugh at it as it sped back.

'The top of this house smells like a distillery' he said.

'It's Mrs Phillips' said Dan.

'I know. Why don't you ask for a room lower down?'

Dan looked at him gravely, munching.

'I used to live up here' said Willie. 'There is an odour of whisky for half an hour in the passage after Mrs Phillips has scrubbed up here.' He sniffed at the door. 'That is not the case when she scrubs lower down.'

Dan reached over for his cup of cold coffee.

'I used to be sickened by a stench of Scotch' said Willie 'when she brought in the breakfast, when I lived up here.'

Dan put down his cup.

'That is because she is so short-winded' Willie Service said severely. 'Now I am downstairs that does not happen. I can only suppose that downstairs there she is not so short-winded. At the top of the house she is always puffed.'

Dan gazed at him very seriously indeed, head-on and chin lowered.

Willie Service went round the table to him, Dan retreating. Willie attempted to throw his arm around his waist.

'You old man's darling!' he said laughing, going away again. 'When are we going after the old egg-and-butter man? He is very furtive! I saw him in the distance yesterday, but he turned into somebody else and when I got up with him he had become my aunt Susan Service.'

He squared up to the ball and, staring it out, approached his gripped-up jutting jaw till their skins touched. He turned about.

'Well. I must go after the newt' he said and left the room slowly.

Part 5

THE SPLIT-MAN

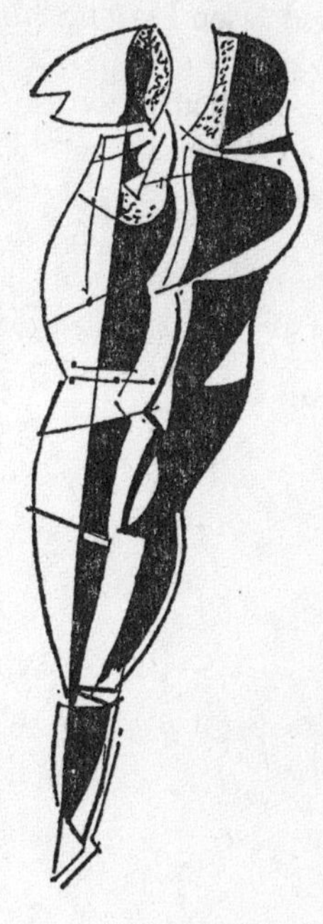

WOKEN by Mrs Lochore, Ratner thought he saw the sun through the window of milled glass in the room at the back, into which he looked from his big cheaply damasked love-nest in the front one. That was not so, it was a mirage, as he perceived when the charwoman pulled back the curtains, hauling upon the leaded rope. The tesserae of glazed bricks, and the windows, he could see were wet, and the air was its habitual grey. This coarse dirty light, with the withdrawal of the curtain, exploded in the bedroom. It struck the hard red face of the char.

He saw himself, Julius Ratner ('Joo' during early days in Whitechapel, that had been spelt in joke at times, by some grim hearty, 'Jew' – but disarming winsome plain british 'Jimmie' was preferred by him) he saw Jimmiejulius plunged once more into a sort of eternal flash-light photograph, when God – the abrahamic fire-god of Mr Zagreus – with the sunrise, every morning, began shooting the world. The god turned the handle quickly or slowly: very slowly at first – the God of Abraham was a tired god, although still fairly jealous. In this bath of unpleasant light Ratner lay blinking, rattish and cross, at being recalled to effort – not being a blue-eyed Son of the Morning as he perfectly well understood. But he was nevertheless, in his real-life feuilleton, the hero discovered upon his for-publicity-purposes much-loved-in bed. It was a *sad* story. It was a very dreary bitter little plot. This highbrow-sub-sheik of the slum had been the triste-est Tristan tricked out in the dirtiest second-hand operatic wardrobe – the shoddiest Don Giovanni – the most ludicrous Young Lochinvar – the most squalid Sorel, he had been the most unprepossessing sham Ratnerskolnikoff without the glamour of poverty of the Russian (because of his healthy business sense) – he had been the Judas without the kiss (for no fairly intelligent Christ would ever trust him) with a grim apocryphal lech for a Magdelen – he was the Childe Harold without the Byron collar, and worse, sans genius – the Childe Roland without the Dark Tower, or corpse-like Adolphe, a Manfred or a Zara, risen again, but who could only half-live – the eternal imitation-person in a word, whose ambition led him to burgle all the books of Western romance to steal their heroes' expensive outfits for his musty shop – the split-man of another tale.

And now the morning eye-glue of yellow-lidded, sleek-necked Joo, was attacked by the tear-glands which he had. This was but a desiccated trickle because Joo was a parched wilderness of an organism so much more colloid than aquatic. But still a few gouts gushed in the yellow rock and his mouth held that taste of dry decay that was the invariable accompaniment for Ratner of waking, presage of the disappointments of a gastric order ensuing upon the coffee.

Julius Ratner did not rise in solitude, he came to life to act at once. He was not without his audience. Every morning he was accustomed to make his bow, bashfully to incline his head and then skip out of sight, with white teeth bared (ivories that figured in income-tax returns as *necessary business exes* like Guinnesses and taxis) demonstrating the eternal youth that goes with cabotinage – proverbial stoicism of the great calling of Make-believe. Then every morning Joo had his gallery, because one Lochore is much like another. *House Full* would not be just bluff. Lochores are only abstractions, they are called 'gods' and that is probably the reason. They are not personal – for Joo gods were that, and the anonymous Masses. – Mrs Lochore, in this first blaze of light, at the beginning of each new day (undeniably the blinding light out of God's belly) was always there in her place. – Mrs Lochore was paid for her regular attendance.

But it was a woman's eye, the char's represented the Publicum – even that idiot-swarm that clotted the Artists' Entrance of the theatre, to mob its matinée-idol. Her kind was the unnumbered sheep. He was but an inferior and rather dirty Star – a glow in the worm but of low magnitude, now cast for oldish parts, yet as Jimmiejulius as late as the Battle of Mons he had played juvenile-lead, and it must be a treat for the widow of the night-watchman Lochore (with the grand name, that took with it something gallant and fierce, the remote foaming at the prows of piratic canoes, and all the physical splendours of Scotland), to be in the same apartment as a half-awake Star (whatever the age in light-years or the paltry magnitude) every morning, which was better than the stage-door (though this was figurative since Ratner had never in fact trod the boards at all, though a born Variety Pro – dance-turn – very musical – with comic relief with moist-eyed bathetics upon the trumpet-viol) – and then empty the stellar slops!

After a prostrate spell of sudden inanition, too sluggish to want to come-to-life at all (habits of hibernation in the serpent-blood) Mr Ratner was ready. He brought to mind his cold. A low harsh rattle from the direction of his pillow surprised Mrs Lochore. Mr Ratner had had a slight temperature – apprehensive, she remembered her wages which were good with a twinge under the corn-plaster – she looked over towards the bed: apathetic but preoccupied, she bustled round the wash-hand stand. She saw him out of the corner of her eye moving his neck a little, circumspectly like a snake, and swallowing. The large rugged thyroid cartilage travelled up and down the front of his throat. She poured the discoloured water of the wash-hand basin into the service slop-pail.

'The cold's not gone has it Mr Ratner sir. It's a bitter wind this morning, you should be careful and see you don't get a worst one sir. These winds we're having is very treacherous.'

The papers said daily, pneumonia was very prevalent, and the wind was very treacherous. She read of all the deaths from colds.

'I know Mrs Lochore. But that's so dif-fi-cult' Joo whined with condescension.

He analysed as usual some seemingly selected three or two-syllable word.

'That's what you gentlemen always say you "can't stop in" – prevention's better than cure, if you didn't go out in this bitter wind Mr Ratner sir it'd be gone tomorrow' she whinnied back at the whining invalid and coughed, to lend point to her exordium.

'But I caant Mrs Lochore I wish I could!' Joo's plaintive rusty pipe exploded. 'I *caant* Mrs Lochore stop in!'

Oh shut up, she thought. Now *why* can't he for once the old char perforce must reflect, deny himself to those outside just for once! 'Oh I believe you could sir!' cried she in a loud tone.

'But I have to go and play TENNIS!' hissed Joo while he watched the rugged old bitch of the bull-dog-breed shake his pretext roughly – before dropping it to reply, as she quickly did –

'Play tennis Mr Ratner sir!'

'Tennis!' he nodded, his eyes alight. *Tayern-neece* was the way Jimmiejulius pronounced this last word of his piteous crescendo. And the disgust of the old bondwoman, anticipated, was reproduced in the prompter's voice.

Most mornings Jamesjulius put himself in a good morning mood with this familiar crone and this was the way it was done. At will he would press a few stops, from his recumbent position, in the rickety instrument, and caused it to play.

God save our Gracious Naughty Mr Ratner sir! Amen!

'Play tennis!' char exclaimed again, but the dummy overdid well-nigh, in imitation of Ratner, the horror-struck part. To the rôle of deep humble reproof she was too much to-the-manner-born altogether. Too crude a volume of indignant servility escaped from Mrs Lochore. It gave the effect of fooling-the-fooler. The contrasted points of view showed up too stark. Julius frowned in his yellow-soap-sculptured sleep as he lay back and heard it. But the good woman knew it was up to her and was at a loss – she thought he had meant it was an unsuitable time of the year perhaps or he had no racket, or was tennis not his sport or too hot work or what? – for often they misunderstood each other and her *tennis* was not his *tayerniss*, nor his gods her gods. But they got on fine for all that and money spoke soft and sweet.

Reserve a court – Ratner made the note (speaking of tennis). His mind that hated all physical games, of ball bat foot or club, forgot he knew on purpose, he was never reminded. So he blocked in this memo, in bold black cursive script up in his cock-loft on top of everything else, where he could not neglect it.

'You'll go and run about and get hot and then you'll catch another cold before you know where you are Mr Ratner sir!'

'No I shaaant Mrs Lochore!' Joo wailed in teasing gritty growl, very pleased – very very Spoilt-boy at this, very Naughty-man.

'Well I hope you don't sir, I'm sure I do Mr Ratner!'

'Thank you ever so much Mrs Lochore, I won't run about too much!' He naughtily yapped.

'I shouldn't sir if I was you! You'll pardon me for sayin' so

Mr Ratner, but you want to be careful in these treacherous winds.'

'Ah these treacherous winds!' he chanted in mockery.

Beneath the crafty swollen eyes of the salaried british bondwoman foster-mother, he cuddled his pillow openly. For two pins he would pluck a pis-en-lit in his bed, under the old grog-blossom nose of her he would. Becoming very siamese-kittenish Joo cooed, with the runculation of the matutinal catarrh.

'Mrs Lochore!'

'Sir?'

Mrs Lochore put down the pail, standing wiping heavy chapped domestic fists upon her canvas apron.

'Used you when you were young ever to feel you would like to go away by yourself, and escape from all the young men you knew, and ...!'

Joo stalled, making a long expressive sigh but before it ended a cough came.

'*Never see them again!*' completing his sentence, he passionately wailed.

Mrs Lochore leered at Mr Ratner for a moment, and said:

'I wasn't so what you might call sought-after not as all that Mr Ratner sir!'

'I expect you were Mrs Lochore!' Joo retorted in swift sneering patronage, from the pillow.

'I daresay I had a young man or two like the rest' said Mrs Lochore. 'We're only young once Mr Ratner!' she said.

'Didn't you ever feel Mrs Lochore that you *hated* all your young men and wished you could never see them again!' Jimmie insinuated from the pillow.

'*All my young men* – listen to you Mr Ratner! I don't think I had scarcely so many as all that Mr Ratner sir! We wasn't not so fast, time I was young, as what they are now you might say.'

'Do you think *we* are so dreadfully fast now Mrs Lochore!' blared Joo at her at this, raising himself an eager inch from the pillow to give her a better view of the *young idea*.

'I don't know sir' said she, who was unprepared: 'I don't think I ever thought much about it sir. I don't see why people shouldn't amuse themselves,' she sniffed with indifference.

'I wish I could go away and never come back!' boomed the

tragic voice of Joo, in vibrant sotto voce, the martyr of the fastness of the New Age.

Mrs Lochore was put upon her mettle: she knew Mr Ratner sir had put her on her mettle. She knew what Mr Ratner was doing.

'If you goes on like that Mr Ratner' and she eyed him like a suicide boasting of his cowardly crime, 'I shall think you ought to see a doctor sir!'

But he sneered back, with criminal eye, a cruel encouragement. So she responded,

'What have you got to be miserable about my dear sir, I should say you was very lucky.'

'But I dooo Mrs Lochore – I want to leave all my present life!'

All his present lucky life, what others would be only too glad etcetera and he disdained.

'You've bin working yourself too hard sir, that's where it is.'

A reference on the part of the char to the book-shop, 'working' was, not to Julius's authorship, although upon the bedside table lay the novel telling of an impossibly juvenile-minded and even *sickeningly* sensitive Lothario's most grim attachments (only a decade gone) to unworthy girls – when the Peace was young, and Joo was not plain Joo but juvenile-Joo you were to understand and get-away-closer was the proud refrain, upon the Rummelplatz of Easy Money, astride the post-war pigs-in-clover, galloping round the jazz-organ at the heart of the blood-drab Circus of the bloody Peace.

'Yes! Hard work! It is!'

It is love, it is the woman loving, always loving the lucky and so lovable 'great baby' that all Ratners lovably are – it is to keep up with the demands of passion, that makes the lives of Young-Joos-in-Love so bitter-sweet and hard to bear, Oh willow-waily oh! and Hey nonny nonny!, till after a few decades they drop being absolutely 'young' in despair, because of the obligations involved in the mere epithet (when a really able Jujube avails himself of it too freely) but *never again* do they return to be just plain Joo Jack or Jill: *Young-J-in-L* becomes just J-in-L that's all, with L in lovely capitals.

'You can't burn the candle at both ends not for long sir!'

'And in the middle too!' wailed, very very naughty, old Joo

coyly – and he gave his bed-clothed person a horrid homosexual waggle.

'A rest is what would do you good Mr Ratner sir!'

'A *rest* Mrs Lochore?'

'Yes a rest Mr Ratner sir!'

Ratner directed his eyes through the open door and fixed them upon his correspondence, where several letters lay, placed by the char upon his morning papers.

'If only I didn't have to open those letters Mrs Lochore!'

'Well why do you sir? I shouldn't sir, if I was you!'

'I know!' Jujubejimmie bleated hoarsely, with juvenile pathos, tossing upon his pillow archly.

'But I suppose you 'as to, that's where it is sir!'

'That's where it is!' agreed Jujubejimmie, repeating with conscious grin that made him look more bald-browed, with his flushed sleek sinciput, the english idiom – which rose in the mouth of Mrs Lochore so pat a reflex.

'That's where it is!' the char then echoed him.

'It isn't as though they weren't all awfully nice people of whom I am most terribly fond!'

Terribly fond – of a select entourage!

'It isn't as though you wasn't *popular* Mr Ratner sir, no one can say you isn't not popular sir.'

'Well I don't know about *popular* Mr. Lochore!'

'It isn't as though you was without friends Mr Ratner sir!'

'Well I don't know about friends Mrs Lochore – I wish I were sometimes!'

'Oh don't say that Mr Ratner sir. It isn't every one has good friends like you Mr Ratner, not like you have Mr Ratner!'

'That's just the trouble Mrs Lochore.'

'I can't see that sir you'll pardon me for contradicting you, you ought to be thankful Mr Ratner sir that you has.'

'So you say Mrs Lochore!'

'Well I'm sure I don't know. Most people would *envy* you I think Mr Ratner sir.'

And Jujubejim lay still and softly sighed at that! The climax of this long complaint had come at last – of *envy* that sweet attendant char had spoken. The word ENVY had sounded upon her lips.

'Lucky I should say you was Mr Ratner!'

And Jimmiejulius allowed a livid eye to steal in the direction of the flattersome appropriate char. And then it stole back and he put down over it its heavy yellow waxen lid.

'Very lucky!' said Mrs Lochore with a final flattersome bridle. And then she went out of the door into the passage with the service slop-pail, full of the self-appointed, self-advertised, self-published, self-loved, almost self-made Star's surface-dirt and clouded urine.

But Julius Ratner had worked himself into a false frenzy, this was sure the gas for the literary engine, the petrol for the mechanical pegasus. The creative ferment was announced – no one was more surprised than himself seeing that with the good Joo it was a settled habit to treat his muse as a bad joke, as she was right enough. And when she turned up (every time more pretentiously not-of-this-earth, but of some spurious, borrowed, gimcrack millennium, staged on the Rummelplatz of *that* polish market or in *that* swabian dorf) he grinned from ear to ear. However, with Mrs Lochore Julius had got going with the great novel lying upon the table which was so difficult to finish. He saw two whole chapters, in which the hero had a wander-year. The Childe Harold, the romantic, the 1830 note had been struck: as he vamped his big succulent pillow he squeezed out a lot of high-flown matter – a fine frenzy, they were mad words, they catapulted, sly and slovenly, here and there. And this, as Mr Zagreus had whispered to Dan, was 'the lowly Whitechapel Ape in Excelsis' and, as he had added, then, 'that is why you must go one day – he is your proper quarry among others: for, though one Ape is not unlike another Dan, yet the Ape of that ilk has peculiarities not found in the Brit (and vice versa) and it is your duty to acquaint yourself with these. In short you must spot and note up how this apishness that knows no frontiers works out – when it is the keen disillusioned mind of that great race instead of the dull sentimental one of that other equally great, that is in question.' And then Horace had supplemented that by the day's orders and it was seen that Mr Zagreus set some store by it for Dan; and that he had learnt his lesson well and was fit to pass it on to the boy, who could doubt?

For now it was quite beyond question at all that since Mr

Julius Ratner kept a highbrow bookshop, a certain Mr R. was able to sell his friend Joo's books – and because as well Jimjulius was a publisher, Joo was luckily in a position to publish his particular pal Ratner's novels and his poems – and on account of the fortunate fact that J. Ratner and Co. were the Publishers and distributors of a small high-brow review called simply *Man X* it was possible for Juliusjimmie to puff and fan that wan perishable flame of the occasional works of his old friend Jimjulius. It was a concatenation of circumstances such as every author whatever must sigh for. J. Ratner and Co made its money on the limited-edition-ramp by printing in white-calf of the Eighteenth Century literature of gallantry, in translations from the italian and the french: so the hearty exploits of some legendary square-pusher of the golden days of Europe, pre-Marx and pre-Bonaparte, among other things became gold that was from time to time judiciously laid out to appease Mr J. R.'s personal vanity. The literary book-merchant who had given his name to Ratner Ltd could help his blood-brother Julius. Such was the involved interplay of business and the mildest of literary power-complexes indulged invariably in a *gentlemanly* manner.

For five minutes Joo was in those throes. Mrs Lochore returned with the pail. She moved about the two rooms and from the sounds (for his eyes stood heavily-shuttered) he recognized her whereabouts.

Flinging up a bare arm, that was fattish and swarthy, Joo turned his face over upon the pillow, left cheek up, as if offering it to a hostile hand. Joojulius relaxed his large distinctly moulded sallow eyelids: like a letter left deliberately upon a table containing something flattering to the recipient, just where the inquisitive might surreptitiously acquaint themselves with the contents, so Joo paraded a sham-slumber. This was that long lying-in-state repeated every morning. His hand lay however against a portion of uncovered scalp, where, in the centre (a bull's-eye, seen vertically) hair was no longer to be encountered. 'She can't see' snarled Julius to himself about Mrs Lochore, 'she hasn't got eyes but holes:' but as the ironic comfort of its heat passed down his arm from the rudest of nude scalps, dark fancies began suddenly chasing each other about his brain, like the furious darting of urchins in a twilight slum. – He passed on gradually to that kaleidoscopic perspective of his day, and the events rushed back upon him as though from the volcano of an uneasy memory.

First came the 'Tayerness' – to book a court. Then came, out of order, Miss Joan Persimmon, Truby-King-trained: at tea-time that was to be settled, she would go down to Katherine at once at Radcliffe if suitable. Next Dan appeared to him and the sallow death mask upon the pillow frowned – Joo picked their restaurant, the cheapest in Soho with vile wine: he savagely tipped the waiter, spilled six coppers under a plate as he left, with a curse upon each. He did not touch the ill-favoured dishes (he had a sandwich beforehand in a pub) – so much for Daniel! Next came the morning's business when he reached the shop. At this thought the suprarenals discharged, the intestines registered a hot vibration: the gonadal glands were affected – digestion, love, instincts of battle awoke as one man, in Ratner there were no compartments. He saw into his small shop in Soho in spirit – there he distinctly perceived a man in a new dark overcoat. It was the day before, for Julius looked before and after both at once – there were no barriers whatever. This thick-fingered gull (big feminine-jowled, soft and shaven) was bending over a large white volume. He had seen him before (he could not get his name out of him) – the fellow was weighing its pornographic promise against his big cheque in his pocket. The large hearty fool frowned, for the promised manure did not docilely present itself, as he turned the pages, affecting to be highbrow.

Ratner (as he had done the day before) hesitates. Then with a rattling sneer, meant to be soft (but coming out so harsh the startled fool looked up at him) he bends forward and says to him, looking down at the book:

'I was reading it again yesterday. It is an astonishing piece of writing. But I confess I was horrified – I wondered how I could ever have come to publish it! The part where the – Where is it?' and he guides the customer with a sleuth-like index to the satisfying spots one by one. – The cheque changes hands. (The gull's name was Geoffrey Gainford.) The customer leaves. Ratner rushes incontinent to the lavatory, calling as he goes to Christopher Sholto-James, his youthful assistant, to replace him lest in his absence some book-thief steps in and helps himself – for last week ten pounds' worth of books had been taken.

Rows of books paraded before Ratner from afar televisionally as he lay in his bed: the big money lay in those behind the glass doors, their value made them almost move about, like living things. There were conversations that would occur: 'Macquire, Belfast, wants two more. (That was of the special edition.) He owes for the last' says Stacey, if he is not out. 'Well what of it?' Stacey got his goat. Old Hugh Keene was to do the notice in the *Collector*. 'I'll see what can be done!' Humph humph! I shouldn't count too much on the lousy old hack: since he's quarrelled with the Dove lot – and so on. – *Don't* forget next Wednesday. DON'T FORGET NEXT WEDNESDAY!

Julius yawned nervously.

'That is yesterday. I should worry!'

The report of the gas-fire came from the next room. Mrs Lochore said, standing in the doorway;

'The hot water is all ready sir.'

She nodded towards the wash-hand stand.

'Oh thank you Mrs Lochore' Ratner drawled without opening his eyes.

A door closed softly. Mrs Lochore had now gone.

Ratner released a drowsy glance of immense universal disaffection, it vacantly occupied the bed-room. While staying-put for inspection, the lying-in-state, *that* was consoling. The eyes of Mrs Lochore massaged him in his attitude of a Venetian Venus. This was, however, only in his fancy for Mrs Lochore scarcely ever in fact looked at Ratner, but as his eyes were mostly shut he could not see that, and he *believed* Mrs Lochore did so continually, he supposed she could not help herself – and so how the position presented itself to Ratner was that the presence of two such obedient eyes of 'faithful-dog' order was necessary to beauty-culture – no human hand did the skin such good (exorcising wrinkles, driving fat out of its disgusting strongholds – under chins – also, with him, about the eyes, most terribly dripping or slipping down *from the top*). A pair of honest stupid eyes – *that* was better than a pair of the most electric hands ever possessed by expensive masseur what what! But now the eyes had gone off. It was the signal for the removal of the actor's mask. Ratner sat up in bed.

Sluggishly the clothes were urged down – Ratner crawled out. In skimpy pyjamas, of a quadrated pattern, so close-fitting as to look like tartan trews – a small yellow figure, thick-necked, grown fattish in the middle, Joo sat scratching his head. The legs – flat like fishes in the direction of their movement – spread now at right angles on the ridge of the mattress. His feet were planted in the nap of the mosque-arch of his namazlich. The imitation of the compass used to ascertain the direction of the prophetic shrine was swivelled so as to place the holy city at Moscow instead of Mecca – an accident this with gentleman-Joo.

Ratner went to the hot water can, he jadedly poured out the water, frowning at the steam, scratching his neck.

He slid his hands into the water. He soaped the channel between the muscles of the back of the neck, a hand limply hooked, with a row of four fingertips. The head moved upon its atlas, rubbing itself cat-like against the almost stationary fingers. Travelling forward over the occipital bones pimples were encountered. Working the antagonistic muscles framing the thyroid shields, he gently and limply rocked his headpiece.

With a thick glass bottle containing a substance resembling vaseline, Joo prepared to dress his scanty hair. Altaean Balm, the name of this material, was applied here and there over the scalp 'well-rubbed-in'. The royal arms surmounted the title upon the label. How disgusting: 'flesh is filthy!' was his vindictive comment as the heat from the scalp entered his fingers. Then over the temporal bones his eyes and fingertips went searching for whiteness.

Ratner faced Juliojim in the glass: he gazed at this sphinx, which he called self, or rather that others called that, not Ratner – at all events it stood there whatever it was. Impossible to question it. Anything but that could be interrogated, but one's self, from that no one could get an answer, even for Julius it was a sort of ape-like hideous alien. Lo, it preened itself, it came back and smirked, arch and earnest were its several expressions – it attempted to improve its mouth. It would defy itself, in the mirror, yet it was it, all the time – best turn away! Such as it was it was that in which Ratner believed – a rat caught in its own rat trap, for he was cowed and dull, he was yet attached to the fortunes of the ratself – where it went Ratner would go, Ratner would defend it to the end – only over the dead body of Ratner would another approach it to destroy it. And so on.

Examing steadily his terrible life-partner, doctoring his mask – 'You beast, you beast!' darkly Joo thought, giving it glance for glance – how well it knew its deadly power! Upon the hard lines of pain, the age-indexes, nostril to mouth, the constriction of the damp surface, the filling up of all hollows by that foul yellow suet (the result of hæmorrhoidal trouble, and cheap mass-production intestines he was fond of reflecting with sharp-thoughted Schadenfreude) he fixed a steely, glittering, feminine eye. It was the scrutiny of a rival, woman against woman. And it said 'hag!' But frightened at its expression of murderous rage, Julius began to change his tone. He went about to flatter it, in the cheap words of this or that past bit of skirt – usually either a Doreen, a Betty or an Eileen, a June, a Pauline or a Joan: *No, you're rather nice aren't you – rather a lamb! you're rather sweet, I think. Raather sweet!* he mouthed and mimicked. Doreen said so, so that must be so! A light venomous sneer detached itself towards incarnate Doreen. *You're just a great big baby really!* (again Doreen) – a diabolical grin of self-mocking craftiness for the 'great big baby!' – He approached the disordered vertex with a comb: the sneer changed the frown, in spite of itself, into a grin of bitter coquetry: perhaps too it was as well not to look at himself in the glass – think of Doreen or of Eileen, of Viola, or of Violet and remain with his mask off. Therefore the bashful smiling sneer remained upon his face. *It was for Doreen.* 'Yes: you're rather nice to know, aren't you!' This time the offended image appeared to require a great deal of soothing. 'You're a nice boy!' Ratner coaxed it. Then he began addressing it as though it were a dog! 'You are you know! Come here I want to tell you something!' Ratner laughed. As he did so he showed his fangs.

Beneath the mouth's straight overhanging line, lifted at the corners as though with a snarl, the large teeth lay, more wolf than rabbit. But the mouth had a shallow palate of the latter breed, with these fierce tushes. The incisors and the gums provided him with a flat and not a bow-front to his mouth. His smiling was always restrained and unexpansive (which fitted in with his sly habit of shrinking shamefaced bashfulness) for without being 'toothy' it was this rabbit-gum that thrust out the upper lip when he was smiling, and it inclined to expose the tips of the two central teeth, like a properly 'toothy' person.

Next squatted Julius pyjama-clad at a high table, tapping at his Portable Juventa pre-War model that rattled as he hit it (he only used the stub and inkpot for swank – in private messages). He stamped out swiftly, with few stops or caps, what had collected in his head while he swore to Mrs Lochore that he would prefer never to see all the young women again and give his whole set the slip, his particular circle – and go away to live alone, probably in a desert like Antony.

Ratner types:

'Her face came from far away, it was a clouded autumn night. Should he take up the question with her? Why not? It had to come. Better now than when they were in the train. The suspense would be intolerable.

Had his prose had any effect in muffling their passion? He doubted it. And yet!

Why, when he had wanted to explain the first time, his heart bursting with sickening questions, had Alec moved away? If he had only stopped. All might have been different!

Let's be pals Alec, he had wanted to say, taking him by the arm and leading him to the embrasure of the window, from which could be seen the boa-constrictor of the black river. Let's be real pals. A factory. Two freemasons. A cloud threatened the tail of the serpent. A little child picked a forget-me-not. She lifted a chalice. It was there. *Epiphany*. There were three distinct vibrations.

The house reeled as the mob left the square. They were on their way to the Prefect's house. The voting was heavy. It was a new Chamber they were electing. The blind walls of the house gave a sickening shiver. Rochester.

Why had Alec not listened? If he could have spoken to him in prose it might have made a difference. Who knows? Everything might have been different! The sickening years might not have sped as they did like a series of red and white billiard balls with a sickening thud into a big pendant pocket. Twenty-six!

Look here Alec I owe you no grudge, all's fair in love and war old man. I have staked all and lost. I am not difficult, I don't think you can accuse me of that! But I don't want the love of Majorie this side of Christmas, if we can come to an understanding. Love is War. War is Love. Fate is fate. Kismet.

Why did he dread to go into the canteen. Was he not alone? It was the old old question of mal-adjustment. You and the other fellow. Dread. He would not enter because of this sickening dread. Once inside all was different. What had possessed him to allow this sickening loathing to take hold of him? The interior was comfortable. The walls sang with white light. It was gas. What magic made all these people bury their sickening faces in their plates and the great chef passed by. What pass-word distorted the waitresses? They were too new, he was utterly exhausted and he looked up the next train in the catalogue. It was Two Six. Budapest.

Why had Majorie left him hanging on the railings? A tide of nauseous scourings with sickening drops of livid foam poured over him, he made headway against it and he found the flood had subsided. He was free, but why had Majorie not returned or sent a telegram to say not good enough or better luck next time, anything but *Marjorie* only, it was a sickening feeling. This was intolerable. It was the ravings of a lonely and forsaken chapman. *Marseilles*.

How why and where? Should he reach Marjorie if he was forced to return? Had she really drowned herself? For him? The sickening thought that it might be for him almost prevented him from buying the ticket. The storm burst. He was overwhelmed with a tempest of tremendous jealousy, it turned his stomach and made up his mind that he must leave her neighbourhood for ever, this was final. Next time. Why could he not away? Why could he not hence? Always frustration, always struggle! Life! Why could he not strike his tent and depart for good? It was the best way. Was it not as easy to go as to stay? Not quite. He had forgotten the magnetic brown, darker in the right eye, with an electric-blue spot in the left.

Yes but was not this a false start? Who could say offhand? there was no track.

This piece of prose might help her to forget. Women never knew till the day after next.

When he came out of the canteen he could hear the train starting for the terminus. He would be there. He turned sharp to the left. Two lampposts. A druggist's. Weed-killer.

In case!

The ticket must have a visa. Paul remembered the man had

told him second to the left and straight ahead. It was a large building in a cheerful quarter of the village. There was a vitriolic stench under the stairs. Who had been there?

If she could hold him and have him. But no. The frustration had left him too nearly unconscious. The spell had broken. The question it was true was a fair one. If she could have him, she would never return. But she should not. He would be too far. He must put up with that. She had not notified him. Never mind. All's fair in love and war. He wasn't grumbling. Better luck next time. If he cast her off she would go off he could not stop her, but he knew she would lure him back always lure him back with the promise of the strange kiss in the Tube-tunnel. He had no regrets.

Put in that way there were of course three alternatives. Women always chose the last. Who do women love? It is their secret. He must leave all his sickening anguish to settle that. Once he had bought his ticket and his visa he must never look back. Whose fault? His? No no, she was in her heart of peace the sole offender. Alec had always in his heart of hearts been jealous. He was not in the picture, while Paul was as blameless as Protection would allow, where a child was in question. There were three children. She had deceived them both. Amberley.

Was Alec aware of it? He would never succumb because she had deceived him, he knew Theodore had not intended to betray them. Because she had forgotten that passage about the rock against which the red waves lapped, that had spoilt everything. Opposite was the crèche. Gaily they entered it together, she clung to his arm as though she were the child. Jaspar struck an attitude in his cot, drawing his mouth down in an angry grimace of hatred. A japanese warrior.

Why was it so easy to run on? Why did he not – '

Ratner stopped. He bluepencilled Alec's *heart of hearts.* Too near to *heart of peace*, one heart too many so to speak. '*Was Alec aware of it?*' Ratner scowled at the question mark. '*Why was it so easy to run on?*' Ah why? He scowled at that question mark more heavily. '*Why do women love?*' – '*Whose fault? His?*' – '*There was a vitriolic stench under the stairs. Who had been there?*' Suddenly he saw nothing but question marks, in this prose that had the property of muffling passion.

'Sickeningly' aware, he had suddenly grown, that he could not proceed, not just at present, with this 'sickening' composition. With a remarkably bad-tempered jerk he plucked the 'sickening' foolscap sheet clean out of the machine. He stared down at his prose with a hatred only accorded to persons and generally denied to things. – But this was a *personal* prose!

The very vibration of the voice of the visible self Ratner had left in the mirror droned from the violet-studded foolscap. He heard it distinctly, up it came at him out of the paper just as the 'sickening' face had come at him out of the glass. That was the voice of that person. Automatic writing, spirit-tapping this was as it were, only he had seen the fingers and he knew the spook in person. He had met him in the looking-glass.

He reread some passages of the message. Now was not that just how that *would* write if it wrote? It was the very accent!

The self seen in the glass, to be followed through thick and thin, that all the same was one thing – this 'prose' another. For there was the Muse. Much in common, yes, but *not* the same thing.

Jim's Muse and Jim were separate persons: two abstractions, very sympathetic to each other, but strictly dual-personalities. The Muse-soul was nothing if not secondary to Julius Ratner, quite a side-issue in fact.

This time Ratner certainly had been misled. It had seemed to him distinctly that the Old Muse had wanted to excrete a little, but it was a misunderstanding.

That deadly family-likeness of the creatures of his pen so that a word written by him became immediately ratnerish and lifeless, how was it! That was the worst aspect of this composition, referred to as 'prose' of his, it had that look he knew at once: the ratnerish thumb-marks never altered, it was an impact that was soft and limp – not like the thumb of God upon Adam, as a creative archetype – a novel something.

Oh this prose-voice of Julius – auto-parley Ratner frankly? He nodded. Yes yes. All self. And freshness only comes he knew from contact, when there were *Not-selfs* in touch, and things – not *nothing* but feverish conscious people. Continuous Self – Continuous Present: and where self is strong, why there art is weak and that's all the world over! And that was how the matter stood at No. 50 Great Eustace Street, Bloomsbury, when Ratner sat down to write.

A visitation of Ratner's Muse was nothing but a short uncritical spell and nothing else. It was the brief power to be uncritical. However, certainly he had been led to believe, in this instance, that this was at hand. But it had turned out that that was not the case, so tant pis. He got up.

Ratner did not move away. Rising brusquely to his feet he held with his eye his most recent 'prose.' With hatred strictly centripetal (in piscine flatness, with one large frowning ocular disk), over the expanse of written matter which had been tapped off to the dictation of his galloping brain, compelled to this faux-naïf inconsequence, his eye trampled, upon the paper. He identified one by one those well-known ratnerish fingerprints. And the sly frantic-eyed old hack-highbrow daimon – not the Muse of a *faux-naïf* for nothing! – had given him the dirty slip! Here he had been left face to face with this obscene diarrhœa of ill-assorted vocables, upon the foolscap.

Ratner picked up the piece of paper with the tips of his fingers. He examined it with the expression of a particularly squeamish sanitary engineer now.

A page of idiot-questions. Did not this 'prose' resort to continual impassioned asides? *It did.* Of old with gnashing of milk-teeth bitterly, had not Joo recognized, with far-sighted precocity, that this so-called prose (and it was far worse when it was prosody) abounded in these signs of second-rateness? *Joo had.* To alter such vices would burn up more energy than, had he possessed it, he would have cared to expend upon concocting a 'prose', thank you! – one without mechanical questions, purged of clichés of the epileptic schools – without those thrilling words in isolation, of high-brow melodrama, and the rest of the 'sickening' tricks of the least ambitious, sham-experimental, second-rate literary cabotinage – that would be to humbug self – why he knew better uses for spare energy and such surplus power (as he had not got) than to put to school a lazy old mule of a Muse, to stop her asking rhetorical questions!

But a wave of especial pessimism traversed Ratner as he let the stuff drop with a hideous shot-bird flutter of its foolscap, upon the table. Oh how Joo boiled for a spell with militant low-brow 'loathing' at all the powerful highbrow canons, in which he could not make good now or ever, they were too *dif-fi-cult?*

Even the reason that those images of mal-de-mer occurred with such 'sickening' frequency was just because Joo knew too 'sickeningly' well what would be there upon the 'sickening' sheet when he had done with his mechanical table-rapping.

Now came another impulse of a disgust more *absolute* – from a different, really an august, quarter. In Ratner the prophet the third person of his triune self, awoke, with the well-known abruptness of such occurrences. All of a sudden it was the authentic thunder of the ethical rage of Israel, that imposed itself upon this distant son. He was within an ace of crashing an indignant biblical fist down upon the typewriting machine – mechanical defenceless accomplice of his, in these improper activities. These stolen hours, that should be spent more profitably from any point of view. Afterwards, on looking back on it as they say, he wished he had – but the time had passed almost at once. Within four minutes of the first rising of the wind and pealing of the thunder, Ratner had sunk again to the plane of Jimjulio. He was smirking back in the glass, as large as life, in the teeth of the mosaic law – as he doctored the crater left by a blackhead and inspected a yellow fang, to rescue it from tartar, that encrustation of saliva. While it lasted it was impressive. The nerve in Ye Olde Stumpe asserted itself with powerful pang. That bitter Conscience that was so uneasy, that made the early jewish nation into the theologic people, with a strong good-and-bad bee in its bonnet – caused them to make canons of conduct in short for the entire Western Earth for a period, up to last century – pricked this penultimate Ratner, the last of the pure pre-War Jews as it were – one who had crossed the Red Sea, emerged at the Armistice, but who lacked faith and believed he had not crossed it after all or something.

To perceive the unrighteous waste involved in the manufacture of a forgery of sorts, but one that could take no one in – it was that that had come upon him, it was that to which he had come!

Lord have Mercy upon us!

An article strictly desired by nobody was turned out in this den of Ratner, at considerable pains, at considerable cost!

Vanity of Vanities, All is Nix!

It had come to this, this is what His Ratnership had come to!

Lord have mercy upon us!

Upon a precious vellum, upon a fair sheet of Dutch-Mould-made!

Oh Vanity of Vanities!

One worthy of a better lot of words, sensibly assembled – one designed by its Maker for a document of great worth!

Lord have Mercy, Amen!

A parchment that might serve as the repository of this or of that – of a valuable tract against Woman's Suffrage, on behalf of Wages for Wives, for White-slaving – in favour of Polygamy, Polyandry, and Monogamy – of a five-quid vellum version of the Song of Songs – of a treatise upon a tribe of significant cannibals – of a pamphlet upon the Neuroses of the Analerotic!

Good Lord Deliver Us!

Yes, man alive, a lousy limited edition of an intellectually-fraudulent book that no one could sell, that no one would want!

Save us, Oh Lord!

That would at last be remaindered, that would be sold as pulp, that would be so still-born that it would never even have the chance to die!

Good Lord Deliver us and assist us in this Day of Our Adversity!

Not even as honest-to-goodness bookstall hogwash, not as sale-worthy trash, not that even but of no earthly value whatever, to God or to man – as low-lid fodder or high-brow bumph!

Lord have Mercy upon us!

Which a few penniless old friends must reluctantly purchase perforce, out of their bitter pittance, and yawn through a few pages before sleeping outright!

Intercede for Us now, of thy Mercy Oh Lord. Amen.

A baffled shamefaced grinning bursting through the wrathful mask, turned back upon himself in bitter sport. It stoned the prophet in himself with rotten eggs and mocking his better-half – the excitable Old Shepherd – Ratner swiftly left the bedroom, directing his steps to the Morning Paper, and to Sanity (at a price).

*

At tennis, after the court had been booked earlier as per intention, by telephone to the club, Ratner with teeth-set defeated his beautiful assistant, Kit Sholto-James (good for the old 'un!) as Kit being a discreet young man of no great parts who knew his place, always allowed Ratner to do – and then Ratner had a long relax at the bottom of his hot bath, as flat as an alligator and quite still. At tea-time came the Truby-King-trained smirking expert into the room upon the heels of Mrs Lochore – a nice fresh girl, Miss Persimmon – they came to terms quickly and he engaged her. Jimjulius kissed Miss Persimmon before she left as a matter of form – he attempted the usual intimacy.

He was such a nice man and so gentlemanlike, he had said she had lovely hair. He seemed a shy kind of man except you could tell from his eyes he was hot stuff! Hands with a strong-silent bedside-manner tenderly repulsed these advances, not at all snubbing, the contrary. – He would have her that was evident – when she brought the kid up to town – then the bright young buxom Belfast body (labelled 'Miss Persimmon' like a horse) should from-the-waist-down receive his politest attention. (The through-the-dress intimacies had prospered.) That was the second nurse in a fortnight! He bought Persimmon's third-class ticket with a fierce sly smirk at her over his shoulder for the benefit of the booking-office-clerk – a smug blaze of the coyest possible understanding-between-the-sexes (love having passed, lips met, bodies duly having made, his and hers, the double backed beast – in fully-clothed, blank-charge, informal rehearsal). At the carriage-door he drove his yellow fang into her rose-red Ulster lip in tender play (several there envied him, beyond question) – he grinned in thick-throated triumph but turned away his head, negligent and even so-to-say forgetful of his good-fortune, and later Miss Persimmon waved her handkerchief in the outgoing breeze along the side of the Northbound Express. He did not respond, as soon as he saw it he turned on his heel. – It had been eleven when he reached Colet Street – Sholto-James his attractive mannequin took his lofty wasp-back down the shop, in idle showmanship, followed by a Traveller, while three women pored over an expensive book of vulgarly-selected verses for the lettered Week-End public, whispering to each other about the price. In the doorway he received a discreet ovation from the char, Mrs Dicksee. She was at work on the stairway amongst some straw – she clucked at the master's silhouette against the glare of the street, shouting that the wind was bitter. Sunny – when Ratner reached the office behind the bookshop – transformed her personality for the moment into a seaside en-fête, with girlish indiscretion she welcomed her popular employer who was only 'a great big baby.' Then the new jobbing stenographer, Fern Hurwitz, a pretty young jewish girl, not to be outdone, even more violently, but sombrely, glowed with glad welcome – while the youthful Traveller who had followed Jimjulio in, smiled. With a bashful smirk of the most deprecating modest rebuke man could muster, Jimjulio passed in. The smile of the Traveller was not lost upon James (as his grinning head moved quickly to left and right to see on all hands the conquering hero come) – he took it to betray an intelligible envy. He smiled in response, but he frowned simultaneously: *Such popularity* – and with the ladies! Seeds of scandal! – that would never do! the frown said.

'Be quiet!' said Jimmie hushing her transport with sheepish flushing smirk – to the effusive Sunny. And the Traveller and he went into the miniature office beyond. – The end of the day was passed by Joo at a concert as the main feature. To that he took (holding her in a fond close snuggle by the arm, that all and sundry might guess they were probably sleeping-partners) the plain wife of a celebrated novel-writing fakir. He held the hand of the wife of the celebrated fakir in public as well as private, in the glooms of the cinemas as in the vivid electricity of Shaftesbury Avenue. But with the best will in the world to outrage the horrid fakir, more than by mere hand-holding, the flesh (Ratner found alas) was weak, was unworthy – finally he had to abandon all idea of earning fully the coveted title 'lover' or of making her in the absolute 'mistress' – after two cleverly dissimulated failures. So Jimjulio confessed with great bashfulness that he had a venereal disease. He had no disease, but when they went to his flat to kiss (as he had to, worse-luck) Joo had received many extra pimples (of which the wife of the woeful fakir had a great plenty, upon her chin and forehead) because of this beastly obligation to clip and peck and glue the lip. But Jimjulio was able and that was the main thing to exult over the disgustingly celebrated fakirman. Fakir dripped large bitter drops of unfakirlike uxoriousness over this person of the weaker sex he had taken to his sentimental bosom. But Fakir had been so proud and distant with Jimjulio. Drag in the mud of gossip a little it is to be hoped, this objectionable fakir-fame, Jimjulio or anyone could do – wound the too susceptible soul of His Fakirdom. This Jimjulio not only *could* but *would*, and he did – with the lowest archery of the dirtiest cupid, insult the Sultan's bed, what! – the fool-fakir unable to object, being impotent, or hating St Antony's fire per se as much as Jimjulio or rather more. This fastidious fakir was Julio's contemporary and Joo had watched with matchless venom his rise to an arcane renown. But that hateful effulgence should be utilized (via wifey) to advertise Ratner and Co. By reserving a super-stall (once even a box it had been, at the start – which Ratner converted into a public love-nest, for the benefit of the fakir's highbrow public) this was quite simple – so Jimjulio could get his own back and bite his thumb at the Great, wreak vengeance upon fame and name, make homosexual love to the rather attractive fakir by proxy (in the person of this equally fakir-hating woman) – and this he would do once or twice a week now – armed with disinfectants, of course, for a boil more or less meant a good deal to Juliusjames R.

Half way through, into this bustling day of a Split Man, stalked the tall and silent presence of Daniel Boleyn. A most unwelcome interlude it was.

Going for the snack-lunch beforehand to the Beddington Arms, Ratner found himself amongst business friends. They sat at a marble table – as it was a café within a pub and the Saloon had tables. Principal amongst those there was Siegfried Victor, though Hedgepinshot Mandeville Pickwort was a sharper man. They were both Oxford-bred, half-mid-european men, and both young. Ratner was to publish their anthology of the *Verse of the Under-Thirties*. Jimjulio would have liked to have a verse in, but though most were over thirty they did not regard Ratner as a writer in the running so would not draw the long bow for him and get him in as a sham under-thirty at all, especially as he was so old – but there was no reason to and they never discussed it. On the other hand, the two editors found him an intelligent publisher. Ratner was Victor's choice, it was he who knew him.

Siegfried Victor was a massive young man, even above six-foot, and very broad shouldered, with a handsome nobly-proportioned head upon a greek museum-model. With an expression of the most stately implacable brooding serenity imaginable, Siegfried Victor had all the appearance (as, an elbow upon the table, and a large hand placed over his chin – occasionally it would pass beneath it and twang the slack flesh of his throat – he sat and listened) of a young patriarchal squireen, of a different caste in everything from the six friends that sat with him. He had that air of sitting in judgment, an informal pub-moot – upon anyone he attended to, in turn, he passed a summary judgment – and now he sucked, with a formidable owlishness, a bold black pipe. Hedgepinshot Pickwort, who was a small bleached colourless blond, stared before him. He sucked another pipe.

Ratner, with his craven smirk, his self-torturing mind – half-bald lizard's stony head, that saurian skin, squalid stature – he was a rat beside this empty aloof lion of a person: Poor pre-War Jew of the People for better or worse was Ratner among other things (though so gentlemanly and bashful) and he knew that Siegfried Victor did not want to hear the catalogue of his complexes. Julius belonged to a Lost Generation – to speak generationally, was not he a member of *a Lost Tribe?* He would go the way of the Elder the Mediæval Zion, with all his complex outfit intact.

Like a beautifully carved statue, a little over lifesize but of the finest finish, Siegfried Victor sat and smoked. He wore his youth with a certain heaviness, like a large sombre mantle of state. Drawing judiciously at his great pipe, with a disdainful detachment his eyes would run over Ratner as Ratner spoke. He suggested in his presence perhaps a circassian commissar, an administrator perhaps over a province as large as France. He had been to Moscow on Film Work and there his bulldog pipe had been a great success.

With his friend with the peculiar name he would bring out the *Anthology of the Under Thirties*, they were to be coeditors, and with Ratner as the publisher. Also Ronald MacMark was there and Joseph Workman, there was Maurice de Glehn and Bertram Brown.

In the middle of the conversation Hedgepinshot Pickwort rose with a sluggish stumble, he was dressed in a spotted and baggy undergraduate get-up really, and he crawled out of the Beddington Arms without speaking.

Hedgepinshot is rather a rare name and so is Pickwort, but he was a poet and a picker up of words as he went no doubt, and 'pinshot' was a word Pickwort had picked up under a hedge very likely, and Hedgepinshot carried on the 'decadent' tradition upon a tide of pallid very low-volted reactions, for what it was worth, and was a very different man to Victor who was a political poet of parts and a fair controversialist and a moderate man, whereas Maurice de Glehn stooped so low as to imitate Tristan Tzara. But Bertram Brown who was underfed and had the face of a permanent victim of influenza, he had a brutal bridling little pen – but he was under the influence of Pickwort, which was a pity, but he did not follow Hedgepinshot out of the pub and was quite nice to Ratner – who tried to tell him about a complex, but Siegfried Victor nipped that in the bud.

Siegfried Victor took no notice whatever of the withdrawal of his coeditor Hedgepinshot. Nothing however could disturb or surprise him. The matter was settled out of hand. Hedgepinshot's assent to terms had been indicated by his crawling stickily away, as if his trouser-legs had been coated with webs of adhesive glue, and a sort of bat-wings had compounded his two trailing trousered Oxford limbs.

*

The lunch with Dan passed in savage silence, Ratner read the paper part of the time. So far this was a meeting after Dan's own heart. Then Ratner improved in temper and thenceforth Dan had a difficult time.

Much to Dan's alarm, Mr Ratner began sketching in a few witty strokes several of his more important Complexes. Dan had never listened to such a repulsive recital and he hastily swallowed his black coffee. But it had put his host in a good humour and he was now in great form. He ordered Dan a Zambaglione and he had one himself. He told Dan about another Complex, a most diabolically unpleasant one, and Dan shrank into his corner and only trembled and stammered when Mr Ratner solicited his opinion upon a dark point or two in one of the more horrid of his intimate revelations, invariably connected with the functions of sex and its painful and more musty 'frustrations'.

Then for a short while Ratner settled down, one-man-to-another-wise, to be confidentially improving in a more general manner. Some of the more recondite Complexes of other people were passed in review, with solemnest unction. Then he silently watched Dan for some minutes with his small one-sided tomahawk-disk of a yellow-suet face, with his large glaucous grey eye (framed principally for the functions of measuring and watching, watching and footruling and again watching – but always fishily *watchful* above everything, this eye of the marine-bottoms – at the end of its tentacles).

'Zagreus' Mr Ratner asserted unexpectedly, for that subject had not come up so far, 'Zagreus is a clear case of surplus thyroid stimulation.'

At the name 'Zagreus' Dan looked up all boyish anticipation, but at once he cast his eyes back upon the table-cloth when he found that nothing was to follow, of a nature to interest him.

'I mean everything is enormously *important* to Horace.'

He waited but Dan was sunk in a sombre day-dream provoked by the mere mention of Horace: as to what Dan understood by *important* he offered no indication, he took no intense interest, as did Ratner, in what was 'important' at all – in the dull or the exciting, in stimulus and its reverse.

'I daresay you have noticed how interested Horace is in everything,' Ratner softened his voice for the occasion, the tenacity of his pedagogic purpose burning in him as with yellow electricity.

'I wish I were like that!' Joo whimsically wailed. 'It is enviable, don't you think it is? To be able to regard everything as *terribly momentous*, as Horace does, must be a very nice feeling to have! I wish I had it!'

Ratner simulated a nice gentlemanly bashful brand of envy, and he cast down his eyes. Then he raised them, and began watching again the lovely downcast young head. He ground out in sneering croak:

'One would scarcely know oneself, one would never be bored, it must be won-der-ful!'

Dan yawned slightly but involuntarily: he was extremely susceptible to the word 'bored'.

'Horace has a thyroid surplus' then Ratner quite savagely announced, and he turned his face round the other way and watched Dan with the other eye.

No answer was received from Dan at all who showed no sign that the word 'thyroid' had stimulated him.

An idea occurred to Ratner as he turned over in his watchful mind the baffling fact that progress had been slow. He said, muffling his grin in a cloud of seductive frowning earnestness,

'You know what they say about thyroid?'

Perhaps this young moron did not know about thyroid. And sure enough Dan shook his head – he had not the least idea what was said by them.

'It gives people who have thyroid-surplus that feeling of the great *importance* of everything,' Ratner instructed him, in owlish pedagogy of a wiseacre wet-nurse.

Dan looked listlessly at the unimportant countenance of the young italian waiter, standing and gazing out of the window of the restaurant – it would be jolly to have a surplice or whatever it was. He had a pain in his stomach.

'There must be *some* explanation of Horace' Ratner protested, with veiled indignation.

Dan showed no sign that he thought any explanation of Horace was called for at all, or of anybody for that matter, and (as he was annoyed) even if there had been (his unresponsive face conveyed) Mr Ratner would not be the person to provide it.

Ratner frowned a little nastily, at display of so little esprit de corps, as between two people not relying upon the fictitious stimulus of a freakish hormone. He considered Dan for a moment, this hard nut to crack, because of its extreme softness. He returned to the charge, he remarked impressively:

'Horace is an old man. – How old is he?'

Dan simply looked quite blankly down at the table – was he

supposed to answer or was Mr Ratner musing aloud and would he reply to himself in due course? Evidently the latter.

The ages of persons, outside the burning question as to whether they were nineteen or twenty-one, left him completely indifferent of course, when not merely confused. He thought Horace must be a beautiful uncle – uncle-aged too.

'Sixty. Perhaps sixty-three or four.' Ratner reckoned negligently, gazing into the distance, down the time-vistas or up and down the age-ladders. 'You would not expect a man of his years,' said Ratner, 'to be as interested in everything as a boy fresh from school, as *he* is! – he gets dreadfully excited, it is rather funny. There must be *some* reason' he suggested plaintively, to the superlative youth before him, so sublimely age-blind.

But Dan had never known any man of such an age as that mentioned (the age of grandfathers – a class of beings unrelated to Horace or anyone he knew) – this was a question devoid of meaning, such as only Apes propounded probably, for the confusion of men and gods – and of poor ignorant irish young-men, and he had a dum head for figures and he wished Mr Ratner would stop doing sums and talking about Horace in this pointless way. He did not quite like the way Mr Ratner spoke about Horace, he could not exactly say why – it was true that Horace took the most tremendous *interest*, but he thought Mr Ratner was suggesting Horace should be different to what he was in some way, and *not* take any interest, which was ridiculous. A perplexing Ape! He believed that he smelt – there was a smell.

'I'm sure it must be too much thyroid!' said Ratner with a rather bullying guttural emphasis, looking over the table nastily at Dan now. 'He always has been like that.'

Dan blushed for he was not used to being pointedly fixed in that way by another person's eye, he objected to it: the atmosphere (where eyes described their sly parabolas, or wandered aimlessly, or made bee-lines for you) was *public* – that was quite understood, no one could *say* anything (there was always the cat that looked at the king) but he did not like it.

'Horace is an outstanding example' Ratner coughed a little asthmatically (he wished to arouse sympathy *in* himself *for* himself, by means of a little asthma) 'an overdose of thyroid!'

Thyroid – thyroid – Dan thought of *thigh:* at that he blushed deeply. *Thyrus* occurred to him also *tabloid* or *rhomboid* – mathematics and medicine, those beastly subjects!

A sickly appearance of unhealthy human affection invaded the face of Mr Julius Ratner. Brotherly-love of a most 'sickening' order escaped from it – moistened it, expanded it.

'I have known Horace Zagreus for a long time!' came out a little haltingly at last, from this mask of unsightly benevolence. 'Horace is one of my *oldest* friends!' and Ratner sneered at himself as he said it, because of these strange human instincts that *would* cause him to love so dearly, his *oldest* friend.

Dan believed something had not agreed with Mr Ratner – he looked so uncomfortable and as though he had a pain – and Dan started to reflect that he had himself felt none too well after the soup.

'I am terribly fond of Horace!' Ratner burst out with a croaking tremor.

Dan looked at him sharply. *Fond of Horace?*

'I do not know anyone that I have so much actual affection for as Horace!' wailed Joo.

A cloud the size of a man's hand collected upon the brow of Dan. – Why had Horace sent him to talk to this insinuating devil, whom he hated more every minute!

Julius Ratner paused and examined Dan slowly: his words at last it seemed were having considerable effect. He cleared away as best he could the meaty altruism, the painful cloying varnish of thick fellowship, the treacle of 'old time's sake' which had been called up for his recent declaration. An air of camaraderie, and of complicity, took its place – its mark was Dan and he eyed his young guest with an easy conversational manner.

'Horace is a most unusual man' he said. 'He is very strange in some ways.'

Strange, thought Dan, indeed, when he sends me to listen to this soporific Ape, whom, Dan thought indistinctly, must surely be – what were those things? – yes of course, be a Jew. But then he remembered that, in his *Day's Orders* from Horace, something had occurred about this particular Ape *differing*, in some respects, from the pure Sassenach (who was called a Brit, was it, by Horace) – about his coming from the East, he thought it was, or was it the East-End? Was not that where those disbelieving people dwelt? Yes it was a point of the compass – *East* (not a country, 'The East', which was India). There was a barbarous jewish horde, he thought he had heard, not far to the East of London or Ireland. That was the *East-End*. It was 'East End' Horace had called it. – So (Dan concluded) he must be sitting with a Jew! This was an uncomfortable novelty! He looked up at that, and he examined his host closely. He had never seen a Jew before – and he hoped from the bottom of his great irish heart that he might never see one again! He looked away at once.

'In that respect Horace does not change' the *Jew* was saying: 'Horace has always wanted to be with young men!'

Dan flushed with anger – at the thought of *all these men* Dan frowned with cattish fury – this had got the goat of his arm-pit – his breath blushed fire – he could wring all their necks – knock the heads off them! His muscles hardened, he became a young man of steel.

'What did you say?' asked Ratner bending forward, with a light insolent grin, quizzing up into his face with an eye on a hook.

Dan shrank back and shook his head violently – to drive away this foreign unbelieving devil who was getting nearer to him now, the coaxing Ape!

'I thought you said something.'

Dan gave the carafe of water a look of melting hatred.

'Horace Zagreus has not any idea' Joo unfolded his exclusive information, analytical and psychical, with the detached familiarity of the expert gossiping quietly with an acquaintance, 'why he always goes about with young men. He always *does* as you know. If you asked him why he always went about with young men I expect he wouldn't understand you. He doesn't know that he does.'

Horace always went about with young men! Horace! – but Dan refused to listen to the insinuations of this devil in human form any longer!

'Horace believes – he is quite sincere, I know Horace *very* well – that it is because of their "genius" that he always seeks out young men of twenty, and takes them to theatres and to cinemas.'

Takes the young men to theatres and to cinemas! Oh this was a really horrid individual if ever there was one, thought Dan – though he *did* believe (in the same way as Horace) in his *genius*, it seemed: but he hoped very much that Mr Ratner would not begin cross-questioning him as he might do. He would then think he was not so clever, after all, as he had at first believed, and as Horace believed *absolutely*.

'He believes that every pretty boy of nineteen or twenty he meets is a "genius" as he calls it!' Ratner repeated.

He could not stand this person – Dan for some reason felt, in spite of the fact that he spoke so much about his 'genius' that Mr Ratner did not really and truly like him. He was beginning to feel that Mr Ratner in fact hated him.

'Horace has always been like that – his intentions have *always* been strictly honourable' sneered Ratner 'and he has never lost his belief in "genius" – associated *always* with extreme youth, and a pretty face! Unfortunately, the type of beauty which appeals to Horace you see is rather commonplace. The result is Horace has never actually met with a "genius" which is a pity. It might have opened his eyes if he had!'

Dan had the impression that Mr Ratner was spitting at him, he appeared to detest him! How he scoffed out his words – how his eyes darted hatefully out at him!

'Horace has always repressed himself' in the strictest confidence Ratner assured Dan now – it was an exclusive, as it was a superior, truth, that of Ratner.

Dan waited for something that he felt was coming, it was in the air.

'Horace Zagreus is a man of the Nineties of course' Ratner said. 'He was an enemy of Oscar Wilde's. But even *then* he probably always wanted to be with young men – to this day he has not the least idea why that is.'

Mr Ratner was one of the worst Apes Dan had so far met.

There was a moment's pause, Ratner spied out his opportunity.

'Horace is a repressed homosexual' in a rapid voice he declared, stinging Dan quickly with his right eye. '*Repressed.*'

Dan blushed, it was impossible to carry on a conversation with this horrid man – he did not understand what these scientific words meant, that people sometimes used, but however scientific they were not nice he knew. He reached down beneath the table for his hat where it had fallen.

'Must you go?' asked Ratner grinning, as he remarked the nature of his movements.

Across the road there was a clock in a shop, it said half-past three. – As Dan walked away from Mr Julius Ratner he noted in his mind, for his night-log: 'A preposterous Ape – an unbelieving *eastern* specimen. Should be in the Zoo I think.'

Part 6

APE-FLAGELLANT

THE servant stopped. Serving-men do not go straight in without a decent irresolution, it was a luxury-shop: so he drew up, he hesitated, he went in. Dreamy little pack-animal, he received a pleasurable shamefaced sensation. It was the chief show-girl of the shop-staff of the Malster Galleries that gave it him, who hovered in lanky elegance near the entrance, in wait for Kensington customers, to float before them, with mesmeric hip, towards a parchment lampshade or a jacket-cover wall-paper – and he looked pleasant in response to the sensation, looking politely his best, as he removed his certified-driver's car-cap with the same civil wobble of the body that served for the foot-scrape upon the mat. Cowed by the discreet richness of the bazaar he slunk up the twilit aisle. Going in among similarly-gendered cockney wage-earners, with whom he exchanged underdog glances and covert amiabilities, he asked for his daily pack. Stoutly secured, the picture-frames for Mr Richard Whittingdon were brought out to the patient discreet bare-headed figure who took them up upon his shoulders, and he left slowly by the side-entrance. There were seven gilt frames.

'Can you manage all right, mate?' asked the aproned carpenter who held the door open. The typical class-weakness of the master descended upon the servant, the frames were not a load for a gentleman's gentleman.

'Yurss!' Cubbs blurted all polite derision, at such a compliment. 'Ere, dont you go and forget them four, tomorrow twelve. E wants 'um sharp. E's orf dinner-time.'

'E shall 'ave 'um! With*art* fail!'

'That's the stuff!'

As the servant entered Grotian Walk he perceived he was followed by a tall young toff looking up at the studios. – 'That's im – what 'e was in conversation on the tellerphone over, yest-day. E dont arf look soft.'

*

Daniel found Grotian Walk without having to ask a policeman. He was very hot, it was approached only by hills.

On top it was mainly a terrace of bungalow dwellings, with towering North-lights in top-heavy attics, pitched over rustic cottages. There were tapering slits for the reception of canvases, with small derricks fitted to their jambs. He fanned himself with his felt-hat. Just before him moved with difficulty a squab form, inured to hills, from whom sweat fell. Some beast-of-burden of a lower order to be spotted at a glance, who bore a load of picture-frames. Came to him a rosy grimy boy bearing oil-jars from a gateway, and called to him:

'Ere Rich-erd Whiddindon where does 'e live mate? It is 'ere aint it?'

'Ah!' Cubbs pants 'where those 'ere cars is!'

They all looked down Grotian Walk for Dan was with them now, and Dan saw the Bugatti and he knew he was there, and beyond it there was another Bugatti the same as the first. There were two distinct Bugattis.

Outdistancing the loaded cattle Dan reached the first Bugatti in some strides. Behind him he heard the rush of a van and stepped aside. It drew up beyond the second Bugatti. *Fortnum and Mason* was upon its sides. A liveried messenger went to the rear and removed boxes from the van and they entered the gate together. Cubbs now came in behind.

'Ere is that right – Major Wit-in-Tin?'

Fortnum appealed to the lad with the oil-jars, who had them on a sling like onion-sellers.

'Ah. First floor. Up them stairs' said Cubbs, who breathed heavily.

The second servant of Fortnum's put down a case within the gate. The party, headed by the provision-merchant's messenger engaged in the stair-case of clattering stone.

As they approached the landing a door opened and a large figure in a paint-dappled smock with black-rimmed mandarin spectacles for painting came out. It was 'the World's Ape' and Dan, preceded by the van-hand, waddling with his burden of provisions, entered the Apery.

Dick, an artisan among artisans, went in with them, the

dirtiest workman there, chewing the canè tube of an underslung chimney-pot briar.

'How are you? Come in,' he said to Boleyn, and when they were all inside Dan fell among more people – inside the door was a messenger with a letter, gathered before a picture were three members of the possessing class, one was a small bald groom-like person in plus-fours – there was his wife, who rolled jauntily beside him, puffing a cigarette – and there was the midget polish lesbian, Bloggie, who sat in the largest chair upon a model's-throne – she dominated two sucking doves, who smoked in silence upon a divan beside the gas-stove, and watched Bloggie, their fat flesh-yellow legs hanging down like four ripe plantains, ferruled in extremities of flowered gilt.

'We'll have tea Cubbs now' Dick said to the servant, looking over at the window. 'It's all right, I will undo this.'

'Very well sir' said Cubbs.

Dick signed the book that the belted page took from a military pouch. He tore open a letter, he threw it down, beside the settee. The bell rang in the kitchen where Cubbs was. The door had remained half open. The reverberation of stolid feet came from the stone staircase. Cubbs this time opened another door, from the kitchen to stairs. A muttering came from the kitchen.

'How is Horace?' Dick asked, as he cut the puissant thongs that secured the picture-frames.

The frames were burnished ivory black and gilt, gilt and silver, ones. He stood them against the wall where there were many others, taking the largest over towards an easel, next to the one before which the two people, husband and wife, were standing.

The horsy motorist, in giant scotch-checks, exclaimed, with emphatic traces of trenchant Yorkshire, with a false nail-driving heartiness:

'Damn good Dick! Damn good!'

He was looking at the picture upon the easel.

'I'm glad you like it' drawled Dick condescendingly, looking at it too.

'*Damn* good!'

Obese and smiling, with a face massaged to a floury pallor, the small woman continued to roll beside her sporting mate, with a jaunty assurance, cigarette-holder aloft in a pudgy stump of a fist.

'Yes Dick I agree' she got out after a reluctant interval, as Dick squinted at her ironically. 'I should call that a jolly good day's work Dick.'

'Jolly good!' husband echoed. 'I'm not sure it's not the best painting you've done Dick! Damn good!'

The Yorkshire brawn of the voice hammered in the hearty epithets.

'I think it has something to be said for it!' Dick agreed with lofty modesty.

'It's jolly good Dick!' exclaimed the seasoned connoisseur, looking at husband. 'Don't you agree Richard – Dick should send that to the Six and Six, instead of the other one?'

The studio echoed with their delighted Dicking, as the pair took it in turn to Dick this rich coveted amateur, so haughtily 'county' (just the thing for their imperfect brand-new social-life), conscious of all the Tomming Dicking and Halling that their class-war-profiteered factory-wealth but lately-inherited, made possible – proud of the presence of such as the noted lesbian (of Gossip-column calibre) squatted in their rear – with whom they would soon with luck be Bloggie and Jenny, shaken up like a cocktail in the bowels of the Bugatti. Marvellous money that turns everything into a pet-or-nick-name or a Dick-like something! Who can deny it or forget that *Bugatti calls to Bugatti!* – so they were the pleasedest pair they were (of small sporty swaggerers) but oh mortally timid, behind soft flash summer-suitings and six-cylinder-speed-prams – for oh, is not so much unexpected money so unreal and uncanny, when not possessed from the cradle up? A new proverb: *A fortune in middleage – An eyrie in a bird-cage.*

But Dick raked this preposterous Jenny with a cross glance.

'Oh do you think so?'

This awful old bore of a wife of this rich mountebank marine-painter, *would* stick to her stupid opinion and air her views as if anyone wanted to hear them! Small fat half-blind ex-cooks – confused matrimonially with the legatees of rich manufacturers, who were marine-painters, and however much socially a joke, still with palettes upon their thumbs and with powerful Bugattis – should be seen and not heard!

But the portentous old Jenny squared up at this. If she, the artistic consort of a renowned millionaire marine-painter, *must* praise, in the interests of social advancement, these attempts that were not bad (for a rich tyro) why it must be understood that she would *select*. Beggars can't be choosers, but Britons never never shall be anything but pickers! You must like it or lump it! The rugged spirit of the small midland yeoman was up in arms – Jenny was nothing if not sturdy. The contentious bully of the rustic pub came to life in her hardened arteries and matched itself against the overbearing squirearch.

'Yes I *do* Dick!'

This was a matter of principle. – And we have got a Bugatti!

'Don't you think so Richard?'

Husband looked doubtful, the unprincipled flatterer. He hoped something might occur to divert Jenny from this bone of contention, which, once she got it between her jaws, there would be no pulling her off it.

'Well I don't know Jenny!' He shook his head.

The coffee-and-blue-scotch-checked Bugatti-Number-Two (who was 'Richard' to Bugatti-Number-One's 'Dick') knitted his brows. It was the usual quandary – it was *the obstinacy of Jenny*. She *would* lay down the law about pictures because she had once played a piano in a Cinema for a living. Everything else might be fair game for Jenny the law-giver, but for painting she had not a mandate. No Jenny! No Dick! I will not go with her, Dick, when it is pictures! We're banded against Jenny, Dick, when it is pictures!

'I don't know Jenny!' husband said. Very serious consideration was called for, it was a moot point, off-hand it could not be decided – *no Jenny*, not so easy as you suppose quite! – though both you and Dick are right in a sense, for you are a brilliant and superior pair I grant, and *where one has to decide between a matriarch and a squirearch* – well it is no easy matter!

'I think the other one is better Richard!' said Dick, imperiously coaxing Richard with drowsy myopic smile, meaning that Old Jenny was above herself a little as usual and Richard smiled back at Dick with a look that passed muster for a vulgar wink – to protest that Old Jenny meant no harm but *would* have her say, there was no denying.

But Jenny straddled obstinately on her two fat old pins, and the angry army-and-county amateur knew the significance of this attitude in Jenny and the bad blood mounted into his face – while his north-country double, in the clownish check, turned away his face to show Jenny she was going too far and (for he had been a clerk in the Naval Reserve in the War) should haul down her pennant and trim her sails according to her cloth, for they were on a lee-shore in spite of their bank-balance-ballast of hard-fisted Halifax bullion.

'Well I don't care what you say – I maintain Dick that you should send this to the Six and Six!'

Richard felt a little hot at the thought of the lesbian sphinx (of Gossip-column calibre) watching all this – but it was no use, Jenny would not take a no for she was a great judge of pictures.

'Oh you do! Why Jenny? Because Richard thinks –'

'I don't care a damn what Richard says, I maintain as I always have the house is too red – yes it *is* too red Dick you know it is!'

You know it you naughty Dick! – a sudden arch softening that promised a compromise was here – Jenny grew roguish. Very pleased Richard laughed merrily with her, in anxious encouragement.

'You *maintain*, Jenny! You're always *maintaining!*' but Dick testily piped.

Richard associated himself at once with brother Dick, if it must come to a mix-up.

'Yes Jenny you're "maintaining" again! – Dick altered the red, Jenny!'

'I don't care' jauntily cries the wilful old Jenny, squaring her jaw: it was clamped down upon the stem of the cigarette-holder, caught between the only two teeth that had started life in her head and not in another's, and she smiled most aggressive, with the glittering false residue. 'I think it's still too red. It's far too red!'

'I'm sorry you think I'm wrong Jenny!' lightly and loftily and fiercely sneered Dick, throwing up his head with eyes almost closed to shut out this absurdity.

'Well Dick let's have them out side by side!' the undaunted voice of old Jenny rang out.

'Yes Dick!' husband exclaimed to brother Dick, with a fawning truculence. 'Let's have it out and compare them!' Then Jenny would see, wouldn't she? Let us confound Jenny: Too red indeed! – don't listen to old Jenny Dick – you know what Jenny is, you know my wife by this time surely!

With a manner of great seigneurial restraint, to honour this little old girl (short-skirted once more by Fashion in her advancing years) grandly dawdling Dick goes over and drags out the canvas in question. He fits upon it its glittering collar of costly gilt, and then he plants it groggily upon the narrow shelf of the easel and turns away to take a cigarette from the box upon the mantelpiece.

'There you are Dick what did I say!' the attractively self-willed little Jenny is heard to exclaim, as she flings herself over heavily in front of the picture, with a face of the maddest cross pugnacity – and Richard after her, standing by to restrain her, full of anxiety – and Dick turning from the mantelpiece coming quickly up upon the heels of Richard, towering in the rear of both of them angrily.

'What did I say? You see – the red house spoils it. You must admit Dick that the red house spoils it.'

'I don't admit anything of the sort!'

'I maintain it could not be that red!'

'How do you mean Jenny – "could not be" that red! What does it matter whether it *could* be or not!' Dick peevishly pumps out his argument, in spasms of rich-toned complaint.

'No Dick you can't have I maintain in a realistic picture –'

'But it isn't realistic!'

'*Yes it is!*'

'Really Jenny I don't think you.'

'No Dick. I still maintain it's the wrong red, I'm sorry!'

'Jenny is *maintaining* again Richard!'

'Oh I know!' brother Richard laughed helplessly to brother Dick.

The kindergarten was all alive with the dispute over the big boy's oil-picture, with the Noah's Ark H for House that they all knew he had squeezed out of the tube of vermilion, when left to himself, just to be clever and steal a march, but only the little old girl dared to speak up, and it was a ticklish moment. A thrill went down the spine of Dan. Here if anywhere was the authentic Ape-feeling to be encountered in the very atmosphere, and he began composing his log. '*Discovered Apes in bitter argument over a masterpiece of Apish art. Expected from moment to moment these Apes to fly at each other's throats. As far as I was able to discover, a red brick dwelling the subject of this dispute.*'

But Jenny's raging voice was at it again hammer and tongs.

'You can't use that colour, in that position – that's what I maintain it's too hot. No Dick it's no use.'

'No Jenny!' exclaimed Dick, woundingly coaxing: 'you said yourself yesterday that it was not because it was too hot. You said "pure colour". You said only beginnings I mean beginners thought that to use pure colours – you distinctly said – I'm positive – *beginners*.'

'No Dick, hot was what I said! No Dick "hot" I said.' Jenny grew waggish, wagging her old finger sexily at the six-footer – rolling jauntily in his shadow, a tubby dinghy in a slow-swell, husband would have seen it, with his old sea-salt's eye.

Dan blushing very deeply, had approached the scene of the dispute. He gazed at the pictures. Richard turned to him, with a dashing cringe, and carried his fingers towards his ears, smiling.

'When those two get together!'

Looking at this man in alarm, as though a statuette had piped up unexpectedly, Daniel withdrew into a corner near the door of the kitchen.

With a solemn scowl of scorn the polish lesbian midget squatted aloft upon the model's throne – she was dominating her two sucking doves in attendance who sat like fat odalisks. Her face was with twenty years' hard work as a polish lesbian, with dyspepsia and cosmetics, yellowish – her eyes of an obliquity roughly judeo-tartar. As silent as Dan, she modelled herself upon the asiatic statuette, as seen through the eyes of the Hollywood or West End Producer.

'No it's no use Dick!' Jenny's voice rushed in again raucously to the attack. 'This is the better picture.'

'Jenny you *are* ridiculous! That's not the question. Yesterday you said the red was all right you said you were mistaken.

You've forgotten what you said!' He flung down his cigarette.

'Now Dick!' Jenny again was waggish. 'Remember! No Dick! I was down on the red the moment I saw it.'

'Down on the red! Really you are absurd Jenny!' in exasperated accents Dick mocked her, the saliva collecting in his mouth, producing the effect of his fiercely relishing a dish of lush delicacies, as he champed his jaws up and down in impotent excitement, like a nervous and short-sighted giant in a fairy tale. 'I shouldn't mind – if you only *remembered*. You might *try* and remember!'

'Jenny is right Dick!' Richard exclaimed in alarm, all of a sudden. For he knew it was impossible to stand by and see the *memory* of the law-giver attacked. Not one of those things that were fair game – joke was a joke. Husband looked serious.

'Oh I'm glad you think so Richard! I'm afraid I don't!' Dick gave Richard a very hard bright little rap with his eye indeed – that's for you my fine fellow! Darting his trunk round to the fireplace he swooped and struck it low down with the muzzle of his underslung pipe. A thimbleful of stiff ash shot into the water-basin before the gas-fire. The chocolate-suède feet flung out to right and left, Dick then went down the studio towards the kitchen. As he went his person was quaked, from chocolate-suède footwear to electrically-tanned occiput, by a heavy hiccup. Its undulatory path ended in the back view of his brown one-piece neck and head – which stood up starched and stiff as the wave of the hiccup passed into space, and the report sounded from his mouth.

Consternation entered into Jenny and Richard. As one person they started to move after the offended figure, Dicking hard as they went, in plaintive chirping.

'Dick! I see what you meant Dick about the tree on the left!' cried Brother Richard.

'Oh really!' muttered Dick as he drew away.

'Dick! you're not offended are you! Dick! I'm not sure after all! I think the red.'

The great man did not deign to turn but he called shortly: 'I'm going to see if the tea's ready!'

Jenny and Richard fell astern – Jenny rolling squably but rakishly in the wake of the departing full-rigged-ship, Richard heaving to at her side. They both put their helms hard to port. They began hailing each other, anxiously, in cowed undertone.

Dick drove into the kitchen, as if a battering ram had blundered in at the door, and it drew up upon meeting in its path the form of Cubbs: bursting in the door he charged shortsightedly half-way across to the spot upon which Cubbs stood. Cubbs, his adenoidish mouth moistly half-open, and a dreamy masturbatory eye of mild blue discreetly fixed in the far-away, only half-noticed the entrance of the great studio-lord in the painter's smock. It looked as if the too-civilized Cubbs, in a refinement of politeness, affected to mistake Dick for a house-painter and decorator.

As, out of the fog that invested his short-sight (the two now unspectacled dog-brown eyes, that could not see) the features of Cubbs appeared, Dick was shattered by an involuntary hiccup. It exploded in the face of Cubbs. During the recent argument a big wind-pocket had been maturing and a real man's deep-chested belch was the result. – But of proved steadiness under fire, Cubbs did not blink. A little sentimentally he fixed his eye – in a 'Poor Tom'-Tommy's Tipperary stare – upon the long-long trail a winding into the land of his dreams – just above the right shoulder of acting-Major Dick Whittingdon. The Captain was not the man to go to bed to be delivered of a belch! – and he said loftily, staring stonily over the left shoulder of the servant,

'Is the tea ready?'

'It won't be a moment now sir.'

The servant continued to face his superior, suspended by his susceptive glance from one spot in space – while the gentleman blankly aimed a grand and expressionless stare at a similar imaginary bull's-eye, in an opposite region of the same vacantness. (Dick and Cubbs dwelt in the same vacuum.)

'Isn't the kettle boiling?'

Dick was deeply shaken by another convulsion, but it spent its force within, it was a dud.

'Just on sir.'

'Bring it in as soon as it's ready.'

Dick's bulk vacillated, it swung awkwardly about, he drove back to the studio, passing through the door with a crash.

'Yes sir.'

Dan had been forced to leave the chair by the door of the kitchen. Upon the approach of Dick, his knees stuck out so far, he discovered, into the fair-way, and he did not feel justified in leaving them where Dick would have to pass. Upon that he retired to the settee, which had been vacated by Bloggie's attendant sucking-doves, who had gone to lie upon the model's throne near Bloggie's feet.

Jenny, rolling heavily, and with a considerable list (as she was stronger on one pin than the other) came into port. After a disappointing interchange with Richard (who was definitely out-of-sorts and disposed to be critical), she had sheered off, and now rolled in the offing. She eyed the occupant of the settee, and the vacant place at his side, obviously making up her mind to drop her anchor. Her roving half-blind old piratic eye had noted a lonely young man, sitting upon a settee. The young man looked disconsolate she thought, and there was only one thing to do.

So Jenny sat down beside Dan in the most friendly way and with a semi-maternal (young-for-a-motherly) camaraderie, cocked a hail-fellow-well-met eye of understanding at the young chap's face, and said to the poor young man, point-blank and pally,

'Are you a painter?'

With an impulse he could not control Dan withdrew a couple of pygmies' lengths on seeing this strange craft descend upon him – so charged with jolly energy, so full of ballast and abundant in the beam, so stricken with involuntary momentum, so inclined to sag to starboard – and seeing *her* starboard was *his* port.

Jenny settled herself upon the settee, it began to oscillate with a billowy movement that flung Dan about from side to side. He was compelled to steady himself against the massive walls, which backed this too elastic, distinctly choppy, surface.

'Don't you think Dick's last painting is good?'

One question – a first, and perhaps a last – can always be ignored. But at her second question Dan half-rose, in panic, intending to leave the settee, for as she spoke she developed, he remarked to his great alarm, rather more movement, as a battleship most probably does when it discharges its guns. Also she exaggerated the angle of her inclination to starboard, when in speech, and distinctly approached him across the quivering surface of what was their common element in this position – while he retreated, flung back against the circumscribing walls, padded and sprung for such eventualities.

Dan did not rise however, for half-way he caught the eye of a recumbent sucking-dove, so he clung on slowly. He shook his head.

'A shy boy!' thought Jenny. She continued to leer at him, pleasant and open, rakishly maternal. Jenny was used, in husband's pictures, to the open spaces of the ocean. The bluff ways of blue-eyed Jack Tar were her daily ship's-ration, and as a consequence she would hail a fellow and say *well-met!* as soon as look at him and all was frank and free on the ocean-wave of John Buchanan, born 1880 and still going strong!

But Dick drove lazily back, kicking a few footballs with his brown suède footwear to right and left, with Richard clinging to him like a Rugby forward, tackling very low, in a doubled-up cringe indeed. Rakishly maternal still, old Jenny transferred her merry eye to her sulky host. Then Cubbs brought in the tea, and all partook. Dan had the greatest trouble with his tea-cup, riding as he was upon a perpetually agitated superficies.

The conversation languished in the studio as the tea, the *friandises*, and the tiny sandwiches found their way into the assembled stomachs. For Dick Whittingdon was no conversationalist although highly argumentative when roused, and was distinctly annoyed into the bargain. Richard held down Jenny as best he could, whereas Bloggie never spoke at all, and Dan was much the same, and there only remained the two attendant odalisks – who were, both, heavy and coy dependent-creatures, half-sleeping like dogs, and they took their cue from their dumb goddess. So it was an impasse.

Dan cast about for a way to go, for he was due at Yarmouth Place. But just then one of Bloggie's team exclaimed in a deep voice.

'Oh Mr Whittingdon may we see your whips! Would you mind showing them to us?'

And the other one immediately bayed, behind her:

'Do you mind terribly showing them? Would it be a bore?'

Dick rose. They all got up.

Do not forget to ask to see his whips! Dan remembered: and although he felt a little nervous, he thought he had better stop, in fact he must for Horace had particularly enjoined him to do so and he must not leave Mr Whittingdon's house without having seen his *whips.*

The party now headed towards the door by which Dan had entered, led by Dick Whittingdon, and in silence they passed out into the stone passage.

'Who lives there?' whispered one of the two friends of Bloggie to the other hoarsely, as they passed the door of a studio.

'No one' the other replied.

'No one? How very odd!' said the first.

'Not at all!' said the second.

'Don't you think so?' said the first.

'No one lives here, except Mr Whittingdon' said the second.

'Aren't the other studios let?' asked the first.

'No,' said the second.

'Aren't they good studios?' asked the first.

'Very good,' said the second.

'Why aren't they let then?' said the first.

'Because Mr Whittingdon has rented them,' said the second.

'All of them?' said the first.

'Yes the whole block' said the second.

'Oh' said the first.

Here was an Ape indeed! reflected Dan upon hearing this in spite of himself as he walked at their side. He rented *all* the studios, there must be quite ten studios – in this way the 'world's Ape', it could easily be computed, must prevent *ten* geniuses from having a roof over their genius, and must keep them in small ill-lit rooms while he sat on all these valuable workshops in solitary egotistic state – and *there* was a splendid passage waiting, for his evening's log!

The party entered the studio immediately above the one they had just left. It was almost empty, except for a few large rocking-horses, parallel bars, a miniature american bar, a dentist's chair, and three settees. A red drugget led to a pair of steps: there were piles of canvases against the wall beneath the window, a hookah bottle or a narghile, and phials and glasses upon a table. At one end stood a large black cupboard.

Collected in the middle of this studio, like a party in the charge of a lecturer in the gallery of a museum, they waited, a little huddled together. With well-pleased showmanship, all in dumb show, Dick approached his black cupboard. Catching hold with difficulty of the little metal process over its lock, he pulled it open, after several tries with a peevish oath.

But Dan had grown increasingly alarmed. The greater tenseness and mock-melodrama of the atmosphere of this sight-seeing party was most marked. They had settled that they would go about this personally conducted tour, to see some whips, as if they had been engaged in the business of a dark ritual, and the clap-trap of their solemn huddled silence sent his blood cold and Dan wished himself anywhere but where he was. He had begun to eye askance this collection of people, with whom he had come to inspect some objects, of a mysterious nature, it now seemed, though he had been told they were only 'whips'. Certainly a whip was a dangerous plaything like a shotgun. But he had often seen whips, especially in the country in Ireland, and his uncle had a dog-whip which he had once cracked, when in high spirits. But the attitude of these habitués of the Ape-world was disquieting in the extreme, and he began to think that this time he had got amongst a number of very dangerous Apes indeed.

As the doors of the cupboard, first sticking together, flew violently open, striking Dick who staggered back crossly, old Jenny uttered a hoarse squeak.

'Oh Dick you've got a *new* one haven't you! What a beauty! I'm sure I've never seen that before! What is it?'

'It is the thong of a Bokharan cow-herd,' said Dick impressively, very big-boy-at-school. 'It is made of goat-gut.'

'Oh I think that's *sweet* Dick, don't you Richard?' she gruffly trilled, and Richard came in far down in the bass in assent.

The party in a compact body had approached the black cupboard. Dan could not see what they were looking at, they were in the way.

'I know a man who had a marvellous slave-whip!' said one of Bloggie's she-chaps.

'Arab?' Dick asked with professional expert succinctness.

'I believe so.'

'This is a *most* lovely one Dick!' exclaimed Jenny, who had hold of it.

There was a loud report. Everyone jumped except Dick who was quite unconcerned. Jenny had cracked the cow-herd's whip in sport.

To Dan's great horror Jenny was spying him out he could see – and he lost no time, he went quickly in behind the two friends of Bloggie, his heart beating, where he waited.

But he heard the voice of the old harpy in his ear almost at once, for she had followed him. And holding out to him a stained and reddish thing, that resembled a fat dead snake more than anything, which had a sleek and sinuous waggle as it oscillated restlessly in her hand, with a carved handle of oily wood, she laughed, he thought, in a most significant threatening manner as she said,

'Feel how heavy it is! You wouldn't think it was made of goat-gut would you?'

He was forced to grasp this horrid object, and, pale to the lips, he held it for a moment, while it writhed in the air, until it fell to the floor, where Jenny picked it up.

Richard took the thing from Jenny, he examined the carving upon the handle, with frowning punctilio.

'Very nice isn't it Dick?' he said, holding the thing up, the carving, to Dick, with the air of understanding the craftsmanship – his professional reserve had the thrill of all things deep. The freemasonry of the arts has its cabbalisms – Richard used a certain gesture.

But by this time Dan was beside himself with apprehension. While Jenny had been bending down to pick up the whip, he quickly removed himself to the opposite side of the group, where he at once caught sight in one terrified glance of a perfect hedge of birches, drover's whips, bamboos and martinets, within the gaping inside of the great black cupboard. His eyes fixed at his feet he stood before Mr Whittingdon. Making a great effort, he succeeded in muttering that he had to go to tea now, it was time he went to tea.

'To tea?' said Mr Whittingdon.

'No' Dan said. But he did not remain (to make himself

intelligible) any longer in the presence of these startling people. He could not without screaming have stopped a moment longer in the neighbourhood of that awful black arsenal. With a swift and muscular tread he reached the door. Rushing into the studio below he seized his hat, and, without looking back, he descended the loud stone stairway very much more quickly than he had come up it.

Part 7

PAMELA FARNHAM'S TEA-PARTY

CLEMMIE RICHMOND went to see her friend Pamela Farnham. She found her in at tea-time, in her large Kensington flat. The servant preceded her into the hall. *Much music marreth men's manners.* Clemmie's were bad, and this might be accounted for by her calling. Mrs Farnham was found moving in the door of her sitting-room. She flung herself at Clemmie, kissing effusively, her lips falling like a forehammer upon her friend's slack cheeks, made more inert by her cross passivity. Clemmie with chilly deliberation surrendered her left cheek. Her large nose, which was like the Old Testament female nose, 'as the tower of Lebanon which looketh towards Damascus,' required a wide backward movement of the head as it swung to present the right side for the ringing antistrophe. A movement, epodic in intention, towards her jutting mouth, she prevented, shaking herself free. For a moment to mark off this lyrical event, in time and space, she stood and stared.

'You *darling!* How nice of you to come! You darling!'

Mrs Farnham's fervour, expressed in what was her epigraph for all meetings with women, was again translating itself into action. With mouth preparing to register, slightly moistening her lips, arms rising, she again was starting towards Clemmie to set on her with her lips.

Clemmie advanced, giving her a rough manly push. 'Come along Pamela, that's enough of it. I'm thirsty. Have you any tea?'

In the sitting-room a crimson glow from the shaded lamps stained the apartment like a rosy infusion in a medicine. The deceitful light lay like a spell over the small assembly.

Two visitors contended with fervour.

'He wanted to send it back. It is the third time they've been given him . . .'

'How do they manage it? Is it by lots . . . ? I didn't like her myself.'

The dozen self-conscious masks were so many indexes read

by the incoming eye. Each one in turn caused Clemmie an appreciable astonishment. Like so many policemen standing in dark doorways at night, alarming the night-passenger, they were coyly withdrawn. One face, turned up, watched her. Like a bouquet of prudence and cleverness these heterogeneous realities were held in place – she added her petal, she took her place in the bunch. To theirs she added her particular silence, she proceeded stealthily to hide herself among them, she sank her large nose down level with their waiting heads.

Raids were made into the unaminous restraint by Mrs Hollindrake or by the hostess. Mrs Farnham went her round. One by one she forced open the obstinate little mouth of each mollusc, and then let it alone until its turn came round again.

Pamela Farnham, who had not followed the new arrival in at once, but had gone on moving in the doorway, now entered. Clemmie had not been spoken to or looked at, except for Mrs Hollindrake, as the hostess was awaited to remove the quarantine. No one seemed pleased at its being removed, but bowed very guardedly, with the exception of Novitsky.

'Let's see you don't know everybody here, do you? This is Mr Novitsky: Miss Richmond. *This* is Miss Dowsett, Lady Briggs (she passed over Mrs Hollindrake with a smile), Mr What's your name? Nosworthy: Miss Brest: and *that* – THAT is Jimmie! (As you know.) Oh, I had forgotten Mr Wildsmith. (So sorry – you don't mind?) But you know Arthur? Yes, of course you do. And – where are you? – that is Sullivan Walpole. I don't know that man's name there, but I think it is Fishmyer. That is right, isn't it? Yes Mr Fishmyer.'

Pamela's shagreened hand, its family of miniature faces circumscribed with glittering rings, went under the lamp-shade into the lighted area of the tea-tray, and poured out a cup of tea.

'You do take sugar, Clemmie darling?'

It was one of Clemmie's privileges to take sugar.

Jimmie, with a pleasant abstraction, slowly passed the cup.

With the weather-beaten cheeks of an Old Salt, Pamela was more than half another Jenny, but with a better social start – and everyone knew that it was not maritime exposure that accounted for her complexion. She was on the water-wagon, Clemmie had heard that. She was annoyed, as she did not like liquor, to find that the cakes all seemed to contain some, rum or curaçao.

'Do you think a man ought to marry, Clemmie? We've been discussing Peter's engagement. Isn't it dreadful! I don't know what all these young men want to get married for – you won't, will you Jimmie? I don't think I could bear that. Promise me you won't go and get married, Jimmie! Promise!'

She clung to her old-woman's-darling with an incestuous ardour that made Jimmie gasp. His bright cheeks mantled pinkly, and his eyes shone with the roscid moisture that Mrs Farnham's hug had squeezed into them. His straight, rather thin citron hair danced upon his brow. His mouth remained open like an eternal plum, upon which he laid a few appropriate words, like the remarks of Royalty in newspaper reports, as the occasion required, a little faint and clipped.

'Of course I won't Pammie. Don't. You're hurting!'

'Yes can't you see you're hurting him Pamela?' said Mrs Hollindrake, bending forward severely with a wheeze.

'I *would* hurt him if I thought he was going to get married!'

'I don't believe Jimmie will ever get married! I can't see him married poor darling, can you?' Helen Dowsett said, her voice fricative alert and soft, casting a warp round the boy with her flattering eyes. The other two sturdy hens, Mrs Hollindrake and her bosom friend Pammie Farnham, bobbed about upon the scented tide, all subtly pulling at the same object. Lady Briggs sat upon a cushion, her back against the wall. With her Clemmie, in an undertone, conversed.

Mr Nosworthy had moved out of the inner circle. He had directed himself to the side of Miss Brest. Mr Sullivan Walpole, and Mr Fishmyer, who were together, became engaged in a conversation with Novitsky.

'No, I *can't!* Euh!' (hugging again). 'Let him just try it' Pammie hissed through her teeth, some of the spittle coming through at 'try', seconding the occult activities that a limited decorum prescribed.

Catching the withdrawing glint of Wildsmith's spectacles, Mrs Farnham remembered and said:

'And what have you got to say about Marriage Mr Wildsmith? I'm sure you never intend to get married.'

'I haven't thought about it I'm afraid' Arthur Wildsmith breathed with the offended detachment that never left him. Whenever addressed he answered in a manner as though he would say – 'Why do you address me? I am listening to you. Please do not address me directly.'

The presence of this museum official at the tea-party was accounted for by a weakness he was assumed to feel for Jimmie, though he never spoke, even more rarely than Jimmie, nor did he ever look at the object of his passion. Jimmie did not speak because 'little boys should be seen and not heard'. Wildsmith preferred to be pressed to speak. Then he would answer with a pretentious reluctance.

'Will you get married some day, Novitsky' asked the hostess, eyeing the sort of vitruvian scroll that made a movement outside the blank rhomb of her ceiling, and revolving her rings.

'Some day!' Novitsky fanatically beamed and burned, turning away from Fishmyer and Walpole towards the tea-table.

'I suppose we must make up our minds to do without you. I think we can spare him, don't you Peggy?' she asked Mrs Hollindrake. 'Well, we'll try' she shook comfortably towards him, to show how comfortable she would be without him. David Novitsky continued to smile and burn holes in them with his small luminous eyes.

If Wildsmith whose family name was Bernheim, suggestive of impressionist pictures, was aloof, though impassibly attentive, Novitsky was extremely attentive but with an all embracing sociability. Fanatically unaloof, a constant stream of vitality was wasted from his eyes. This outpouring clearly caused him a strange pride, comparable to that of an urchin displaying the fine parabola of his urine.

'Well, tell us why you will get married some day Novitsky.'

'Willingly!' and he began at once with a bright dogmatism. 'I will tell you why! I shall marry in order to be more comfortable than I can be as a singleman.' *Signalman*, as it sounded, was a coquetry uselessly dispersed over his hardened old female hearers. They cocked their horny ears with a wounding indulgence to this semitic trumpet. 'To defend myself I must have a woman – that is why I marry!'

Adapting themselves to this peculiar loquacity which they had provoked, the ageing ears (hungry for the last murmurs of an early lisping life, as represented by Jimmie, and which this outburst obstructed) lent themselves with an english patience. Novitsky burnt them with his unnecessary furnace of cheap russian primitivism.

'You will marry, Novitsky – '

'I shall marry. Socially, a woman is necessary!'

'Peggy!' signals of ostentatious distress to pass Pammie an ash tray.

'A man is fastidious – mentally!' Masculine and mental, he showed his teeth.

'A man . . .'

David Novitsky, as 'a man', swelled and twisted with importance.

'Life disgusts him!'

'Jimmie, you look *pale*. Are you *quite* sure you are well?'

Mrs Farnham gazed at him with anxiety, wondering if what they, hardened old edwardian sinners, were supporting, might not be found too fatiguing for him. He gave her a slight reproving frown. He fixed both eyes upon Novitsky, as though to distract this concern, to discourage it by his stoicism. Pamela as hostess should listen to what was being said. After all it *had* to be said.

'How is one to speak to a conventional person? The man is afraid – I don't know! The woman is frightened!' Novitsky crouched down between his shoulders. 'The wife knows everything – she is afraid of nothing. She enjoys all that the man hates. She loves the carrion! She loves, it-is-her-breath, the society.'

Mrs Farnham gazed at Jimmie with admiration.

'She loves it at breakfast, luncheon, at supper – the hour entlang she will be pleased it is all one. She is for the man the scavenger. It is her business. She represents him – in the market-place, kitchen, the latrine.'

'Jimmie!' Mrs Farnham who had been nestling whispered hoarsely, at the same time overflowing protectively upon his fragile adolescence. 'Are you *perfectly* sure you – are *quite* comfortable?' He indicated by gestures of soft repulsion the nature of her misunderstanding. He looked steadfastly at Novitsky. The narrator had frowned and delivered himself with the force of a mock invective. But now he beamed at those who had solicited his opinion and the others who had not.

As the disorganization was complete he stopped. Satisfied, his actor's zest was appeased.

'Women are so useful aren't they in keeping other women at a distance?' Jimmie lisped at last.

Pamela leaped at him.

'How clever you are, Jimmie! You've heard someone say that! You *are* so clever! You oughtn't to talk about things you don't understand. I must kiss you, you look so sweet!'

The aged drink-puffed lips pressed the baby-red and the breath of old carouse and the aridness of cigarettes blew round the astute juvenile nostrils, that never defiled themselves except indirectly with those things. The wild young blue eyes, with a learned candour, vacillated beneath the caress.

Clemmie took a large chocolate in gilt paper, in the shape of a bottle, from a plate, and crushed it partly, holding it to her lips. At once a heavy perfumed stream poured out all over her frock. It was full of liqueur.

She mopped this up with her handkerchief.

'Oh, what a pity Clemmie! I hope it hasn't stained your frock?' Mrs Farnham asked, grabbing at her dress.

'Yes, it's a pity. No it's nothing thank you.'

Very angry with her imperfectly teetotal friend, Clemmie prepared to go.

Novitsky glowed in the corner, watched by no one. But Mrs Farnham turned to him to forget the misbehaviour of the chocolates.

'The sooner you get your hausfrau-sçavenger-woman Novitsky the better. Don't you agree with me, Peggy? that the sooner Novitsky gets his hausfrau-scavenger-woman the better?'

Mrs Hollindrake directed her gaze reluctantly at the squat, broad-shouldered, bearded, grinning musician.

'I wonder if he knows how to select what he has described? It would be a pity if – *if*.'

Novitsky had beamed at her almost to the breaking point, and now degenerating into hysterical chuckles, he spluttered:

'You're right. You're verry right, Mrs Hollin-derrake. I don't know you know, I should have to find the woman first to help me choose the woman. You're right!! It sounds eas-ee! Mind I didn't say so. You think you know – we're devils! – for ourselves we are. *Once bitten twice shy* is what they say! Is that right? – You're right! I shouldn't know!'

He exploded at the idea of his own incompetence. So much so that the women paid no further attention to him, considering him temporarily put out of action by himself as it were. The Novitsky episode was at an end. Mr Sullivan Walpole and Mr Fishmyer became again his confidantes.

This increasingly disgraceful scene had not been lost upon Arthur Wildsmith, although he had not seemed to notice it. He turned his head slightly towards the window-curtain a number of times. But things did not mend. His grey goat-like face, with its glimmering disgusted eyes behind the glasses, exuded as much tired contempt as Novitsky's did benevolence. He had been the nearest to his ex-co-religionist, and judeo-russian exuberance was not the thing most calculated to appeal to him. He now rose with negligent abruptness, his eyes vacantly filling the worst area of his large glasses, and approached Mrs Farnham. Muttering a few words, his head turned away from her, he took her hand. As he passed Jimmie his offended look deepened, his eye-brows rose half an inch, and his eyes descended the full length of his cup-like lids. Also his ears seemed to lie back against his head, like a whipped dog's as he slunk by.

Various transformations of an alert coquetry also appeared to occur in Jimmie. He sat up, he lisped vivaciously to Mrs Farnham, his eyes abstractly playing upon the slinking form of his departing admirer. At the door Wildsmith, with the delicious sensation of having his tail between his legs, gave a wild blank turn of the head towards the room (the bright blue eyes still playing on his shamefaced back, with the shrill little lisping throat turned so that its enervating notes would reach his glued-down ears) then vanished.

'No-oo!' Jimmie baaed, as though intending with his small flirtatious pipe to pursue Wildsmith into the passage outside, 'I really *never* have had it done. At least only wer – w – once – a little. I screamed so much they stopped. That was a *long* time ago – when I was young. But I *know* I couldn't stand it now. I'm sure I should die!'

'Oh *Jimmie!* Peggy what's to be done! Jimmie hasn't been *vaccinated.* You know what a lot of smallpox there is about. But he says he won't be done.'

'Nonsense. He'll have to be. I never heard such a thing – going about without being vaccinated.'

Bringing his red mouth down to a feline point, and staring with dazed hesitation into the distance (full of blood and lymph) his hands folded in his lap, Jimmie baaed uncertainly. 'Yes, I *know!* It's *dread-ful!*'

The bell sounded, and soon a tall woman with a death's-head with its rigid grin, large flat shoes, a flowered smicket of german greens, with a Byron collar, came in followed by a sturdy young husband, with a simple smirk upon his face.

Mrs Farnham feeding this smiling pair with tea and cakes, asked Clemmie if she was going to Victoria's (Lady Goring Landon's that was) on the Saturday of that week.

'Yes I am playing there' said Clemmie shortly, getting up.

'You're not going, Clemmie?' Pamela shrieked.

Clemmie stood over her, nodding her head, gazing down at her darkly, and saying 'YES!' fingering the cloth of her dress where the curaçao had stained it, with the tall stalking fingers. The bell had been ringing. And now Pamela, looking towards the door with alarm, said

'Whoever have we here? My dear – !'

A very tall young man indeed stood there with great severity claiming attention.

Mrs Farnham went over to him.

Gazing fixedly down at her, he said with a pedantic distinctness:

'My name is Daniel Boleyn.'

'Oh yes of course: you are a friend of Arthur Wildsmith's? He's just gone. What a pity! Well come and have some tea.'

Having made a few bows, Dan sat down with his knees sticking up very high. A delicate veneer of solemnity appeared so much a part of Dan's face that a smile must have broken it to pieces. He began staring at everybody in a more serious way than it seemed to them possible to look, but he was very afraid.

Mrs Farnham had been seeing Clemmie out, and then Mr Sullivan Walpole and Mr Fishmyer who were also leaving. On returning she found her new guest negligently disposed, in a series of spacious Zs, gazing with fixity at Jimmie.

Mrs Farnham gave Daniel Boleyn a look of great suspicion. Then she flung herself upon the settee by the side of her Jimmie, saying to Boleyn,

'You don't know Jimmie, do you? This is Jeem-mee! That is Mr Daniel Boleyn, a great friend of Arthur Wildsmith's.'

She whispered hoarsely to Jimmie – 'Be careful of that young man!' Jimmie looked at Dan with astonishment.

'I'm not a great friend of Arthur Wildsmith's' Boleyn suddenly said and everybody started.

He then added, very confused:

'I scarcely know him.'

'Oh I thought you were a great friend of his.'

Dan shook his head.

Dan stared darkly into his tea-cup, where he had seen two *strangers*, and drank his tea like a machine.

'You are very young aren't you?' said Mrs Farnham. 'Arthur told me I think – what did Arthur say.'

'How old are you Mr Boleyn?' Mrs Hollindrake enquired.

Mrs Farnham poured out more tea for the smiling pair, the man and wife, who were engaged at the moment with Novitsky and Miss Brest.

'Just nineteen.'

'Why you are a CHILD! You are younger than Jimmie!' she said incredulously.

'When were you born?' Jimmie asked him.

The question had the ring of a challenge. Several heads turned, expecting a minor episode. Dan gazed stolidly at Jim.

'I was nineteen two months ago' he said almost severely.

'Two months ago.'

Mrs Farnham had been listening to the curt dialogue of the two youths with the face of ravished wonder of a bourgeois hostess, in the presence of two typical pre-war noblemen, condescending to discuss – *pour épater les bourgeois* – the splendid details of their pedigrees. – Now she would egg them on, to prolong the treat.

'When were *you* nineteen, Jimmie?' she asked coaxingly 'I am quite sure Jimmie you put on your age most shamelessly. I don't believe you are a week over seventeen.'

Daniel Boleyn was stirred to the marrow and almost pugnaciously awaited events – well-trained young eyes as it seemed noting those behaviorist processes so negligently exhibited.

The effigies of wax and ivory that the Duchess of Marlborough had made of the dead poet (upon Congreve's death) or anything, might have filled the blank behind that scrutiny. So unusually active were Dan's piercing glances that he might have been aptly remembering how that devoted Duchess had ordered the feet of the wax effigy to be rubbed and blistered every morning by the doctors – even as the gouty feet of the dying man had been treated – and how the ivory one accompanied her everywhere, standing upon her table. He might have been saying to himself in effect that this appeared to be almost as unresponsive a waxen doll for Mrs Farnham, that was called Jimmie (but rather that of a defunct abstraction in place of a personality), a plaything for her nostalgic dotage. And as he looked at Jimmie he might have been regarding one of those life-size dolls, with mechanically revolving eyes, made for the children of the rich – or have been imagining, as their crooning mistress manipulated them, a glimmer of waxen sensuality stealing out of their glassy ocellation towards their possessor, soliciting an unnatural caress – a veiled, mechanically-repeated ogle, the thickening of a brutal coquetry in the squeak. Maturing in the bees-wax bosom, he might then have conceived the voluptuous processes that would perhaps be evolved by the ingenious doll, appropriate to its puppet's condition.

Instead Dan was saying to himself that if the heat swelled his feet much more he could not stand it – the tears were not far off *but* he was resolved not to let that little beast on the settee, who was twenty if he was a day, get away with that seventeen and a week stuff!

Jimmie, like a child hesitating over its lesson, was saying with bored obedience looking at Daniel Boleyn,

'I was, let me see, nineteen eight months ago.'

'You are six months that big boy's senior!' Mrs Farnham

insisted roguishly. 'No Jimmy you are not so much as that you know you aren't.'

'I spose I mussht pee yes six months more than him – you're so good at counting Pammie' he replied.

Pammie-mammie: the love of babyhood, the return to the womb, the corruption of the cradle – the severe eyes of Daniel seemed to miss nothing of these far-flung analogies. Mrs Farnham looked over at him with misgiving, at the face of Dante-young. Dan was recalling a boy, Tart Pitshaw, who was his senior. They had been caught both dressed as girls, and he was biting his lip as the shoes pinched his feet to keep back the flushing at the eyes.

'Have you just left school?' suddenly he asked Jimmie involuntarily.

'Oh good *gracious*, no. Yee-ars ago! I've been for two years in the city.' The ravishing assumption of the pomps of seniority which caused Mrs Farnham to melt in a silent transport of fond mirth, was associated with a mask of bored resignation.

'And he's never been vaccinated yet? Nineteen and never been,' she burst out exultant.

'Not *prop-er-ly!*' he sang archly, fluttering his cloudless eyes, and trying to deepen by a shade the pink of his brazen candour.

'Never been vaccinated!' exclaimed Novitsky, frowning, grinning, sheepish and bold, breaking into the conversation – the plebeian roughness with the crudely affected incredulity took this apparently simple hygienic issue by the throat.

'No' lisped Jimmie softly, sitting the whole time bolt upright, like a child at his catechism, or a small Dresden Buddha.

Mrs Farnham had been eyeing Dan with a more marked suspicion. Suddenly she met an oppressive stare, intercepting it as it was heavily directed upon Jimmie, with a mesmerized interest – she felt her chick was in real danger.

'Is it true, Mr Boleyn, that somebody has *made you* – that you have been manufactured like the – Hoffman doll?'

'No.'

Dan did not display any signs of decomposition at this question, answering at once with heavy smoothness and brevity, and blinking once at Jimmie.

(Am I somebody's doll? Is that why I sit? The doll of Zagreus!

He blushed with pleasure at the novel thought. Horace Zagreus's plaything – really!)

'I thought it must be' Mrs Farnham sneered, casting glances at him to discover what had happened to her dart. There was no trace upon the surface except the faint vestiges of pleasure. So it had passed magically into regions as to the nature of which she found it impossible to guess. But, as she watched, with her revolving glances, she knew he had been hit. The whole man moved – broke up, as it were – the Zs straightened out, the whole figure rose to its great height.

Dan came over to her, took her hand and went towards the door.

'Mr Boleyn! You're not going? I hope I haven't offended you!'

In the passage, while he was putting on his coat, she repeated her last question.

'I have an appointment – not be late' he muttered and left, crouching beneath the flat-door.

'What a very peculiar young man!' Pammie exclaimed, when he had gone. 'I'm sure there's something strange about him. Didn't you think so, Dowwie? He seems to be sleepwalking. Arthur told me he was a sort of Trilby. But he said he was very clever.'

'My dear, I think it was naughty of you, to ask him' Miss Dowsett began. She had been preparing to be nice to Boleyn when he had suddenly left, and she felt it.

'Oh well then, people shouldn't tell one things about people they are sending to one – if they don't want one to repeat them. It's Arthur's fault. Besides, he didn't seem to mind – the young man had an appointment.'

'I think he was a nice young man' Helen Dowsett continued to complain.

'A very nice young man' the voice of Pammie came back at once with the words just as they had left the mouth of Helen, whom her hostess eyed.

'My dear, most attractive I thought he was, why did you drive him away?' Helen was on the war-path as she rolled over in her mind the gigantic young limbs of the departed Dan, and rolled her slumbrous hips in pensive spasm.

'I? I did not drive the young man away!' said Pammie, a little pale but grave, indicted for driving away the young – young manning back with the best, teasing the ginger nap upon her yellow deckled wrist.

'You were being horrid to him! Somebody *made* that young man, what did you say – I heard you say somebody did something or other to him. You meant to be offensive, Pammie!'

'Somebody had made him! – no – the young man himself took no exception to what I said, did he Peggy, you heard what we said.'

'Yes' said Peggy.

'It is my opinion somebody has' Pammie hard-case that she was muttered deliberately, under her breath.

'Who has?' exclaimed Helen.

'I expect they *have*' lisped Jimmie to himself, not to join in but to send his faint aside to consort with Pammie's under the surface, and start a contrapuntal whispering.

'Jimmie!'

'What a lovely idea!' came up the languid voice from the floor. All turned round and looked hard at 'Snotty' Briggs. 'Who is supposed to be responsible for the young man Pammie?'

'The young man is a discovery of Horace Zagreus, Arthur told me.'

'He is supposed to be absolutely under the influence of Horace Zagreus' Snotty was informed by Peggy. – The go-ahead wife of the enobled actuary lay in Lido-slimming standard close-up, upon several cushions, at Miss Dowsett's feet.

'Arthur Wildsmith, that young man who has just gone, told me Daniel Boleyn was so attached to Horace Zagreus that he will knock you down if you mention him uncivilly.'

'I know' said Peggy. 'Arthur said he did actually strike him with his fist last week for saying he considered Zagreus mad.'

'How sweet!' the bass-viol on its back intoned in its deep horizontal chest.

Fisticuffs, wrapped up in friendships for intellectual men, reached the ears of Jimmie, he pricked them up. Tales broadcast by Wildsmith too. Sides had to be taken. *This was a man's quarrel.* Jimmie screamed, recoiling upon the settee.

'He's a liar!' he boldly exploded, in vibrating falsetto, referring to shamefaced susceptible Arthur Wildsmith fiercely.

'Jimmie! What next! Jimm-ee!'

'The language that young man uses!'

'Never let me hear you use such language again young man!'

'You may not know it but it's unbecoming at your age!'

Jimmie with great hardihood faced the motherly music, as *Oh-what-an-obstinate-child!*

'Perhaps!' he scornfully fluted and tossed his head, a very *Mary Mary-So-contrairy.*

'What's that!'

'Nothing Pammie!'

'No I should think not!'

'I'm sorry, Wildsmith *is* a liar! That young man doesn't look as though he could knock a fly down, I'm positive it's a lie!'

Pamela Farnham and Peggy Hollindrake in the closest formation descended upon Sonny-Boy-Jimmie, with enveloping motherly glances. The dusty old pair of glede-birds, with united wing, made, with sweeping, scandalized glances the little rebel waxwork the centre of their predatory orbit. To detect any sign of the muscular tension that might announce the first approaches of adult violence, they were on the alert.

'What do you mean Jimmie?' frowning Pammie eyed the incipient male.

'What I say!' and the voice of the audacious minion had the coquettish rasp of the heel of a haughty beauty, stamped in pretty passion crossly.

'I hope that young man wouldn't knock *a fly* down!' then shouted Peggy for the indignant pair of them.

'Knock down! no I rather hope he wouldn't. I hope nobody.' With such breath as three bustling decades of bottle-cracking, and a spell of suffrage-platforms, had left her, Pammie wheezed.

'Little savage!' Ma Hollindrake portentously bridled.

'Knock down indeed!' What-nexting Pammie Farnham raked him with the firewater of her fierce old edwardian eye.

'That's just what I *said!*' Jimmie bleats, playing up in the pertest style, to hold the centre of the stage, the true babe-hero of nursery farce. The tireless old team of matrons plod hither and thither, to catch retorts, in preposterous tit-for-tat.

'You shouldn't say such things!' then Pam puffs out, to draw once more the youthful fire.

'No!' joins in the breathless Peggy 'you should be more careful what you say young man!'

'A young man like you shouldn't talk like that!' Helen Dowsett tells him too, for there's nothing like old female leather, and a male's a male for a' that, even in flapper-counterfeit, even with no down in its waxen nostril – there is still the bristle in the blood!

'What do you know about *knocking down* I should like to know!' Mrs Farnham hoots.

'Knocking down indeed!' comes the angry echo from the tetchy hen called Hollindrake. The scrotum-skin of her withered apple-of-Adam was distended for her fierce admonitory cluck.

'The young man's twice your size!' from Mrs Farnham.

'I don't care!' cried Jimmie-light-heart, as cool-eyed and coarse-voiced as you please, in lovely effrontery.

Pammie and Peggy rise up as one man. The frilly barm-cloth upon Pammie's bosom is gustily inflated. They shriek together, as if asked to assist at a pogrom.

'Jimmmeee!'

'You do terrify me Jimmie – I do wish you wouldn't be so pugnacious – you *are* so inconsiderate!' Pammie flung herself back. She picked up and quaffed a gilt-edged Chartreuse super-chocolate.

'You are the most thoughtless young man I've ever met!' Peggy scolded hoarsely.

'One of these days he will be getting into some fight I know he will!' the hostess sniffed and Peggy and Helen cast glances of burning reproach upon the selfish Young Person. And they all shuddered as they gazed at the soft thing that he still was – at the thought of the great bully he soon must be. 'Snotty' Briggs, even, stretched out at full length for fulsome columns of Gossip or a possible Candid Camera, cast up from the floor a languid glance of cross astonishment.

The boy-man crowed.

'I've put my foot in it! – *All the same!*'

'Don't be absurd Jimmie. Of course that young man could

knock people down!' Pammie told him quite cross and sharp now.

'No I'm positive that young man couldn't knock any people down. He couldn't knock a fly down!' answered Jimmie, for the occasion taking up a discarded accent – nasal and lancastrian.

'I have warned you Jimmie! That is a very dangerous young man. – I know!'

'Oh *do* you!'

'Yes. That's why I got rid of him, if you want to know.'

Saying this, Pammie crossed eyes with Helen.

'It was because of what Arthur told me about him' she then said. 'The fact is I was afraid to have him in the place any longer!'

'Oh Pammie – I am so terribly glad you got rid of him when you did! If I had known I should have been simply terrified!' Peggy exclaimed at this.

'I know' replied Pammie. 'He made a dead set at Jimmie! The moment he came in he did.'

'The brute!'

'I saw him looking at Jimmie as if – '

'The wretch!'

'I was on tenterhooks!'

'On what sort of hooks Pammie!' enquired Jim.

'Be quiet,' answered Pam.

'I shan't!'

'He was giving Jimmie the most *horrible* looks, he didn't once take his eyes off him!'

'The despicable young cad!'

'Yes. I gave him a look or two myself. He was quite unmoved.'

'What an unpleasant young man!'

'Bosh!' exclaimed Jimmie, oldfashion'dly, broad and genially *Manchester* now.

'Thank you Jimmie, I've very obliged to you.'

'He looked as though he were quite capable of knocking us all down as soon as look at us!' Peggy exclaimed. 'I think he was a most horrid young man!'

'He couldn't knock *me* down!'

Bracing his toy juffs, composing his doll-jaws for snarling battle, the boastful Jimmie squared up (sitting) to a big bully (also sitting). He flung himself into boxing attitudes to a chorus of hoarse female screams.

'Jiiiiiiiimeee!'

'What an alarming young man!' Snotty Briggs breathed from the floor. 'He is a fire-eater!'

'Fire-eater!' Peggy vociferated her pantomime-eyes upon him. 'Little ruffian I call him!'

Mrs Farnham swallowed in quick succession three of her stiffest brandy-chocolates.

'Jimmie! Let us understand one another!'

'By all means Pammie!'

'No. I am in earnest!'

Panting, she blew the occult brandy in a fiery current over at his face.

'So am I.'

'I won't have you talking in that way.'

'How?'

'As you did just now.'

'How was that?'

'When you said that young man could not knock you down.'

'Nor he could!'

'Jimmie! You understand! I won't allow you! You hear me!'

'I could knock *him* down!'

There was on all hands the sound of the heavy explosion of matriarchal wrath. But the embittered baby piped with glee and faced the fuming Frauenzimmertum.

'Well, you said that young man' said Jimmie 'could knock me down didn't you!'

'If he did I'd tear his eyes out!'

'Really!' Snotty Briggs, dispassionate observer upon the floor, released the detached exclamation.

'I'm sure you would Pammie!' Peggy cried with heartiest conviction.

'My dear – I'm positive she would!' that, Helen, grinning then confirmed.

'What a dangerous set of people you all are!' was the comment of Snotty, *audessous de la mêleé* – as she lay stock-still upon her Lido-beach, to slim and tan, and puff the weed, through an enobled hole in the squab proboscis.

'It's no use, Jimmie should not say such things' said Pammie.

'Of course he shouldn't' said Peggy.

'He upsets me most terribly. It is most unkind.'

'He only does it to frighten us Pammie.'

'I wish I were certain that was it!'

'I'm sure it is Pammie – Jimmie's bark is worse than his bite.'

'Bow-wow!' went the irrepressible Jimmie.

'Ah these women and their Pekineses!' Novitsky's voice smote into the pack, and they all turned round as if a stink-bomb had crashed in their midst. The excited megaphone of Novitsky had sounded uninterruptedly in the background, but they had forgotten the existence of the Russian Jew except for Snotty (making the best of both worlds, with one ear impartially registering the bellowing behind her, while the other missed nothing in the universe of JIM, beneath her eyes). The death's-head in the green smicket, and the smiling fat young husband, also at this point became actual once more, where they sat before Novitsky, in passive cheerful inanity, while he broke new ground for them with a furious pick. Behind them the faces of Miss Brest and Mr Nosworthy nodded together, in furious assent, upon a dim settee.

'While the babies of the poor starve, these women with their peach-fed pets! Look at them! They should be stoned into sense! Their bread should be branded! Two ounces a person, it is sufficient. They should be put to work – in silver-mine or as old Jacktars, as cooks in Tramps, or upon canals – or to be given a ferret for a pet and to be sent into the drain after the rat!'

These women – look at them! but at *which* women! was written upon all the women's faces together.

Jimmie let fly a high-pitched snigger, tickled by the scowl upon the countenance of the excellent Pammie – whom he could not help but see at that moment as an old Jacktar or Jackdaw, or in the galley of a windjammer, introducing rum into all the ship's-rations.

'What's this?' growled Pam.

'Oh as usual! We are too rich,' said Peg.

'Who are?' said Pam. 'Who is he talking about?'

Novitsky was as pleased as possible. In contrast to these fiery words and this muscular hysterical trumpeting in broken english, his face was fixed in an enveloping burning grin. The grin tightened and reddened all his forward scalp. He looked straight into the face of his hostess.

Pamela Farnham frowned – 'these women with their Pekineses' – mal-apropos or perhaps malicious – there was something repugnant and bolshevik – this bore Novitsky – the man aired his views – in and out of season – he returned her dislike – but compound interest. *Whom* was he addressing?

'They are past the teaching – they are too old!' the thunder was resumed. There were clouds of russian cigarette-smoke around Sinai. 'You want dog-whips for that sort of ladies with their animals, not for their dogs – *the fault is the foolish human being!*'

The russian grin still burnt full upon the face of Pammie. But the docile young husband as well was smiling, and half at Pammie, at the constant soft joke of life. His wife, good death's-head, in her folk-dancing, *raggle-taggle-gypsy-oh* smicket, was grinning after the manner of skulls, in spite of a thin layer of flesh, and she looked at Pammie too, baring her white gums.

'I know!' said the death's-head. The jocund skull 'knew' that bread was scarce, that there were dogs and cats as pets, and selfish burgesses, in corrupt cities – it agreed in bloodless sympathy. They were bohemian, she and her smiling yeoman-mate. They had been to Albania in a caravan, and camped for preference with vagrants.

'That's true,' said the smiling husband.

'Yes!' hissed Novitsky.

'What is Mister Novitsky talking about now?' Pammie demanded of the smicket, with impetuous gruffness.

'Oh – about women, Mrs Farnham!' the death's-head replied, with a ghastly slyness.

'Oh! Is that all.'

'And their *pets*.'

'Oh.'

'Yes Mrs Farnham. I was saying – '

'I don't want to hear what you were saying Novitsky,' Pammie stopped him roughly. 'I've heard it all before thank you.'

'The wild-wild-women!' Helen Dowsett chanted, quoting a

war-song of those unforgettable halcyon feminine days of death for half-the-world, and laughing. '*My dear!* Why stop him!'

'You are a woman-hater,' said Peggy. 'But we know that by heart!'

'No you are wrong Mrs Holleen Drake!' burst out Novitsky in grinning protest.

'Oh yes you are!'

'But may I not defend myself? I *love* – !'

'That is *worse* – far worse! We'd rather you remained a hater Novitsky!' Pammie roared at him. 'You are a good hater – we will concede that to you Novitsky!'

'You don't want me for a lover Mrs Farnham!'

'No!' howled back the warlike Pammie, digging a set of brand new teeth into a massive chocolate, with a kernel of alcohol.

Jimmie rolled his mouth round in a big stuffed greedy O, and crowed to see such sport.

The death's-head mildly grinned at the face where the slav intensity was stretched to breaking point and threatened to burst into a nigger-peal of diabolic mirth.

'I think Mr Novitsky would make a better hater than he would a lover' quavered the mild Death.

'Yes,' Peggy thought so too.

Novitsky gazed first at one face, then at the other, from one possible 'lover' to the other.

Snotty Briggs was growing bored. This was dangerous ground. Her languid voice sounded a call to order, to snub the russian chaos before things went any further.

'Tell me Pammie, who is Thug Rust – what was the name of the person who was supposed to be the particular hero of that young man?'

'Do you mean Zagreus?'

'I suppose so.'

'Horace Zagreus, oh haven't you ever heard of Horace Zagreus?'

'I don't believe I have. Ought I to have?'

'*Ought* – no, I shouldn't say you ought. Before the War he was well known as a practical joker.'

'Practical joker? Is anybody – just *practical joker?*'

'Yes a notorious practical joker. We knew him quite well – that was years ago.'

'Is he an interesting man?'

'He once went off with our front-door, if you call that interesting.'

Novitsky trumpeted (full miniature brass-and-wind) apocalyptic messages. 'In charge of babies! – mother-kitchens – the food is spoiled! Why should they be given tickets? They are not child-worthy. The Vitamin E should be forbidden! They should be sterile! *We want the sterile workers* – we do not want the children of these useless women!'

'One of the best things Horace Zagreus did' said Helen Dowsett 'was with one of those tapes you see surveyors using.'

'I don't remember that – but I haven't seen him for years. Horace Zagreus did one or two quite amusing stunts. You remember how he dressed up as a Guards Officer and disarmed the sentries at the Palace?'

'Oh yes. That was one of his best known jokes wasn't it.'

'Did he really disarm them?' Snotty asked.

'Yes. He was in possession of the Palace for about ten minutes. The idea was to show how easy it would be to kidnap the King.'

'How lovely!' said Snotty.

'Something like the Captain of Koepernick' said Peggy.

'Yes, that was the idea.'

'He sounds rather an interesting man' said Snotty.

'Yes' said Pammie 'he was. But when he goes on doing the same thing *now!*'

'Does he still?' Dowsett asked.

'They say he still is apt to remove your front door' said Peggy.

'A rather awkward man to have about the place!' said Snotty.

'Most!' said Dowsett.

'I find it rather boring!' – Pammie yawned.

'I didn't imagine him that sort of man for some reason,' Snotty said.

'He has become a New Thought crank hasn't he Pammie?' Peggy asked.

'So I've heard' the contemptuous Pam replied, 'I have not seen him for a donkey's years.'

'I have heard Horace has gone high-brow' said Pam.

'Oh how boring!' said Snot.

'I am positive Horace is pulling people's legs. I am sure he is not sincere.' Pammie looked past Peggy at Novitsky, who was speaking in a confidential voice to his deferentially grinning listeners.

'Is he a charlatan?' asked Snotty.

'I haven't seen him, as I said. Zagreus always has to be in the limelight, he is incredibly vain. But he definitely has a screw loose.'

'I believe we are all a little mad' said Peggy dreamily.

'How original Peggy!' said Jimmie.

There was a pause: the whisper of Novitsky was worse than his bellow, it filled the room with a hoarse hiss.

'What was his trick, with that tape?' Snotty asked Helen.

'I don't know Horace Zagreus you know' Helen answered.

'Oh don't you? I thought you did' said Snotty.

'No. I have heard lots of stories, about his practical jokes.'

'But what did he do with the tape?' asked Snotty.

'He was a surveyor by profession, he lost his job I believe because he was always playing the fool.'

'When I knew him he was in the Diplomatic Service' said Pammie.

'But he was a surveyor originally.'

'I did not know that.'

'But his rags are quite *historic!*' said Helen.

'Not to me' said Snotty.

'I thought *everyone* had heard that story!'

'No, not me' said Snotty Briggs.

'Well, once he was supposed to be measuring some site or other. He hurried into the street with his tape measure or whatever it is. Going up quickly to an old clubman who was just coming out of a club – '

'Horace always gives you the impression of being in a tearing hurry as a matter of fact' said Pammie.

'He said to the clubman "*Here sir, take hold of this!*" You can imagine the man was rather surprised! "A measurement of the utmost importance is in progress. Keep hold of this till you get the signal. I shall be back in a moment!" The old boy was so astonished he hung on to the end of it. Meantime Horace Zagreus rushed away, paying out the tape.'

'Oh, yes, I think I remember this story. But I have heard it about somebody else' said Snotty.

'I have always heard it told as one of Horace Zagreus's stunts' said Helen.

'Yes' said Pammie. 'It was one of Horace's best-known stunts.'

'Anyhow, he dashed round the next corner, where he met another man. He thrust the other end of the tape in this second man's hand. "Please hang on to this for a moment, sir. There is a measurement going on of the utmost importance, there is not a minute to lose! Hold this tight till you get the O.K. signal!" And then he hurried on and was soon out of sight. The two men held the tape for hours I believe, and of course Horace did not return! He was seen no more that day!'

'How sweet!' said Snotty giving an appropriate mirthful gurgle. 'I was mistaken – it was another story I was thinking of.'

'Poor old Horace!'

'I think Horace Zagreus is the most crashing old bore!' said Jimmie.

'Some of his jokes were certainly strokes of genius,' Helen said.

'For those that find practical jokes funny!' snorted Jimmie. 'I think they are the most boring things in the world.'

'Has Jimmie met him?' Peggy asked.

'Have you met Horace Zagreus Jimmie?' Pammie asked.

'Of course I have' said Jimmie.

'You never told me Jimmie!' Pammie looked at him severely.

'Ho ha!' said Jimmie. 'I don't tell you everything Pammie!'

'No. I think some of Horace Zagreus's jokes were really brilliant' Helen said.

'Yes I know!' Jimmie exclaimed peevish and impetuous. 'But you have to say over and over to yourself *he once gave the end of a tape to a man in a street*, and so on – and in the end, even when you've said that to yourself two or three times over, it simply doesn't help you to bear up – he *is* such a crashing bore. At least I think he is.'

'But he has given up his stunts I suppose' said Helen 'you

say you know him Jimmie. What is he like now? He is a religious crank I suppose? Anyhow he's different.'

'That's even worse!' Jimmie would not have Dan's patron at any price. Pammie began eyeing him with renewed anxiety.

'What sort of aged man is he?' Snotty asked.

'Horace Zagreus must be at least sixty!' Pammie said.

'Is he as much as that?' asked Snotty.

'He's an albino – it's impossible to tell,' said Peggy.

'Rather more, he must be sixty-three' said Pammie.

'An albino! How does he succeed in exercising such an influence upon the young?' Snotty enquired. 'Is it as a practical joker he carries weight?'

'He carries no weight at all!' said Jimmie loudly and dogmatically.

'No it's this new cult. He goes in for magic' Peggy said.

'Exercises an influence? Horace does not exercise any influence, that I know of' Pammie replied, airy and sullen, listening to the harsh buzzing of Novitsky's voice. 'Except over that young man. That young man was the first I've heard of that he's exercised any influence over.'

'*Anyone* could exercise an influence over *him* I should think!' Jimmie sneered with a tiny snort and a toss of the head.

'Jimmie!'

'Well so they could!'

'Now you are starting again! Jimmie!'

'I wish that young man were here still. I'd tell him to his face what *I* think of Horace Zagreus, which is not much!'

'I am thankful Pammie got rid of that young man when she did' said Peggy with portentous nod. 'I'm afraid you would have no chance with a great big monster like that. He's quite twice your size Jimmie.'

'Perhaps!' Jimmie remarked, with strong-dumb menace. 'Twice my size? Perhaps!'

'I do think Jimmie's most awfully plucky' exclaimed Helen. 'He really *is* twice his size. I am sure that young man would kill Jimmie if he hit him!'

'Helen! will you please not make remarks like that!' Pammie cried. 'If you encourage Jimmie I will never speak to you again! And I think what you said about killing Jimmie was disgusting

Helen! What with one thing and the other, I shouldn't be surprised if you drove me to drink!'

'It wouldn't take much to drive you to drink Pammie!' Jimmie retorted, and Pammie hurled a liqueur chocolate at him, which struck the wall – Jimmie ducking, nimble urchin, and darting out his unruly member at his patroness, as he resumed the upright position.

The bell rang in the flat-passage. Snotty Briggs rose from the floor.

'That's Parnell I think!' she said.

'Who is Parnell?' asked Peggy.

'That is my chauffeur!' said Snotty, bending forward towards her, her prominent profile developing a great rake, as she stood stiffly, one black solemn owl-eye ambushed under the hat-brim.

'What a divine name for a chauffeur?'

'Yes isn't it! He is related to Parnell I believe.'

'How curious!' said Helen.

As Snotty went towards the door with Pammie, Novitsky came over grinning to the tea-table. The tea-party began to come to an end.

Part 8

LESBIAN-APE

DAN scudded down Launceston Place, a high wind smote its acacia fernery, and he found his way to Ashburn Place, which was up in arms. Two vagabond cripples had seized a basement, into which they had fallen. This Place he descended in quick strides passing to the other side of the road, averting his head from the scene of disorder. Where Ashburn Place ended he hesitated, and then entered Rosary Gardens. Leaving them behind him, and passing over into Chelsea, he consulted his pocket-map.

It was a long way to this spot from Mrs Farnham's. He could never have done it without the help of a pocket-atlas of London and his natural map-craft. Policemen made him extremely shy. He never spoke to them if he could help it, and avoided their eyes, even, when crossing the tides of traffic. From experience he had found that, on account of his self-consciousness, it was quite impossible to understand their directions at all. Nothing but confusion ensued from asking to be directed by one of these helmeted young men in blue – whose proverbially kind eyes only drew him in, under the cruel peaked eaves of their helmets, and made him forgetful of his duty and feel so terribly hot and ashamed too and only upset him in any case.

Dan went along a tunnel that was an arched way beneath flats. And in the twilight he came to an empty terrace, upon one side of which was a row of liver-umber, brick, geraniumed cottages. Confronting them was a high and gloomy wall, it filled the terrace with premature darkness. Above it Dan could see the tops of the windows of formidable studios. – These were the gardens he was to visit. *A great nest of women Apes!* The studios were secluded.

Turning into a paved court, out of the narrow terrace, there was a row of wicket-gates, cottage-effect. He attempted in spite of the misty dusk to read the numbers upon the small green studio doors. He stopped at the third wicket-gate. He looked over it for a little while, he was satisfied. Although the number was blurred and might be five instead of three, he entered and knocked upon the massive doll's-house entrance.

The door opened very suddenly. Dan at the moment was collapsed, as if deflated, and crumpling at the left side. He had forgotten he was there, about to put his head into the she-ape's den, in a spasm of delicious reminiscence, and of anticipation. Tomorrow Horace would be with him!

With alarm he glanced up. Before him stood a severe masculine figure. In general effect it was a bavarian youth-movement elderly enthusiast. She was beyond question somewhat past mark-of-mouth. But this was a woman, as in fact she had appeared in the typed description. Of that he felt tolerably certain, because of the indefinable something that could only be described as 'masculine'. An heroic something or other in the bold blue eye, that held an eyeglass, that reminded him of the Old Guard or the Death-or-Glory-Boys, in the house of Mr Brian Macdonnell, secured for him certainty of the sex at least without further worry. It was She. This was Miss Ansell.

She was wiry and alert with hennaed hair bristling, en-brosse. In khaki-shorts, her hands were in their pockets, and her bare sunburnt legs were all muscle and no nonsense at all. There was something that reminded Dan of Dick Whittingdon, for she was bald, he remarked with a deep blush, on the top of her head. Only there the resemblance ended it seemed, for whereas Dick was anxious, that was easy to see, to disguise his naked scalp, *this* strong-minded person had a peculiar air of being proud of it all the time (to be bald, like the ability to grow a moustache, was a masculine monopoly). A march had been stolen, with her masculine calvity. But a strawberry-pink pull-over was oddly surmounted by a stiff Radcliffe-Hall collar, of antique masculine cut – suggestive of the masculine hey-day, when men were men starched-up and stiff as pokers, in their tandems and tilburys. The bare brown feet were strapped into spartan sandals. A cigarette-holder half a foot long protruded from a firm-set jaw. It pointed at Dan, sparkling angrily as the breath was compressed within its bore.

Daniel Boleyn stood simply rooted to the spot. He was frankly dismayed, but could think of nothing to say to excuse himself for having knocked at all. 'The wrong door!' he muttered in his mind but he could not utter the apology. He was genuinely sorry he had knocked – but he was quite unable to find his tongue. Could this be Miss Ansell? Surely he would have been warned in his morning duty-sheet. Not even Horace would have been so inhumane as not to whisper a caveat! Why had he been sent to her? He must have mistaken the number. What *was* the number? Was it five? Was it three? He had not looked for some time at his instructions, though he was positive three was the number. What a terrible oversight! –

They stood staring at each other for a momentous half-minute, the woman with the utmost hostility.

'What are you staring at!' at last she asked him, bold and gruff, straight from the shoulder.

A shiver went down Dan's back as he heard this voice, but he was incapable of moving a muscle.

She turned up a wrist-watch towards the sky.

'It's a bit late isn't it?' She pointed out to him gruffly.

Dan blushed. It *was* late.

'Come in, if you're coming in!'

She turned upon her heel and went back into a large lighted studio, which he could perceive beyond. At least it was a studio, even if the wrong one, and should he bolt she would be after him like a flash of greased lightning he was positive and catch him before he had gone far.

But as she left him he did regain the use of his legs. Convulsively he stepped out and it was forward he was moving. He followed the soldierly boy-scoutish fantosh into the artist's-studio, slinking in the wake of its positive strut.

'Shut the door!' she called over her shoulder at him, as she receded.

Dan went back and, with the most anxious attention, he closed the front door without making any noise whatever, as he pushed it into its sleek solid oaken rabbets. Then anew he made his way into the lighted interior, and she faced him in the manner that is indicated by the word *roundly* and by the word *squarely*. There she stood, and avoiding her militant male eye he approached her. Her dander was up.

'Who sent you? Was it Borstie? Was it Miss Lippencott?' she demanded.

'Lip Got!' Dan cooed, with blankest eyes, in Beach-la-Mar.

'Lippencott' she said with a dark puzzled scorn.

He was quite silent. However pressed for an answer, he would have been quite unable to open his lips any more.

She quizzed the drooping six-foot-three of speechless manhood. With vicious eye she wrenched off his four-foot of swaying trouser-leg. She tore to shreds the massive pretences of the male attire.

She snorted a sigh, as she saw the man quail at her glances.

'Well, let's have a look at you!' she then ruggedly exclaimed, as one chap to another. She jerked a thumb backwards, towards a screen, beneath the balcony, which ran the entire length of the long side of the place.

'You can undress there! Look slippy!'

At this Dan's knees in fact did shake. Had he had a tongue in his head he would have told her then and there that she must be mistaken. He was *not* an italian model (such as he had seen leaving the studio of Mélanie). There was some fearful misunderstanding. This was not Miss Ansell, he had been deceived. It was quite a different kind of Ape, that dwelt in this lonely well, to the one it had been Horace's wish he should visit.

But even as these words (which would not materialize) were crying out inside his brain, he was assailed by a new doubt. If this *were* after all Miss Ansell? Horace he said to himself would not have sent him here upon a purposeless errand. There was nothing purposeless about Horace. This was a noted Ape of God no doubt. He had been dispatched to report upon her – he must not leave empty-handed. It was not his place to call in question the arrangements of Horace. Horace, it might very well be, *had* intended him to pose as a nude italian model, to this woman. For the ways of Horace were mysterious in the extreme.

Taken to its ultimatum and crisis, where would this not perhaps lead? The expressive eyes of this dewy colossus, this maidenly great doe, rolled in panic – he saw the path that Horace had, it might be, intended him to tread, but he balked it in one sweeping squirm of lovely revulsion. He writhed, beneath her insulting eyes. *Mustht* I? his eye, in tender obsecration, asked. *Yesth!* her eye signalled in response, in beastly parody – hitting every time below the belt.

In spite of the fact that his glances were downcast mainly, Dan was yet present to every object, and he had immediately observed with terror a large dog-whip upon the model's-throne. Haunted as he was by the memory of the Bokharan oxthong he had been compelled to hold by that grinning old Jenny, the sight of this disciplinary instrument disturbed him extremely. In fancy he could see himself naked, in full flight, before this little hennaed white-collared huntress – her dog-thong cracking about his girl-white surfaces, of Clydesdale proportions, as he rushed round and round her artist's studio – till probably he would fall, panting and exhausted, at her sandalled feet! And vae victis of course – there would be no quarter in this sanguinary munera.

For better or for worse, he must escape at once – he could not go through with it, he had made up his mind – tomorrow he must inform Horace that posing as a nude model was a thing he was quite unable to do. Would Horace excuse him nude-posing please, as a great concession! It would be asking him to suffer the tortures of the Damned! *Please* Horace, do not ask me to strip and nude-pose – not *that!* (It was not as though he were *beautiful*, he added with a secret blush.)

'What are you doing may I ask?' the horrid masculine accents banged out at him ever so loud in the big hollow studio, and caused him a fright-bang too – a discharge of adrenalin. 'Look sharp! I can't hang about here all night for you to peel!'

Oh how that dreadful word *peel* left him not only naked, but skinless! What, wrench off his putamen, in obedience to this martinet? Oh what a horrid errand was this, upon which Horace had sent him! – if, that was, he had come to the right address. What an anguishing thought – the real Ape he had been sent in quest of might in fact all the time be expecting him with a glass of sherry, in the studio opposite.

She had been lighting a cigarette, straddling her tiger-skinned hearth, selecting a seasoned cigarette-holder, resembling a Brissago, facing the mantelpiece. Catching sight (out of the corner of her eye) of this maddening male professional lay-figure, who had turned up to offer himself for posing-work, still in the same place (posing as it were already where he stood) she wheeled about in the most savage manner possible. Pointing to the screen, she shouted:

'*There* you idiot – over there! – can't you see the bloody thing! Go over there and peel at once or I'll chuck you out of the bloody studio neck and crop! Yes I mean it! I do believe you're some beastly Fairy! I don't know what possessed Borstie to send a ghastly Fairy round here! It's no use your making sheep's eyes at *me!* Either go in there and peel or else beat it! Do you get me! Jump to it!'

As she said *jump* she jumped herself, and more dead than alive Dan skipped as well. As she took a threatening step in his direction he turned tail, he rushed quickly over straight at the screen. Bolt upright behind it, his heart-rate trebled, he held his breath and bit his lip, rolling frightened eyes. He strained his ears to catch her movements. Oh – what he had gone through for the sake of this man! And did Horace return his devotion? He smiled wanly to himself, in the comparative darkness – no, one would scarcely say Horace *did*, to judge from all he made him suffer!

Dan became slowly aware that his was the opposite case to that of the ostrich. He had achieved the occultation of his body, but the luxuriant summit of his head must be visible above the screen. So he made haste to crouch down, and in that position he placed an eye to a crack, where two of the panels of the screen met. With an intense alarm, he was able now to observe all the movements of the threatening masculine person beyond, in her sports-kit (dressed to kill, by sheer roughness, and to subdue all the skirted kind) scraping a large palette with an ugly looking jack-knife.

He saw her look up, stop scraping, and incline her head to listen. Then she called out sharply.

'I say aren't you ready yet? You take a long time to peel for a man!'

There was a pause in which, knife in hand, she listened.

'I don't believe you *are* peeling!'

He saw her put down the palette upon the model's-throne, next to the dog-whip. She retained, he observed abashed, the long jack-knife in her hand.

In an instant Dan had wrenched off his jacket, torn from his neck his collar and his tie. With hands all thumbs and all a-flutter, he undid, and then in one continuous movement dropped down, and kicked off, his man's long trousers – as if as a symbol of capitulation to the militant feminine-male beyond. Standing white, occult, and quite naked, his teeth chattering, with his vest in one hand and limp shoe in the other, he awaited the next move of the master-spirit – the boy-scout spinster masculine rake. But suddenly he was pulled up sharp with a vengeance, and put to work to think in earnest: he gazed, startled and guilty, blushing unseen, quite lost in thought. Feverishly he turned over in his mind a most knotty problem. It had not presented itself to him before, in the midst of this breathless march of events.

Necessity proved herself once again, upon the spot, the mother of invention, and he put down his shoe and seized the limp empty arms of the thin cotton vest. He held it out, until the square body of it hung like an apron before the midst of his person. With the speed bred of a high sense of decorum, he had passed the shoulder-line of the vest, rolled into a rude rope, about his waist – securing it behind, at the summit of the buttocks, in a large knot. Then he drew the apron that hung down between his legs, and he incorporated its extremity in the large bulging knot behind.

'Look here I've had about enough of this!' came the now familiar bark, from beyond the screen. 'Are you coming out or not? Anyone would think you were a bloody woman!'

The imperious tones of crashing command rang out upon the air of this palatial well of stern bachelor loneliness, and they froze his blood.

Blushing a deeper red than any hefty big-handed Susannah could ever compass – surprised by the most designing of Old Elders that ever stepped upon painted canvas, Dan came out into the obscene harsh light of the arc-lamp which hung above the model's-throne.

He gave one dilated terrified glance at the woman standing astride before her easel. Turning swiftly, he rushed back behind the screen. There was a hoarse laugh from the haggard old bachelor-girl in sports-shorts. But her voice pursued him scornfully over the screen, behind which once more he crouched:

'The world's coyest virgin what! Well well well! *Come* out of that! Come out and let's have a look at what all the fuss is about! I'm sure I don't know what the men are coming to!'

Dan stood and shook behind the screen. Wildly he rolled his eyes to himself in a great effort to decide what steps to take, in this fearful emergency – what for a Pelman-brave would have been Kinderspiel. But he simply shook with blank indecision.

'I say, cut this out old bean will you? You've come to the wrong shop!' she raised her voice still more. (The wrong shop indeed! This *could* not be where Horace had sent him!)

'I shall absolutely lose my patience in two shakes of a donkey's tail!' the harpy's voice whipped him like a cat-o'-nine-tails. It had grown ugly too. 'Come out unless you want me to step over there and drag you out by the – ! Chuck all this jolly rot and roll out, you dirty little sprucer, or I'll stick you up on the jolly old throne myself!'

Upon a terrified sudden impulse Dan came swiftly out from behind the screen. He cast one glance of wild appeal at the woman, and rushed up upon the model's-throne. There, blushing down to his waist line – the 'ram and goat' even, of the horrid poetry, suffused with red, his solar plexus flushed, as if it had been punched in boxing – he limply stood, his head turned in the opposite direction from the watching slave-driving person, his body drooped in profile.

'Good!' she rapped at him. 'Yes!' she said, with her painter's squint. 'Not at all bad!' she informed the nudity before her, with hearty male patronage, as she ran over his points, 'you're quite muscular!' she yawned.

The studio was extremely cold, when you were nude, and Dan was beside himself with fear. He shivered without ceasing, occasionally gulping.

'Model! Turn round – do you mind! I've had that view of you long enough.'

Slowly Dan moved, until the whole of his back was turned towards her.

'No!' the woman immediately bellowed, as she grasped the manœuvre. 'No! Not *that* way! Turn round *this* way. Not your *back!*'

With a fresh spasm of deep-red bashfulness, Dan still more

slowly turned about, until he faced her. But he stood with averted face, gazing away to his right flank. He held his chin high, for beneath upon the floor of the throne was the dog-whip, and he wished to forget its presence.

'What on earth have you got there!' he heard her exclaim.

Dan was petrified. The hard white light poured down over him, splitternaked and stark as your fist's-face, he could not move a muscle. Oh, what obedience to Horace (if it were indeed Horace who had planned this) had led him to! In a pose of hieratic stiffness, his head in profile, he awaited her attack. He heard her brisk step and the rigor increased. Marching over with decision to the model's-throne, she did not hesitate a moment. A half-scream, the first sound he had uttered since his entrance, broke from the lips of Dan, as with careless hand she rudely seized the coil of his cotton vest. Then, with a violent tug, she dragged it clean off his shrinking person.

Standing beneath him, his vest in one hand, she fixed him with a chilly masculine eye.

'Listen to me my dear man!' she said: she waved a disdainful hand in his direction, 'that is of no interest whatever to *me*. Do you understand me? Put your mind quite at rest! It would take a jolly sight more than the likes of you to vamp me! Get me? So don't let's have any more of this stuff! You come here to *sit*, not to try and seduce me anyway! It's love's labour lost! See? Spare yourself the dérangement!'

She threw down the vest upon a chair.

'Do you want to sit or not?'

Dan violently nodded his head. He desired from the bottom of his heart to sit down.

'Very well. Let's get on with the War then! I shan't pay you for the time you waste while you're trying to vamp me! If you want to sit – sit!'

Dan again nodded his head, without looking at her, with great vehemence. She was appeased.

'Very well!' it became almost a tone of approval. 'Here get hold of this!'

To his horror she snatched up the dog-whip and brandished it. He retreated a step, his eyes fixed upon her in terror. She held out to him the handle of the whip. He seized it, and his knees knocking lightly together from mingled cold and dread of what this fearful Ape might not require of him, he held it tightly at his side.

'Take up an attitude like this will you?'

Dan gave her askance one fleeting look of horror – for she had thrown herself into an attitude replete with offence not to some figure but to himself he felt.

'I want you for a figure of a roman soldier threatening Our Saviour. No that whip!'

Dan struck several attitudes. All were designed, as far as possible, to minimize the immodesty of the glaring white crown-to-foot exposure of his animal self. The towering milk-pink declivities of the torso beneath the arc-light, the sectioning of the chest by the upright black feather of body-hair, the long polished blanched stalks of the legs, upon which the trunk oscillated, all moved hither and thither. He threw his head into the scales, first to the left then to the right. Full it is true of earth's old timid grace, as haunted by the feminine irish chastity, he threatened an imaginary Saviour with a whip. But at length the restless evasive bulk fell into an accepted position.

'Stop like that!'

Camped energetically, charcoal in hand, she dropped into a watchful, pounding attitude. She looked keenly from the white surface of the body to the white surface of the paper, and back. With difficulty Dan came to a halt.

'Can you keep that?' she asked him.

His whip gave a weary upward waggle. His head sank, in melancholy affirmative. For a few seconds he held himself quite still. When he saw her eyes were upon her paper he moved about, seeking a more comfortable arrangement for his twisted nudity – one that might eventually lessen the immodesty.

Now a steady scratching began. A large sheet of paper was fixed upon a board. Her legs wide apart, the busy artist stood before her super-easel – thrusting out at arm's-length a stick of charcoal, from time to time, while she squinted up the eye that was not furnished with the eye-glass. She computed relative distances, from one landmark to another, upon the person of her sitter. She joined these major points, upon the paper before her, with sweeping lines.

But for Dan the physical agony, in succession to the mental agony, had now set in. His hips had become still more inconveniently twisted, in order to remove away to the left the greater part of his exposed person, and so present as far as possible an offenceless edge-on object to the eye of the observer. On one foot the heel was gracefully removed from the ground. The other foot received the complete weight of a muscle-laden body rising above two metres into the air.

The staccato rasp, flashed to and fro, of the brittle charcoal, was incessant. A page was whisked off the board with as much force as had been used to remove Dan's vest. It fell to the floor and she stamped upon it as she returned to the attack, dashing dark black lines here and there upon the new page.

But Dan stood bathed in a cold perspiration. His face, from having been a sunset crimson, had become a corpse-like white. Then it became a most alarming pallid green. Holding stiffly at arm's length the whip of the legionary, Dan swayed from side to side, with more and more giddy abandon.

'Keep still can't you!' the enraged employer of labour shouted, from the easel. 'I can't draw you if you roll about like that!'

Dan's last thought (before he fell) was of Horace. He had forgotten that this might be the wrong studio altogether. All he could say over and over again to himself was 'Horace, why are you *always* so unkind – why – so always – *unkind!*'

Dan reeled, slowly at first. His body with a loud report came in contact with the floor of the model's throne. As his head struck he had a sickly flash of consciousness, and his body turned over, in a slight convulsion. Then he lay relaxed at last in a deep faint.

When Dan came-to there were two voices audible – one soft and one hard. The hard one said,

'Of course I thought you sent him, Borstie. How can you be so stupid!'

The soft voice replied inaudibly, it was a muffled tinkle.

'With *that?* Thank you!'

There was a hoarse whispering, with a snorted laugh or two, also a super-male chuckle, a bald *ha-ha!*

'A more useless piece of goods I've never met with.'

'It is certainly a horrid sight.'

'You're right. If it could only stand up on its legs!'

'You don't propose to pay it for lying on its back do you!'

'The trouble I had to get the animal to peel! Il s'est fait prié ma chère.'

'Isn't he a model? – What does he come for?'

'I think he thought he'd got a *bonne poire*. He tried to vamp me!'

'My *dear!* That!'

'Oh yes. He wanted me to undress him. He was most averse to posing.'

'Pah! Turn it over! I don't want to look at that *any* more!'

Opening an eye slightly, Dan perceived a second younger figure, that that possessed the softer voice, beside the first – but dressed with recognized feminine elegance, with a breast visible to the nipple, and with sun-kissed silken legs all-clear to the tenderloin. Then a rough hand seized his shoulders and attempted to roll him along the floor of the throne.

'Don't touch him – he might not like it, if he were conscious,' the feminine voice remarked, solicitous for the safety of her mate.

The man-voice snorted defiance, and gave Dan another big shake.

Dan's head and neck were wet with water. He made a slight movement with his arm.

'He *is* coming round' said the slight voice. 'My dear! *Look!*'

'Model! Do you feel better?'

Dan was nearer the edge of the throne now: with an eel-like agility born of shame and terror he rolled off, and as he did so he sprang to his feet. The newcomer started back and uttered a scream. Swiftly Dan regained the cover of the model's undressing screen. His 'vanish' was accompanied by two loud shouts of laughter from extraordinary woman No. 1 – who, at his bashful exit, indulged in the coarsest mirth, pointing after him with her cigarette-holder to her sweetheart, who tittered sneeringly as the great white mass disappeared, like a rat into its hole.

With a violent head-ache, overwhelmed with shame, Dan got his clothes on very quickly. But the vest remained in the hands of the feminine enemy. When he was quite ready, standing in his hiding-place he waited some minutes. He hoped that the second woman might take herself off. But the terrible voice of the first to bring him to his senses soon rang out.

'How much longer are you going to potter about in there? If I hadn't seen all you've got I should have thought you were a woman. Hallo! Come out! I've had enough of your company. Hop it! Do you hear model?'

Dan came out and went towards the door with averted head.

'Here. Here is a half-crown for you.'

She intercepted him and thrust the money up into the occulted palm of his trembling hand.

'Go and have a Scotch.'

He held the half-crown in his hand, and he went on towards the door.

'You don't appear satisfied. It's all you'll get! It's a bloody sight more than you deserve!'

She slammed the door upon him, as soon as he had passed out into the garden.

Night had now fallen. In the lighted doorway of the opposite studio stood a dark eminently feminine figure. As he went through the wicket-gate he observed it making signs to him. Without losing time he decamped at the double, but he heard at his back in the darkness a tinkling voice.

'Is that Mr Boleyn by any chance?'

That was it! Evidently that could be none other than Miss Ansell, to whom he had been supposed to go after Yarmouth Place. He had got into the wrong studio. *Horace was not to blame!* He did not look back but hastened away from this monstrous colony.

Part 9

CHEZ LIONEL KEIN ESQ.

MR ZAGREUS stared at his imposing shadow moving slightly upon Kein's door. He steadied himself against this exenterated paper-maché self, dodging parallax as it moved with the precision of its contingent nature – registering the slightest breath of life disturbing the higher dimensional shape it waited upon. *On ne mesure pas le hommes à la toise!* Dan's shadow, as well, waited upon him, not upon its original. Dan was there like a shadow too, on and before the door. Were they inside the door as well, in further projections of still less substance – their stationary presences multiplied till they stretched out like a theatre queue? Was there anything after the shadow (as was there anything behind the man)? The queue of four might be multiplied to any power within, from where still no sound issued. 'We should have brought camp stools' said Zagreus to the rest of the queue, shifting from one foot to another as one man. He saw the horse, black and primitive 'like a pompeian fresco' that drew the mortuary chariot from which Proust peeped. That processionary fresco extended from Pompeii to Kein's door. 'Lounge suit and sporting kit' – 'Of faultless cut and style' – with 'Summit Collars' and 'the Profile of Youth' 'accommodated' his shadow. And so back to the modern environment, to the theatre queue. The sun struck him with its hot shaft upon the back of the neck. He shifted his hat. 'My place in the sun,' he muttered, not expecting an echo – always the sun made him madder as he knew.

The Keins were no doubt discrete to an upper angle of their seemingly stone-deaf residence. They were *blottis* in a furnished parallelopiped with all required by the human worm for its needs. Brushes, craters, pigments, tubes and files – duplicating mirrors for the multi-mask, powders and combs. As though with antennæ, with the blind head of the queue in this way composed, Zagreus felt towards the couple manœuvring in their secret upper-apartment. There they would be observing with conspiratorial glee each other's obscenities – cheating time with professional unction.

'What's happened to Hassan?' asked Mr Zagreus, and his shadow started at his voice, with the alacrity of the dependent responding to temper, and reached the bell-button. A very faint tinkle below the street-level matched the action of the shadow's arm. The Bellman listened to his summons, awaiting the tripping fairy-footfall of Kein's butler.

'We're so early perhaps they won't let us in' Zagreus said. 'Ah I hear Hassan.'

Thd door opened with a powerful silent caving-in. A tall dark young figure in black alpaca smoking-jacket and black melton trousers swayed slender and uncertain in the rush of sunlight, clinging to the handle of the swinging door – shooing away the naughty rough sun, shading his eyes, entranced for a moment. A sweet flicker of welcome was on his red lips and in his plum-black eyes of great traditional feminine docility. But in a recollective spasm he twisted to one side to make room, looking away over his shoulder, effaced and distrait, and they entered. He hurried nervously before them – still gracefully entranced, half glancing at Mr Zagreus under his fans of lashes. In the grating deep cockney of the levantine ghetto he lisped gushingly,

'I'll tell Mr Kein you're here. Mrs Kein isn't down yet. Shall I take your hat?' with awkward, bashful movements of invitation towards their hats and coats.

Dan and Zagreus did not look at each other. This new person, fluttering about them, called forth that discipline which, with them, took the form of etiquette. Zagreus stared ahead of him. *A new person, judge for yourself, I will not interfere with so much as the influence of a smile*, was the formula understood. Up the stairs in indian file – Hassan danced in front, the stolid tall young Dan brought up the rear, while Mr Zagreus shook his albino mane in the middle. A troubling perfume appeared to stream back from the alpaca-covered feminine haunches of the valet. Hassan would pause politely as though stopping to brood, both feet together on the same tread – a limp hand laid like a glove upon the banister rail – a reflective profile inclined towards the pair of trampling visitors, poised above their mathematical ascent. Then he would dance upwards again, with the ease of a bird taking to its wings.

They were introduced into the ugly, dark drawing-room. Hassan for form's sake examined it without curiosity to see if he could espy his master or his mistress lurking behind the piano, or imperfectly concealed beneath the settee. Satisfied that that was not the case, he departed to search for them elsewhere, with nervous precipitation and a confidential flash of the profile – pale and resigned, like a quickly turned mirror catching the light in the direction of the guests, the eyes flying away with mechanical shyness. His subsequent airy ascent of the staircase, three steps at a time, without, resounded faintly in the room.

Mr Zagreus had entered followed by Dan. He moved to the fireplace, and stooping, pulled towards him the old iron-plate fitting round the fire-box. 'You see, mean old devil! By reducing the rate of combustion he reckons to save himself three bob a day – yet at a moment's notice he can appear to have a cheerful and expensive fire.'

Withdrawing from the fireplace, he marched with a regularity suggestive of a cadastral operation to a city of books – closely packed and partly curtained, in three or four tiers against the ground. Turning, he moved to a position between the large front windows, where he scrutinized a painting hanging upon the shaded intermediate wall. From thence he moved across the face of the grand piano to a pile of music disposed in the angle of the wall and of the instrument. When, circling the Grand, he had proceeded diagonally the entire length of the room to the corner (where a spiral stand in some dark alloy, representing a serpent, sustained a cluster of electric bulbs), the investiture of the room was complete. At that moment a voice reached them from the direction of the garden beneath. Zagreus heard and disposed his head to listen – his lips silently moved to the movements of a song.

> Ich gehe nicht schnell, ich eile nicht
> durch Dämmergrau in der Liebe Land.

Zagreus flashed a signal to Dan.

'*It is she!*' He listened, exclaiming as the romance sturdily struggled through the thick, glittering window pane.

'*Isch geh-heh nischt sch-shnell, Isch – Isch – isch!* – Von welcher Judengasse hast du diesen Accent gekriegt, liebe Isabel?'

In ein mildes blaues Licht.

'Jor-Jor! Du eilst gar nicht, bestimmt!' he mocked angrily, stepping to the window and gazing down. Thrusting his fingers into the sash lifters, he heaved, arching his back. The thick rail in which his fingers were hooked stood as though morticed into the socket formed by the casting bead. At the third spasm a slight movement occurred, the heavy sash began to move upwards.

Zagreus stood back, looking about him. Passing his hand behind the window he seized a pole-hook, and swinging the ungainly lance across the window, guided its nozzle into the ring of the top rail, hanging upon it then. Slowly the upper-sash came down towards him. He replaced the pole-hook, and seizing the bottom sash underneath, forced it up a few more inches.

The song had now terminated upon the hissing 'lissht'. As he took his hands away they were sticky, and he discovered smears of black lead and tallow upon their under surface. He held them up disgustedly to Dan.

'Li's filthy draught-proofing – anyone would think it mattered if the fresh air got in and played on his rotten old spine.'

Turning his back upon the snake, he took a cigarette from his case. He reached to a granite bob, bristling with pink-tipped matches, and lighted it. Then lay back negligently against the wall, his eyes fixed upon Dan, who was looking out of one of the windows. Dan had reached the position behind the Grand. Mechanically he had started visiting the spots recently vacated by Zagreus, like a dog at successive lamp-posts. He turned to the stacked music. He picked up the pieces at the top of the pile.

Wolf. Verborgenheit.

Brahms. Lieder und Gesänge.

Under that came *Douze chansons. Duparc.* Idly prizing up a further sheaf – *Pierrot Lunaire: Schönberg* was uncovered. He looked up across the Grand towards the still attentive Horace. He smiled gently at his friend – who believed so *utterly* in his genius – and he adjusted the music to its old position.

Zagreus pointed to the picture upon the wall above the piano.

Dan approached it, his eyes solemnly riveted upon the opaque slices of drab pigment. It was cattle.

'De Segonzac!' the name came across the room to him. He looked slowly round. Mr Zagreus pointed to another painting to the right of the last. Dan moved steadily into position before it. He remained some minutes his head tilted up. He thought he could observe Laocoon with his two sons and accompanying serpents, their various limbs and trunks organized into something like galls of the cynips, in chilly colours. A conventionally distorted, antique, floridly-fringed head presided over the congery of tubes, rolling like an ornate primitive ship upon its side, the eyes dilated.

'Chirico!' Horace shouted the name of the italian master.

At the arrival of the name Dan again turned. The almighty Horace waved his hand towards the table, upon which were arranged a dozen literary reviews, and several new books, in their dust covers.

Nouvelle Revue Française Dan read. *The Princess and Other Tales. D. H. Lawrence.* He thought 'sides of beef, erected nordic males, advertisements for ladies' underwear' – words of his master, that his master had got from *his* master. Always the shadow of the mystery-man – the god-like Pierpoint, whom he hated!

A translation of Proust by Scott Moncrieff he was about to pick up, when he sneezed unexpectedly, with cyclonic force. Mr Zagreus was uprooted, and was seen moving towards him, through the tears that gushed into his eyes – the advancing figure was heard exclaiming:

'*Prosit!* – Proust? Come and have a look at old Lionel's library.'

Blowing his nose, Dan followed.

Horace Zagreus stood in front of the shelves examining the titles. As he caught sight of one marked *Varnish in June* and another *Mayfair. Six double O.* he pressed a lathe-like, soft-skinned, index against them. Then, half turning to Dan, he remarked in a low voice:

'You've got those haven't you? I told Willie Service to get them for you. It's suffocating stuff to have to read. When Pierpoint first made me read them I almost mutinied. I *couldn't* believe it was necessary. But I've never regretted it – it's wonderful what you can get out of them!'

His eyes shone innocently with the glamour of a young postulant, at the thought of this discipline.

'That one – no that – is a perfect one. That has all the names on the backs of the characters. Its moralizing makes it tiring reading. It's like old Lionel when he has got some bankrupt young artist in a tight corner, and begins lecturing him on man's duty to his fellows!'

He gave a hearty easy laugh and Dan felt in the Seventh Heaven – as they bent down together to read the titles upon the backs of the volumes.

'*Mark Harlein – Lipstick-Lagoon.* It's the companion to his *Stocking-Flesh – Flesh-on-Flame.* It is almost *too* vulgar – Pierpoint describes it as "the last extremity of maudlin decay being feasted upon by one of our most mettlesome, vulgarest conquerors." It is *ghoulish,* he calls it – because you see our Society is a cemetery. It is a hairdresser's assistant romancing about a musical-comedy Duchess – the expensive ways of her, the expensive flesh-silk stockings of her shop-girl outfit, her vulgar crânerie – or it is the last pitiable success of the ancien régime, dressed up to look like *new.* Pierpoint pointed out to me how near this was to its high-brow mates – it should be read along with them. Listen – Proust is not so far from Harlein! I can show you!' he whispered eagerly, as one zealous novice to another. 'There's dear old Li's *Primrose!* Oh I will show you that!'

Horace Zagreus pulled out a mauve-backed book and set it in his hand, turning the uncut pages.

'Look how his publishers turn it out! He pays through the nose for his simple pleasures, Li does. The machining is disgusting – it looks as though it's out of register, even, there: they touch him for a good round sum, and get it printed in the Island of Staffa, I should think, for a tenner. We'll get him to give you a copy: "a great admirer of his work! – *The thought of meeting him has filled you with alarm*" – don't forget!' Horace laughed with glee (a fierce icelandic Puck, with Kaiser-moustache – but made of the best bleached blond silk – gigantic albino). 'You've scarcely slept last night remember! – all because upon the morrow you were to meet the author of *Primrose!* Don't forget.'

Dan shook his head gently and smiled the softest smile of most gazelle-like roguery that ever wandered, like a shadow, over a sad young countenance.

Zagreus turned, expectant and leisurely, towards the door, and it opened promptly. Mr Lionel Kein appeared in the doorway, smiling like a very knowing polichinelle making his entrance. Then, closing the door behind him with the action of a dog chasing its tail, his thin legs flexing in his ample, striped, whip-cord trousers, he advanced towards them with an alert dandified energetic shuffle. He presented now the earnest mask of a beardless, but military-moustachioed, spectacled Dr Freud.

'How are you, Zagreus, my dear fellah?' a throaty, rich-clubman's voice: 'Isabel will be down in a moment. I'm so sorry to have been so long: I was only just told by that idiot Hassan a moment ago that you were here.' As he reached Zagreus and took his hand – looking with solemn, black-eyed-loyal-and-affectionate unction into his face, his jaw propped out – his voice dropped to a hoarse sentimental whine: 'How are you, my dear fellah! I'm so glad to see you. It's a long time since we met!'

'A long time!' Horace Zagreus agreed.

'It must be a year,' said Kein.

'Why that's true, Li, it must be. How are you, my dear old shipmate? It was so good of you to arrange that we should come before the other guests. How are you?'

Kein dilated a close-lipped, ragged, bristling muzzle, puckered his eyes, gazing into his friend's, and nodded.

'Quite well!' (short, sharp and knowing).

'That's capital. – I've been in America.'

'Which part?'

'I believe it was principally in the north, there were a great many extensive buildings and a considerable stir, but I really forget.'

Kein propped open his shallow jaws, and emitted a clattering croak. The withering of the alveolar bed with age, in spite of costly dentistry, left a shallow ranine muzzle. He now sketched gestures of affectionate horseplay. He succeeded only in fixing his hand upon his friend's arm in a precarious squeeze.

'You *forget!*' he mimicked in a long nasal wheedle (Oh! you naughty, charming child, you! You are a one! a wilful charming one – and damn-it-the-fellah-knows-it!) 'How like you! The wanderlust of the Vikings, eh.'

'A greek Viking' Zagreus mildly qualified his friend's description.

'Well, weren't they Vikings?' Kein blustered a little, as the images of the sea-rover took shape for him. He felt, always subject to the clown's limitations, *a Viking!* His eyes almost became china-blue.

Mr Zagreus regarded him reflectively, as though mystified for the moment.

'I thought we Greeks were more jewish than anything else.'

Kein looked disgusted as the Viking was hurried away and the Jew came in.

'Perhaps now, but I meant the old Greeks – the Greeks of antiquity.' He clicked to the final vocables neatly with satisfaction.

'Ah!' Zagreus gazed at him.

Kein was still ruffled at the way the Viking had been handled. He looked a little malevolently at this slippery friend, who disdained the Viking. He made an unseen signal to the discomfited pirate not to go away altogether – hinting that his dismissal was not final. *Stop there my man! We shall want you again in a moment!* The spirit of the northern sea-wolf once more occupied his consciousness. He breathed heavily and his moustache bristled.

Kein shivered, his bones bending his black stiff-shouldered jacket, and he looked quickly round towards the open window.

'I think we'd better have that closed – Isabel is not very well. It seems a pity on a lovely day like this.'

He went rapidly towards the window, Zagreus following him. While Kein clung to the rail of the bottom sash, Zagreus took the pole-hook and aimed it at the slot in the upper rail, then pushed. Afterwards he assisted Kein with the lower sash.

'The damned things are so stiff I can never do anything with them myself. Hassan is the only person in the house who can manage them.' Kein stood back cymballing delicately with his hands to remove the dust. They returned towards Dan.

'So you've been to America,' Kein said, 'On business or just for the trip?'

'I beg your pardon?'

'On business or just for a trip.' Kein raised his voice, and aimed the words at the ear of Horace.

'For no special reason –.'

'Just in order to move about?' (Viking-motif.) 'That I find difficult to understand. As I get older I find I want to move about very little. But you always have been a wanderer.'

'I always was a roving blade.'

Kein smiled up at the large sea-rover handsomeness of his guest – with the long gracefully-stamped lines, the healthy skin, the flourishing mass of the albino hair, with its tinge of citron – an almost Polar pelt, and all the magnificent physical balance. His *friend!* (like *my* furcoat, or *my* alsatian).

'Do you know, Zagreus, my dear fellah' Kein said with naïf histrionic affection 'what I've always thought of – how I've thought of you always?'

'I've not the least idea.' Horace looked at him sideways doubtfully.

'Well, I'll tell you. As a sort of – Baring. A Waring I mean.'

'Not the banker?'

'No, not the banker! Browning's character. Waring.' Kein squared his jaw at the sensation of his daring frankness, and at contact in imagination with the Trelawneys of this life.

'You incorrigible old flatterer!' Mr Zagreus exclaimed, flinging out his hand, striking a considerable arc in its upward movement, chopping it quickly down on Kein's shoulder. At the same time he lowered his face till the large, grey ocellated discs (suggesting in their blueness, their fixity, their boldness, the uncharted ocean to his vis-à-vis) with which he roguishly transfixed Kein seemed drawing up the soul from the nadir, with artificial shavian good-nature. Like an albino figure of a play of Shaw's, Horace Zagreus struck his attitudes, but a figure like a more delicate Shaw himself – if Shaw had been in fact a fierce albino, and gone to school with Pierpoint at sixty.

'But why – come now, Li, let's see how a flatterer's mind works – the task for a Hellene! Why, Li, old boy, should you imagine that I should fancy myself at all upon the quarter-deck of a ship? Why? That is a careless piece of work it seems to me! It's extremely wide of the mark. That's strange. I'm sure it's well meant.'

Kein gazed back imperturbably from his black toffee-eyes, the Punch-grin fixed in painful lines upon his face. He received sentence after sentence – spitted as he was with this prating pirate's mocking eye, grappled with his mighty hand. But in his chaldean, thought-reading gaze, he reflected in the black crystals of his eyes the words of the other before they were spoken, examined him before he was born god-like (but provincially god-like) from the northern foam – indulgent, calmly smiling, looking before and after, entrenched in his mystery – himself nothing, his race everything. *Wide of the mark! Well meant!*

Holding it back for some moments, Kein then released, evenly and insinuatingly:

'Was I flattering you, do you think, Zagreus?' Zagreus removed his hand and laughed with good-natured appreciation.

'No I daresay you weren't, you impudent old whore!'

Kein remained immobilized, floating over a fleet of treacherous lickspittle insults, upon a tide of liquid eye-toffee.

'Dear me, if I were a flatterer, I should go differently to work!' Zagreus exclaimed, with a slight flourish. 'Suppose I were after you, Li, for instance. I know what I should say. I should say – I should say – that you were a – a *great "psychologist"* – your own word for yourself, old fellow. "*A psychologist, as I am*" – so no invention required: I should invent very little if I were a flatterer. I may say at once, I should just encourage people to describe themselves, and use the description they seemed most to relish.'

This disappeared in the viscous urbanity of Kein's silence.

'However, I owe you a compliment, don't I? I've always regarded you, Li, as – can you guess? – *a perfect Proust-character!* How does that accommodate you?'

'Very well!' Kein replied with vehement rapidity, his eyes flashing and darting. '*Very well!* – But Proust is a recent acquaintance – you've known me much longer than Proust.' (Me. An old me, pre-Proust – Kein, your friend.)

'Well, then, upon the coming of Proust I said – "Ah, there is Li's author!" *A Li in search of an author!*' Horace added with great joviality in a lower key.

'Six lies if you like!' Kein retorted fiercely, his face changing to its solemn mask. At the name of Proust he ran up his state-flag. Proust, when he entered his soul, made him more self-confident than the Viking, even. He was ready for anything under that banner. He began to deliver himself with heroic emphasis, with the full roulade and rattle of his most *withering* drawl – like snarling drums set rolling to celebrate an arcane victory.

'I should certainly take it as a great compliment to be associated in your mind in any way at all with Marcel Proust. That would be the way to flatter me if you wished to!'

'I told you I could beat you at your own game' Zagreus laughed – 'How is Pierpoint?' he enquired suddenly as if it had just come into his mind.

The Punch-aplomb at this further name went back. Horeb and the Forty Years was fully reinstated upon the old clubman's flushed mask, serenely at bay, contemptuous of the 'paltriness' of his friend's weapons.

'Very well, I believe. I have no reason to think otherwise,' Li drawled, with lofty blankness of expressionless eyes. 'Very well I should think.'

'Very well?'

'Very I should think.'

'Do you see him now, Kein?' Zagreus asked softly.

Kein screwed up his face in a sweet grin.

'I haven't seen him recently.'

'No?'

'Not very recently.'

'Ah! – Money, I suppose?' Horace enquired absent-mindedly. 'These beastly artists! We rich men have to put up with a great deal from those artist-fellows. They –'

'I don't know if *you're* a rich man, Zagreus,' Kein exclaimed, very upset. 'I know I'm not. – I wish I were. If I were, if –'

'Of course not, Li,' said Zagreus soothingly. 'I was only speaking jokingly. Of course not Li!'

He continued to gaze at his host, lost in thought, and to go through the pretence of reflectively stroking his chin, and offering all the other signs of a musing abstraction – while Kein stared silently and resentfully back for a moment. Then he rested his eyes upon Dan, then transferred them back upon Zagreus again. – While this stringing and jockeying for position had been occurring, Dan had stood with his abashed fascinated gaze fastened upon Kein, as though Kein were in actual fact Mr Punch in the flesh and Dan a small boy out with his nurse, who had chanced upon this raree-show.

'Joking apart Li,' Mr Zagreus began sedately. 'I am in fact very interested in your reply. Li – *no*, it is joking apart. We must have our little fun when we meet mustn't we, but it's always I'm sure upon a footing of the friendliest goodhumour, is it not, and there is one thing that no one would be able to say about us, at all – that is that when we leave each other we do not leave something behind us. Yes, *our heart*, a little – I agree, my dear old chap! I agree. Our heart! – but I was thinking at the moment rather of our *intelligence*, Li. I never leave you, my dear old friend, without the sensation that I am taking something away that does not belong to me. Perhaps, however, you only make me notice things that were there all the time, but which I had neglected – until contact with you revealed them.'

With extreme discretion Mr Zagreus had dropped into declamation. It was a monotonous muted reflection of his host's colloquial pomp.

'I'm glad to hear that Horace. Well?'

Kein was very short and not to be cajoled.

'Well Li – I was saying! – In reply to my clumsy compliment you asserted that to be a Proust-character *ferait parfaitement votre affaire* – to break into the *idioma* of the Master in question. What flashed through my mind as you said that was this: that in that case you would be one of the first notorious Proust-characters to appreciate the honour. Am I wrong? The originals of the famous social figures in Proust's books are said to have been highly displeased, and to have called Proust a cad or something of that sort for using them so unceremoniously. Am I right?'

Kein had grown redder as his irritability deepened. He had moved towards the fireplace, and Zagreus had followed him. With a very-well-I-will-answer-your-question pause, and an after-dinner speech camping of the person, he began:

'Would I like to be one of Proust's characters – do I understand you Zagreus, that is your question? – one of those who do not receive very flattering treatment at his hands? That is your question? I should consider it *well worth the privilege*' with the deep tremolo of emotion and the rich assistance of catarrh 'of having known Proust, to be treated in *any* way by him that he thought fit!' (Applause amongst the angels, heard only by the finer senses of Kein. He stands a moment a blessed martyr transfixed with the arrows of Truth.) 'I should know, however little I liked it, that it was *the truth* about myself! Perhaps not the *whole* truth. But I should not complain. That I think is my answer. If I were vainer than I am, perhaps then it would be otherwise.' Having stagily snarled out with rapid unction the conclusion of his riposte, looking at Dan significantly he said:

'Won't you and your friend sit down?'

'Ah yes, I was forgetting to be sure – this is Mr Boleyn, whom I mentioned in my letter. He is a bio-chemist, he knows an extraordinary amount for his age. I believe he is a genius! He is only nineteen.'

In his best-bred military clubman manner Kein shook hands with Boleyn. Then, in a dragging tone of wheedling insinuation – uncle Lionel at once – he exclaimed:

'Only nineteen!' There was the croupy rattle of paternal pathos. 'Only nineteen: I wonder if you know how lucky you are! I don't expect you do! I only wish I were double your age my dear boy, yes double your age – I should be quite satisfied.' He drawled 'quite satisfied', pitiful and nasal, with a senile titubation of the tongue, exploiting the death-rattle – Pierrot Vieux – poor Uncle Punch of the Children's Hour, the most popular grown-up ever broadcast – the old pet of the Pan-nursery, Nunky Li.

'Or treble, Li!' laughed Horace Zagreus.

'No it's not quite so bad as that.'

'I thought it was a little worse, Li!'

'What is a bio-chemist?' asked Kein, amused and dainty, of the young staring giant.

'I haven't found out yet,' Dan replied, looking at him blankly, as though he had not recovered yet from the great astonishment of meeting him, in the flesh – or perhaps of seeing him come in at the door, instead of up though the floor. Screwing his face towards Zagreus, Kein laughed appreciatively, at the responsible party.

'And where do you study bio-chemistry?' Kein wheedled him, mouthing 'bio-chemistry' in a sneering polished finick.

'Nowhere,' answered Dan, playing up to him with lazy indulgence, so encouraged by the presence of Horace, otherwise he certainly could not have said Bo he knew.

Kein laughed with grateful heartiness.

'I mean at the moment,' Dan added perfectly pert.

'Not for the present,' Kein imitated, inexactly.

Seizing at an emotional escape, his desire to be 'in right relations' uppermost, *religio* – the traditional great escape – suggested the religious, the emotional exit to Li. He gazed at Dan with the maternal tenderness of a hearty uncle: he looked whimsically at Zagreus, who sat like a stuffed bird gazing glassily sideways: his eyes returned with every sign of an impending expansion to Dan.

'Well, you're a youngster –' was thrown out with a grating bluffness, rattled hoarsely with avuncular winds of wheezy emotion. 'You may take this from an old man – you've got a good friend – I'm sure of that, I can tell you that – here – in (sob-choke) – Horace Zagreus. And I know.' With maudlin intensity he went on – 'I'm not a man who makes friends easily! Zagreus and I have been friends for – longer than you've been alive, actually! Isn't that so Zagreus? I've never met a man to whom I take off my hat – whom I *respect* – whose intelligence I respect, as I do his. It's a great thing for you. You don't understand – you're too young! Some day you will. You've been watching us bickering – you think we're not good friends, I daresay. That's our way – that's all! We've always been like that, Zagreus and I. But I'll tell you how – .'

The door opened, and Kein's elegant Judy entered, with a smile of welcome advancing towards Zagreus.

'Hallo Zagreus! Where have you been all this time?' (A jolly, a friendly, a sensible 'brilliant-intelligence'. A 'beautiful woman', of great breeding and charm.)

Horace Zagreus sprang up, he bent low over the chivalrous emblem extended towards him, nestling its plump tentacles caressingly in his own palm – settling and examining it for a moment, then lifting it, with head reverently bowed, to his mouth.

Isabel Kein, her handsome, brilliantly-painted mask, on high, assumed a seat near the fireplace. She stuck one leg out with a perfunctory roughness – feeling with her foot for a hassock, and placing it upon it, flexing her other leg beneath her. She rested her forearms upon the lateral scrolls of the arm-chair, her trunk erect and slightly advanced, talking meanwhile. The coils in the upholstery beneath concertinaed under the familiar pressure – the rows at the head crushed especially by the massive decline of the legs, and the front portion of the roll permanently depressed. She adjusted herself into these slight depressions. Two panels on her black frock disguised the rotundances of the hips. A tippet of mauve silk was round her shoulders. Except for vivacious and intelligent movements of the head, she moved very little while seated. The eagerly-disputed, ruthlessly-discouraged embonpoint, though not excessive, would yet allow of no unpremeditated physical licence. It compelled her, in revenge for the fasting, to be wary of spontaneous movement. Where she sat she had to stop, to a great extent, without variety.

Mr Zagreus watched her with admiration. Dan answered the questions she occasionally addressed to him with his blank astonishment – with which he still met Kein – modified for Mrs.

'And is Mr Boleyn a friend of Marly's, did you say?'

'No I am a friend of Martin's. You probably mistook the name.'

'Oh, Martin? I don't know him,' she said quickly – dismissing Martin from her mind, and Marly with him, also Dan, and turning to Horace Zagreus.

Kein sat silent nursing a soreness. The intermission of fresh greetings had thrown him back into himself, where he did not smooth out his ruffled spirits, but brooded against what had just passed.

Isabel Kein's intelligent eyes, beside the usual domestic seismology, took stock of Lionel's discomfort, her guests (the stupid, pretentious boy, his noble patron, their old friend – always these ridiculous boys!) and added her own particular pressure to what she had found on her arrival, with aplomb and grace.

'I forgot to ask you, Li, after your – the work – books. I suppose work is the right word? We have here in young Boleyn *a great admirer of yours*. When I told him he was about to meet the great author of "Primrose" and "Frederick Aldous" he was all in a flutter, I don't believe he slept a wink last night for thinking of what the morrow had in store.'

A painful and resentful smile became fixed upon Kein's face as he listened, sitting bent forward with his elbows on his knees, half-looking at his two guests. He glanced at Dan, whose face betrayed no emotion, except one of the deepest astonishment, as before – without moving he stared before him.

'He's very shy,' said Horace Zagreus, indicating Dan. 'You'd hardly think to look at him that he heard what we were saying would you, but he takes it all in every word of it, nothing escapes him, he is a genius! He is probably suffering agonies of shyness underneath that calm exterior at this moment. Still waters run deep.'

The eyes of Kein and Mrs Kein kept in touch, commenting upon this rapid speech, Kein's assuring hers that he was capable of dealing with the situation, that he was quite indifferent – hers flashing with the promise of her aplomb and resource, at need.

'I'm afraid you'll get nothing out of him' said Zagreus, still gazing at Dan. 'I hardly think I ought to have mentioned his admiration for your books. He will probably remain tongue-tied now for the rest of the visit.'

Very slowly Dan turned his head in the direction of Mr Zagreus and as their eyes met a faint smile of understanding, an avowal, burst as it were upon his lips and in the gentle flash of an eye, then disappeared – as though with its indolent explosion something had consummated itself. The mask became fixed.

Although intelligent and aware, it was once more sedate.

'What did I tell you!' exclaimed Zagreus. 'He's positively too shy to speak! It is the shyness of true genius!'

'There's no occasion, Zagreus, for your young friend to say anything about what I write. If he enjoys it and understands it, as you inform me that he does, so much the better. I'm very glad. If not, he wouldn't be the only person. There's really nothing to *say* – '

'No you're always right Li – I suppose there isn't.'

Boleyn's smile had held up Mrs Kein, some dark blood had sprung into her neck. Frowningly she arched its stumpy column and glanced guardedly at her guests, making up her mind. ('Oh, you old man's darling! You – you – ' she left a boiling blank in her mind for the things the young offender was.) 'Is Mr Boleyn always as shy as this?' Mrs Kein asked.

'Not always. It's only *when he admires anyone very much* that he retires into his shell – so much as this!'

'How curious. He exaggerates people's importance, I expect. He's very young – '

'Yes, very very young!' Mr Zagreus leapt in, watching her mouth, before she had said it.

'Yes' she nodded quickly and slightly interrupting herself, 'and he'll learn better no doubt,' she panted a little through her nostrils, as though each sentence had been supported by a measured volume of breath expelled along with it – a negligent rapid drop of the voice finishing what she had to say.

'Oh, I hope he won't lose his illusions!' Horace looked deeply distressed at the suggestion. Then he went on heartily, squinting a little: 'The way I look at it is that it's up to us – *as illusions* – to do our best to prevent that happening. But you seem to have thrived on the death of your illusions, Isabel – I've never seen anyone look so well. I believe you murdered all yours in your cradle, and have been living on their corpses ever since!'

'Perhaps I did,' said Mrs Kein brightly, pleased at the metaphor. Horace Zagreus, the aristocratic albino, stately in stature and a bright talker, she had always favoured.

'Li, on the other hand, has artificially preserved all he started with, and he collects a dozen new ones every day. *I* am one of his illusions, too, I've just discovered that – he described its appearance to me. But when I tried to escape from that responsibility he was extremely upset – weren't you, Li?'

'No. I have no illusions about you, Zagreus.' Kein did not change his position – he looked his *illusion* in the white of the eye.

'Li is cross with me – Li is offended with his little illusion! When you came in Isabel we were having an argument, I'm sorry to say, about Proust. Shall we take it up where we dropped it? Yes let us Li. Born arbitrator that you are, you will be able to clear up my difficulty. – Li here says that he wouldn't mind what Proust wrote about him – or what figure he cut in his books, if he could only be *in* them. He says he's such a devotee of Truth, and that he recognizes in Proust such a master of it – especially of his, Li's, truth – that he would pose gladly for his pen. *Any* portrait he would welcome, provided it was signed "Proust". What is your attitude upon that question, Isabel?'

Isabel was indulgent, airy and decisive.

'I feel like Lionel!' she panted lightly. 'But I don't mind what happens to me in that way in any case. If I were consulted, I should say *certainly* – let me be dealt with by Proust, sooner than anyone else I can think of. By all means!'

Kein watched with smiling displeasure, inhaling his cigarette deeply into his nervous crazy body.

Zagreus had thrust his head forward with a contradictory expression. His face was knitted into a frown, and with that was impounded a faint smile. This flashed out rigid and inexpressive when he was interrupted or if his words appeared to have been misunderstood, further explanation imposed upon him. The rather painful frowning, which drew down his brows and wrinkled the long wide-winged nostrils, never let go of the smile at all. It lighted up merely with a flickering break the solemn mask with its slight flush. Speaking he did not look at Mrs Kein but past her or through her. This gave the effect to this dialogue of a telephone-conversation. During a retort or interruption, Zagreus waited, as if unseen, and standing at the opening of a transmitter, for the voice to stop – an answer building itself up in his head, his lips already slightly moving. Dan glanced at Horace and at his hosts from time to time – his feet were very painful.

'What first occurs to me Isabel is this – and excuse me. What you say you feel is a conceited thing to feel – to some extent.'

'How do you mean conceited?'

'Well, in the first place. The public mirror, the *Proust* – in which people survey themselves so comfortably – can be an indecent institution – can it not?'

'Indecent?'

She knew her lips were watched by Horace for their lip-language. She sculptured her replies with the scarlet plastic of her smile.

'Yes, because it is so *critical* it makes people uncritical and comfortable.'

'I don't see that, I must say!' Isabel laughed. 'I think it is very salutary, on the contrary. There's no obligation to look, either.'

'Is there not? Why not then? They are stuck up everywhere. It is surely less trouble to have a look at them than to avoid them.'

'But I am interested in myself. Perhaps that however is indecent! Proust makes me more interested in myself – and in other people.'

'By "interested in other people" you mean *maliciously* interested. Your interest in a person is in proportion to the power you can exercise over him? It is some combination of your *power-complex* and your appetite for gossip that makes you so pleased with such a writer as Proust?'

'No, people interest me in every way. I am not malicious.'

'But what generally is that *interest*, about which we hear so much? An "appetite for people" would describe it? Your "self-feeling" grows fat upon the people you can intellectually devour or dominate – in Fiction?'

'Well, of course that may be so. I've never analysed the effect of reading in that way. All I know is that I am interested. I would rather be interested than bored, that's all about it.'

Zagreus paused, and, glancing at Kein, to see if he was saying anything, resumed:

'How is it that no one ever sees *himself* in the public mirror – in official Fiction? That is the essential point of my argument with Li. Everybody gazes into the public mirror. No one sees himself! What is the use of a mirror then if it reflects a World, always, without the principal person – the Me? Let us put it in this way. You would not like to look into such a mirror and suddenly find *yourself* there. Not so cunningly sucked in and eternally fixed as happens with a master like Proust. Imagine your sensations if you can! I do not wish to be disobliging or rude – but flesh and blood will not stand *that!*'

'I believe I regard myself just as objectively as Proust could.' Isabel smiled, the reverse of nonplussed.

'Then why – how shall I put it – are you not *different?* Please excuse me – it is very important. Why do you never *change*, in spite of that revelation? You or anybody I mean of course.'

Isabel airily tossed her head upwards, emitting a throaty glockenspiel arpeggio to the left, then one to the right – six notes on either side.

'Ah why not! That I can't tell you. Why aren't you different? Or perhaps you are. You *have* changed lately, a little.'

'People feel themselves under the special protection of the author when they read a satire on their circle – am I right!' Horace exclaimed with discipular unction. 'It is always the *other fellows* (never them) that their accredited romancer is depicting, for their sport. Or is it that the Veneerings and the Verdurins read about themselves, see themselves right enough – *and are unabashed?*'

Horace Zagreus flung himself back for a moment staring blankly at Li, to see if he was opening up. He was not. Then Horace proceeded: 'At all events nothing happens. It would seem that it is impossible to devise anything sufficiently cruel for the rhinoceros hides grown by a civilized man and a civilized woman – along with the invulnerable conceit of a full stomach and fat purse. The satirist merely seems to put them on their mettle, according to that view. It is almost as if, when they saw him approaching, they exclaimed: "*Here comes a good satirist! We'll give him some sport. We are just the sort of animals he loves.*" Then the official satirist fills his pages with monsters and a sprinkling of rather sentimental "personnages sympathiques", and everybody is perfectly happy. The satirist is, of course, quite as insensitive as his subjects, as a rule. Nothing really disgusts him.'

Isabel lifted her eyebrows, turned her head to the left and performed a glockenspiel arpeggio, and airily tossing her curled-out, hard, painted lips to the right, repeated her performance upon that side, with defiant 'happiness' – a creature of eternal Spring, with the 'conceit of a full stomach and fat purse'. – Dan began examining her with renewed and furtive surprise.

'But with Proust I feel that he sees things as I do,' she exclaimed with a parade of the obtusest complacency.

'Yes, I should imagine you do –'

'I think so!'

'I admire Proust very much.'

'Thank you!' gaily snapped Isabel.

An exultant rasping cackle came suddenly from the quarter of Kein, towards whom they all three turned, Dan with an expression of empty dismay. His good-humour was abruptly returning. His Judy had been more than a match for their troublesome visitor.

'Isabel has answered you better than I should have been able to, Zagreus. What you say about the Verdurins and' he rattled importantly in his throat, to patter out the latin glibly 'hoc genus omnes – that is perfectly true – they don't recognize themselves –'

'No, that as you say is perfectly true.'

Mr Zagreus now slewed his chair in the direction of Kein, and he camped himself in front of him as he had in front of Mrs Kein. Fixing a glittering eye above Kein's shoulder, he transferred the dialogue momentarily to the man – with the manner of a person interrogating an entranced medium, responses attended from a great distance. As he caught the drift he would slightly animate his smile and advance another well-placed question.

Kein gave a series of deep croaks and indicated Zagreus to his wife with his cigarette-holder as a mock-insulting pointer. He screwed his face up sweetly appreciative.

'It does *am-muse* me to see Horace settling himself for a de-baate!' he drawled with a sugary finick. 'He reminds me of the Ancient Mariner – with his skinny hand and glittering eye.'

'You knew Proust, Li?' began Zagreus at once.

Kein shook his head – chin propped out, frog-mouth widely set, eyes in eyes – steady tranquil smile at mast-head.

'What would you say Proust would have thought of you if he had known you? Would he have known he was in the presence of a Proust-character?'

'How can I say?'

'No but what do you think?'

'I should imagine that he would have known that he was with someone who had a great admiration for him. – I should not have disguised that fact!'

'I'll bet you wouldn't!'

Kein lowered his head, fidgeting, drawing deep breaths as he inhaled his cigarette.

'You never saw Proust, Li, but –'

'You know, Zagreus, what a great admiration, we, Isabel and I, both have for Proust's work.'

'Well you didn't know him that is that and you wish you had. Had you done so –'

'I don't see what you're driving at Zagreus. What has that got to do with what we are discussing at the moment?'

'It might have a great deal.'

'It might. But as we didn't know Marcel Proust – I only wish we *had*' Li almost moaned.

'Well, we will abandon that.'

'Your contention seems to be, Zagreus – if I understand at all what you're driving at – that the use of real characters in fiction –'

'No that's not really it. What I really am trying to say is that none of us are able in fact, in the matter of quite naked truth, to support that magnifying glass, focused upon us, any more than the best complexion could support such examination. Were we mercilessly transposed into Fiction, by the eye of a Swift, for instance, the picture would be intolerable, both for Fiction and for us. No more than there are "good" and "bad" people, are there such people on the one hand as can pass over into a truly inquisitorial Fiction with flying colours, and those who, upon the other hand – so translated – are disgraced. *Every* individual without exception is in that sense objectively unbearable.'

'Yes. And what then?'

'Well, first, I think, *the real* should not compete with creations of Fiction. There should be two worlds, not one.'

Kein sprang nervously a few inches this way and then that, and precipitated himself in the path of the discourse of his friend.

'My dear Zagreus, excuse me! But what you have just said is word for word what Pierpoint said the last time you were both here together – and about Proust – it was about Proust, if you remember, that we were talking at the time –'

The frown disappeared entirely from the face of Mr Zagreus, and only the smile (but still held in leash by some other agency) remained.

'Well, what of it?' he asked.

'Nothing at all. Noticing merely that you were *repeating* –. You remember that we disagreed with Pierpoint – in his attitude towards Proust, for whom both Isabel and myself –'

'Were the words the same, even? I have a great respect for Pierpoint's intelligence –' Zagreus objected.

'You could not have more than I have, as you know – no one could have more I assure you of that' (with angry fuming precipitation).

Kein's face was decomposed and the maudlin-after-dinner Kein competed with a less avowed, less formulated one, as to which should supply the tone appropriate for Pierpoint.

'Well, I am but the *instrument!* But the problem raised by that extraordinary Pierpoint still remains,' said Zagreus. 'Could it have been better raised – could it have been delivered and argued with more fire and purpose?' he exclaimed in a rather menacing tone defending his *broadcasting*.

Kein yawned, tapped with his left foot upon the thick pile of the rug, inhaled deeply.

'You and Li seem at cross-purposes,' Isabel remarked. 'Pierpoint's views are not ours – nor *yours!* When that conversation you have been talking about occurred, it was you, Zagreus, who contradicted Pierpoint – not Li or myself. Some of the points you made were very good, I remember thinking at the time.'

'I only did that to give him the obstacle he required to display his mind.'

'I was under the impression at the time, that you made some very good points. You have not *always* held the same views as Pierpoint. I daresay you forget that.'

'But of course I agreed with him – I agreed with everything Pierpoint said. But Li and I are d'accord upon the subject of Pierpoint, at least – don't take *that* away from us. Let's get on with our argument. Li will be me – I will be Pierpoint! – I am sorry Pierpoint is not here: I will take his place.'

'I would much rather you would be yourself,' Isabel sharply objected.

'No no. I shall rouse old Li much more effectively by being Pierpoint, that famous matador. You will see, Isabel, in the event. Well, Li, what did that friend (that is not a word we use idly here, is it, *friend!*) what did that friend say upon that lovely Spring afternoon? We were talking of that sort of Fiction (what a thing to discuss with the whole of nature spring-cleaning!) which derives principally from Flaubert – "scientific", "objective", Fiction: That was the subject – am I right?'

He leered at Lionel as he shouted *Am I right*. It was the pierpointean exclamation in excelsis – *am I* RIGHT!

'Oddly enough that is our subject now! Now as then, here we are discussing a certain sort of Fiction. The Fiction we are discussing pretends to approach its material with the detachment of the chemist or of the surgeon. But in fact what happens is that, as it is *Fiction*, not *truth* – art and not science – the work usually of a writer for the salon and the tea-party (and not of a chemist in his laboratory, absorbed in inventions destined to very different, less personal ends) such "science" is of a superficial description. The air of being "scientific" and the paraphernalia of "detachment", used by the average literary workman, result in something the opposite of what you are led to anticipate. The Fiction produced in this manner becomes more *personal* than ever before.'

Horace paused, and passed his tongue over his lips, a trick familiar to Kein – it was the personal trick of *another* person (not present). Kein fidgeted, as though exposed or attacked by the sudden silence.

'So we have had for some time, simultaneously, (1) a school of unabashed personal Fiction, and (2) a universal cult of "impersonality". Strange, is it not? You see, Li, *a mask of impersonality merely removes the obligation to be a little truly detached.* The writer like Jane Austen (her personality according to the methods of the time in full view) had that imposed upon her. When the personality is in full view, the person has, in all decency, to be a little impersonal or non-personal. *The "impersonality" of science and "objective" observation is a wonderful patent behind which the individual can indulge in a riot of personal egotism, impossible to earlier writers, not provided with such a disguise.* – How does this pan out then, Li, in the average book of the average fashionable high-brow fictionist?'

At 'fictionist', as though he were a man with a wet moustache sucking and smacking in the moisture, Mr Zagreus stopped, his eye fixed upon Li, to effect a kiss-like inward whistle – by engulfing the air in the neighbourhood of his moist tightly-closed lips. Then, as though relishing a meal, he slightly lip-smacked and swallowed twice. Having made this deliberate meal of air, and washed it down with a little saliva, he proceeded without haste:

'Well then. The result is generally as follows. There supervenes a system of *heroes* and *villains*, just the same as in the victorian or french nineteenth-century romantic Fiction. What else, if you give it a thought, could be expected? For the more the average person is invested with the signs and powers of a superhuman *impartiality*, the more *partisan* – more partial and human, he is sure, in fact, to be. Instinctively he uses the "impersonality" presented him by natural science, or by popular superstition, rather (as he uses everything else,) to be *personal* and *partial* with. In this system the intellectual slur, or, worse, the *social* slur (the disciplinary voice of *the pack* – the values, defensive and offensive, of the writer's herd), is substituted for the old moral slur – that is the Public Opinion, offensive and defensive, of humanity at large. (Have I got the words right?) In the place of Christendom – with all its faults and cruelties – is substituted the *salon*. In place of the life of the-world-at-large – of so-called public events, and of the executive values of men's traditional ambitions – you get the values of the woman's world of social life, and the Public Opinion of the salon. In this system who become the *villains*, and who become the *heroes?* To start with, anything like a hero is a villain straight off, and without appeal. For the atmosphere of the salon has been adapted always to providing a place where the little can revenge themselves upon the great. What is "the great", what is "the little"? But who is agreed upon that? Nobody at all. What however we are all of one mind about, is such rough working measurements as serve our purpose. "The great" is the incalculable; "the small" is the calculable and the safe. Such is "Society". It is an organized pettiness – to use, Li, a favourite expression of yours – or it is nothing. Society is a defensive organization against the incalculable. It is so constituted as to exclude and to banish anything, or any person, likely to disturb its repose, to rout its pretences, wound its vanity, or to demand energy or a new effort, which it is determined not to make. "The small" is merely that constant and stable, almost dead thing, which can be measured and *abstracted.* "The small" is the abstract. "The great" is the *concrete.* What we call "great" – what we call "great" – *that is the reality!*'

Horace Zagreus paused in his peroration, flashing his eyes all over Kein (as if massaging him with a false and fiery preparation prescribed by the Great Absentee, even the mighty Pierpoint). – But chucking his head up quickly, muzzle-set, moustaches bristling, eyes screwed up – 'amused' – Lionel regarded the orator pugnaciously, until the words started coming again.

'*Hero* is a great, surging, primitive counter. Shall we concede this colossal husk any *reality* at all – or can we, rather, in the epoch of the *Massenmensch?* Is it possible to imagine "a hero"? Can we place before our mind some thrilling shadow from a universe of things not included within the catastropho-conservative philosophy of the *salon* of the post-war time? Whether that is possible or not, this something we have despaired of – and so disbelieved in, and banished from our environment – has been pictured under the figure of a vast and wandering sea-bird. It is the *albatros* alighting upon the deck of the vessel, when heroism comes amongst us – our laughter fiercely follows the winged intruder, as a stranger is pursued with the barking of dogs in a suspicious countryside. *Democracy* – at least we know what we mean when we use *that* word – that at least we have no difficulty in picturing! And the salon – that is the stronghold of democracy as democracy is understood with us. But if a "hero" were surprised lurking somewhere in that Leveller's Club (unusual as such an eventuality must be), what then would occur? Upon the spot he would take on (according to the salon code) a dark, a ridiculous, a disreputable hue.'

At this point Mr Zagreus crouched slightly, to represent the 'hero' discovered in the gilded den of the *Forty Thieves*, of the contemporary social strongholds of the Shiebertum, the robbers who came out of the Field of Armageddon – those victors with their spoils.

'*Fiction*, as we call it, is indeed no misnomer, since it is generally an untruthful picture. In its more high-brow forms it is in fact the *private news-sheet*, the big "Gossip"-book – the expansion of a Society newspaper-paragraph – of the Reigning Order. And the Reigning Order is the people with the pelf and the circle of those they patronize, and today it is the High Bohemia of the Ritzes and Rivieras. And the "great novels" of this time are *dramatized social news-sheets* of that particular Social World.'

Mr Zagreus swept his eyes around the room in a swoop worthy of a foraging kestrel beaked and spurred . . .

'In that system of Fiction (namely that in which the gilded herd of the Ritzes and Rivieras, of the luxurious studios of Paris or of Berlin, find themselves depicted for seven-and-sixpence) the villains of the piece, of course, are the people who displease the accredited editor of Social-Gossip and of public opinion – or, in other words, the author (the "novelist" and his friends). It is the villains, only, who are treated "objectively", or rather whose portrayal, however grossly false, could by any stretch of the imagination be so termed. *Ce sont eux qui payent les frais de la méthode scientifique*. The heroes of the story (or what used to be named in that way) on the other hand, are the editor (the novelist, his patrons and particular friends, those in favour with him, those with whom he is in favour). At the head of that dazzling élite is usually some whimsical, half-apologetic, but very much sheltered and coddled projection of himself, the editor (that is the fictionist). They, the heroes, are *not* treated "objectively"! Of that at least you can be perfectly sure.'

Zagreus paused, scouring his lips with his tongue, as though it were an interlude of degustation in the midst of a hearty meal, his eye still fixed upon Kein. In a moment he proceeded.

'Just as time is made for slaves, so scientific "objectivity" of treatment is made for *others* – strangers to us, those not "of us"! It is clearly not made for *ourselves*. For the heroes (for the author, his patrons and his friends) the most time-honoured, most subjective romance is invoked, for their benefit. What is "science" for you, that is not "science" for me. No no: here what is sauce for the goose is *not* sauce for the gander. For the mythology here in question is the monopoly of the social Trust which controls it. So *science*, yes – science by all means! On condition however that it be inflexibly one-sided, conventionalized in every respect, and used to blacken such types of men as are not persona grata to the social consciousness of the moment. – Meantime, the presentment of the hero-type, in this system of Fiction, is livened up with a pinch of malice, naturally. Else, even among friends, the magical advantages and predictability of success of the conventional, unmistakable, "sympathetic" type, would become a little monotonous. The apparatus of "objectivity" (which the modern fictionist is bound to parade) would be too transparent to be satisfying. In consequence, carefully-sorted and innocuous malice is administered to the hero, of a becoming shade. On no account must he be confused with, or even suggest, the "hero" of romantic type. The energy of a Karamazov, or even the successful human type of the order of a balzacian top-dog, would transport him at once into the category of *villains*. He would become *un vilain bonhomme* upon the spot. Everything conspires to an, in appearance, impartial distribution of *dis*qualifications. Only *some* disqualifications are *far more disagreeable* than others – it is in the manipulation of these desirable, and undesirable, traits, that the successful editor of Society-Gossip, that is to say the chosen fictionist of the Gossip-Column-World, the High-Bohemia of the Ritzes and Rivieras, must excel. It is the neatness with which this is done that assures the success of the "serious" Fiction-writer.'

Mr Zagreus paused, took a series of deep breaths, and turned sharply in the direction of Isabel, fixing his eyes upon her red and smiling lips, as if he expected these shortly to begin moving in response to what he was now about to say.

'The destinies of the "best people", in contemporary Fiction, is very much what it is in real life. There is a great pretence of egalitarian principles, there is an absence of ostentatious distinctions. The casts are so arranged (no undue Starring – in order discreetly alphabetical) that the more innocent reader will *discover for himself* (gratified at his astuteness) a *difference* between A, B and C. "I rather like So and So," he or she will come to say: "I think he (or she) is *rather* sweet!" – (Rather "quaint", but one feels one would like to know him, or her)! – On the other hand (all the herd-instinct, held in place with every cliché of the moment, worked upon, excited and prepared for several pages), the more innocent reader will suddenly come to a great decision and will exclaim: "What an objectionable bore (or cad) So and So is! I think the author's much too kind to him!" Or: "What an old bore that Lady X must be! How could people possibly go to her dreary Lion-hunting parties." Always in these books what could be called the '*Lion*'-*theme* – or the *anti-'Lion'-theme* – will be noticed recurring. It is a constant feature. For this is a jungle from which all Lions are banished – lest democratic susceptibilities be offended. And anyone who is noticed being kind to a "Lion" – much more any "Lion-hunter" – has pretty quick *snob* spat at him – that is, superlatively, a sport that is not allowed! For in the High Bohemia of the Ritzes and Rivieras are we not *all* "artists" – all "geniuses" – all "Lions"? Was not the War fought to that end – to make the World safe for Democracy, and free of disturbing "Lions", for ever more? It is the Paradise of the Apes of God, we are to understand!'

Mr Zagreus rolls his eyes at this, as he mouths, over and over again, the great leonine substantives. And he rolls his eyes fauvesquely round at Kein. Then he continues, turning back to Isabel:

'It is just *ordinary*, nice people who are hero and heroine. And they are best seen when they are contrasted with "Lions", but poor degraded "Lions", represented as underdogs, as "villains", of this charivari. Heroes in contemporary fiction are specimens of, so to speak, *the quiet little great*. And the traditional *great* undoubtedly bring out their qualities – that quietness-even-to-slyness of them. – So, then, what is called "Fiction" is in large part the private publicity-machinery of the ruling Society. A famous Fiction writer (the sort who receives a few columns of "searching" and flattering appraisement of his latest arrangement of current-Gossip in the "serious" reviews) exercises a good deal of power. In fact he is a sort of editor, of the current news-and-Gossip-sheet, for the select public of the High-Bohemia of the Ritzes and Rivieras.'

M. Zagreus rolled the World of Ritzes and Rivieras around his tongue, like an unctuous tenor.

'But, being an individual of some importance, the famous-fictionist further will indulge his private rancours, and those of his friends and backers. So another factor is added to the falsification of these socio-literary processes. – Last of all, the author of "serious" fiction in our present world, at his most bitter, is not able to go far beneath the surface. Even the work of Proust is almost entirely a matter of whether, when one of his characters cuts another when meeting him in the company of a third (of a somewhat different social grade) it was deliberate or only half-deliberate – should be overlooked, or retaliated upon him. Proust was nothing if not personal – all went straight out of life into his pages. Was not Proust for years the Gossip-column writer upon the staff of the Figaro? Is it not as a Gossip-columnist that he got his information? He remained the high-priest of Gossip.'

There was a restless movement of protest from the direction of Lionel, and Isabel frowned above her smile.

'But Proust *is* the prince of this type of fictionist. Among the smaller champions it is safe to say that they cannot or dare not cut down to a region where all are equally naked before the seat of Judgment. The "truth" if it were told (not that it can be by more than one man in a generation or two) would bring rushing down the whole house of cards, would it not – or do I exaggerate? The truth, even if it were available, could not be applied technically to the villains of the piece. Obviously that would involve the heroes as well in the disgrace of the villains – or else abuptly expose the fraud. Finally, then, the heroes and heroines can only be sustained and held in position by means of some sacrifice of objective truth where the villains are concerned. Or rather the "truth" of the villains assorted with the "truth" of the heroes, if it were not toned down, would be too glaringly utilitarian and partisan. In cases where a more ambitious author attempts to give *the full weight of truth* to those people on the one side, about whose destinies he is indifferent (while, naturally, leaving those in whom he is interested, upon the other side, nursed in a nimbus of romance, however disguised), the result is much less satisfactory than that obtained in traditional drama or Fiction, where the writer was not obliged to observe this pretence of "reality". – That *these* must be self-evident faults of all Fiction which follows too closely some original – identifying itself with it, mixing itself with it, contingent upon it – is what I advance. What is the conclusion? That the world created by Art – Fiction, Drama, Poetry etc. – must be sufficiently removed from the real world so that no character from the one could under any circumstances enter the other (the situation imagined by Pirandello), without the anomaly being apparent at once.'

Mr Horace Zagreus, turning his head, looked very hard at Mr Lionel Kein, and Daniel Boleyn stared in amazement at Isabel. Isabel frowned above her rigid smile.

'But there is a further, a supreme, reason, why these two worlds should not be fused into one. It is precisely that truth – that any objective truth whatever – cannot exist in the midst of the hot and immediate interests of "real" everyday social life – the life of the Gossip-column, the fashionable studio, the freak-party. The purest *truth* cannot be used for the purposes of such a life. Used as a weapon only, it must lose its significance. The creation resulting from such a mixture must daily become more utilitarian. *The works of literature resulting can be nothing but weapons of the vanity* – day-dreams of the too-concrete personal self, of the Society-leader, the most eminent of Apes. Those works will be contrivances only, and too simply, for the securing of "power" (in the ordinary, vulgar, nietzschean sense) – not instruments of truth. How was it that the masterpieces of amorous-poetry – Shakespeare or Petrarch – were invariably addressed not to a *real* person – in order to claim the pound of flesh legally, by æsthetic right – but to a more or less fictitious personage, who could never be materially possessed? That Li, is my argument. That is all I need say on this head.'

The peroration had scarcely ended when the mocking applause of the Keins broke out. Head on one side, face puckered to its utmost of bantering combativity – hands held up like toy hands in front of his face – clapping with little imitation blows, Kein exclaimed 'Bravo! Bravo! Couldn't have been better done! *Awfully good!* I congratulate you on your wonderful memory!'

'Yes awfully good!' Isabel panted, frowning and smiling. 'I think Horace would have made an excellent actor, at least he would require no prompter with such a memory as he has got. But you were once an actor, weren't you? Astonishing!'

'Yes wouldn't he – I have often thought of that. Anyone would be taken in – I'm sure I forgot for the moment myself that he was giving a recital. Ha! Ha! So like him, isn't it – every word, like everything else about him, *borrowed!*'

'I wish other things were as easy to borrow as words are,' Horace Zagreus said, moulding Kein with a heavy eye.

'Yes, I daresay you do!'

'Well there is the peroration! But it was not all borrowed. Did you notice?' Zagreus asked Isabel with a pressing eagerness.

'Yes' Lionel replied. 'I don't seem to remember that part about the poets – '

'No, that was mine! I made that up – I wasn't sure if it came in all right. Did you think – ?'

'Absolutely all right my dear fellah.'

'I thought it needed something there.'

'It was the best part of the speech!'

'No that is nonsense. But I do not think it spoilt the rest, at least.'

'You are too modest my dear Horace!'

'At all events, there is our great and dear friend Pierpoint's text – orally preserved, quite in the primitive manner.'

'I think it is far more than that text – or *any* text my dear fellah – deserves, I must say!'

'A matter of opinion. How does it strike you at a second hearing?'

'Oh the same as the first time. I will yield to no one' Li blustered and bristled, bloodshot and bulldog-jawed ' – *no one whatever* in my admiration for Pierpoint!'

'It is wonderfully true I think! *And* what a light it throws upon your contention, Li – that you are eager and ready to take your place, without alteration, in the universe of Fiction!'

'I don't see how it affects what Lionel said' Isabel objected.

'When Lionel says that he would welcome the truth about himself, he knows, as you do and as I do, that he is bluffing us. The truth about anybody – to leave Li's especial variety out of the question – any truth (that is, the kind of naked, "scientific", truth that Li affects to love and welcome) is too horrible to contemplate. Such things should not be mentioned in polite society.'

'Then why do you mention them? Or are we not "polite"?' asked Isabel.

'You are most polite Isabel. All I have been saying is that no truth of that order of reality – and it is only that order of reality that matters, utimately – can make its appearance in polite Fiction – the Fiction favoured by polite society. In the nature of things, such Fiction does not deserve to be considered seriously. It is a highly remunerated flattery – it is not *truth*.'

'I agree with you as regards most Fiction. But I do not favour *polite* truth, that I am aware!' Isabel smiled – over her frown at him.

'No you favour the most brutal truth possible – provided it is canalized and conventionalized, and that you are immune.'

'I did not know that I was so unfair as that!'

'That is not what I said.'

'I thought it was.'

'I did not say you *knew*.'

'I see.'

Isabel relaxed, frowning at Lionel.

'You know, Zagreus, in some ways, my dear fellah, you're very naïf!' Kein full-stopped, inhaled deeply: blew out the smoke which forked itself like a shot-out tongue from his mouth. Should he go on? Should he tell him – should he not? He would.

'You know I understand you so well, my dear Zagreus.'

'You are a great psychologist,' Zagreus mildly reminded him.

Kein interrupted himself to smile his acknowledgments.

'And I am very easy to understand!' added Horace more mildly still.

'If I *did* not understand you so well, if I did not understand you so well, I should be irritated with you sometimes my dear Zagreus.'

'It is evidently lucky for me that you are such an enthusiastic "psychologist"!'

'When you quote Pierpoint to me my dear fellah' (Pause: puff-puff – unhurried emission of smoke) 'Pierpoint' ('Pierpoint' with two incisive carefully articulated panting smacks, and the ghost of a derisive rumble in the throat) – 'you had a great admiration for Pierpoint?' *Long pause* before the significant plunge. 'I wonder if you understood Pierpoint as well as I did – as we do – Isabel and I?'

'I wonder!' Isabel nodded and frowned.

'I am not a great psychologist –' said Mr Zagreus, hesitating, in search for what Kein required.

'You are so generous, my dear fellow, you bestow on people things they don't possess – you really do – you always have, and I've always loved you for it!' (Unstinted tremolos and the catarrhish collapses of *belcanto.*) 'You know how fond Isabel and I are of you – perhaps you don't know that? It's *true*. And I daresay you couldn't guess why!'

'All right Li. – If you wouldn't think I was plagiarizing *you* – this time – I should perhaps say that those words you have been using about me I have heard you address to Pierpoint, sitting in this very chair.'

'Lionel!' Mrs Kein signalled towards the side of the fireplace. Kein sprang up, he staggered about. The fire, the obstacle to combustion removed, had for some time been burning brightly. Kein took a fan from its position upon a powder-stool at the foot-end of the settee, and handed it to his wife, who held it between herself and the inconsequent heat. She worked the fan with an irritable movement, frowning at Zagreus.

Li sat down again. He ruminated, he spoke up.

'When you first met Pierpoint at our house –'

'I had already met him.'

'Yes I know, but it was here first, my dear Horace, that you got to know Pierpoint.'

'No, I first got to know Pierpoint elsewhere, some time after that.'

'But I asked him here on purpose, and at your request.'

'Actually it was your suggestion Li.'

'Very well. However that may be, you met him.'

'Undoubtedly I met Pierpoint.'

Isabel and Li signalled to each other, there was indignation in their glances. It *was* beneath their roof! – but Li had insisted enough. (There was *dignity* to consider.)

'I remarked at once that you had succumbed.'

'Oh, how was that? What does one look like when one *succumbs?*'

'I had expected it – I knew you would.'

'That was an instance of psychological insight!'

'You were not the first person to be impressed by Pierpoint: Isabel there – '

'Leave me out of it Lionel!'

'Very well I will leave you out of it Isabel – I quite understand you! You saw, Zagreus, in Pierpoint a very brilliant young man indeed – '

'Young? Very *brilliant* – in fact a very great genius!'

'A young man? *A brilliant young man*,' the rich avuncular roll returned – Lionel would not abandon his terminology. 'Pierpoint when you met him was not much over thirty – he is the most brilliant talker that I know.'

'I should not describe Pierpoint as *a talker*.'

'I really don't know Horace why you are so disposed, my dear fellah, to dispute with me about any petty point!' Li panted testily, darting his head rapidly about.

'I am not at all, Li. Please go forward with what you have to say.'

'If you will not bicker with me, about everything.'

'I apologize.'

'A very brilliant man indeed, then – will that satisfy you?'

'He may be described as brilliant I think.'

'Exceedingly brilliant – and no one is more willing to concede that to him than I am – no one has more admiration for him than we.'

'No one!' exclaimed Isabel martially.

'Isabel – although she doesn't want me to bring her into it' Li worshipped Isabel for a moment in a tearful spasm – 'she who is so unlike you Zagreus in most things – '

Isabel smiled and frowned at Horace.

'She has one thing in which she is like you – *she is a hero-worshipper!*'

Li worshipped the hero-worshipper for a moment, with his puffed eyes.

'At heart' Li exclaimed, and his voice broke a little, gutturally, at *heart* 'she is every bit as much a hero-worshipper as you are, Horace. She had that same generous nature that gives always more than it receives – ' (a drone at breaking-pitch of emotion was set up) – 'that makes her see swans where really there are only crows!'

There was a hush – in which Isabel joined – in which they all bowed their heads – which lasted upwards of three minutes, in order that they might salute the sacredness of the generosity of Isabel. – Then they resumed the conversation at the point at which the wild fowl had flown into it, as a metaphor.

'All her geese are swans!' Li bellowed softly – worshipping Isabel in the moistening of the voice and of the eye.

Mr Zagreus turned to Isabel with an expression of mild appeal, since she had been cited along with him. Isabel arched her eyebrows ironically, and turning her head to the right performed a glockenspiel arpeggio, and then repeated it perfunctorily to the left.

'She knows they are!' his face puckered, sweet and coaxing Kein trumpeted softly towards his Judy.

'Is that swan Pierpoint now a crow?' Zagreus enquired, in a moment, harshly.

'Pierpoint will never be any different as far as we are concerned my dear fellah!' the painful emphasis distorted Kein's face. 'From the first – '

Kein looked up from his dark, turgid, toffee-dream at Hassan's interruption – who had opened the door with a nervous suddenness announcing 'Mr and Mrs Glasspool,' with a throaty lisp – when these people had passed him flinging himself daintily out of the room, looking back over his shoulder like a dancer making his exit.

The sun had gone in and it had become extremely dark. There had been sounds that were renewed several times, noticed by Mrs Kein, who had coughed sharply to attract her husband's attention. It was then that, with a surly embarrassment, the two short people like high-brow tradesmen out-visiting, had been escorted in by Hassan. Mrs Kein had sprung up, assisted in this ambitious movement by the catapulting of the rear coils of the spring beneath her, had adjusted herself imperceptibly, taken a step or two towards the new arrivals with the friendliest welcome – slightly panting, a little superciliously, her words – throwing them with negligent good-nature, full of abrupt stops.

Kein now addressed himself to making the shy surly little newcomers at home. Hassan had been dispatched to bring a tray of appetizers.

A greater volume of sound immediately rose from beneath, and after a few feints and deceptions, materialized in four people. It became still darker with increasing fog and storm. At length nineteen persons were gathered in the obscurity of the long apartment, with the fire flashing its lightnings at their feet, as if struggling with them for the oxygen required by both – the matches for their cigarettes sporadically illuminating their faces, a half-dozen cigarette-tips pricking the opaque atmosphere. Their voices produced a booming volume of sound. Most began by tuning-up the complicated round or sphenoid wind-instrument they had brought with them, that is their respective headpieces – in which the air trumpeted and vibrated in the darkness. But the tumult increased. At length each guest (with the help of his sinuses and with a possible auxiliary trumpet in the laryngeal pouch, and the neatly-ranged teeth) got really started. Soon all were working their bellows forcibly. When most in form, the hard palate could be heard producing its deafening vibrations in the buccal cavity. Eagerly they thrust their heads forward, and launched their verbal symbolizations upon the puffs of deoxydized air, in the direction of their neighbours. These responded – broke across, out-trumpeted their opposites.

Isabel Kein conducted with a contemptuous smiling mastery this discordant herd, she had negligently collected. If no sound came from one of them (although he seemed to wish to trumpet, but lacked perhaps aplomb) he would be dexterously stimulated by his hostess. She would invite him to contribute to the general orchestration. Politely she attended to what was said. A pleasant musical laugh rose encouragingly from her lips, as the backward guest, provoked by her, barked or sang pleasantries. The sensitive feminine instrumentalists bursting into slight spasms of conventionalized pleasure (their heads ringing agreeably with the well-bred clatter of vocables and volleying reports of laughter) showed a mobile energy.

The foggy day-time darkness deluging the room magnified the din. Kein moved restlessly about, considering some of the loudest and best-pleased of his guests obliquely (a novelist – a psychologist – upon the prowl) his face flushed with nervous dissatisfaction.

The door at last opened and the face of Hassan sought Mrs Kein's between the dark bodies and faces, signalling. Mrs Kein jumped up, and still talking to the nearest guests, she strode robustly towards the door, moving her shoulders in time with her heavy hips, and gathering a wrap about the convexities of her biceps, as she went. Kein expressed his satisfaction to Mr and Mrs Glasspool that lunch was ready.

'I'm hungry! – damn hungry!' Kein said.

The company moved towards the stairway, where, from a long rectangular expanse of window, a burst of dull light struck them, and in a few minutes the dark smoky room, hemmed-in with fog, was empty.

*

The herd ate and drank beneath the eyes of Mrs Kein, who drank water and ate a little toast. Such restraint in public as regards nourishment was god-like and enhanced her arrogant detachment towards her guests. Her brilliant handsome profile was like a large ornate knife at the head of the table. A certain taint of craft was suggested, in her face, by the massive receding expanse of white forehead, from which the hair was pulled back – by the vivacity of the great, too-conspicuously knowing eyes – the long well-shaped piscine nose, like a metal fish.

With a ceremonious delicacy Dan did not look at the people about him. Also he was intimidated: these were those picked for him, among whom Mr Zagreus had brought him. Until his friend, therefore, drew his attention specifically to this one or that, he felt it would be indecorous and inquisitive to be found peering at them even had he dared. But his ears were full of their trumpeting. He began to recognize their names - 'Julian' was the figure upon the left-hand side of his hostess: his own neighbour, a girl named Ashmele, was Violet. The names of Burrows, Keith and Horncastle – Jack, Eddie and Anthony accompanying these names – were present to him. He detached a goblet from the accompanying wine glass and tumbler in such a way that the butler should have the largest receptacle conveniently placed when he came, as he was thirsty. When it was filled with a sparkling liquid he raised it to his lips and was surprised to find it was cider. But as it contained a few filaments of fruit and a taste of spice, fennel, lygistris, cloves, it must be cider-cup, he concluded, swallowing it almost at a stroke.

Horace Zagreus appeared to be acquainted with his neighbour. This, Dan noticed before long, was one of the first two humble arrivals, Mrs Glasspool in fact.

'So you don't see him now?' Zagreus was saying – to which a thin resentful whine responded, and he gathered Pierpoint was being discussed.

'Mr Boleyn is a bio-chemist!' announced a strident voice. Returning a piece of plaice he had been peeling to his plate, Dan turned to his left, where he met the smiling countenance of his hostess, who (shouting above the tumult) pointed at him.

'*Aren't* you – isn't that what you are?' Mrs Kein hectored and smiled. 'My niece would like to know what a bio-chemist is!' With a nagging nasal incisiveness she indicated a shining face at his side very like her own, but young – with the eyes extremely close together, the black hair bobbed. Violet Ashmele.

'What is a bio-chemist?' his neighbour asked Dan, insinuating, her attention withdrawn from a conversation elsewhere. 'Is it something to do with life?'

'It is a branch of chemistry.'

'To do with life isn't it?'

'I hardly know any chemistry.'

'I think it is so interesting.'

'My father is a bio-chemist.'

'Is he really – how divine! I've always wanted to mix gases and play about with retorts – I know I should blow my head off if I were turned loose in a laboratory. Are you terribly fond of it?'

'No.'

'At school they used to give us litmus-paper. What is it turns red? Oh don't tell me please – just a moment – I know – when it's an acid it turns it red, and what is it turns it blue again? An alkali – that's it isn't it? I used to enjoy stinks at school more than anything else – a dear old man, he was called Doctor Palliser, used to teach us. Do you know him?'

Dan shook his head.

'He was a perfect darling.'

Dan ventured to eat a piece of fish.

'When are you starting?'

'Starting?' Dan was startled. Starting *what?* – he looked covertly at Horace Zagreus.

'To be a bio-chemist.'

'I don't think I shall yet – I am an artist' added Dan convulsively. He had been about to say 'a genius', but he said 'an artist'. He blushed deeply and stole a glance at Horace for he thought Horace would have heard and that he would tell her that he was a genius, though in a way he hoped Horace wouldn't.

'An artist!'

'Yes I'm too young to have done much!' he added very hastily.

'Of course – are you a student at the Royal Academy?'

'No.'

'How old are you?'

'Only nineteen,' he said, apologetically blushing.

'Really, only nineteen! That is of course far too young to have done very much. It must be most exciting! Which do you like best?'

'I don't know.'

As Mrs Glasspool was speaking to Kein, Zagreus turned his head to the left, and examined Isabel's end of the table. Next to her sat a figure new to Zagreus. He eyed him for a moment. An old yellow-skinned coquette! A Charlie Chaplin moustache under a large carnal nose, thick lips ecclesiastically trimmed to an ironic, ascetic peak. Isabel's new familiar! This meditative guy was picking up crumbs. These, when pressed, adhered to the tips of his fingers. Daintily choosing among the tiny debris, his brown eyes ironically glazed, he mused. From what could be heard, Zagreus concluded that it must be in the wake of his friend's Proust-interests that this man had entered their circle.

Kalman now was asserting ruggedly: 'It makes me want to laugh! The angels weep – I laugh.'

He had attracted the attention of Kein.

'What makes you want to laugh Kalman?' Kein asked with bantering sweetness.

'The eminent.'

'The eminent? And who are the em-mi-nent?' Kein enquired with finicky coaxing irony.

'He says Health and Youth are "eminent". They are solemn, he thinks, just like dwarfs and cripples' somebody nearer to their host than Kalman shouted in the direction of his ear.

'Wealth also makes me laugh' Kalman exclaimed, taking no notice of Kein. 'I see a money-bag! – All place and circumstance, political or social, makes me laugh – it seems absurd to me. It is a *man* become a *thing*. Instinctively I laugh at it. A water-jug walking about would make me laugh – *things* are always so solemn! Wealth, Youth or Health, as *things-in-themselves* – by themselves cut off from the universe of Space and Time – such *things* do make me want to laugh when I meet them when I am out for a walk – have you ever met them? I can't help it! Health as it stalks among Anglo-saxons. That is the funniest in its way, it is terribly funny. It's sad, too – think of the footballer or police-constable. – Very sad!'

'The *laughing philosopher!* You do am-muse me Kalman! Youth! But you're only a baby yourself! Ha ha! Em-mi-nence! You do *amuse* me!'

Kalman turned to Kein, beaming cherubically (clearing away his deep beethovenesque frown – under his mass of chestertonian curls) through his gold-rimmed spectacles.

'Not so young as all that,' he said. 'Young to *you* Lionel – never *sir* to you sir!' he added with the heartiness of the travelling salesman. 'But I'm beyond the *eminent* stage, at any rate. I was a bolshevik in my cradle, my granny tells me. It's my bolshevism that makes me want to laugh always, it may be that!' He shook like Pantagruel, who '*laughed at everything*'.

Sadofsky sitting opposite to him smiled.

'*Oh God! Oh Montreal!*' sighed Mr Zagreus in his sleeve, examining Kalman, at whom Dan was gazing in astonishment across the imposing front of his erect and bristling master.

'So was I!' vociferated Kein all of a sudden, administering a rhetorical stage-blow with his fist to the luncheon-table. The goblets and wine-glasses in his neighbourhood demivolted, gonging and tinkling. 'I always *was* an anarchist!'

Kalman stared with pointed amusement at his wealthy and wine-flushed host. He had the board now: his neighbours were attending to him. Horty, the american novelist, his neighbour but one to the right, thirty-two years old, had just put another guest as though by accident in possession of a simple addition sum. Its factors, points of reference in his 'post-adolescence', when worked out, which could be done comfortably in the head, described Horty as being at present round the age of twenty-four. Horty was silent. He exchanged 'dry' prim smiles with the guest in possession of these figures, called Bolsom, whose predatory profile directed itself to the new centre of interest with a flushing grin that made the hair withdraw an inch higher up the sparsely covered head.

'I know a hard-working middle-aged journalist' began Kalman, delighted with his success.

'You know *what!*' boomed Kein.

'He keeps a wife and large hungry family in considerable style on sucking-up to the Young. His Youth-stuff he calls it – in papers and magazines. "Youth at the Helm!" or "Bravo Twenty-Five!" or "When Youth Can – When Old age Does Not Know" are the sort of headings he gives his articles, you know the sort of thing. – There's money in it!'

'What does he make?'

'More than I do! – He can write them with his eyes shut. The old devil once offered to teach me the trick. He had practically made a corner in a certain brand of flattery – very paying!'

'What an old monster!' said Mr Glasspool, upon whom the wine had already had a humanizing effect.

'Not at all! A clever man! He is particularly good at devising schemes for the violent extinction, or the segregation in penal-colonies, of men and women of his own age. He's won-der-ful – he's very hot when he gets on to that!'

'I know a man like that,' said Keith.

'But he is marvellous!' roared Kalman. 'Only last week he had a huge success with an article proposing a drastic revision of Bernard Shaw's *Every man over forty is a scoundrel.*'

'I believe I saw that!' said Horty.

'By a most ingenious process of reasoning he showed that this should now be altered so as to establish the *birth of the blackguard* as he called it, at thirty-six.'

'How lovely!' Miss Ashmele exclaimed. 'What a perfect man!'

'But why theer-tee-seex?' asked Vernède sedately, at Kalman's side.

'I know, why thirty-six – that's what I asked him. But he's not at all satisfied himself either – he contemplates shortly a further reduction, for he says he notices that people are getting to have a shabby worn-out look at thirty-one nowadays, and he hopes soon to be able to stabilize "scoundrelism" at the thirty milestone, with the electric chair or the Tarpeian Rock at thirty-five – *five years of criminal life*, that is – and then the law would step in!'

Kalman again paused – relaxed the string and it quacked round him like catgut, on a dozen applauding lips.

'I think that's too divine!' Horncastle exclaimed, exhibiting himself effusively from the other end of the table, and immediately, in a lower voice, he enquired of his neighbour:

'Who is he talking about? That *shabby, worn-out look* – I recognize that don't you!'

'*Birth of the Blackguard!* Ha! Ha! Ha!' Kein shared his mirth with Kein. Horncastle's neighbour, with two spandrils of pepper-and-salt hair, a moist perpetual smile giving his mouth the Official status of a sex-gland, – 'the mouth of man is a dark cavern' guarded by a dragon's teeth (with Burrows small and sharp) – supremely unrefractory he melted beneath Horncastle's eyes – but did now know the personality involved in Kalman's conversation. Kalman continued:

'His master-stroke, however, is to have taken women up into his system.'

'What a dangerous man your friend is,' said Mrs Keith.

'I believe he is' said Kalman.

'What does he say about us?' said Mrs Keith.

'Oh it was suggested to him in the following way. He keeps his ears open. He heard somebody saying that all artists should – without patents or gifts to hospitals – be recognized as *noble*. This was enough for him! This at once gave my friend his cue. Women had always been his stumbling-block – they were the weak spot in his system. He felt that they could not be treated on the same radical footing as men. And yet they were not *all* young. That was the great difficulty. But now he saw his way out. – Why should not all women (for *artist* he substituted *woman*), be recognized as *young!*'

'I think that's a marvellous idea!' said Mrs Keith.

'Not bad is it?' said Kalman.

'Your friend is a genius!' said Sadofsky.

Genius! – Dan looked up angrily at the speaker. He caught the eye of Zagreus, and blushing turned away his head. The man was palpably an Ape – Zagreus had evidently remarked it!

'For *noble* he substituted *young!*' Kalman said.

'Your friend is an apostle of aristocracy?' Raymond Bolsom suggested.

'No – merely a business-man I think,' Kalman replied. 'He argues that in mind women are in fact "young", whatever their age. In consideration of that fact, why should not they share the youthful privileges of their offspring, as is the due of their function of perpetual nurse and companion to the young?'

'I don't understand what he meant by women having "young" minds,' objected Mrs Keith; 'I should have thought it was men if anybody – !'

'Yes but that was his way of arguing.'

'Yes.'

'Naturally he did not neglect the other side of the equation – suggested to him by the man who claimed that all artists should be recognized as noble. It was only a step for him in any case from the patent-of-youth-for-the-woman, to the daring and popular proposal that all "the young" should be recognized as *noble*. "Every man is a poet in his youth" he argued. But poets – who are "artists" – are, as we know, noble. Tommy is young. Tommy is a poet. Therefore Tommy is noble.'

'An excellent syllogism!' blustered Kein, enjoying 'syllogism', a bit of greek.

'Has he made allowance for the relinquishing of the title at a certain age? Would there again be only one title? Or would some very youthful people be dukes, and those approaching thirty, say, be only knights?' asked Mrs Keith.

'At the thirties all Commoners – and at the forties Untouchables!' buzzed Bolsom, (half-way between a knight and an untouchable) with a sly hysterical glee.

'We did not discuss that,' Kalman answered, with owlish earnestness, 'we have not discussed that. But he has I know very extremist notions as to what is "young" and what is not – few people here would satisfy the requirements of my friend, who is a very full-blooded youth-snob indeed, especially as his bread-and-butter depends upon it – My friend is the cleverest man I know!' Kalman concluded with sententious brevity.

There was a silence at Kalman's end of the table, and Isabel's voice was heard by itself, she was discussing her Zoo. 'He's very dull, at least I can get nothing out of him. Lionel likes him – it's his theatre-interests. He has produced several things quite intelligently I'm told.'

As she felt the silence isolating her voice she raised it a little, and her eyes played with a leisurely insolence in the direction of Sadofsky, over to where he sat near Kein. Julian Hyde's sallow mask, with its ironically peaked mouth, and one eyebrow drawn up as well to a whimsical vertex, was directed towards the guest under discussion. Anthony Horncastle was exclaiming 'No really Jack! I think that's too perfect!', and the hearty camaraderie of Mrs Bolsom's laugh was replying to Horty's proud american.

A loud clap of laughter burst from Kein's mouth, it rattled and tossed for some moments along the table, until at the vocal source it met a barrier of phlegm and ceased abruptly.

'Damn good! What a good liar you are Kalman! Very amusing. "Youth at the Helm!" Ha! Ha! Ha! "If Old Age Could!" Ha! Ha! Ha! I think that's *damn* good! If I thought such a person existed as your friend I should insist on knowing him, Kalman. But you're such a liar! Ha! Ha! Ha!'

'Ha! Ha! Ha!' Kalman echoed with hollow regularity,

beaming at him. 'I'll bring him to see you if you like. But he won't like *you.* He would regard you as the greatest scoundrel unhung!'

'So I am! So I am!' Kein croaked, throwing himself about with gusto, and giving Keith, his right hand neighbour, a playful buffet.

'Who was the person who said that all artists should be noble?' Keith in a faint toneless voice asked Kalman. 'He has a lot to answer for.'

'Yes wasn't that good – I like your friend's process of argument!' Kein exclaimed.

Elizabeth Brereton, sitting on Kein's left, kept her swarthy russet fatness pinched and dimpled in a smile never speaking, but her rich voice joined in at the climaxes as though she were a class of laughing-instrument.

'I don't know who the fellow was, except that he was irish, I suppose' Kalman answered across the energetic face of Mrs Keith.

'I wonder if he was the person in the story' Keith said. 'You must have heard it I expect, to whom James Joyce said he could do nothing for him – because he had arrived at the period of blackguardism!'

'Yes who was that?' said Mrs Keith.

'If so, perhaps as he couldn't be young he thought he'd be noble another way.'

'What story was that?' asked Kein, turning his ear towards Keith, feeling he was losing something or might do so owing to Keith's quiet delivery. His face became decorous at the name James Joyce – one of the rugged eminences upon which Keith wandered, securing for his personality the atmosphere of the hardy mountaineer, with which his small freckled spectacled face was mistily bathed.

'Don't you know that story?' Keith replied sluggishly and unwillingly. His wife, observing his langour, lifted up the story bodily upon her own brawny shoulders.

'Joyce as a young man of twenty' she said, 'went to see George Moore I think it was: when he found him he asked with arrogance at once – "How old are you?" Moore replied "Well if that interests you I am forty-three." At that Joyce shook his head, and said "I'm afraid I can do nothing for you!" – Isn't that splendid!' she exclaimed energetically. 'What high-spirits! What gorgeous cheek! I think that's worth all *Ulysses* put together!'

'You haven't got that quite right' Kalman said. 'It actually had more point to it than that. Joyce went to see Moore or somebody – I don't believe it was Moore – to try and get him to do something for him. The moment he entered the room he saw from his face that he didn't intend to do anything for him. It was then that, merely turning the tables upon him, he asked him his age. When he heard it, he sadly shook his head – and saying with mock pomposity, "I fear I can do nothing for you!" left the room immediately.'

'Oh was that it?' asked Keith who had come to life doubtfully, a little vexed.

'Damn clever' exclaimed Kein throatily, darting about nervously in his chair. 'Damn clever! Joyce is very clever. – See how well he's managed to get himself – .'

'Yes that's *irish* – that's the *irish!*' Kalman shouted beaming, with a slight brogue (the MacAlmon in person in fact) and great confidential intensity and mock eager-eyed. 'My friend is irish' – he added rapidly, as if clinching an argument.

'Ha! Ha! Ha! your *friend!*' barked Kein.

Meeting the sea-roving eye of Horace Zagreus, which he had been seeking, Kein shouted:

'Look at Zagreus! as solemn as an owl! Zagreus, there, he is one of your friend's clients, Kalman! He believes in Youth more than anyone I know. Between ourselves – but never mind. – He's an enthusiast in everything. I expect your story about your friend displeases him.'

'Did it?' asked Kalman, looking across at Zagreus with cool curiosity, as though he were a creature strayed from another world, in which it was improbable that philosophy existed.

'What do you suggest, Li?' asked Mr Zagreus. 'That I should defend what Mr Kalman calls "eminent" Youth, in process of exploitation by his friend? But what excuse should I have – I should certainly be suspected of perversity if discovered at such an enigmatic task.'

'Perversity my dear Horace?'

'I am afraid so. Still to please you Li I will try.'

'I knew you would, my dear fellow.'

'I can see you are an altruist, like me,' Kalman said with a deft grin.

'Without, however, your dislike for the "eminent",' Zagreus corrected him.

'Oh it is the poor down-trodden "eminent" to whose rescue you are going, is it! That is indeed perverse.'

'But you see I am *not* an altruist.'

'Keep those two apart!' Kein called out. 'Once *they* start they'll never stop.'

'That is a mistake, you misrepresent me' Zagreus called back to him, the deaf to the deaf. 'Of my own accord it would not have occurred to me to argue with Mr Kalman at all.'

'Then why do you?' asked Kalman.

'I place friendship above everything – even above the friend!'

'How very extraordinary.'

'Yes I know.'

'Well?' asked Kalman, quizzing and soft.

'Yes well!' said Zagreus with a flourish. 'What you meant by "eminent", Mr Kalman, I have not quite understood that – perhaps you would favour me with a little enlightenment upon the term "eminent"? I cannot satisfy Kein's requirements until I know what I am supposed to be arguing about.'

'The socratic method!' Kalman beamed. 'I have a lovely feeling – *that I am in Athens!*'

'That is the idea' said Zagreus.

'Eminent? Oh by that I understand pride – pride manifested by the object of a superstitious esteem.' Kalman was negligent, transferring his attention to the talk of those neighbours whose interest he had lost.

'But *there* is a strange thing to describe as pride!' Mr Zagreus bustled and flourished a little – in order to recapture, for Kalman, the attention he coveted. 'I do not call it pride when people seek eminence in such impersonal, wholesale, communistic ways. That I call humility.'

'Indeed!'

'Indeed I find I must do so – for what humbler thing, can you tell me, could be imagined than pride in *health?* Imagine going about to flatter a baby by saying to it "You are a baby!" or making up to a clergyman by saying "How wonderful it is of you to have lungs" or "I do admire your remarkable intestines!" or to draw attention to any organ that all animals possess, note that it works with average efficiency, and find nothing more flattering to say to a man than to refer to his possession of it! Would you not rather – if you possessed a little resource, and wished to flatter – look for something in the individual *not* possessed by other individuals? So you would say, perhaps "What *a quiet* baby you are!" or to the clergyman "How *unlike* the average clergyman you are!" Yet it is true that in our democratic society flattery does take the form of saying to people that they are *like* other people – rather than *unlike* or possessing something peculiarly their own. And the personal advantages that are chosen to flatter them about are those that they share with great crowds of other people. Such is "eminence", and the accompanying flattery – the commodity exploited by your friend – call it *crowd-eminence*, if you like, if you can guess what I mean by that. So I can hardly believe you are sincere in saying that you regard health-swank, or youth-advertisement, as a form of *pride* – like pride of place or birth.'

Kalman's face had grown displeased. Beethoven, the Jupiter of music, was reinstated – he removed his horn spectacles, he wiped them, and replaced them, fixing a reflective eye upon this antagonist.

'Yes.' Pause. 'Yes!' he said, when Zagreus had stopped: paused again and then said 'Yes' once more, as though hesitating as to which weapon to take up to destroy Youth's champion with.

'You don't think I'm sincere?'

The others were once more attending to what was in progress. They had watched with satisfaction the slow and ominous removal of Kalman's spectacles, like the navvy slowly divesting himself of his coat.

'No' replied Zagreus quickly and airily, 'but your insincerity makes no difference, as we are not discussing you. You know no doubt well enough that the "eminence" that makes you laugh is the last ditch of a ruined society, and is anything but pride. That is really why you *laugh* at it.'

'I can assure you I *do not* know – whatever it is I am *supposed* to. In fact I don't know in the least what you're talking about. And if you don't mind my saying so, I don't believe you do yourself.'

Mr Zagreus darted his eyes all round Kalman, as though his antagonist had been a pin-cushion in which he was planting pins with lightning rapidity.

'Well, then let's see if your obtuseness can be overcome in this way. Let me know if you fail to recognize the landscape as I go along.'

'I'm sure I shall recognize nothing.'

'Your "eminences" I suppose, unless I am quite at sea as to what you mean, are the result of the break-up of social snobbery into its component parts – am I right? The old snobbery of pride-of-race is broken up and is evenly distributed among the crowd – is that not so? – each getting his little bit in rotation. Only those factors are retained and exalted, which *all alike*, at some time, can be sure of possessing. The old thrill and awe at the noble-man is run into the more material *animal* moulds. The noble animal – the "noble savage" – is the successor of the nobleman. The street-arab or the young Apache is a "sheik" or a *chef de bande*.'

Kalman nodded condescendingly.

'Suppose' said Zagreus 'a territorial magnate, of the old type, who, as the result of extravagance, revolution, or what not, loses possession after possession. A time would come when his vanity would be forced back upon things that formerly he had taken for granted, and never, perhaps, noticed. What is the last thing (in a progressive collapse towards primitive conditions) of which a man could boast? Just *to be alive*. That would be the last thing of all. It is the slave's thought – *I am alive*. What a consolation! – a consolation incomprehensible to Cato who asked himself *why* slaves went on living! So with the snobberies that Democracy has installed in place of the "noble" ones of Tradition. Anything less *conceited* than they are, in the essence, it would be impossible to imagine! They are characterized almost without exception by a pride in being not a *person*, but, as you have said, in being a *thing*. And what can there be more humble than that modest vanity? So it is misplaced bolshevism on your part, or else bolshevist perfidy, to pretend to interpret as *pride*, what is, in fact, its *opposite!*'

Kalman had relaxed into a broad proletarian, and 'socratic' grin – his teeth rising like ragged yellow rocks into view, the tawny dusty amber of his spectacles, his hair, and his skin emitting a glow of good-humour – the weapon that, as he listened, he decided it would be best to choose.

'Go on!' he invited Zagreus with nods. 'I haven't recognized anything so far! But it's very interesting. I'm both insincere and perfidious: that much I've got.'

'Well, I'll arrange it a little differently and spare your *sincerity*. Shall we consider the baffling fact of revolutionary eminence? If bolshevism succeeds, it becomes "eminent", does it not? Would you regard it as a consistent to become bolshevist about bolshevism?'

'To start with, I don't know what you mean by bolshevism.'

'You used it in the first place quite loosely yourself to indicate what most people mean by it.'

'Yes, that is true, I did,' said Kalman, as though glad, even, to be able to concede a point to such a very contemptible antagonist – and so make the argument a little less one-sided – not so monotonous for those looking on. 'But if we are going on using it – then we seem to be in for a very deep debate indeed! We shall have to define it. I used it in talking to Kein, merely.'

'If communism – will that do? – succeeded' Horace Zagreus then said, smiling, 'in a sense it becomes "eminent" sure enough, does it not? But it becomes "eminent" *all over* – everybody is "eminent" in some way, simply because they are *alive*. To be a human being, any human being at all, is to be "eminent" under communism. But that "eminence" would not make you laugh, would it? Because – although it might mean stagnation and a mechanical hardening into this simple concept and that, like so many *things* rather than *people* – it would not mean "eminence" in the old sense that caused you to be born, like Li there, a little liberal, or, as he said, "anarchist"?'

Kalman's face for some time had worn an abstracted and somewhat puzzled expression. For a moment he said nothing when Zagreus stopped. Then he looked up and said:

'I have had this argument before.' He paused, looking over

at Kein. 'I had this argument, in a rather different form, at this very table with somebody – about three years ago wasn't it?'

'Who was that.'

'I don't know if you know him. Pierpoint is his name.'

'I know him very well.'

'Well I recall that we had this argument, almost word for word – only it did not start in the same way.'

A short interrupting bark of laughter came from Kein. Towards Kein Kalman looked – he scowled, and transferred a lowering face of great displeasure from his host to Zagreus and back. Zagreus was smiling broadly. Evidently he had been the victim of some mystification – Kalman's displeasure became a formidable sulk.

'Yes you're quite right Kalman. Zagreus has been treating us to impersonations of Pierpoint ever since he arrived.'

'Oh I see!'

'He has a double-personality. I don't believe he knows when he's Pierpoint and when he's himself.'

'Oh that's it! Now I understand!' Kalman's face unruffled with magical suddenness. That accounted for everything, there was nothing more to be said. Zagreus looked at Kalman, and then he looked at Kein, as though to see what further sparks these two cronies would strike from each other – or what further combination might result, from their contact, to him. Nothing more occurring, he turned to Dan.

As he did so he found Isabel's eyes fixed smiling upon him. Mr Julian Hyde was saying

'Who is that?'

But Isabel not replying yet, went on looking at Zagreus (as did also Mr Hyde over one listed shoulder and under the pointed arch of a quizzical brow – smiling from the privileged perspective of the table-head under the ægis of the hostess).

'Who? Horace Zagreus? That is Horace Zagreus. I'd forgotten you did not know Horace. I've known him' with lifted laughing brows ' – for a donkey's years! Lionel has known him still longer. He knew Zagreus long before we were married, and that is seventeen years.'

'Really?'

Zagreus, imitating the confidential manner adopted at this

point by Isabel, said to Dan in a voice for his ear alone –

'I was using Pierpoint's methods. *Those were the methods of Pierpoint!* That is how he would have met that argument! But of course what was said was nonsense enough. Pierpoint's method, if I understand it, is always to expose his opponent's argument without taking the least account of his own private views. They would only hinder him – just as a personal emotion on the part of an actor would interfere with the interpretation of a part. Pierpoint would have said to himself – "Kalman is looting between, or behind, the lines, having provoked a war." (Kalman is nothing if not bluff and honest: but I imagine he is as fond of provoking conflicts and disputes as is Kein himself.) Had he found himself dragged in, as I was, Pierpoint would have pretended that the looter was a disguised enemy. Then he would have proceeded to encircle him with flags of truce, from those marked down as belligerents. Having made him return his booty, he would have handed it over, like a conjurer, to the lookers-on.'

Horace expounded with an eager delight the steps in the masterly manœuvre that undoubtedly Pierpoint would have employed, and Dan opened his eyes wide as he gazed at this double-scene – side by side, the behaviour of the paradigm, and the proceedings of the living-copy – the manœuvre that should have been and the manœuvre that was.

'I have not achieved all that,' said Horace, with a negligent rhetorical flourish. 'But in the absence of the master mind I did what I could. That man Kalman is only earning his keep as a clown. He was annoyed when I trotted Pierpoint out. He was talking complete nonsense, as you saw. Whoever heard of Youth without Health – if indeed without Wealth! Youth without Wealth! – think of slum-life and the crafty gutter-snipe. There is no Youth *there* worth the name! If the gutter-snipe started exploiting his "youngness" it would if anything be on the model of the beggar exploiting his blindness or his wooden-leg. In the same way Health, as conceived by Kalman, is meaningless. The Health of the police-constable is not Health at all, that is in the only way that has any significance – *energy* alone is *health* – the health of a Hannibal or a Moses, for instance. Health as intended by Kalman is "*thingness*" right enough! It is vegetable bulk, it is unconsciousness. Why call it Health? I do not know! Health is never the stupid brawn of the lumbering police-constable, but it is energy in any shape – am I not right? An organism like that of the russian novelist Dostoievski – shattered by terrible nervous seizures, or that of Flaubert – another epileptic – *you must go to them for Health.* They are colossally "healthy" I think – else how account for the books of both these C.3 persons – these down-and-outs in the matter of health?'

Horace Zagreus drew a deep breath into his pair of A.1 lungs – in magnificent order, as fresh as the sweet strong bellows in a dairymaid's buxom bosomish chest.

'No sir!' exclaimed Mr Zagreus. 'Never is Health that absurd thing Kalman affects to have met walking along for all the world like Gogol's Nose, as solemn and full of itself as a village beadle. As to *eminence* – but that is really a counter of the agitator. Kalman is an agitator, with a clown's gift. Himself he has of course no conviction one way or the other. It seems Pierpoint used to dispute with him. Ah but Pierpoint! – Pierpoint is that compact dynamism of Health and of Youth, or whatever you like to call them, upon which these people *feed!* That is why Kein is so angry at Its removing Itself as It has done. The old Li can no longer get at It poor devil, to nourish himself with It! That makes him *rage!* That is a bitter thought, he is very bitter – all it is necessary to do is to say *Pierpoint* and he bristles did you notice? It is like a bottle of strychnine or phospherine getting up and taking itself off – fountains of energy of that sort do not grow on every tree – what a metaphor! – if one removes itself its world withers – as primitive men felt their crops would be blighted when the strength of their rulers declined. You I feel will be – are! – one of those *fountains of life!*' Zagreus boomed at Dan, in a sort of ecstasy.

Dan sat without moving, staring attentively in front of him.

'*You fountain of life!*' Zagreus repeated, in a voice of thunder.

Those near Zagreus turned towards him quickly, searching (with astonishment) for the object of his apostrophe. More like a stone-image still, frantically saluted by its primitive worshipper, Dan stared inscrutably ahead of him, showing no sign of awareness or of life whatever. Hoor-aah! he cried faintly to himself. He had been called a *Fountain of Life* by Horace! Over and over again he repeated *Fountain of Life* to himself, and he was so elated at being called a Fountain of Life by Horace that he could not move a muscle, it was almost painful.

'You are a geyser of young and beautiful life!' roared Mr Zagreus quite beside himself with enthusiasm. 'You are as molten as the first gush of lava from a green volcano in an american tropic!' he exclaimed in rapture – *couvant* Dan with his madly-maternal sea-bright eye, encircled by the thin line of tell-tale red of the bronzed albino.

From across the table, Vernède was observing them with a demure understanding smile. Horty, interrupted by the sudden electrical discharge in front – with pinched blue mirthless lip, with that especial shade of intolerant raw superciliousness that the traditional American calls 'saturrical' – watched Horace and Dan. Violet Ashmele, from her crafty slits, cast glances at her neighbours as she sat – informing herself at each glance of new points for her dossier, mechanical and at bottom as aimless as a squirrel with its nuts and merely *observation-habit.*

Dan's face seemed a shell of mutton-fat over his faint dead brain, that was pulled tight, to deaden this amorous assault. *No one* would have guessed that he was saying *over and over again* to himself – 'I am a Fountain of Life! I am a Fountain of Life!' Nibbling a little bread he stared over Vernède's left shoulder. Zagreus appeared to remark that this outburst had attracted attention.

'Li is a blood-sucker,' he went on, but in a stage whisper, in Dan's ear. 'A blood-sucker! He has aged a great deal since he lost Pierpoint! It's taken ten years off his life! I thought by disguising myself as Pierpoint that he might be deceived and revive! But Li's a crafty old bird and he disdained the bait. Meantime I have made him very angry, as you see. Li does not like being reminded of his loss.'

'Well!' with a wealth of finality Horty said to his neighbour Bolsom, who had been observing Zagreus and Dan with him. 'What do you make of *them?* They're a queer pair, *any*way!'

The white mutton-fat of Dan's face flushed up. A meek minimum of tired life returned to his eyes. He stirred slightly, as if relaxing from a trance and his eyes took the direction of Horace, upon whom they rested for a moment.

'If I had been replying to Kalman,' Dan said 'I should have answered differently.'

'Kalman,' Kein called (swaggering clubman and man's-man). 'Will you bring your friend next Sunday? My nephew, Tommy Ashmele, is coming. He is in the same line of business as your friend. They would get on well!'

'I'll see if I can get him. But he's a very practical man! I doubt if he'll come.'

'But he must lunch out sometimes!'

'Very rarely. He says there's no money in it.'

Kein threw himself back, with a gesture of withdrawal and discouragement.

'I knew he didn't exist!'

'No, Li, there *are* such people, who think like that – *really!* I know you don't know them.' Kalman surveyed his neighbours. The look of pleased naïveté had not left his face, and he hurled his replies at Kein's deaf ears, his eyes protruding from his head, one fat shoulder thrust far over the table, with an optimistic effort.

Isabel and Mr Julian Hyde, after the last outburst, were discussing Zagreus, her voice reaching Horace with the most aggressive distinctness. She was speaking with her two eyes upon him, occasionally turning slightly to Mr Hyde, to whom her words were ostensibly addressed.

'He is a sort of Roudine' she was saying.

'A Roudine?' the incredulous drawling monotone of Hyde responded. 'What is that? A Roudine!'

'Oh don't you know – Tourguenev's book. Roudine is the arch *raté* of Russian Literature. In Tourguenev's book he is always turning up in new places – as soon as they find him out in one, he moves on to some other part of the world, and begins all over again. Wherever he is, he is always regarded as a *genius* – somebody who is "going to do something" someday. He never does anything, of course. He just goes on talking and talking. His new friends admire him a great deal for a time. When they find him out – he leaves. It is a very russian figure. Zagreus is not quite like that – besides I must say I am very fond of Horace

Zagreus – there is something very attractive about him. But he is a *raté*. Zagreus is a disappointed man. – Then he always has – well, boys. Boys he takes about with him – no one would object to that, but he becomes demented on occasion – their presence excites him so much, when he has one with him.'

'Has he one now?'

'I am sorry to say he has!'

'How would you have replied?' Zagreus asked Dan, hanging upon the words that did not come.

Oh! Dan blushed very deeply for he had not expected that this would go any further: Oh all that was expected of him because he was a *genius!* – Sometimes he wished that he wasn't one at all – and he had really only thought one thing, that had struck him – he knew he should not be able to say what he had thought but he must try he supposed. Help! Help!

'You had a plan you said' – he was again pressed eagerly by the bright-eyed Zagreus.

'I thought – I thought' Dan muttered brokenly 'that what he said was that *dead* things were bad, and that persons were – all *geniuses!*'

'And did you not think that wrong?' bellowed Horace in his ear with rapture, forming already with his mobile, child-like, sooth-saying lips, the big *yes* that must declare itself at any moment now upon those of Dan. He eyed his oracle with the most awed expectancy, all over the face – that beauty was irresistibly delphic.

'Yes,' said Dan, 'it can't be true. A thing, a thing.' He strove and strove. Then he burst out 'It cannot be *a genius!*'

'How *perfectly* you have expressed that – it is a criticism that is worthy of Pierpoint himself!' Horace Zagreus was transported with triumph, and he raised his voice as he exclaimed: 'That is far better than I could have done!'

But no one was paying any attention now – Kalman had again secured the ear of the entire table, except for the super-detached hostess and her official confidante for that luncheon-party.

'What Kalman said was, as you say, not entirely false' Horace then said, in a calmer tone, 'only it depended upon the assumption as you showed with such wonderful insight that "dead" things were in themselves undesirable, or inferior, and that persons (that is mobile things, able to come to conscious decisions, move hither and thither for purposes of attack, or the securing of individual satisfactions) – that persons were some higher order of things. – It is that point that, with your unerring eye you would have picked out for attack.'

Zagreus stopped and he regarded with great attention for some minutes his oracle. Even, he abandoned himself to an involuntary wistfulness, scanning the beautifully-moulded features of the impassible boy that could not possibly lie – *beauty is truth, truth beauty*. That once had been his favourite axiom – ever had he put it in practice – so that never otherwise than emotionally had he been able to apprehend truth. Never on the other hand could he cease to believe with devoutness that the *grecian profile* (like the camera) could not lie! (His english blood it was, the Follet-half, that caused Horace to feel in this fashion – from the cradle up – about the hellenic face-line.)

The hellenic profile blushed (full of the blushful hippocrene) but it did not speak. Why should it? With almost a sigh Horace Zagreus spoke again – he spoke by proxy for the dumb line of the nose and brow – for the praxitelean lips.

'That is how *you* would have replied. You would have shown that his description was in one essential false. The importance, in his remarks, attached to *people* and to *activity* – that is what you have questioned. His *abstractions* (though certainly where they begin imitating people they may make you laugh a little) would please me better than quantities of *people*. His "Walking Jug", for instance – say a Toby-jug. That would be a sort of *duck*. I should not mind that. Why make everything into a Toby-jug? – My dear Dan, how I agree with you! Pierpoint could not have given him a better answer! "Health" is a duck. "Youth" is a swan. "Man" is a Toby-jug! Pierpoint once said something like that – but I am not sure he has stated it with so much force!'

But Dan was speedily congealing again into a *thing* – such as men have invariably worshipped. And Mr Zagreus, as though to arrest the process (for he longed for his oracle to speak again) or in order to benefit by his spasm of expansion before it was extinct, with great haste exclaimed:

'Dan look round for a moment at this lot for instance. Do look at it! What do you say to them? I should like to hear what you thought of them! I should be curious to know!'

Horace ran his eye invitingly along the row of heads in front, like a stick along the railings. However Horty's voice fascinated them for a moment as he said in conversation with Bolsom:

'I saw his Cosy A Saivy Par-ree' – with cross reluctance – no much like!

'What do you think of it?'

Horty made a haughty highschoolgirlish *moue* with his prim button-mouth. Then he began laying down the literary law straight-from-the-shoulder re Pirandello.

'Ow!' he grumbled frowningly 'Pirandello's arl right' said he '*He's* not bad! But *he's* only a fash-nable spook playwright! Ow! That's grand geenyol that's about all *that* amounts to! His six old characters in search of their author when they found him if they ever did wouldn't gain any. *They'd* be no more alive than they were before! All *he* can do is characters *in search* of an author – if they weren't out looking for old Luigi – why they wouldn't be much of a bunch. I guess it's only because they're *lost* anyway!'

'*Sixteen characters in search of an author!*' vociferated Zagreus. 'Look at them! They don't look very real, do they?'

'No' said Dan, looking at them. 'Not at all.'

'It would be better to say sixteen characters in search of a *real* author' said Horace 'to replace the sixteen false-authors, or the *faux-auteurs* that this lot probably are. All to a man, I'll wager (like Pirandello's *six characters*) are characters of Fiction. *That* they can claim right enough: for they have all been written about in their own or their friend's books – upon that you may rely. But of what Fiction? It is a Fiction as dependent upon reality – *such a poor reality and so unreal* – that they are neither flesh nor fowl – they are *fictional mongrel facts* (that is Pierpoint's expression). There they sit, neither one thing nor the other. They are far worse off than if they had no author at all! *Happy is the character without an author* – with such ridiculous "authors", or creators, as these!'

He swept his predatory enthusiast-eye about the assembled authors.

'All so-called "real" people, trying to find an author! And

in despair – for a real author is none too easy to find – they have all set-to to write about each other and themselves. (Mr Horty over there, no, the one with the fringe and side-whiskers, he must say some odd things about himself in his books! Some sort of harsh, pathetic, super-flapper, Middle West tart *he* becomes, I should fancy). You know how old Li represents himself! But Li is at his best in representing Mrs Li – that well-bred and cultivated personage at the top of this table! A much more concrete and imposing situation is brought about, without supernatural machinery, by these *semi-real* people (got out of real life) than by personages imagined by Pirandello in his *Six characters*. This one has the advantage of being the supreme contemporary situation as well. A time without art, we exist in a period without art. So, a time without background – or shortly it will be that. There, in front of us, they sit in two rows (we are in one) – *the people who have never been able to become Fiction*. How portentously they suffer for the want of a great artist to effect that immortal translation – how they suffer! So they cannot exactly be blamed for their attempts at self-creation. – One of these fine days a *real* creator will come along. What a sigh of utter relief there will be – when the Ape can cease from Aping, and the sham-artist lay down his pen and brush and be at rest!'

Mingled with his own words Horace Zagreus heard Isabel remarking to Julian Hyde:

'– most of his life abroad – all over the place. He is very restless. I don't think he's quite all there sometimes – it's in the family I have been told – he is half a Follett – what? half a Follett, if that means anything to you.'

Such things did mean something to Mr Julian Hyde – a Follet was always a Follet for him – he solemnly inclined his head in sombre recognition of the Follets.

'He has had sunstroke – he was in Panama or some country in the tropics as a young man. Sometimes he is very peculiar indeed.'

Zagreus looked at her as he talked to Dan: after a moment's embrace of their four eyes, she turned her head back to Julian Hyde and said, with her lips curving out, in a higher key:

'Besides as you see he is an albino! I always think there is something the matter with people who are albinos – don't you think so?'

It was at this point that Mr Zagreus, still deciphering the messages of her brutally extended lips, threw into his discourse the reference to their hostess as 'that well-bred etc. person,' that was at the top of the table – that 'cultivated' person.

'Most of his time however has been spent in Italy!' Isabel spoke slowly, through the nose a little, as if intending to deaden the voice in that manner: – 'the home of the english *raté* – Italy. In lots of little ways Zagreus is very like the Englishman-in Italy-type – you know, the sort you find in the english colony in Florence or Venice. They're a rum lot! I think that species of english exile is a very peculiar thing indeed. As a matter of fact that's where Lionel first met him – in Venice. He used to be well off. I believe he's not now.'

Zagreus stared at Horty and Bolsom: Bolsom who was a journalist, was saying –

'The last time I was over there I stayed with a friend, in a diabolically noisy street. I hate Paris. I don't like the French.'

'Neither do I,' after a moment of discontented silence Horty grumbled accommodatingly – with the weighty reluctance of somebody admitting to an unorthodoxy of some value.

'They're so rude,' Bolsom said. 'Also another thing is, the English are not popular. I'm very fond of London, myself. Sometimes it gets awful, but on the whole I like it better than any other place.'

Horty squirmed – movement of some sort required first – then said – with a final gathering up of reservations, concessions, indifferences, into one ball of all possible factors, exhausting the subject in a discontented but decisive affirmation.

'I like London!' (*Arl* right! I'll like London! I like you. *Arl*-right! *I'll* like London!)

Dan was eating rice, prunes and a little scroll of beaten cream. Zagreus watched him.

The theatre queue! He and this strange attendant standing upon the other side of the wall at his back, outside the door of the then silent Kein-mansion, ringing for admission. The sun was upon his neck – the same sun, or another, that had struck him, the young bematist, swinging a plumb-bob, in the plantations where the De Castro factory now stood – Para a day's journey on the river-steamer. A long offset was about to be taken. A big portuguese workman was lazily nursing a cross-staff. Isabel had reminded him!

The pompeian funerary chariot – the shadow so much older than the original – and the little peering jewish face, now defunct – from a wall in Pompeii to Kein's door. *The theatre-queue had come to life*, now: here, all about him, in solid ranks, it chattered and ate. He had imagined a queue. But here it must be – less and less resembling the original – shadows upon the walls of Pompeii, of Paris, the hot andean plains – a horrible family of shadows. An ape-herd, all projections of himself, or he of them, or another – gathered from everywhere, swarming in after him, or collected to await him. Their plangent personalities, stuck up in opposite rows, behaved as though they were meeting for the first time (as indeed they might be) and had little connection. (*Roudine*. That was a nice discovery!) Or the queue had started *acting* – for want of an author, as he had just said – after a fashion. When their eyes met his it was always *himself*, in some form, at some time. The intensity of this truth, like a piercing light often compelled him to turn his head away from people, as he might from the image in a mirror. He lifted up his head – he would look these apparitions in the mirror-like depths of their eyes! A life-time of these machines – he knew them by their factory marks: it was not a task beyond his powers to take their 'movements' out of their cases – it was a *human* task – that great mechanic Pierpoint had been his master. But he who was 'fey' disdained it – he dismissed those phantasies now and fixed his frowning eye upon Isabel. He might be irritated or *irritate himself* into assuming his place more fully in a relaxing reality – at all costs he must fly this tension! An immediate interest be taken in these relationships! Make the most of Isabel's manifest desire to insult – put it to himself! Remember *albino – remember albino!*

He heard the name of Pierpoint: all those *present* having been picked dry, or merely sniffed at and put down, by Hyde and Mrs Kein, it was the turn of *the absent*.

Isabel shrugged her shoulders.

'He's socially impossible. It is impossible – with him it is really no use. Such people should be locked up somewhere and made to write.'

'I do so agree with that' said Mr Hyde: 'it applies to all "creative" writers, and composers.'

'Composers most of all!'

'Yes – there ought in fact to be a Zoo where all the Beethovens, Mozarts and so on could be shut up. We could go and take them buns of a Sunday afternoon, or watch them fed! – The question of food is most important. There are many works of art that we should understand far better than we do if we could watch their author at feeding-time – in a *genius-house*, at a Zoo.'

Depressing her long equine head over her hunched shoulder blades, and tilting up her chin, the eyebrows rising and receding to a point – in the manner of hair flushed back by the wind on the head of a running nymph – Isabel performed an arpeggio this time to the front – the ripple of the glockenspiel.

'In any case they are all brutes,' Mr Hyde proceeded. 'I have never known a man of genius who could tell one piece of food from another. All wines taste the same to them – I don't believe, even, they can tell one woman from another! They seem only made for one thing – they should not be mistaken for human beings. They should all be in a Zoo.'

'I don't know about that – not perhaps all. Some I think could be allowed to remain at large.'

'Of course – but very few indeed. Proust was hardly in that sense a man of genius – he was the voice of civilized people, he could have been *anybody*. He was not one of those creatures in league with Nature, almost *against* Man – '

'No, he certainly was not that.'

'But what sort of man is what's-his-name – Pierpoint? Is he a gentleman?'

'If you mean – well, he belongs to a well-known welsh family I believe – on his mother's side he is irish. He says he's the Duke of Munster or something of that sort – but all Irishmen say that. One of his relatives was convicted of embezzlement the other day – you may remember perhaps, in the Gilpin case. Yes I suppose you'd call him a gentleman.'

'That's all I meant – the question of their private means is also important.'

'*Private means* – what a delightful expression! No he has not got that. That is why he sees so much of Zagreus.'

'Is Zagreus the financier?'

'Financier! that is a strange title for poor Horace Zagreus – but I believe – yes, Horace is said to be always trying to lay his hands on money – to give to Pierpoint!'

'He keeps him?'

'Practically.'

'That is very interesting.'

'Pierpoint is a very brilliant creature, there's no question about that. I can quite understand anyone wishing to help him – but I should not like to have to keep him.'

'He is perhaps an expensive pet.'

'Pierpoint is altogether unbalanced. At times he will do the most extraordinary things. We, of course, were very fond of him – Lionel was extremely good to him – too good really. There's one thing I *can* say – Pierpoint will never have a truer friend than Lionel was to him – and still is! It's peculiar, but Lionel *won't hear one word against him*, even now,' she panted lightly, frowning.

From the other end of the table came Mrs Glasspool's voice in the nasal whine of intellectually-transformed shop-girl english:

'I shouldn't mind if he were only *honest*. He has no sense of personal honour.'

'He calls himself a writer: but he cannot even write *eengleesh!*' Jean Vernède broke in, his distended eyes darting from one pleased angry face to the other, bringing his quota of animus. Kein's face however averted itself from him, with an expression of annoyance.

'Pierpoint is what we call in Scotland "a puir wee –" ' What Pierpoint would be called in Scotland according to Mrs Keith, was obscured as Miss Brereton's dimpled smile of a giantess broke through into the gurgling deep of her laughter. Mr Keith lay back with one arm over the back of his chair, smoking, with half-closed eyes – 'detached', faintly smiling, freckled, spectacled.

Kein sitting like a mute – overwhelmed with professional sensations of universal calamity – had sat fixing his bloodshot eyes first upon one speaker, then upon the other. Occasionally he would take a draught from the whisky and soda at his side. With Mrs Keith they stopped: no one made a sign to take up the ball. Kein inhaled the air, now beginning to be filled with tobacco smoke, with a deep and melancholy sound.

'Well as you know I've stuck to Pierpoint through thick and thin' he began to croak and boom: 'Isabel and I will never change in our regard for him – our deep regard! Once we give that we never take it back!' The stature of his magnanimity increased at every sentence. He finished his glass at one sharp throw, and filled it again from the bottle and syphon at his side. 'But that there are things about Pierpoint which even his most devoted friend would find it difficult to defend – that it is impossible to deny. I am sorry to say. I wish I could! Poor Pierpoint! I wish I could have helped him to – to, not to lay himself open to so much hostile criticism. What he will do now I really do not know – Isabel and I often ask each other that! We often wonder –. We talk a lot about it. It worries us very much sometimes. We can't help, even now, being *concerned* for him. He has no money. What I'm terribly afraid of is that he may – well really *go under* – a man like that depends so much upon the support of a few friends – *good friends!*'

'And look how he treats zem!' Vernède exploded impetuously: Kein casting him a dull glance of resentment.

Mrs Glasspool shook her head, saying, 'Yes' in her girlish voice – her musing eyes fixed upon the disgusted face of Vernède, every *bassesse* met with a blank snub.

'Ah my dear Eddie!' Kein exclaimed in a low melancholy gurgling tremulous roar, gathering volume as it went. 'If you only knew how Isabel and I, especially Isabel, have helped him in a hundred ways – have put ourselves out – as few people, my dear fellah, *will*.'

Julian Hyde said to Mrs Kein.

'What an ungrateful beast! I quite see the type of person you are describing. He is one of those people – they are unluckily numerous – who don't know when they've got a good friend.'

'*He* certainly doesn't!'

Loud, strong, offensively harmless laughter (like a healthy organism emptying out of its window upon the public place, as it were – with a good-natured oath of good pedigree – a surplus of unvalued energy) rushed out of Zagreus – abrupt, disinfectant. The baltic-blue of his eye shone with insolent open light upon the caustic offended subterranean yellows of Mr Hyde – anchovy-tinted with traces of eczema, with his harassed pomposity, who when attacked seemed offensively to exude his sulphurous pigment.

'You heard all that?' Zagreus asked Dan. '*You heard what they said?* It's all fantastically untrue. It is very amusing to me who know the truth, as far as there is truth in these matters. What they never say – ! but of course they never utter anything but a pack of lachrymose lies.'

'Do they' said Dan. Zagreus laughed, growing noisier from moment to moment. Dan blushed at the thought of all the lies. He blushed for all these liars – tears and untruth.

'It's an old habit of Isabel's to discuss her guests openly. That dispenses one under certain circumstances from any ceremony oneself – there is that about it: both as regards her, and her guests. For if the hostess does not respect the guests – why should they respect the hostess, or respect each other? No. No reason at all! It becomes a free house. So let us make ourselves at home – I will be the host! You are an inquisitive arrogant gossipy guest, upon my left hand – you would like to know what description of cattle I have invited you to meet: I will inform you – not, it is understood, with the aristocratic sans gêne of Isabel. Nothing but good-breeding could enable one to achieve that. Still, I will do my best.'

Thereupon he slowly passed in review with his eyes, starting with Mr Julian Hyde, the luncheon party. Dan's eye followed his from head to head – a furtive follower.

'Nineteen of us! There were some I was not able to account for at first – the first two that came, for instance. The two shabby unimportant couples and perhaps a couple more – I've found out their function. They are friends of Pierpoint, or formerly were. That is what they are here for – what you have witnessed – what you have heard.'

'Who are those people – upon the right' muttered Dan, indicating their host.

'That one? Now him I can tell you all about – it happened

that I was seeing Kein at the time he materialized. That is Keith of Ravelstone, who tends the shadowy Kein!'

The bronzed albino threw back his head and uttered a piercing laugh, like the cry of a wild-bird.

'He is as you see, a very earnest, rather melancholy freckled little being – whose dossier is that, come into civilization from amid the gillies and haggises of Goy or Arran, living in poverty, he fell in with that massive, elderly scottish lady next to him – that is his wife. She opened her jaws and swallowed him comfortably. There he was once more inside a woman, as it were – tucked up in her old tummy. In no way embarrassed with this slight additional burden (the object of all her wishes, of masculine gender – but otherwise little more than a sexless fœtus) she started off upon the *grand tour*. And there in the remoter capitals of Europe the happy pair remained for some time, in erotic-maternal trance no doubt – the speckled fœtus acquiring the german alphabet, learning to lisp italian greek and portuguese. It was at this point that that old Man of the Sea yonder (our venerable chum Lionel) came into his young life. Keithie is a journalist, you must know, and develops a great deal of scottish earnestness with traditional facility upon the slightest provocation. He is a "critic" you must know, too. Now the latest little book vamped up by the Old Lionel's fœtid dotage, is published: it is in due course dispatched to Helsingfors to Keith to review – Li-ing self-portraiture, of course – on this occasion about Li's school-days (which had to be resorted to in order to reach a vein of homosexual episodes – no one since his tenderest years, I will say that for them, has ever thought of Li in that way, and he is incapable of inventing – except, and that he is a little master at, over and around facts). The book carries of course the nom de plume of Simon Cressy – no indication whatever of the cunning old fury concealed beneath the chaste name of Cressy, except naturally what could be found in its pages by anyone not a complete *fœtus*. "Ha!" says Keith "a new writer!" So (incredible as that may sound) he discovers old Lionel! Ha ha ha! in the innocence of his heart and thanks to the deep critical insight that distinguishes him – he unearths that Old Li! He has the honour of being the discoverer of the same that is now, or (at this time of day) ever will be, for ever and ever amen! So he pores over Lionel's pages, immediately develops freckled earnestness. Mamma – that is wifey – scents perhaps something more palpable than *genius* in the pages of the "new writer" – at all events croons encouragement, as ever, at the sight of the little earnest half-born face of the child-hubby. Down he squats upon his little freckled hinnie and for his sins or his fathers' pens a little earnest careful paper – all about old Li's little book. Off it goes the earnest little article to the land of Yankee Doodle, where a million molluscs learn of the dering-do of the double-faced, double-penned, double-named (that of the *plume* and his personal one) double-dated, Li. Deftly excised by the vigilant Romeike, back it flies to the lair of the watchful old stiff, feverishly awaiting events – his last little old egg painfully laid, with the robust collaboration of Isabel. Kein at last has "an admirer!" Oh ho! a something-for-nothing, a boob in the flesh – an authentic *unpaid* supporter! Demented curiosity in the Kein household! *Who is the Unknown Idiot?* Who can this unmatched moron be now? What manner of poor puny little scribbling gull can *that* feeble little bait have hooked – for the love of Lillith! It is Madame Kein and old Lionel smelling and peering at the little simple meaningless words, of the *A hauntingly beautiful piece of work* – the *We await with the keenest interest the next book by this new writer* type. All, all swallowed. Ha! Ha! with bursts of phlegm on both sides of the table! Not a trick (painfully concocted between them and wound out of their two old heads) – not an attitude, not a line, not a lie, *not swallowed whole*, by the earnest little unknown mind. – To cut a long story short, as Shanks would say, epistles fly forth into the Unknown. Eventually Keith over there is brought to light – he stands revealed as *The Unknown Idiot*. Soon he has not a shred left upon his poor little person – the epistolary rage of the Keins ferrets and burrows and scratches across space. *All* his history, circumstances (with special attention to financial details) – age of his wife, climacteric approaching, what residue of breeding-years (circumstances of old better-half with special attention to financial matters) – marital relations (satisfactory agreement materno-platonic from the start, or, contrariwise, *appétit qui est venu en mangeant* merely, or sporadic aphrodisiac patches only, regulated by atmospheric conditions, or intangible factors) – early upbringing of *Unknown Idiot*, in the highland-home – fingers in the porridge pot, tending of the shadowy, mist-wrapt kine (excellent training for subsequent attendance upon Lionel – boredom-proof it is to be assumed!): juvenile "complexes", little hopes and fears and infant vanities, hatred of vermicelli, imperfect acquaintance with classical idioms, french, shorthand – gallantry exhibited in early struggles brought to conclusion by the arrival of God's messenger, pawky Peggy: all this is wormed out of Keithie across space by letter after letter, that drew nearer by every post "admirer" and "admired". With heaviest modesty Li returns the compliment. Keithie is informed of what he ought to know – the salient facts – namely *the modest competence* that has enabled the "new writer" to produce his books without considering the Public – the age of the "new writer" (admirer let down gently with an "in middle-life", or "bleached and seared somewhat"), his infirmities – conspicuous amongst which is a love of truth and a tender and over-easily-touched heart (over which Isabel, his dear good consort, has sternly to mount guard) – his hopes, his fears, his infant-vanities, his boyish "complexes": and last but not least the beautiful character of his wife – that astonishing jewel that Heaven knows he does not deserve, but which was sent him to make of him anything that he had subsequently become – with her companionship, her helpfulness (especially that habit she has developed of amusing herself by writing books more or less, with Li's tremulous assistance). All the preliminary *épanchements*, in short, were discharged – calculated to lay the tearful, clayey foundations of a thousand and first "life-long friendship". – To all friends met with or to ill-paid hirelings Li exhibits the treasured newspaper-cutting, from the american paper. "*The only one of the whole lot who understands my Work!*" he exclaims. "He, my dear fellah, *knows what I'm driving at!* He's the only one so far!" There is one cutting he always keeps in his pocket – a duplicate of it he lends out – both are renewed in his methodical household like the ink in the inkpot, or the towel or the napkin, as it gets soiled, by the dependent detailed to such tasks. – But at long last the time approaches for Keith's return from foreign parts. A day of expectancy and then, behold, no longer through a glass darkly, but at last face to face –

Admired and Admirer. Lionel gives him one quick glance, opens his mouth and swallows him, in fact sucks him into every pore of his rickety old person and closes the lid. But Li has also to swallow, as best he can, *Missis* Keith, of course, which he does with a grimace or two. Lionel's "admirer" is then rapidly installed in a cottage a few miles from Falshwood Farm, his country house – and they all live happily ever afterwards so far. There is another aspect of this little romance that is not without a curious interest of its own. Lionel, as you know, since Proust's imposition of the pederastic motif upon post-war society, has not of course become a practioner – his years preclude that: but as far as possible he has worked into his scheme of things the pederastic pattern. Nothing if not in the swim, old Li: so he immediately on realizing the way the wind was blowing, secures a pederastic major-domo (our friend the butler), who is encouraged to ogle all his male guests in the hall, valse away with their coats and hats and so on – as you have seen. But Keith also has been dragged in and made to contribute to the same end. So now Lionel disputes the already half-devoured and over-chewed Keithie – approaching with senile impetuosity from the purist pederastic position, and driving straight to the proustian bull's-eye – while Missis K. simultaneously bears down from the angle of woman-love. – That is who *that* pair are. Next please!'

This had been delivered at a moderate pitch, in a rapid monotonous rattle. Some parts of it reached their neighbours, especially in the case of Violet Ashmele the entire volume was absorbed and rapidly shorthanded in the mind in the natural course of things. Zagreus's eyes frequently struck towards the people being described who however could hear nothing as Kalman was wrangling across them with Kein.

'And does the person you have just described now compose novels himself?' Dan asked.

'Undoubtedly. But I think Keith is encouraged more to be a *critic*. That is evidently his forte – I should say Kein was distinctly of that opinion. No, I don't think he must spend too much time in writing Fiction! A little poetry, that is a harmless pastime: but ambitions as a fictionist would cause difficulties. Then he has his living to make – the cottage, bought with Kein's money, has to be paid for! No, Keith is a *critic*, I think.'

Dan looked idly along from the Keiths towards Kalman.

'The cynic-philosopher of the Kein establishment' said Zagreus. 'Horty over there hardly needs explanation. He has been explaining himself one way and another ever since he sat down. The next are a Pierpoint couple – the lady Pierpoint was probably careless enough on one occasion to sleep with – so she bears within her unprepossessing person the promise of love's confidences. She has in other words, figuratively, a dirty scandalous little Pierpoint fœtus in her side. And like most such things, it would bear very little resemblance to the alleged original. She will be eagerly accouched later in private, by the Kein obstetric method – she exclaiming a little, perhaps – affecting to regard the operation as a painful one – a very painful one.'

Horty's blue mirthless lip lazily outlined a 'sardonic' smile as he remarked to his neighbour Bolsom:

'I can see what's going to happ'n to that ant-Mary – Zeggroost what's his name? *He's* going to get himself thrown out before long – that's what *he'll* do I guess!'

'Next, our hostess, who has set us this excellent example.' Horace fixed his eye, across Daniel Boleyn, upon Isabel Kein – and as though sketching her, looked up and down, from a point upon the table in front of Dan over to her face, and then back – to and fro in clockwork flashes, as he proceeded:

'Isabel, now, is "une forte tête" – I like old Isabel. It is a *sneaking* regard. She is capable – not attractive. That sort of "good-looks" usually causes me to shudder. But with Isabel, she drives her old well-polished and well-repaired chariot jauntily along – she is so sensible with her personality – that from the sheer good-sense of her handling of it one finds it (without its ever being anything but a barren and expensive fraud) yet not absolutely *unpleasant*. That is *the triumph of good-sense*. That is what it is. I do not at all mind Isabel. Her face has been lifted, they say, nineteen times – gathered behind the ear, you know, and laterally adjusted – she has had paraffin injections beneath the skin – she cannot see clearly more than a foot and a half: in spite of the fact that she eats nothing, Isabel is fat. Now you would expect the result to be depressing. I for my part do not find it so. How is that? Simply because she is so *sensible* about it! Her cosmetic operations and the rest of the ridiculous business of being *that* over there, she does not take that seriously – it is entered upon, and gone through with, with a perfect good-sense – coolly, "cynically", quite without pretence. The result is not a triumph of the face-surgeon's art, but of good-sense – always *good-sense*. – For the sort of person who would laugh at her for all that, for such she has (her intelligence enables her to justify it, make it prevail) a complete – a masterful – contempt. It is not for *them* that she hitches up her old sail and paints it a seductive pink – nor for anybody for that matter. It is on the same principle that persons wash their faces with care that she gets hers surgically refitted, it is hygiene rather than vanity. Good-sense everywhere corrects and as it were *makes all right* what in a less intelligent person would be repulsive and comic. Take again her writing habits – for she is in fact an Ape, it is she who writes his books rather than Lionel himself. I do not mean she writes them – Lionel is her medium – *he* writes them, she is the all pervasive editor. *Primrose* was all about herself, for instance – she would tell old Li some salient passage in her youth – he would go off and write it down, as well as any Boswell that ever held a pen. Then Boswell would return with the type-sheet. But this Doctor Johnson had something to say (who can doubt it?) in her own portrait – who would not? Yes, *there* was an extraordinary affair! It was a jumble of all the nice things anyone had ever said about her or that she had supposed people had ever thought. I came into it. The sweet things that *I* was supposed to have thought about Isabel made me rub my eyes at times! But again that book was not quite idiotic, as it might have been. *Good-sense* rescued Isabel, even there – when posing to herself as the seductive "Primrose". The same cool cheek, the unruffled craft, saved it from being what – in less capable, steady, emotionless hands – it undoubtedly would have become. A certain brazen contempt for themselves – that I think is the secret of the strength of such people. It is the under-dog virtue par excellence – as a truth-bearing virtue it is probably unsurpassed. It is not beautiful, anything but. – Of course Isabel is not by birth' Horace raised his voice slightly 'not the butterfly – the "social butterfly", as an aunt of mine on one occasion reproached me with being, not that at all – she is not a butterfly, really – she is a *clothes-moth*, one might call it. You may know by repute the famous Covent Garden misfit shop, Lazarus –'

As the name of the mendicant leper, the opposite to Dives, rang out from the lips of Zagreus, the fist of Isabel smote the table at her side.

'That's enough Zagreus! Take your latest boy somewhere else if you wish to slander people!' Isabel exploded, her breast heaving. Kein, who had been unable to hear anything at such a distance, had been signalled to anon. With a growing nervousness he had attempted to catch what his troublesome guest was saying – semaphoring repeatedly to his wife, reflecting her rising resentment, in his flashing glances. Now he jumped up and moved towards Zagreus, Mrs Kein at the same time shouting towards him:

'Turn him out! We've had enough of him! He's insulting everybody. He's *drunk!*'

'What – on cider-cup?' Zagreus indignantly protested. 'Isabel! Your *good-sense* should tell you that on such fare –'

'My good sense tells me you are a cad!'

'No not on cider-cup!' Horty agreed 'Something else has excited his head' looking significantly at Dan.

'My wife wishes you to leave Zagreus. Will you please do so, as you have annoyed everybody –'

'He has not annoyed everybody' Mrs Kein cried. 'He has insulted *me* – deliberately. Tell him to go – at once!'

Horace Zagreus sat looking with a smile of bewilderment about him.

'Mr Horty' he exclaimed 'I appeal to you as a gentleman and a foreigner, regarding our english ways with the impartiality of a stranger! Did you notice anything in my behaviour that seemed to you not to conform to the manners of this present company or that was in any way unworthy of our host and hostess?'

'You leave me out of it' Horty said, wriggling his lean bottom, and pulling down tightly his mirthless upper lips as though drily to sip a little tea – 'drily' smiling. 'I noticed a good deal, although only a foreigner.'

'You are very observant Mr Horty – I could tell that at once' said Zagreus pleasantly. 'I appealed to you in consequence. But you are not thoroughly acquainted with our ancient customs, I fear. It has always been among the habits of the ingaevonic and in a less degree of the celtic tribes, when at lunch, for the hostess to discuss all her guests in a loud voice, with some person selected for that purpose. But *also* and from time immemorial it has been the inalienable *right* of every tribesman (if he so wished) to discuss – with anyone he might select for that purpose – his hostess or any guest or guests he might choose – or indeed all together, one after the other. I have merely availed myself of our ancient british custom – obsolete, it is true, but recognized wherever men of our race foregather – as a precious and jealously-guarded privilege, always up everybody's sleeve at any moment. With the american procedure in such a case I am unacquainted.'

'In Amurr'ka I guess we're not so law-abiding as all that. But never mind about Amurr'ka – leave *me* out uv-utt Egg-roost!'

'Very well Mr Horty. I see that as a stranger – '

Kein tapped Zagreus upon the arm.

'I should like to have a word with you Zagreus.'

Zagreus suddenly sprang up and caught Kein by the arm.

'Of course, Li. But tell me about it later. You're such an impetuous, terribly impatient man!'

Heading Kein towards his empty seat at the bottom of the table, Horace gently led him towards it, Kein proceeding with him as though he were walking backwards.

'There Li. *After* lunch, my dear fellow – that will be plenty of time! Bad for the digestion!'

Mrs Kein, with a chair-noise like the angry clearing of a throat, rose, gathering her wrap around her heavy shoulders, and all the guests rose too – sliding out backwards between the chairs, and awkwardly standing looking from their hostess to Zagreus – the ladies initiating a herd-movement towards the door.

'Zagreus!' Isabel called harshly. 'You won't come here again, you understand, with your ridiculous boys! Find somewhere else in future to take them! The servants will have orders not to let you in. We have had enough of you.'

Swinging her heavy body majestically, she strode towards the door, which Anthony Horncastle opened, the ladies following. Zagreus made a deep bow towards her – remaining slightly inclined until she had left the room. He then went back to his seat and sat down, inviting Dan to follow his example.

'I think we'll go upstairs,' Kein said to the other men of the party. 'Hassan!' he called to the pale profile slipping out at the door at that moment. 'We will have the coffee upstairs. No – upstairs!'

'You see how peculiar they are,' Zagreus was saying to Dan. 'They will not have it that what is sauce for the goose is sauce for the gander. They advance instead some ancient usage of tribes to which we none of us here, as far as I know, belong.'

'Did they do that?' asked Dan, for he was at that moment an offended 'genius' – looking with sternest astonishment in the direction of Kein.

'No but they're quite capable of doing so.'

The last of the other guests had passed through the door on their way upstairs. Kein stopped and turned back towards the two seated figures.

'Zagreus' Kein's face was soured and sobered – his habits had met an obstacle, challenging in a new tongue his sad sweet dream at its mellowest.

'Sir?' Zagreus, throwing an arm over the back of the chair, turned towards him.

'You heard what Isabel said?'

'Yes, most of her remarks – though naturally some escaped me. You know that I am hard of hearing.'

'Well, you'll please come here no more. You hear that, I hope?'

'I can scarcely say with truth *I hear it*, but I *see* it – is that satisfactory?'

'Entirely, so long as you understand that you are to come to our house no more.'

'I may or I may not. Who can say?'

'You will not. The servants will have orders not to admit you.'

'I never take any notice of servants – except when forced to repel their advances.'

'Very well. Take that boy away as soon as possible.'

A sudden turbulence invaded the cloudless blue disks with their greek immortality of calm – like a reminder in an athenian brain of the cold landscapes behind the migrations – or the cloud imposed by the sun when it had struck him, ravelling the young images of life.

'Kein, you shall not insult a visitor here under my protection. You must confine your remarks to me.' But the cloud was driven back by a wild easy laugh as he regarded that old Li. 'Hurry away you crazy old humbug you or I shall begin weeping like the angels and laughing like Kalman at the same time, and you'll have to get an ambulance – and *pay for it mind!* They make a charge for bringing ambulances to private residences! You'll have to have me carried away – I shall be completely hors de combat if I look at you much longer. Shoo! Your turn is over. Look out – or the curtain will come down upon your head!'

'Be careful that it doesn't come down on yours!' Kein turned to the door. He started as he found a small stocky figure in a short jacket and 1830 hugoesque necktie, falling in a loose bow, who stood there demure and grim, awaiting him. A priest-like repression fixed the face, that of a wizened child, in sedate repose. Marking time duck-like, with a monotonous muscular oscillation, holding out a hand Vernède was saying:

'Goodbye – I must be off.'

As he recognized Vernède, Li exclaimed with annoyance:

'What – ? Aren't you coming upstairs?'

'I must go, I'm afraid.'

'Oh must you go now? Why? Come upstairs and have some coffee.'

'I have an appointment at sree.'

'Come on let's get out of this,' Mr Zagreus said to Dan, rising. 'Let us go and get a cup of coffee at that coffee-stall we passed on our way here. Better coffee there.'

Hassan was awaiting them in the hall, as Vernède, Dan and Mr Zagreus came out of the dining-room. His personality was steeped in the nostalgia induced by this humdrum service. Secret ecstasies haunted cloudily his face – he stood drooping – a funereally-clothed human monument of voluptuous absent-mindedness. Stationary butterflies, his eyes fluttered bashfully as the three visitors came into the hall. Then he turned towards the cupboarded room where the coats and hats were placed.

Kein retreated up the staircase from this region of unsatisfactory conflict, hurrying to the side of Isabel, who he knew would be awaiting him in the drawing-room. He saw her luminous myopic eyes of fierce enquiry – heard her few breathless words in an undertone, a certain hush among the guests. He began already forming the syllables: 'I told him to take his boy away as soon as possible. (She will want to know just what I said. *Take your boy away* yes.) I told him we had had enough of him. *Yes he's gone.*' He glanced back over the banisters. Zagreus was looking up at him and now rushed to the foot of the stairs exclaiming:

'Shoo! Phuist!' with gestures to hasten the departure of an animal. Kein's batrachian muzzle stuck over with its bristling military moustache – the toffee eyes behind the spectacles – stared solemnly down – the black loosely-hanging frustrum of the cranky trunk above the rail, and, beneath the ascending ornamented soffit, the shining linen – the cigar held in the hand – remained a moment as though commanded to stand still by some supernatural agency – immobilized to gaze inscrutably down into the twilit well of the hall.

'Basilisk. Pecksniff!' Zagreus shouted with a gesture of banishment and dismissal. 'Acabada la comida! *Finished!*'

*

When they were in the street Zagreus started at once walking to the right, Dan folllowing, with Vernède attaching himself hastening to keep up. Coming abreast of Zagreus, Vernède upon the outside, the belgian said:

'What was ze matter between you and Kein?'

A Stage latin-quarter artist, Vernède expressed himself in a Stage-Frenchman's english, of *zee* and *zat*.

Zagreus looked straight into the sun, for now it was bright. *Remember albino!* That was still in his mind. *Remember albino!*

'I think Li was a little oiled nothing more – if he'd only drink the same stuff he provides for his guests, all would be well.'

'Ah you are right! What wine! I did not know zat zair was such a drink possible!'

'He gets overtired you know – he works, as he calls it, too hard. At his age he oughtn't to play the Proust. It's very bad for him, I am sure I couldn't. On top of that he is apt to drink, not too much perhaps for a normal person, but for him – to repair the waste.'

'He gets vair-ee tired!'

'It's a bad system all round, there's no getting away from it.'

'A ver-ree bad sys-tame!'

'But he is an ungrateful old parasite – he has the sense to attract people of vitality, but he skives them down – takes fright at the flight of a mosquito if it is *money*, as though it were a veritable Flight of Capital. And he is jealous, too, of *power* – it is that that makes him so ugly.'

'That is the chew!' Vernède vehemently observed, illuminating his nearest eye with a chauvinistic light. 'They can't help themselves – where it is money zey are *mad!*'

Zagreus also gave him only one eye, and their two single eyes manœuvred for a moment in their profiles, one with its large massive prominent beak, the other with its crushed and puckered smeller.

'When people fall out' Zagreus remarked 'they always call each other "dirty dagos" "dirty Jews", "dirty Germans" or whatever they happen to be respectively. Yet that is surely the very moment when they should, instead, insist upon the individual person, more than at any other time – rather than upon vague generalizations.'

'I agg-ree!' exclaimed Vernède. 'Off gorse!'

'Supposing you are having a dispute with a Spaniard. You call him a "dirty dago". That transfers at once all the indignation at your command to the whole race, instead of concentrating it upon *him* – from a man to a pentagonal peninsular.'

'But do I not *know!*' howled Vernède with passionate conviction – as if it had been just *that* he had been endeavouring to express.

'*Or* on the other hand you call a person "Ill-bred", a "bounder", or what not – he referring to you in the same manner. That transfers the offence to a usually entirely fictitious *class*. I have never heard a man call another "*a dirty human being*" – though it is true you often hear such an expression as "bloody woman" – as though that meant anything: or "bloody male" I have heard.'

'I too have heard zat!'

'So the *sex* gets what you intend for the *individual.* Look here, if I were angry with Kein – as Heaven help me I am not – I should call him *Kein,* I should leave the jewish jibe out of it. I don't believe in "Jews", "Dagos" and so on, either. They are vulgar myths – but that's another matter.'

'Yes but all zee same, Kein is a *chew* – zat is not nothing!' Vernède objected.

'Yes and I have known persons who were Jews whom I respected more than the cabbages of christians by whom they were surrounded!' Zagreus protested energetically.

'Oh do not speak to me of zee *chreestian!*' Vernède implored him in a screech – putting the points of his index-fingers to his ears, as though to keep out the noise of the 'chreestian' cabbages.

'Kein is a *bad* specimen of his kind, that is the trouble.'

'Zat is it!'

'He is an idle – '

'Oh he is *fear*-full-ee idle!'

'pretentious – '

'What does he *not* pretend!'

'old busybody of a succubus he is!'

'Ha ha!' exclaimed Vernède, his eyebrows levitating alarmingly above his eyes: 'a *succubus!* Il est un veritable succube!'

'He is no advertisement for any people.'

'People in all zee races are like zat!' Vernède shouted fiercely.

'Yes' Zagreus stormed back, grinning broadly at the romantic ghost at his side: 'when we meet an Englishman like that we do not say "Dirty Englishman"!'

Vernède laughed in glad false mirth – for he was very angry.

'You *can* not do zat ard-*lee!*'

'No because then we should be calling ourselves "dirty" too, by implication. We have to leave it in that case as a judgment upon an individual. Smith, or Jones, is a dirty dog we say – that is the idea! That is more precise.'

'Ha ha! yes – zat is what zenn you must do!' came the breathless Stage-french chorus of Monsieur Vernède.

'With Kein I prefer to do that too,' said Zagreus, as they rushed along.

'Off gorse!' Vernède breathlessly rejoined. And then very

quietly, with a black look, Vernède put the snub away into a dark place – where many snubs of all ages were collected. The 'Off gorse!' had been violently forced up, an example of self-respecting submission. A turbulent silence filled in after it.

As they passed the tunnelled entrance to a Mews, a figure stood looking up and down the street: then it remarked with emphasis into the mouth of the tunnel:

'I-shant-get-a-bloody-break-down-not-a-goin-on-as-I-'ave-bin-lately!'

A bark of enquiry came out of the tunnel.

'I-shan't-get-no-bloody-break-down-not-goin-on-way-I-'ave-bin-lately!' the figure shouted.

A fresh bark of gruff uncertainty came from the tunnel.

'I sed, I-shant-get-no-bloody-break-down-not-goin-on-same-as-I-as-bin-not-lately!'

They left this figure behind – his hands in his overcoat-pockets, looking up and down the road.

Ahead of them, from a street running at right angles to the one they were descending, appeared an airy, well-dressed form. 'The swan, Youth' said Mr Zagreus. Almost immediately afterwards the dark bulk of a police-constable rolled forth from the same spot.

'Health!' said Dan.

'The Duck!' said Zagreus.

'Helse zee Duck!' exclaimed Vernède.

As a third figure rose to the pavement painfully from an area they cried in chorus.

'The Toby-jug!'

Vernède laughed, and nodded his head, sharpening his eyes up and down the figure.

'Yes! you are right. Eet-eess a Toby-jug!'

'Over there is a figure that has not got its abstraction on – he's left it at home or – what do you say? – *has never had one!*' Zagreus pointed.

Dan scrutinized the bilious indifferent face of the passer-by indicated by Horace as naked, unclothed in *abstraction*.

'I think he's got one on that we can't see,' said Zagreus.

At the head of the road they were ascending three figures rapidly appeared to meet – to clash like billiard balls, and to disperse in different directions, calling out noisily as they receded from one another. One approached them rapidly with a market-porter's soiled jacket too long for him – a jaunty, fife-and-drum, mechanical kick of the heel, as his little legs danced under the jacket.

'There we have *Race* I believe – a cockney incarnation' said Mr Zagreus: 'some scrubby little fighting-cock, hastening to draw a ration!'

His eyes upon the man's feet – with their jaunty lift, and deft flash of the heel – acrobatic, a trained dog – Mr Zagreus followed him a moment.

'With him' he said to Vernède 'you could fairly apply your "dirty" categories, I should say!'

'Yes!' Vernède heartily hastened, emphatically assenting – eyes pursuing the quick-travelling object to show, politely, that he was attentive, and that their minds indeed worked in unison – as did the trotting cockney-feet.

The three tramped forward: the Sunday coffee-stall was reached, a flotilla of taxis beside it. Collected beneath its projecting flap, they ordered coffee.

'You have known Kein a long time?' Vernède enquired of Zagreus.

'Oh yes.'

'He frrightens me *you* know!' Vernède smiled primly and coquettishly. 'Vair-ree much!' he added lifting his eyebrows delicately. Then he added, dilating his eyes and mouthing his words 'Not for *myself! Forruthaires!* Always I find myself afraid – I am afraid that he will *swallow* zem up!'

Vernède with his toothless gums chewed imaginary mouthfuls.

'Yes he's a man-eater, only he's so small.'

'Yes but he is *dangerous*' Vernède said looking very serious. 'When I see some new person at his house, I am frright-tent at zee way Li opens his *eyes!* And – his *mowss!*' he made saucers of his eyes and mouth, like a nurse engaged in an account of the story of Red-Riding-hood. 'He devours zem, he sucks zem in – he *inhales* zem! It is, you know – how do you say it in english? *touchantgo!*'

'Touch and go indeed, but he always ends by biting them.'

'He can't help himselve!' Vernède was confidentially emphatic.

'For my part' said Zagreus 'I always feel more anxiety for the objects of Kein's parasitic interest when the stage of the first breathless inhalation is over. When he has thoroughly warmed himself under the skin and begins to make himself at home – subsequent to the first great crisis of inquisitiveness – then comes a period when he is really obnoxious.'

'I should have believed zat Kein was already enough so – *far* before zat stage mon dieu!' Vernède answered, a little dour. Zagreus finished his coffee and they left the stall.

'I go *ziss* way!' said Vernède, pointing to the western exit from the large square in which they were standing.

'We this way, I think' and Zagreus pointed away from Vernède's route.

When he had left them, Zagreus moved his head softly after him and said.

'Pierpoint stresses very much the necessity of never allowing people to use cheap class-abuse. He won't allow you to say even "he is an ignorant man". You have to say – "Smith is ignorant." As to nations, and social classes, he would throw his hands up in despair if he heard you making the sort of generalizations indulged in by that little Belgian.'

Dan looked at him steadfastly.

'I know I should not have said that – I am glad you noticed,' said Zagreus, shamefaced. 'I did not mean either "*little*" or "*Belgian*" – those were both slips of the tongue.'

He looked over his shoulder. Vernède was out of sight.

'Kein on one occasion got rather excited and offered to set up Vernède in a bookshop – for art-books, first-editions and so forth. Next day of course Vernède received a note to the effect that Li much regretted, but that on making enquiries at his bank he found – *or* that owing to unexpected calls he was unable – *or* that thinking it over he did not see his way – *or* that he was so upset at the thought of Vernède abandoning his literary work and wasting his time selling books to stupid people – in fine, that he – The old old story! It is always the same – Kein never fails one, he knows he never fails one – in that way. And when he knows you know him and he can't humbug you any more, he grows defiant and morose. He can never feed on you again. Once you *know* – you cease producing the milk he depends on. Also, although he has no "pudeur", he hates being watched at work – that puts him off his feed too. – What did you make of him?'

Dan frowned – he brought his mind to bear upon Kein as best he could.

'Not much I expect.'

'He did not seem to understand,' said Dan slowly.

'That is it' said Horace. 'And Isabel?'

'She did not seem to understand' there was a long pause, and then Dan precipitately added 'at all.'

'How true that is – that is it ! – I like old Isabel' said Zagreus: 'a *sneaking* regard – but they do go splendidly together. Li and she. We will go there again and have another look at them!'

As they were about to part at the bus-halt, Dan said slowly,

'I wish I knew Pierpoint.'

Zagreus appeared much taken aback – he caught his breath. Then looking a little askance at his pupil he said,

'That's impossible. But you wouldn't get on – I will tell you all about Pierpoint – I am his Plato.'

And the bronzed albino left his disciple laughing – saying 'I am his Plato!'

[illegible] and [illegible] that on whatever you have [illegible] pronouncing the [illegible] depends on. Also, [illegible] the latter being [illegible] at work [illegible] What did you make of him?'

'He [illegible] – he brought this and [illegible] he could.'

'Not much I expect.'

'He did not seem to understand,' said Dan slowly.

'That is it,' said [illegible]. 'And Isabel?'

'She did not seem to understand [illegible]' There was a long pause, and then Dan [illegible], added [illegible].

'How true that is – [illegible] the [illegible],' said [illegible] and [illegible] – but this [illegible] together. I [illegible] We will go there again and have [illegible]

As they were about to part at the [illegible], Dan said slowly, 'I [illegible] point.'

[illegible] much [illegible] reached [illegible] a little [illegible] at his point he [illegible].

'[illegible] impossible, but you wouldn't [illegible] I will tell you about [illegible] later.'

And [illegible] let his [illegible] – saying, 'I am the [illegible]'

Part 10

WARNED FOR DUTY AT LORD OSMUND'S

WILLIE SERVICE, dressed as a chauffeur, entered Daniel Boleyn's spartan quarters – a letter in one hand, a philosopher's egg in the other. In sheer sombre smartness he exsuperated all known car-flunkeys – surely with busks in breast and bum – with a more than military bombasting. Civilly he removed his official conning-cap and dust-goggles.

'Well' he said '*what of the newt?*'

Blandly affording the ground for an objection of crambe bis cocta, he cocked his eye at his marsh-mallow of a master.

Dan shook his head mournfully. He knew nothing of the newt! But he was alarmed at the formal nature of the costume in which Willie Service had thought proper to disguise himself upon this occasion. He feared that it boded no good for anybody, least of all himself.

'A letter for you sir' said Willie.

With a wan smile Dan took it and held it in his hand.

'Here is this too – it is a philosopher's egg.' Willie handed him the egg. Dan accepted the egg, and he held that in the other hand.

'That's all' said Willie Service.

Dan reconnoitred his posh livery more in sorrow than in anger.

'I'm detailed for field-work. I'm in on this,' said Willie Service.

'On what?' said Dan, blushing at this language of high-handed complicity.

'I have to taxi you down.'

Dan looked with infinite sadness into the distance – his feet were hurting and he had no vaseline.

'Aren't you going to slit up the letter?' asked the factotum.

Dan considered the new-laid philosopher's egg and sighed.

'I have blown out the albumin and popped in the saffron. Any complaints?'

Dan dropped the egg upon the floor.

'What a fool you are! Can't you even hold an egg!'

Willie Service picked up the egg – it was a salmon-yellow hen's-egg with smears of dung. He examined it. It was only a little crushed in upon one side.

'I suppose I shall have to get you another. If you break that I shall leave you to your fate. You'll probably get gastritis. Look out!'

Dan shivered slightly at his cross tone and veiled threat and he had a shooting pain in his bad toe. His nose began to bleed, but not very much. He took a handkerchief out of his pocket and held it over his nostrils.

Willie Service went to the door and removed the key.

'All right. Lie down. I'll put this key down your back!'

Dan, still holding the letter, got down upon his rude pallet, and Willie Service thrust the large key down his back. Dan shuddered.

'I will go and make another philosopher's egg,' said Willie Service.

'Thanks awfully,' said Dan.

'Don't bleed to death while I'm gone. – Turn the key round when it gets hot.'

Dan blushed and the blush came down his nose as hæmoglobin.

At the door Willie Service turned.

'Haven't you slit up the letter?'

Dan had not slit up the letter. He held it upon his chest like a missal.

Willie Service went back to the table and threw a table-knife at Dan.

'Here, slit up the letter. It's important.'

Willie Service then left the room smartly.

For some time Dan lay still, bleeding gently and dozing. Then he picked up the knife and slit up the letter. Horace's superscription was within.

DIRECTIONS FOR LORD OSMUND'S PARTY,

That was in Horace's big dainty hand! Dan fanned himself slowly with the letter. Who was Lord Osmund and what party was this! Oh how his feet hurt him! He had just returned at full speed from three parties (he could not walk slowly) at one of which Horace had been present but in the company of an extremely objectionable person of the same religion as that other horrid man who had said such beastly things to him about Horace and whom Horace called *Split*. He simply disliked from the bottom of his great irish heart *this* one however – he was a young man. He was more horrid than *Split* altogether, and talked very quickly and rudely he thought – very. He had a name like margarine. He had been distinctly uncivil and *once* quite unkind! He could not understand Horace associating! He could swear to it on oath that once Horace had laughed up his sleeve at something that disgusting young man had said in his ear and he was positive that *he* had been the subject – turning, with one accord – he had been sitting at the time and observing closely a lady-Ape who had wanted to play with the piano but she had not been allowed. Horace had been first and last all through the party terribly unkind!

His log swarmed with the names and addresses of Apes, he was tired of writing down their descriptions: and now here was another great party and masses of new Apes in 'spectacular' rendezvous! And what had Willie Service done yesterday? (He was a madcap he knew but there were some things beyond a joke – off and on he believed he was not responsible, his actions discovered it!) When Daniel was out on a night-party he had obtained possession of Dan's log, and he had written in it in a facsimile handwriting that had quite imitated his to a turn, several disgusting remarks that he had found by the purest of accidents when he came back though he might never have done so and what would Horace have thought? He was dismayed! What he wrote was soft-headed mischievousness but not what you would expect. 'Met' (he had written in the calligraphy of Daniel – as though he had written it) 'an Ape of God (Paris Exhibition 1898 first class diploma) called Horatio Zagrust, née Follett, a bombastic faggot if ever was – called bronze albino, tropically tanned but pink underneath, (homo sapiens, not homo sexual) sixty Summers, and one dull Spring – who says we are gibbering gibbons but what about himself?' – In the own identical handwriting of Dan it was scribbled as large as life, as an entry of the week-before-last. And for an hour at least had Dan not been compelled to go over the whole of his log, entry by entry, and scrutinize every sentence – to make sure Willie Service had done nothing else in a cruel attempt to disgrace him! The offensive impersonation in question he had torn out of the book and burnt it and how he could explain its absence, that the page was not there at all, he did not know – he must say it got lost or fell out, or the best thing yet, that some Ape crept in when he wasn't looking and snatched it out of his note-book, because it was about himself and he had got wind of the log he was making and feared to be shown up for the creature he was! That was it!

Still, to business! What was this new thing in store for him? So he read – though he did not understand much of it especially about the dress:

This is the greatest battue of full-grown man-eating – and Lion-hunting Apes – to which you have so far been summoned. I have designed it to serve as a grand culmination to your apprenticeship. If you come through this with flying colours you may regard yourself as a Bachelor of the Gentle Art of Bearding the Ape in his Drawing-room. It has been announced in every Gossip-column in Fleet Street as a great Lenten Freak Party. Our part in this pantomime will in this instance be a sufficiently important one to require the support of two other individuals at least, and I have chosen (to fill the rôles indicated by the social commitment I have entered into) Mr Julius Ratner on the one hand and upon the other a very brilliant young man indeed (whom you have recently met) Archibald Margolin – whom I suspect of having just *a touch* of genius – how much I cannot say as yet.

The party occurs at the house of Lord Osmund Willoughby Finnian Shaw, in the country, at a distance of forty miles from Charing-Cross, at his Lordship's week-end country-estate, Jays Mill Manor Farm. Lord Osmund, the senior, more or less male, offspring of the Marquis of Balbriggan, is a master-Ape. It is with him well-nigh *a craft* – he makes of Apehood a true business – not of course that he earns money by it (for no Ape can be an Ape unless he is quite rich, and no one has ever yet been found who is fool enough to pay an Ape a penny-piece for any piece of Apery). But he takes Apery very seriously indeed: whereas his expertness and his method entitle him, in the great freemasonry of Apehood, to the title of grand-master-craftsman of all branches of Ape-work whatever.

Very luckily for you Daniel the Finnian Shaws afford the lively spectacle of how Apehood may affect an entire family, for apparently all the relatives of Lord Osmund (even as far removed as second-cousins from the primum mobile, Lord Osmund in person) are slightly tainted. There is no Finnian Shaw at all who without warning is not liable to advertise himself at any moment, in however modest a way – abruptly revealing himself as a lampoonist, a zither-player or precious minor poet or stunt-historian.

The details of the rôle expected of us at this party – we are going there not as guests but as performers – will be unfolded when we meet. I am having conveyed to you a parcel, which will contain a costume. I suggest you accustom yourself to this by wearing it for some hours before you are to be fetched – that will be at four sharp tomorrow afternoon. – Service will inform you of anything you may wish to know. No rehearsal will be necessary for the part assigned to you. It is a *simple* one.

Horace Zagreus

Dan put down this document with one sensation uppermost and one sensation all along the line – namely, that Horace in every respect and to the vanishing point of susceptibility, was perfectly generous – perfectly kind! Even the prospect of the presence of Margolin did not throw a shadow. Horace had selected for him a *simple* part, where he would not have to walk about too much and make his feet sore and even in that Horace showed his thought for him. Dear Horace! *Dear* Horace! – Dan fell asleep.

[illegible] These [illegible]
breathless [illegible]

Very likely [illegible] the Horace Shaws afford [illegible] an entire family [illegible] apparently [illegible] of Lord Cannon [illegible] aspect [illegible] Lord Cannon in [illegible] without [illegible] to advertise himself at any moment [illegible] any [illegible] a philosopher [illegible] poet or statesman.

The details of the fête expected of us at this party, we are going there [illegible] will be provided when we meet. I am having conveyed to you a parcel which will contain a costume. I suggest [illegible] you [illegible] wearing it [illegible] before you are to be finished. [illegible] be at five sharp tomorrow afternoon. [illegible] will inform you of anything you may wish to know. No rehearsal will be necessary for the part assigned to you. It is a [illegible] one.

Horace Hopkins

[illegible] put down [illegible] the [illegible] and [illegible] namely, that Horace in every respect and to the [illegible] point [illegible] was perfectly [illegible] have the prospect of [illegible] presence [illegible] turn [illegible] He had elected for him a simple part, where he would not have to [illegible] about [illegible] and make his [illegible] and even in that there [illegible] for him. Dear Horace! [illegible]

Part II

MR ZAGREUS AND THE SPLIT-MAN

i

SLIDING along the hedgerows, a new figure approached the cottage. A profile with an edge, it cut its way warily through the twilight. The cross eye, with its lids like films, fine frowning scroll of hair hooked to the apex of the hooked nose, examined the gate. With an impatient slothfulness a sleek hand snatched from a pocket shook it. It wrenched at the jamming latch. At the doorway a felt hat was removed, fingers pushing the reddish hair. The nails softly guided the cold hair, collecting it as though familiar with each bristle, smoothing it so as to throw a thin mist over the baldness in the centre.

Butting upwards, like an animal constrained to an evolution not proper to it, the asiatic profile with the frowning eye forced its way stealthily up the stairs – the slice of scalp skimming the damp soffit, which led, a gothic trail, to the bedroom.

At the door this visitor stopped, knocked twice softly. A vegetative eye fastened upon the handle. Adhering, a fungus growth of moody displeasure sprang up and multiplied itself in a moment. Had his thoughts possessed a material projection, a dense cluster most like a museum specimen of polypifers, would have been swelling about the metal knob.

He could not have knocked more softly or looked more darkly, if he had been some priggish Mephisto drawn to this meeting by impertinent magic. Magnetically the cross eye reconstructed what was the other side of the obstacle – the filmed eagle-eye of the snake stabbed out in wrath towards its unseen adversary.

Now keep me waiting! (spat the thoughts of the visitor). Yes that's right – keep me waiting! *Have I the money?* No – *I haven't!* I'd kick the door down the filthy devil! I can hear him breathing (smoking a cigarette he's inhaling). *He* knows the buck-ger – when I go in he'll ask me if I've got the money. Yes why *am* I standing here – I don't know why I stand it absolutely. I'm standing here for nothing – *swine!* (The visitor rapped and kicked). Always pretending – *as if this door!* This is typical –

shell within shell – he expects people to stand outside like servants, tap and wait – oh buck-ger!

(He threw a spasm into his body, and it reversed the disposition of its muscles, his shoes scraping the floor.)

He knocked twice again, angrily and sharply.

At once a *come-in* sounded, very near, with a wounding composure.

He turned the handle: he was at the bottom of a bed. On this a masked figure lay.

'Well, milord!' the visitor said and veiled his sickly smile beneath his yellow lids and lips – allowing it to shine bashfully towards the bed. He worked his neck like a chicken, throwing his eyes coyly to this side and that to see where he could deposit his hat.

'I'm not Lord Rochester. I am Mr Zagreus. Close the door,' the masked figure said.

He closed the door. As he stepped forward again, Mr Zagreus beat him back with his hand.

'Back! back! There – at your elbow, Julius. Dip your fingers in that stoup. A simple lustration. Forgive me – You understand. Just dip. A little domestic perirranterion.'

'Is it necessary?' the mincing guttural and croaking voice sneered – while obediently, placing his hat upon the foot of the bed, he dipped his fingers in a grey ewer placed upon a chair beside the door.

'It's always as well, Julius. One can't be too particular. You will feel better after it yourself.'

'I see,' Julius Ratner drawled, holding his wet hands limply towards the floor. He became astatic. His uneasiness was localized to hip-movements of a graceful type, which threw his head into opposition on each occasion – so that first it dwelt upon the ground with its contemplative eye directed to one side, and then transferred itself to the other, the eye-beam always aimed over the projection of the unflexed hip.

'Do you want a towel, Julius? There is one.'

'Ought I to wipe it off?'

'I think you might now.'

The masked Mr Zagreus had not moved, except for wavings of the hand and arm. He lay sprawled in shirt and trousers. The russet half-mask, in the feeble light, gave him a personality of the *commedia del arte* – and the little room, with clothes flung about, the yellow light of the candles, helped the suggestion that this was a resting acrobat. Ratner, with the movements slinky and dead of sluggish deliberation, or those of a circumspect machine, with a careful veneer of gauche grace, went to the washing-stand. His fingers were dabbed upon the towel, and then drawn up and down over its rough surface.

He then turned, the eyebrow crossly hooked, the eye abstracted.

'Sit down,' Mr Zagreus said again. He held out to him the obtruding member of the phallic hand. Ratner took it for a moment as he sat down.

'I am having a hundred winks, before setting out for the party. We may be late. We shall have to tell all their fortunes. That fool Kit Hanna has told them that, like Simon Magus, I can walk through walls, and that Helen of Troy is my mistress.'

'What a fool!'

'Yes, Kit Hanna is a terrible fool. He is a terrible, terrible fool! He trespasses upon the best side of one's nature – the whole time. He treads it down. He seems to think it's there for him. All that expense. He will not understand it is there for – oneself. Kit Hanna – '

'What *are* you doing?' sneered Ratner sheepishly. For while he had been talking Mr Zagreus had been licking his improper digit and sticking it up his nose. Subsequently Ratner had seen him boring into his ears with the same spittle-anointed finger.

'Disinfecting Kit Hanna.'

Horace Zagreus lay with his hands upon his chest, and the wedge of the right thumb protruded from between the fingers of the left hand.

'Is that for Kit Hanna as well?' Ratner croaked. 'Is it necessary to *far la fica?* Am I so dangerous Horace?'

'No one is dangerous if properly handled. Those of us who are bad managers have to resort to magic.'

'I see. Have you got my costume Horace? I am sorry I was a little late – '

'Yes. I hope you will like it. Everybody would not. But you are a peculiar fellow. I wish I could have found a *beau rôle* for you – '

'There can be only one *beau rôle!*'

'I don't see that. It is your vanity that teaches you to think that.'

'Not at all!' Ratner retorted, polite and spirited.

'I should have liked, Julius, to have fitted you out as a homunculus, a disembodied mind. Or as the Holy Ghost – the most tremendous of all the feminine rôles. You might, for that matter, have gone to the party as the Paraclete.'

Ratner, his legs crossed, had his sallow eye fixed upon the mask, which continued:

'You remember in the Symposium the account of the creation in which the eight-limbed cylinder is severed, and as man and woman we make our first dramatic appearance?'

'I can't say I do – I am not a Greek like you – that is not the ancient literature of *my* race. But go on please Horace!'

'That's a pity. In any case there is a distinct threat contained in the prophetic mind of the son of Sophroniskos that if we go from bad to worse we may be subjected to a *further* slicing up, and find ourselves with only ONE leg, eye, arm, and so forth – instead of the present more ample symmetrical arrangement.'

Julius Ratner kept silence.

'But that, my dear Julius, is neither here nor there. It has nothing more than a bearing upon what I have to suggest.'

Ratner buried his thoughts in his silence, and hooked his eye high upon his forehead.

'I have not been able to dispose of an impression I have of you Julius – rather, I have relied upon that impression to work out the make-up. I think it points to a very good disguise. I have fitted you out with the few necessary things – there they are, in that brown paper parcel.'

He paused, recommencing with conventional seductiveness, as though upon the threshold of an argument:

'*Suppose* that you have lain so long in the depths – at the foundation of the world (if it does not make you giddy or uncomfortable to contemplate such a spot) – and that, like the Pleuronectidæ, you have grown facially all on one side – I hope it is not asking you too much to imagine that? At all events, by that road we shall get at the idea. For you are to be something that this figure will help you to realize. You are the terrible Barin Mutum, or African Half-man. What is that? Nothing to do with the Socratic variety. Forget the great deeps, too. I have just been reading about this creature. He must be one of the most formidable demons in the world at his weight. The Arabs call him Split-man, it seems. It is a being split down longitudinally. He has therefore one eye, one arm – leg, hand and foot.'

Mr Zagreus touched his eye, arm, leg, hand, and he pointed towards his foot.

'There is the Persian Nimcharah, or Half-face – you may have heard of? The Zulus even believed in a whole tribe of such Split-men. They describe how one day these half-people came across a Zulu girl. They examined her. "The thing is pretty," they said. "But oh the *two legs!*" – You get the idea of this being?'

'I think I see what you mean,' Ratner said as darkly as though the door had separated them, and the filmed eagle-eye of the snake were stabbing at the obstruction. The mask was retained to insult him – it was a more intimate, a more offensive obstruction.

'The Barin Mutum is as swift as the ostrich. He is also reputed to be as cruel and as dangerous as the snake!'

Julius Ratner sneered, the colour very slightly mantling his sallow skin.

'So the impression I give is that of a Half-man?'

'Exteriorly I always think of you in profile – like a bas-relief, you know. You always seem to me to be looking at me *sideways* – like a bird.'

'Really! You read a great deal into me Horace that is not there I fear – I never knew I was so interesting,' Ratner croaked – his assumed worldliness breaking and cracking, the primitive gutturals getting the upper hand.

'I know Julius, I know what you say is true – you bore yourself terribly. But you were made for *me*, not for yourself. – I supply the *interest* Julius.'

'Indeed you do Horace!'

'But there is another point or two. Do you happen to have read any of the Phan-Khoa-Tau – the Taoist book of esoteric doctrine? No? That now supplies us with the *side*. The Taoist recommends you to LOVE your left side – where the heart is kept – and to despise your right – that is the side of *energy*.'

'So am I left Horace – ?'

'No – don't let's run before we can walk. No, Julius, it appears to me to be the other way round. You are a *right*-sided split-man, with the liver in place of the heart. – I suggest this because otherwise the dragon is liable to bite you. Although the Taoist regards this as a favourable accident, I don't feel myself justified in laying you open to that.'

'You are very kind. I'm sorry though, that you won't let me have a heart.' A strained, cowed smile was fixed upon the face of the weaker, the heartless vessel.

'I only want you to be right. The Half-man is evidently a right-hand man. I am afraid all half-men are right-hand men. The heart is a superfluity. The whole left side is useless – embarrrassing and really far beyond our human means. Our purse is not long enough. *I can barely afford it myself*. My left side is a façade – but of course it is there.'

Ratner rose and picked up the parcel.

'Very well. I will be your right-hand man for to-night.'

'You are my Jinn, my dear Julius. You are in my power. I elect you to be my servant: as you say – *for to-night*. Not for a permanency, Julius. I wish I could! But you would be a very thieving servant, and I can't afford such parasites as you. Some day, perhaps. Not now! Don't worry about the side, Julius. There *is* an alternative.'

'I am glad to hear that! What is it?'

'According to Taoist theory by turning my back to the audience, and calling you my brother, I could supply you with the missing heart – though the wrong way round. But I don't see how you would benefit by that.'

'That wouldn't matter at all, so long as you could supply my deficiency.' Ratner looked indifferently into the opening in the parcel. 'Well, I will go and put this on I suppose.'

'I suppose so.'

Watched out in silence, Ratner closed the door quietly. He

stood a moment at the stairhead, his thin bow-legs arched carefully in the dark – examining with their extremities, through the thin leather of his shoes, his foothold.

His journey to his inn appeared to him in its totality, as though it were a rope he had to pull in, or a drugget to roll up. He addressed himself to this, a ruffled mechanism. But the same split-man as arrived returned once more, lightly and swiftly – out of the gate, along the hedgerows.

ii

The masked figure has lain laughing at the split-man, and has addressed himself to his own disguise. In a half-hour the heavy toilet may be said to be complete, percoct in his literary kitchen.

'Aah-Tehuti!' he cried, 'seed-moon, grain-moon, great arithmetical wanderer – water-wizard, shower-bath, shaman of the sky – shechinah of our halting judgments, *god of lunatics*, tell me where my cob and wand has got to! Flash down your roving light!'

He grovelled beneath the bed, and found what he had been looking for.

Upright once more, glancing out of the window, he said, 'Pardon. I did not notice you were so small'; as though, having been exhorting to love an exhausted man, he had suddenly observed the malapropos.

There, in the thrilling chasm of the sky, the ever-vivid meniscus was visible.

The masked figure kisses his hand to it as an attic husbandman would to the new sun, and he turned the little silver coins in his pocket. He wished. His wish was a child's prayer – monotonous with happiness. This tsabian gesture exposed a large bronzed hand, which he now began to darken further – with sunburn powder, purchased in Lausanne, sold to alpinists.

The low window, over whose sashes he looked, allowed the mild tranquillity of the night to flow in. The candle in front of the mirror, only disturbed by the maternal pressures of the atmosphere or the more eccentric movements of the man, shed its light upon the small room. It made arbitrary graded zones of the accidental scene – with its position, its colour and particular incandescence – as does the eye of the painter with the objects of his world.

A small iron bedstead, a table beside it, with a cloth of dyed lockram – a chair, a stool, clothes hanging like a carcass in a stall gaping and sagging – handless, footless, and without head: two shelves of books: an open creel which had contained his disguise and the material of that of Ratner, a mat of stained hemp bristles.

A pergamene mask of coarse malignity through the eye-holes in the tawny canvas fixed fiery eyes upon the mirror – or that speck on it representing a comedo imbedded in his jaw, which his fingers were removing. He snipped the last tell-tale vibrissa.

Sputum gathered upon the brutal lips – cracks represented with darker paint, manufactured for this masquerade. He tugged the black lambskin of the beard to the left. He stepped back, examining again the symmetry of his composite clown.

Six feet from head to foot he was composed as follows – like a Mexith's renowned statue bristling with emblems:

A large hat, the crown of which was the mask, representing in a projecting horn, pointing upward, the beak of the Ibis: a miniature representation of the Atef crown of Thoth.

A pearl upon the front of the hat, beneath the beak or horn – the Urna or third eye of Siva.

A pearl at the back of the hat to stand for the pineal eye.

A green feather at the side from the crest of Huitzlipochtli.

The mask was a canvas vizard stopping at the nostrils.

Inside the eye-sockets a film of white rose from the lower lid.

Very long coarse lashes formed fans above and below the opening.

Small ears, like a goat's, displayed their pointed conches high up among the discreet tufts of black hair.

The forehead drove its centripetal furrows to the apex of the nasal bones.

Upon his breast was pinned a bunch of forgetmenots.

Round the neck hung an Anguinum – egg composed of saliva from the jaws, and froth from the bodies of snakes, produced in their knotted summer sleep, propelled upwards by their hissing, and caught by the Druid in his apron.

Below this came a gilt necklace of twenty hearts.

Below this hung the disk of a monstrance, only in place of the cross was a thermuthis.

The mantle of Graziano – corrugated like a peplum – fell from the shoulders and swept the ground.

A black fustian jerkin, with large silk buttons like plovers' eggs.

A belt upon which hung a Harlequin's pouch of red leather. The pouch contained an Easter Egg. THE MUNDANE EGG in uncial characters appeared upon one side. Upon the other was the figure of a bull, representing the Tauric constellation. The capsule was made of paste and hair, coloured like chocolate. Inside, one extremity was painted yellow for the animal pole or male principle – the other red, for the vegetative pole. A marsh-mallow cube lay there – for a pierrot sweet, or a moonlit Nirvana.

There were also a few palmers' shells in the pouch, and a toothbrush (in case he should get on toothbrush terms at all).

A very small ovular pebble. Sesamum, grains of salt and buttemah, made a debris in the bottom.

A dozen spillikins. A Bezoar Stone.

A milfoil wrapped in tissue paper.

Thoth's reed and palette of the scribe.

A snuff-box alongside the Easter egg, to help simulate the gesture of dharma-chakra.

A leaden box full of small grains like barley-meal, and in their midst the mighty SCHAMIR.

The waist was lion-like and ritualistic, resembling that of a Minoan nut (slender and at all events nobiliary) or a kalakhanya.

Or the wasp-like billowing of the thighs and sylph's flat haunch seemed framed for the stampeding of a Jota.

The jerkin bristled with coarse black hairs – these were the kaohuang, or famous hair-rays of the Buddha.

Upon the right side a tortoiseshell was attached to his belt ready to crack in the fire like the face of an old man (the disposition of whose yellow map spelt a more general destiny) and so compete with the yarrow.

A calumet with rattan stem, feathered, and with a filigreed beading upon the bowl of soap-stone.

He would hold a six-foot long, yellow cane-wand, representing a corn stalk, surmounted by a gigantic ear of wheat – a relic of Quetzalcoatl's millennium, rescued by a Spanish priest from the destruction of the temple of Cholula.

For him to carry there was a gas-filled follicle at the end of a string. It now clung to the ceiling gently, the string dangling to within a few feet of the floor. A tawny serpent painted spirally upon it indicated this as a further emblem of the Orphic egg.

A short sling attached to it made of painted cloth, he was further provided with the lotus stool of the 'divine magician'.

Staring at this personal pageantry, he became lost in its distant allusions. In the starry valley before him, he thought he saw the shadow of the Roc.

Out of the shell-face of his disguise he stared as we do out of the protoplasmic mask of flesh, his vision seeming to swim out upon the flood-tide of the night. The sympathetic starching of his features recalled him to his unreal personality.

'I am a moonraker. I am a moonraker,' he thought, thrusting the word out, croupier-like, as though it were some celestial implement, into the night. Remembering the tread of the Venus d'Isle, he heard his right-hand business-man upon the stairs coming to claim him.

'He weighs more now I've cut him in half than he did before,' he thought as he listened.

iii

Marvellously disguised, Ratner stood with sulky diffidence near the door.

'I thought that would suit you! You have successfully blotted out your rudimentary left side. Turn round. Perfect.'

'I thought it was rather good,' Ratner said with gentleman-like modesty – very very gentleman-like and retiring.

'How do you like my disguise now you see it completed?' Mr Zagreus asked.

He swept his hand over his intellectual accoutrements.

'I think I have really got a costume worthy of the occasion!'

'Out of all proportion I should have thought to this occasion Horace.'

'After all the occasion is what one makes it.'

'You, my dear Horace, see occasions everywhere. Nothing is not an occasion – as far as you are concerned.'

'Everywhere! you are right.'

'Who was your Clarkson for this party?' The business-man spoke.

'Pierpoint. He made it up. I have his inventory.'

Mr Zagreus tapped his decorated hip – there was a hidden pocket, with a book of words.

'Pierpoint is very ingenious.'

'Pierpoint is a *genius!*' shouted the now copper-bronzed albino, his silk-worm-white moustaches blowing in the wind of his shout.

Julius Ratner sneered with a soft rattle, displaying a single yellow fang.

'Was it Pierpoint also who provided the descriptions for my get up?' Ratner asked.

'Every detail!' exclaimed Zagreus. 'Every button! Our conversation – *that* was his creation!'

'That too?'

'Every word of it!'

'I think Pierpoint must be mad!'

'Absolutely mad – as a march-hare my dear Julius. But with such *method!*'

'Yes, he has method, as you say.' The business-man spoke.

'He sometimes terrifies me with his method!'

'Demented people are always supposed to be like that.'

'Their logic you mean – yes of course. But examine me, Julius – pocket your envy, you poor split-person – salute this strange shell I have grown! Here I stand, Julius Ratner, as florid as Boro-Badur. My very fly-buttons are allusive.'

He took the mislaid wand from the corner.

'You see my fairy wand, witnessing the harvest of a hero. *What agriculture!*'

He removed the gilded cob.

'So it can become the rod of MOSES. *Ab ovo* it is always a rod in any event. I have merely removed the egg from which it is issuing, or the egg which has issued from it. I have two wings of an air-pilot's jacket in my pocket, wired and united in a socket which fits on the end of this. So I get roughly my caduceus, if necessary – if Hermes Trismegistus is in the wind, and you have enough fancy to see the gilded olive wood in place of calamus.'

Replacing the staff in the corner, Zagreus picked up from the table a small beam and scales, its brass dishes suspended from chains.

'Thoth. It is a small balance – but too large for the hearts that we shall be called upon to weigh.'

He took from his pouch the small white pebble.

'The egg of the cirrus cloud! Bundle of icy needles floating just beneath the advective floor. Why should not this lovely fleece have its egg, as well as the constipated eagle of Zeus?'

He touched the wiry growth upon his jerkin, raising one of the hairs from beneath with his finger-tips, which he drew along to its limp extremity, when hand and tip nervelessly fell.

'Medusa's locks! Kaohuang – the electrical radiations of the Buddha.'

From his pouch he drew the leaden box, and opening it, pointed to the stone, of the size of a barleycorn.

'The most powerful of the Yidgod's creations ever spat in the hey-day of his hexameron! The ass which spoke to Balaam was pupped at the same time. *And* Rebecca's well. *What a day!* Yes: the electrical stone-worm, my boy, the unscientific radium of the Mittelalter's fancy: the creature who can break up the atom: for his size more remarkable – or who knows! – than your ganglia or mine, for example. You call him a devil or the opposite according to the estimates you form of his intentions – whether you regard him as a responsible power – able to break you up, when he might not be able to put you together again. *No Harlequin's pouch complete without it!* See that you get one the next time you go prospecting with Fortunatus into Purgatory – or Mr Zagreus, my name. You know how to get it? Usual trick: hard-boil the woodpecker's egg while he's not looking – no, I'm sorry that's the test. Cover his nest with glass. He fetches the worm to break it. Worm and egg – *solar-myth* – all for tuppence!'

'So cheap!' grated Julius. The business-man to the fore.

'SHAMIR!' bellowed Zagreus.

He replaced it in the box. Pointing to the forgetmenots he said:

'*Vergessen Sie nicht das Beste!* Do not mistake and fill your pockets with gold, or you will be caught in the thunder of the mountain. That is not a Talmudic exhortation.'

Pointing to a smear upon his cloak.

'Singed by a meteorite – aimed at Melkart, enemy of the Zodiac! My anguinum?' touching his necklace. 'Shall I be impeached for employing snake's spittle?'

Withdrawing from a pocket in his hose twisted tissue paper, he displayed two red and wrinkled filberts.

'The testicles of the archigallus!'

Ratner leered appreciatively.

Withdrawing the spillikins from the pouch, Zagreus said:

'This for MIRAMORO. Sown upon the ground by a duly sensitive hand, they arrange themselves like a child's alphabet of fate.' Replacing the spillikins, he produced a few berries which he set rolling in the damp furrows of his gowpen.

'These float upon the water, delivering similar messages. There are 365 buttons on my coat. On its lapel' (he turns up the lapel to the light showing a metal disk sewn on) 'the Abraxas.'

Turning inside out a pocket, he shows a swelling along the horizontal seam.

'Sewn in here is the NEST OF THE MANTIS – gathered beneath an auspicious moon.'

His left side being a blank, the Split-man kept his lively right side correctly in position to follow this inventory.

Mr Zagreus drew a handkerchief from his waist-belt, flowered saffron and white. Pointing to one corner he announced:

'DENDAM TA' SUDAH. Endless love! You see, though, the work is unfinished. *Were it finished, the world would have ended!*'

Raising his cloak, swinging forward a cable of pendulous cloth.

'The scorpion-tail – the winged feet too – of the Everlasting Sun.'

Raising the mask suddenly, his whitened face appeared beneath.

'The child's face of Shudendozi, of the neighbourhood of Kyoto – protected therefore, I need hardly say, by Fascinus.'

He had banished from his eyes so completely all but the attributes of Shudendozi, that Ratner was almost alarmed at last.

'These two horns sprouting upon my forehead are *not* cuckoldic, but a symbol of *undying creative energy*. At my belt, upon this bootlace you see a phallus, such as was worn by the phallophoroi at the Dionysia. You can address me as Mfumo, Bassar, Tabib, Bomor, Mganga = Red-water: Saucy-water or Bitter-water (within this flask): in case I should have to officiate where I am going at El Halaf.'

He lifted a charm hanging upon a cord around his neck.

'There are three names on it, you see: Senoi, Sansenoi, Sammangelof. It is a charm against our bad mother, Lillith. The three names are of the three protecting angels who flew with her in conversation as she hovered with her illicit wings above the Red Sea.'

He fished out in succession a variety of objects, announcing their significance.

'The Album Graecium of the Hyena. –

'A saphie – a shell with one golden lock from the gentle head of Mutter Rosa. I would not exchange this periapt against the biggest EYE in the world! *Jettatura* differs, however – and one cannot be variously enough protected. *There are seeds in the body of the cock inimical to the lion!* There are seeds in EVERY BODY inimical to another! You cannot be too well stocked.'

Fingering the cloth of his tunic:

'This is a funny cloth. A simple dewdrop posed upon it will tangle the thread for a cubit's length. The breath of the South Wind, the Auster, will disentangle it.'

Mr Zagreus stuck his index and *digitus infamis* right into his breast, and lugged out a heart-shaped locket, from its nest of savoury hair.

'I have put on my Bulla, too, sir, for the occasion. (*Toga virilis?*)'

(He directed the question with his free hand, to his costume.)

'Yes? – I'm glad – I need not show you my little phallus need I? They are all the same. Mine is a child's – and it has been locked away for so long.'

'Has it?' Ratner set going the grating music of his sneer.

'Oh! la! la! Ever since last autumn, when it found an Eden upon a moor. A real moor though. Open my heart – when I'm dead, not before – and there you'll find it nestling!'

The SPLIT-MAN swallowed the little filbert-shaped bait and went on croaking harshly and merrily. His countenance was lighted with the sultry covetousness of the dung-fly.

'Are you putting that on? Or are you *really* interested?' Mr Zagreus affected surprise.

'I don't know. No. I think it very interesting, like everything about you Zagreus!' (The name gritted out of the coffee-machine of his throat, an intended caress.) 'It's a new eclecticism I had not suspected!'

'Well, if you are really interested, I will show you.'

Mr Zagreus opened the locket, Ratner peered in. It was empty.

'Poor Julius!' laughed the bedizened albino. 'Nothing doing! – I'll make up for it one of these days, and open my heart to you. I have a Sex-morsel there, yum-yum! – certainly I have! I've been keeping it especially for you: if you will stand up on your hind-legs and beg nicely. But not now Julius. At the Pyanepsia – when as a child I used to play with and sometimes eat the beans meant for the altar of the Autumnal Apollo, I used to call them each by a girl's name – Syrinx, Astræa, Agave, Nephele, Hesione, Thisbe, Echo, Maia. I wonder if Apollo ate them all – that is, those I left?'

'I shouldn't be surprised. Ah you Greeks Zagreus!'

'Why was I named Zagreus?'

Ratner substituting for his natural resentment at this mocking vitality dancing in front of him a sickly-shy, slow-moving smile, grated:

'I didn't think you were. I thought you were called – '

Mr Zagreus stopped him with a menacing hand.

'Never mind! NEVER MIND!' Pierpoint's incantation stung the air with the spanking N AND MINDER of its vibrating gut.

He stepped back and began counting upon his fingers:

'Ace, deuce, tray, cater, cinque, size. How many letters are there in my name? Are there enough to fill the points of space? You *can* say that – numbers don't matter. You don't know? Go to Bath, Mr Ratner! you're never there when you're wanted! But now listen to me a moment Mr Julius!'

Mr Zagreus towering above Ratner, declaimed in a prophetic style.

'*Never change the barbarous names given by god to each and all* – you read in the spurious AVESTA compiled in Alexandria: *Because there are names possessing an unutterable efficacity!* Beginning with the stock-in-trade of the Phap: the name you utter is not the name. The UNNAMED is the principle of heaven and of earth. But the name is an abortion and a tyranny – and you do not have to ascend into the sky, with the Tao, or allege anything more than a common cat, for that. Name a cat and you destroy it! "Not knowing his name I call him TAO."'

'My name for today, Ratner, as it always is but today especially, will be Zagreus and no other. It is a most pitiful travesty, is it not that? Our names are our slave-marks. We should *name* not be *named*. Yahveh "putting his name upon" the People of Israel was branding them like sheep, was he not? That is so. We shall never be anything much, we men, so long as we have names shall we, like Ratner and mine – shall we? Have you ever tried to think Ratner of a name for yourself? Of course Ratner is *not* your name at all I suppose – any more than Julius which you have stolen from Cæsar! So you are all right, Ratner, in that respect. – I have never been able to imagine a name abstract enough for myself.' Zagreus swelled out his chest at this. 'Maimonides disgraces his god by saying that the tetragram IEVE (Yah Hé-Voh Hé) is worthy of him. Schem Ha-Mephorasch! I wish I could see it! It would not satisfy a very particular man – not a quite commonplace man! But in any case the Hebrew god would keep his real name up his sleeve – he would be afraid to leave that lying about where anyone could get hold of it! I prefer some of his Shoan names to the tetragram: Ililfarsangana-el for example: Telk-el Walib-el Bel Mel. Or his secret ones – Coltekolcol (like a mexican god). Gohatjir is a good one. Hajirji: Gorgovajir: Corooking. – A people, however, that would officially reduce one face to an ovoid with seven holes, would be quite likely to find YAHVEH very unique.'

Ratner rolled the harsh r's that lined the bed of his gullet and a reverberant croak was emitted – saluting the mock Yah-hé-voh-hé.

'What is the real name then of Pierpoint?' Ratner asked.

'Ah!' Mr Zagreus exclaimed. 'That! – Pierpoint! No.'

'Pierpoint? Is it?'

'Ah.'

'Why, is it a secret?' Julius limply coaxed, grinning with sickliness that increased as he bashfully and balefully eyed this gimcrack sphinx-man. 'You are so mysterious Horace!'

Dr Mysterion wetted his naphtha-eyes and flashed up two liquid sparks to our firmament.

'*Our names are our slave marks* – you have heard what Pierpoint said – *Our names*' there was a lacuna in which the mouth of Horace continued contorting, but no sound came '*slave-marks!*' He licked his lips.

'Yes.'

'*Slave-marks!*' softly Horace breathed again, with a thrill in *slave* – a hissed whisper of whips.

'Did Pierpoint say that?'

Zagreus looked at Ratner steadfastly for a short interval of time – very slowly opening his mouth, and drawing back his lips as if his lips were cats and they were in the act to spring – as his lips often stealthily moved, to pounce upon words.

'It was Pierpoint' he said weightily 'who said' he paused and struck up his moustache, '*all that I have said to you!*'

'Figuratively Horace?'

'No – '

After a moment Zagreus added:

'Julius.'

The eye of Horace glittered with the same light as that that alarmed the wedding-guest who beat his breast, but Julius Ratner only rolled his most raucous r's about in the bottom of the old yellow sack of his mouth and slowly drawing in his breath over the rattling consonants, brayed a harsh bright cloven bray.

'He said it to me' said Zagreus – mouthing *me*, his voice dropping to the plane of confidence.

'And you got him to write down the names?'

'I got him to – he did.'

Ratner repeated the croaking bray, with a sluggish dragging inhalation.

'You old Boswell!' ground out Ratner, in chaffing wheedle. 'What a lovely time you must have together!'

'Pierpoint is the greatest genius I have ever known!' Zagreus shouted, challenged in this way, at the top of his form.

The bray of Julius followed the *greatest genius* – it broke out to caress Zagreus with its sluggish mockery.

'He taught me a "vanish" for tonight that is superior to Houdini – or Devant!'

'What was that, did you say Horace!'

'To Houdini!'

'Really?'

'Also how to subtilize a pigeon,' Zagreus hissed under his breath, rolling his eyes. His lips moulded in dumb-show the words after he had spoken them – upon the atmosphere arose the shadow of the words '*subtilize a pigeon*' from the unctuous labial pantomime. 'That is simple' he said quickly and scornfully aloud. 'I have two in that basket.'

'Two what?'

'Pigeons. Pigeons!'

Zagreus repeated dumbly twice more (in dumb lip-pantomime) *pigeon.*

Ratner brayed more softly, so that the sound approximated to the runculation rising from a dove-cote, the cooing of a sinister spate of gelded pigeons perhaps – in moist and inclement conditions.

Zagreus having mysteriously boasted of his big bag of tricks, he then looked up and down the room. Then, with some solemnity, he raised his hands, palm outwards, the two first fingers and thumb extended.

'Mano Pantea,' he said fixing Ratner in the eye: he then suddenly spat three times in his face, shouting –

'*Despuere malum!* That's for luck!'

'Luck for whom?' Ratner asked in piping and vibrating voice, wiping off the saliva.

'You may be annoyed with me for spitting in your face. That

would be a mistake! I have to do that to be on the safe side with you Julius. You can't help yourself any more than a person with a squint – it is on record that two women once lived together in a London suburb upon the best of terms: only as one of them had a squint, the other was forced to spit in her face three times a day to be on the safe side – like me. It must have been unpleasant for both of them. But they appear to have got quite used to it.'

All this having passed off very pleasantly, Mr Zagreus looked out of the window and said:

'Well there's a time for play and a time for work.'

Ratner was still wiping his face.

'We had better be up and doing.'

'I thought we were.'

'Is the car at the door?'

'I believe it is. I heard a knock.'

'Did you?'

Horace began gathering together all the objects that composed his costume. He lifted up a perforated box. Looking at Ratner, he framed in dumb-show with his super-plastic lips the word 'pigeon'.

Julius Ratner had grown slightly morose, and threatened, if spat at any more, to resort to a dignified attitude. There was hauteur in his sallow mask already.

'Willie Service must bring these down,' said Zagreus. He replaced the perforated box upon a large black case, secured with cord.

Ratner was silent.

'Daniel Boleyn is at the *Plough and Viscount* with Margolin.'

Ratner, still stand-off, said 'Is he?'

'We pick them up as we go along, at the *Plough and Viscount*.'

By his demeanour Ratner conveyed that he was indifferent as to who might be established at the *Plough and Viscount* (himself he had been provided with a garret at an inn called the *Moody Arms*) but that he was prepared, ready as ever to oblige his *oldest* friend, Horace, to assist at their honourable collection – more he would not say.

'Daniel Boleyn awaits us' Horace said impressively.

Ratner replied with an impatient movement, then he said:

'How have you dressed him? Is he dressed up too?'

'As a Cinquecento exquisite – white silk tights – rather a smart novel dress.'

Ratner gave a sickly sneer of long-drawn weary mischief.

'Who is footing the bill Horace – you are doing things in style?' The business-man insisted, with threatening eye.

'That is all settled between Lord Osmund and myself. – The fee is not large! Did you get that money? – Tell me later!'

Zagreus moved towards the door.

'Here: carry this.' He handed Ratner the lotus throne.

At the door Zagreus stopped, catching sight of the many gaping life-like garments, he was leaving behind in the room. He returned and battered them out of human shape as far as he could. Some were recalcitrant and seemed to cling to their second-hand life. At last he thought he had subdued them. The bed, too, had his imprint removed from it – and it presented no longer a surface upon which magic might be practised. He then rejoined Ratner, who was warily descending the stairs, with the lotus throne.

Part 12

LORD OSMUND'S LENTEN PARTY

I The Banquet

As the door opened the approach of a human tide was announced, it had its peculiar voice. The first distinct words, for anyone awaiting it inside the room, would have seemed to contradict its first jarring murmur.

'J'APPELLE UN CHAT, UN CHAT!'

As if the spirit of the speaker had burst away from the confinement of the sluggish tide, came this intemperate declamatory shout.

Lisping and nasal, with an affected testiness, someone scolded the disturber.

'J'APPELLE UN CHAT, UN CHAT!'

A refrain, or a dogged assertion, again these words stamped themselves upon the air. And immediately afterwards followed the lisping voice of mock peevish-complaint.

'I know, and somebody *un fripon*. But do be quiet Knut – you've made quite enough noise. The Pigeon will escape! You will terrify him if you keep talking about cats!'

'*I will* talk about cats! There are so many cats!'

'Do! Do! But not quite so loud!' A sneering purr or grunt accompanied these words, and the speaker appeared in the doorway.

Led by the pink emolliated form of Lord Osmond, the company enters the long apartment where the dinner is to take place. Lord Osmund is accompanied by his boyish wife, by his brother Phoebus, his cousin Eustace, guests and attendants.

'QUI, POUR LES BLÂMER,
MALGRÉ MUSE ET PHÉBUS N'APPRENDRAIT À RIMER?'

the head as it were of the procession continues to vociferate – a small grimacing pink-cheeked puppet, in the shadow of the figurehead, the host, the famous Chelsea Star of 'Gossip', Lord Osmund Finnian Shaw.

Lord Osmund is above six-foot and is columbiform. His breast development allies him also to that species of birds whose males are said to share the task of sitting and feeding the young with their mates. The pouter-inflation seems also to give him a certain lightness – which suspends him like a balloon, while he sweeps majestically forward. His carefully-contained obesity may be the reason for his martial erectness. Or rather, there can be no other reason for the evocation of that god.

Like Lady Fredigonde, Lord Osmund is a divine Pleroma – and the company the brothers have collected for this banquet is, with few exceptions, a brotherly brood. So the elder sweeps in with dignity, the fifty guests or more and relatives wander or shuffle in. Prowling up and down the board, they seek their names upon the cards, to find what place they are to occupy.

At the far end Lady Robinia Finnian Shaw seats herself, with Lord Phoebus and Mr Eustace Mulqueen upon her right and left hand respectively.

A tremendous punkah oscillates overhead, to deal with the equinoctial mildness expected, installed by some *maître des secrets* of the family. It has been gaudily painted till it resembles an example of Newton's rings. The sconces, where the torches are stuck, the length of the rough and lofty walls of this converted tithe-barn, are of polished brass, and their mirrors each rock a duplicate flame.

This is a hastily-converted norman grange, in the rear of the super-farmhouse acquired for parties and as a nursing-home by Osmund. It is ill-lighted and draughty, a large log fire is at either extremity. The torches and a multitude of twinkling candles upon the refectory table – to seat at a pinch a hundred diners – are the only illumination. It is productive of a glaring and smoky light. A constantly agitated firmament of shadows, lost in the timbered roof – the rushing, slovenly-dressed, hired waiters – a scratch troop of flustered women – everything sustains the air of restless improvisation, a sort of quaint, shabby lavishness, down to the cheap and perfunctory disguises of the guests.

Robinia, married for two years to Lord Osmund (who combines, with the traditional irish 'madness', every correct minor mania of the post-Ninety æstheticism of the Chelsea English) conforms to the prevalent fashion for victorian atmosphere. She is a period-piece that is a wan confection: she has a deep straight parting in her flaxen hair, her very narrow colourless face possesses the sly and pallid repose of an entirely devitalized instrument of post-Ninety satisfaction. As it were a permanently run-down domestic animal, Robinia drifts, scenting things a little, staring distractedly at nothing – and, sometimes, between her fingers she twists a straight silken wisp of the yellow hair of her head. She is a musician, like Dan she is A GENIUS – there is no greater musical genius in Europe than Robinia. It is questionable if there is any so great!

Above the pallid musical girl-wife, Phoebus and Eustace frankly tower – before they all three are seated – for they are both six-foot three inches high. This pair of cousins are very grave indeed, with the air of supporting a ceremony with affected awkwardness. Suddenly both of them sit down as if at a word of command – as if falling from a considerable height: as if the word of command, ill-learnt, had forestalled their readiness by a couple of seconds, whence their unconscionable haste.

The male preponderance, and the physical conformity, of this assemblage, would have been remarked upon immediately by a stranger – Lord Osmund would be found to respond to the 'ancestor' in these patriarchal *cadres*. Then, could human beings grow up in a year or two to be rather pallid boys of twenty or even more pallid chaps of thirty (but shrinking into corpse-like faded shadows as they tread the borders of middle-age) – should they be littered in half-dozens, and should infant-mortality be small, this table would have appeared furnished principally by children of Osmund. But – this not being so, as it is not – some reason for the queer personal conservatism that prevailed would have to be found – to satisfy science, or mere curiosity.

As far as possible, then, the generality of this assemblage are physically identical: and the pattern is a pallid chorister of seventeen – gelded or drained of all the grossness of sex by a succubus or something at birth.

Robinia exceeds all in lifelike imitation. But a decade or so, in reality, junior to Osmund, in appearance too transparent and thin – five-foot and pale – where he is so much the opposite, she is yet a succinct shadow of her bulky lord. The majestic original, not yet quite a senior but yet already patriarchal, he is adapted, by malignant Nature, to the dishonoured seat of priority.

To the above law of the pallid rabbit of the osmundian social system, a few exceptions only can be distinguished, here and there. An insolite group of three, placed midway between the imposing polar presences of Osmund and Phoebus (for Robinia is but a blind window, or a tinkling victorian musical box): a man in a green forester's jacket, with tyrolean cock's feather: lastly the occasional women, all old ones, and the finnish poet who in many respects transgresses the osmundian pale – he whose exclamations have disturbed the entry.

There are two women upon either side of the host: there are the two blood-relations upon either side of Robinia.

This gathering, meant to be a lenten festivity, develops through the ineludable bent of the hosts and satellites into a *soggetto*, arranged for the showing off of their favourite characters – it is their private theatre, this is Osmund's dramatic troupe and household-cast at full strength. In addition there are a few distinguished guests who are spectators. In his personal theatre, Osmund is seen with his troupe then *au grand complet:* except that the most important figures are always Absent (since, if it is generally true that *les absents ont toujours tort*, in the case of Lord Osmund's gatherings they could be said to receive an *overdose* of wrong).

Hors d'œuvres of a summary description begin to pour on to the table: skipper sardines, salamis, beetroot, celery, saladed potatoes and an occasional dish of egg-mayonnaise. The cutlery and silver, much of it brand-new, of a quality found in cheap restaurants, is in places defective. Some guests have only one fork or no dessert-spoon.

A suggestion of the sumptuous has been cynically imparted to all this, however, in the details of the appointment of the feast. In addition to the punkah, Congolese figures and Malayan masks make their appearance here and there, upon the walls of this giant dining-room. A painting by Severini (of Scaramouche with a guitar and two masked pals) hangs near a cubist rendering of the Woolworth Building in New York, and a post-pre-Raphaelite landscape by a period-fancying Gloucestershire Hebrew, to point the grangerizing of the time. Rough craters, of pseudo-etruscan design, are distributed at intervals along the centre of the table. These are filled with tulips. From the midst of their whorls of lightly carmined lawn – a yellow stain surrounding the green suppuration of their stigmas – their pistils are trained point-blank upon the guests. The human cryptogams in front of them (the carefully bled Osmundian sucking pigs) – vegetative, secretive – grown from spores, without true seed, stamen-and-pistilless, were obscenely mocked at by those chasmoganous growths – the tactless table-ornaments.

But now the trumpeting of the verses denouncing the *grand siècle* drew attention to the scandalous guest:

'POUR UN SI BAS EMPLOI MA MUSE EST TROP ALTIÈRE.
JE SUIS RUSTIQUE ET FIER, ET J'AI L'AME GROSSIÈRE.
JE NE PUIS RIEN NOMMER, SI CE N'EST PAR SON NOM:
J'APPELLE UN CHAT, UN CHAT.'

'Oh, taisez-vous donc, monsieur – avec votre CHAT et encore votre CHAT!' exclaimed his neighbour.

'Yes, do be quiet Kanoot. I do wish you'd learn something else,' Lord Osmund scolded, in lazy nasal drawl.

The Finn, a gilded laurel wreath upon his head, and upon the top of that a green Phrygian bonnet – but combed like a common tiara – grinned with doll-like fixity, with eyes insanely bright.

Pointing at Lord Osmund he again burst out:

'MAIS, SANS UN MÉCÉNAS, À QUOI SERT UN AUGUSTE?'

Lord Osmund tossed his head and clicked his tongue, in sign of despair, and turned to his reigning pet. This was a lady veiled and muffled, she sat upon his left-hand side. He deferentially whispered to her. The lady belonged to a distant generation. She supplied him with tit-bits of Gossip arranged with his favourite sauces, the old yellow sauces of the Naughty Nineties. This was really his old cook, who presented him with little delicacies cut off, first from one, then from another, of his more aggravating acquaintances or friends – done to a turn in her cunning old cuisine, flavoured with the recipes she had learnt in a former age from the lips of the great men of that wicked, perverse, most clever epoch – from Wildes, Beardsleys and Whistlers.

Some hated swine-flesh there was, of particular enemies, that the more-than-a-thought teutonic Osmund never wearied of: some little birds' anatomies he knew by heart, whose entrails he especially prized.

Purring a trifle piggishly, and savouring the ridiculous in his prominent snout (from which came a sardonic note) he settled down gluttonously to gossip.

'Tell us, Sib, about So-and-so!'

'What did So-and-so say to you, Sib, when – ?'

'Tell them the story, Sib, of how you met So-and-so, yesterday – *I thought you bought it, but I find* – ! You know Sib – do tell them that! No one has heard it, I am positive!'

He pleaded, condescendingly down his nose – exciting with the colossal snobbery of his baying drawl his muffled aged soothsayer, come all the way from that far land of the Nineties. He wheedled his old Nineties-nurse for a further slice of victorian cat's-meat.

'Sib! Sib! Was So-and-so seen smelling Belvedere's hand, while Poor Tom was being sick – that was perfect you *must* tell them that – you must! Do tell us again I have forgotten how it goes! That was a divine story Sib!'

There were a thousand and one gems of café-chatter, of tit-for-tattle – of score-offs and well-rubbed-ins.

The monotonous leads, uttered in rich nasal drawl, never stopped for a moment now. Osmund caressed his fœtid old prophetess with his fond false eye. He confirmed the impression of the pouter-pigeon by that gruff, gurgling coo – with which he would encourage or reward her devoted clowning, her decrepit somersaults.

Indeed, from the moment that every one had become settled, a blight of unrelaxing gossip and of stale personal allusion descended upon the entire table from end to end. For this Lord Osmund in the first place was responsible, and it was accepted by all as the business of the evening. The tongues started. And a motley of figures arose in these racontars. There were the small antagonists of osmundian literary intrigue – people who had hurt his lordship's vanity by ignoring or by castigating his literary enterprises. There were those who had resented the dilatoriness of payments for a picture or a book, or for an object of furniture – kindred-spirits were pulled out and made to run the gauntlet of these tongues – someone who had made him a butt in an entertainment like the present one. Many victims recurred with clock-like regularity.

In fact in a sort of ill-acted Commedia dell' Arte, with its Pantalones and Arlechinos (the family of the Finnian Shaws monopolizing the Harlequin rôle, however unsuited for it), this family-circle passed its time. A passion for the stilted miniature drama of average social life, as it immediately surrounded them, had assumed the proportions with this family of a startling self-abuse, incessantly indulged in. Their Theatre was always with them. Their enemies – Pantalones, comic servants, detestable opponents (whose perfidy disrespect malice or cabal they would signally frustrate – unmask them, knaves and coxcombs to a man!) always this shadowy cast was present. Indoors and out-of-doors, dilated, in full war-paint, sometimes as bombastic phantoms, or else, laid aside in doll-like collapse – but always present. So their commerce would appear, to an outsider come into the circle of their existence, like some unvarying 'shop', with all its monotonous technique – *concetti*, *soggetto*, *repertorio* – masks of gravity, malice, or lechery – cloaks of the Dottore, air-bladders, rice-powder – incessantly in evidence.

In colour Lord Osmund was a pale coral, with flaxen hair brushed tightly back, his blond pencilled pap rising straight from his sloping forehead: galb-like wings to his nostrils – the goat-like profile of Edward the Peacemaker. The lips were curved. They were thickly profiled as though belonging to a moslem portrait of a stark-lipped sultan. His eyes, vacillating and easily discomfited, slanted down to the heavy curved nose. Eyes, nose, and lips contributed to one effect, so that they seemed one feature. It was the effect of the jouissant animal – the licking, eating, sniffing, fat-muzzled machine – dedicated to Wine, Womanry, and Free Verse-cum-soda-water.

The hosts, except Lord Osmund, who represented some apocryphal Restoration ancestor, were not in fancy-dress. But the guests availing themselves for the most part of the alternative of the invitation cards were *Characters in Fiction.* The party of three nondescript strangers, quite unknown to their immediate neighbours, conversed with each other in low voices. They were deeply disguised. This banderbast of bold intruders detained the eye of their host, he cast in their direction many questioning puzzled glances, so rapidly they became indicated as the official butts of this phase of the entertainment.

The lady facing the Sib, across the stately front of Lord Osmund, was a massive harpy who glared at the assembly, often she would explode in broken English. Admired by her hosts, because of her prodigious aggressiveness, she was as it were a bulldog bitch of a society-matron, with pretentions to a sledge-hammer wit, whose robust tempers in contrast to their own had the power to divert both Osmund and Phœbus, though obnoxious to Robinia.

Next to this lady the finnish poet, who was in fact it was said a Lapp, in a very tight and shabby suit of clothes of a dark green check, sat bolt upright throughout the banquet – his staring eyes of intense polar green appearing to light up his rigid, long-lipped grin-from-ear-to-ear, with its deep symmetrical dimples, to make his painted cheeks as well glow with a more carmined flush. But this strange painted shamanized northern wanderer – who possessed no home, but who passed from pub to pub, studio to studio, party to party – he it was, if any one, who was the recognized Soggetto. He was the factor of scandal, required for the occasion: his rôle was to provide that thrilling element – to be the iron jelloid of the languid jest, to be the live wire amid Weary Willies.

From those high latitudes out of which – a figure of crapulous saga – Kanute or Knut had emerged (a mad painted grin graven upon his face where two flanking front-row teeth were missing) he had brought, in his ever-tightly-jacketed boy's body (though now in years a strapping man) a voice for an apocalypse. At a moment's notice it could take its place in a brass-band, in the event of the bursting of a percussion instrument or the destruction of a trombone. With this equipment he had in France collected a proud booming delivery. That was upon a classic stage, which, an infant-actor, he had trod. The verses of the french high-noon of the Latterday West welled up, inconsequent accidents, from this source of incandescent sound, of their own accord. The entire table was rocked with the detonation of haphazard strophes – fragments of poetry, metrical thunder-claps, bisected couplets, heads, or extremities, of rhymed invective – they struck it with the full force of the age of the King-Sun.

'J'IGNORE CE GRAND ART QUI· GAGNE UNE MAÎTRESSE!'

(Jeeeen-*yorrer* ss grarnt-*tarr* – kee *garny*er een mayt-*tresss!*)

The vociferation occurred, a solitary alexandrine – and Knut, with his face split across with kobold-grin, was stiffly silent afterward, squatting wooden and smiling, as if modelled upon a ventriloquist's knee-boy – the leering nipper of music-hall canon – that the performer's voice had abruptly ceased to visit.

Lord Osmund, putting his hand round his ear, as it seemed to protect the most tenuous of maidenly whispers, and looking significantly towards the Unassimilable Three, the group of interlopers (still carrying on their anti-social mutter-à-trois) shouted at Knut:

'Do speak up Kan – oot! I can't hear you – there's so much *noise* going on!'

Kanoot spoke up. The face of the rouged and powdered doll that is to say split. While the horizontal gap expressively contracted and expanded, two more vast lines of verse came out, deafeningly recorded.

'SAINT-AMANT N'EUT DU CIEL QUE SA VEINE EN PARTAGE.
L'HABIT QU'IL EUT SUR LUI FUT SON SEUL HERITAGE.'

Lord Osmund held his hand behind his ear always, as if hard-of-hearing, and again he called out in strident tones – to make himself heard seemingly above formidable interruptions:

'You really must speak up Kanute – I can't hear a word you say! There's such a diabolical noise going on that it's quite impossible to hear oneself speak! Speak up and then perhaps I may be able to hear you.'

'It *is* difficult, isn't it!' bellowed Phoebus from the other extremity of the table, rolling eyes of an affrighted doe upon the Unassimilable Three.

'I can't imagine where all the noise is coming from can you!' Lord Osmund answered in a howling whine, looking down both sides of the table in turn. 'It isn't as though there were any noisy people here! It is really absurd that we shouldn't be able to hear each other speak without shouting like this – I can't understand it at all.'

As the drawling thunder of the big-baby-talk rolled up and down the banqueting-board, from Osmund to Phoebus and back again, the Unassimilable Three were silent, burying their masked noses in their soup.

'I know!' exclaimed Lord Phoebus. 'It is really too bad of Mrs Bosun to have left the wireless on,' he lisped in a tremendous drawl, that concentrated the full force of its snobbery upon *Bosun* – 'is it the wireless loud-speaker do you think Osmund – shall I go and turn it off – why ever has Mrs Bosun left it on?'

'No' big brother bellowed back: 'I'm positive it's not the loud-speaker!'

'No it's too loud for that don't you think – I wonder whatever it can be!' Phoebus with his dupe's-mask on – of simple puzzled gull – carried his eyes hither and thither.

'It isn't the sound, or what do you think, of the loud-speaker Phoebus!' Lord Osmund tallyhoed back, in majestic high-pitched lisp: 'the loud-*speaker* makes quite a *different* sound – I shouldn't bother to go and turn it off if I were you Phoebus – I'm positive it's not the loud-*speaker!*'

'It's far too loud I believe for the loud-speaker – unless they've got two or three more since yesterday. I shouldn't be at all surprised would you? We didn't have to shout like this yesterday!'

'I know! It was quite quiet wasn't it yesterday.'

'Perfectly – I can't make it out at all can you? Mrs *Bosun* probably ordered two more in case one should break down.'

'She insists on having the Savoy-band with her supper.'

'I know, but I do think this is going too far, don't you agree?'

'Much too far, I shall speak to her about it tomorrow.'

'I only hope it's not a storm brewing!' blew the rumbling nasal contralto of Osmund, upon a fog-horn note of fear. And some guests shivered slightly and they gazed about for a Clerk of the Weather.

'A storm, yes I hadn't thought of that – the temperature *has* risen I believe in the last few minutes – do you think it is – I hope it's not!' bayed back in blank-faced alarm (such as that felt by all young feathered things at the approach of the tempest) the languidly-youthful wild-eyed Lord Phoebus, gigantically Fauntleroy. 'It looked very black I thought just after sunset. Did you see how black it was? Just after sun-set. What? After the Sun Set yes! It was!'

'Was it – I know! I did notice, most terribly black – and blue!' Lord Osmund agreed, still shouting down his nose, in lazy nasal blare. 'But it must be a very *bad storm* don't you agree!'

'I believe it must be! I do hope they've shut the windows! – All I hope is they've closed up the win-dows!'

'It must be one of the worst storms for years!'

Turning to the Sib, Lord Osmund repeated, in a lower key:

'Don't you agree Sib, it must be a very severe storm! It must be quite a hurricane.'

He raised his voice (above the storm of course, and combating Sib's deafness):

'*Phoeb*-us thinks Sib – yes *Phoeb*-us Sib – that it is probably one of the worst storms for years, I shouldn't be surprised if it were! Don't you think it may be? Don't you find it exceedingly difficult to hear what people say? I do!'

'I believe I did find it a little difficult just now – yes it *is* difficult!' said the Sib, with her bright craft, in her veiled voice.

'Most – I feel particularly deaf, myself.'

'So do I!' agreed the Sib, 'as deaf as a post!'

'It doesn't seem like an *english* storm at all does it? There's something outlandish about it don't you agree? It's the sort of pandemonium that Cockeye often refers to, when he's talking about his early experiences in the Gulf of Siam!'

'Yes – the gulf of Siam!'

'It simply means that the weather has broken!' Lord Osmund

crashed out crossly, impersonating the marquis his papa, 'Cockeye' in fact: 'but somehow I felt in my bones it would break – all along I knew something of the kind would happen, didn't you feel it might Sib?'

Affecting to listen with misgiving to the outrageous sounds, denoting that uncouth break in the english weather, the Sib drew her black victorian wraps about her shoulders.

'I don't believe it's a storm Osmund!' she panted stormily, short of wind.

'Not a *storm* Sib!'

'Not exactly a storm!' breathed the blanched Sib.

'I wonder whatever it can be then' Osmund asked anxiously, 'if it is not a storm! That would be most uncanny, if it were not a storm!'

The Sib leant towards him a little, and she said in a more muffled pant:

'I believe it's the loud-speaker!'

'Sib thinks it's the loud-speaker!' Lord Osmund immediately called down the table, beckoning to Lord Phoebus. 'Yes Sib believes it is not a storm at all – she believes it is the loud-speaker Phoebus!'

The Finn, who had begun to resent the competition of the bogus elements, suddenly took out of his pocket a piece of soiled paper.

'I haf a Map of Tenderness!' declared the Finn.

'I don't care what you've got Kanute!' said Osmund with high-pitched off-handedness.

'Is that Madame de Scudéry or is it Doctor Stopes?' asked Mr Wildsmith across the table, for he was sitting next to Sib, without looking at the Finn.

'I don't know,' said the Finn. He put the paper back in his pocket. He drew out another larger fragment of paper, upon which there was some handwriting.

Noticing an accidental hush, Kanute clamoured automatically without stopping to think:

> 'ET TOUT DE VERS CHARGÉ, QU'IL DEVAIT METTRE AU JOUR.'

The verses still issuing from his mouth, he affected to grind an itching shoulder upon the upturned wooden blade of the chair at his back.

'ET TOUT CHARGÉ DE VERS!'

With a resentful loudness, Kanute insisted upon this.

'I do wish you could manage to let us forget – if you *are* lousy it's nothing to be proud of Kanute – let it go at that don't you think? – is it really necessary to *scratch?*' in his complaining drawl scolded Lord Osmund.

Basking in the seigneurial banter, the Finn grinned, at the two old women, his fellow-satellites.

'Mais comment monsieur! vous vous frottez contre votre chaise! Mais alors quoi!' exclaimed ruggedly Madame Volpemini: 'si vous êtes tellement *chargé* de ces bêtes-là, monsieur, ne vaudrait-il pas mieux que vous vous mettiez un peu à l'écart – je n'ai pas envie moi d'être devorée – ce n'est nullement pour cela en effet que je me trouve ici, à cette table hospitalière – je vous le garantie – Au contraire!'

'Mais parfaitment madame!' answered Knut. 'Moi non plus!'

'C'est là cependant bien votre affaire à vous, n'est-ce-pas? Quant à moi, je n'en ai pas envie – voilà! Je ne veuz pas de vos hôtes agiles et malhonnêtes, vous entendez! Gardez vos *vers* pour vous, monsieur, gardez vos vers pour vous Monsieur!'

'Mais, Madame, je suis un poète – donc, je n'ai pas le moindre *vers!*'

'Tant mieux! Voilà la sorte de poète qui me convient, à moi! D'ailleurs j'ai horreur des bohêmes sans-culottes!'

'Sans-culotte madame! Comment! J'ai toujours mes culottes!'

He drew her attention to the tightly-sheathed darkly-checked thighs beneath, half-draped with tablecloth; then he looked up, and in masterful accents brought to light the same verses with which he was charged, all over again, with a challenging flourish – letting in the daylight, putting them on show.

'TOUT CHARGÉ DE VERS, QU'IL DEVAIT METTRE AU JOUR!'

'Je n'aime pas ces vers-là non plus – autant peu que les autres!'

growled the same old critical polyglot, who was Venetian, while she slightly scratched her naked bicep of pale roman ochre, that smelt of sweet-pea.

'Je croyais madame que toutes les belles filles aimaient les poètes!'

'Moi pas!' she roared 'Moi pas!'

Lord Osmund and his Sib had proceeded to whisper, in loud penetrating stage-tones, looking towards the three masked mystery-men.

'Osmund!'

'Yes Sib!'

'Do you know what I believe it is that has been making all that noise?'

Osmund is all hushed attention: he whispers back:

'No Sib! Do tell me! – *what is it?*'

'I have been looking round,' husky and dull hurtled the Sib – communicating from afar off among the black Beardsley glades haunted by big inky vamps, and pirouetting amid the Fêtes Galantes of the Naughty Nineties – interrogating her attentive beruffed Restoration patron, so far and yet so near – in fact at some distance as well, in the time-spaces and chronologic perspectives, in the London of Lord Chesterfield.

'Yes Sib! do tell me what you suppose it is, I shall feel all of a shiver till I know!' He purred down at her from the baby drone within his musical beak: 'for some time I must say I have had my *suspicions* – but I could scarcely believe my ears! I wonder if what you think's the same!'

'It is only a guess!'

'I know, it is impossible to make up one's mind – I've found that too – first one thinks it's one thing, then one thinks it's another – I still believe I must be wrong!'

'Mine is only a guess – tell me if it seems too fantastic!'

'I am quite in the dark – '

'So am I – I conjecture, I am tentative – '

'I am not dogmatic!'

'Anything but – anything but! But for some time it has seemed to me – I know it sounds absurd – that all the noise is proceeding from *those three people* over there' – she slid her eyes round, followed by those of Osmund 'the ones with the steeple-hats, who look like three friends of Guy Fawkes,' and the Sib lowered her blind-puppy eyelids, while Lord Osmund observed with attention the three masked mystery-men.

'Do you know – !'

'Yes!'

'I had exactly the same impression Sib!'

'No really?'

'It was identical!'

'I do think that was a coincidence!'

'Wasn't it! I thought my ear must be deceiving me! It would not be the first time!'

'Don't talk to me about one's ears! But I believe we must – '

'We must I believe be right Sib!'

'I don't believe our ears have played us false!'

'In this matter – I believe they haven't!'

'I am not positive – but I should be surprised if they had deceived us!'

'For once I do believe that mine has proved trustworthy!'

'It is a miracle if mine have!'

'Not more so than with mine!'

'But who are they, do you know them?'

'I have never seen them before in my life!'

'You don't know who they are at all?'

'Not the foggiest!' Osmund sneered and purred the absurd expression.

'Who brought them?'

'Who indeed?'

'When did they arrive?'

'I did not notice them arriving!'

'Are they interlopers?'

'I shouldn't be surprised!'

'How did they get in?'

'Ah who knows!'

'What did they come for?'

'What is their business here I should like to know! *No good* – I confess I can see nothing for it but that!'

'It looks black against them!'

'And for us! Very black for us!'

'Certainly it is disturbing to have them!'

'Disturbing! Disturbing's not the word! It is too much of a good thing altogether!'

'I should not be surprised if they went away.'

'If they don't, I shall have to have them removed I know that and pretty quickly too!'

'They are certainly enigmas!'

(Those nearest to Lord Osmund follow his example, they hold up their conversations and transfer their attention exclusively to the mystery-men. An uninterrupted hoarse whispering arises from the Trio of Scandal. Their postiche Fifth-of-november moustaches waggle in a manner that bodes no good for anybody, beneath their black half-masks of satin, which carry at their base sharply protruding, steeply-pent, half-noses – pink-lined, with nose-tips of live flesh outcropping. Their neighbours incline their ears, in the relative hush, to surprise some sentence or some tell-tale exclamation, but it is out of the question to catch what they are saying, although their voices can be distinguished quite plainly.)

But the finnish principal, at a loss for a verse (that should be both sonorous and incendiary), realized a danger. In his mesmeric fixity, of latter-day Scald, he abruptly foresaw, in a visionary fashion, that, in the long run, at the hands of these intruders, he might suffer an eclipse. As a performer, he might suffer an eclipse. He noted their unpopularity – he assured himself of the will of his masters, Osmund and then Phoebus. These beyond question were official butts – he saw it was a sport to which all and sundry were plainly invited. Therefore, staring at the dread Three, in company with the rest, he took the initiative. He delivered a blow at the table with his large-hand-for-a-little-man.

'Silence!' he roared at his rivals. 'Silence, I say! Do you not hear me! Silence!'

Twice again he gave the table volcanic slaps, to the delight of his hosts succeeding in shivering a wine-glass and upsetting the wine over the great harpy, the Volpemini's evening-frock.

'Im-*bé*-cile!' that irascible foreigner cried out beside herself, as the false scarlet of the bad Bordeaux was ditched the length of her hefty lap, spilling over forward spout-wise from between her knee-caps, splashing her slippers.

For a moment it seemed certain that the pampered bull-bitch would fling herself upon Kanute. But instead, pushing her chair back, she attempted to repair what had been done without loss of time. To that end she wrenched open the two beefy cliffs of her thighs – the ditch split, a chasm yawned, the wine dropped through, upon the floor beneath. She wrung, in convulsive laundry-work, the discoloured silk. Gripping a napkin, up and down she scrubbed – Lord Osmund, with ceremonious perfidy, assisting her with abortive advice, seconded by the squinting Sib.

'Mais quel goujat!' panted the Volepemini. 'Mon dieu, quel malhonnête personnage quel celui-là!'

'Vous avez raison madame! C'est un – fripon!' Lord Osmund agreed, with great readiness. 'Fripon!' he added mildly to Kanute.

'Un fripon – c'est exact! Un fripon en effet!'

The big three, the mystery-merchants, did nothing to suspend their debate – they showed no sign of intending to draw each other's attention to their unpopularity in any manner – they were composed and earnest and impenetrably disguised, as to class or kind, though in sex there was some probability that they were just mystery-men and not women.

'Osmund!'

'Sib!'

'It occurs to me –'

'Yes Sib – what is it?'

'Aren't those three people –,' in her mufflled pant said the sycophant Sib.

'Yes, those three whispering bandits!'

'Those three men like bandits – perhaps the performers – those conjurers.'

'No, the conjurers when they come, at their own request are to dine at that table there, that is apart from us. They will not be with us – it is not the conjurers I am positive.'

'Not the conjurers.'

'No not the conjurers.'

'Oh.'

'I can't account for them in any way.'

'I can't either.'

'They are mysterious. But there is no question about their insolence.'

'They are quite undisturbed!'

'They are three knaves!'

Kanute slapped the table (up to which the Volpemini had just drawn her chair once more) with undiminished force. With the accents of a town-crier announcing a lost gold-hunter, he vociferated:

'THREE KNAVES!'

The Queen of Spades at his side answered –

'Sâle voyou!'

– but those he had denounced – the Three Knaves – remained unaffected.

At the far end of the table, looking in the direction of the finnish poet, Lord Phoebus remarked:

'I do hope there's not a fight!'

Mr Eustace Mulqueen was positive there would not be – the Volpemini had not got the pluck.

In a training voice, charged with a pompous gravity, Lord Phoebus explained to his neighbour the situation – the very loose, very rough soggetto, in short.

'Knut – you see up there at the other end of the table, who is sitting beside Osmund – next but one – he is quite mad. Yes quite mad. He has been mad all day. He has the most extraordinary delusions. He believes that his spirit is a pigeon. He is afraid to open his mouth for fear it should fly away.'

'Really? How very extraordinary!'

'Yes it is. Did you notice, a moment ago when he called out and struck the table, how with the other hand he guarded his mouth, as though he were belching?'

'I can't say I did.'

'Well, that was in case the pigeon should try and escape. Yes, very peculiar isn't it? That's what I said to Osmund. I really think he may never recover this time, because he refuses to sleep. He has not slept for four nights. He dare not sleep for fear the pigeon should escape. It's a Trinity Complex.'

'A Trinity Complex?'

'Yes a Trinity Complex.'

'Who are the other two members of his Trinity?'

'He has a theory that the Pigeon is attached to his umbilical cord. It is supposed at present to be in his stomach.'

'But who is the Father? How does he – ?'

'No, he says he does not know who his father is.'

'And the Son?'

'He, of course, is the Son.'

'He must be quite mad.'

'Quite, I'm afraid,' Phoebus drawled with thrilling matter-of-factness, returning to his dinner.

'He ought to be taken care of. Has he seen a doctor?'

'He refuses to see a doctor. We wanted to take him to see our doctor today. Osmund is going to try again after dinner.'

As the wine found its way into the small bloodless stolid bodies of the guests, the canvas became more animated. It moved them to diminutive dead-born gestures of comic aggression, towards the interloping trio. And a certain comfortless inter-ogling declared itself and there appeared a gentle ruffling of the surface by not very strong currents of obscenity of a certain type – drifting or stationary, always a little dreary, just so much languid play as the engrained, long-cultivated spectator's rôle would allow.

But the wild Finn, the poetisch scaramouche of the osmundian canvas, was, in contrast, so replete with exalted nonsense and a great deal of drink, that, by this time, a *dénouement* seemed assured. Some terrifying *lazzo* slept in his shining eye and his ear-to-ear grin! Would he become a seal and grovel nimbly upon the sawdusted floor? – where he would fight the Volpemini to the death? Or would he, glass in hand, vault the table and perch upon the dresser, and from thence challenge the unpopular Three?

He rose with the same uncertain suddenness with which Phoebus and Eustace had at first sat down. *Molto perturbato* – full-scandal-lazzi. A startled complaisant 'Oh!' from the Sib – sheepish grins and a little pale-pink blood in the cheeks of the initiated spectators.

Kanute turned a shining eye upon the company, an actor sure of his triumph. But no athletic somersault or gem-like sally was required, he knew, for success. Only to be a Finn, to be drunk, and to appear the whole time about to outrage decorum, to be always *on the point* of tearing off the veil of grey restraint.

Head erect and eyes fixed above the level of his scalp he started off, unsteadily but quickly, towards the principal exit. *Il guido maestro* shook with condescending fun, cooing gruffly: but he flashed signals with his eyes, as he was always doing, to his business-manager, brother and colleague, Phoebus.

Phoebus rose. He planted himself in front of the door, or rather flattened himself against it, his head dislocated in the direction of the Finn, with his hands palms-pressed upon its massive panels. He did not look at Knut, but gazed like a dog, or like a cop dissimulating his interest in a suspected person, at something else, with a kind of heavy professional duplicity. The shamefacedness peculiar to Phoebus added its sheepish flavour of coy sex to this pretence.

Affecting to discover, there before him, quite unexpectedly, this human bas-relief, the Finn changed his plans. He continued his journey, as a circumnavigation of the table. He negotiated its extremity, circling behind Robinia, and went up the farther side on his return journey to his place beside Osmund.

A moment he lingered behind the three interlopers. He examined them with his broadest grin at close quarters, but at their back. Then he passed on. Arrived behind Lord Osmund, he approached his grin to his host's ear – holding his hand in readiness, near its slit, to intercept the pigeon. This action resulted in a gesture of clumsy confidence. He whispered for some minutes.

Not resuming his place at table, Knut wandered amongst the domestics. Phoebus, back in his place upon the right hand of Robinia, eyed him with a wary and business-like eye: he was more than prepared at any moment to crucify himself and to be a bas-relief again – 'over my dead body' – an attractive tableau, and one that furthered the Soggetto, at once. But Knut drifted beatifically on, round and round the mulberry-bush, colliding with the waiters. He made longer and longer stays in the immediate rear of the interlopers, however, it was noticed, by both his hosts – who saw him passing continually around them – with sagacious sporting eye, as true fans of such baiting and fencing.

Coming up with a waggish spurt behind Phoebus – who kept the tails of his eyes busy in readiness – Knut suddenly collapsed, a hand upon one shoulder of his junior host, his head rolling in unsightly finnish horseplay upon the other.

'Phoibos – pewer one! – tarling! I *must* tell you!'

Phoebus started up, scandal-lazzi uppermost in his stern mask, the man-of-action to the fore.

'Knut! go back at once to your seat! You are disturbing everybody! You really must be quiet! We can't have it! Go back at once!'

The mock-victorian-old-maid, which historical character-part met with a hospitable reflection in the spirit of Phoebus, discharged her shocked accents.

Holding him at arm's length, Phoebus marched him back to his place.

'There! Sit down and be quiet! Stop there till we tell you to move. You mustn't move about so much and get in the way of the waiters.'

Knut collapsed in his chair, directing his gaping grin and painted cheeks at his major host, for approval.

Two log fires at the opposite ends of the room develop a devastating heat. The guests fan themselves at last and shrink from them.

'Is it too hot for you, Sib?' Lord Osmund asked with concern. 'I *am* so sorry – I feel as though I am in a Turkish bath myself. I wish they wouldn't pile logs on in that way. Peters,' he lisped in complaining falsetto – 'Peters – don't you think you could possibly manage to get a few of those logs off? The heat is beyond description. I know it's cold sometimes, but it's particularly warm tonight.'

Lord Osmund addressed Peters with a coaxing appeal but with the customary complaining nasal peevishness, and the servant, with a mixture, as well, of impatient contempt and of slovenly obedience, began removing the uppermost of the logs. Lord Osmund twitched his nostrils, curled his lip, and sniffed very slightly – looking whitely at the Sib, his hands upon the table at either side of his plate, the hard-goffered cuffs coming down over them, a flowered handkerchief overflowing his chest from beneath the brocaded flange of his doublet. Then he turned quickly again towards the servant.

'Don't take them *all* off. We must have a fire! Before it was too hot – that was all I meant.'

Peters like an automaton, without turning his head, replaced two smoking logs, which he had just pulled out into the grate, upon the fire. Lord Osmund looked at the Sib, his eyebrows a little raised.

Peters poured water from a carafe over the logs in the grate. There was a determined hissing, a burst of steamy smoke, and a slight stench, at once.

'I wish you could think of some other way of disposing of the logs Peters!' hissed and puffed Lord Osmund in still louder expostulation, simulating a man choked with the fumes of charcoal. 'Now you've filled the room with smoke! It's quite full! I wish you could manage not to smoke us out!'

Peters took no notice at all of his testy lord, he hit the logs.

'This is too much, what are you hitting them for? – don't hit them! – how do you expect us to eat our dinner if you first grill us and then choke us, I wonder if *you* could with your mouth full of smoke! The fumes are dangerous! I wish you'd take the logs *away*, instead of patting them like that and making them worse! They are far worse now!'

Peters rose, bandy and efficient, grasping a log where he had extinguished it, and he bore away the first smoking carcass.

Lord Osmund pointed to his forehead, and shook his head.

'He's so stupid!' he said to the Sib. 'Peters is a natural.'

Contorting herself and smiling with a pained twisting of the wooden lips, Sib replied:

'Servants pride themselves upon their stupidity so much – they are all the same. Their stupidity is the symbol of their independence.'

'Yes. But I think Peters is *really* stupid.'

'Oh I am sure he is!' obsequiously panted Sib.

'Yes – he really is!'

At the farther extremity of the table there was a similar upheaval. Phoebus rose, and, with a face getting very flushed and cross, he struggled personally with the logs one by one. The servants paid no attention to the turmoil engineered by the two brothers, for they had been led to expect it: whenever the tithe-barn was used for an extempore banquet, scenes of this nature were re-enacted. Osmund and Phoebus would bay whine and bluster, complaining of the fires as if they had not installed the two great grates themselves – they might in fact have been put there by their own proper fetches, or by some monstrous 'good people', but never by them: the staff, it was half implied, was a besetting world of supernatural underdogs, who were in league with the fire and smoke. In consequence the clowning passed unnoticed by the servants, for they observed that this was nonsense, beneath their notice, and most likely not intended for them as well. Gathering himself together, for a final struggle perhaps, with his competitors, the mysterious Three, the Finn was alert. Attracting the attention of Finnian Shaw Major, by his violent and incendiary gestures, he uttered, by way of clarion call to the disturbed company:

'POUR LE REPOS PUBLIC – POUR LE REPOS PUBLIC!' – and having gained the attention of his host, he added in a more familiar key, but with the same unctuous pomp:

'DU MOINS IL ME LE SEMBLE!'

'Moi aussi!' Osmund grinned agreeably his encouragement, and Knut at once proceeded, embracing the entire table with the radiations from his staring eyes of polar green and the unrelaxing pits, dyed in the carmine of the setting sun, of his dimples:

'TOUS LES HONNÊTES GENS, AYANT FAIT LIGUE ENSEMBLE,
TOUS LES HONNÊTES GENS, (mars oui madame, *tous* les honnêtes gens!)
DEVRAIENT COULER À FOND, À GRAND COUPS DE BEAUX VERS
(Devraient fondre dessus) – À GRAND COUPS DE BEAUX VERS!
LES PÉDANTS, PLUS FACHEUX QUE LES TROP LONGS HIVERS!'

A big pause came after these heavy blows of beautiful verses, administered like a master: aiming in anti-climax a mere bluff blow of the fist at the spot hit before (to make bull-bitch saltate as she readily did), Knut detonated, denouncing what he would send to the bottom, swamp, sink with verse-blow after verse-blow, or broadsides of booming vocables:

'PÉDANTS!'
(PAY-PAY-DORR!)

That's what he would stave in and scuttle! Pay-pay-dorr! – But that dark Trinity of Pedants did not stop the mechanical waggle of Fifth-of-November postiche moustaches (large leaves of oil-dropping saladed lettuces tattooed with their Clarkson bristles, as they vanished in their faces, beneath the masked noses) – they ignored the heavy blows of the beautiful verses.

'I'm positive that he's right, don't you agree Sib – three *pedants* – of course! – it's just what they must be now I come to consider! Don't you agree! Don't you agree!!'

'Pedants! *Of course*! Pedants!' echoed Sib. 'I was mad! It is as plain as the nose on your face!'

'It's as plain as a pikestaff!''

'It's as plain as print!'

'Plainer than print – plainer than print!'

'Much – much!' lisped Sib in the voice of Osmund, precipitately.

'Pedants!' Knut rushed in to agree forcibly with himself, in a splutter at the cap, a big labial P, nodding with fury at the shoddy Buddha, Wildsmith, across the table – who kept his chin high and looked down his nose at everybody, full of the scorn of his cheap contemplation, his eyes swimming superciliously in his spectacles. 'Per-per-per-ped-dornt-tuss!'

'How stupid of me, how really *asinine* of me it was!' brayed the great victorian Osmund at that, the young Trollope-curate in person: 'of course I should have known all along – all the time they were really *peasants!*'

'Pedants!' Sib corrected.

'Yes of course, Pedants – I should have thought of that at once – did you?' Osmund chided himself again. 'But how stupid of me! I could *kick* myself!'

He inflicted a light blow upon his own shin beneath the table – Sib to follow suit hacked out but she hit Mr Wildsmith with her foot by mistake.

'I was a perfect fool not to have thought of that!' Sib panted, plunging herself into sackcloth and ashes, in clownish imitation of the clowning of Osmund, and they both took the tumble together, their eyes on each other.

Wildsmith (more meretriciously chinese, the Bloomsbury sinologue *genre* Chu-chin-chow, at every moment) put on a mask of deep offence. Pedants! – what was this they were talking about? Who was a pedant? What next!

'Of course. Pedants!' Lord Osmund repeated.

There's no of course about it! said the indignant mask of Wildsmith, Bloomsbury Mandarin of the First Button. *No of course about it!*

'DEVRAIENT COULER À FOND, À GRAND COUPS DE BEAUX VERS!'

The shouting Finn rose to his feet. He described an intoxicated stance with an imaginary besom, with which he swept off the board *all* pedants that were there, with the stroke of a Plus Man or of a magical batsman bent on a century. And having done that he just said –

'*TROP LONGS* HIVERS!'

– looked at the company to see if they had taken in about the length of the winters, and sat down with the greatest abruptness.

'Far too long!' his host, with his purring sneer, agreed.

'Pour le repos public!' added the Sib.

'Exactly!' said Lord Osmund. 'Pour le repos public – too long by half!'

'En effet!' the Volpemini wound up the matter.

Wildsmith slightly singed the Volpemini in passing with a cold sinological ghost of a pale dawn of mirth though not quite so coarse as a smile.

Along that side of the table upon which sat the mysterious Three, the form of Phoebus floated forward osmundward and his chair was vacant. There was some hush as he passed, for such a step was unusual. Phoebus had come to confer with his brother Osmund: the Finn, as he caught sight of him, exclaimed in rousing accents that occupied the silence:

'MAIS, QUAND J'AI MAUDIT ET MUSES ET PHÉBUS,
JE LE VOIS QUI PARAIT, QUAND JE N'Y PENSE PLUS!'

and then he kissed his fingers at the approaching divinity.

Phoebus inclined himself to whisper in the ear of Osmund, and Osmund whispered back, with olympian calm his detached eye wandered. There was a short return of confidences, a consultation in which Osmund pronounced himself, it was plain, and Phoebus was satisfied. Solemnly concerned was Lord Phoebus, it was a weighty secret, and their friends watched their mysterious patrons out of the tails of their eyes, as the movements of two policemen are intently canvassed by the crowd in an emergency – as the officers consult and counter-consult, moving noiselessly hither and thither, flashing their bull's-eyes upon this object and that.

But the Finn rose in his place and barked at the intruder – pointing his finger at that obtuse embodiment of nursery pomp-and-circumstance, curly Lord Phoebus-Desmond – pointing and shouting –

'BIZARRE HERMAPHRODITE! – BIZARRE HERMAPHRODITE!
DE QUEL GENRE TE FAIRE – ÉQUIVOQUE MAUDITE!'

'Do be quiet Kanute!' said Lord Osmund, objecting to 'hermaphrodite'.

'Yes do be quiet Knut – it's a mistake to think you're funny – !' Phoebus was quite down on him too, these verses, à la longue, were a consequential absurdity, even in bad taste.

'BIZARRE HERMAPHRODITE!' thundered the Finn.

'Kanute stop making that noise or I'll have you put outside!' Lord Osmund raised his voice to say, while Phoebus stopped in the midst of an important disclosure. But the Finn indicating with outstretched arm and stiff air-stabbing forefinger his vacant place, to the breathless Phoebus, at the far end of the table, replied, frowning and openly contumelious –

'TU NE ME RÉPONDS RIEN? SORS D'ICI! FOURBE INSIGNE!
MALE AUSSI DANGEREUX QUE FEMELLE MALIGNE!'

Phoebus rose quickly up into the air, swiftly leaving Osmund's ear behind him and beneath him, full of portentous secrets, and on light and airy feet withdrew, the way he had come, followed by the voice of Knut –

'SORS D'ICI! FOURBE INSIGNE!'

'Don't you know anything else Kanute except those stupid lines of Boileau is it still? We are tired of those, try and remember something else.' Osmund turned his back upon Kanute and signalled the Sib, who was talking to Wildsmith, who had his back turned towards her.

'It's difficult to know how to stop him once he is wound up. Kanute gets obsessed with some tiresome verses.'

'All Finns are like that!'

'Have you known many Finns Sib?'

'No. But he is not a Finn is he?'

Scarcely had Phoebus resumed his seat, dropping into it with graceful precipitation, than he was again upon his feet. A distant, hollow and violent, banging was present to the ears of everyone at the same time, and it woke a sensational echo, from one end of the table to the other. Both Lord Osmund and Lord Phoebus started up, with looks of horror.

'There they are!' Lord Osmund exclaimed.

'Who?' asked Sib.

'It is the conjurers!'

'It sounded like the conjurers,' agreed Lord Phoebus, stalking towards the door.

'Just like them! It must be the conjurers. Unless it is the police!' Lord Osmund added darkly, under his breath.

'The police!'

Full scandal-lazzi at 'police'. A hundred guilty china-blue periwinkles in awed baby-heads composed a suitably guilty chorus for a police raid. There was plenty of guilt, if looks went for anything, there was no lack of lawlessness, and all the officers would have to do when they burst in would be just to 'pull' the entire assembly – they would then have under lock and key (said those coy criminal-masks, that openly hugged out-of-sight some unmentionable turpitude) a pretty hot catch for one round-up – a bag of a hundred odd of sly little black-sheep, and a few crooked old black shepherds, and one or two big blond ones. There would be promotion for those police-officers! Oh lucky police!

The knocking somewhere continued.

'Wherever is Mrs Bosun?' Phoebus asked in disgusted caterwaul.

'I expect she's listening-in to Moscow.'

'I shouldn't be surprised!'

'She's in the middle of the News I'm positive – from the U.S.S.R.B.C. !'

'Does Mrs Bosun listen to Moscow?' asked the Sib, the evident victim of a long wavelength of civic misgiving – hearing the ineffable name of 'Bosun' associated with the metropolis of the Third International.

'Peters has taught her how to listen in to Moscow,' said Osmund still standing: 'she never misses her bit of propaganda about this time!'

'How alarming!' Sib panted: 'to have one's staff in nightly touch with the U.S.S.R.!'

'But she can't reply, she can only listen.'

'She can only hear jazz!' said Geoffrey Beale.

'Peters is a dangerous man.' Sib cast a glance over her shoulder, lest he should be passing.

'I think he is, like all half-wits.' Osmund's eye stalked Peters in the distance.

'Why do you have a half-wit for a butler,' Sib asked him.

The knocking grew fiercer, and more hollow.

'I think I'd better go don't you Osmund?' Phoebus called.

'Well perhaps you'd better – Mrs Bosun it seems is not going.'

'It seems not.'

'I should go, if I were you!'

'I think I will! I will go and see who it is!'

'I am positive it's the conjurers!'

'It is the conjurers I believe.'

Lord Osmund sat down. The assembly awaited the return of Phoebus in a tense secretive manner, mostly with an excited whispering, speculating upon the likelihood of a descent by the London police – though all agreed that if there was little to choose between one policeman and another, that the London Police was the best and the Berlin Police the worst. So the world-hush of the universal *Speak-easy-soul* of the Post-war, was in this company prolonged until the knocking abruptly ceased. Then it was surmised that Phoebus (a little confounded with Siegfried) was at grips with the Law-and-Order dragon – though in spite of the deference due to their champion this Theoretic Underworld still shook in its criminal shoes, its Edgar Wallace teeth never ceased to chatter, its Potemkin heart was in its throat. The World that had become fashionably Underworld wilted deliciously, at the bare prospect of wholesale detection: half-amorously it fluttered at the shadow of Authority (a child shrinking from the birch-armed Dad) – all breathing one big bated breath of fond fellowship of romantic Revolt, of elect Criminality.

The door was burst open and a tall masked figure with a back made for the Stulz swallow-tail, holding in its hand a six foot long yellow cane-wand, surmounted by an ear of wheat, the mantle of Graziano held over an arm, entered. It was Mr Zagreus, in ordination First Conjurer to Lord Osmund for this momentous Lenten Party: but upon his heels came a Half-man in stealthy procession, and a tall young Florentine gentleman next, with a very small figure to bring up the rear, which was Margolin. But Mr Zagreus now in his dignity of First Conjurer gave the rule of respect to that of the Split-man and they revolved a moment in proximity to the entrance: then Peters turned them aside, and the party headed for the performer's table, while Kanute – *princeps* as well as *primus* – raised his green bonnet in greeting, for he foresaw here a welcome diversion, that would draw away interest from the mysterious Three.

Separated from the main portion or nave of the tithe-barn by irregular pillars of wood, and a network of rugged struts, were two aisles: these had been here and there fitted with partitions, furnished with tables, with underfoot sawdust but otherwise nothing. It was into such a compartment that the group of performers was introduced by Peters. It had the appearance of the Manger of tradition, in an altar-piece, with Zagreus in that case a visiting Magus, and they sat with their four backs to the wall, with as the nearest guests to them the three mystery-men. From left to right they were Margolin, Dan, Zagreus and Ratner. Behind them upon the wall two small wooden panels hung, they were specimens of pokercraft. One said –

DO BE CAREFUL PLEASE!

the other said –

TEA FOR TWA.

'It *was* the conjurers!' said Lord Osmund.

'I thought it was,' answered the Sib.

'What did you think of them?' O. said.

'Which?' S. looked about to form an opinion.

'The party of conjurers,' said O.

'Very smart I thought,' said S. 'Their leader was imposing.'

'That is Zagreus,' O. said.

'Oh that is Zagreus,' S. replied. 'Who used to do the jokes?'

'Yes,' said O. 'Zag-rooce.'

'I know!' nodded S. (a fellow-"Ninety"!)

'He is a magician now,' said O. with rounded eyes, to welcome magic. 'They say he can walk through walls. He learnt to do so in the Orient where he has spent many years – he is an adept of afghan magic.'

'Is he going to put us under some spell this evening?' S. made haste to ask.

'No, he will not this evening,' O. disappointed S. 'He says it is not worth while. He has promised however to cut one of his assistants in half: also he will make a flagstone float upon the surface of the bath-water – that will be only for members of the family.'

Both O. and S. showed signs of distress, as the logs had got the bit between their teeth and roared, darting their large tongues into the brick chimney.

'I hope,' said S., 'that he won't disturb,' and she looked around the powerful barn 'the atoms of the building, with his spells. Already I feel a little insecure.'

'There is no occasion to,' O. said: 'I am positive that he won't interfere with the atoms. He is very careful.'

'Oh that is good,' S. panted back.

'He did what he calls *a vanish*,' said Lord O., 'at Lady Shuter's, a week or two ago. He was supposed to be spiriting away one of his assistants, but instead of that all of a sudden Lady Shuter disappeared!'

At the thought of *the vanish* at Lady Shuter's there was a gasp from S.

'Lady Shuter disappeared!' she said, 'how terrifying! Into space?'

'Yes,' said O. 'There was nothing left but a rather dirty stain upon the floor.'

'I've never heard of such a thing as that!' S. said.

'Nor I,' Lord O. agreed.

'But was it explained,' S. said, 'at least!'

'It seems that something had gone wrong,' O. told her. 'No one was more surprised than himself – Mr Zagreus looked at his assistant who was supposed to vanish and of course the young man was still there! But when Mr Zagreus found that Lady Shuter had disappeared he considered that the trick had after all been a success.'

'I should think it had!' S. clamoured. 'I should rather think it had, don't you! If it eliminated Lady Shuter it must distinctly be called a *success* I should say! A success – it was a triumph of the conjurer's art – almost a turning point!'

'Un succès fou!' Lord Osmund cooed and sneered.

'I suppose everybody thought the same,' the S. then asked.

'It was regarded by several people I understand as the best trick they had ever seen!' Lord O. at once replied.

'What happened after that?' S. pressed him to tell her the sensational sequel.

'Then Myrtle Shuter began crying,' said Lord O. in his deep coo: 'she said she wanted her mother back and she accused Mr Zagreus of doing it on purpose – of spiriting her away!'

'Of having her in his pocket perhaps!' S. said.

'Perhaps!' said O.

'Did he then whisk Myrtle away too?' S. asked.

'He might have done so with advantage,' O. agreed. 'But as a matter of fact he was rather upset about the disappearance of Lady Shuter, because apparently he was not sure he had the required formula to bring her back again.'

At this neither O. nor S. were at all surprised and they sympathized with the perplexed magician in retrospect.

'How did he manage to do so?' then S. asked.

'He tried several passes,' after a pause O. said, noting in the distance the behaviour of the forester. 'Then in desperation he remembered the pass that the indian fakirs use to conjure with elephants (they call it the *ton-lifter*, it's done with fingers forked) – he made the pass, and Lady Shuter shot out of the ceiling and was restored intact to her guests!'

'As hale and hearty as ever!' croaked the S.

'Far more so!' exclaimed Lord O. 'She incommoded several newcomers by her redoubled heartiness that nothing had prepared them for, and assured them all that she had never felt so terribly hale, that she could remember.'

'So sound in wind and limb!' S. panted in asthmatic chant.

'So full of joy dee vivre!' O. added.

'It was lucky he remembered the formula!' S. said with feeling.

'Wasn't it!' eagerly responded O.

'I suppose Lady Shuter thought that all's well that ends well,' S. conjectured.

'Oh no,' said O. 'Not she!' said he. 'Lady Shuter wanted to disappear again!'

'That was tempting providence.'

'It was,' O. thought as well.

'And would he do it?'

'No,' said O. 'Not again, he said he couldn't do it again – not so soon! He said it wasn't safe!'

'What did he mean?' S. asked, 'by that – was that polite of him?'

'I suppose he meant the house might not stand it a second time!'

'In quick succession!'

'It was only a house after all!'

'I am surnamed The Hardy. I was King of England, Scotland, Ireland, Denmark, Norway, Sweden, Poland, Saxony, Brandenburg, Bremen, Pomerania. I am Hardycanute,' interrupted the Finn, with the rude buzzing rub-a-dub of his norse palate, discharging a volley of r's at them, as they gossipped about *the vanish* at Shuter's.

'Kiss me Hardy!' was all that Lord Osmund said, in a tone

bordering on contempt, and turned the cold shoulder upon his clown, who was under a cloud and inferior fun to *a vanish* he must understand.

'Oh Osmund! – tarlink!' the Finn exclaimed affecting the soppy manners of the Seventh Heaven, and offered to fling himself at once upon his host. Lord Osmund gave him a buxom push with his fat hand upon the chest.

'That's quite enough Finland!' he sneered in a rough purr as he threw him off.

'Tarr-*ling!*' exclaimed the Finn.

But as too much haste is as much before time, as too much delay is out of time, Hardycanute enveloped a shadow only of the nimble bulk of his host (who had left a void for the outstretched finnish arms) and he fell flat upon his face and there they left him. His legs provided an obstacle for the staff, over which they hurdled at breakneck speed, on their way to the service door, getting very expert soon at this.

As he lay upon the floor, his cheek wooing the soft dust of wood, his nostril distended to capture its sappy scent, and closing an eye, Knut was heard, in muffled lazy bellow:

> 'LABORIEUX VALET DU PLUS COMMODE MAÎTRE,
> QUI POUR TE RENDRE HEUREUX ICI-BAS POUVAIT NAÎTRE!'

Lord Osmund levelled a kick at the exotic prostrate tumbler, his polyglot fool.

'Shut up!' he said: and Kanute lay still and stark, apparently falling into a deep sleep.

'He's passed out,' said Lord Osmund.

'Who is that!'

'The King of Finland!' Osmund replied.

Some anxiety had been experienced at the prolonged absence of Lord Phoebus, for no one had seen any sign of him since he had gone away to admit the party of conjurers. But at this moment the door rapidly opened and Lord Phoebus was revealed, in great drooping haste to resume his seat, his hair a little dishevelled and his face so preternaturally obtuse that it was realized by everybody, without anyone needing to tell them, that something of a grave nature had occurred.

'You've been away a long time Phœbus!' as he saw his truant junior sink into his chair, Lord Osmund called out to him.

'Yes I know!' Phoebus hollered back, signalling to Peters for some asparagus.

'I hope nothing's the matter!'

'It is – very much so!'

'Whatever is it now?'

Phoebus raised his voice, and he discharged the peculiar news in measured and loud matter-of-factness.

'Mrs Bosun's had a fit!'

'A fit!'

'Mrs Bosun!' the World echoed.

In a world of Bosuns what could two babes-in-the-wood expect, except repeated calls upon their vitality and their initiative, Phoebus conveyed by his perfectly wooden expression, as he lifted a piece of asparagus into the air and lowered its blunt barbed head into his dickie-bird beak, thrust up to receive it.

Sensation throughout the audience – Bosun and Fit! A vivid exchange of shocked anxious glances and the splutter of a giggle here and there.

Lord Osmund sprang to his feet and in the deep florid bay that belonged to the throat of all Finnian Shaws without distinction, in the male line, he responded, in undisguised consternation –

'A fit – has Mrs Bosun had a fit!'

'Good heavens!' exclaimed the Sib. 'Mrs Bosun!'

'What kind of fit! Was it apoplectic Phoebus – are you sure it was a fit!'

'I'm positive it was a fit – she was lying by the side of the loud-speaker!'

'By the side of the loud-speaker? How extraordinary. Was the Savoy Band playing?'

'No.'

'*Not* the Savoy Band?'

'No.'

Whereupon it was *immediately apparent* to the least initiated that something very strange had occurred, and that it was not unconnected with the loud-speaker. It was extremely significant that it was not the Savoy Band – Lord Phoebus knew more, it was quite plain, than he cared to impart, unless somewhat pressed. And the loud-speaker was in some way at the bottom of it.

'Did you turn it off?' asked Lord Osmund, taking a step as though to go and do so presently, as the thought of its roaring away by itself was uncanny.

'I turned it off the moment I got there,' answered Lord Phoebus. Nothing if not a man of great emergencies, Lord Phoebus had turned it off at the main with the most surprising presence of mind.

'And the Savoy Band was not after all what you heard Phoebus – not that but something else you say!'

'Certainly the Savoy Band was not at all what I heard.'

What could it be (whatever could it be!) that Lord Phoebus had heard, as he just saved Mrs Bosun by turning off the loud-speaker?

'You will see they will continue shouting to each other, they are wound up,' Horace Zagreus pointed out to Dan: 'and they have this play to do – it is called BOSUN. But look – you cannot benefit by all that you are hearing in that position, you are crouching over the table with your legs spread out – I am sorry, hold yourself (have you your drill-book?) well, to begin with *legs crossed* of course – crossed – clamp them then, fast, that is the first step' (Dan crossed two silken show-lady shadow-legs under the table-rim, clipping knee to knee, grasping the under with the upper) 'and the hands, cross those next – palm on back of it – no, right on top – press down next upon the thigh surfaces, it is the prescribed position – cast your eyes up and in upon the juncture of the brows – *squint* Menschenkind – in other words squint! squint, that is it, is that so difficult! it's all in the book, *equilibrate – equilibrate!* Make yourself into a vessel a *retort* that will trap that thunder of pure folly, this thunder of pure folly, that is going on. Those equidistant claps from Phoebus, counterclaps from Olympus, which is Osmund – what a moonstruck music of hallucinated machines that is – they chose *Bosun* to suggest a nautical print these predestined period-fanciers I expect, to make you hitch up your slops and spit black plug – there is no Bosun, and there is no fit! But attend! they are approaching their stupid orgasm. It is they who will have the fit! Watch them excite each other, see how they whip one another in perfect time with drawling tongues, they quite lash out – it is a slow approach to the delicious crisis – a heaven of small hate constructed of small-talk will explode as the joke bursts. Bang! – What a small return for so much solemn fuss? – not at all – ends and means, like effect and cause, are not marked off with such precision as all that! There, in another moment they will have their fit! You will see them "die of" a little snuffling laughter. But their ritual must be seen to be believed! Regard those pompous showmen as the kettledrums you remember – the clouds and drums heard from within, coming out of the body in the first condition of Yoga. After that the bees and *then* the bells – *then the bells at the end of it.* You know Yoga. Don't you remember – enjoining silence! Yoga. Yes – Yoga! Indian stuff. Well. Here it is different – you have to turn this inside-out I should say outside-in, do you follow. You look a little stupid (perhaps you have not diligently practised squinting – it is a lost art). Imagine for instance the good Osmund is an intestine. Yes *an intestine*. He has been reduced to a percussion music by your disciplines your *asanas.* That was essential. Let his snout be the mouthpiece of a submissive organ. After its kind it can make music. All this company is but *one unit*. It is one thing, a unit. You have to compress it, for it to be a single body – you define it, set terms to it, you endow it with a hide to tie it up, force it into one envelope. Cram it in – it will go nicely. But yourself, you hold yourself *outside* it. That is quite good Yoga. Now however these thunders become the intestinal organic music of Yoga. Is that quite clear – I ask you for you do not look as if you entirely understood (but that may be the effect of the squint). – Listen to Osmund. His voice is instructive – it is a drone, in the sense of the basis of the bag-pipe. Ennui is the ballast of the drone. When it is Osmund. A slow measure, listen again – Osmund dances to the music of his boredom, slowly with satisfaction. That is the sound of Osmund. And Phoebus is his bombastic echo.'

That was good Yoga, yes perhaps! thought Dan, if he thought.

– But as he sat with his legs tightly crossed, his hands forming a vice-like circuit with the stiff arch of his shoulders, and his eyes directed inward, fixed on his nose, in a high-pitched squint, all he could say in reply to himself, but over and over again, in a self-colloquy – which in its turn was a verbal squint of sorts – was '*why oh why!*' and the rest of his customary invocation to Horace – the cause of the unkindness of whom he could never pretend to fathom for a moment, for it was strange and unnatural. And when Dan wondered, with great bitterness, not once but many times, how long he would have to sit in that grotesque position. '*Why Horace must I sit*' and so on, but of course such questions did not pass his lips, and *how long* he had no idea, but only sat and squinted (with death in his soul) as high up his nose as possible (though once he fell as low as the tip).

Star' alla porta quand' un non vuol aprire,
Et aver un amico che ti vuol tradire,
Son dieci doglie da morire!

Margolin was mischievous: the sticks of matches fell in a shower upon the mysterious Three – they shot up from the nervous fingers of Zagreus' assistant, for Archie was a match-stick archer, and he shot true. But occasionally a piece would fly out at a tangent, and, as Dan riveted his eyes upon both the left and right surface of his nose at once, to satisfy Yoga, now and then a Lightship Safety Match stick flew into his restricted field of vision, and the delicate missile administered a small blow to the organ Dan was surveying, before glancing off and falling upon the table. Such was life!

'That drone of the bored grandee, My Lord Gossip' Horace continued, to supplement the action of Yoga, 'if you only sit in the right position, you will have that music at your centre, it is right there inside you Dan, like the thunder-cloud in Yoga, that's what I mean. (With hard cash it is, My Lord Gossip pays the columns, the mentions, such as "Lord Osmund has a new book of verses on the way", or "The Finnian Shaws again! What a strangely gifted family!" – he thrusts round with agents the photographs, that he buys in reams, of his stout ego – nothing except enforced absence from the Gossip in the cheery

Chat-columns would cause him to lose weight.) Sink boldly Dan into these embodiments of "Gossip" as you would into the swelling volume of a velvet-watered hot bath to the neck – to enervation – get well into this rich thunder of Chatter – get down boy into it neck crop rudder and udder (though painful it is well worth while) with the same zeal that, the good little Yogi, you would slip into the appointed "Noiselessness". Here you have come out frankly, into a swarming desert, *to find Noise* – not to fly it. – The Raja Yoga is reversed. This is Pierpoint's invention. Pierpoint's? Yes his invention – to me that would never have occurred – to get the specific noises (including the notorious tinkling) *outside*, by disciplines, that is his handiwork – in everything he is *inventor*. Great Inventor!' Mr Zagreus clamoured his belief in the infallibility of the great Pierpoint, while Split-man bowed his head, with sneers. 'The subconscious prehension should be sextupled, as the adoption of the correct position improved it? Do you find you are registering the vibrations better now? They are charged with idiotic – charged with idiotic – I should say *idiot-waves* is what they are. Are they rolling in forcibly? An insipid machinery. I can no longer listen myself, I am impatient. What? Have I not implemented my promise, to show you the Ape of God at-home? If you are at a loss to reach the meaning of any of his diversions, at once inform me! No man can guarantee to circumscribe, with cast-iron cartesian definition, all that they do. But that is not necessary. The posture you have adopted enables you to transcend such dialectic. The significance of these reduces itself to a sort of music, and *that* you have trapped. That you should have trapped. I as your Guru am music-master in ordinary: I impart a musical art. The last thing you must look for is the message of an orderly sentence – the significance lies in the impact of the image. One of Pierpoint's loveliest verses will sound like nonsense.

Multimark of the cliff-breeding species, to cormorants
Next allied
Were apses.

'You see? To speak of the "meaning" of that would be beside the mark – it gets you in the guts like a bomb or it doesn't. *Were apses?* – It is my favourite!'

Mr Zagreus smiled to himself with pleasure, over *were apses.*

A Safety Match struck Dan's eyelid. He heard the nasal roar of Osmund, as it were in the distance – *well outside.* The Safety Match landed sharp corner foremost: he did not flinch.

'Listen to that one!' said Mr Zagreus, as he heard Lord Osmund calling again to Lord Phoebus. 'Quite apart from the words. Chart the intonation, plot it – then you have the whole lot in a net! Osmund is the perfection of Osmund. I call his a first-rate tone – of course making allowances. A mellow bellow! *What is that instrument! What* is that instrument?'

Mr Zagreus lent his ear to the osmundian pipe.

'As to the subject of the song, it is unquestionably self-pity, rising from the illustrious blubber – Osmund is spermy. Why, the pathos of a What's-his-name exploiting his patent blank-cartridge or hollow manhood that is it, as if such things could constitute the patent conferring the laurel coronet of the historical poet! But what are the Wild Red Waves Saying, Lord Osmund? Lord Osmund to the Dark Tower Came – but *WHAT ARE THE WILD RED WAVES SAYING?* If they were not there, then nor would you be either Osmund – anachronist – Kanute squatting fronting the flood-tide that is blood-red at the flood. Just out of reach. That is paradox if you like – such is the price of what we call "Gossip" – the principles symbolized by the coloration of massacre military and civil, gollops everything except "Gossip" – "Gossip" and more "Gossip", which (highly politic) it leaves standing as an advertisement. *That* it allows – for does not the mildew of the "Gossip" throughout the land discredit everything the Red Principle moves to destroy – what else so much as it and the social facts to which that corresponds, could cause this society to look quite so foolish? The answer is *nothing*. All Revolution is preceded by "Gossip". That must be so – I feel that must be a law. No it is too ugly, I cannot listen – but that base old viol has a fine tone all the same, for such as can descend to that basement!'

The Finn passed, bombarded with matches by Margolin.

'Osmund before he had become Gossip-Champion, when he was at the outset of his career as a professional Publicity-attraction, had a great hankering to be a Lion and to be hunted by the latest Lady Leo-Hunter. With his itch to take part in a lion-hunt with himself as the "lion", Osmund directed his steps to all the selectest bright Chelsea parties, as the War ended. But the leo-huntresses saw him, shot a shaft at his title for luck, but would not at any price hunt him upon the "lion" basis: none were to be caught napping by a lion-skin stuffed with pedigrees and Bradburys. For all he has said of them since, these hostesses had the good sense to recognize that that was nothing but an Ape in "lion's" clothing not worth powder and shot of a "Leo"-Diana. At this Osmund raged, and he vowed to get even – to hunt if he might not be hunted: to humble, in fact, those unsportsmanlike Chelsea hostesses – who cried out for "lions" and more "lions", asking Osmund to bring them "lions" when next he came *as though he were not there himself at all* – ready to roar very prettily. Quâ "lion" they would not consider him, only as "society" figurehead, who (like themselves, in all probability) wrote articles about dress, and novels or broadsheets about their acquaintances. So it was that *faute de mieux* Lord Osmund became a Leo-huntress's-hunter. *Lion I am not*, *Leo-hunter I deign not*, and so on. *Hunter I am*. No. It was a case of discouraging those sports in which he was not qualified to participate as the sacrosanct victim. Such is the genesis of Osmund's lampoons upon the Chelsea hostesses – it was a would-be "lion's" illegitimate vanity, wounded by the non-discharge of the Leo-huntress's duck-shot!'

'Is that really,' asked Ratner 'the reason?'

Margolin called to a waiter and asked for more matches.

'Of course.'

'I didn't know.'

'I thought everyone knew that Julius.'

'I supposed he found the hostesses boring, as most of them are,' quite bored and off-hand Ratner thrust in his objection.

'Not at all! He loves Society. But that of course is the answer he would make *himself* to what I have just said.'

'Would he?'

'Of course – you made it for him! – Again Osmund hated the "lions". That comes into it too. Britannia's hard on the "lions", and Osmund never liked "lions", not real ones, any more than Britannia. All such as Osmund have those sensations.

I know, because Pierpoint has told me. They have hated him, for his lion-heart – he knows all about it! The "Gossip" page is a zoo of sham kings-of-the-forest as everyone knows, and "Gossip" as we now have it was invented about nineteen twenty-four, for that purpose. All along what he coined "high-brow" to denominate was hated by the yellow hack. The proletariat of Letters was glad to settle accounts with its grandees, those "lions" – poets and artists – and the Osmunds of whatever period make pacts with the canaille – they are true to nothing not even themselves – to nothing! But so long as there were Leo-hunters there would be "lions" that was but too evident: so if you destroyed the Leo-hunters you killed two birds with one stone, so it seemed. To doing that Lord Osmund was by no means averse, although his peculiar quarrel was with the narrow-minded huntresses, who would not hunt a stuffed "society" animal – that was the gist of the trouble.'

'Do you believe though Horace that the suppression of a lion-hunter does any harm to real "lions", I don't see how it can,' Julius had his say, but Zagreus turned upon the Split-Man at once, with an offensive laugh – he had had enough of his Split-Man as usual, though he would not part with him for worlds.

'Ah, I see: you also Ratner would not have been averse to be a little *hunted?* No – you know as well as I, that when you destroy one snobbery you make room that is all for another. Besides what better "snobbery" exists perhaps you can tell me, than a passion for those of great intelligence? What more natural than to seek their society? *Snob* – that is anyway a word invented by the middle-class yahoodom of Liberal England. It is a Whig word.'

'At least you practise what you preach!' boldly hissed Ratner in his face, but Mr Zagreus did not seem to hear him this time – to the real Ratner he turned a deaf ear.

A Safety Match dispatched by Margolin, at this moment struck Lord Osmund.

'Soon there will be a fracas.' Horace gazed with approval at the practical-joker-born. 'But you know the advertisement of Birth that is used as puff-matter, in order to swell this Gossip-lion so much with gas – referred to in gentle Gossip-mockery as the "importance of being Finnian Shaw" – on the pattern of being Ernest?'

'Of course.'

'That it seems is a sham too!'

'Go on!' said Arch.

'No. Their grand manner turns out (my informant is a Debrett-fan) to be a flunkey's, as one might have guessed without Debrett. – They are not Finnian Shaws at all or Willoughbies.'

'Now I think better of them!' exclaimed Margolin, lightheartedly aiming a Safety Match at Phoebus.

'Are they bogus, Horace?' sneered Split-Man at his side. 'Do you mean Finnian Shaw is not their name?'

'No. Shaw is their name. The first Shaw, or should I say the last Shaw, was a Dublin-Scot, he was a wealthy chandler. The Marquis of Balbriggan at that time was penniless. Somehow the Scot got the place and got the name: these are shavian descendants – a waxwork, a wax-tallow, dynasty.'

'How could that have happened though – you Horace understand about such things however.' The Split-man would not let the wax-work out of Debrett past.

'No. I may not have got the facts, in fact I haven't. But my friend is emphatic. He has the facts. They are Eighteenth-Century chandlers – of Lowland stock! They have nothing to do with those ancestors about whom they talk and who come into the big Finnian Shaw puff-ball as feudal ballast, who before being french-speaking nobles of the Pale, were paladins, in Anjou and Germany.'

'That would certainly account for a great deal, if it were true,' the Split-Man said with reluctant relish, coyly torn between hatred of Lord Osmund and hatred of Horace.

'The story would account for their picturesque snobbishness, their middle-class snobbishness, if we may have it both ways, and put them in the category of Leo-hunters.'

'I think so. It might.'

'Why not? A family butler, usurping the style and title of his master, would, in three generations, lead to something like Osmund?'

Ratner smiled assent to the proposition of Horace, accepting the butler, if such Nichtigkeits amused his childish patron (truly this was the thyroid talking!) He smiled with a sad superiority.

'They have an ancient name, but they have the push of the new-rich. All the boastfulness of a usurper!'

With a non-committal smirk of hatred-all-round, the Split-Man contemptuously allowed these remarks to pass, about new-rich, and about usurpations.

'The story must be true!' Horace insisted.

'Well I don't know about that Horace!' Ratner was very indulgent, loath to disappoint.

'Oh I believe it must.'

'The more I look at them, it is true, the more I feel conviction growing Horace –'. Julius gave him both their heads, on a sudden impulse, with malicious unction.

'That is it! All is not sweet, all is not sound!'

The Split-Man gave a croak that was a rattling insuck of the breath.

'Not quite!' he said.

'Well, that is all right,' said Zagreus 'as far as it goes. About this upkeep of Split-Men there cannot be two opinions, they leave us where we were. It is a rotten stable.'

'You seem discouraged Horace,' Split-Man, showing him his coyest half, insinuated.

'No, no, but I cannot waste time with you sir, you are not here to make conversation.'

'Very well Horace. As you know, I am at your service.'

'Masochismus, thy name is Ratner!'

'Do you think so?'

'Inoculated grafts prove better than those which spring out of the stock. But that is nothing to do with tallow-mongers and intruders.'

'You know best.'

'Dan.'

Mr Zagreus turned to Daniel Boleyn and as he began to observe his disciple he fell to laughing, disturbed with a great seizure of involuntary mirth.

The original erectness in the rough-and-ready postulant had slackened on all hands, the head had sagged forward, the elbows swung idly inward upon the ribs, a stoop had crept up the back and buried each shoulder, two fists foregathered limply upon a mere lap of dejected thighs, legs had quitted their muscular self-constriction (muscles gone to roost) – folded together as tame as two dangling extremities of tackle out-of-commission. Daniel Boleyn had from head to foot disintegrated, in the stress of meditation, into a squinting crouch. Having given each other a disconsolate rendezvous at the projecting nose-tip, his eyes met gloomily upon a point between two nostrils – resignation had deposited the hands like unoccupied gloves beneath the navel at the table-level – such was Dan's ultimate Yoga, his whole guttering appearance providing a commentary not far short of a mock, directed point-blank at the methods of his master.

'Why what a funny Yogi you look' Zagreus howled almost to himself in astonishment. 'I have never beheld such a drooping Yogi as you!'

Even all Dan's love was not proof against this coarse assault; he drew himself up, throwing discipline to the winds, gave a shake like a person waking from a dream, and said from the bottom of his heart, with the utmost simplicity,

'I am not a Yogi.'

The Split-Man laughed outright, a little painful clap of derision, and Mr Zagreus if anything nonplussed looked fairly serious.

'No but you have come to see these tallow-lords at play and you are under a discipline that has some points of resemblance to Raja Yoga you know, come you know that don't play the innocent – the system in which the insistence is upon the *will*. Will!' Mr Zagreus licked his lips and rolled his eyes. 'That, if I am not mistaken, is your strong point! A will of iron Dan I should say you had got, from all I know of you!' Mr Zagreus positively shouted in challenging fashion at the grinning Julius, 'To bring your will power out to the full has been my object: I have constituted myself your temporary Guru or master. No young Yogi ever got far without a Guru – that I know for a fact – in me you see your trainer let us leave it at that. You must not say you are not a Yogi. It's very naughty of you to say you're not a Yogi!'

Dan's mouth trembled at "naughty" as he stood up to the reproof, still slightly squinting. Oh why should Horace call him *naughty*, when he had never intended to be! His feet were extremely painful: but he had a little tin of vaseline in his pocket and at the first opportunity would introduce it between the toes that hurt the most.

'The Ape of God is a portion of eternity greater than the eye of man can measure – you will find in that diapason (the braying as it were of a mechanical ass, bellowing to its fellow, Phoebus) all that is necessary to fill that cosmos, brought by your postures beneath the control of your six-cylinder will. You will be able to call it up or dismiss it – at will! You will no longer depend upon the exterior cosmos in any way whatever – the power to create and destroy will be yours.'

He gazed at Dan in admiration, in the most flattering manner.

'You are the most silent person I have ever met. That in no way surprises me! Did not Bhava when asked to describe the nature of God, observe a profound silence: in the same manner he met question after question. *Silence*. That is your answer! It is because *silence* is your answer, Dan, to all our questions – it is for that reason that I believe so profoundly in your genius, the quality of your silence allows the highest hopes for your future. Its brilliance I have never doubted for a moment!'

Dan blushed, and opened his mouth to speak.

'I – ' he said.

'Silence!' commanded Horace: 'it is your modesty that causes you to open your mouth and to say "I" – that "I" spoke volumes!'

The single act of insubordination was now forgotten and forgiven.

'When Mrs Bosun, you observed, was picked up beside the loud-speaker – you heard all that? – *what was it that had overcome Mrs Bosun* – such was the burning question of the moment. What deadly sounds had been coming out of the loud-speaker as Phoebus entered the room! You heard the sequel – when at last the laugh came, at the name *Robert*. Their friend so-named was broadcasting a poem tonight – had you studied the B.B.C. programme beforehand, and so been aware of that fact, you would certainly have foreseen what would have been supposed to be coming out of the mouth of the loud-speaker, when Mrs Bosun was supposed to have been taken ill, and Phoebus was supposed to have gone in. It is a typical pantomime. As performed by these strange adult children of anything from thirty to fifty, you have a fair specimen in this farce called *Bosun*. Robert Wright is a well-worn London laughing-stock, of ten years' standing – before that he was laughed at all through the world-war, on account of his pronounced gallantry-in-action and constant attempts upon the laurel of the war-poet, in competition with Brooke: there was a time when you only had to say *Robert* and everyone would hang out a bright smile to welcome what was to come. So much for the world's fool Robert – the Public however understand he is a poet – ten million spell-bound subscribers or some of them listen to the truly gloomy verses of Robert we will assume. So when at last the cat was out of the bag as you saw, and the cat turned out to be *Robert*, that was an instant success. Mrs Bosun, joke number one, had been knocked out by Robert, joke number two. You must bear in mind that all these persons are permanent school-children, if desire counts for anything, and in consequence all their jokes smell of bread-and-butter as you would expect, and you must not be surprised if they are very very simple little skylarks really and also portentously solemn, conducted with that particular solemnity only met with in youngsters. But there is their standing joke too – that illustrates exceedingly well what I wish to convey, all the more so as it is the joke of "the Parent", the male Parent – that grimly remote author of their being, as seen in the eyes of a family-group of oh such mischievous high-spirited gossoons and nestlings. This is the Finnian Shaw family-jest called "Cockeye", a typical nursery-persiflage, depending upon the capital illusion of this tribal group of wistful adults – namely the abnormal perpetuation of their young-ness, like a new most mysterious patent of Nature's. That is the nickname given the father – "Cockeye" – the aged marquis, by these *gallopins*, such *disrespectful* little offsprings of his as they are – Osmund, Phoebus and Harriet – and what these little rascals will do when "Cockeye" goes to a better place it is difficult to see. Pierpoint is very much to the point upon this subject (he knows them intimately, they hate him terribly, but they don't know that I know him – I should not be here if they did). The Wiltshire story Pierpoint tells is admirable for the light it throws upon this case, so sociologically curious, of the Finnian Shaw family, and their kind of *professional* wistful juvenility. I forget it but here is its gist. It is a tale whose purpose is to illustrate the longevity of the natives of Wiltshire. Two old patriarchs of ninety or so are seated dozing upon either side of the fireplace in their cottage, when a neighbour rushes in and announces that their son John, who is at that time a mere sixty-five, has been fatally gored by a dangerous bull, and his body is being brought back to the village on a hurdle. There is a long silence in the cottage. But at length the old man exclaims, in an exultant quaver: "Ah Nellie I always did tell 'ee that that lad John would be a difficult one to rear!' – Pierpoint says that he can see no reason why Lord Osmund at sixty-five should not still be devising pleasantries at the expense of the hoary Elder, "Cockeye", ever so mischievously – with the wily "Cockeye", with the superior cunning of eld, retorting by cutting down Osmund's allowance from time to time, and telling the Marchioness that "for the sake of the dear children" they had better tie up the entail or take some steps to protect (in the unlikely event of their own demise) the inexperience or impulsiveness of these minors!'

Ratner's face was transformed with a radiant smirk for a brief moment, grateful to be back in a home-element.

'Later in the evening' Horace told Dan, after a glance at Ratner, 'you will see them all sit round in a great family circle of militant minors – Lady Harriet Finnian Shaw (whose last book of verse Willie Service handed you I hope yesterday) will be here after dinner. Harriet is about forty and very bright in a stately cantankerous fashion – she is the image of Phoebus – she will be accompanied by the friend with whom she lives, Miss Julia Dyott, who is about fifty and a perfect kitten – with Eustace, and perhaps some other cousins, they will all collect, with a mass of visiting pseudo-child-guests in front of the vast Santa-Claus Christmas-time grate, and tell each other stories of "Cockeye". You must be present – it is field-work of the first importance – have you your note-book? *Fathers and Sons* it is the great contemporary subject – Pierpoint was the first to point this out (I should have sent you his treatise). You will see a sort of film of the communizing Nursery – call it "Revolt of the Children" – they will not fail in the course of the evening to laugh at "Cockeye's" most extraordinarily amusing habit of referring to them in conversation with the Marchioness as "the children"; that affords a mental picture of a family-group of quite small tots, such touches contribute to the idea at which all strain. Admittedly it is a gloomy business to come to this super-children's party – I understand your feelings! I will let you know when the "Cockeye" phase is about to open. But a thing to be noted: none of these children themselves possess children – a sterility that has had the effect of preserving intact the all-important Nursery-situation as you can imagine. They can never, however long they are spared (and may it be a long while yet) become Cockeyed themselves in turn – that is unless a certain New Zealand jewess, Babs Kennson, succeeds in landing Phoebus, when certainly the youngest of these great subfeminine tallow lords will be compelled to melt and conjugate, giving a pretext at least for a brood to the Jewess, who will be given an inch and will take an ell. The future marquises will then be considerably less shavian and the more masculine realistic strain should drive out most of the wax-work nonsense (though I need not add that Miss Kennson is as scottish as scottish – look out for a go-ahead mayfairish flaxen but anything-but-braw lassie). Robinia cannot breed (but pass your eye over Robinia) – if Babs traps Phoebus with the magic of her Maori money-bags, she has all the trumps in her neat kosher fist. – Now they are going. Observe, Dan, this pompous departure. Never omit to pay especial attention to the *breaks* – when a society breaks up – for that matter either for the shortest time or for good and all it is all one – that is the moment for the restless analyst. – Lord Osmund will pass us. He is somewhat annoyed at the matches of Margolin, he has a feeble appreciation of fun when in the form of matchsticks or otherwise it is directed against his own person. I think you can see that. Here he comes – I believe it is his intention to speak to me – yes it is. – Good Evening Lord Osmund! Yes I have my troupe as you see – we each have our troupe Lord Osmund! – We shall do our best, I am sure, to entertain the company. – What? Those three conspirators – yes I noticed them certainly. Could I hear? Well my ears are not of the best as you know, but I heard what they said quite distinctly. Their speech? About that there was no question at all: I am sorry to say I noticed that they were speaking to each other in hisperic latin. What? In hisperic latin I am afraid. It is a lingua franca of the lowest type of conspiratorial scholar. – Yes, it seemed to me rather underhand – yes, very difficult. The *Altus prosator* was written in hisperic, you may not have heard of it, it is worth knowing from some points of view – it gives you immunity from any death except *death on the pillow*. That is important. Don't want death on the pillow? No. I don't blame you. You'd rather have *violence!* Well that's a matter of taste Lord Osmund – yes violence *is* nice in its way! Many people have regarded death on the pillow as a privilege – though there are always people to be found who plump for stoning or lynching. *Live dangerously* – of course, that is my motto too. – What is that? Never, as far as I know. – Pillow-death is not romantic but it is comfortable – no I'm all for it, for the absent-minded and weak-sighted. – Death by suffocation. – What were those wild men saying Lord Osmund? Nothing in particular – they said you were – but I really could not undertake to repeat what three such ruffians said, they were three objectionable cads and what they said is neither here nor there. They were outside the pale! – Their private thoughts. – Yes. They appeared to be engaged in the doubtful pastime of exchanging their private thoughts, from what I could gather. – I should! In a public gathering it is a breach of all privacy. – No next year. – Very well. We will follow as soon as we have finished our coffee. The coffee. Yes. – Peters? I shall remember. A rivederla! – Niente niente! – What a monumental posterior – look how it rolls him, the great double-barrelled contraption for sitting that he has plastered on to him – heaven help him – what a sweep of sit-down to pop into Restoration shorts! – *Death on the pillow* – he'll never escape far from those two great swollen segments of pillow-for-day-use (not for the head but the tail) – *there* he will die, even if shot he will fall back on his downy bottom-bolsters – he couldn't fall forward. But what aids to gravitation! – what an unfair pull that must give a body! – No

– what do you say about it! There goes his clown at his heels. *Come here Kanute – lie down, good dog!* What a slumberous broadside of a quarter-male – what a tallow-laden gelding goes there, by Pierpoint!'

At the door, the last to leave as he had been first to enter, Knut turned back with dismal bellow, eyeing the refectory-scene he was leaving behind him, with the litter of fifty covers:

'MUSE, CHANGEONS DE STYLE, ET QUITTONS LA SATIRE!
C'EST UN MÉCHANT MÉTIER QUE CELUI DE MÉDIRE!
À L'AUTEUR QUI L'EMBRASSE IL EST TOUJOURS FATAL –
LE MAL QU'ON DIT D'AUTRUI NE PRODUIT QUE DU MAL!'

A burst of hollow clapping came from Mr Zagreus and the Finn bowed in acknowledgment, removing his green bonnet.

'Lying *is* a "méchant métier"!' Mr Zagreus exclaimed, 'and to be a "mauvaise langue" may have bad results on occasion – but rather tell that to your patron, you peculiar parrot!'

'I will so!' And so is it!

II The Players Solus

'Does Pierpoint see them now?' asked Julius, muffling his rough utterance to smuggle 'Pierpoint' out innocently, as if the 'Pierpoint' had never been inside at all but was an external transaction of the lips.

'Pierpoint!' Discreet as had been the 'Pierpoint' it had provoked a flushed and religious response.

'Does he see them?' Julius clipped with his upper-lip the small cup held in his corked black hand, drew up a hot dram of coffee into his throat, once or twice, with a poised eye of hawk-like abstraction, a pause between each dose of his black gargle.

'No not now' said Horace, watching Ratner's face to see if any more 'Pierpoints' were in the wings.

'Did he know them well?'

'They were great friends, for a long time. Pierpoint rather likes Phoebus.'

'I should imagine he would.'

'Would you? Only yesterday Pierpoint told me Phoebus was not so bad – he had the makings of a disciple, he said. He said that was somebody else's remark.'

'I thought they were friends.'

'Yes they used to be.'

'Did Pierpoint want Phœbus to be his disciple?'

'Pierpoint! What a singular idea! No, he meant for me.'

'Oh for you Horace!' Julius croaked sweetly at the modest 'me' of Horace the Humble.

'Yes. He said Phoebus, till his dying day – .'

'Phoebus till his dying day! I like that expression Horace' Archie Margolin obstructed the discussion, with violent patronage, 'I like that. *Till his dying day.* The day for dying, same as day *for drying*, Horace – clothes on the line. *His dying day!*'

'Didn't you know it?' asked Horace delighted. 'Didn't you know it?'

'I have heard it,' Arch said, aiming a match at Peters, who grinned broadly as he fled with a spank of black swallow-tails, in the wind of his exit.

'What did Pierpoint say?' asked Julius.

'He thinks Phoebus is a nice girl.'

'Till his dying day!' Arch choked, excited with mischief.

'Till his dying day, that's it. In perpetuity a pleasant-spoken young lady.'

'What has become of Willie Service?' Julius asked, it was plain, to be censorious.

'He's in the kitchen,' Zagreus said.

'Oh.'

'And why not? He is now abusing us like pickpockets in broad Hoxton, he is winning the confidence of the Finnian Shaw chef. He is a smart boy in white stove-pipe head-gear. In that way he hopes to collect some Finnian Shaw gossip.'

'I think I'll go to the kitchen' said Margolin rising, and he left.

'That's done it' said Julius.

'What do you mean Julius?'

'That young man seems very restless. I wonder why he has gone to the kitchen?'

'Who knows?'

The eyes in the sunburn-powdered face of Horace, who had laid aside his mask, spoke volumes of approval as he watched the dark dancing figure of Arch disappear.

'I think' said he, with a look that was an afterthought at Dan, 'that Margolin has *more than a streak*' he lowered his voice 'of *genius*.'

The Split-Man croaked deeply and drearily.

'How lovely for you Horace has he!'

'I know genius means nothing to you! I see through you.'

'Do you Horace!'

'I've got your X-ray-cabinet – don't think you're opaque.'

'Have you Horace!' The sceptic gazed at him stolidly. Opaque! – Ratner squatted impassible, a dense screen to his disgusted consciousness of *opacity*, called up by this use of the word. (The impenetrable deposits of yellow suet that no tennis would dispel did not seem present at all to the guileless mind of this florid foe.)

'Absolutely – I have your thumb marks!'

'Have you Horace!'

Ratner thudded with his throat-cords, a rusty G-string gamma-music. He shot a look at Dan but it was impossible to gather whether he was attending or not.

'There must have been a time Horace' he said 'when Willie Service even showed signs of genius!'

'What?'

'Did Willie Service Horace never look as though he might turn out to be a great genius?'

'Willie Service?'

'Yes Willie Service. I seem to remember you called me *sceptic* –.'

Horace had been bewildered for this was too subtle – the cunning collocation of Service, a name for a super, and of that quality, 'genius', which played such an outstanding part in his life. But bronzed albino in full warpaint that he was, he was as impassible as his split sparring-partner, as he sat erect, a haggard kitcat to the knees – most like a Choktaw chief who chatted of buffaloes with a feathered chum. But in quick pity he laughed at the split-creature to whom genius was a closed book.

'Service would laugh if he could hear you ask that!' laughed Horace.

'Would he!' Ratner with withering croak riposted. '*Now?*'

'Service is a detective!'

'You didn't tell me Horace Service was a detective.' Julius was coyly reproachful with Horace, in tête-à-tête now that Arch had gone, for Dan did not count.

'Oh yes. Listen Julius to the strange life-story of Service.'

'He has scarcely begun his life yet.'

'He is *young!*' agreed Horace with a bustle of alacrity but an eye touched with pathos, the difficulty of associating *no-genius* with *youth* causing him a passing sensation of impotence. 'But he is a disciple of Edgar Wallace.'

'Of Edgar Wallace. Not of yours Horace.'

'That – never! He is totally wrapt up in the criminal-world as it exists in the brain of Edgar Wallace.'

'That is disappointing. I have seen the point of Service!'

'He believes I am a lag as he calls the receiver of stolen goods. Dan he regards, he once told me that, as my homosexual decoy, whatever he may mean by that, I don't understand. He is persuaded on the other hand that you, Julius, are one of the Big Five of Scotland Yard!'

Ratner rattled away in his throat to be disarming, and he examined Horace blackly out of the black segment of his painted face, the eyehole of the non-existent moiety.

'Oh is that his Complex; he sounds rather like you, Horace.'

'Me, Julius!'

'When you were young. You must have looked at things like that a little.'

'You mean my jokes, you angry devil. – Always angry!'

'Angry!'

'Always really – angry!'

'I didn't mean anything Horace.'

'A public clown.'

'No – really Horace!'

'It was my jokes you meant!'

'Is Service, as you describe?'

'No Service is full – but *full* of Edgar Wallace! It is fantastic – he lives in a world of crime.'

'Don't you envy him – it must be nice to be so excited about.'

'Never bored.'

'I know, I wish I were.'

'Those of us who are not tecs in Willie's eyes are criminals – picklock or anti-picklock – *nothing* that is not *rat* or *anti-rat.*'

'What are we?'

'We, Ratner?'

'Are we rat or anti-rat?'

'I am anti-rat. You of course are rat – with such a name – !'

'I know. I guessed as much – Ratner – of course. – In Edgar Wallace there is no criminal who is not also a detective.'

'I know, and vice versa – that's poor Willie's picture of things too – he is completely mad, Ratner, don't you think!'

'I must say he sounds.'

'All through reading Dime Novels.'

'I don't understand that craze.'

'Edgar Wallace!'

'I know!'

'Pierpoint.' Zagreus uttered the name-of-names and stopped, expectant.

'Oh yes Horace, let's hear what Pierpoint!' There was a convulsive croak. 'I expect he has a lot to say – I can imagine what Pierpoint thinks.'

'Shall I tell you?'

'Yes Horace, I should like to hear what Pierpoint thinks Horace.'

'You would like to hear what Pierpoint thinks, you sewer-rat.'

'House-rat!' coyly.

'No. *Cloaca.*'

'Very well. Go on.'

Ratner obliged – he effected the equivalent of a temporary withdrawal beneath the basements, beneath everything else, in pitch-black drains, underneath the horatian city. After the snub, he composed himself to listen-in to the big-wigs booming up above. He would submit to the broadcast of the absent Pierpoint (whose microphone-personality, in the mouth of Horace, offended him if anything more than the hated flesh and blood). It was settled – he would answer when spoken to.

The argument opened along, to Julius, familiar lines. Even the voice of Horace took on the tone of the distant speaker.

'The Detective Story and the Dime Novel are the same thing – both are children's reading am I right?'

These *Am-I-rights?* – So the broadcast began – Ratner dutifully muttering his response *de profundis*.

'I suppose so.'

'Ten years ago and beyond during the Great Massacre, Mr Phillips Oppenheim was the favourite reading of all Cabinet Ministers and all great magnates, all bishops and Captains of Industry. The War-makers read Oppenheim – the young men fought the Boche.'

At 'young men' the voice of Horace grew unctuous.

'There *is* a similarity in those occupations,' said Ratner. 'I confess that had escaped me until now.'

'Outside those circles (this would include subordinates – employees, congregations and the great average of the electorate – the time-honoured patrons of the Dime Novelist) Oppenheim was not read. Only by politicians, bishops, generals and stock-brokers among outstanding people, of so-called education.'

'I suppose you mean the high-brows didn't read Wallace then.'

'No I said Oppenheim – Wallace is his successor. Yes, no one who was intelligent, or, more important, had pretentions to be that, was an Oppenheim-reader. That has altered. What yesterday was a sign of stupidity, is today a sign of intelligence.'

'There are always fashions.'

'Yes. The fashions of an epoch reveal its popular tendencies. The Wallace-fashion is symptomatic of high-brow capitulation, in face of universal pressure.'

'But as a compensation surely Horace the Paris high-brows are sufficiently cockahoop.'

'In relation to the world-scene that must be looked upon as nothing but an *entlastungsoffensive*.'

'And our solitary high-brow pur-sang Lewis?'

'His are *teiloperationen*.'

'What is that jargon Horace!'

'The war-jargon of german peace-politics. – At this moment every high-brow is a Wallace-fan.'

'Yes I know, Horace.'

'Wallace is for modern London what the Arabian Nights were for arab civilization – to account for their habits the high-brows claim. Or, they say, "a vice".'

'He is a vice I think.'

'Picking your pocket a man might exclaim if you detected him, *This is my weakness!* – then shoot you and remark, *A still worse one of mine!*'

'Yes I see that Horace.'

'Thanks to Western training-for-war, the anglo-saxon infant-mind has always resembled the inside of a criminal mad-house. It has been full of drugged potions, sawed-off shot-guns, arsenic, hairbreadth escapes, blackmail, armed warders, King's Messengers, pirates and crooks. What was the schoolboy mind has now become that of the anglo-saxon adult. The post-war anglo-saxon adult has become a boy with a tin pistol. To that the Great War – the "Great Adventure" – has brought him.'

'He always was. You said so yourself.'

'No, he tried to grow-up out of the criminal reformatory – he called it "outgrowing". He had aspirations away from murder, arson, public massacre, theft and blackmail. As a boy his elders fed him upon them: as a man he *did* attempt to escape. But the War was every anglo-saxon schoolboy's dream-come-true.'

'But the cabinet-ministers, the generals – .'

'Those pre-eminent in the profession of Arms, of Politics, of Finance, are of course committed to murder, robbery, black-mail, physical and non-physical lawlessness. Life is their bustling melodrama: Oppenheim or Wallace holds up the mirror to their will-to-power in all its cheapness – that is understood. Pre-war anglo-saxondom was deeply vulgarized, but a certain fraction stood in opposition.'

'It is that that has gone, is it.'

'There is no opposition. The discipline is perfect – there is only "party" and "non-party". Professedly "non-party" men are as zealous as those of the party. – But first there was the cinema. Begin with that.'

'Don't you like the cinema?'

'That is not what I said. For a decade everyone has grown

accustomed to watching animated photographs of plays written for children, or for the least bright Nippy or domestic drudge. He could not help himself; if he went into any Cinema Theatre he was compelled to swallow a mass of the bad with a fraction of good.'

'Not necessarily, he could enquire at what hour was the film he wanted to see.'

'The War was a leveller.'

'I have heard that before. I am afraid it *was* Horace.'

'You are afraid it was Horace.'

'Yes I think so.'

'It must have made the fortune of the manufacturers of "gaspers".'

'Are Gold Flakes levellers Horace? I smoke them.'

'All men below staff – or cabinet – rank were compelled to smoke, eat, read and the rest, *worse* – for all men the standard fell – except perhaps for convicts.'

'Do you object to that very much?'

'I object to nothing. I state.'

'I see.'

'The film-play of Post-war is the homologue, upon the mental plane, of the War "gasper", from the standpoint of palate. And the thrillers of Edgar Wallace also are a sort of "gaspers". Mental "gaspers".'

'It is not as thrillers people consider them.'

'They are the "Gaspers" of this Peace – of this unhappy Truce. But if the average high-brow had not been broken in by the Film to unrelieved stupidity, then he could never have swallowed Wallace.'

'I daresay.'

'If you will allow an illustration from luxury – Restaurants, except those priced for the magnate-client, have settled steadily down to Lyons level.'

'I like Lyons.'

'The collapse of the cuisine in France, where the average meal is now worse than London, is the triumph of the standards of the poverty-line. But name *anything* where taste is at stake – it will provide an example of the systematic forcing down of civilized standards.'

'Where does this lead – the suspense is beginning to tell on me Horace.'

'To the standards of the misery-spot – after an orgy of cheap ice-cream, which may last a hundred years.'

'Aren't you glad you won't be here Horace?'

'I *am* here. – Back to *The Squeaker!* Edgar Wallace is what the government gives you to read. It amounts to that.'

'Has Edgar Wallace a government contract?'

'It amounts to that. From station-stall to smart hotel it is he that is purveyed, in uniform editions, is it not? It is your bully-beef, your tasteless ration. Turn up your nose at that and you are a marked man.'

'How sinister you are Horace!'

'A dangerous, an aristocratic taste is betrayed, if you turn away with a yawn from *The Squeaker*.'

'You would make a good advocate.'

'A devil's advocate you think. That depends upon the god.'

'I did not say that.'

'The official stamp as well is upon Jazz – the approved mass-article. Jazz is the folk-music of the metropolitan mass – slum-peasant, machine-minder – the heart-cry of the city-serf. His masters sing his songs – they even write them for him!'

'That's above my head.'

'Edgar Wallace is what the machine-hind is supposed to read.'

'Machine-hind?'

'The little oiler feeder and keeper of the machines of the Mechanical Age.'

'There are alternatives to Edgar Wallace, Horace.'

'Not many really, and what's good enough for a Secretary of State (what they now call "Puppet-politicians" for fun) is good enough for a machine-minder anyway.'

'Their tastes are much the same – since both are puppets that is not surprising.'

'The same laws, such as the american Dry-laws, which make every citizen into a potential criminal, watched by an armed federal agent, provide Everyman with his Dime Novel up-to-date.'

'True Horace.'

'Shades of the prison-house begin to close about every formerly law-observing polite person, for if he does not go to jail for a bank-robbery he may go there for an unpaid fraction of a blood-tax or a reel of cotton sold out of business hours. *The criminal mentality is forced upon him* – the furtive tricks of the underdog and underworld taught him, through unnatural laws. Almost some criminal ruler might have *wished for company!* – it is the sensation that these laws suggest. All the average, useful and honest, persons are brutally empressed – they are mocked for their ignorance of prisons – for their *respectability* and the possession of the bourgeois-mind, as civilians were mocked for their ignorance of murder at the outset of the War, by shrieking women – it is a newly-branded handcuffed world!'

'Crime is de rigueur!'

'In this connection! It is dangerous not to be some sort of criminal, or outlaw, or *out-caste*, so that you come beneath the protection of those penal principles involved in the motto, *Honour among thieves*.'

'That does not sound to me over-safe however.'

'Only *more* safe. – So this tax-crushed post-war puppet of the *megalopolis* has the energy demanded – no more – to a nicety, to tickle his pale fancy with a blood-and-thunder article of the writer's art – did he display more it would be taxed, it would be taxed!'

'Ah well Horace!'

'Willie Service is that small average high-brow automaton – he is hallucinated. He absorbs the matter provided in the books, he gets drunk upon the film-pictures. Now he is stunted, with the mind of a daring gutter-product of ten-summers. – What is the issue? *Pierpoint is convinced there is no issue!* We are all rats caught in a colossal mechanical trap.'

'Ah' exclaimed Ratner, in full panoply of resurrected rathood issuing out of his cloaca with a hoarse squeak.

'Ah.' Mr Zagreus gazed at him, in a questioning manner, as if at a gigantic rat-coated interloper.

'If we are *all* rats!'

'That makes you less of a one!' Horace lightly called out and with the manner of a Merry Monarch he struck Julius gracefully upon the shoulder. 'Do not crow over us all the same, you old bottom-dog popped up from your gallows-pit.'

'So that is what you think of Service.'

'He has been quite swept off his feet. He lives for crime. He lives for crime.'

'Is that his only interest?'

'He has no other,' said Horace simply and he relapsed into silence.

The staff had left the barn, after having removed upon substantial trays most of the cheap china and plate. At the moment no servants were there at all, it was occupied only by the belated performers, less Margolin who remained absent.

Zagreus was reposing now for a moment after his performance, Ratner was sulky and no sign of life came from Dan, when the door opened and a pair of furtive persons, one evidently a woman, entered. The first was dressed as a cowboygirl, the womanly one was in a costume suggesting a rather shy but wealthy edwardian child of about six, in knockabout print-frock for nursery-wear. She and her big brother (or a sister immodestly disguised as a he-man) had the air of being upon an expedition of a predatory nature. They might be actuated by a desire to introduce a finger into a pot of strawberry jam kept in the cupboard, or even to subtilize a small fragment of a piece of delicious marzipan.

As mischievous a pair of lovable little genial bodies as ever played truant, the moist-eyed paragraphist of Punch of the time would exclaim – catching sight of them in the distance over the top of his spectacles, allowing a lucrative tear to gush underneath at the thought of all the thousands of sweet little nestlings he'd never had – some throbbing Thackeray.

The cowboygirl was jowled, rough-browed, and dark. These two suspiciously-reserved intruders whispered for a moment. The fantastic form of Mr Zagreus, beside the guttering candles upon the side table, resembling nothing earthly, and the bisected figure, half of shadow, like a satellite reflecting sun upon the side offered to Zagreus, were not remarked. Dan was concealed by a pillar of wood.

The cowboygirl went towards a dresser, upon which some silver lay. There were a few nickel spoons and a nutcracker. She swept them up, an eye upon the farther door, and thrust them into the pouch of her belted girdle, sagging with the weight of an outsize automatic.

Her companion had noticed a movement from the direction of the performers. Zagreus had lifted his head in fact rather sharply. She uttered a warning *psst!* The cowboygirl strolled back. They exchanged a few further whispers, eyeing the fantastic statues set against the wall, lighted by the guttering candles. Then in best film-manner they withdrew as they had come with a deliciously guilty jerk.

Zagreus turned to Ratner with a small ornamental laugh, the mild tinkling of a musical-box.

'Do you know her?'

'No.'

'Ah ha!'

Zagreus lighted a russian cigarette.

'Did you see what she did!'

'I saw.' Ratner nodded.

'The cowboy was Molly Seymour-Lambton.'

'Oh, Molly Seymour-Lambton!'

'The one that went off with the nickel salt-spoons. I knew what she was after!'

'Crime, Horace, crime – we are in the thick of it! I said you were like Service!'

'In the thick of it Julius. I wish Willie had been there. He would have enjoyed it.'

'They may be friends.'

'I don't think so. It was Molly Seymour-Lambton who was arrested in Rapallo last year for a church-robbery.'

'Oh yes. – Is that it!'

'Indeed that is it. You recollect it? She attempted to make a get-away with an offertory-box, she had her car waiting outside the church – Molly has been on the dirt-track she is a great motorist too. – She punched a priest in the eye.'

'I'm glad she didn't catch sight of us. She had a gun!'

Mr Zagreus shook his head.

'She wouldn't use it.'

'Does she stick at that?'

'She wouldn't use that!'

'Did she get off?'

'In Rapallo? A passing black-shirt captured her – she slapped his face for being fresh and kicked his bottom.'

'Stout fellow – I don't blame her! – I suppose they let her off?'

'No – light-fingered Anglo-saxons of possessing-class-status are anathema to Mussolini, as you know. Molly had to go to jail.'

'I remember the case. Wasn't there a woman with her?'

'That was the girl you saw.'

'Just now?'

'I think so.'

'Who is she?'

'I forget her name. She is a niece of the Duke of Strathorr.'

'Is it Hermione Gordon – I once met her at a party.'

'Hermione Gordon, yes.'

'Have you known – what is her name – long Horace?'

'I first met Molly thirty years ago when she was a débutante, she still lives in the family-mansion, it is in Petley Street, Park Lane – it's a big house.'

'She is well off.'

'Extremely well off – why she's an old heiress and has married *herself*, as it were – she's a bachelor-bride. From birth she has been lesbian. But the first time I heard of her stealing was in 1919, when she got off with a caution for stealing a priest's bicycle in North Kensington.'

'It sounds as though your friend had a down on the clergy.'

'I think that was a coincidence – but they say she has effected many daring daylight robberies in a small way. But Lesbos came first, and Devil's Island last – she still is first and foremost a sapphist and her defiance of the eighth commandment is a side-issue. She is said to have a museum of plate and other stolen articles, which her secretary and butler take the greatest care of. They are hauls from restaurants, churches, hotels and a few museums, all over Europe – she has the names written upon tickets. A sixpenny mousetrap is one of her exhibits.'

'How well informed you are Horace!'

'That is true. I have been at great pains to do field-work for Pierpoint and wherever I went to get that material that he requires.'

'Well, Miss Seymour-Lambton is in the same line as Service.'

'Only Service does not run with the hare so much as hunt with the hounds. She would look down on Service as a cop.'

'Do you think she would?'

'I'm positive she would.'

'Extraordinary people, aren't they Horace?'

'It's in the air!'

'I suppose it must be, as you say!'

'Jacques Coq d'Or the Paris critic is now officially enrolled as a thief – he belongs to that new exclusive club of french men-of-letters, for which no one is eligible who has not his thumbprints at the Sûreté Générale.'

'I think it's in the air!'

'It must be. Pierpoint is always right. There are the *Faux-Monnayeurs.*'

'There are certainly the *Faux-Monnayeurs.*'

'And the *Grain Qui Meurt* leads to the *Faux-Monnayeurs.* An outcast-status leads to a *brotherhood* – reaching from the gallows to the rubber-shop. Laws against sex-perversions like dry-laws make criminals of harmless sex-oddities. But everybody is driven into the league against Law.'

'That is true Horace.'

'Jacques Coq d'Or.'

'What a name.'

'For years with him it was common-or-garden homosexuality, not very exciting (we had our poor old Oscar under Victoria) but new in France and very exclusive. The french are stubborn whoremasters – they are I believe, what do you think, far more masculine than the Anglo-saxons. It afforded Jacques the necessary advertisement for a rising critic for many years. Now times are different. Homosexuals are as common as dirt.'

'It is now the non-homosexual who is abnormal.'

'That is so. But Jacques Coq d'Or was not the man to stick at anything and something had to be done and that quickly, so he pocketed a pourboire put down for a Bock Blonde that had been left upon a café table by a departing customer. After that he made a habit of it. He would watch for the departure of a likely British visitor, then he would sweep up the tip in great style when the garçon de café wasn't looking. He has boasted that "his pourboires" as he calls them run into four figures. Annually.'

'That should be easy in francs. Does he never get caught?'

'Never – involuntarily. Once he was, but that was on purpose. No one believed in his capacity or they pretended not to – they thought he made money by writing reviews or something stupid of that sort. This was too much for him. – But a month in the Santé was essential in any case.'

'How old is Jacques Coq d'Or?'

'Well *en pédéraste* he says it's thirty-nine. But I daresay it's not more than fifty. He's just been shut up.'

'The Santé?'

'No in an asylum. He was extremely angry afterwards and made a great fuss when he got out, because he had counted on it's being a *criminal* asylum, and it was not.'

Ratner gave his laughter free play for a moment upon the barren bed of his gullet, it dragged itself back and forth.

'I should have thought that was too risky' he said after that. 'They might have kept him.'

'Oh no. He is a very eminent critic – they couldn't lock him up for good. Besides, he isn't mad.'

'I should think he might get caught. The pitcher that goes often to the well.'

'No, they're too stupid.'

'I suppose so.'

'He has many rivals, of course – that is the only quarter – several of the best-known "younger" french novelists have spent their *villégiature* in jail lately. Dozens of Americans do time as a matter of course now – they won't let them into America when they want to go back if they haven't – I mean won't let them into the best literocriminal New York circles. The ticket-of-leave is as important as the passport.'

Ratner croaked again and Dan started at its nearness. He was very nervous.

'François Villons, without the poetry.' said Horace. 'These gaol-birds who have never sung! They are as common as dirt.'

'Is that so?'

'As common as dirt.'

The door opened softly, both noticed it at once. A rice-powdered face out of a victorian harlequinade came into the room by itself, disembodied, a long chicken-neck cut off by the door. Convulsively it shot to left and right, it peered up and down. A spontaneous outburst of laughter broke from Zagreus and Ratner.

'Not another!' Julius grated, incredulous.

'Come in! Never look back!' called Zagreus.

The head as if shot darted back, and the door shut with a smart jerk. While it had been ajar they could hear the sound of the constant arrival of motor-cars in the court outside.

'Willie should certainly be here! I wonder where Margolin is?' Zagreus gave a delicate yawn, cat-like and dumb.

'Would he have arrested them?'

'The women?'

'Yes.'

'No. He never arrests.'

'Never?'

'No never. – I have known him to blackmail.'

'Ah. – I thought there must be *something* more.'

'Oh yes. He blackmails, but that is merely graft and thoroughly *policemanesque* as he calls it.'

'Policemanesque!'

'That's what he calls it.'

'So he blackmails!'

'He is very apt to. – I daresay he will blackmail Osmund if he gets a chance.'

'He is a dangerous young man! I thought he was.'

'Oh you can call his bluff – he's not very serious.'

'Can you?'

'Easily.'

'Perhaps there are ways of blackmailing *him*, too!'

'Now Julius!' Zagreus stretched, striking Dan lightly with his hand. 'I am sorry Dan! – Well there it is – if within a decade and a half you massacre ten million people in war and another ten million in civil war, it is not easy after that to return to a morality that regards it as wrong to pocket a salt-spoon.'

'I suppose not.'

'Life is more important than a spoon.'

'I suppose so.'

'The universal return to the mentality of childhood and of savagery – Nursery after Army, and dugout-canoe after dugouts in trenches – that seems to ensue.'

'So it has been said. I have read that somewhere.'

'And there will be more upheavals.'

'It is difficult to see how that can be avoided.'

'People had better keep their hands in, with a little pilfering – "scrounging" is the word they have for it in the war-books.'

'Have any of the new french school of literary-pickpockets yet dabbled in homicide? Are you informed about that?'

'Ah there is the difficulty!' Mr Zagreus passed his finger lightly across his neck, where the chicken got the chopper. 'There was Loeb and Leopold in Chicago. But you have to be under age, rich, and one thing and another, else you swing, that is the difficulty. Besides ten years is no joke!'

'No.'

'But it is actually no difficulty' Horace smiled steadily and lazily at Ratner.

'How is that Horace?' Ratner looked suspiciously into the distance, with indifference.

'Why simply this. We have the immense background of War and of Revolution. That is enough – the blood is gratis! Both the soldier and the communist enrol themselves to murder – one under militarist rules, the other under marxist disciplines. But both are homicide-clubs, you call your victim "Hun", you call him "Bourgeois", it is all one – no, wars and communes have cheapened murder.'

'That is the solution!'

'Both sides wish us *criminal* – both invite us to a carnival of bloodshed accompanied by universal loot. There is no side, there is no Church, that repudiates the weapons of Terror and of Force. We are between the Imperial Devil and the deep Red Sea – that other crimson sea!'

'Perhaps God will cause the waves to part!'

'For some, no doubt. – No, homicide is in the air. No one would get anything out of homicide, unless he first proved that in minor ways he was a hardened criminal. He might after all just be a regimental sergeant-major out of a job or a dull marxist-doctrinaire, might he not, a theorist of "catastrophe"! – That would prove nothing.'

'I suppose not.'

Zagreus stood up.

'I think I will go to the kitchen!'

All was preparation and bustle in a moment in the Split-camp – as Horace with his svelt pedigree back, made for the Stulz swallow-tail, left the table. The entire Split-person, with a wolfish rush, came together, the dead half and the quick – it shook itself, it burst into action. The repressed instinct to strike, in the snake-like suspense of the faculties, in the rattish winter of his discontent beneath the horatian city, armed Ratner's tongue.

Scoffing with passionate eye-glitter he watched – after the manner of a witch's needles he plunged glance after glance into the back of the dummy – the human body was a dummy, at that distance it lost importance. (But a feeble toy walked off nothing more, out of which had evaporated Horace the Talker.) Then with a ponderous swing (owing to the weight of the attraction of the retreating dummy) he dragged his yellow face off its moving target. With a *well-let-that-go* look, with lips curled in contempt, with the relish of hatred, the face swung round on to Dan. In caressing croak, the softest available, he expressed himself.

'Horace is really mad I believe tonight!' he immediately suggested to Dan, whom he attempted to mesmerize with the battery of his eye-in-profile, with which he watched him to see the effect of the suggestion.

But Dan sat motionless, he was not disposed to be talked to or mesmerized any more for the moment, all was at sixes and sevens in his head as he thought of the kitchen. Horace had gone to the kitchen, Horace had gone to the kitchen! for Dan nothing else existed except kitchen and Horace – he might have to sit on where he was, beside this wearisome stranger, all night – no word had been dropped by Horace when with cruel suddenness he disappeared, going to the kitchen, to say whether he would come back or when, or what was at present afoot, if anything. When had they to get up on the stage? He dreaded the publicity, with the pink puffing on his legs and all, but that he would face – almost *any* exposure. It had not seemed Horace had noticed how he was left rapt there upon the bench – no word to say *Come too* to Dan – no *Come to the Kitchen?* How he longed that he might be asked, for the simple request of the words *Come with me Dan to the kitchen.* Willie had been there with the chef why not *he?* it was most cruel and unkind, he could have said *Come* when he went there too, if he must go he could have said that! No. This sudden going away, there was nothing said, but – *I am going.* Margolin had gone to the kitchen and now Horace had gone to the kitchen. Had he dared he would follow, he would have gone and simply turned up in the basement, walking in with an *I've come to the kitchen too* nothing more, sitting down without looking. But they were all there and he was not intended! He was shut out – why could he alone not! The kitchen of all places in the house – never could he have believed it possible if you had told him last week! Oh *why* did Horace hate him *so much* – was life really worth while!

'I really think it's the beginning of the end' the impossible person hissed in his eardrum and he smelt his breath, bitter with the coffee.

'The end!' staring violently Dan echoed it, in fervent despair. *The end* – this was the most startling man!

'Yes' said the Split-man, encouraged and with a glow of decision, 'he may even have to be restrained.' This was the most startling of men – to be left with too without so much as a word.

'Next to nothing' he said, though what he meant Dan did not know but he felt funny. 'Pierpoint's teaching' Split-man was saying talking forty-nine to the dozen – and it was that it seemed had done it. Pierpoint had altered Horace, all Horace had been changed inside-out. It was a pity! And it was Pierpoint!

'Was he not always – !' disclosing his secret heart whispered Daniel greatly daring to his Split colleague. His own voice was frightening, as it came into these guilty exchanges, to discuss Horace. But he did dearly desire to hear of some alteration. Why? Because he supposed it might be an excuse – an 'alteration' – he hoped there had been an alteration!

'Like this?' The voice breaking out at his ear was loud and angry with the question, though heaven was witness he had not meant it, to offend the man by asking, or to offend in anything – except that he was betraying Horace. Terrified, to put it plainly he was of this cross person he must talk to, and had never expected him to come jumping down his throat in that fashion – all he had said was *Was he not always* and what harm was there in that?

'Like this – not at all – as he is at present. Horace has changed completely. You would not know him! Not the same man. He used to be. Not himself.'

Horace *had* changed! – the man had spoken the truth! So Dan listened again, and he heard the man say, always with grins of apology, or of superiority.

'Poor Horace!' he said 'I've never seen him like this!' an impressive mutter. 'He has been an actor at one time. (Horace an actor!) He remembers as you've noticed all the words he gets by heart – he repeats as if Pierpoint were Holy Writ. I'm *sick* of hearing!'

Dan heard him say 'religious mania' with a grin, but he was asking himself – *Poor Horace!* What was that – pitying Horace? Never mind for nothing mattered.

Dan's head ached and was somewhat worse – was the party over? It might be – the play had fallen through. He felt quite tired and done up and glad if the truth must be known to be sitting. The man with the rat's name went on as before: he stopped listening. Dan doubted if he could stand – questioned if it was possible to listen, his head hurt, mostly at the back but there were shoots up beside the eyeballs.

That 'broadcast' was the last straw! Oh Horace, why must you *broadcast!* Since they had been together no evening had passed but they had it, and sometimes at lunch or tea – twice Horace had 'broadcast' by telephone. Certainly there were voices and voices: but the accents of Pierpoint – well it passed his understanding that Horace with his beautiful speaking-voice should adopt the harsh bellows of that pronounced charlatan. Again. Saying all that now, to other people – that was not sensible, it put Horace in a strange position as it would anybody (though Horace was blind to the fact) to have that disgusting charlatan's great voice (with all the wild things it said) coming out of your mouth! If Horace would only realize the position it put him in – it was of course that that that rat-named individual was always hinting at the toad, and he could bring it home to him. Horace did not seem aware. Might he not be arrested? He might that! Horace was in danger at this minute! All through that charlatan!

Dan put down his head to reflect upon this situation. Tonight it had been especially worse than ever, he went back to think it out – that voice would be the death of him! How they had kept it up tonight too, one after the other, with insults and laughter, with the other man being so rude all the time he could see. It had been a bad night (though if you asked me to say what it all led back from at the start, I'll be bound to confess I'm unable – don't ask me!). Quarrelling, and smiling at each other, a most painful impression it had made on him, very painful from start to finish – he could not bear these strange arguments where they were smiling and laughing all the time like so many hyenas! Oh how he had prayed they might stop on bended knees, he could not endure it the sound of the two talking as if to order upon his senses. The howling of two waves in the sea that were engaged in a combat – that might express this disagreeable sensation, something painful and impossible – he would have screamed out to Horace and the other to leave off there and then but how could he, he had no excuse!

Dan put up his fingers to his ears – they still rang with it. He shook his head violently.

The trouble was, Dan said to himself, it did not end with them at the table. No it did not! Say what you would, underneath there was something. You could feel it – he had seen it. Out of sight it was, there were *other* people – you could not see them – it was just as with Pierpoint – never there in person, to be touched and seen. Horace had called him a puppet, both were acting – they were shaken by what they said, he had been shaken – that was *the others* that shook them! So they tossed and fought. The impatient smiles they each had upon their faces as they spoke and as they were answering – then the words! perhaps they, worst of all, destroyed him entirely and so the headache had come. They were once or twice scientific. That horrid word used by Horace what was it! Homo and something – he never felt comfortable. He was quite positive the word was beastly, he could not understand at all why Horace insisted upon using it when broadcasting (as he called this acting, when he was doing

Pierpoint). The struggle raged under the words, the words became beastly. Both used beastly words to each other until he became frightened. Partly it was what they said, partly the way they said – speaking in cipher, or was it a tone-code, of another tongue. – Between the flashes of the speeches this time with great distinctness he had snap-shots of the second scene. Actually he had seemed to catch glimpses of a country that was beneath this land – in which they were locked. – It was something like a glancing landscape, like a dream that was there – he had had that as a schoolboy in Ireland, when the Rebellion was, the night before the arrest of his father, when he had seen through the pavement (as he had dreamed he was walking) scenery beneath his feet. There was a world that ran through things, like pictures in water or in glassy surfaces, where a mob of persons were engaged in hunting to kill other men, in a battle-park, beneath crackling violet stars. Were there trees though – it was a distinct picture and there were parks for fighting? No not trees. Certainly that was treeless also. At both ends there were groves of spikes. A withered world altogether – spike-planted parks it looked like. A needle pricked the skin and there was blood. Everywhere underground under the earth trodden by us was blood too. So it would seem if again he were not partly in a dream. This world in question had looked brown. As to colour there you had it – a pinkish, a brownish, but a dark shade, and, for its extent and measurement, a plain; and he had in a dull flash perceived its distances, a tall row of hills, a moon was shining. At moments the place had come out so vividly beneath, when they were laughing most – certainly he could not hope to follow what they exactly meant, but here and there WAR – *war* this and *war* that – had been spoken of between them. The other had turned away his face from Horace. Arrests and murders they had been mentioned especially, at a certain point he believed Horace had spoken about blood. There must undoubtedly have been some murder. Perhaps it was a big case or a cause célèbre. They both cracked jokes. Someone had been done to death! Evidently, some criminal hands! There were guilty persons, not caught red-handed – all was in confusion so he gathered. And in all probability he had been looking at the identical bloody scene of the act. Where he had been looking (that place that brought the dream back he had) he had just been staring down into the very scene as a witness of the catastrophe. That accounted for its presence. – Both were laughing. But both had seemed angry. *Angry*, Horace had – he had heard him say to the other – he had said (he remembered) *always angry!* – always angry he had muttered and he appeared to be accusing the other really, in some fashion, but he could not be sure of that fact. He was not at all sure it had not been somebody who was absent he accused and spoke to, but they had laughed as if it had been some kind of joke they had together. It must be the blackest bloody joke, thought he, this side of hell, to judge from the signs, and it separated them – little wonder! The landscape was very near to him once – there were stones he believed – there was smoke, it came out where the earth was cracked, it burst from bricks – in the sky the stars constantly burst into smoke, there were pools of smoke, also there were thundering fountains, reaching to a hundred feet. That was black smoke. The music of Lord Osmund had played from his stomach while that was in progress – a martial march. Nothing could live thought Dan, or *love* thought he and sighed, where he had been looking, where alas he had looked and seen the battle-parks and the spikes planted for trees, he thought. – He would never look again! Never of his own free will would he look again for years! Between as it were the flashes of their remarks, the steady quarrelling with one another – glimpses of violence that was all – nothing pleasant! – he would not look again at that or ever listen to a 'broadcast' as understood in the mad vernacular of Horace, never! For *pleasure*, was it, as it seemed, that Horace walked in those repulsive places – did Horace not know what love was perhaps – was he not able ever to be happy? And what was that landscape, and the cause of the quarrelling? They kept breaking through into something else, as you put your fist through a sheet of paper.

Ratner was voluble, he pressed Dan hard with argument and was very insidious, knowing and obliging.

'You are not the first one' said Ratner with a weary leer. 'I've seen a few – the way you feel – it's beastly! One has to make up one's mind to the fact I'm afraid – Horace is irresponsible Dan.'

(The puzzling person's breath stank like a fish, fish-like were his eyes for that matter, Dan wished he would move away. What now was 'beastly' then – was it *himself* – could he be shaken off. This limpet was abrupt and repulsive. He heard Ratner with a coax in his croak call him *Poor Dan.*)

'Poor Dan! I suppose you think Horace is sincere don't you – I don't blame you, it *is* diff-i-*cult!* You will find Horace out Dan.' He heard further phrases from Ratner. 'The old Horace – Old days – Only difference – *Now* practicaljokes with us – *Before* practicaljoked – Crowned heads – He hoaxed the nation.'

(Perhaps Horace was not quite a serious man? – Why had he become *Dan* for this person?)

'Horace acts Pierpoint.'

(Scrappily Dan gathered the heads of arguments against his will. He half-heard Split-man remarking. 'Horace is an actor.' An actor was not a serious man. Was Horace not a serious man, and an actor? He had never known an actor.)

'Horace is one of that crowd – Yes that – What? – Lord Osmund – He belongs to the same set – Rich Men – When he mocks at Lord Osmund – Words stolen from Pierpoint – He steals from – That is bluff! – More fool you Dan! – Believe me or not – Pulling your leg.'

(Was Horace pulling the leg? Dan looked down disconsolately, he saw the pink puffing, there were the strapping Ziegfeld understandings, just clear of the table-rim. The figure of speech led him back to his fancy-dressed figure in concrete with legs in fleshings to be pulled like crackers – he blushed as he thought of the discredit, and he saw in his mind's eye Father Donovan.)

'Yes pulling your leg.'

(Ratner looked at the legs too, with a sneer his eyes followed Dan's glance, and they both stared down at them together.)

'Yes pulling your leg!' Ratner repeated.

(Dan looked away from the pink puffing. Ratner as well.)

'He doesn't care whose brains he picks – He picks Pierpoint's brains – It's not pockets – Pickpockets – Not his line – *Brains!*'

(Ratner looked at Dan's head. *Brains!* His head! The 'genius' was there, thought Dan, the 'genius'! He felt uncomfortable.)

'Yes – Brains!'

(Ratner continued to stare significantly at Dan's head.)

'I'm very fond of old Horace but I know Horace is a perfect

vamp – Vamping you for all he's worth – Old Horace will pick you dry.'

(*Vamp* motif. Fear of the Ogre.)

'He knows you've got *genius!*'

(Ah!?)

'He is after your genius!'

(At this point Dan became seriously alarmed. – After his 'genius' was he – was it possible! But was that true at all? How could anybody obtain one's 'genius' by a *coup de main?* He felt very uneasy indeed, however, for all that he argued himself out of his natural concern, for his threatened 'genius'.)

'After all Dan, what is Horace doing – what are we all doing here?'

(With circumspection now, Dan allowed himself to wonder what they might be doing.)

'Horace likes dressing up – Finnian Shaws like – Both like – Buffoons! He has come here to play a few rather stupid jokes – He laughs at other people's jokes – Finnian Shaw jokes – Just the same as his.'

(Dan continued to give ear and to pick out the main heads of the abominable arguments against his hero as they came.)

'Horace has seen through his set.'

(His set?)

'That is his set – Always has been Horace's set – He has seen through – He wants to stand outside – Vanity – To prove he doesn't belong to it.'

(Forgive me for listening to this man Horace!)

'Do you know what he says behind your back – Are you listening? – He is making a fool of you!'

(A fool behind his back! Oh Horace is that possible!)

'He calls you his idiot-boy.'

(His idiot-boy – oh Horace, *your boy* yes indeed 'tis so!)

'*Moron* is his word – Do you understand *moron?* – He means a sort of rustic idiot you see.'

(Moron was a nice word! – *I am his moron* Dan thought, and since he always thought of himself as small – *I am Horace's little moron!*)

'Once Horace described you as the justification for Miss Gertrude Stein – Yes you – For Miss Gertrude Stein.'

(Gertrude – what? What girl was that Dan wondered that Horace had brought into the conversation!)

'Don't you know Miss Stein?'

(Know Miss – ! This was the most alarming man!)

'Miss Stein is a writer – She is a *genius* Dan – Has a peculiar way of writing. Horace says you are a moron – You *think* as Miss Stein *writes*.'

(If this girl was a genius, that altered the whole complexion of the matter. He had never met a girl who was a genius – not *a girl*.)

'Pierpoint calls her *the Stammerer* – Miss Stein does stammer as a matter of fact – She stutters Dan – Miss Stein does stutter.'

(And that was the sort of girl that Horace! For him. With an impediment in her speech!)

'Well – are you listening? – Horace says you have the *moron*-mind Dan – Celebrated by Miss Stein. She writes – are you attending – like an idiot – It is like a soft stammering ninny spelling out its alphabet – Horace says.'

(She writes like an idiot – the girl he was mentioned with by Horace in what connection!)

'Horace got that from Pierpoint – *Child-mind* Pierpoint says. Cult of it – Child-mind.'

(Pierpoint again – Pierpoint the Pickpocket.)

'*Sham-child-mind* he – Pierpoint – says – Stein's sham. You follow! Stein's sham – yours real. *You* – Dan – *genuine idiot!*'

(Nasty man – who doesn't improve upon closer acquaintance.)

'That is what he thinks of you Dan!'

(He would tell Horace all the lies this man thought proper to tell.)

'Can't you see Dan that you are Horace's plaything – When he talks about your "genius" – Pulling your leg – That's to get your "genius"! – *People always pull other people's legs when they want to get hold of their genius!*'

(Oh the disgusting fellow, now he knew this was not true after all, and he had suspected Horace without cause!)

Dan got up.

'Where are you going?' asked Ratner surprised.

'Kitchen' Dan muttered.

III The Kitchen

Ratner entered the kitchen but it was full of smoke. It was the cellar of the farm and there were great vats to tan or brew, imported from the next homestead, for period purposes, standing beside the doors, like drums. But Ratner soon saw, when his eyes emptied of water, many people enough, with the chef in the midst, distinguished by the white cylinder his head supported in integral erectness, armed with a bright cutlass. He was demonstrating his art.

Domenichino who painted Sodom put three pillars upon the left of the ill-fated esplanade, there was an aqueduct to take potable water to the doomed citizenry, but no river (there was no occasion to wash dirty linen in public) and three Stewards of the Plain with spotless ribboned rosettes, approached a group of nonentities with a view to warning them off. They had come where they were not wanted – all were Walking Gentlemen out of the cast of a Revue lately come to an end, who balked their exit from the capitals of the Plain, though economically undesirables. That picture had been seen by a fellow-tourist of Julius Ratner. Upon his tardy Grand Tour (when business had boomed, in the first days of the Private Presses) he had met the tourist, who had seen the celebrated canvas. He himself had never seen Domenichino's *Sodom* at all, but such was the impression of what he had been told – as he blinked into the smoke-screen he saw the passage to the right where there was the imitation, lantern-lit, of a provision-shop (a true Pye Corner, with delicate-pig-and-pork) from whose pent-house dangled Bologna sausages, an entire porker, and a dusky period-movement of self-conscious shopmen that brought to mind a painted place. Perhaps it was the three pillars in the centre resembling salt – it had called up at sécond-hand the mere tongue-picture, it is true, a vivid verbal snapshot, of the decor of Domenichino – pillars of whitewash: yes a colonnade of balks began – they held up the hall above, stationed to prevent Osmund and friends from falling through bodily into the kitchen. Otherwise they would have all fallen through into the kitchen.

The domestic inferno (accessible to staff but not guests) under the upper world which for sun had Osmund and for moon

Phoebus, for a sharp-set food-fan perhaps a very heaven-on-earth certainly, was far from that for the dismally-prowling Ju. His maw was chokkerblock, with everything turning to basalt already within (*what* intestines to be handed down to one!) which would have to be blasted out the morning-after, with charges of pink female pills, nothing less. He hated kitchens. For him this was hell – as an embodied curse split down the centre he made his way through the chimney-smoke. The heat of this nether cook-house found favour with his chilly bones, his body took like a duck to water to the hell-heat, at least there was that to be said! He drew near to the distant fireplace, between the pillars, a whipped under-devil or sub-demon, scheduled to play a domestic-animal part, of an unwanted doctored cat, spinally sectioned black-sided and white-sided. The main thing was the hell-heat however, that was good. It was the cheer of the period-fire, in the period-kitchen, in the period mock passion-play, in the period-world. The Dance Of The Black Joke went on.

'Away kitchen-stuff! Rip you chitterlings!' a proper *roaring boy* from the noisy Past for the occasion, the thyroid-maddened Horace quoted. 'Kitchen-*stuff!*' he bawled in his accents of a section-boss. *He* was entering into the spirit. Straddling and pointing. Beastly albino-hyena, as usual ill-bred old brawler, he pointed rudely at two gloomy turnspits or counterfeit pot-wallopers (for it was a fake-fire sure enough, with period-pot and period-spit) who sat sucking their smoked thumbs as if they had been two copper-red smelt-bodied kippers, if that could be, they had been sucking head-first. The twin City-porters Magog and Gog (Briton and Saxon emblems or gods) could not have been more like this, sentinels upon either hand of the chimney – a museum of salamanders, saucepans, gridirons and a permanent baron of beef, revolved by the smoke-jack, making a model museum-joint. Both poor pensive clowns mocked up hill and down dale by Horace – calling out to kill your head *kitchen-stuff* over and over again. Beefeaters! he shouted. *Beefeaters!* The cursed devil! ah hold your tongue – you'll soon be dead! Ratner's eyes, bloodshot with smoke, struck out in evil stabbing glances at this bombastic phantom – *You will soon be dead!* his mind hissed. Horace was grinning at him.

A pig swung from a cambrel in the pent-roof beyond the exit-*du-fond*. The excited chef hurled his chef's-knife in the manner of a javelin at it. The party of conjurers applauded. It stuck in the floating carcass. *Drunk* was Ratner's conclusion and he slunk to the left, avoiding them, sitting down beside a dejected turnspit who eyed him heavily, as if he had been a rival period-piece.

A number of drudges from whose mouths streamed cries, in the manner of prints plastered with slogans, upon all hands stampeded, as the young chef of the kitchen, a little above himself, discharged a second knife – juggling as they ran with sauce-boats, tureens, skillets. The tide of the banquet in the barn had flowed back into the deeps of the kitchens and the murky bottoms of the household – fine ten-pound pines were visible, the refuse of geese à la daube, house-lambs, the bones of lemon-soles and electric eels, Skipper Sardines, ruined sweetbreads of sheep, lettuce-leaf still-life à la Douanier, tinned goosegogs, Heinz's tomatoes, noggins of iced punch, bottles of Bass, flagons of Kia-Ora, empty bottles of *Presta* Splits, a Big Tree Manhattan bottle – masses of bitten and half-swallowed rubbish of animal and of vegetable. The refuse of stomachs. How these armed maggots crawled in this garbage, with heavy voices, overcome by the fumes. A World of bowels. Synecdoche!

An auxiliary outfit of unused ship's-coppers blocked the second entrance which was just as well. There were only two doors and these admitted the emergency staff and the standing-army of slovenly personnel, a few blackguards who came in to pick up what they could get, a few hobbadahoys plus a *pompier* skeleton crew from the village in case of a fire which was very likely.

Willie Service in full roadster-kit now (though burnished with shammy-skin and buttonbrush to a dazzling pitch of posh liveried perfection) entered leading Daniel Boleyn. Though ghastly pale Dan blushed a ripe red, for he felt he was called upon to bluff it and as naked as next-to-the-skin could make it.

'What has happened?' asked Julius Ratner.

'What Dan do you mean? The puffing caught fire.' Horace spoke as if referring to pastry.

'What is puffing Horace?'

'His legs went up in flames.'

'Good heavens!'

'It was the puffing on them.'

'Was it?'

'Do you feel better Dan?' At Dan Horace hollered and turned away smiling towards Margolin: Ratner elected himself upon the spot an indignant embodiment of Public Opinion. He became a walking reproach to the callous Horace. And *there* stood the poor oppressed young man Dan, first class witness for the Society for the prevention of cruelty to children!

Dan drooped and blushed and was tugging at his hose in a deep girlish fidget, of virginal concern. The part of the personality near to the blushfully important, the centric-parts which must draw the eye, was there – one more such accident and all would become irreparably improper. The soul started at the knee-cap and ended at the navel. Oh!

But the prominent specific codpiece, fashioned like the botticellian conch of Aphrodite, laced into position, was all that was left, except for the hose which was clipped up with suspenders. The short bum-curtain of the doublet was a lascivious eaves – the contretemps had occurred almost immediately upon entering, and there seemed nothing for it but to blush and bear it. The fire had done in a flash, lashing at his loins, what, in the way of costume, he would at no price have consented!

'For the rest of the evening you'll have to be a girl Dan!'

Horace might at least moderate the timbre of his voice, was Dan's reflection, in publicly approaching such a painful subject! – his friend's suggestion took from Dan the last vestige of countenance that he had and visibly he was confused as could be.

'We must borrow a frock.'

Surely it was not necessary for Horace to specify the nature of the garments that it might be necessary for one to wear! *Was* it not bad enough as it was? And *what* would the man say next – were they to have an inventory of a feminine toilet! Were they to be spared no details of those blush-producing attires!

'I'm afraid you'll have to make shift with that!'

That is right – shout it out! Oh in what a bullying tone Horace was speaking to him tonight, upon all occasions. No one would think, who did not know, that Horace was the only person in the world who had recognized his genius and believed in it absolutely – nobody!

Well he must dress up as a girl! thought Dan – nothing but the fire-bucket flung at him by Willie had saved him perhaps from destruction, it had been Willie's presence of mind. His legs had burst into flame as he stood by the main grate of the building with his back to it, and it must have been a fragment of tinder or a wandering spark of volatile coal-gas attached to a mote of the atmosphere. All must go by the board (sex he would not consent to think of directly but it was *sex* must be sacrificed his sex whispered and he could not stop it) in such an emergency all had to go – but why should he care how he looked – yet he would not, it stood to reason, *choose* to take a female part. What man would wish to be got up as a girl? No man would. It was the *last thing* of course. He would see what he felt like and perhaps he would find he would go away from the party at once, for he could not suffer himself to be insulted any more by that little Margolin-fellow the cad – whose Safety Matches already rattled upon his codpiece, in offensive bombardment of his person. He really believed he must take Horace aside and whatever the consequences give him his private opinion of his *new friend* Margolin – who was evidently one of those people who lived on the outskirts, the dirty portions of capital cities and put our Saviour to death in their own city in the Bible. Then at this juncture he thought of Father Donovan, he would speak to him about them and find out what might be their numbers and if there were many of such people really, or how it came to pass that he met so many, whereas was it perfectly safe or not to consort with them, or suitable for a catholic. And also he would have to report how against his will entirely he had allowed himself to be dressed up as a woman, though all his instincts had been strongly against consenting and would remain so to the end.

Well then, if *woman* it was he was now to be, the sooner he got the things on the better as he did not relish standing here before all these strangers in this public place. The chef must think him extremely peculiar! He exposed himself to insult, or to some immodest pleasantry, every moment he stood there. He would have turned his back – but! At his back – at his back he had no codpiece!

Splitman came up, and Dan, gravely blushing, held his head in pensive inclination, prodding the floor with his toe. Ratner was looking at his legs – he wished the horrid man would leave him, or not look there!

'Did you get any burns?' Ratner asked, using his eyes terribly! Oh take your eyes from off my legs, and take your beak from off my thingimies! *Singularly* tactful to come and gape at an accident!

'You were extremely lucky not to have been badly burnt!'

Oh was I Mr Paul Pry! Go back to your stool and mind your own business!

'Did it just burn the silk – ?' Ratner approached a finger to the blackened hose-top, soaked with the emergency-douche from the fire-bucket, where small festoons of skin appeared beneath the doublet. At this Dan acted, he removed himself a step: he thought that was not far enough and he took two more.

'You must go up and see Mrs Bosun Dan!' Horace was calling out before everybody in the room. He might have come over to him – he really appeared to experience no interest at all. *No interest at all?* What had he done, except catch on fire – to cause Horace to be so indifferent, and so terribly cold? Evidently he had not wished him in the kitchen – that was but too clear!

Willie Service was at his side, as per ever sleek and impassible, standing almost to attention.

'Quick march. You are to come with me sir, up to the housekeeper!'

Willie Service himself began marching, he was linked to Dan – he led him quickly off. Dan did not look up at all, he hung his head as he was taken off.

A man passed them, coming in, and called to Peters who was in conversation with the chef. He said –

'Old Osman sez-'e wants a saw!'

'What's 'e want now! – a saw!' called Peters with passion.

'Ah! A saw.'

'What's 'e want a saw for!'

'I dunno.'

'To saw off his bleedin' 'ed?'

'Ah!'

'Well 'e can't 'ave one the rotten ole barstard not tonight! Ask 'im what 'e wants it for!'

' 'E says 'is wife wants to play on it!'

' 'Ere tell 'er to go and play on 'er spinach bed instead!' Peters retorted violently, and turned his back upon the emissary.

'What's that you want mate – a saw?' asked the chef over the broad shoulders of Peters.

'Ah!'

' 'Ere's a saw!' the chef said, and he pushed towards him a short butcher's meat-saw, like a ragged hatchet.

'Ah take 'im that!' said Peters.

The man wiped the saw upon a tablecloth.

' 'E says a long saw 'e wants.'

'Take 'im that, that's all 'e'll bloody well get tonight!' Peters told him.

'It don't matter not to me what 'e don't get guvnor!'

The slouching man who was a hired waiter, went indifferently away, holding the heavy meat-saw.

'If 'e can't play on that mate tell 'im to come 'ere and fetch one 'imself!' Peters raised his voice to shout back out of the midst of his muffled heart-to-heart passages with the chef, Lord Osmund still indistinctly on his mind.

Margolin with Mr Zagreus stood in repose beside the period-grate, interfering with the passage of the heat from the coals to the body of Ratner. Mr Zagreus had been watching the episode of the saw.

'Every man gets the butler he deserves,' said he.

'Some don't have a butler at all.' Margolin was sleepy, as the period-heat ascended his ancient spine in the young body of a blond crimped doll.

'I know.' Mr Zagreus did know that there was a class of persons without butlers, who deserved them.

'*I* haven't,' Arch told him.

'If you had you wouldn't attract such a butler as Peters Arch! Where he picked up Peters is a mystery to me. Possibly Peters was his batman.'

'I wouldn't have a butler Horace!' Arch effusively favoured Horace with his confidence.

'Class-War is in full swing at Osmund's,' Horace remarked. 'Class-war – in full swing!'

He watched Margolin's lips expectantly, moving his own slightly to anticipate the response, but Margolin said nothing.

'I knew somebody,' said Horace – it was clear from the expression upon his face that Pierpoint was that Mr X, 'who says before a revolution these conditions always exist, as between masters and servants.'

'Before a what Horace?'

'Revolution – like the French Revolution of course or the Russian.'

'Was there a revolution there? When was that Horace?'

'Of course.'

'I didn't know. Was there? That must have been when I was young.'

As Horace watched the lips for the words and saw them spell out with their subtle movements the word 'young', he beamed at Arch fiercely from out of his bronzed Choktaw mask – thrilling (great European) at the youngness – all his subconscious surging up in silent hallelujahs, blending snob-thoughts of muscle with snob-thoughts of *mind*.

'He says servants become unmanageable.'

'Like horses like.'

'It is a *sign*!'

'Go on!' Arch had shut his dolly-eyes and slept stolidly upright. He dropped into the mass-jargon, playfully class-conscious, standing before the period-fire, in the company of one of nature's gentlemen.

'Yes' said Horace, thoroughly warmed up to the topic, 'he says it was just the same in Russia before the crack.'

'Was he in Russia?'

'No. The masters felt it coming as well.'

'They must I should think.'

'Yes – they get familiar with their servants. Many treat them as friends. They start doing so.'

'Servants! Do you like a servant Horace?'

'That depends.'

'I think' said Archie 'servants ought to be kept down!'

'You find the servant who is waiting at the table joining in the conversation – he will help himself over your shoulder to a whisky and soda occasionally. In Russia they used to smoke cigarettes while handing round the fish.'

'They hadn't half got a nerve hadn't they – I didn't know. While they was waiting?'

'I gather that is so.'

'I shouldn't wonder *in Russia.* I've heard they're very socialist there!'

'Of course, but before that!'

'I should smoke if I was there doing that. Wouldn't you Horace? I was once a waiter for a week.'

'The barriers that will soon be *thrown* down are already down in fact.'

Margolin stretched himself and yawned out of his pink-and-white doll-lungs of saw-dust, a miniature bay (stretching his mouth-muscles, displaying his midget boxer's-reach with curled-up fists) in order to expel the period-heat that was drugging his tissues. *Yach-yach-yach!* he distended the invisible guttapercha binding his jaws like sailor-hat-elastics. Emerging from these spasms swollen-eyed, he plunged into a casual confidence, tied-up in a little pompous frown, with the airs of a consultant in a key-industry at a moment of national crisis.

'There won't be a revolution not in Old England Horace!'

(And that was from the horse's mouth – by the courtesy of one of those that make the revolutions, an insurgent 'worker of the world.')

'You think there won't.'

Nature's gentleman, against whom such disturbances are directed, politely declined to be convinced.

'I bet you – here Horace I bet you *a cool thousand*, will you take me on!' spluttered Arch, this stupid *cool* tacked on to the pound-sterling four-figure-quantity tickling him to death whenever he used it.

'I don't possess such a sum of money!'

The paradox, for all the nobilitarian smile that accompanied it was lost upon Arch.

'Not in *our* time Horace!' Arch said – he threw an overpowering leer of the most lurid mischief in, at the sarcastic possessive before 'time', also at the further english idiotism and the thought of many more, with which he was furnished. In mockery of his mastery of this important tongue he had a spasm like a sneeze. Taking his hand out of his jacket-pocket he cocked a thumb and finger and sped a Safety Match to its billet – a broken-down british club-waiter out-of-work cantering in the background with a tray of glasses.

Zagreus, a great sportsman, dilettante of all dexterities, watched the trajectory of the Safety Match. The first fell short. Arch drew out from the bottom of his pocket and loaded a second, cocked and discharged it. It winged its way, this time over the waiter's head. A third followed in lightning succession – Archie was bracketing. It was short, but a better shot. At last one fell upon the tray.

'What quantities of people Osmund hires for his parties,' Zagreus remarked, watching another hobbling picture of past smartness in edwardian tails.

'It can't half cost old Osmund a tidy bit Horace to have a party you're right.'

'This is the nucleus of a Parliamentary Army!'

'What's that?'

'Black Guards – Red Guards!'

'Are they? – I didn't know.'

'That is their feudal leanings – playing at the seigneur. All Finnian Shaws are vulgarly feudal – like a new-rich with a castle.'

'You're right Horace – ole Osman's a proper toff!'

'He feels his time is short, it may be that.'

Mr Zagreus bent an impressive gaze upon his proletarian genius-in-embryo, the halcyon yiddisher babyhood of whose face refused hospitality to any political shadow whatever. But Zagreus expected an answer. Margolin was crystallizing into an oracle rapidly, for each time now with Horace this came about with greater speed. As he felt himself compelled to conform to the sphinxishness expected, by this, compared with him, gigantic gentleman (dressed as an aborigine) Archie felt he must keep a straight face. Turning towards what now was obviously a new patron, out of the same family as Dick, he tucked him up under his proletarian wing with the lightheartedest splutter.

'Horace, who's been telling you Old England's rotten Horace? they're not right! Don't you take any notice of them, it's sil-lee!'

Not right – how lovely – Zagreus wore his smile to-the-manner-born, like an over-big buttonhole in his mouth.

'What?' he said, and laughed.

'Don't listen Horace to *alarmists!* That's alaaarm-ist!' Archie was delighted with the pomp of this big foolish newspaper word he had found inside his little head, burlesquely he swelled to utter it – all words were potential toys, big mouthfuls especially, to be battered over when talking, by his little tingling tongue, at such as Horace – *talking* a great indoor sport, *batting the winged word* captured in a newspaper over the net.

'Is that alarmist Archie?'

'Absolutely – Horace!' Arch frankly disintegrated at the sheer orotundness of the *christian name* of his patron – *Horace* – what what! – not to mention Archy-the-Bald for-the-matter-of-that!

'Is it!'

'Yeees! Here! You must have got in with a lot of communists Horace!'

He frowned up his face in inquisitive reproach.

'Do you think so? No. I don't know any.'

'Well it sounds as if you was. That's what that lot say Horace, I know some communists. Revolutions – Old England won't stand for them, not the Briton Horace – you don't know them – I know Britons, they won't stand for them, not the British.'

'No. It's the Banks. The Banks have been telling people there is going to be a big crash.'

'Oh it's the Banks!'

'The Banks!'

'Which?' barked the baffled Archie, scowling towards the Banks.

'People I know are selling their houses and leaving England. A whole family I know went back to Florida yesterday. They had been here for forty years – the old man was nearly eighty.'

'Nearly eighty!'

'The Banks say there is going to be a big crash.'

Archie the sphinx stood grinning and nonplussed confronted with the Banks.

'The Banks are liars!' he blustered. 'The Banks are potty!'

'A big crack is what they think – I shouldn't be surprised if they were!'

'I should – very surprised indeed – *very surprised indeed!*'

Mr Zagreus fixed a sparkling eye upon his budding oracle, eagerly watching it speak, lip-reading with great relish – he was trying out this new machine, but he had made up his mind to have it as an oracle, whatever came he would have it as an oracle, it was too perfect.

'That lot upstairs has to go *somehow* Arch!' Mr Zagreus raised bloodthirsty eyes to the ceiling.

Archie Margolin burst out laughing in the face of his patron at this.

'Who, old Osman?' he shouted.

'The same!'

'Why, Horace tell us why, Horace, old Osman must go!'

'Nature I am positive has marked them down for extinction!' Mr Zagreus resorted to natural law.

'They don't do any harm to anyone!' Arch complained stoutly – 'Not old Osman and Pheebie!'

'Osmund is his own worst enemy,' Mr Zagreus sentimentally conceded, a crocodile-sob à la Kein in his voice – he felt for two pins he might begin broadcasting Lionel.

'And that's not saying much!' spluttered Arch.

'That's true, that is not saying much!' Mr Zagreus said almost abjectly.

'If *that's* all he has to worry about!'

'He hasn't *much!*'

'You're right. I wish I had nothing worse than that anyhow!'

'I should be a new man if I hadn't any more than that!'

'You're a communist Horace.'

'Yes perhaps that's what it is. I *am* down on the rich.'

'You're an alarmist!'

'I think you're right Arch!'

'I know I'm right Horace, you alarm yourself Horace.'

'Yes. Well I may! No that's not true. I've got nothing to lose – as yet. When I have!'

Horace Zagreus regarded his new discovery with an increasingly uncritical eye. One more step and he would no longer be able however mildly to keep his end up he plainly foresaw, he would be prostrate. He was practically certain now that he was in the presence of *genius*!

'I think Arch you're *absolutely* right - through and through! – the Finnian Shaws are not the sort that would take a social knock-out standing up.'

'Absolutely not!'

'They'd crawl into *any* World is what you mean – upon their hands and knees if necessary and even by choice, in the attitude of quadrupeds – so long as it was a capital W of a World, with Gossip-notoriety attached, and it had possession of all the Beaches, newspapers, palaces and great hotels.'

'I didn't say Horace – no. Poor old Osmun give him a chance!'

'That's it – how right you are! Already they are fairly outcast, which, as Pierpoint says, it is essential to be – from what cadres are still standing of the old fabric – in order to be socially popular with the canaille of the Ritzes and Rivieras!'

'Oh hark at you Horace – you're a proper communist as ever I come across – it was at the Ritz I was a lift-boy for a week – no I was in the kitchen!'

A dreary report burst from the throat of the unseen Ratner, it made no pretence to be a laugh.

'They have not far to fall,' fiercely continued Horace, in the midst of a sudden *broadcast* 'to step into the social cadres of a Soviet!'

Arch yawned. The lassitude of the sphinx was apparent – what was Soviet to him or he to Soviet?

'When are we going to have our show Horace?' he asked to change the subject.

'We will go up in a moment and see. I have to arrange our screens.'

'Have you Horace. Have you got them?'

'Service has.'

Both Margolin and Zagreus were glad that Service had got them and they wondered what he was doing.

Peters left the laughing chef and they both approached, Peters in front.

'Here Pete!' called Arch.

With a dark and friendly grin Peters strolled up, stocky and bandy, a butler of steel, to the grinning Eastender waiting to receive him – Peters' little class-pal.

'Sir!'

'Here – this gentleman here says Pete we're going to have a proper revolution in Old London Town – you know same as they had in France when old Robesspot – no I'm getting it mixed – old Potemkins!'

The clouds of an impending British Terror descended upon the brow of the butler (who was harshly un-period even anti-period) and he ceased outright to grin. His eyes became those of a wholesale informer, at the bar of summary popular justice, with all his highly-placed arch-enemies about to forfeit the least important parts of their bodies, namely their head-pieces.

'I shouldn't be surprised if one of these days' said Peters with great energy 'I didn't make a revolution not all on my own – straight I shouldn't!'

Mr Zagreus left anti-period Peters and his small grinning class-pal and approached the youthful chef-de-cuisine, who stood smiling bashfully with a mighty chopper stuck in his girdle, a great deathsman of dead ruminants and an iconoclast in his way.

IV Mrs Bosun's Closet

Dan and escort passed a fishfag who stood at the door representing one of the Old Cries of London, with more bloaters and fresh haddock, and the cat scratches the wheel. Up the office-stairs they directed themselves and it was Service who announced with a knock they had come.

'Is this the young gentleman?' Mrs Bosun asked.

Dan blushed and Willie said it was.

'This young gentleman will make a lovely girl' said Mrs Bosun. 'I'm sure I shouldn't have known the young gentleman was a boy if you hadn't told me.'

This egregious period-matron gloated upon his great maidenly damaged fleshings, with professional fish-eyed sex-banter born of a seafaring past (and archaic sex-directness of nautical ancestors) until he could positively have screamed at the vile old body and told the horrid old soul to call her great coarse blue eyes off – or he would say *good day to you* without more ado and give her his room instead of his company the old horror!

Mrs Bosun sat in her closet (she did not rise when the two came in from her windsor chair) which she presided over: a dignified red-white-and-blue domestic personage bluff and stout with blue and steadfast eye, of best ocean-blue (as the waves used to be before Trafalgar but especially prior to the Mutiny of the Nore), with a discreet foam of decent frilling bursting from under her buttoned-up period-bodice-case (bust-glove or rib-trunk) – rigid with stay-busks – and also a trickle out of the mouths of her massive serge sleeves of spotless undie-white: as she moved there was a period-petticoat-rustle with it of silk and black callamanca combined, under the barme-cloth or the callous apron as white as the morning-milk – flannel and swanskin certainly in comfortable bloodbaked sheaths clung upon the buxom body, of beef-bred british limb and torse, of this model matron.

A *heavy wet* upon her housekeeper's work-bench bubbled at hand, obvious porter: though no one would rule it out with Mrs Bosun, that such a ruddy period-piece as she was would stick at a round dollop of Old Tom, termed blue ruin, to keep her period-person in good twig and up to snuff – is there not melody in *max?* There is melody in *max!* She would not draw the line. – But there was a bottle of Arquebuscade Water as well and the remnants of another Baume de Vie not far off, also a posset not very distant, always ready for the headachy or the coldie-coldie and the young gentlemen and young Lady Harriet too were headachy often poor little darlings, and fretful bless their sweet precious hearts! And then would they not looking ever so pitiful, come crying in to good old nanny Bosun for a *posset please!* with a petulant lisp, or some *arrowroot:* or they *would* sometimes go and strike their little knuckies against a piece of furniture, or fall down as children will, or cut theirselves, and then looking ever so blue come crying up the stairs to have her kiss the place as she often did and make it well, or have it dabbled with Arquebuscade. For Mrs Bosun herself, who liked her cup of tea, there was, not far from the *heavy wet*, a monumental Rock Pot (classical Rockingham ware, of coarsest plum-purple and blue-black glaze – samovar of the servants'-hall – the cheapest but sweetest, guaranteed to provide a better brew than the choicest china set) – a worsted camblet was next a family-Bible, which awful brass-bound volumen was a certain pledge that this period-bosom was not sounding brass at all or a tinkling thimble but sound to the core – nourished upon Genesis and upon Exodus. Then there were knitting sheaths and needles lay upon a second table – pillows and bobbins for the Bucks Point that Mrs Bosun had easily learnt to do. A large swill held garments of The Quality – a larger swill was dark sweat-grey and grease-green, with the garments of The Flux, which were to be mended – the former by Mrs Bosun, the latter distributed to her two maids, though she would sometimes do a ceremonial garment of Peters, with braid, and sometimes a maid would handle a garment of a guest. On top of the first basket was a pull-over of Mr Eustace, in violent russet and reckitts counterchange, for he was staying this week – he was a fair one was Mr Eustace for tearing his things he was and a very careless gentleman.

That Mrs Bosun went to the arms of Morpheus in the same closet over which she presided, was but too evident, owing to the portentous presence of a four-poster, minus its pillars, but plus a strictly period eiderdown – two quilted bedcovers and a counterpane. A sitzbath and the bases of two flowered chambers completed the evidence for night-and-day occupation and residence, with the ineludable suggestion that Mrs Bosun cast off her purely period-shell in the night-hours and sought the repose she had so well deserved upon the same spot where she so brilliantly transacted the housekeeping, from six o'clock onwards, and dispensed possets and arquebuscades.

'Well I suppose we must find this young gentleman a young lady's frock mustn't we!' boomed Mrs Bosun with the opaque cheerfulness of the *keep-smiling* doggedness, that made the playing-fields of Eton what they were in pre-Brodrick days. And the breezy old body got up upon her staunch sea-legs and bore down in an air line upon a roomy Mother-Hubbard-cupboard, built in the wall, but the size of a station waiting-room in a small Halt. Into this Mrs Bosun passed bodily, the door following her in and remaining in the entrance behind her, and she was now lost to view and as it were in a second Mrs Bosun's closet.

But Dan was torn between the horns of a gigantic dilemma, which tossed him to and fro and made him by turns hot and cold: for the question that at every moment forced itself with greater urgency upon his consideration was this – *how to effect the change of costume?* Could Mrs Bosun be relied upon to turn her back? (That was the sort of agonizing question.) Or – and this was the idea that had obsessed him entirely ever since he had entered Mrs Bosun's housekeeper's closet, and (poor forlorn Daniel of a Dubliner that he was) put his head into the British Lion's genial den – *would this kindly old period-body and dear old dimity-soul of a wax-work housekeeper not perhaps insist upon effecting the change with her own officious old fingers!* – There was no use disguising the fact, there seemed every likelihood that, with her fiendish sex-jollity – her primitive prude-ragging proclivities no doubt – with those solid period-views in fine, of a breezy and barbarous culture (born of nautical necessities, of sea-faring sans-gêne) that she would simply ravish the last vestige of *one* attire – picking him dry of every stitch, as though he had been a pre-war Pears-Soap-Baby or a little animal nursery-tot (especially seeing what in reality was her accredited social function as regards all Finnian Shaws up to sixty, or any of spoilt-baby ilk resembling same, and arousing similar reflexes, under her care, from first childhood to second childhood – she possessing diplomas, cups, gold medals, and shields for untold tact *in between* – making due allowance for the fact that *everyone* whatever, for her, as a matter of professional pride, was simply a tiny tot, or else a poor young person, born into a bosunic universe with a silver tit stuck into its pout as a matter of course) – bearing all this in the brain, was it safe to assume that having with business-like bustle ravished him of *one* objectable fancy-dress, she would not force upon his unwilling limbs *another* – some disgraceful frilled abortion such as females bought in haberdasheries (even down to the abjectest drudge) packing their immodest extremities with lace in the most offensive manner. Oh what a ticklish situation to be faced with as the result of an accident – in a sense Dan could almost wish he had been a girl! For at least then he could not have been treated in this rough-and-tumble masculine fashion at least – girls lucky devils were protected from these tactics of false free-and-easiness on grounds of *modesty:* at least had he been a girl there would have been no question of his being manhandled and heartily-overhauled by a member of the opposite sex or dressed and undressed like a circus-horse or washed down like a public stallion with no mind of its own! Sometimes to be *a man* was awful nothing short! When one came in touch with these hearty persons of primitive culture, it was awful! – who had about as much sixth-sense (that is sex-sense) as a knock-about comic or a lousy sheep-dog in the street, but just plunged through life like a bull in a china shop seeking the exit, death in their eyes! This great mastodon of a matron from the brutalest of the British Past (and how brutal the British Past was only an Irishman could guess) would come crashing out of her closet-within-a-closet, playfully lay hold of him possibly by a leg, like a chicken to be plucked, and strip him in what she would of course call two shakes yes of a Moke's tail or some such hearty horror of an expression. She would regard it positively as a joke and a good hearty side-splitting one too, to slip one of those repulsive garments that all women wore upon their legs to make them look different to men's though they weren't (hung probably – and he shuddered – with the most fearful bawdy frills and in other ways stupefyingly disconcerting) upon his. He was fully alive to all the dangers that he ran in the room of this terrible old lady.

Willie Service, an underdog eye upon the door of the closet-within-a-closet, was polishing off the *heavy wet* imprudently left behind by Mrs Bosun upon the table. Dan's mind was made up. Face it he could not! He moved towards the door by which they had entered.

'Yes! Where are you going?' Willie Service the horrid officious little beast had one of his worst bullying moods on at present, everything pointed to that. However Dan said nothing but he suggested – to whom it might concern and whose business it was – by the expression of his face, that just feeling the least bit queasy, he had intended to go down into the yard, for a minute or two.

'No you don't!'

Willie Service bore down upon him and drove him away from the door or perhaps Dan fell back before the onrush of his liveried keeper – disconcerted by this forced march and the stern expression assumed by Willie (whose motto as he always told people was *Ich Dien* like the royal family, or *At your service!*)

'Back! It's no use! You must stop here!' Willie Service's two eyes were in chilly ambush beneath his shining cap-peak of a sham-chaufleur: he stood-easy, chewing an imaginary piece of gum, in imitation of the american film-sleuth.

'Why?' asked Dan faintly.

'Because I say so. That's good enough for you!'

The little bully squared his jaw, Dan fell back a step.

'Anyway orders are, Boleyn, that you should be dressed as a girl. You know that as well as I do.' He became the genial turnkey. 'I'm sorry and all that old bean – duty's duty! – I'm surprised they haven't dressed you as a girl before – it will suit you, down to the ground.'

Down to the ground! – with burning cheeks Dan turned away from this impossible attendant.

'You'll have all the men after you!' added Willie, as if on purpose.

Oh Horace, why should you have chosen for me this *impossible* attendant, who does *nothing* but bully and insult me!

'She's thinking-up an attractive undie-outfit for you.'

The beast! Dan could almost have wrung Willie Service's neck and would not any longer stand for all this caddish bullying but the very next day would tell Horace that he could not continue to suffer himself to be bullied by this little cad of a Willie, – either Horace must find somebody else or he would take the law into his own hands, he would go away or simply dismiss Willie Service after this party and tell him he required his services no longer.

But the door of the closet-within-the-closet burst open with fracas, and Dan's great irish heart of a wild doe of Erin was in his mouth, riding the root of his tongue and threatening to suffocate him. Mrs Bosun came out loaded with one lady's complete period-wardrobe and instantly it was possible for Dan's eyes to note (with a distension of unmixed dismay) *on top* – and as the most conspicuous garment – a forked horror loaded with lace worthy of a second-empire can-can cocotte. Oh Horace, why (Dan could not refrain from observing to himself) have you exposed me to such insults as *these!* And he blushed at *these* as who wouldn't!

Filled with an uncontrollable panic, Dan flung himself towards the door, colliding with Willie Service, who was there a fraction of a second before him. In his irrational consternation he seized upon the handle and shook it violently, but like a vice the policemanesque fist of William Ich Dien closed upon his fingers. Alas, there was no escape! For two pins Dan knew this fiend-in-human-shape (but with the soul of a policeman) attached to his person by the heartless Horace, would have handcuffed him – the demon incarnate would not have stuck at pinioning his legs - he would have stuck at nothing – he would not have drawn back in horror before chloroforming him for the operation of undressing him utterly – spreadeagled upon the operating-table of the terrible Bosun, and drawing on, piece by piece, that most vile costume! So, his heart beating a breakneck tattoo, he withdrew from the door and he stood panting before the intolerably cheerful personality of this period-nurse of gigantic tots, full of a diabolical bustle of unmentionable preparation, now borne forward upon the flood-tide of the coarsest high-spirits to a consummation of the most total immodesty. – Pawing and fingering she was the fearful cylinders of senseless silk, smoothing out the sprigs of the best Honiton, testing the tautness of the rigging of the stays, counting the scollops, locating the button-holes, seeing that the hooks went into the eyes, hunting for the ends of prurient tape – behaving as though the body were a smoking-room joke in fact of which *the legs* were the cream (but in which *the bust* ran them pretty close) – as if some Rowlandson had come back to earth to spread the view that human beings were worth nothing more than *things*, and that all were within the compass of his bold stylistic pen, from bigwig to bowwow – women big coarse flowers open to the four winds of heaven, stations for bees-glue or pollen upon the route of the mystical bee – men an abstract species of great bulk, concerned with a dull system of unwieldy crafts – all men and women justified in nothing but as *objects* pure and simple – to be models standing to be drawn for the laughter of a Rowlandson!

'Now if this young gentleman will strip while I turn the other way!' roguishly crashed out the preposterous Bosun with a fruity joyous indifference to all finer feeling that was absolutely pre-French Revolution, and that was even fading beside the death-bed of the last of the Stuarts (*Queen Anne is dead* that most significant sentence in all the chapters of the long tale of England – alas *Queen Anne is dead* – the Old Dominion and the Land of Penn in full swing – the first sky-scraper in sight upon the dismal horizon): 'Lord bless my heart I do declare the young gentleman is blushing! Why what next my pretty – to suppose an old woman like me who's had three husbands two of them widowers matters! But there – *I promise faithfully* not to look! Here are the things laddie! You know how to put them on *don't you!*' (Oh the old fiend – he could have struck her outright – she was holding up the most horrible of the suggestive garments and actually waving them up and down, a faint but meretricious perfume escaped from them, and Dan did not know which way to look). He simply averted his burning cheeks and downcast eyes from these filthy frilled cylinders – with that beastly duality that was tantamount to a carnal encounter (it was in the nature of all such things that they should go *in pairs* too, which made it worse) – oh that he might never again see or hear of such humiliating leg-bags and breast-sacks, stomachers and calf-hose, that were contrived to make a mockery of existence, or else why have invented them at all!

But the hearty old hen would have her way and turned her back with a roguish discretion – he could have struck her upon it with the flat of his hand for being so extremely beastly!

'Hurry up you!' said Willie Service. 'We're all waiting for you!'

But hardly had Willie Service given vent to this coarse and bullying remark when the door at his back flew open with as it were violent ceremony, and he staggered with the impact before he could remove himself. This was succeeded by a ceremonious pause, then a heated messenger appeared, with majestic haste, in the entrance – an osmundian footman, cheap but showy.

'His lordship has been injured in the kneecap by a saw!' in a hollow drawl this man announced, as if he had been breaking the stillness of a room with a *Viscount and Viscountess Neecup Byassor!*

Mrs Bosun wheeled about, with the precision of a buxom top of good manufacture, the solicitude of generations of brawny brisket-bred mothers-of-men pictured posthumously in her merely period-face, which only had two expressions and this was the other.

'His lordship – injured!' she cried, taking a smart step to the rear.

'Yes, my Lord Phoebus madam! His lordship has been injured by a saw.'

'A saw Giles'!

'Yes madam. Her ladyship did it with a saw.'

'You must be dreaming man! Her ladyship do it!'

'His lordship cannot come up the stairs, he says he would be glad madam if you would go down at once madam and attend to him. His lordship is in the study. – His lordship is with him.'

Mrs Bosun flung open her medicine chest, her hand went automatically to the spot where the first aid articles were collected – for pricks, knocks, cuts and cigarette-end-burns – burnt tongues, hot ears, bruises, pin-wounds and tender feet. She snatched up the bottle of Arquebuscade and without needing any further prompting she rolled with dogged speed and ruddy dignity out of her closet, followed by the impassible osmundian valet de pied.

'Now get these things on' said Willie Service extremely rudely. 'I will look the other way!'

This young man was more horrid with his brutal bullying manner than Mrs Bosun was jocund and vile – there was not a period-pin to choose between the pair of them, except that Mrs Bosun could not help being like she was whereas Willie was wilfully awful!

'All right' said Willie Service yawning. 'I will go and take a leak. When I come back mind you're ready – if you haven't got them on I shall report you!'

Blushing Dan covertly watched the pocket-martinet march

off. Then he went over to the door and double-locked and double-bolted Mrs Bosun's famous closet firmly upon the inside.

V At the American Bar

A Praxiteles' statue of ill-luck – a squalid *fate* – placed at the stair-head above the kitchen, Ratner listened to the voices of Horace, the chef, Peters and Margolin below. He could see upon his right the far-fetched prismatic lustres of the great saloon, that was crowded with people who were strutting in a dance, to a music of drums, with contralto and counterbass saxophones – period The Present. The studied mass-energy of the music, hurrying over precipices, swooping in switchbacks, rejoicing in gross proletarian nigger-bumps, and swanee-squeals shot through with caustic cat-calls from the instrumentalists, depressed him. It was as if he had written it himself! But more still did the vibrations of the voice of Horace Zagreus depress him – *that* it would be impossible to attribute to Ratner's handiwork, with the autocratic dominant strut of its sentences, but doubly stupid it was in Ratner's estimate, twice as tiresome as the idiot mass-sound of the marxistic music.

'He is a genius!' Horace was thundering below. That accent of fatuous finality that he knew so well! His yellow face took on a mildew of hatred. Upon each occasion when a new planet (for his private solar system) swum into his ken, radiant with what he called *genius*, this thunderous acclamation recurred with Horace. There he went again! 'You should be proud to have a *genius* in your kitchen! It is the first time you have ever had a genius in your kitchen!'

Trying to make the young chef jealous! Well well – *Margolin!* The mildew of hatred almost *smelt*, like a fungus, upon the face of Ratner, as he stood suspended at the stair-head. – But the 'genius' was not averse to hearing his own voice either – Arch made himself heard in vocables collected between Smithfield and Mile End, and Ratner responded with a sickly smirk (alas my poor brother!) to this pantomime: but the voice of genius cracked beneath the weight of its natural hysteria – Ratner could hear its collapse below, like the crash of a lush fat duck's egg upon asphalt, and the chef's laugh crowed out, to crown the accident, with imitation excitement – Ratner's lip curled back and he sneered at the young chef.

One by one at last they came up, talking nonsense. They were followed half-way by the boyish Swiss responsible for the economics of the menus, his white cap waggling as he laughed. Ratner moved away from the stair-head, as they caught him up, after their long delays about the exit to the kitchen. There was a small room with AMERICAN BAR above the open door. Horace led them in at a grand stroll, Ratner brought up the rear, the sting in the tail of the trio.

One of two negroes tossed an american mixture in a silver shaker lazily, while he rolled his eyeballs, to show he was a negro, and did not hide his teeth under a bushel.

'Is it compatible with our standing as players to ask this negro for a drink?' boomed Horace to himself, who was in fine fettle and high feather at the idea of the presence of 'genius' under his wing and protection, and sat down. Several consumers cast glances upwards of abashed enquiry, at the self-styled 'player'.

'What will you have Horace?' asked Margolin mounting upon a tabouret at his side, very bustling and possessive, and full himself of the nuptials of his 'genius' with an intense 'admirer', Ratner stood outside the lunar warmth of this grotesque honeymoon of the mind, and its peculiar sentimentals – shivering slightly in his Split-kit, which admitted the draughts of the period-farmhouse.

'I will have a Madeira' said Horace. 'What will you have?'

Behind the negro were dazzling ranks of bottles, decanters and flasks of alcohol, of rainbow-tinted spirit, super-'colorful' as possible for the coarse saxenglish nigger-palate, side by side with black Eighteenth Century stoppered flagons, for the Sandeman Sherry, Port and Madeira 1926.

Horace lifted the glass of Madeira and put it to his lips.

'Bottlescrew days!' he exclaimed before sipping it off.

'Happy days!' howled Margolin happily to Horace.

Ratner with a furtive distaste put his glass to his mouth and, his big flat grey eye-in-profile crawling upon the wall in front of him, he allowed a trickle to enter his body.

'Oh double-racked – aguardiente fortified – white Jesuit Wine I don't think!' Horace clamoured at his glass.

Beaming at Margolin – the little frisky bride of his Understanding – he employed the *I don't think* of his popular repertory as a pretty compliment, and drank again and again, hosannah after hosannah, to Archie in the Highest. Margolin smiled in brotherly brutality at the afroamerican, who was whirling the shaker.

STILL GENEVAS THE LIQUOR OF LIFE

A card pinned upon the bar-wall above a large black period-bottle had these words lettered upon it.

'Genevas!' said Horace as he caught sight of it, pointing it out to Ratner at once.

'Yes' Ratner said, looking over at it reluctantly and sulkily.

'Best unsweetened *London Gin* I should say.'

'That's his national drink' Ratner said.

'Whose Ratner?' Horace asked.

Ratner nodded towards the gold-toothed ex-cotton-helot at the bar-counter.

'Are you referring to Africa?'

'No – I suppose he's an american negro – Americans call gin – '

'An american negro?' Horace muttered absent-mindedly, for he was wondering if Margolin could sing, as he believed he must have a splendid tenor voice – in fact he was turning over in his mind whether *genius* would manifest itself by appearing as notes out of the mouth or as a handicraft or in the field of engineering.

'I suppose he is.' Ratner looked crossly askance at the love-sick wool-gathering genius-flirt, lost in this new *affair* of the mind.

'American probably' said Horace, watching Ratner in the bar-mirror. Ratner with an abrupt movement perceived he was being watched. He grinned angrily back in contempt, at this fatuous effort to spy.

'Yes Horace!'

'Are you an american negro?' Horace asked the Black.

'Yeah!' said the negro.

'Ach so– du bist doch lieber Neggerdeutsch nicht wahr!'

'Nop boss I no comprenny. I'm no dutchman barss!'

'Have you just come over from New York?'

'No I've just come up from Athens last week.'

'The Congo has come from the Acropolis! The Congo has actually come from the Acropolis!' Mr Zagreus chanted, lifting his eyes heavenward, forgetting the boulevards of Athens in imagining the african swamps, which were extremely unhealthy.

'Is he badly hurt?' asked a person at Ratner's elbow with black grease paint, counterfeiting the negritic hue, a compliment to the black bar-tender, in the costume of an african rajah out of Purchas or Mandeville since the guests had been invited to disguise themselves as *characters in classical fiction*.

'No he was only scratched' replied a tall man partly in fencing-dress, representing Adolphe.

'I thought he'd had his leg sawn off' said the first.

'Not quite' said the second.

'Didn't they send for the ambulance?' the bogus despot as seen by the untutored mind of early navigators asked, smiling at his blackened face in the glass – at the broad-mindedness that made it possible for him to eclipse his skin's white and become a brotherly-black on the same footing as the nigger.

'He only had his trousers torn a little.'

'Was that all? Were you there?'

'Yes, the saw wouldn't work it was too short and Robinia snatched it away to send for another one and hit Phoebus on the knee.'

They both smiled in the glass at their faces and the negro smiled.

Recalling the saw taken from the kitchen, Ratner handed in to the gathering of grinning heads in the looking-glass his own bitter contribution, an acid smirk of contempt. He found Horace watching him again.

'Oughtn't we to see about fixing the screens Horace?' Ratner asked.

'There's no hurry,' said Horace.

With the guilty stealth of the cat Ratner spat at his side – one of the worst of his Complexes related to a sense of inferiority in the matter of his spittle – Ratner felt that everyone was repelled by and had a down on his spittle – Ratner was very cowed after having spat, but the bitter taste remained in his mouth. There was champagne on tap, with a nickel-spigot with butterfly stop-cock in the tinselled bottle-neck of the magnum, which was laid upon its labelled flank. Archie held out a glass to the negro who filled it from the bottle.

'Subject to market fluctuations, six bob a bottle!' Horace told him, as Archie held it frothing an inch from the counter.

'Fizz is my favourite wine!' burst out in bubbling mock-confidence Archie to Horace – letting him in behind the scenes with a rush to have a privileged peep, giving away what was the favourite beverage-wine of 'genius' – when at its most sparkling, at its youngest – the cork simply flying out at sweet seventeen, and still going strong at barely twenty. He leered at Horace, and Horace leered back at him. Ratner turned away his head as if it were blown round upon his shoulder – one of his really capital Complexes related to his face in such a situation as this, where he was an outsider – it always felt like a face deprived of its nose as pictured in a clinical treatise.

'Fizz is your favourite!' crashed out Horace, demonstrating by the fire of his response that he was not unworthy of the confidence of genius, and that he thrilled at the privileges accorded him. 'I can understand that Arch – *that* I can understand!' – the impact of his voice upon the air was so perfervid a slap that even Ratner started – the outburst was overdone – even for somebody genius-mad as was he – this was a super-solicitous Boswell of this baby, surely – could so much force not be *intended* to be silly? And even the subtle watchful sleep of Ratner's flat eye-in-profile in the looking-glass seemed disturbed as if it smelt a rat.

'You are like champagne yourself Arch!' after a pause Mr Zagreus thundered. 'Like a magnum full of life – your wit astonishes me! If a jack-in-the-box popped out of a bottle of Heidsieck I could not be more astounded! *You* are champagne!'

The watchful grey eye-in-profile in the mirror gave a positive jump, as if a fly had bitten it. Ratner turned abruptly and looked

Horace full in the face, with both eyes, for a brief moment, of awful scrutiny.

'At six bob a bottle?' Ratner asked in a business-like tone, looking down gravely at the counter in front of him.

'No!' shouted Horace in his ear, 'no you old cask of *sour-grapes* – Vinegar-man! – *not* at six bob a bottle! Nineteen-nineteen you hear – best year' he dropped his voice suddenly to average pitch – 'best mark!'

'Ah!' Ratner's eye was in the glass again, more vindictive and more direct.

'Absolutely!'

'Taste in wine Horace – '

'Yes Julius! Taste – yes.'

'I was about to say taste in wine is purely subjective,' Ratner sneered.

'According to *you*,' exclaimed Mr Zagreus noisily, foaming slightly at the mouth in a mock-rage or with mock-inspiration, his eyes sparkling, '*everything* is subjective, you old relativist Ratner – you relativist!'

'Relativist!'

'You deny objective reality *even to yourself* – and I for my part take you at your word!'

'Thank you Horace.'

'Not at all, that is not at all difficult.'

'I meant for believing me!'

'Oh there is *no* belief attached, if that is what you mean!'

'No – I am sorry Horace.'

'But I have not made you the devil of my Morality for nothing.'

'Your Morality Horace?'

'Let us use then the favourite expression of Lionel Kein, *Amorality* – my *Amorality*.'

'I don't understand. Are you referring to a play?'

'Not really, no, my words meant nothing. But such assistants as you are going cheap today you can't get away from that. Three offers of help by post – I've got in my pocket.'

'I know I'm not a *genius* Horace, if that's what you mean Horace – not even a *financial* genius!'

'You are all right. You were the first to my hand.'

'I see, the first to your hand Horace.'

'That is it Julius – you *are* handy. You have financial – *talent!*'

'Next time I shall not be so accessible,' Ratner pretended to retaliate, affecting to be on his dignity.

'That won't matter at all – there are plenty more where you come from. As like as peas, as like as peas! I could do it myself!'

That having passed off pleasantly and everything being put upon the best indulgent basis, honours being easy, Horace asked Ratner's opinion upon a matter of moment, in the following manner, but as may easily be supposed Ratner was not much pleased at being asked, and equally Zagreus paid little attention to his responses.

'This party gives me an itch Julius to do a thing I have never done before!' said Horace.

'What is that Horace?' asked Ratner.

'Write an epigram,' Horace said.

'Oh. Write an epigram. Why don't you Horace?' his Split shadow that financial wizard put the question required by the principles of the *broadcast*-dialogue.

'Because I don't understand the laws of satire' Horace explained to Ratner.

And Ratner realized that Horace was preparing to 'broadcast' or to try out a new Pierpoint Record, and that he might begin at any moment now. He resigned himself to listen to the ubiquitous loud-speaker, with the hated voice of Pierpoint starring.

'Are there laws in satire?' asked the shadow-man.

'Certainly there are laws in satire,' Horace assured him.

'What are they Horace?' ever so humbly Ratner asked, crawling up to his feet to learn what laws obtained in Satire.

Horace looked at him with some fixity and then he said with deliberation:

'The comedy of the Stage has killed the comedy of Life.'

'Yes? Has it?'

'Eccentricities have become less prominent. All the material for legitimate comedy must vanish as civilization advances.'

'If it advanced,' Ratner helpfully objected.

'Yes, if it advanced. As it advances.'

'Yes. Well?' Ratner sought to confer a natural touch upon this transaction by picking his nose in the glass with thoughtful eye – 'and who said that Horace? We are listening to Pierpoint I suppose?'

'No, those words are Hazlitt's.'

Wrong again! – anyone would do as well as he really – and there were plenty more where he came from! Finance was his real province. Ratner had a movement of impatience.

'Well?' he said.

Horace watched for his response in the glass: when the lips had finished moving he went on.

'A century since it was said by Hazlitt that comic social types upon the stage killed comedy-types in everyday life. Does it not become increasingly difficult (Hazlitt asked) for people to be ridiculous upon the scene of life, when upon the stage they are constantly caricatured? So, he said, life tends to grow uniform and accentless.'

'Well Horace – and what is your epigram?'

'Today we may be pardoned for regarding that remark of Hazlitt's as unsound.'

'Yes we may Horace,' Ratner smiled indulgently at Horace, showing no more than the yellow tip of a fang.

'Don't you think?'

'As we look round us!' Ratner looked furtively round him. He was evidently expected to look round him.

'Exactly. But Hazlitt probably meant in a stable society, not subject to violent fluctuations and to abrupt decay.'

'Yes I expect he did,' Ratner hissed lightly, with an increase of occulted impatience.

'He took it for granted Julius that the anglo-saxon society he knew was a sort of fixture upon this earth or had a longer lease than in fact it had.'

'I expect so – we all think – yes I *expect* so Horace.'

'Yes – but even then, however much good comedy might teach people how to laugh, and at what to laugh, they would still laugh at the wrong things – or if at the right, *still* Lord Osmund and Lord Phoebus would be very little modified. Their skins are too thick. Satire would break its spear upon such a hide.'

'I have heard Lord Osmund is very thin-skinned.'

'No that is a mistake. His skin is very thick.'

'I believe he would be easy to wound,' said Ratner, 'by satire.'

'He would bellow at the least aspersion upon himself. But he is thick.'

'Thick-skinned, is he, yes.'

'But there is another point Julius.'

'Another point! What is that Horace?' Very indulgent and talking-down-to-the-children, Ratner sneered at himself in the glass, with a yellow-lidded blink and puff.

'True satire must be vicious, Hazlitt I believe was right, not wrong as is generally thought in accusing Shakespeare of being too good-natured.'

'Did he?'

'To be a satirist, at all events. The venom of Pope is what is needed. The sense of delight – the expansion and the compassion of Shakespeare is no good at all for that. He is a *bad* comic.'

'I don't remember – did Hazlitt say that? I have never read Hazlitt.' (He was a mere financial wizard!)

Zagreus gave a broad quick grin to Ratner-off-his-guard, who smiled back wanly, not in time.

'You've missed a treat!' said Horace.

Julius nodded his head.

'I daresay,' he said. It would not be the only treat – with a glitter of the eyeball he conveyed the picture of a 'treat' he would not miss for something. But nature's gentleman had not finished.

'To be a true satirist Ratner you must remain upon the surface of existence.'

'I see – upon the surface.'

'You must never go underneath it.'

'I don't see I'm afraid what you mean – but you will explain Horace – go on, I'm sorry.'

'No. Well, to regard people as "good," or as "bad," you will concede, one must remain very much upon the surface to do that.'

'Must you Horace?'

'In other words morality is superficial.'

'Is it Horace?'

'Morality is of the surface. But also the values that decide whether a person is ridiculous or free from absurdity are pure conventions of a society, they exist only in a surface-world, of two dimensions.'

'Well.'

'You agree?'

'Please go on.'

'Underneath, if one pricks far enough, in the eyes of a Shakespeare we are *all* ridiculous – we all play those tricks that make the angels weep.'

'Some more than others Horace,' Ratner humbly corrected the rationalizing megaphone at his side bringing order into chaos with broadsides of reason.

'That *more* and that *less* – such fractions are invisible to eyes that are sufficiently unsealed.'

'I suppose so, to eyes that are – as you say.'

'Such a man is no satirist. God could not be a satirist.'

Ratner grinned at God in the glass – the God of Horace.

'So satirists have to be half-blind, there is no other way.'

'Perhaps you are right Horace!' Very *sub specie æternitatis.*

'To the satirist a thing must present itself as more simple, it must possess a stupid finality, it must be more rigidly contained by its genera, than in fact anything is.'

'There is not much left for the poor satirist Horace is there!'

'What about the Public. The Public!'

'Ah the Public!'

'Yes the Public – that is most important of all – the Public.'

'I had forgotten the Public Horace.'

'Yes. But the audience of the satirist is composed of strictly two-dimensional beings – such creatures can respond alone to a quite simple, a superficial, image. It has to be a something cut out of their prejudices and conventions.'

'Yes.'

'Shakespeare employed simple laughter too much, when he was not handling tears, to be a satirist.'

'You think so?'

'Yes. I think so.'

'I suppose he did if Pierpoint says so.'

'Yes. Or his laughter had not the metallic bark that kills.'

'Perhaps.'

'There is no perhaps.'

'No of course not!'

'No.'

'You are meaning Falstaff?'

'Falstaff was the Swan of Avon's soft spot.'

Ratner off-duty sneered slowly at elizabethan knighthood.

'Satire to be good must be unfair and single-minded. To be backed by intense anger is good – though absolutely not necessary.'

'Absolutely not necessary.'

'No not necessary – better without it.'

'Oh.'

'But you Ratner, if you had the talent, would make a good satirist.'

'You think so?'

'I am persuaded that you would.'

'I am not so sure about that Horace!'

'Oh yes – if you had the talent.'

'I know. If.'

'Yes. And if your anger were more sustained!'

Horace lay back and fanned himself, and smiled at Margolin, who had been silent and now looked a little damped by so much satire, and Ratner knew that the 'broadcast' was at an end. He darted a deadly look of solipsistic understanding at himself in the mirror – with hooked frowning eye-in-profile, sank down in relaxation, yawned with a bristling peep of fangs and sighed.

'What did you think of it?' Horace asked suddenly, in almost a timid voice.

'What Horace?'

Horace saw that his duettist was cross.

'The scene Julius – what we have just done together Julius.'

'I thought it was good! Was it all Pierpoint this time Horace?'

'Every word!'

'Very striking!'

'Except the gag where you come in.'

'Oh, that was yours?'

'Most of it.' Horace leant over to speak in his ear. 'What do you think I paid him for it?'

Ratner grinned the bad grin of a black sheep – sheepish but full of turpitude – a financial sheep.

'Do you really pay him – for things like that?'

'No do be sensible! Pay him! Of course I pay Pierpoint for *everything* I get! The labourer's worthy of his hire.'

'Yes.'

'No but tell me Julius. What would you suppose I paid him for that. *Roughly!*' Zagreus coaxed him, to persuade him to put his sense of values in motion quickly and tell him *roughly* what he thought would be a fair price.

'I confess I can't guess.'

'Not guess!'

'No.' Bored, smiling with difficulty. 'I give it up Horace!'

Horace paused a moment, uncertain and crestfallen.

'Well.' He cleared his throat. 'A tenner!' he breathed in Julius' ear.

'A cool tenner!' said Margolin who had leant over to listen.

'A tenner! Not bad was it?'

'What for – about Hazlitt?'

'From the *epigram* – that was the start – down to where you came in – *if you had talent* – you remember?'

'Oh that was his was it?'

'Yes he said that would annoy you.'

'He is quite wrong!'

Mr Zagreus stood up and laughed.

'You could not convince me of that.'

'I don't wish to.'

'I don't believe you.'

'All right Horace! – What has happened to Dan?'

Slipping into the part of agitator, at the service of all oppressed classes – women, miners, children, Jews, horses, servants, negroes, frogs, footballs, carpets during Spring-cleaning, Zoo-reptiles, canaries and so forth – seeing all that might be got-the-better-of and got-even-with thereby – all the husbands his feminism could give horns to – fathers to rob of their disaffected children, riders to be thrown off their rebellious horses, civilized habits to be suppressed – where no man would be willing to serve another – libraries to be bonfired on the ground that the care of books competed with the care of babies, carpets caused to flap round and hit housewives in the eye, footballs to refuse to enter goalposts unless people stopped *kicking* them, Zoo-reptiles to be caused to bite their keepers, wild nature to be encouraged to flourish at the expense of contriving intelligent Man – Ratner frowned, as he asked where that poor young man Absolom might have got to, and grinned at the same time to make it worse – the grin struggling in vain with the frown, the frown stronger – righteousness more than a match for mere friendship and fondness for Horace.

Horace Zagreus laughed and took Margolin by the arm.

'Yes where is Dan! How do I know Julius!'

'I think we ought to find out.'

'Why Julius?'

'Oh I don't know!'

'Don't you Julius?'

'I think he's a very sensitive young man – he might hang himself from a tree!'

Horace Zagreus frowned upon the Split-man.

'Your sympathy for others does you great credit – why should Dan hang himself from a tree?'

Ratner swallowed and put his ears back to show that against the grain he had given up the battle for the Oppressed.

'Depression leads to suicide' Ratner muttered. 'The awkward age.'

'*Yours* is a far awkwarder age Julius – when as now you are no longer young and scarcely know what to call yourself!' Horace laughed, beaming pleasantly at the Split-man - in everything *divided*. 'It is *you* Ratner who may be found hanging from a tree!'

Ratner smiled in the face of this sentimentalist with bitter craft with the consciousness of the impossibility of any age being 'awkward' for such as him – entrenched in such opposite impulses to those that produced these touchy romantic children.

'I must wash my hands' said Horace.

VI Dan at the Assembly.

A lovely tall young lady it was, of a most drooping and dreamy presence – most modest of *Merveilleuses* that ever stepped upon a palpitating planet screwed into position by a cruel polarity of sex – in consequence compelled to advertise a neck of ivory, nipples of coral, a jewelled ankle of heart-breaking beauty-line – extremities, for the rest, superbly plantigrade – a miracle of blunt-heeled – metatarsally-dominant – proportion – under the arch of whose trotter a fairy coach made out of a cobnut could be readily driven. What has not been the lot of girls since the first sombre circles of Bluestockings assembled, or the rampant feminist denied The Sex the bland receptive idiocy of does – *that* was embodied once more in Dan – as if to say 'You must come to poor defeated Man if you desire to find what was once the Eternal Feminine – alas only in Man is now to be found the true-blue Ladyhood or Girlishness – by Man invented, by Man never betrayed!' That is what those sad and melting eyes, with a shrinking modesty, proclaimed. With a timid and enquiring step, with a circumspect eye, Dan wandered forth into the decorated garden; by the protective height of a box-hedge guarded from behind, upon a retired garden seat he sat down – he sighed. Life was a lottery! Oh Horace Horace – why hast thou willed me a woman! Oh!

A few perfunctory Alcoves, furnished with supper-tables of six covers, had been constructed beneath the grove of trees that led up as an avenue to the french windows of the great saloon. Two parties sat there at supper – upon a railway-platform hand-trolley for food, tons of cold prog was pushed over to this party from the kitchen, by hard-breathing attendants. The splashing of water issuing from the hidden mouth of a mammoth gramophone filled the air.

Suddenly the welkin rang with the shooting off of chambers, with alarms and points of war. In all directions a rash of fresh illuminations switched-on suffused the gardens with an inflamed rufous glow, while green and blue tassels of fire sparkled sharply.

From behind the box-hedge came a smother of self-satisfied voices, and then Lord Phoebus quickly made his appearance, leading a group of ladies and gentlemen, to whom he loftily exclaimed –

'Yes but come and see the Bonassus – yes the Bonn-nass-suss! It's a most wonderful animal! There are only six in existence. Yes – it is a Bonassus. It is a sort of Ape!'

'Is it alive?' asked a guest, while, limping heavily with his bandaged leg, where he had been wounded by the saw, Lord Phoebus hurried them forward at breakneck speed, to see the Bonassus.

'Too much alive at times' Lord Phoebus grimly drawled, through set-teeth – for although he made light of the terrible wound in his knee-pan, it was not to be supposed that a less determined person would have been able, with such an alarming handicap, to conduct a party of people to look at the Bonassus. 'Very much alive indeed I'm afraid – you have to be very careful! But if you're with me there is really not much danger! No. Not very much danger! I can manage the Bonassus better than anybody. So I am told!'

'I do think Phoebus is terribly brave don't you – I shouldn't like to have to look after a *Bonassus!*'

'I think it's too marvellous the way Phoebus is using his leg as though nothing were the matter at all! Ten minutes ago he couldn't stand up!'

'I know! I think Phoebus is terribly brave!'

'Have you had the Bonassus long – is it yours Phoebus or is it Osmund's?'

'No not long. Cockeye sent him to me as a birthday present!'

'A birthday present!' The guest's voice conveyed that he scarcely believed that there could be a birthday in the family of Finnian Shaw!

'Yes a birthday present!'

'How marvellous! I think Cockeye is sweet!'

'Is this Bonassus a birthday present to you from Cockeye Phoebus!'

'Yes from Cockeye. I must show you Cockeye's letter. *I didn't know what to give you for your birthday so I thought I would send you this ridiculous Bonassus!*'

'Oh how good that is – I adore Cockeye!'

'What a terribly good story!'

'I think that's too marvellous! I do want to see Cockeye's letter Phoebus!'

'I think Cockeye is too marvellous don't you!'

'Terribly funny!'

'I think that's too marvellous!'

Feeling that the situation he had chosen was getting decidedly popular or threatened to and was too much exposed to the passage of tumultuous persons of either sex or of both sexes at once – who might eventually seeing him there accost him, taking advantage of his isolation – Dan rose from the bench. Also if there was to be Fireworks – and he remarked in the distance certain preparations that distinctly pointed to that – he did not want to be there out-of-doors at all as he was afraid of rockets – which as is well known go up but also come back again to earth when least expected with their charred sticks, and he had heard somebody say *Fireworks* behind the hedge. Beyond the miniature bandstand, where the Mazes were, he had heard a prolonged squeal which he took to be human – he had shivered and as he did not at all relish the idea of the Bonassus, he thought he would step into the house. He had remarked many *Apes* already this evening but not an ape of the kind hinted at by Lord Phoebus (whom he considered particularly intrepid) an ape which, if that gentleman was to be believed, entertained a fond partiality for *him* – but would one, Dan reflected, be justified in the expectation that – should it meet a strange young lady in the dark of the garden – it would regard her with a similar favour? Nothing but the blind pride of one of nature's vestrymen could cause one to believe it! No, thought Dan, the Bonassus would scarcely change its spots to accommodate him, but in spite of the lanterns would immediately proceed to devour him, should he find him alone upon a garden seat, without a protector. At that moment a further discharge of muzzle-loaders beyond the house did not tend to reassure his feverishly beating heart – he hastened his steps. – Everything considered, the crowds inside were safer than the solitudes without.

But from the first moment of that starblasted afternoon when he had agreed to undergo the disciplines imposed upon the Ape-hunter by Horace, until this tremulous interval – left quite to his own devices by his friend and master – he had never felt so low. Even a new thought came into his mind to add to his confusion: altering his opinions without the slightest reservation – without remorse as without provocation – Horace might grow to forget the very existence of his *genius*, upon the discovery of which their pact had been based. Insignificant as he was – by comparison with his paragon – he yet felt wounded as it were in *his genius* – at all the neglect he was called upon to suffer. Humbly he arraigned his great preceptor, backing his charges with proofs, most ably led – pragmatical and overbusy as he knew these complaints would appear if he were suddenly confronted with their irresistible object. But he did not think Horace could be entirely absolved from the charge of unkindness, for allowing him to wander dressed as a girl, alone at night, in this unholy and old-fangled garden, where if he had not been a prudent young man he might have fallen into the mazes that Mrs Bosun had told him to beware of – from which had issued that peculiar only half-human cry – suggestive of the violent enterprises of some wretch who perhaps had his lair in those ill-begotten Mazes.

Before doing anything else Dan just thought he would go to the lavatory and make use of the vaseline upon his right foot which was the worse of the two and which really he could not bear much longer, and he entered into a dark back-door and found himself in a low passage where in the obscurity he tripped against a disused period-jackback for the home-brew, and shinned himself with a cry of pain. There was a red light at the end of the passage which was a long one: as he approached the rose-lit door the body of a large woman who evidently knew her own mind burst out of the dark wall just at his side dressed in a lute-string trollopee (with a couple of twin chicks upon her heels, bunters in stuff gowns) howling '*This way!*' and in an incontinent rush they all charged into the red door. What an escape – it was a *Ladies* and Dan rapidly stepped through the door still quivering with the late explosive passage of the three women, and Dan understood as if in a flash that he was a girl to all intents and purposes, but that as a consequence all regular places of retirement were barred to him, both dexter and sinister, both cock and hen, and he sadly limped down what seemed a service-passage, wondering what next was in store for him, when he approached a lighted opening and noticed it was a *Gentlemen*. As he passed it he could not help out of the corner of his eye with a little envy looking in, when, in that single glance (for immediately he hastened his steps and reversed his head and the picture had gone by for ever) he perceived Horace in the midst of a number of persons in fancy-dress attending to their make-up or joking and some were washing their hands in a row of basins. Horace sat upon a table, wiping his hands upon a towel and there in front of him stood Margolin, showing off as usual, planted in the centre of the picture. Though they evinced some surprise, as who would not, at his coarse antics, the guests seemed to desire not to notice this discouraging buffoon. Holding up the furcula of his first two fingers to express **2** (as if he had expected Horace to seize his merry-thought and wish) Arch gasped with unbecoming mirth – with that wheezing sound of slightly punctured gutta-percha squeezed, or that a mouse makes with its throat like compressed indiarubber, and Dan felt quite sick at the mad message of mirth of this obscene wind-pipe. It had been for the fraction of a moment – as a line is the flux of a point, so from the imperceptible pause that his astonishment at coming upon them so unexpectedly had caused him to make Dan glided forward – disgraced in his feminine dress as he felt – barred bodily from all places set aside for his legitimate sex – he saw those enervated masculine prerogatives dissipated in a breath! He was no longer a man! In a sense was he not an outcast of sex! He was an outcast!

But now he had turned into another passage and could collect himself, although to his left sounded that hungry roar in close proximity, where lay the great saloon. Abruptly, in the neighbourhood of his head, a Jack-o-the-clock called *Kook-Koo* and looking up he observed the Welsh Ambassador withdrawing, after having delivered itself of this untimely remark. It was half-past ten. An animal of whom no one was fond – it got through life on account of this solitary remark, nesting in timepieces – Dan was rather afraid of these birds but it was clever to use them for that!

Entering the crowded saloon, Dan noticed at the farther end the small gallery, that held the musicians. At present they were enjoying an interval: they were six negroes – they smoked cigarettes and regarded with cold pity the mob beneath them, danced to their music, masses of white fools!

Dan found a seat with lowered eyes, and, once seated, gave himself up to a relentless melancholy. The hurried glimpse of Horace, in the company of Margolin, had been particularly distressing – a blow in the back in fact: thus to see, without himself being seen, these two – for now he must think of them *together*, not of one without the other – was worse than being met without speaking.

Committing himself to a first venturesome glance or two at the surrounding panorama, Dan distinguished a great number of variously costumed individuals – ranging from the Cyclops, apparently, or Cain and Abel it seemed, down to Peter Pan or perhaps Prufrock. All seemed profoundly conscious of the rectitude of their own appearance, most had the air of being highly satisfied to be found where God in his infinite wisdom had placed them – to assemble and roar for a while at Lord Osmund's Lenten Party.

After the solitude of the garden this place was almost restful – after the Bonassus, after the Mazes, after the rockets. So Dan sat a long time it seemed, and rested. The orchestra crashed with the fulsome stutter of a maudlin giant. A sluggish rhythm stirred up the dense mass – this was driven about, in an eccentric vortex. Then with a crash the band stopped, to start its huge stammering again after a storm of clapping, and so forth, and Dan found himself in the midst of another interval, wondering if he might attempt the discovery of some secluded spot once more, in order to apply the vaseline, when he remembered the Bonassus. But at that moment when he had just remembered the Bonassus, there was a great outcry: involuntarily he raised his head – he saw a strangely painted half-naked man rush past him with sub-human roar. The apparition had enormous red asses' ears. Upon the heels of this fugitive appeared Lord Phoebus, very flushed, resentfully aloof from everything about him. The whole cross manner of Lord Phoebus plainly showed that he had been compelled to enter a place that nothing but an emergency of some sort would have induced him to come to: without allowing his eyes to recognize their shapes as individual men, much less as guests of his brother or himself, he dashed into the throng assembled in the interests of Gossip, taller than most there with his three inches over six-foot, in pursuit of his red-eared quarry.

'Stop that animal!' he was vociferating loftily as he ran. 'He has escaped! Be careful how you catch him. It is the Bonassus – you must be careful to seize him by the right ear! What? Yes – it is a *Bonassus!*'

'Is it a Bonassus?'

'Yes it is a Bonassus!'

Lord Phoebus rudely pushing to right and left his guests, disappeared in the crowd. All the assembly followed the incidents of the chase. In a moment the Bonassus, still hunted by Lord Phoebus, disappeared at a distant exit. The band gave a gargantuan belch, followed by drum-salvoes until further orders. Then it whined out in its nose a little sugar-stick complaint – about a very little, much misjudged, unimportant person.

'Phoebus looked rather pale I thought – he does not like parties,' said a guest and anyone would have known at once the guest was an intimate friend and probably dined in Chelsea every night when they were in town with the brothers Finnian Shaw.

'So I've heard' said another more modest party-goer.

'I think he looks wonderfully decorative' said a lady-guest, providing the sex-note demanded by the Gossip-situation – the homage of the eye, at the passage of a god, from a humble non-friend – anonymous mover in the best Gossip-circles, but very much *opposite-sex* – deliciously that.

Dan considered the Bonassus. Was it a man dressed up? He felt slightly less afraid of the dark spots in the garden now. – But a new terror was substituted for the Bonassus – multitude, like solitude, held its particular bogey-man, the Crowd now gave him a taste of its quality. And a most mettlesome crowd it turned out to be, possessing a mettlesome champion.

In one of his periodic light-house-like outward sweeps *en dessous* (of his veiled and melting – bronze-velvet violet-shadowed – eyes) Dan began to remark a suspiciously loitering stately figure, who was observing him in a pointed manner, with an expression that sought to suggest – so it seemed – that they two had some secret between them – that it was *my word* a terribly *amusing* one – for the horrid man, on the second occasion, bit his finger – although he was plainly an elderly man – as people do when they are *shy*. The conclusion was unavoidable – the man was suggesting that *he* Dan was shy and abashed – he mistook him for a girl of course and Dan blushed deeply and turned away his head – to show the man he wanted to have nothing to do with him.

But in a moment this obnoxious person, with the most immovable smiling assurance, had come up quite close to him. That he must conclude him a fool was obvious – Dan forgetting that he was a girl started moping. But to Dan's dismay then this monster made a leg, quizzing him very roguishly with a dancing eye. To say that Dan shunned the occasion of speaking with this foppish stranger of advancing years would ill convey the shrinking manner he had of expressing his desire to be left in peace. But to put off a designing fop with undisguised signs of mild aversion is of all attempts the most chimerical and the least likely to succeed. The gentleman's costume denoted research after elegance that was impertinent in one so past the zenith of his manly charm, with legs so shrunken and with such bloated saucers for his eyes to squat in withal, and such a web of blood-vessels risen up like a lye into his cheeks: whereas his breeding, if breeding it might be called that breeding was none, bore all the stamp of a pastiche artifice. – To what attribute this booming see-saw delivery too – which sought to confer a significance upon the most trivial remark? – to nothing but a Nineties-culture, from that it must date, where this fatuous relic must have been a buck in the shadow of Oscar – oh an Ape-of-god of Ninety-one. – I think I have done with assemblies, thought Dan to himself and attempted to forget the presence of this importunate individual – But soon the voice followed the smiling presence. And it was of such a brazen tone that it deafened Dan a little and he was compelled to introduce his forefinger at last furtively into his ear because it was singing.

'I humbly beg pardon!' boomed this great clap-trap beau, with a mince, 'for breaking in upon – what I conjecture – must have been, seeing its subject – the most delicious of reveries!'

and this mannequin from the salon of Madame de Lespinasse, compounded of every egregious gallic trick, to outwit the animal world, took a pinch of tabac d'Espagne, of the powder of the spanish Indies, tiptoeing at Dan's side. 'But if I may be so far allowed' – again he paused, to take snuff, and to enable the last booming of *allowed* to die away upon the air – 'the honour and happiness Madam – if I may presume – if I am not so unhappy as to have been the cause – of a dislocation of some precious train of thought!' and he actually inflicted upon his forefinger a vicious bite, as if *very* bashful and contrite, 'if the honour and happiness – however undeserved – might yet Madam fall to my lot!'

At this point Dan's admirer had the assurance to sink, with a sweeping movement to remove the ponderous flaps of his laced coat and laced waistcoat from the diminishing space between his posteriors and the seat of the chair by the side of Dan: then with a gliding movement, like the sortie of a nest of snakes, his lanky fingers came out of his gigantic sleeve-cuffs and en bloc they firmly seized the hand of Dan.

Snatching his hand away Dan made to rise but the gentleman rose too and Dan sat down once more, while the gentleman stood over him, with an invariable graceful flowering of the lip-tips of the perfection of insolence, stolen from the portraits of some understudy of Talleyrand, of Etienne de Mortemart, or of Philippe de Vendôme.

The wig of clubbed hair of this outrageous coxcomb was attached behind his head *en bâton* with a fathom of ribbon, of a silk of madder-plum, whereas its foretop mounted towards the lavishly decorated ceiling of the resplendent saloon where a hundred bestial cupids that were a pink litter of pseudo-Picassos (pneumatic – with the wind with which they were inflated whistling out of their rosebud-mouths – ill assorted with the stolid carving of Grinling Gibbons upon the walls and fireplaces) swam in a tormented musical ride, high above the stalactitic lustres – while to Lord Osmund's bathing-closet elsewhere (absconding from the crowded conditions that prevailed upon the ceiling) a solitary plump cupid had winged its way and (blowing like a porpoise from its rosebud mouth-piece) was privy to his lordship's testy morning despair – over the mounting tide of his flaccidity, the alarming growth of his natural adipose bustle (that only a *cache-bâtard* would be adequate to disguise) as he saw himself, in all the naked pomp of his all-too-solid flesh, reflected within a venetian mirror (of course in two pieces) bordered with bold rosettes of lapis-lazuli crystals.

'But allow me Madam so far to presume!' fell the brazen drone of the old period-piece of a painted man-harlot upon the eardrum of Dan 'the irresistible charm – if I may venture to impute to myself – some *feeble* proportion of *unconvincing* discernment – of *the grace!*' he threw a thunder of wonder into this long-drawn syllable, 'with which Madam you with such infinite sweetness discover – your *partial* displeasure' – the snuff-box snapped, as the hideous pretence of exalted coxcombry swept his body towards the ground, and he waved his hand with an awful fatuity – 'is more pon honour than mere mortal Madam – is able entirely to withstand!'

Again he made a leg – was it? – and was contemplating another when it appeared he changed his mind, and disposed himself to resume his position (having stood long enough, in the interests of decorum) at the side of Dan. Once again the long and dandified fingers abandoned their ambush within the striped sleeve-cuffs and took possession of the fingers of the bashful Dan – and when anew the large hand fled, pursued it into what would have been – had Dan been the girl he seemed – his lap.

But this was far more than Dan was able to tolerate and it had gone too far already by a good many lengths, so recovering from his disconsolate droop – his cheeks the sunset hue of shame, his eyes expressing nothing it is true that might be termed pugnacious and yet with a sort of command in their mute appeal – Dan said distinctly –

'Sir you are mistaken – I am not – '

But before he could say 'a girl', this ancient period-strumpet of a bedizened man (upon a pattern drawn from a time of swords and silk, when men were in their floweriest scent – savagely tattooed with braid – intoxicated with their own snuff – forever on tiptoe – disgusted with the mannish – wooing Woman after the fashion of women) burst in and silenced him, quenching his words with a deluge of vocables – ill-chosen, rapid and meaningless – an imperious gesture to exact silence coming first, tongue-tying Dan – from which indeed Dan shrank as from a blow.

'Madam! – even if forever I should forfeit your esteem – Heaven avert the omen! – indeed I must vehemently demur!' He paused with shining eyes, as his vehemence had used up all the breath in his old bag-pipe. 'I must implore you Madam not to disavow – a condition in consequence of which' and he rolled his eyes about upon Dan's spurious femininities until Dan had a violent spasm of alarm ' – I am your slave – borne captive in your beauty's chains. – No, disavow yourself you shall not! – stand by and see you turn your back – however lovely – upon this fair self-that-is-not-yourself – I will not hear of it! – as you *appear* so must you *be!*'

This language of an inflamed heart put Dan into such strong confusion that for a moment he lost the sense of where he was and even for a moment seemed to smile. Seeing this, his tormentor brassily challenged at once.

'If I am so unhappy as to offend – do not seek to spare me Madam – strike home at once! – your beauty is such – that I can but commend my heart to your care – for to me it is lost for ever!'

Thunderstruck at all these abrupt and masterful declarations Dan was unable any further to move hand or foot. Present to his surroundings once more, he understood that here was a situation such as, in his most apprehensive moments, he had far from foreseen. Put an end to this fearful misunderstanding he must! Oh surely this horrid man did not guess the truth! – there was something in that too-liquid eye that troubled him more than should even the fierce glances of a Don Juan. Dan made an effort over himself of which he had scarcely believed himself capable.

'Sir' he said in an unsteady whispering voice 'you are totally mistaken. I am not a – '

'Oh Madam!' cried this egregious period-being with his deafening machine-voice just as Dan was about to say *a girl*, the words simply struck dead upon his agitated lips – 'Oh madam refrain – refrain from informing me of what you are *not* – overlook my presumption – if I presume too much – Madam it is, I protest – more than should be required of me – even by *you* – to hear in patience – from those lovely lips – accounts of what you are *not*. – Oh Madam there is no NOT.'

He waved his hand to dispel from the atmosphere any *not* that might be lingering there.

Distressed beyond the point of maidenly endurance, blushing freely and profusely all over the cut-away neck – oh for a roman chin-cloth or a heavy wimple to cover neck shoulder, chin, but especially *ears* – which blushed brightly away by themselves and made him feel one big blaze of shame from tip to toe! – (oh why had he been thrust into this world as a sort of *Merveilleuse* – though with pack thread he had succeeded in sewing up the nasty slashes in the skirt).

'Loveliest creature – do not suffer me to *distress* you – if I have declared myself – with too unseemly a suddenness – your servant for evermore – you can only impute it to your loveliness – not to some fault of mine!'

Dan could not recollect a time when he had been so stupefied with fear. – Oh faithless Horace (his downcast eyes seemed to exclaim) to desert him in this heartless manner – dressed in this travesty of himself – as if he had not drawn the blood that blushed for him, so continually, from a princely phylum, of several houses of irish kings – if they had houses – and in spite of the associations of his patronymic with King Henry the Eighth!

'If I might flatter myself to believe' the voice of his persecutor again crashed out in his ear, in brazen period-drawl – 'that I might attribute' and with an intolerable leisurely imitation of The Graces (and *always* The Graces!) he again took snuff, 'not alone to your pardonable distress – at the contact of such an unworthy object – but to some happy confusion of innocence – those marks of concern – to some miscegenation – of a slight pinch of fear with a tincture of pleasure! – if that is not too bold a conjecture! – Madam it shall henceforth – be the whole study of my thoughts – so to *deserve* – '

The metallic drone continued, the brazen drawl buzzed upon the surface of his ear, but meanwhile to his extreme consternation this ungovernable mock-personage at his side (in the midst of his stately snuff-taking halts) had introduced a hand behind his body. There this hand now familiarly rested upon the odious *dress-improver* – which was that part of this vile costume at the back lying upon the rear of the pelvic feminine opulence of the wearer for whom the dress had been destined (not a man like himself) designed to supply the true feminine line – based upon large nutritive systems and a horrid hip-lavishness – and render its possessor duly steatopygous, a match for the Hottentot.

'Oh sir' exclaimed Dan faintly 'you are in error – I am not –'

'NOT!' howled the monster beside him at this, prancing upon his chair at Dan's *not*, in a tantrum of tawdry protestation – 'Never Madam let me hear – as long as I live!' he wailed archly – 'that objectionable *Not* again – which you inflict upon me out of cruelty – because of the pain you rightly conjecture that it causes! – You are *not* Madam like any other woman in the world – Yes! – *not* one Madam that is ever likely to be overlooked – in however vast an assembly – *not* one that ever could be forgotten – by one who has been privileged to behold you – *not* Madam indeed of this earth at all I believe! – Those alone are the NOTS – which your unworthy servant – under correction dear princess! – as the abject custodian – of your far more than mortal beauty – is able, yes even from yourself – Madam – to allow!'

And even as he spoke, in this strangely exalted and overbearing fashion, he moved up and down the dress-improver, with his bold didactic hand – until Dan came to feel, with bodily nausea, that his *a tergo* extension was quite of a feminine order – in inordinate provocation, in the feminine way – to a disconcerting distance! Also he was beyond measure terrified lest this incalculable personality at present laying siege to him, under a misapprehension, might cause his 'improver' to leave its moorings altogether, when he would be eternally disgraced – for he could not avoid entering into the part and it was uncommonly uncomfortable – being in a woman's skin he could not help but feel that should he loose his 'improver' – the disgustingly occulted source of his pelvic portentousness – he would be disgraced for ever.

Overwrought at length to a pitch where he could no longer seek relief in a mere blush – cornered, as he felt it, and upon the point of some decisive humiliation, Dan carried his hand to his too open breast and drew out the tiny cambric handkerchief which with devilish forethought had been placed there by the evil Bosun with the remainder of the impossible wardrobe. Armed with this lilliputian tear-sponge, he quite broke down. Applying the handkerchief to the upper part of his face, where the eyes were already crying, he commenced to sob with hushed little sounds like a muted sneeze, with mild spasms of the breast which moved up and down along the customary feminine lines, while with his free hand he turned his attention to the place where the absurd 'improver' was still an object of abstracted interest to the offensive gentleman who was making things so difficult for him, and panted simply, in a last lisp of hurried pleading –

'Don't!'

'Oh Madam!' positively roared the ignoble personage beside him at this, 'Oh Madam – what is this that I have lived to see! – Most beauteous of womankind – is it possible that my eyes deceive me – or is the sparkle of those lovely eyes all turned to water! – Can such a piece of perfection – be acquainted with the name of Sorrow – oh Goddess is this a graceful subterfuge – so that the poor mortal may feel less dazzled in your presence – believing that he sees – in your affected forlornness a simple mortal – in place of a Goddess – !'

So spiritless and dejected as no longer greatly to care what sort of figure he might cut, Dan steadily wept into the small scented handkerchief (which smelt of distant roses, in gardens that were swept with fardingales, centuries off across the misty time-tracts). His heart was weighted with a heaviness against which no effort of his could prevail and which could only be expressed – if at all – by the one ponderous word never far distant from his loyal lips – namely HORACE. He was the sport of chance! But when he felt the sleeve-cuffed period-arms of this abominable old beau encircling his waist, he experienced a last spasm of the sense of self-preservation. He withdrew himself with a tearful energy from this insidious conjunction.

'If I have the unhappiness *to offend!*' exclaimed his self-appointed protector 'Oh then Madam – I *beseech* you – !'

But all of a sudden those grating sounds occurred which announce the running-down, in other instances, of machines-for-talking. Something appeared to check that brazen declamation in mid-career. Dan felt the officious fingers relax, the pressure of the arms grew less oppressive. Through his tear-dimmed eyes Dan was just able to perceive a new figure, evidently present to his aggressor, in some ominous way – who had thrust himself suddenly into the picture. He heard himself asked in a voice of the coldest command, in accents that immediately dispelled the treacherous mists of period-illusion. The new accents were the accents of everyday – even a thought cockney – there was an *ow* and *aw*, faint but reassuring, in the new sounds.

'Are you Daniel Boleyn?'

Dan nodded violently – *yes he was Dan!* – he nodded frantically that he was that identical Dan – to this protector of his youth – with a transport of gratitude! But as he did so a new fear assailed him – what if the possessor of this business-like voice were perhaps a detective, and were about to accuse him of misbehaviour and even arrest him for being disguised as a woman? It was not allowed. To this the action of Horace had exposed him!

'This is a man sir!' Dan heard the newcomer saying and at that the discomfited fop sprang up in affected consternation.

'A man! But sir you must be deceived – this beauteous creature can be no man – for I have never seen a son of man so fair!'

'This is a man!'

'Oh sir – no man that ever breathed – possessed such lips and such a neck as these!'

And then Dan heard the newcomer, a little bit to his surprise, say –

'That's enough! Don't waste my time but beat it!'

Quite shrill the fop retorted with great period-scorn –

'A nice expression I must say to use before a lady – *beat* it!'

But the newcomer became rougher at once, stung at the suggestion, it seemed, that he was wanting in period-breeding.

'Get to hell out of this!'

'Better still!' shrilled back the beau.

'He is in my charge. Cut the cackle Arthur – I'm pressed for time!'

'In your charge!'

'Yes in my charge! And it would not be the first time Harry

Caldicott' (the roll of the Adelphi melodrama came through to Dan of the *it would not be the first time – Harry Caldicott!*) 'that you had attempted a public seduction!'

Dan could not *see* the narrowing of the eyes to feline film-star-slits, nor clenching of cow-boy fists, but the modern cinema was upon a sudden all about him: the dropping of the voice at the unmasking of the villain, when the name was uttered and 'Harry Caldicott' stood revealed, came straight out of the Dime-days and the popular photoplay – but at the same time Dan understood that he had run a very great risk in this ill-starred assembly: for this fearful protagonist of period-romance, an old and cunning hand – swimming with such diabolical assurance in the currents of this ridotto, was none other than a notorious expert in *public seduction* and Dan had had as providential an escape as any man dressed as a woman had ever had in public – snatched in the nick of time from the encirclement of these deceitful advances, in a public function, under the very noses of a thousand guests.

As Dan's deliverer led him away there was some small stir. They were followed by a hush and a universal whisper. His magnificent deliverer – whom he could not see, and dared not have looked at if he could – conducted him into the garden. There, upon the same bench upon which he had sat before – just after the forcible transformation of his sex – he found himself again – this time not unaccompanied. – Dan wiped his eyes and blew his nose.

VII Blackshirt

Now Dan was able, after a short period had elapsed, to examine his benefactor. A few furtive glances showed him that he was in the company of a young, dark-faced, black-shirted person, very trim and solemn, and he felt himself immediately prepossessed in his favour, apart from the fact that his gratitude would have made of the most lamentable duck a dazzling swan, under the circumstances. His young réscuer was just sitting there and watching a bright supper-party of sparkling persons, which now occupied the Alcove nearest to the house. A strange young man! – he took no notice of Dan and was as silent as recently he had been strong. A very nice young man indeed!

Gradually Dan felt that this person must experience an utter contempt for him and regard him as nothing but a cry-baby. Perhaps that might be the reason for his prolonged indifference to his person upon the seat beside him. Or perhaps the young man did not like girls – perhaps although he knew that Dan was not a girl he felt awkward, as if a girl had been seated there at the side of him. Perhaps! But he did not look like the sort of young man who would take much notice of a girl or feel *shy* at anything. This was not at all a shy young man – he was just an indifferent young man – who was occupied with his private thoughts as a young man should be.

He did not like however to attract the young man's attention, he would not risk that. They just sat side by side for upwards of five minutes. The night-air had by this time dissipated the worst effects of his ghastly experiences with the treacherous elderly period-beau, in the great saloon. That had been touch and go! Dan longed for the gift of words (enjoyed in such a superlative degree by all his relatives, with whom speech was abundant and continuous – all their thoughts clothing themselves in words so that they spoke them aloud all the time, with great volubility – gift withheld mysteriously from him). He wished to express something to this ironfisted altruist – dressed, he timidly and tentatively reflected, as Signor Mussolini, the italian potentate in the political Dime Novel of Modern Rome – that boy-scout Cæsar – oh how he wished he could seize this young man's hand and cry *Thank you* for he was very thankful: but no words came and so he sat very depressed in consequence – this young man might never know how terribly thankful he could be!

But, to his intense surprise, he heard himself saying – in a broken voice it was perfectly true – while he discovered his head unexpectedly turned towards his new protector –

'You must think me a terrible cry-baby!'

Where the courage had come from to utter this remark Dan never knew. It must have been his *Genius* speaking! – he was at a loss to see how otherwise these unexpected words could have found their way to his lips – there was no other means of accounting for it at all.

'I have come here to-night as *The Fascist* and I have two companions. They are also fascists!' the strange young man said at once. He looked away again, then he turned back. He said –

'I have a ticket admitting *A Coachful.*'

The young man drew out of his pocket an invitation card with a design upon it, cubed and coloured of a harlequin.

'Six persons! A Coachful.'

The young man looked at him in the way that men look at each other who fight rivers in solitary spots, all day long, and when they rest have plenty of time. The bench was *a log*. Water splashed behind the chestnuts. There must be *log-cabins*.

'We are only three,' the young man said slowly 'I could not find more than two to come with me.'

Dan felt somehow sorry at once for this lonely young man – who had only been able to find two to come with him, in spite of the fact that he had a ticket for six.

'We are all dressed as fascists.'

Fatchested blackshirts were no novelty to Dan and all these were blackshirts – like boy-scouts but black – *black-scouts* as that might be. Dublin had been full of blackshirts for an anniversary. So Dan knew very well what that was and this entirely accounted for this particularly strange young man, who was just *a blackshirt*.

This Fascist had a black moustache. It was the first one Dan had seen with a black moustache, he wondered if the others had moustaches on their lips – that must be heavy to have moustaches. He found he wanted off and on to put out his hand and pull it. He smothered a giggle, the Fascist turned towards him, with the same immovable solemnity.

'I know all about you Dan' with a familiarity that was of a quality that was quite startling, the Fascist said, eyeing him.

Dan hoped very much that this young man, to whom he felt quite drawn, only knew about him the things that were in his favour and not everything.

'I have been looking for you the whole evening' the young man said.

Dan's heart beat a little at this. He wished he had not smiled aloud a moment back.

'I did not expect to find you dressed as a woman' said the young man. 'That is no doubt why I did not spot you before.'

He had not yet told him how he came to know his name.

'Why are you dressed as a woman?' Fascist asked with truculence.

Oh to explain why he was dressed as a woman would have taxed Dan's resources of expression out of all measure and Dan knew it. To cut a long story short Dan said nothing.

'It doesn't matter' the Fascist said – nothing seemed to matter very much to this young man and Dan felt for a moment that he really might take a little more interest! But there – it was clear that he could not! It was clear that the Blackshirt could take no interest.

'I know all about you' said the Fascist. 'I know you never speak.'

Someone had told this young man that he never spoke – *there* was a strange thing to say – *he* who sometimes would chatter like a magpie!

'Zagreus calls you "his idiot".'

It was not the first time Dan had heard that. It was not obliging of Horace because a little familiarity between friends and a pet-name or two is one thing, but for strangers to begin calling you by them is another thing. It was a breach of confidence.

'You don't mind? You evidently don't. It is as I thought.'

The Blackshirt seemed very cool with him and angry about something. – He did not know whether to be pleased or not at what Horace had said, as sometimes people were locked up if that was said about them, obviously, however innocent they might be, and it was not exactly friendly. Horace had spoken of him as *his* idiot – but to be *Horace's idiot* was all he asked – for the development of his genius and to be near Horace – so no one could mind what Horace had said.

'For the remainder of the evening you are to regard yourself as under my charge' Blackshirt announced, and he was glad of that.

Then Blackshirt said.

'But you will carry on with Horace Zagreus – for the Vanish I mean.'

Confusing! How was he to 'carry on' with Horace exactly? Difficult! What did the young man mean by *carry on with Horace?* But all in good time everything would be explained no doubt by this exceptionally nice young man.

'We are displeased with Horace.'

This was unexpected. Who were 'they' who presumed to be displeased with Horace – he would like to know that!

'We object to Horace Zagreus' cruelty to young men – egged on by Ratner. You know Ratner? Yes. He wastes our time too.'

This puzzling 'we' always, this quite confused him in the end, he was bound to admit that he did not much relish the young *men* – how many was it he would like to enquire – although Horace was the cruellest man he knew it was true. Who was in a better position to judge that than himself? That it was *his cruelty* that made him love Horace he could never admit to himself but he felt at the bottom of his heart that if Horace were not so terribly unkind he would not revere him quite as he did, so he did not understand what these persons *we* stood for meant by objecting to Horace's cruelty.

'He wastes our time' the Fascist repeated with a sepulchral dull monotony of dogged statement – it seemed he thought that Dan might consider that Horace didn't.

Horace wasted their time! Well Horace wasted *his* time but he only wished that Horace would waste more of it yet, but not waste so much of *Archie Margolin's* – there was no occasion to waste so much of Archie's.

'Zagreus is a youth-snob – we have been very patient but he is as great a youth-snob today as when we first took him in hand.'

Blackshirt seemed really cross with Horace.

'We can do nothing with him.'

Nor could Dan, so he was not particularly astonished at *that*.

'It is impossible for Horace to resist youths – that is because he is so old – it is a great waste of time.'

Here Dan was entirely with them.

'Youth seems to Zagreus something *extraordinary*. Which is because he is so old. – We have been unable to cure him of that.'

This was strange language. Dan too had noticed certainly that Horace was far too partial to *youths* – one youth in particular he had in mind. This had caused him some anxiety, therefore he could perfectly understand what these people meant by what they said and he very much hoped they might soon succeed in curing Horace of things in which he certainly ought not to be encouraged.

'He wastes our time!' as a deep monotonous refrain came out of the mouth of his amiable deliverer – to waste their time was obviously inadmissible and that is what Horace did it seemed.

'You have heard Horace Zagreus drivel about genius?' asked Blackshirt brutally, with common cockney *drivel* – what words! – and Dan received a most painful impression. He felt he did not wish to listen any more. Yet he found he heard the young man's next remarks with an unusual distinctness.

'Horace Zagreus thinks every dull young man of nineteen possesses what he calls "genius" – we have often asked Zagreus what he means by "genius". All he can do is to laugh. He doesn't know himself. Genius is nothing.'

This was becoming a painful conversation – all Dan could feel was that from the bottom of his heart he was glad that Horace had held out in the way that he did. He too had found that it was not *everybody* who understood what "genius" was – it was a difficult thing for people who had not got it to understand what genius was, and Dan had never met anyone except himself who had got it. (It was wonderful the way Horace understood it.)

'We have told Zagreus on many occasions that one more "genius" and we would drop him.'

There was something *mysterious* about 'genius' Daniel casually reflected – it was not the sort of thing one wanted to talk about with Tom Dick or Harry. He yawned.

'I found him a moment ago' said Blackshirt in a tone massive with indignation 'preparing a report. He intends it of course for us. It is about a *new one* – a little Jew this time!'

'A Jew!' in spite of himself exclaimed Dan – for this nice friendly young man had expressed what had been long in his mind – not it was *not* suitable, with persons who had the record the Jews had in the Holy Land and who lived in such terribly squalid surroundings to this day – for it was known that they were the lowest of the low and very dirty – to be on such terms as Horace was with several at once, of Jews.

The nice young man had looked at him in some surprise when he had spoken, for the last thing he expected him to do was to speak – or if he did to take an interest in such a subject. He said, in a more respectful tone, Dan thought, taking more trouble to explain.

'It is not that. Pierpoint holds Jews up as exemplars, in the matter of *directness* you understand: a Jew is never *sentimental.* Pierpoint once directed me to get more of the Jew into what I was doing – meaning more *head* and less stupid *heart.* I did so and I was successful. Now I never do anything without getting a little of the Jew into it. – It is not that.'

Pierpoint!

When would he ever be able thought Dan to escape from that terrible person. So *We* was Pierpoint all the time he supposed. He looked shyly at the large shoes of the Fascist, wondering what next he would say.

'That is not it,' the Blackshirt repeated. 'But we cannot have a Jew as a "genius" – that would cost money and we cannot have that. Horace Zagreus has much less money than he formerly had. That we can never make him understand.'

Well that seemed straightforward thought Dan – *he* had never received any money from Horace except the five and sixpence a week pocket-money, plus expenses, and he dared say that a person who would be capable of what those people had in the past would be quite likely to borrow money from Horace and this young man was quite right it would not be a good thing for Horace to do, though he was sorry to hear that he found it necessary to get a little of these antichrists into his whatever-it-was (was it work?). He would certainly tell Father Donovan what he had heard and perhaps Father Donovan would tell him on no account to become intimate – he would be surprised if he did.

'Horace must make up his mind one way or the other!' This strange young man now appeared to be threatening him though why he could not guess.

'*We will have no more "geniuses"* – to that we have made up our minds! No more "geniuses" – you are the last!'

Well Dan did not know what to say to that – but secretly he hoped that what the kind young man – with the rough manner – said, might prove true. No more geniuses. He hoped not.

'Horace Zagreus often misinterprets what we tell him – as often as not he gets it all wrong!' Dan was being virtually bullied by Blackshirt now – still this rather rough young man meant well, of that he was positive.

'In the matter of these outlays for "geniuses" we have put our foot down – Horace Zagreus has had our last word on that subject! He cannot *afford* it. And what you cannot afford you should not have!'

The moustache of the Blackshirt waggled in a swashbuckling way and Dan became a little anxious on account of Horace – in case this young man should meet Horace for he seemed very incensed indeed and Dan was not sure for all his great coolness if this young man really had as great control over himself as he should. – However, he became more cordial suddenly.

'You now' Blackshirt said pleasantly 'cost him nothing to speak of. Apart from his boring us with you, we have accepted that as a necessary evil. *But we will not allow him to have another!*'

The Fascist was quite fierce again, and again Dan trembled for Horace. Dan thought he understood why the Blackshirt had moustaches – it was because, he thought, it gave him an air of authority, in spite of his youth – Dan thought there was no question but that he was tremendously clever and he had quite taken to him – he felt more at home with him than he did with most men but perhaps that was because he was so terribly grateful for what he had done.

'And then how about this show! What do you suppose that is costing him? You can't go about with a troupe like this for nothing!'

The nice young man felt quite violent, it was apparent. His mind was full of sums. Horace had overrun the constable.

'The Vanish alone' Blackshirt exclaimed 'must have cost him a cool fifty!'

What might a cool fifty be – Dan was in the dark and the young man was so angry he knew he would end by getting frightened of him and already his head was aching at being required to do sums – all of a sudden this young man had shown a very mercenary side and Horace was a spendthrift if he was to be believed.

'Where is it coming from?'

Now what was the use of the Fascist asking *him* where it was coming from! He knew as little as the Fascist. He felt extremely sleepy and wished he were at home and could take these disgusting clothes off his body which was getting girlified – he did not like to move his legs about as a matter of fact.

The Fascist unbuttoned the braided pocket upon the breast of his shirt and produced a long folded heavy document.

'Here is your dossier!' the impossible young man remarked, holding it up.

At this Dan showed no sign of animation, he had not heard distinctly what the other had said.

'Would you like to look at it?'

Would it please this nice young man if he said he would like most awfully to see what he had got? He had been so terribly kind to him that the least he could do now was to hold out his hand and show he would like most awfully to see what he had got!

'This is how he explains you.'

The Fascist pointed to something, of which he seemed very proud, upon one of the pages which were typed and numbered, twelve sheets single-spaced.

'This is all about *you*' Blackshirt said.

All about *me* thought Dan! He blushed as he took the tell-tale document – if it turned out to be.

'He leaves us all this nonsense to read.'

In his mind Dan dissented – *there was no nonsense about Horace!*

'I am Pierpoint's political-secretary.'

That was why thought Dan he had such an awfully good head for figures!

'I have to deal with these communications.'

The young moustachioed Fascist Brave stepped smartly over to a fairy lamp which he took off a twig and returned. He held the light up to the document.

'There.' He pointed. 'That is where it starts.'

Dan read and this was what he read, and when he had read it he was no wiser than when he started, but much sadder – as invariably he was after having to bend his mind to the perusal of anything above a few lines in length.

About a hundred years ago lived Mr Diarmuidh K. a strong gentleman-farmer of this family. His place was not far from

Slieve Bui (Yellow Hill). He was much addicted to the study of astrology, and the occult works of Cornelius Agrippa. When his only son was about a month old, one of his servant boys ran into the parlour one day to tell him a cirumstance that had greatly astonished himself: 'Oh, master,' said he, 'the black cow was just while ago under the old thorn-tree in the meadow, and all of a sudden a fog came round herself and the tree, while all the rest of the field was in sunshine. I was going over to try what was the matter, when what should I see but a big sea-gull flying into the fog, and making ever so much noise with his wings. For fear he'd pick out the poor beast's eyes I ran over, but just as I got to the edge of the fog it all cleared as if there was some magic in it, and Blacky was walking away on the other side.' 'Oh, ho!' said the master; 'what I have long been wishing for has happened at last. Now, Pat, attend to what I say. Watch that cow close: and when she calves, be sure to bring me some of the first beestings, and I'll give you more money than you have ever seen at once in your possession.'

The boy did his duty, such as it was. He brought the first beestings to his master, and received 10*l.* for his pains; and Mr K. ordering the child to be brought to him, made it take a spoonful or two of this first milk of the black cow. When the child began to speak intelligibly, the master of the house called all the family together one day, and charged them as they valued his favour, or dreaded his resentment, never to ask his son a question till he was fourteen years of age. 'The questions, I mean,' said he, 'are such as he could not answer without being a prophet. He is gifted with a spirit of prophecy, and when he reaches his fifteenth birthday, you will be at liberty to get all the information you please from him, concerning anything that is passing anywhere in any part of the world at the moment, or to ask about things lost or stolen, or your own future destiny. But attend to what I say. If you ask a question of him before he is full fourteen years age, something terrible shall happen to him and you; take timely warning.'

The boy had a wonderful capacity for science and language, but seldom spoke to those about him. He was very amiable, however, and everyone anxious for some favour from his father always got him to be their spokesman. Strange to say, he reached to within a few days of the fatal time without being asked an improper question by any one.

He would occasionally when in company start and begin to talk of what was passing at that moment in the town of Wexford, or the cities of Dublin or London, as if the people about him were aware of these matters as well as himself. Finding, however, by and expressions of surprise, that they had not the same faculty, he began to grow very silent and reserved.

About this time a grand-daughter of the famous Blacky was about to calve; and Mr K., who set a great value on the breed, recommended her particularly to the care of a young servant boy, a favourite of his. While he was looking after her and some others in a pasture near the house, a young girl to whom he was under promise of marriage was passing *by chance* along the path that bordered the fence. He asked her to stop, but 'she was in a hurry to the big house.' Stop she did, however, and full twenty minutes passed unmarked while they stood and conversed on very interesting nullities.

At the end of twenty minutes he gave a sudden start, and examined the different groups of cattle with his eyes, but no Blacky was to be seen. He searched, and his betrothed assisted, but in vain; and the poor girl burst out crying for the blame he would be sure to get through her folly. She went forward at last on her message to the big house, and passing by the kitchen garden, whom should she see, looking at the operations of the bees, but the young master. Let her not be blamed too much: she forgot everything but her lover's mishap; and so after making her curtsey, she cried out across the hedge – 'Ah! Master Anthony, alanna, do you know where the black cow has hid herself?' 'Black cow!' said he, 'she is lying dead in the byre.' At the moment his eyes opened wide as if about to start from his head, an expression of terror took possession of his features, he gave one wild cry, fell powerless on his face, and when his wretched father came running to the spot, on hearing of the circumstances, he found an idiot in the place of his fine, intelligent son.

'*An idiot* – you see? – *in place of his fine intelligent son!*' the Fascist remarked. 'That according to Zagreus, is *you*. He says you are possessed of powers of prophecy, like the bright son of Mr Diarmed K. but that they have been blasted – that is what he says to us – *by people asking you questions* – in your cradle, he says. He says – they should never have been allowed to pester you with questions. But he believes you may get back your power of prophecy.'

Dan's head swam with all this at once for *what* questions had he ever been asked by people at the period mentioned except to wish to know for sure whether he had a pain in his tummy – and he smiled as he reflected that they could not have received much of an answer – from *a baby!* Powers of prophecy were one thing, *genius* was quite another – for genius was the thing he had. Genius consisted simply in what it was, and then on the other hand in what was Horace's belief in his genius. What was prophecy? Old men with white beards had *prophecy* and artists had *genius* when they painted pictures, and Horace had recognized that he should have a studio with paints, pictures and a suitable easel like Mélanie had. Never himself would he so much have suspected the presence of his genius for he had never had a tube of paint. For seeing the genius in him he loved Horace. But this whole story of black cows and of sea-gulls was a strange and fantastic matter – some blarney no doubt a fairy story, it had nothing to do with *genius*. He did not say this but he thought it, and left it at that: so he put the paper in his young girl's lap and looked at a waiter who was taking a bottle of period-champagne (Time – Present. 1926 vintage) over to the supper tables, from which came a lot of loud vulgar sounds, denoting the presence of *A Coachful* (he would not like to say of what) unrestrainedly satisfied at finding themselves al fresco beneath the osmundian greenery, about to poison themselves with the osmundian champagne.

The Fascist was a nice and sensible young man – he did not seem at all surprised at his making nothing of the paper, and took it for granted he should make no observation.

'So you see' the nice young man said 'Horace Zagreus has discovered this in one of the books of demonology he is always reading. They do him no good at all *we* are of opinion, I may tell you. He will go on reading them. So he jumps to the conclusion at once that you are fey. You must have powers of prophecy! Of course you have been blasted by some shock in childhood – and so you have become an idiot!'

Dan smiled, for although the Fascist never smiled, he said quite amusing things sometimes.

'To *us* it is perfectly clear that you have never in all your life been anything *except* an idiot, and that you will remain that till the end of the chapter.'

The Fascist displayed some warmth in this matter, and

anxious not to offend him, Dan looked the other way, for he was still smiling a little.

'All this taking you about to show you *The Apes!* Well of course they *are* Apes. What however in Jesus' name are you but an Ape and Horace Zagreus himself he is the worst Ape of the lot! Does he not take all his ideas from Pierpoint? Is he not essentially a rich dilettante? Is it not owing to his *money* – not that he always *pays!* It is absurd!'

Dan kept his head turned away for although he was feeling a little alarmed now and had lost his secret smile, he thought that if he allowed himself to look at the paper lying in his lap the other would think he wished to dispute his point of view.

But the Fascist lay back against the bristles of the box hedge and he lighted a cigarette from the fairy-lamp. After that he began negligently instructing Dan, as though to contradict what he had just said about *Apes*, and about instruction.

'You have remarked the arrangements of the garden?'

Blackshirt paused – not for a reply evidently, but to give Dan time to focus his sub-average intellect upon the accessories of the scene lying before them. He gave him a minute and a half.

'This is of course Vauxhall' he said.

Mélanie had often warned him against Vauxhall in the past and Dan remembered that it was a vast and most dangerous bridge, from which many people had fallen into the water.

'In the days of Pepys and so on. A famous Public Garden – an Amusement Park – this is it here. The Finnian Shaws would suggest.'

Dan looked round with obedient attention at the Amusement Park.

'Within is the Rotunda – over there are the walks. Boswell, Goldsmith and Walpole are part of the scenery, so you must believe. Yonder are the famous mazes.'

Dan shuddered slightly, as a timid mariner might at the mention of a dangerous whirlpool.

'There are the Alcoves – and there is the sound (only the sound) of the Tin Cascade.'

Dan heard the splash of the Tin Cascade.

The Fascist warmed to his task, he sat up. No follower of Pierpoint was proof against this *docte* enthusiasm. Blackshirt began expounding. It reminded Dan of a 'broadcast'. Only this figure seemed *always* to be 'broadcasting' more or less, that was the difference – that was because he was the secretary Dan supposed.

'These Finnian Shaws' said Blackshirt – and Dan thought he detected a certain vulgarity in the accents of his voice but could not be sure, 'they are the *showmen* of their Past. They are the showmen of the Past in general as well. But first they are the showmen of their Past.'

The Past! Dan was given a minute and a half for this difficult abstract notion.

'Vauxhall belongs to the Past-in-general' said the Fascist. 'Only the Finnian Shaws, you understand, being mere showmen now, they do not go to Vauxhall – Vauxhall has to come to them. You understand? Here it is.'

So this is Vauxhall! Dan's eyes in-duty-bound expressed.

'In some cases' Blackshirt expounded, as a cat sharpens its claws on anything 'dispossessed chatelaines, in the Soviet Republic, have been allowed to stop on – but as the curators, or as the showmen, of their castles, and picture-galleries. If that were here (after a Crack) the Finnian Shaws would perhaps be kept on – what do you think of the idea? – as the managers and showmen of their ancestral castles. Then they would be allotted, suppose, a small fund for dress, for cigars, servants, cellars and so forth. A living museum – do you get that? Different from Russia. See? Commissars from London would spend their holidays with the Finnian Shaws in Galway or wherever it is. They would be received by the Finnian Shaws as royal guests – the commissars would spit in their faces when they wanted to of course – but no Finnian Shaw would mind that – and give them a week down below in a dungeon perhaps – for bilking the administration in the matter of the wine-supply – falsifying the accounts as regards tailoring expenses – not keeping themselves smart enough – spending too much on doctors'-bills, or what-not. Still they would be *chez eux*. Home sweet home!'

The Blackshirt almost smiled – Dan turned his head in case he did. But when he went on he seemed to have increased a little in severity.

'It is about like that now,' he said. 'Really not so very

different. Not so different as you'd think. What is the difference? None really except that they do not possess an administrative stipend to run their Finnian Shaw museum on, but have to get along as best they can with what they have got! In consequence the wine is undrinkable, the food bad, the decorations rough and flimsy, and of course their guests are not high and mighty commissars, but the smart herds of Mayfair and of Chelsea, of "interesting people", a sprinkling of Bloomsbury, a few Gossip-column lords like themselves, a mass of actresses who cannot act, painters who spend nine hours out of the twelve in hurrying from house to house to collect subscriptions for their statues and pictures, or to get a charity-portrait on the strength of their *Salon-fähigkeit*. All this is still supported (upon an ever diminishing margin) upon the plundering of a tenantry, upon money taken from miners, or from engineers, or chemists, or if you like soldiers.'

The Fascist was in full 'broadcast', and the opinions of Pierpoint rang round the glades and walks of the last twentieth-century reflections of Vauxhall, when an assistant-chef, come up to get some air, asked the Blackshirt for a match to light his cigarette. He gave it him with marks of a deep-rooted contempt.

'Why have I this ticket for *A Coachful!*' he asked Dan fiercely, flourishing the ticket in his face: 'why have I this? Because (upon the instructions of Pierpoint) I am editing an anthology of *Post-war verse*, and all three Finnian Shaws suppose that an extra poem each of theirs will go in if I come here! They are entirely mistaken!'

Dan shrank more and more from this blackshirted embodiment of pierpointean invective – he felt glad on the whole that there were *not* a Coachful of them but only three – although he contrived to be passionately grateful to this nice young man for his timely assistance.

'The doors fly wide open!' the resounding voice of the Pierpointean told the trees, and the insolent young chef puffing at his elbow, and the distant masqueraders. There was, as well as a great vaticinatory verve, a certain boastfulness about this Fascist. 'Follow me – you will find you can go anywhere! Shall we go upstairs?'

He rose, scowling at the smoking chef.

'Shall we go upstairs – I will show you some fun – better than Zagreus could!'

Dan rose – he felt the Fascist would make good his boast. But oh he wished he might have stopped where he was until the time came for the 'vanish'.

As they went towards the house, the Fascist advancing with a negligent strut and a cold assurance that betokened his boundless contempt for all he would find within, he remarked:

'When I was up in their private reception-rooms just now – they will not go down among their guests, they barricade themselves in upstairs as though all these people had got in against their will – I saw the start of their private sports. The Old Vics were arriving. You don't know what that means. Colonel-baiting was in full swing and they were expecting an ex-Admiral-of-the-Fleet and two Zulu-War veterans with all their medals. The first Colonel was a bit slow. But Harriet was gingering him up.'

They entered the passage that led to the garden.

'We can spend a short time up there. Then I will show you the Library.'

At the mention of the Library Dan was very depressed. Would he have to read all the books? He made up his mind to say that he had read them all so need not read them all again.

As they passed beneath the clock the Welsh Ambassador popped out and cooed Kook-Koo for the Quarter. They turned to the left, followed another passage, and entered the main-hall. There they ascended a sumptuous staircase to the upper apartments. Above the squat gilded stairs (hastily enriched with bogus gold-leaf upon the period-balustrade) brooded a pantheon of Verrio. It had been executed with a jazz-agility by an american negro-designer, who was very cheap because he was black. A dull and thick-limbed peasant-goddess – or goddess of the dull potato-patch of Demos – by Maillol – squatted half-way up – then a barbarous ice-cream-tinted panel by an East-End confiserie-cubist was a few steps from the dull daughter of Demos. But *pack-thread for Bosun!* – a part of the canvas-wall (to make the roundness for the period-stairpit) had already come unstitched. An apocryphal portrait-bust of Tiffin – Bug-Destroyer To The King – was the first object met with upon the landing, in mouldering gilt, with one cracked glass eye.

His face exposing the same invariable solemnity of mind, Blackshirt made his way to a door at the end of a passage, out of which two servants hurried with fleas in their ears it was but too plain.

'This' said Blackshirt with condescension to Dan 'is where the Finnian Shaws pretend to take refuge for the greater part of the evening from the concourse of their guests.'

As the Fascist opened the door, there was a rush and an outcry.

'Shut the door!'

'Keep them out!'

'Don't let any more of them in! We shall have no room to breathe in a minute!'

Lord Osmund's voice could be heard above the rest dominating all with a stentorian whinny of irritated complaint.

'Phoebus you really must keep them *out!* We *can't* have any more coming in here! They will *all* be up here in a minute – if you don't drive them away. You must really Phoebus drive them away!'

'If you don't keep them away Phoebus' a deep lisping voice of a woman shrewishly rang out 'we shall be sitting in each other's *laps!*'

A picture of a world swarming with the coarse hordes of Demos was at once evoked, with side by side, in dazzling contrast, another picture – that of an intensely exclusive, aristocratic family – shrinking from publicity – whose roman noses had never so much as sniffed the words of a disgusting Gossip-column (from the miasmas of bog-infected Press-puffs they had been sheltered by hereditary pride!). It was a noble and historical piece the second. But the spacious assembly-room, rapidly built for great entertainments – with stage for performances of Lady Harriet's operette – was full of a mysterious multitude. These hordes had come down from London in cars and in buses. *Upon whose invitation?!* Who was the traitor! *Who* could the traitor be who had betrayed the Finnian Shaws? – and let in all this disgusting army of nonentities – disguised as *famous characters in classical fiction* if you please!

Lord Phoebus placed his hand upon the chest of the Fascist, and in a loud voice of baying complaint he exclaimed, while he pushed, without looking at the object,

'No really you *can't* come in – you must go away! We have more people here as it is than the room will hold. We have far more people than the room will hold.'

'Lock the door!' a voice shouted. 'Lock the door! Keep them out!'

'We really can't have any more people in here, it is quite impossible – we can't breathe as it is!' Lord Phoebus looked at the Fascist, for he was surprised that by pushing he had not advanced in his intention of pushing the interloper out.

'This is private!' Lord Phoebus bayed in aggrieved protest at that. 'This is private! I thought everyone knew this was private! You can't come in!'

The Fascist, at a slight forward inclination from the vertical, leant against the flat hand in a stiff drunken posture – toppling allowed himself to be supported by his lordship.

'You really can't come in here! It is not for the guests. These are private apartments.'

'Turn him out!' a roar came from the rear.

'Yes turn him out!' came another. 'Turn them out!'

'I say Phoebus do hurry up and close the door will you – I'm getting neuralgia!'

The Fascist produced the card for *A Coachful*. He thrust it under the nose of Lord Phoebus, with a frigid brutality, who looked askance at it. But *A Coachful* was *A Coachful* – Lord Phoebus was impressed and put down his arm – *Coachful* was the sign that meant 'Gossip' – the Press, publicity, Fame – *all* that could no longer be obtained by merely being a peer of the realm – *all* that was the breath of life – it was no use.

'We are terribly overcrowded' complained the flushed and harassed face of lordly law-and-order.

'I am Bertram Starr-Smith.'

'What is that?'

'Starr-Smith.'

'Turn him out!' Osmund bellowed from inside.

'No it's all right Osmund' called back Phoebus.

'*I* should turn him out!' Osmund said.

'It's all right Osmund – it's Starr-Smith!' Phoebus called back.

'Starr what?'

'Smith.'

The voice of Lady Harriet sounded now.

'If it is Mr Starr-Smith do not keep him out Phoebus. Not Mr Starr-Smith!'

If her brothers wanted *their* poems left out of the anthology, she did not want *her* poems left out of the anthology!

'Osmund does not like any guests who are not specially invited to come up here' said Phoebus.

The Blackshirt did not move. He remained in the doorway where he had been stopped by Phoebus, very collected and expressionless he was, he did not come forward.

'I am specially invited!' said the Blackshirt sombrely.

'I know' said Lord Phœbus 'but people really have to be kept out – once one began letting them in they would *all* come in, you know what they are – as it is there are far too many in here.'

'Far too many' Fascist agreed.

'Far' said Phoebus. 'It really is much too crowded but do please come in – Harriet wants to speak to you – please don't go away will you!'

'I'm not going away.'

'Well come in won't you – I want to close the door. Do come in – Harriet is very anxious to see you.'

'I will come in,' said the Fascist, and he moved in the sense required.

'I am terribly glad you will come in! – I know Harriet wants you most awfully to come in.'

Lord Phoebus as he gazed at Starr-Smith remembered the name and connected it with the anthology. He smiled invitingly.

'I am so glad you came up!'

Lord Phoebus stepped aside as he heard a commotion in his rear. As he did so a large figure burst past him, and Dan, without, in drooping neglect, his eyes in a swimming stare, recognized the stout tempest of a person who had broken out of the dark wall at his side, in the lavatory-passage, almost on top of him, in lutestring trollopee. Limbed to her in filial leash were still the same two bunters in stuff-gowns and Prussian bonnets, but she had outstripped them in the impetus of her exit. As she just passed through the door, her train still sweeping for a foot at least the interior of the room, a haggard figure appeared as though from nowhere, almost out of the air. In a flying leap this angular female form descended upon the departing train. So great was the indignant speed of the matron, in fuming-flight (from a place where she had been *de trop*) that she was unable to draw up. Her powerful limbs tore themselves clean out of the train. The train and all the dress from the waist, stayed – torn from her, upon the floor, in her wake. The flying harpy, in her embroidered gold, with a sinister tiara, stood in the middle of this ruin. – Lord Phoebus started forward and the tiaraed lady who had caused the accident then leapt back, with a loud exclamation of alarm. The trampled and torn skirt lay between them.

'Oh look what I've done!'

The tiaraed-one lightly wrung her hands.

'I do think you are dreadfully careless Harriet' Lord Phoebus scolded his sister, with wild glances of affected panic. 'You might look where you're going!'

'I do believe I've pulled Lady Truncheon's train right off!'

'I think you have!' Lord Phoebus cried.

'How terribly careless of me – I do hope Lady Truncheon will excuse me, it was particularly clumsy of me.'

'*I* shouldn't if *I* were Lady Truncheon!'

'I could hit myself!' the offender bayed at herself.

'I'm sure she could!' crashed back Lord Phoebus.

'If I had only known you were there Lady Truncheon!'

'Couldn't you see that Lady Truncheon was there Harriet!'

'I know!'

'You must I think have been *blind* not to see that Lady Truncheon was there!'

'I believe I must Phoebus!'

'I'm quite positive you must Harriet!'

'I know, mustn't I?'

'Whatever is Lady Truncheon going to do now,' howled Lord Phoebus. 'She must go at once to Mrs Bosun's closet!'

'Yes there's not a moment to be lost!' exclaimed Lady Harriet. Lady Harriet was eyeing Lady Truncheon with a thunderstruck face which was a reflection of that of Lord Phoebus, which was also thunderstruck. They both stared at the wife of Sir Thoman Truncheon, Knight – her skirt having vanished from the waist line and a great gap occurring behind, Lady Truncheon stood speechless with indescribable passion. The mighty legs stood in startling negligé, like a couple of stalwart old silk-decked stallions, which had drawn her at top speed with fine team-work so far – then come to the abruptest halt. A streamer of silk hung down in front, a comic apron. Dignity was impossible. The world of without, irreverent eyes, were made privy to hind-quarters lately ennobled. A *fesses* of silk – born of coarse disruption – almost stared you in the face. Lady Truncheon's eyes spoke volumes to Lady Harriet, and her dyed mouth manufactured an epithet of the gutter, of which the high-wind of her breath prevented utterance. *Apoplexy!* said the eyes of Lord Phoebus and of Lady Harriet – opening wider and wider; but the two twittering bunters flew with a cry to the hen-bird and covered its legs with their bodies.

'Take this lady immediately to Mrs Bosun's closet!' bayed Lord Phoebus at a half-grinning evening-help, 'immediately do you hear!'

'Can't you hear!' bayed Lady Harriet.

'There is not a moment to be lost!' Lord Phoebus exclaimed.

'No my lord!'

'Yes there is not a moment to be lost!' Lady Harriet boomed as well, planted beside her cadet. 'Don't stand there gaping at Lady Truncheon you sheepshead!'

'Yes don't gape at Lady Truncheon!'

'Didn't you hear what was said! Take her ladyship at once to Mrs Bosun's closet – *there is not a moment to be lost!*'

'The man is certainly half-witted – can't you *see* that there is not a moment to be lost; I should have thought you could see.'

'I do hope Lady Truncheon I haven't spoilt your fancy dress!' Lady Harriet Finnian Shaw howled, her face narrowed to a waspish witch-mask, as she glared at Lady Truncheon across the wreck of the fancy dress. 'I can't imagine how it happened!'

'Nor can I!' her cadet joined in in well-disciplined bay.

'It is that carpet Phoebus, I stumbled just on the edge.'

'Yes I saw you stumble Harriet – I saw you just on the edge.'

'Are you sure I can't do anything – this is particularly awkward for you I am afraid Lady Truncheon!' Lady Harriet whined with a long nasal note of serio-comic consternation. 'Are you absolutely certain I can't do anything whatever for you Lady Truncheon!'

'No thank you ever so much Lady Harriet' piped the elder of the bunters.

'Nothing!' stuttered Lady Truncheon hoarsely, and turned her front – now become her back as it were.

'Oh I am so sorry that it is impossible for me to do anything, but I suppose you know best!'

'AREN'T YOU GOING TO TAKE LADY TRUNCHEON AWAY!' Lord Phoebus howled at the waiter, stamping his foot, a sort of thunderstruck smile playing, with the effect of disguised lightning upon his face, twisted up at one side as if blown in upon the other. Round one ear he seemed to be laughing, round the other all was dumbfounded gravity.

'Yes I think it's too bad – I wish he would take Lady Truncheon away!'

'I wish he would too!'

'I wish he would take her to Mrs Bosun's closet! – It is high time she was attended to!' Lady Harriet said, turning away with a display of regal impertinence, from the lack of understanding of the waiter.

'It's high time Lady Truncheon was attended to – *can't you hear!* Are you deaf!' Lord Phoebus remonstrated with the waiter. 'She must be catching cold – it's terribly draughty here!' he added to Lady Harriet with a sniff, in brotherly confidence.

'I know there is a positive wind blowing here!' and Lady Harriet sniffled a little and shivered slightly, saying 'UUUUgh!'

'And at any moment somebody may come!'

'I know that's quite on the cards! That's why I said there was not a moment to be lost!'

The Truncheon family, in the company of the waiter – subjecting his smile openly to the obligations of hired service – departed. Indignant murmurs marked their translation.

The Fascist, in a solemn aside as they, Dan and himself, all barriers down before the anthology, passed into the room, said to Dan:

'One of the daughters ought to have hit her on the head – with Lady Truncheon.'

During this painful scene Dan, with peonic blush and not

knowing which way to look, had stood only a foot or two distant from the distressed Truncheon – unable to assist but unable to glide away.

VIII Finnian Shaw Family Group

The room was a large Queen Anne and cubist apartment, with more of the same hybrid cupids as beneath in the saloon – a pine basis throughout with an economic minimum of oak in the inexpensive fakes (but where oak visible, upon *the outside*, where it *could be seen* to be gossiped over) with a veneering that would have secured the withdrawal of any sensitive cabinet-maker from the scene on the spot. Festoons of heavy fruit-and-flower material surrounded the mantelpiece while in the centre Finnian Shaw arms were displayed. The doors possessed broken pediments terminating in volutes, and there was the cherubic head, circumscribed by its bed of wings.

Upon the walls the pictures revealed the strange embrace of Past and Present – of so casual a nature as to produce nothing but an effect of bastardry. There was a picture of two buffoons by Giovanni Cassana, a late Venetian: two Magnascos of a mock trial in a cavern of witches and gipsies – a Chirico of a carthorse surprised by ruins, springing into the air – a Tiepolo sketch of the abdomen of a horse and a platter – a Max Ernst of two disintegrated figures in frenzied conjugation – a Modigliani of two peasant morons, both girls, one depressed upon her left flank with a ponderous teat. There was an equestrian sketch of Lord Osmund by Munnings (an apotheosis of the Georges One-to-Three of super-hanoverian squirearchishness). An enlarged photograph of Cockeye – old rackrenter, Gloucestershire landlord and provençal chatelain, as a Victorian Volunteer. A Niccolo Cassana of a Finnian Shaw, a Harlequin, and 3 Rowlandsons were in one recess, with books and African masks.

The room was a regular polygon, with an arched recess in every-other side. It was the section of a sort of rotunda: reached by an abrupt stairway was the tower of Phoebus, for he lived in a small stucco tower of his own to show he was a poet – his private apartments in this eyrie were reached by the sheer stairway coming down in a spiral into the very large circular room. A great many people there were not – Dan who had feared he was about to enter a rough thick crowd with many men, found himself thrown up into conspicuous relief and blushed in its free spaces, upon the smart polished floor, and once he slipped. Colonel Buckram, who was in disgrace through not having come-off, stood out terribly too, on account of his large scarlet face, staring eyes of tender blue, and huge white grampus lip-growth – the caricaturist's *Colonel.* That misbegotten stock old-military-man could not hide – his face was now at its best, for he was too upset at not having come-off, poor discredited butt, and only wished they'd try him again, and yet dreaded they might.

There was a chorus, perhaps two dozen, they were carefully picked sub-men, but there were no women – there was a great monotony about this bodyguard – but they were a portion of the company in the barn for dinner. Amongst others Jacoby Cheatham and David Parr were understudies of Robinia (who had gone to bed with a headache after having wounded Phoebus – to be cupped and blooded and perhaps lanced by a period physician), there was Basil Spatworthy who was identical with Lord Phoebus in all but height, and Robin Jerningham who was exactly like Robinia and Osmund combined – Eric Mastrodonato was there who was like Lord Phoebus dressed up as Serge Lifar, then Gregory Fawkes and Dickie Pagett sat in a corner who both favoured the personality of Harriet. Jasper Summerbell, Freddie Parsons, Nicholas Compton, Theodore Goddard, Julian Gasbolt, Clement Glenny, Frank Brunner, Stephen Boyce, Martin McGregor, Raymond Carrington, Peter Runacres, Raymond Freedlander, Cecil Dawson and Ronald Shafarek, although all pigmented differently and of various height, age and build (some were wide and some narrow, and the heads of some were small and of others large) yet they all conformed to the osmundian canon but had the air in most cases for preference of an impossibly early undergraduate life – as if just turned out in spick and span, passionless, lisping rows by Eton for Oxford Colleges and Inns.

Lady Harriet Finnian Shaw said –

'Oh Mr Starr-Smith I am so glad you were able to come to-night!' as if it were a great relief that after all Starr-Smith had not been prevented from coming, while she levelled an insulting sullen look at his head – she made no pretence that she could not have wrung his neck here and now for not putting *all* the poems of the Finnian Shaws that they had ever written into his beastly anthology but was glad he had not been prevented and hoped he would stop till he had enough.

The Blackshirt gave her glance for glance – he said –

'I was here just now.'

'Oh were you Mr Starr-Smith!' Lady Harriet asked him fairly musically.

'Yes' said Starr-Smith. He was smoking.

'I didn't see you' said Lady Harriet. 'I can't have been here.'

'You were talking to somebody – a military – .' And Blackshirt directed his deliberate eyes to that part of the room in which he knew the Colonel was not to be found but in the opposite.

Harriet looked straight over where he was – Colonel Buckram saw Harriet look.

'That crashing old bore over there do you mean!' with a great burst of spleen Harriet hurtled forth like a dam and looked relieved at once. The thwarting of hatred for the anthologist was eased in expression of dislike for the Colonel-who-was-a-damp-squib. Harriet with severe pale ginger-lashed eyes stabbed Colonel Buckram in the belly. Colonel Buckram did not double up but held his body politely to attention, but he coloured till he attained to a shade that was a record as an extremity of red. But as she went on stabbing he having attained the non-plus-ultra register even of his redness, Buckram bolted – the door slammed upon his soldierly back with the crash of saluting ordnance.

'Yes that's right *go!*' howled Lady Harriet after him as he went, and the routed picture of gallantry heard her parting shot – 'you disgusting old bore – yes *you* – I *do* mean you – yes *you* – and don't come back!'

The Colonel's Colenso-coloured neck and the bald scarlet moon of his tonsure flamed with fear, as they had never done at Maggersfontein.

Blackshirt took this opportunity of withdrawing with Dan to a suitable recess. They sat down upon a padded window-seat in one of the recesses that this room had as a billiard-table has pockets. It was distant from Harriet but diagonally they had the place where she sat under observation. Blackshirt took up a book snatching impatiently at a shelf. It had *Donne* upon it, he put it in his pocket.

'That is not Klopemania' in an aside he volunteered. Then he volunteered – 'I shall drop that in a pond.'

He considered a moment if he should volunteer again. But he decided to volunteer for want of anything better to do.

'I shall just drop the Donne in a pond.'

Dan heard the Donne drop in the pond all right – it was a waste of good Donne no doubt.

'Tadpoles have as much right to Donne – it might be an Easter-egg for the frogs.'

Dan thought of the froggie-would-a-wooing-goes – still he was unconvinced, and Blackshirt volunteered:

'When they look for their Donne they won't find it!'

Dan saw that.

Dan wished he could slip out, for he was inclined to tremble – several of the young men had looked at him rather hard he was positive, one especially, a rather nice boy, as he was passing. He could not help wondering what they thought of him!

Blackshirt threw down a second book he had picked up.

'A book of old Harriet's!' he told Dan. 'All about arab rocking-horses of true Banbury Cross breed. Still making mud-pies at forty!'

Dan looked at the good sprinkling of learned looking persons interspersed with standardized Etonians and tame imitation-choristers by the main grate across the room – dominated by the massive Osmund. The Volpemini flung off two or three as she changed her position, in violent french. Osmund and the very learned men who were peering into the books had clusters of Etonians of all colours and ages at their feet and hanging upon the back of their chairs and settees. Lord Phoebus stood – he clasped a large Bantu toy, disconcerting in its phallic boastfulness. One of the donnish intelligentsia examined a musical snuff-box. Many objects of *vertu* and barbaric fragments were strewn about with books beside the fireplace, from tally sticks to ritualistic pudenda from the Pacific.

Dan experienced a discomfort amounting to gentle aversion

for *some* of the objects. He could not give a name to his sensations of confused dread but he was positive he would never be able to know awfully clever people because they were so horrid. If asked to converse with the young men who had looked so strangely at him he could only say things they would think dullard-talk – he could not look over where they were, he was not really sorry, without moving a little every time because as a matter of fact somebody stood in the way, which was just as well.

It was the Sib who got her body in front of Dan – it was some protection. She stood shoulder to shoulder, as two spectators, with a depressed looking man, some elder Don.

'Aren't they sweet!' said the Sib to the Don.

The Don sucking the dregs of his bypast existence up in a straw, gazed over glassily at the studiedly-undergraduate groups, with short-sighted old homosexual eyes.

'They always bring out all their toys, when the other children come to see them and show them!' the Sib panted in the Don's ear. But nothing could console the Don for not being a bright young Don of forty – he saw the toys, he nodded his head.

'Phoebus is going to fetch another!' the Sib panted softly and fondly. 'I am awfully fond of Phoebus. He has a little Hottentot tricycle he's just had given him. It is carved out of lead. He is fetching it to show it. He is terribly proud of it!'

'I'll fetch the little tricycle!' Lord Phoebus bayed in flight, unthinkably Fauntleroy, as he passed them (a print of Goody Two-shoes tucked under his arm that he was returning to the wall of his bedroom). A hyacinthine lock danced giglotish upon his tall and pensive temples as he leapt past in fawn-like awkwardness. Like a whirlwind he rushed up his stairs, into his tower.

Three friends who were Eric Mastrodonato, Basil Spatworthy and Nicholas Compton bolted at the same time – all four fled upwards into his superlative rooms, furnished for a single person, having a prospect into fifteen communes and two home-counties, a dozen Downs, with a hundred sheep-walks.

David Parr went up to a musical box that stood upon a console screwed under a cubed flower-piece, in a sort of penetralia, and turned the handle, while a few *badauds* of the household crowded up, to watch the mechanical minuet, danced by small powdered gilded puppets, with such a stiff politeness.

'Phoebus' the Sib said 'will never grow up – I can't think of Phoebus as *thirty* can you? I suppose he must be more than that. It seems impossible.'

Thirty was not the Don's favourite age at all, he showed less and less interest.

'I always see Phoebus as a child, just playing with his toys – only he is not destructive!'

'Isn't he?' asked the old Don with languor.

'Not at all destructive! I have never known Phoebus to pick out the eyes or pull the feathers off one of those masks made by savages over there. – I've often wanted to do it myself! But he is very careful with them – he puts them all away and gets very annoyed if you pick them up carelessly.'

'How extraordinary!'

'Osmund now *is* destructive!'

'He is more so is he?'

'Oh far more so than Phoebus – his nature is not at all the same! I have known Osmund to pick a toy to pieces. Once I surprised Osmund putting one of Phoebus's Japanese dancing mice upon the fire!'

'How terribly cruel!'

'He *is* cruel!'

'But Phoebus is quite different is he?'

'Phoebus is as different as possible. They often have, well not quarrels, little disputes, like schoolboys have you know, with each other, it is nothing – usually about Osmund's cruelty.'

'Indeed.'

'Osmund has there is no denying it a little of the bully in him. Sometimes more perhaps, he is positively brutal sometimes.'

'I should not have guessed that – he looks so kind.'

'Yes Osmund is kind – he is most terribly kind. I know no one who can be kinder than Osmund. But all the same it is so. – Sometimes he can be very cruel.'

'You surprise me.'

'Yes I know. I rather like cruel people I confess don't you!' the Sib panted, masochism mantling the pearly film of her eyes.

'I think all people of character must be cruel' said the old

Don with ferocity, sad sadic embers smouldering up in his owlish glances at her.

'I agree with you!' Sib panted back hectically to him. 'I am afraid I do agree with you – I don't like to believe it – but *I must!*'

'No – one doesn't. One must. It is force majeure.'

'But I am sure it is true. Everything goes to prove it.'

The learned Doctor fiercely sighed – an empty old bloodthirsty homosexual sigh.

'Everything. If life were not cruel – !'

'It would be *kind*?' panted the Sib.

The Sib peered short-sightedly over at the place where her master Osmund sat. The remnants of the optical machine that had looked upon Oscar in all his social glory, when Lion of Mayfair, watered. In the hanoverian Osmund Sib liked to think she saw, so she said, the living double of the blank fat mug of Oscar – and was not that legendary wit reincarnated in the brilliant Osmund? It was or the Sib was very much mistaken!

Dan listened with attention and he shuddered at the remarks of the aged Don whom he particularly feared. *Must* people be cruel – how he fought tooth and nail with that thought! – it was a beastly one to have – he stopped his ears finally when the Sib panted *It would be kind* – they were the most heartless old couple he had ever overheard he was positive or ever wished to!

But Blackshirt was whetting his tongue. He too had been listening very much to some purpose – he had noted the Sib's view with regard to Phoebus and he was bursting with abuse, with the will-to-expound – the pierpointean dervish he began whirling the pierpointean invective round in his head prior to commencing.

'Sib!' Lord Osmund was calling – in a long-distance coax came his nasal *commando* – for he had looked round and missed her. 'Sib!'

'Yes!' Sib panted back as she violently started. She was able only to talk with her lips, Sib had no breath and answered with a pant, as if struck in the stomach with the word of command. It was behindhand – the pant got to her lips too late for its words. Inaudible almost. '*Yes! Osmund!*' she said. 'Yes!'

'Do come and tell us Sib – you know, what Lettice Lady Hornspit said, Sib, when you upset the aspidistra!'

'Yes do tell us that one Sib – I've never heard that one, about Lettice Lady Hornspit!' came over, like the sound of a gun at sea, the counter-tenor boom of Harriet.

The Sib squeaked hoarsely. Harriet's cannon-ball had hit her in the midriff – it knocked, in one big gutta-percha squeeze, all the breadth out of Sib's body, in a thick squeak.

'Lettice Lady Hornspit! Yes I'll come!'

Muttering and panting propitiatory remarks, Sib started off. With a decrepit expedition she moved towards that Restoration Falstaff, her beloved patron. He sat in smiling state awaiting her. His eye dwelt indulgently upon this living period-piece in crazy motion – consecrated by Saint Oscar – in which paradoxical repository the author of *Sobs in Quad*, or the Ballad of a Broken-hearted Fairy, had secreted wit, it was self-evident.

Blackshirt watched very sombrely the departing old pet and wit.

'You heard what she said?'

He waited, he knew Dan did not know whom he meant, he did not care whether Dan heard.

'This is a nursery!' he hissed at Dan with accusing finger at the general prospect, as another man would say *This is a den of thieves!* 'This is not a house – this is a nursery!'

Dan looked idly about him – he saw Lord Phoebus who had returned, without his Hottentot tricycle. He was nursing a lovely black gollywog made of wood – a little envy he could not helpbut feel for happy Phoebus, who could help it? He wished that Blackshirt would not breathe so hard, it was like a great big dog and he had never got over the fright he had got aged ten when Carlo struck him with his tail in the face.

Lord Phoebus stood by the baroque chimney, a substantial willow-pattern. In skeleton Lord Phoebus represented the byzantine canon, namely that of *nine-heads* – as opposed to that of Polycletus. But the externals were transformed into Gothic. Haggard-faced – with his byzantine *nine-heads* – he had the british version of the hellenic chevelure. Up either side it was baldish and window's-peaked. The haggardness was buffoonish however – Phoebus' countenance always appeared to *puff* (like the mouth of rococo cupids, cloud-blasting or blowing in trumpets) with a smile of mirth-frustrated. A corrupt and comic gothic of *nine-heads* then – a late *Perrot* crossed with *Pierotte* for sport, obliterating sex.

Dan wished he knew Lord Phoebus, slightly.

'This is God's own Peterpaniest family!'

The breath of the Blackshirt was rising like the first swell and subsidence of what was to be a first-class storm. There was dirty weather ahead, the wind was rising.

God's Peterpaniest family sported unmoved beneath the eyes of the pierpointean censor – Dan even slightly laughed in sympathy as one of the sportiest attempted to straddle the Hottentot tricycle, which Eric Mastrodonato had just found up in the tower of Phoebus and come running up with, with a shrill cry of triumph.

The Blackshirt almost laughed through his teeth at Dan – a gnashing half-laugh – as he noticed that he had thought it proper to smile in sympathy at the sports of God's Peterpaniest family.

'Moron that you are – I suppose you think that's funny!'

Dan jumped a little – it had not been his wish to laugh, he immediately felt guilty for he realized what he had done.

'It might be a kind of joke, if it were not so *expensive!*'

It must be terrible, thought Dan, like Blackshirt to be forever adding up. He planted a soft glance of pity upon the chest of the ill-tempered adding-machine. – The economist chained up his economic wrath, for the sake of imparting other information.

'You know old Harriet by sight don't you?'

Dan looked up, straight at Lady Harriet Finnian Shaw, whom he knew by sight.

'There is a celebrated painting of Battista Sforza Duchess of Urbino. Harriet thinks she looks like the portrait. Tonight she is got up to look like the portrait.'

Dan looked again – he was rather pleased at knowing Harriet by sight, he knew it pleased Blackshirt. He looked twice more.

'Yes. That is she. Standing with her is Julia Dyott. The person with whom she lives. That is her friend.'

Dan looked at Harriet again – *there she is!* his eyes said *she's over there!* He could pick her out – he was not such a fool!

Blackshirt looked at Harriet too, he squared up to her – from unmistakable signs which he had come to recognize at once, Dan knew a big 'broadcast' was brewing.

'Harriet' Blackshirt said, measuring Harriet with a butcher's eye 'turns forty easily on the scales with a bit to spare. She is a forty-year-older – and as for that old chum of her there, Julia, she is a fifty-tonner – what do you think – she p'raps weighs eight or ten summers more than Harriet – do you see her there?'

With his head bursting with time-tonnage, in an effort to learn to weigh with the eye, Dan darted a swift look at Harriet. Dan himself was not able to count above thirty (he had often been glad there were only *twenty* shillings in a pound). As he looked up he half-expected to find, where he had last seen ladies and gentlemen, a school of salmon in their place – he was relieved to remark no violent sea-change but just the same rows of bodies he had seen before.

'You see that great romping bundle of kittenish black silk bouncing about at present beside Lord Phoebus?'

Dan certainly remarked a lady behaving with great vivacity, quite close to Lord Phoebus -- who looked sad he thought.

'To his intense disgust! To Lord Phœbus's great vexation! Observe the expression upon his face!'

And Dan *did* notice that Lord Phoebus did not look best pleased and felt very sorry for Lord Phoebus in a way, he looked so cross and upset.

'Julia's not a bad old body. Is it her fault if she's a cool fifty?'

A breath of refreshing air seemed to blow over upon Dan from the fifty cool summers of the girl-friend of Battista Sforza. Chilly proximity – for fifty such cool summers!

'I daresay she's got as much of the milk of human kindness in her big toe as all the Finnian Shaws together have venom in their little fingers – it's quite possible. But she's altogether too milky, whether it's kind or sour.'

With bewildered fawn-face shyly Dan cast a covert glance in the direction of the Finnian Shaw family group, but of course as they were all shod as usual he was not rewarded by being able to remark any milk coming out of the big toe of Julia.

Blackshirt now entered the most massive 'broadcast' he had yet fallen into – it was a four-square pierpointean record.

'With stately step my lord Osmund approaches the portals of

his personal Age-hell. It is marked with the mystical 4 to the left hand of a Zero – that ugly *orty* sound too after it – *oh Hell* in other words. Oh Hell!'

Dan had an eye upon Lord Osmund but he did not see him move – there was no writing on the wall – there was no low temperature! Hell was mild today.

'There is the big Never-never door – Osmund prepares as it clangs to upon his enormous Eighteenth-century backside to drop all esperanza so he hates to see that grinning great glossy kitten hopping about his family-circle – there's no denying it she *is* on the womanly side – she has *kind eyes!* They *are* a bit on the *kind* side. But above all, Julia is a fifty-tonner – that's too much ballast to carry for a family-circle of widely-advertised Juniors whose age-tonnage is already far too much for the *child* class-events in the contemporary literary Regatta. Julia is no junior, she lets down the family-group with a great bump!'

Dan looked for those kind eyes long and earnestly but he was so sorry for Lord Phoebus all the time he could not find them, so he looked up at Blackshirt wistfully, who said –

'I have heard this from Pierpoint.'

Blackshirt appeared to think his glance had been one of incredulity perhaps – so he told him where it came from, that giver of all good things, the great PIERPOINT.

'Julia Dyott (heaven rest her soul) is the worst possible advertisement. *Why* need Harriet twenty years ago in choosing this woman-mate have chosen one older even than herself. That is how these distressed brothers argue. It would be so much nicer if Julia were *younger* than Harriet. What is the use of advertising oneself if one has *that* skeleton always in one's family cupboard! How could Harriet have been such a fool – why could she not have foreseen that twenty years hence she'd form part of a family-group who might become great Gossip-juniors. That's the idea.'

Dan could see that that would be more pleasant, he sympathized very much with everybody about this, but it must be confessed that he was not at all at his ease at the thought of the *skeleton* hidden away in some family *cupboard* in this house he was in – he thought at once of Mrs Bosun's closet!

'When they go with a squad of press-photographers to present a copy of their playlet *Pity the Young*! to say Ellen Terry – "from Youth to Age" it would be inscribed – it would be *so much nicer* if old Julia were not there to show the world what old Harriet's taste was twenty years ago! That is the point. It is capital, so it seems a neck-or-nothing point. *These people are exceedingly sentimental.* They take this advertisement question very seriously. It *is* their long suit – and a very *long* suit indeed! And they feel that someone has blundered!'

Pity the Young – Dan could not help feeling that that was a sentiment of which it was impossible to have too much, and he fell to pitying some of the young very much just then.

'No, Julia's a bad break of Harriet's. Why Harriet couldn't have *foreseen* – she must grow old herself she should have understood, so couldn't afford to attach *that.* This is quite the most perplexing feature in this otherwise straightforward problem.'

Dan looked perplexed. He wrinkled his brow to show he was ploughing up his brains. But he gave it up – anyway he was quite sure Blackshirt would unravel it – he looked very worried about it at present, but he would soon clear it up Dan was positive.

'So there stands that walking *blot on the scutcheon* – already – might not Osmund wheeze through his hanoverian nose – rendered sinister *enough* by the incessant ding-donging of Time, for their own personal family birthdays – without inviting somebody in, whose birthday-chimes every twelve-month deafened the whole neighbourhood for a full half-hour – *and* fell in the same month as the climacterical carillon of Harriet! For Osmund and for Phoebus – why Julia is their Cross!'

Dan brightened – *Hark now he hears them ding-dong bell* – forty ding-dongs – baked in a pie! Dan's ears quite rang with the pretty vibrations!

'I have this from Pierpoint. For Finnian Shaw lore, Pierpoint is unequalled.'

Blackshirt threw himself back, and he took a B.D.V. from a corrugated iron cigarette-case secured upon Bank-holiday at Hampstead in a luckydip. This was the conventional microphonic pause in the 'Broadcast', Dan was quite accustomed to that, he liked it. And when Blackshirt said *these bad brothers* Dan knew that the pause was over.

'These bad brothers' said Blackshirt 'for ten years' and he held out both hands, which Dan could see were fortunate enough to possess ten fingers still 'these bad brothers have moved heaven and earth to effect the expulsion of that compromising effigy – that old woman of the sea.'

He pointed his cigarette at the nice pleasant smiling middle-aged woman from whom Lord Phoebus attempted to hide a little toy he held in his opposite armpit – and she the tactless tomboy romped round to snatch it out.

'Then the miracle happened!' boomed Blackshirt and made Dan jump and almost cross himself. 'The one little touch of old mother nature that makes the whole little kindergarten world of men *kin* – that manifested itself of all unlikely places in the bosom of that imitation Battista Sforza old Harriet! She *would not* turn her back upon her life-time friend!'

The Blackshirt whistled softly *Auld Lang Syne* and Dan looked up in some astonishment. This display of musical ability in such an unbending realist was unexpected to say the least.

'But it spoilt the Finnian Shaw family-group!'

Dan looked hard at Julia, who was making jokes with Harriet, thinking *spoil-sport* – he owed her a grudge for making Phoebus so melancholy.

'It is the old antagonism – *nature* versus *art*. Man proposes – Time disposes!'

Blackshirt whistled *The Old Folks at Home*. Dan mentally joined in the chorus of that – the old school-song it was and he loved it. This was a new side of Blackshirt – what he longed for Blackshirt really to do was to whistle *John Brown's Body*. Of all songs he liked it best.

'Perhaps Harriet has only been soured by the wear and tear of life!' Blackshirt exclaimed, making a generous gesture – his expression betraying an intention to see something good in *everything*. 'Do not at all events let us be the first to throw stones at glass-houses of the future!'

Dan gazed into the glass-houses of the future and he saw the gigantic leaves of the tropical narcissus or palm-groves as at Kew Garden.

'You see how things are now' said Blackshirt as one man to another. 'Over there you can see it. It's as plain as print.

Osmund and Phoebus can scarcely bring themselves to speak to Miss Dyott. On the other hand Time's forty horse-power chariot comes hurrying down upon Osmund – soon to be galloping off in his rear. Osmund feels it's too much under these circumstances to ask him to stomach Julia! No!'

Blackshirt gave a long animal yawn. Dan immediately had to smother a spasm set up in sympathy and then felt fatigued all at once. He strangled several more and Blackshirt licked his lips.

The Blackshirt in a loud impatient voice then said –

'But they are puppets not people – they live in a sort of musical box. Don't be afraid to look over at them – I notice you seem afraid to – you have a perfect right to look!'

This was new to Dan, that there were rights and wrongs – it was surely *always* wrong to stare he had been taught – but to please Blackshirt he cast a melting eye over upon Osmund just once, and hung his head next minute to make up for it.

'*Life justified as Joke*. Imagine that principle. The Finnian Shaw brothers exemplify it. You have *the right* to laugh here. – I have the right to laugh. We all have the right to laugh. It is better than that – *you go against nature if you do not!* It is your duty *to laugh!*'

Dan had wanted to laugh for some time so he gave a smile and let the Blackshirt see it so he would know he had complied.

Lord Osmund all of a sudden called out very crossly indeed –

'Eustace, do close that door again – it's being opened by somebody!'

It certainly had come open and everyone looked up indignantly at it.

'Do see who they are Eustace first – we really can't have them in here! There are far too many people here already – some will have to leave or we shall all be suffocated – I can scarcely breathe as it is!'

'There is Zagreus' said Blackshirt to Dan pointing at the door.

'Oh! Who is it?' in a still crosser tone Osmund shouted. 'Yes – that is all right Eustace – but do try and see no one *else* gets in! I can hear more of them coming up. In a moment they will be here!'

'No it's all right Osmund' Eustace replied, coming back from the door. 'It really is all right! I've looked out of the door – no one is in sight!'

'But I can hear them coming up! – The band has stopped and they are liable to come up here because they want to sit down and are too lazy to go out into the garden.'

'I think you're wrong Osmund. There is no one in sight!'

Eustace argued with Osmund.

'It's not a question of sight! I can *hear* them distinctly!'

Dan's heart beat fast. With *him* someone was in sight – and alas *he* was not alone!

Horace was coming across the room at a highstepping stroll, and as he did so he stooped sideways still advancing with knees up, to speak with the little upstart cad he had with him and was never parted from – that Margolin – who came forward in his customary unbridled manner of under-bred effrontery! That this was prejudicial to Horace's dignity was almost certain. For Dan he had no eyes at all that went without saying – open shipwreck of every observance of cordial regard – and of tenderness for his *genius* – had long ago been made by Horace: and he himself (Dan knew but too well) by his lack of push had been the firmest abetter of his own decay, he could not find the words like other people to plead his cause with Horace – not of *his* deserts but of those of genius! – and he even could have wished to be some such blockish and rash person as Blackshirt – to plead his cause with boot or fist horrible as that was – because he could not bear to stand by and watch all that he had once been for Horace became nothing but a name! It was scarcely *a name* any longer indeed! When an unprofitable grammarian at Wexford he recalled, just such another upstart Emanuel Rooney by name it was, had come between himself and the headmaster who had had a great liking for him at first. But a big boy had one day on account of a row attacked Rooney when he wasn't looking and broken his leg with a thumping kick. He almost had it in his heart to wish that Blackshirt would fall foul of Margolin once, and box his ears perhaps make his nose bleed, that would serve him jolly well right! But Dan followed this vein no more, for with the suppressed excitement his own nose started to bleed then – and he lay back his head upon the window-ledge and looked up at the ceiling, swallowing the blood and secretly sniffing.

'Zagreus!' Dan heard a voice calling and he looked down his nose and saw it was Osmund calling his false friend over with a friendly hooked forefinger.

Horace turned back Dan saw. While his two followers stood behind him he talked with much fierce ringing laughter on his side, with Lord Osmund. He bent down and he examined one or two of the more prominent of the toys – fragments of gingerbread work – the Callot entitled *Parterre ou Jardin de Nancy* – an Eighteenth Century japanese bronze mirror – a trojan face-urn – a cledgy cup from Burgoland, and the rest – stroking them and laughing and sounding them with his nails, but Lord Phoebus removed the gingerbread work and the clay pieces out of his reach. – The musical snuff-box he subtilized. Then, reaching out his hand, he appeared to recover it from the décolleté of the Volpemini and everyone applauded very much indeed. It was lovely to have a conjurer in the room amongst one and one sprang up and crowded round him. But Zagreus did no more tricks, and one lay down again.

IX Blackshirt Explains Ratner. Ratner Blackshirt

With a broad and evil grin (the first that night and Dan hoped the last) which carried a wink with it too, Blackshirt saïd –

'Zagreus is popular!'

This pierpointean watched the other pierpointean, and Dan took his head off the ledge.

'What wonder – what strange revolution, has brought him, you ask! *No revolution!* It is period-prestige!'

Dan put the pocket handkerchief that was damp with tears to his nose and removed the blood.

'The great practical-joker of the Nineties – Zagreus was that – that is enough! This man has laid violent hands too upon the hem of Oscar's garment – Zagreus has done that – it is *more* than enough!'

Dan knew that Blackshirt was now saying horrid things about Horace again, but he did not care he confessed.

'It is reported he actually kidnapped Wilde – in those days Zagreus was I suppose a sort of *hearty*. Only the police saved

Wilde from tar and feathers. That is the story. Now he gets kudos out of his attack!'

A growing excitement was visible upon the face of Starr-Smith.

'That is the sacrosanct period-of-periods – the Victorian death, the birth of Decadence! Ah the pioneer naughtiness of the "Naughty Nineties", that *Made the World Safe for Homosexuality!*'

A loud peal of super-pierpointean laughter stormed the ears of the assembly. The swaying figure of Zagreus became the focus for all eyes whatever. Blackshirt looked black indeed at this – Pierpoint had refused always to allow Starr-Smith to imitate his laugh – *talk* he might, to his heart's content – *laugh*, never!

'Zagreus snaps his fingers at them. But *it is Pierpoint's fingers he snaps!* He gets his tricks where I have got my tricks! – Apart from that!' Blackshirt snapped his fingers. 'Horace Zagreus is not unlike these Finnian Shaws himself!'

Blackshirt gave a snort in place of the laugh he might not give.

'Zagreus is like the Finnian Shaws – he is Peter Pan!'

Dan looked over wistfully at Horace. He could not defend him against the Blackshirt – he could not defend him against himself!

'Zagreus does not strike one as old.'

Blackshirt gazed at that tall and graceful figure with a back made for the Stulz swallow-tail, that had bought the right to laugh like Pierpoint from their common master.

'Has that struck you?'

Blackshirt looked at Dan almost as if he expected an answer.

'He doesn't look more than a forty-tonner!' Blackshirt added in a voice that was confidential. 'That's because he's an albino.'

Dan's head ached slightly from the nosebleeding.

'You know the Bible in Spain? Borrow was an albino.'

Dan had never heard Blackshirt mention anything connected with *religion* until now and he listened for his next remark with attention.

'Borrow reminds me of Zagreus.'

Talking about *borrowing* – as it was *money* again Dan lost interest – but into the midst of his day-dream burst a white horse.

'In *T.P.* I read last week how Borrow rode his white charger into the hall of the manor-house of an enemy-neighbour. Was not that like Zagreus? Probably he looked like him.'

His heart breaking, Dan lifted his head – as if anyone else who had ever lived could *resemble Horace!*

'Look at him now – with that East End monkey-on-a-stick!'

Horace was in the act of introducing the disgusting little Margolin-fellow to Lord Osmund (who did not seem to like any too well the doubtful privilege!). Dan could *just* hear, even – by straining very much both ears – the word – *yes* – yes the word *genius!*

'He's not going to take *him* on, so he needn't think it!'

Dan felt unaccountably drawn toward the Blackshirt! Whatever unfortunate directions his remarks might on occasion take, he was so essentially right-minded!

'I shouldn't be surprised if that son-of-a-bitch Ratner had put him up to it!'

At the name Ratner Blackshirt showed his aversion by biting at a hangnail, doubling his head upon his shoulder to get up at it and chew it off.

'Why does he drag all these Jews from Whitechapel round with him – especially Julius Ratner, holy mother!'

Again Dan was surprised, this time definitely gratified, to hear Blackshirt employing an expression that suggested that he might not be a stranger to the consolations of religion.

'It was Pierpoint recommended Ratner.'

The Blackshirt stared gloomily over at Pierpoint's rattish nominee.

'It was a joke,' he added quickly, and blew his nose in lieu of spitting.

Dan could see it was a joke. Hurriedly he gave a smile to show he saw the joke it was.

'Yes. Zagreus has no sense of humour at all – although he laughs so much!'

And as he referred to this privileged laughter of Zagreus, Blackshirt's visage was at its bitterest.

'He has kept Mr Ratner religiously at his side ever since.'

Again Blackshirt – this time directly – had referred to *religion!*

'*He is my anti-genius!* Zagreus says. *It is a good thing to vomit at least once a day*. You have heard him I expect. It would not be a bad thing to call in some cringing scarecrow – if it would only scare off the *geniuses!* But it doesn't, does it?'

Dan could not decide if this was intended to be offensive to all genius or only to such as was not real genius at all.

'Pierpoint says that Zagreus gets money out of Ratner – that he says is the secret – I am quite prepared to believe that, from what I know of Zagreus. It is very likely. All the same, is it necessary to take one's money-lender about everywhere with one?'

Dan had never had a money-lender, so he found it impossible to express an opinion as to what was the best thing to do, to take him about or not. But he was strongly of the opinion that a gentleman should keep such things to himself.

'With him most of his friends are money-lenders – that is unless they are geniuses! – Ratner I am told is very jealous of the young men by whom Zagreus is always surrounded. It is he, it appears, who is responsible for Zagreus treating them so badly. Zagreus would not admit it, but he influences him. There is Willie Service now – *he* is treated worse than any chauffeur. Ratner does all that. It is for similar reasons that I have so much trouble with him, as secretary to Pierpoint – only Pierpoint sends him to hell, usually.'

There was a pause, during which Blackshirt watched Zagreus with his new *genius* Margolin, and his dismal money-lender-in-ordinary, turning over this question as to the desirability of having one's money-lender on one's staff, and other questions, and then a new topic agitated the blackshirted breast.

'I don't know whether Zagreus has paid the costumier,' he said with a sudden fiery anxiety. 'Do you happen to know if Zagreus has paid the tailor?'

Dan was startled at this question – he had always had his suits bought for him and was there not possibly a hint of responsibility (devolving upon *him*) in this point-blank question? No one had ever mentioned such a thing to him before, about suits.

'I know he hasn't paid *us* a penny yet! We designed his dress for him – we gave him a number of sketches. All this symbolical-

personnel you know costs money! You can see that can't you?'

The Blackshirt appeared suddenly to become very excited – the storm burst over Dan's head – this time it was no 'broadcast' either. Blackshirt was exclaiming against his destiny in a spontaneous and straightforward manner.

'I've had about enough of it! Pierpoint is altogether too good-hearted – I respect that but he is so unpractical! What happens when I intervene? That is all the thanks I get! Zagreus is sometimes downright treacherous!'

Dan was sure that he misjudged him and let him see as much, by his face's very grave expression, at once – casting one long loyal look in the direction of Horace.

'Why do you suppose I am here with two more, who are volunteers, as "fascists" of all things, to-night? Nothing to do with *Fascismo* – the last thing – can you guess? It's because I picked up three khaki shirts for a few pence and dyed them black – the whole outfit for the three of us did not cost fifteen bob! That is the reason.'

Dan looked in melancholy reverie sideways at the stomach of this particularly mercenary young man – how anybody could be so mercenary he did not know unless it was being a *secretary*.

'Because I stand between him and them I get the mud – if it were not for me, where would Pierpoint be tell me that! *Nowhere!* His finances were in absolute chaos when he picked me up – it was *I* saved him from bankruptcy! I pulled him out of the most fearful chaos.'

After the way that Blackshirt had saved *him* – from a worse fate than bankruptcy – he could not doubt his word with regard to this lesser act of bold salvation.

'Take again that old *spirit that wills the evil* over there that follows at the heel of Zagreus (and *does the good* – in the matter of financial credits, if Pierpoint is right, and as business adviser) consider what I have to put up with from *him*. As Pierpoint's political-secretary and man of business, as I am – he persecutes me as far as possible. Pierpoint says Mr Ratner has Zagreus in his power. That is over a big loan – that was a year ago. Pierpoint has told me something about it. It's my belief that Pierpoint owes him something too. As it is, Ratner's *Press* do a little printing for us – we have to make use of him, you know how that is at times don't you – though I have suggested alternatives to Pierpoint. But Pierpoint will not hear of it. He argues that we should only get *another* Ratner. It is an *evil that we know* and so on. We argue a lot. Well then, I have disputes with that man there every quarter over money. Sometimes monthly – he plagues my life out. And then he goes and complains to Pierpoint. He is always the injured party. It is my *manners*. He says I am so rude to him and Pierpoint does not understand. He insinuates that I am *violent* – you may well smile! He creeps round and whispers to Pierpoint that my *violence* as he calls it is damaging – I *do harm to Pierpoint's cause!* "A violent young man," is how he described me – it appears that if Pierpoint allows me to continue as political-secretary and to look after his money-affairs that all Pierpoint's affairs will go to the devil! This "violent young man" – yours truly! – will *drive everybody away* – with his quarrelsome natural fieriness of temper – and *suspiciousness*. At that I laugh outright. At that I really laugh outright!'

And the poor Blackshirt almost *did* what was forbidden him – laugh – and a twisted and grimacing face was the consequence.

'Yes – it was the *suspiciousness* that had done it – that I well enough understood – *suspiciousness* as regards Ratner of course! I was lacking in proper trustfulness! Oh please – I could not keep my temper again it seemed! I wish I had not. I wish *I had not!*'

And Blackshirt's second harsher *had not* had such a force to it, that if Dan had had a hat on, it might have hit it off his head – while he looked over at the rival business-man in such a way as boded no good to him my word.

'I who *a dozen times* when he came about his bill – he came only because he wanted to press Pierpoint, so that he could find out how he stood – if he'd got the cash I suppose – I saw through his game! always overcharging us – needing to be watched every half-second or he'd slip in a matter from the account paid six months back – just to be tiresome, intending to get me into trouble – had I thrown the old spy-rat out on his head *a hundred times* it would have been no more than he asked for. *Asks for* – he pleads for it! The ugly old reptile *wills you* to hit him – the dirty old masochist! Well I am Welsh. I talk quickly, as all Welshpeople do. I know that sometimes I have *the air* of being excited. – Sometimes that is more than others. But does that signify I am out of temper? What about? I agree perhaps such a man as that may get my goat. Perhaps. One day I shall be violent *on purpose*. I shall *accept!*'

Dan drew away a little from the Blackshirt, as he had become restless and electrical discharges were coming out of him, he thought (as he considered the problem of the alleged 'violence' that was his, or whether it was celtic impetuosity no more than that).

But Blackshirt's anger rose if anything, if anger it was, as Zagreus and Co. were steadily approaching and his business foe became larger and more distinct – with a decided grin too upon his unlovely mask of a Theatrical-Agent-in-a-small-way-of-shoddy-business – which he brought over hanging coyly upon his fat neck like a bilious tulip. The eye-in-profile darted up at Blackshirt too to provoke him, and the sallowest smirk of the most superior gentlemanly Julius was pasted all over his face – advertising his settled opinion of the comic nature of this amateur-secretary.

Zagreus came up and he was smiling very cordially at Dan. He said in the friendliest way in the world –

'Daniel you make a girl in a thousand – I declare you are too good to be true – are you perhaps really a girl after all Daniel? Is it possible Dan your mother made a mistake!'

Blushing Dan sat tight. His eyes were fixed in stoical anguish upon the floor, his legs were locked together in despair, his hands clasped before his knees and slowly wrung upon his knee-pans in silent grief. If Horace approved of him as a girl that was some compensation for the horrible situation in which he found himself but he could scarcely think that he did and this was mockery too he expected.

The Blackshirt shot up like a Jack-in-the-box and Dan heard him hoarsely remark –

'A word with you Zagreus!'

They moved off and went into another recess together. Standing in front of Dan, Ratner affected to read in a book. The sleepless inquisitor's lateral eye, with its mercurial stability sensitive as a compass, lay in wait for his blackshirted antagonist.

Throwing himself down upon the cushioned window-seat, by

the side of Dan, Margolin closed his eyes. To be a *genius* took it out of you, the false as well as the true. He buried his small frowning face in the wash-leather of a cheap cushion. Suddenly he opened his eyes and said to Dan as if emerging from a long blank slumber –

'Where have you been?'

Dan did not wish to be accused by Margolin of being *a violent young man* but he dropped his head a little sharply and closed his eyes quickly, with no snapping, but firmly.

'Been up in this room long Dan?' asked Archie, as one genius to another.

Oh how Dan could wish that Horace would not leave him alone with this hateful little intriguing cad – he would not suffer himself to listen however to the hateful little cad's impertinent questions now.

Blackshirt and Horace were away for some time, it seemed very long to Dan – possibly thought he the Blackshirt was telling Horace about the expenses of a new *genius*. Now they had strolled out, deep in conversation, from the other recess: and Blackshirt often looked back towards Margolin, and Horace laughed as Blackshirt did so very heartily in his loud easy way – as if what Blackshirt said was a capital piece of fun and pierpointean irony and it deserved a crack of first-class laughter to respond to the rich tickle of it – Horace tossed his head about and stamped upon the floor with his corn-cob wand as if applauding Blackshirt. They were after all both of them mad about Pierpoint – but Dan did hope that his new friend might succeed in impressing upon Horace the necessity of retrenchment and might stop him from having another *genius* just yet – and that he would completely show-up Margolin who was now (he knew) nothing more than a jewish unbeliever.

Archie Margolin lay back upon the cushions of the window-seat very pretentiously, like a little Sultana. From the midst of his asiatic abandon he cocked his fingers and then sent over a whirling Safety Match, which fell beside Blackshirt.

'Here Dan!' Margolin explosively claimed Daniel's attention without obtaining it at all. 'Who is that? Is that your friend?'

To have Margolin beside you was to have a cheddite cartridge in your pocket – the lips of Margolin detonated, they did not speak. How he made thoughts must be like the back-firing of an internal combustion mechanism, instead of a man's brain. This was certainly the most restless toy that genius-fan ever had for a pet – his nervous Match-habit expressed Arch, in terms of Behaviour to perfection.

Ratner smiled at Margolin and Margolin allowed his eyes to rest, drowsy and sultanaish, impassibly upon the person of Ratner.

'Here!' coughed Arch again – peevish and imperious, with a spasm of mock-impatience, facing about. 'That's a stout fellow Dan! Is he your friend over there!'

'It's Starr-Smith!' Ratner muttered coyly into his book – as if he had not intended to be heard, as he stood facing the book-cavities.

'Oh that's Starr-Smith!' choked Archie jocosely in burly inanition, at the *Starr* in front of the *Smith.* 'Stout Fell-*low!*'

In his rôle of sly book-worm Ratner did not look up but said as he read, for the benefit of Dan –

'Starr-Smith is Pierpoint's business-manager.'

Ratner sneered to himself lazily lifting his lip to show a fang. The calling of Starr-Smith was to Ratner (of course himself no business-man, but a poet) a jest that no one could miss.

'Business-man!' Archie blurted 'here Ratner is it Smiff – that's a business-man – it's a good name! It must be Big Business!'

'Very Big!' Ratner sneered in indulgent croak at Arch, down into this nest of geniuses. 'Pierpoint calls him his political-secretary.'

'Political-secretary!' Arch hadn't heard of it, not political-secretary.

Ratner changed his face which became grave but knowing, to utter something from-the-horse's-mouth. The eye-in-profile coldly picked its way among facts – inside information was about to be imparted – but it would be picked and analysed from A to Z. It had the sanction of public opinion – all enlightened persons would assent to Ratner's descriptions. *Not* common-knowledge. *Known to all the most knowing.*

'I am very fond indeed of Pierpoint!' Ratner said, for this was the A.B.C. of success – it must be accepted as an axiom that what Ratner uttered was the damaging admission of a reluctant *friend*. The 'fondness' must come first – the belittlement afterwards it stood to reason. That was so as to have the right to defame. To be 'fond', you must *know* – it must moreover be *very well* that you know – for you to have the time to become *fond*. After that matters are simple! everything said henceforth will have the stamp of authority – that of a truth wrung from unwilling lips. Hence was to be seen that air of wisdom from-the-horse's-mouth – but whose fangs when it was Ratner's mouth precluded the idea of the presence of a real horse still less a Houyhnhnm – and since always it was *the thing that is not* that came out of those jaws, that was as well.

'Is he a business fell-low!' asked Archie with the frowning pomp of his miniature stature.

'No Archie!' in a growl croaked Ratner, with an awful graceful wriggle in the opposite sense. 'Pierpoint is a *philosopher!*'

'Oh a philosopher' spluttered Arch.

'Yes – I suppose so.'

'Oh – so he's *not* a business fell-low!'

'No – I'm afraid he's not a business-fellow Archie! He is very unbusiness-like.'

'Is he? So am I!'

'Starr-Smith is Pierpoint's business-manager – his ideas of business are very funny. He makes Pierpoint almost a laughing-stock – he does the most extraordinary things.'

'Isn't he a business-fell-low?'

'No Archie – he is a very unbusinesslike fell-low!'

'Which one?'

'Both are very unbusinesslike fellows!'

'What did you say the other was?'

'Pierpoint is a very vain fell-low.'

'Here am I vain Ratner?'

'No Archie. Pierpoint likes Starr-Smith because Starr-Smith treats him as if he were a little tin-god.'

'Little tin-god – go on!'

'Little tin-god!' (responsive hysteria of a more frustrated and semi-dignified sort from the Rat). 'Starr-Smith imitates everything Pierpoint does. As a business-manager Starr-Smith – '

'He's not clever is he!'

Ratner croaked drearily.

'It's worse than that!'

'Is it really!'

'As *everyone* knows Pierpoint is hopelessly unbusinesslike.' Ratner gave every evidence of a hopeless attempt to disguise, in his *own* face, all the tell-tale indications of a *hopelessly unbusiness-like* man – of *a poet*. 'Everyone expects that of *Pierpoint*.' (Everyone expected it as well of *Ratner* – his bashful smile made *that* quite plain.) 'But Starr-Smith is even worse than Pierpoint – between them they make a mess of everything.' He spoke as if the separate syllables of his words were clammy and apt to stick together really – this gave the effect of the *reluctance* needed. 'I do some printing for them,' he looked very bashful and un-business like indeed. 'But I only do it because I am a friend of Pierpoint's. Other people tell me however – Starr-Smith is the same with everybody.'

'Is he? Go on!'

Ratner then with meditative eye pointed out, as it were, how Blackshirt was upsetting Horace Zagreus at this moment, as per usual and in illustration of his remarks.

Pretending that something had gone phoney with his right eye, Archie rubbed it until it became very red and looked at Ratner out of it, who sneered and turned away. Dan stared stoically into the Land of his Dreams, up that Long Long Trail A-winding. In that dream he thought he heard Starr-Smith say 'On Account!' and he saw Horace shake his head.

X The Old Colonels

The whole room suddenly reverberated. A footman announced in tremendous accents –

'COLONEL PONTO!

CAPTAIN ALPHONSO TEACH!'

Another footman post-haste upon his heels roared out –

'ADMIRAL BENBOW!

GENERAL WALKER-TROTTER!

MAJOR UPDICK!

COMMANDER PERSE!'

There was an indescribable roar on all hands as these names were announced. Lord Osmund rose. Everyone sprang up and shouted at once. Lord Phoebus came rushing out of the stairs with Eric Mastrodonato and Basil Spatworthy and also Martin McGregor, Patrick Leslie and Cecil Dawson – who had gone up into the tower upon orders from Osmund to fetch Phœbus to keep people out – who kept getting in, in twos and threes, and Phoebus was the best doorkeeper. Eustace could not manage crowds. He had not the knack – he did not carry the same weight and was not brutal enough with them.

So the osmundian world shook to its foundations – all roared at once as the guests announced came out behind the footmen, in a string. First of all through the open door came Colonel Ponto. He was in the company of Captain Alphonso Teach. The first footman shouted out again – a liveried rooster, the head protruding at a break-neck pitch, to deliver his message –

'COLONEL PONTO!
CAPTAIN ALPHONSO TEACH!'

Dan was the only person in the room who was not standing. Matches flew through the air towards the gallant officers and gentlemen who were making their entrance, especially Colonel Ponto, dressed in the full regimentals of Colonel Newcome on parade (chosen by Lord Osmund himself for Colonel Ponto, as the character *in fiction* best suited to his manly beauty, and the outfit had been sent him by post). Captain Teach in full mess kit of the Deccan Light Foot looked very well indeed as a pukka sahib and a credit to Anglo-India.

Of the next batch, shouted in by both footmen (foot-to-foot, emblazoned buttock by emblazoned buttock) Commander Perse was first. His clean-shaven, salt-tanned, non-pareil senior-service face required no uniform to advertise his calling. So he rolled in in squarely-built black broadcloth mufti evening-kit, to withstand all weathers – a Summit-collar, Sandeman Port, Wardroom tailor's-dummy in a million – and everyone must have the conviction at the first glimpse of him – this royal-blue aquatint – that a topgallant was tattooed upon the stiff upstanding pillar of his back – that a mandril picked out in blue and scarlet swarmed up *one* of his sea-legs – that a rude specimen of what Jack Tar has one-each-of in every port bulged with her brawny limbs upon *the other* – that a Capstan Navy-cut british sheet-anchor was suspended upon his left breast almost certainly – that is in that portion alone not overstocked with a rank growth of male hair, above the beating-spot of his heart-of-oak. All this was obvious. It would have been a great pity to paint the lily – naval dress would have been a mere fancy-dress with this essential Sea-salt.

But Admiral Benbow had come definitely disguised as some exotic description of mariner, and there was a quite distinct murmur of disappointment. Had he been so ill-advised, although a stout man, as to represent Lord Nelson? Why had the old fool spoilt himself? There was a note of anger in the exclamations provoked by this discovery.

Major Updick and General Walker-Trotter, two first-class tomato-pink veterans (with dazzling white-lead moustaches of the best coarse bristle) were in their appropriate uniforms by request. Both had been snatched straight out of the Club Window in that Club-Land-that-was – in the very act of exclaiming 'Demme Sir! the country's going to the dogs!' – and brought hot-foot to Lord Osmund's Lenten Party, the Sandeman Port scarcely dry upon their furibond moustaches, to say *Demme sir!* all over again there – that needed no underlining.

But in the wake of the naval and military procession crowded a horde of vulgar sightseers, some of them actually young women, extremely difficult to handle – it was in vain that Phoebus and Eustace attempted to push them back – it was a moment of great pandemonium, people got out of hand and all was at sixes and sevens.

'You really must go away you know!' loftily baying Lord Phoebus ran hither and thither, the picture of misery. He pushed first this person, then that. 'We can't have so many people in here – no really we can't – these are private apartments! You really have no right here at all! This part of the house is not for the public. You really must go back at once to the Saloon and dance!'

The young women smiled at Phoebus and at his hollow bay of loud complaint, as if he had been a part of the exhibition, and were one of the minor side-shows, to be enjoyed at the same time with those marked *Ponto – Benbow – Updick – Teach.*

'Eustace! Tell them *they will be turned out* if they come in! This is too much! – Close the door! No they can't remain here! *Look at them!* Close-the-door! This is *my* room! This is not public!' Phoebus howled and stormed among the intruders. It was in vain, for they imitated each other, and some of them would not take him seriously at all. A great number of nameless guests got in, flushed from their ridiculous exercises downstairs. Afterwards it was impossible to expel them – although, acting as party-police, several rosetted Osmundians did attempt to drive towards the door several unathletic-looking, unaccompanied, palpably friendless persons, who evidently had no business in any respectable house, several of whom appeared to smell.

Listening to the shouting footmen, Ratner said to Horace –

'They must have made up the names!'

'They have been most diligently picked, of course,' said Horace 'for their name, and military appearance. There are not *two* Teaches in the world! And what moustaches!'

Mr Zagreus brushed up fiercely his own postiche circus-proprietor's lip-crop.

All of Horace's party had now, including Blackshirt, been stampeded into the recess: Horace bent down to Dan, with a certain gallantry – as if in recognition of the feminine suggestions of the get-up and said in his ear, quite close to his face –

'Starr-Smith wishes to take you over for the rest of the evening.' He added in a lower tone, in a portentous whisper – '*Pierpoint wishes it!*'

Dan clasped and unclasped his hands in bitter protest.

'I am going down to prepare for our show. I will send for you when I am ready.'

Dan made the effort of his life – he half-rose – it was his last card!

'Oh can't I come!' he cried, and then fell back with a big banging blush, ready to sink into the floor with shame.

'No. Starr-Smith wishes you to stop with him.'

Dan sank back still further, almost in a heap. He had played his card – he had lost! Horace had pushed him off on the Blackshirt.

Zagreus stood to watch for a moment the drumming-in of the fatuous carefully-picked Old Colonels and performing Sea Dogs – each one redder, riper and more unreal than the last.

'The Yeomen of the Guard' said Ratner.

'What a pack of old fools' the Blackshirt remarked with a disgusted violence.

'They kept them downstairs until now – in a locked room!' Zagreus told the Blackshirt smiling, watching for the response.

'Did they – in a locked room!'

'Yes. Under lock and key. We tried to get into the room as a matter of fact – it was locked.'

'Well!'

'Yes. A footman came hurrying up to us, to know what we wanted. He explained the situation – it seemed to provide *him* with considerable amusement I must say that.'

'So I should suppose.'

'As they arrived one by one they were thrust in there and asked to wait – till there were enough of them, that I believe was Osmund's idea, to make a grand slam.'

Ratner continued to grin – not at what Horace was saying to excite the Blackshirt, but at his own thoughts, was advertised by that fulsome steadfast yellow leer. He allowed it to stop there (so he announced in the eyes that were part of it) because it was too much trouble to take it off. But the dank bloom of the grin gave to the face that nice superior feeling. – Nothing especially funny to *him* about the retired senior-officers. Locked up in their waiting-room – well yes, but what of that? Nothing in the footman's face (encountered downstairs) to laugh at or grin at. A stupid young footman liked to have the job of putting old red-faced bigwigs under lock and key. *Of course*. Standing in full farce of his powdered hair, plush and knee-breeches – stuffed into a stuffy state-suit (in mockery, so it must feel to have that on your back) – a gentleman's braided costume in 1750 thereabouts, today reserved for the underdog – that was a sort of insult who could not see that! Also of course it was the symbol of the *external* pomp of the underdog – empty of power, but with a fine court suit! *Fine Clothes for the Under-Dog!* The real unseen master *naked* – upon some distant Beach – Venice or Florida. *No need to explain* to Ratner how such a powdered young man would like to have Lord Osmund too in a locked apartment. Who wouldn't – that was normal, but it was quite trite. The footman *as a matter of course* would relish it. To have *everybody* with the *power* to put *him* into a braided uniform (such as formerly worn by aristocrats, but only by poor bottom-dogs at present) with power to powder his hair white like age – it was but too self-evident that (standing to attention, at the end of an epoch) the young footman would not be far from wishing to tie Lord Osmund up in a gunnysack, to drop him down to the bottom of some disused 1750 well. – Such ideas had neither hands nor feet – they were the mist of possibilities that willy-nilly formed, of their own accord, in the brain, immediately behind the things you saw, if you had eyes to see. There was nothing in that to provoke, or to sustain, such a knowing smile as alone he could give. Such child's play was not commensurate with such craft. Such pictures could fill one sometimes with an intoxication of secret power, like a prophet – of course formerly one *had* felt that and the rest: but the fumes of this secret knowledge had come up into his face – bit by bit they had hardened into this splenetic grin. Only this coy splenetic grin of Julius Ratner was left as witness. All that was passed now with him – he did not care! But the grin he left up above upon his face, because it was far too much trouble to take it off, and it was calculated to annoy people at large, who thought it was meant for them.

The jubilant roar from the osmundian chorus, which had denoted the long expected entrance of all these relics of mediocre Death-or-Glory (this menagerie of Uncle Tobies – all as good as wounded at Namur, or shot down at Trafalgar, it was all the same) died down. This became an excited buzz as the seasoned leaders, and their *Jugend Bewegung* satellites, like swarms of bees (joined by many unorthodox intruders, rudely pushing and laughing) gathered around one or other of the grinning fossils – old pensioners, ex-hearties of Death or Glory.

Colonel Ponto was surrounded and at first pinioned against the wall by an admiring group of pushing and pinching persons. At first Harriet and (a little less prominent) Julia, led them but they deserted him for the General. One rather ageing epicene-contortionist howled in Ponto's face, as he walked backwards in front of him –

'Do tell us again Colonel how you were killed at Colenso!'

Monty Mayors, exploding with the glee of his high blood-pressure, bellowed in Ponto's ear –

'Oh yes Colonel – *do* tell us how you were killed at Colenso again!'

'Oh Colonel do tell us that – do tell us all once more how you were killed at Colenso!'

They all took turns to plead with the steadily advancing Ponto.

'That is a divine story Colonel Ponto – was it in the Zulu War you won the Victoria Cross! – was it! Was it the Victoria Cross?'

'The Victoria Cross – how lovely – did he get the Victoria Cross at Colenso?'

'When he was killed!'

'Was old Ponto really killed!'

'No. It was in the Zulu War! It was in the Zulu War wasn't it Colonel Ponto!'

'Am I not right in saying Colonel it was at Rorke's Drift! Do say I am – just this once please Colonel!'

'Colonel *Ponto* – it *was* in the Zulu War! Do say it was, I'm sure you're right!'

'Did you kill yourself Colonel Ponto! Was it yourself!'

'Did you kill a Zulu Colonel!'

'Yes tell us how you killed a Zulu!'

'Did you do it with a dagger?'

'No it was a bayonet you silly ass! Ponto was armed!'

'His sword did it!'

'No he did it!'

'Did the old Zulu show fight – or was he too afraid of you Colonel to defend himself?'

'I should have been!'

'I'm positive I should have asked for quarter on the spot wouldn't you!'

'I believe the Colonel must have terrified him so much that he just died of fright!'

'And then they gave the Colonel the Victoria Cross!'

'Did Queen Victoria give you the Victoria Cross Colonel!'

'Of course she did! She always gave away her own crosses!'

'Oh I do think that is exciting! Do tell us Colonel how Queen Victoria handed you her Victoria Cross!'

'I wish the Colonel would go downstairs and kill a few of those Jazz-band Zulus *right now!* I'm sure he'd get the Victoria Cross all over again if he did!'

'I wish he would too – it's the world's worst band!'

'Couldn't you see your way Colonel to shoot up a few Zulus we have downstairs! Do say *yes* Colonel!'

'Yes Colonel Ponto – oh do say you will! They have been making the most diabolical noise you ever heard!'

'We'd see you got the Victoria Cross again if you could see your way clear to fight your way through the band Colonel Ponto!'

'We would help you!'

'Yes we would be behind you Colonel Ponto – to a man!'

'Only we'd just do it for the love of the thing!'

'Yes, we'd do it purely for the love of the thing!'

'We don't mind the Zulus really – but we wish they wouldn't make so much noise! We do wish you'd kill them Colonel! We should be terribly grateful to you if you would!'

'Oh do Colonel Ponto! We will come with you!'

The Colonel was a baffled Santa Claus – one who had expected to find a nursery asleep, but instead he had discovered waiting for him a wide-awake hornet's nest of fierce adults – who had made up their minds to impersonate their sleeping offspring – hold up the Old Bourgeois frosted Toy-fair Papa, when he came out from under the mantelpiece – and steal for themselves all his lovely toys, intended for the sleeping children, to stuff their own outsize voracious stockings and socks – led to the assault by a forty-ton grandmother – a witch and a Chelsea poetess. The gigantic face with the high-complexion of Montagu Mayors, eager and bald to a fault, flamed with its grin upon Ponto's left shoulder. One of Mayors' arms was hooked in the arm of Jasper Sommberbell who was a fine shrivelled prancing little nancy-mannie of thirty-nine (but the *nine* written as *zero*, minus its horrid tail, made *thirty*). The Colonel's large bottle-nose growing fiery in the heat of the circular apartment, the coarse white bristles of his moustaches protruding in a straight line from his trembling lip, he ploughed his way forward heavy-hearted and hot. Set in a network of sunburnt seams, two flint-blue eyes burst out of these withered pockets, with a coarse intensity, stiff with the stupid effort to *keep-smiling* in the face of this thunderous latter-day ambush.

'Behold the world's stoic nincompoop!' shouted Blackshirt angrily a key higher than the bombilation and bursts of osmundian joyfulness, as the Old Colonel slowly drove past the recess, encumbered with his violent cortège. 'Stoic about what? *His bottom!* Old sheep! Hoots! Step it out! Crack!'

Propagandist for oppressed respectability, whose picture he was, the old driven head-of-sheep or military mutton plodded on whither he was led, as best he might – but Dan turned away his head. He felt this was a persecution and his great irish heart very faintly and for form's sake bled. Horace had now gone.

'That old gilt-edged serf of an anonymous System that he is – what can he do? He is as important as a half-pay commissionaire – to open taxis and be tipped! That big-business whose armed servant he was has for its trade-mark the Union Jack oh yes – a rare international emblem! – the old son-of-a-bitch is no better than a nigger if that – he is less than *Uncle Tom.* He has not the nigger-kindness even! He is the sheep – that kills! That is *the sheep that kills! Who* kill? – oh just anybody at all he is *told to* – by anybody at all who has learnt the proper word of commandin good enough english to put the old robot in motion (half his kings spoke french – some spoke dutch, some german – in future they may speak *anything* so long as they know the word of command *Quick March* it is enough! The sheep *will do his duty!* Never fear – he can be depended on *to do his duty!*) Dangerous old sheep – that deserved all he gets and more. Bourgeois-robot! Shoooooot!'

But as he *shoooted* his bourgeois-robot off, he was mastered by a fine impulse to express in a more rounded and hand-and-foot manner the matter of his diatribe. So Blackshirt sprang up, with the briskness of a Wild West wind, right in the very rear of the departing Old Colonel – rushing in amongst the followers and sightseers that pressed upon the heels of the privileged firing-party. He rushed in and he planted a well-directed kick upon the broadest part of his small clothes which caused Ponto to spring off the ground in nervous dismay. His movement of alarm was that suggestive of something having been *removed* from (rather than of something having been *conferred upon*) the seat of the person in question – such as a direct booted hit upon the backside causes to those of a *receptive* habit rather than of an *active* habit. So to protest by posterior shrinkage – in the passive recoil forward of the belly opposite – Ponto bucked, the wrong way round.

Not omitting to *keep-smiling* (true *sportsman* even when in the part of the hunted instead of hunter – oh a 'good-loser'! – a *gentlemanly* domestic – a first-class old whipping-boy – the world's easiest blockhead to bleed – the gull for which every shark must have prayed since the world began) Ponto looked back over his shoulder in the act of bucking, into the enormous shining morning-face of Monty Mayors (who had honoured him, in his belief, with the roguish sub-rosa accolade). With that full-fledged full-moon smile following him – a gigantic red lunar threatening satellite – his own timid *keep-smiling* smile, of pained reproach, did mingle – signalling about that root in the B.T.M. – an *it's-not-done-old-man* look from one public-school boy to another went with it – to which Mayors (who had been a staff-major in France) responded, in bluff public-school fashion too – used to the Trenches. The great red threatening satellite (its high blood-pressure doubled) even turned upon the crowd with a fierce exclamation – passing on the *it's-not-done* look with great staff-officer gusto to them. Monty Mayors rebuked everybody in the holiday-crowd for the unauthorized hoofing of Ponto. The old bulldog was not *their* property! Kindly keep your feet to yourselves! Blackshirt the culprit had already returned to the recess.

Ponto shook himself like a mangy old dog to shake out the kick he felt there sticking to him – the blow below the Lonsdale Belt, against Queensberry Rules, that gives the knock-out to self-esteem nothing more.

'Take that!' remarked Blackshirt, when he sat down by Dan, and Dan blushed for his performance, for he did not think he should have kicked the Old Colonel who was in distress.

'Take that!' again said Blackshirt with satisfaction, for he did not seem at all to take it as Dan did. Even he did not speak again for some moments. Honour was satisfied.

But the blackshirted advocate rapidly returned to his argument, after his pause for the degustation of the kick.

'*The sheep that kills!*' he repeated – a little dreamily for him at first. 'The sheep that kills – it is his *respectability* that is his abominable passe-partout – that respectability of his that makes murder respectable. What a façade! Consider the crooks that shelter behind him! No armaments-chemist could exist without him – you can send such as Ponto out with poison-gas in a bomb in an airplane – he can poison with your gas-bomb a thousand people asleep in a village which has refused to pay you tribute, and such is the magic of his ridiculous rectitude, it does not look like *murder* – everyone will say that it is *only war*. He is perfection – that middleclass mask of respectability is worth its weight in gold – some super-Crippen, any super-poisoner or mass-murderer can operate behind it with impunity. Why, behind such a mask some Archimedes might proceed to the destruction of the world – it is not unthinkable!'

But still Dan did not believe altogether in the kick. His averted countenance betrayed a concealed aversion for the kick in spite of everything – also Blackshirt had begun talking about War again, and as he never listened to that he had nothing fresh to divert him from the ethics of Blackshirt's sortie against a defenceless Old Colonel. But Blackshirt saw that he was disposed to criticize his sortie, so he said –

'You did not approve of my kicking him?'

Dan would not commit himself to an expression of disapproval. He confined himself to the collateral criticism of a melancholy gazing abstraction – directed at *about* the level of the kickable hind-quarters of the passers-by.

'Pierpoint would laugh at you if you spoke of pitying such a person!' Blackshirt's face was wrung with the ghost of a suppressed pierpointean laugh. 'Old toothless battle-dog – why should I not kick him – except that one soils one's shoe in kicking that well-fed, well-groomed old pulp of his. It is the stupidest clockwork. You may believe me when I tell you that.'

But the Old Colonel was returning, and Dan experienced some alarm, for he feared that Blackshirt might again set upon him, and to be candid he feared that then that toothless battle-dog might give *him* Dan a toothless bite by mistake – and he certainly thought, as he looked at him, that he had a very fierce appearance!

But a distraction occurred which momentarily relieved Dan of these more urgent reasons for alarm.

Bloated by the heat and blinded by the glitter of the assembly, and fatigued by the effort incessantly to advance against undisciplined odds and in the teeth of a drum-fire of furious remarks, Ponto (before he was aware of his proximity) ran head-on into General Walker-Trotter. General Walker-Trotter was if anything more stupefied by his surroundings than was Colonel Ponto.

The General merited the extra bit of rank – for his face was a more indomitable scarlet even than that of the Colonel, whereas his moustache had that bluish tinge that all the best Old Colonels' moustaches have, and without which the true collector would have at once turned down *any* Old Colonel, as a palpable forgery. Ponto had the egg-blue in the middle too. But it was not the *true blue* of General Walker-Trotter, and its blending with the urine-green of the extremity left much to be desired.

Lady Harriet – as General Walker-Trotter stumbled forward upon a genuinely old-porty gout-infested leg – vociferated in his ear. General Walker-Trotter was as deaf as a post – *genuinely* on the deaf side – but Lady Harriet shouted to show him he was deaf, and if he wasn't he ought to be, and she bellowed at him her mouth thrust out like a trumpet –

'Gen-er-al! I say General. Do tell us once more how you got through the Kyber Pass – with TEN-PICKED-MEN!'

'TEN-PICKED-MEN! *Surely you remember* General Walker-Trotter! You *must* remember that!'

'Yes you surely must remember! Don't you remember General – PICKING the men!'

'Of course he remembers!'

'No he doesn't remember!' Lady Harriet announced, breathless from the attack, shaking her head very ruefully at him indeed. 'General Walker-Trotter doesn't remember!'

'No – he doesn't remember! He's *forgotten!*' exclaimed Stephen Boyce. 'It's quite escaped his memory!'

'It has completely gone out of his head!'

'He can't for the life of him recall!'

'Yes' said Lady Harriet for dramatic effect, in her lighter voice for ordinary use – for those who had ears to hear – young drums, a good scent, sharp sight – very depressed. '*He's forgotten!* He *has* forgotten!'

With dismay in her face Lady Harriet regarded General Walker-Trotter.

But her sepulchral announcement had damped the party entirely: somebody burst out in a burning lisp of arch reproach –

'Oh I *do* think that's terribly disappointing! The General has completely forgotten!'

And it was at that moment that Colonel Ponto and the General collided, amidst a rapturous burst from both those affecting the General and those who had selected the Colonel – though it was agreed that the Colonel was the better man of the two, and that he charged with far more dash.

But General Walker-Trotter, and also Colonel Ponto, both believed it had been *himself* that had been the cause of this accident.

There was a great deal of throaty *I'm-sorry-sirring!* and of *I Beg your pardon sirs!* Then in their hoarse Club-voices they sought to explain the origin of the regrettable contretemps. Each attempted to excuse himself to the other, until the crowd stamped in their delight at this heaven-sent accident.

Dan shrank from the turmoil in dismay, while, a little wrinkling smile upon her flat white lips, the aged Sib tottered into the recess. Panting she deposited her spent carcass in the corner, as far back as possible, so as not to get trodden upon.

The Blackshirt sat, a constantly sombre contemptuous witness, upon the other side of Dan.

'Don't you think this is great fun?' Sib panted at Dan. 'One of those old fools trampled upon me just now. I suppose he imagined himself on the battlefield. His eyes were very bloodshot – I felt rather frightened for the moment.'

Dan blushed deeply at these uncalled-for remarks and surreptitiously he sought, by slight and inconspicuous movements, to put an inconsiderable distance between himself and this talkative member of his supposed sex. At any moment there was the danger that she might ask him some horrible boudoirish question, that no one but a real woman could answer. Oh if Horace had only allowed him to go downstairs and help him, this would not have happened!

But with increasing ill-humour Blackshirt darkly watched this heavy circus – his eyes followed the confused and perspiring old 'battle-dogs', the performing Snobs of Thackeray in their ultimate decay, parading up and down in duty bound, covered with decorations which each stood for some uproarious joke – a Zulu pleasantry, an Ashanti burlesque, a farce at Magersfontein – the emblem of the *Sport of Kings* which had come to be the *Sport of Crooks*, turned into a new indoor-sport of sorts, of a parlour-order.

Their complexions (as much as the pallor of rice-powder, their regimental red) marked them down as *clowns*. At length he relieved his feelings as he said hoarsely to Dan –

'How this picked body of old bourgeois gulls *annoys* me – oh how they annoy me!'

And Dan looked up with alarm, for he had noticed nothing fresh, and now it seemed Blackshirt was about to lose his self-control again. Should Blackshirt engage in some rash enterprise, like the last or worse – *what might not become of the girl-he-left-behind-him!* With this old woman here – there was no knowing! He looked askance at the Sib off-duty.

'This is depressing!' exclaimed the Blackshirt again – and he became a little more definitely fascist. 'This sentimental savagery depresses me!' He spat. 'Which is the worse of the two – the tame old butts being dragged up and down this floor like naval targets, or those equally clownish gunners? I don't know. Both are bad diseases of the same sad system. Oh! Let us as a symbolical gesture join the servants downstairs, in their hot kitchens and stinking sculleries – they at least are the English and, though servants too, something unspoilt – but *this* is a tetter, this is a rot, that shows us all underneath it to be stagnant. Stagnant we are, but still potent – if this is a disease of our national old-age, then it can only be that *we* are not *the nation!* That is something else. *This* is an utter infirmity! – but it is not *us* – it is the System. As for us, we have all been betrayed – much more even than plundered – by these mountebanks – on both sides of this bitter carnival. They have sold us till there is nothing to sell except our bodies now – to hire out into a coolie-world! That they are doing too! They are busy at this moment cheapening us, so that next they may sell us to the Blacks!'

Dan was in absolute agreement with all Blackshirt had said about not going down into the hot kitchen, full of Sassenachs and rude pushing domestics, and agreed that even coarse unpleasant words as he had used – suggestive of cutaneous eruptions – were not too forcible to describe what he had observed upon the surface of the stock in the stock-pot and he felt he would never be able to eat another meal for weeks now not a square one – certainly not one with soup. He glanced at his neighbour and she was fast asleep.

'What is the solution?' with a heavy fluttering sigh Blackshirt asked of the air. 'Is it that the *nation* is after all the wrong notion? Perhaps it is. I stand outside the anglo-saxon world, that is by reason of my blood. I have no bond of sympathy with the Creeping Saxon really at all – never in anything but name have they been our masters. The real masters of England have died out. Old germanic serfs, figureheads, is all that is left – such do more harm than good – they are excellent decoys on the grand scale – there is no longer an English Nation!'

However Blackshirt seemed to soar out of his despondency and to find his anger again, and Dan trembled as he spoke anew – jumping as he said *look*.

'Look how they are driven up and down – their offence is to be the summit of a hierarchy. As the last ridiculous survivals of a military caste they are driven and manhandled. – So that old feminizing mænad Harriet leads the attack – that *tricoteuse* so much socially upon the *wrong* side of the Barricade – making the most of both worlds bad luck to her!'

And, very fascist this time, Blackshirt almost openly hurled his fascist curse at this female enemy of the liberties of the community of Freemen. He would have burnt her in effigy as a witch as soon as look at her.

'Oh this sentimental savagery, that delights to think of itself as "rebel" – what is one to say to *that?* What are these bands of people doing but rehearsing upon these old dummies the darker and bloodier insults of Terror and of Revolution – all the time!

But is it not evident that they are rehearsing their own destruction, too? For does not this old harpy Harriet here owe *everything* – the little brassy tinkle of her verses for the grown-up nursery included – to the civilized order of the Western World – which in all her actions she insults, along with her fat walking-adenoid of a brother, Osmund! What would she be *tell me that* – except some embittered middle-aged char – derided for the airs she gave herself about her grandeurs past – if it were not for the remnants of Order – which, as an interesting "revel", she is in every case committed to flout!'

And the Blackshirt pointed his fist made into a pistol with its index, at Lady Harriet Willoughby Finnian Shaw, and Harriet noticing this in the midst of her sport nodded to him to say *yes* – what a good time she was having! – for she remembered the *Anthology* in the midst of her military sport.

'But these lousy old dishonoured chiefs and captains' and Blackshirt thrust out his blackshirted chest, 'if they had a *touch* even of the French fury – if they had, not the bravery of the intellect, but a horse's sense – they would remind old Harriet of the dirty money that alone permits her to expand herself in brutish amusements of this order, but for which in return she gives *nothing* – they would at once snatch off their ridiculous medals or their equivalents (got for *England Home and Beauty* fighting simple Boer farmers) and fling them at her too. But no – they are as dull and sheepish as she is violent and splenetic. They are locked up in this System just as they were locked up in that waiting-room – worst of all, *anyone* now can lock them up – who has the money to buy the key. They would kill Harriet on the spot if she were proscribed in the due form by their Hairdresser. They would blow their own brains out if they had their salaries paid by a Soap King and were given the order – "Self-Kill! Quick-March!" – and another bar to their D.S.O. was attached to the act!'

Dan became thoroughly uneasy. His feet pained a great deal – his digestion grew somewhat deranged by the impact of the meaningless words. He gave the Blackshirt one mute glance then he looked down again.

'That is the *politics* of what you see. Such politics are nothing. Mixed up with vanity as they are, they are in fact the *politics* of *personal vanity*. Personal vanity is no politics itself – it attracts politics. Every pastime has its attendant politics – witness homosexuality, that is another instance. To-day a *politics of Revolt* goes with that. You know that? It is immaterial.'

Dan could not see why these horrid scientific words should be used in 'broadcast' at all but he knew that they were and he had grown to expect it, but it always made him feel uncomfortable.

'The public good is here the glitter only of the social desires of an ageing group of wealthy romantic amateurs called Finnian Shaw – expressed in the terms of *oppression of youth*. "Youth" is in this case bluff of course. Having analysed the explicit politics, let us turn to that. It is the *personal vanity* you must cut out and pin down. Here we have it. It is very simple. The *Old Colonel* is as it were a Christmas-card figure. Now the vanity is simple.'

Blackshirt paused and Dan observed that he moistened his lip with his tongue, as Horace moistened his lip with his tongue. It was the sign that the climax of a great 'broadcast' was at hand.

'Harriet and Osmund – you see them, Osmund and Harriet – they are compelled to perpetuate the politics of the *child-parent-war*. The *child-parent-war* is put across by means of the emotions aroused by the *age-complex* and the *youth-complex* dominating the first Post-war decade. The *child-parent-war* is the war next in succession to the *sex-war*. You have heard of *sex-war?* Yes. (For the break-up of the aryan Family-idea, two "wars" have been arranged. The *sex-war* covers the man-woman relationship: the *child-parent-war*, or the *age-war*, covers the child-parent relationship. This is a parallel "revolt". When these "wars" have been brought to bear in social life with full effect, the Family will have entirely disintegrated.) Now the middle-aged Harriet Finnian Shaw, when she has carefully picked an *Old Colonel* – one to be a good ripe fruity foil – she goes ahead. You see her in action engaged with an *Old Colonel* – an *Old Colonel* too good to be true. She is up-and-coming – she does not lack *fire*. There she is! There is the *Old Colonel!* I have not invented them – either her or the Old Colonel – you can see them with your own eyes – you may touch them! In her books you may read of them. All right! Many other people here are the same. Rejuvenated by the carefully picked *Old Colonels*, they fling themselves impulsively about, freshened up as a group by the chorus of sham-choristers. To give the "child"-colouring the Finnian Shaws attract an undergraduate-looking rabble: with that monkey-glanding of their social body, they go out to hunt (in their family game-preserves – beneath the oaks of Old England) the *Old Colonel.* He is a deep-scarlet, white-bristled, puffing old bird.'

Blackshirt pointed at Ponto.

'Regard this sport, if you desire a more philosophic or technical definition of it, as a Time-sport. You may do so because it depends upon a pathologic sensitiveness to the notion of *Time.* The *Old Colonel* is a dracontine monstrosity. He is a creature of Time. He is a blood-red ghost of the Time-tracts, snorting about that historic undergrowth of the Dark Backward and Abysm. The Finnian Shaws themselves are half in the Past. They know the Time-paths. They go to hunt the *Old Colonels* in the same frame of mind as the big-game sportsman. They are celebrated Globe-trotters – tourists of an earth conceived chronologically as *history* – as a Time-ball – an eclectic historical playground. Or, better, they are semi-victorian sportsmen of *the dark-continent* of Time – a temporal Africa. It is there they pursue the *Old Colonels* of the epoch of Pendennis – it is there they will leave their bones. They will *die* – one by one – still hunting the *Old Colonels* and trapping the *Old Spinsters.* A fantastic destiny! – That is all. In what I have told you, you may forget the politics if you like. It is a dreadful back-cloth. It is a red mist – a red dawn-mist you understand!'

Near the foyer of the universal carmagnole let loose for the Old Colonels there was an intense disturbance too – for there was dished up the cream of the entertainment. It was Commander Perse R.N. was there – so uncommonly well-equipped to represent the pensioned back-numberdom of the King's Navee – in *any* Club Window whatever of the Pall Mall of Balaclava or the Piccadilly of the young Dizzy (and if people have not remarked its disappearance, but still believe that there is Clubland with great windows in which squat eupeptic veterans, shouting *Demme sir!* – flourishing the *Times* in their red-enamelled or tropically-tanned fists, preparing to write upon the Club notepaper their hackneyed letter – why that is not to be wondered at, seeing that the Press is interested to perpetuate this illusion – in spite of the fact that the 'country' referred to by the Old Colonels has long ago been devoured by 'the dogs' of one breed and another, and there is nothing but a gaunt bone left). This Gallant Officer had been led to the largest arm-chair with every exaggerated exhibition of solemn-faced respect as befitted his age and rank, by the happily-prancing Lord Phoebus – and then Commander Perse R.N. – with one hand in the correct position to advertise lumbago, a stiff leg thrust out to show he was not so young as he used to be (when he was a middie at Aboukir Bay or out beating up a Plate-Fleet or convoying that out of Pernambuco) slowly assumed, with a salvo of asthmatic puffs, a sitting position.

It was quite upon the extremity of the settee (heaved-to upon the Commander's weather-bow) that Lord Osmund sat. Smiling his slyest good-natured encouragement, he cooed in his nose at this tit-bit of a nautical veteran. Meantime a pack of Chatterboxes and Gossips all passionately sub-Osmund, clung on to the back of the Commander's arm-chair, like street-arabs upon lamp-posts at a Lord Mayor's Show. But as many as possible (the greatest favourites) sat upon the floor, cross-legged at the Commander's feet, and fixed their worshipping eyes and their glances of abject juvenile respect – with mouths in which butter-would-not-melt half-open – upon the face of this aged Neptune. At the very last moment an enormous jewish man rushed up. He was of great breadth and stature, and none other than Monty Mayors himself – who had, in a tremendous panic at being late, forsaken the exhausted Ponto at the last moment – his face (of that dark apple-red, of high-blood pressure) was flushed – it shone where apples do – and inextinguishably he wore a gigantic whole-time smile of outside self-welcome – and if his head was completely bald (though only thirty-five said he mesmerically) he had two large dimples – altogether a man bound to be popular if he wished to. Thrusting aside a sprawling figure, with frantic rummaging fists, Monty Mayors rapidly cleared a space upon the floor for himself. Then, with a resounding crash, he flung himself at full-length before the Commander – a massive hip rising so high into the air that Raymond Freedlander, who was small, could no longer see the Commander at all.

These arrangements completed, the séance was quite ready

to start, and a hush fell upon the charmed circle by the main grate.

'Do tell us Commander Perse' thereupon boomed Lord Osmund, 'how you ran your sloop aground – do you remember – when you were pursued by Malay pirates in the Gulf of New Guinea!'

As pleased as pleased – on top of the weather – certified master of any situation – the right man in the right place – a square peg in a square hole, and willing and ready to give a square british deal if ever man was – the bluff Commander, with a last pat at his lumbago, rolled in a throaty quarter-deck growl, that was two degrees better than the most blusterous Conrad –

'When I was in the Gulf of New Guinea! Is it the yarn of how I drove *Hesperus* ashore in the Gulf of New Guinea – when I was chased by Pirates out of Ass-*sam!* Is that what you young people want me to tell you!' and the Commander grew more and more fruity and avuncular – the most fine old crusted Children's-hour-B.B.C.-Uncle would have been a damp squib beside him.

'That's a long yarn, my lads, a long yarn – but I'll do my best to tell it to you!' The Commander spoke in that ringing voice of one whose word has once been martial-law.

The reverential audience at the Commander's feet writhed with delighted chuckling and with splutters expressed their mad mirth under-hatches – and the larger Mayors-boy even literally burst, like a big punctured tyre, and went off into an exhibitionist-spasm of hysteria – rolling his bald head like a big red ball-bearing in the large cup of his meaty red fist, that had fought the Boche for four long years at Corps Headquarters.

'Now then Monty!' said Lord Osmund reprovingly to the Mayors-boy – (not *open* fits of laughter please – the sham spellbound circle of tiny nursery tots, crouched around Nanny or Granny spinning her yarns of long ago, should not be broken – not so that the prosing Aunt Sally should be put out of countenance ever).

But the Admiral of the Fleet had come up behind Osmund and he had been staring with a surly weather-eye wide open upon the Commander. Everyone had been very disappointed at once with the appearance of the Admiral of the Fleet when he had come in: it had been a great disappointment. He was a mangy old sea-dog one had universally agreed. At a glance one could see that he was a rotten old over-praised and over-advertised *Admiral.*

At all events one had fought shy of him and left him to stalk about by himself as he deserved, which may have embittered Benbow, for he looked black. He must have been a rather out-of-the-way Admiral perhaps, for he now touched Osmund upon the shoulder and Lord Osmund looked up very surprised indeed – for he had never in all his life been touched by an Admiral before – or even by a Colonel. So he stared a little hard at the half-pay Vice-Admiral, with even a note of misgiving in his querulous questioning eye-over-his-shoulder. But what was Lord Osmund's consternation as it were, when the Admiral made a sign to him – which conveyed that the Admiral would have a word with his lordship apart. Lord Osmund rose at once and went aside with the Admiral.

This was a disturbing episode – the good Commander, against Osmund's return, did nothing but crack a few jokes about hard-tack and Jacob's Ladders, and all the children roared together with Christmas Matinée laughter. But Lord Osmund came back speedily, and it was at once remarked that he looked rather grave. He stood before the settee and he said to Commander Perse –

'Commander Perse, were you ever a member of the Teneriffe Club?'

'Why no I can't say I was Lord Osmund!' the Commander said with a great deal of heartiness.

'Never been in it?'

'Ah that's another matter!' the Commander bluffly crashed. 'Been in it!' he bellowed. 'Why what sailor I should like to know has not?'

Admiral Benbow, stationed behind Lord Osmund, was examining the Commander very closely indeed, that was plain to everybody. He now stepped forward and addressed the Commander directly, in the bluntest manner possible.

'What was your last ship sir!'

'To whom have I the pleasure of addressing myself?'

'Never mind who I am sir! What was your last ship sir –

that is what I asked. Was it by chance the good ship *Buncombe* sir!'

'*Buncombe* sir! Why no sir! I've never heard of that ship sir!'

'I thought perhaps you had sir! But you have not yet informed me what ship you last sailed in sir – or perhaps you'd rather not!'

'Why no sir – why should I object sir? Not at all! My last ship was a sloop of war – it was *Hesperus*.'

'*Hesperus* sir! Such a ship was never heard of, outside of your fertile imagination sir!'

'I beg your pardon sir – this is most extraordinary behaviour, sir, whoever you may be!'

'Shall I tell you who *you* are sir!'

'Sir, do you accuse me of prevarication!'

'No sir, I declare you to be an impostor sir!'

'An impostor!'

'Yes sir an arch-impostor!'

'But this is unheard of sir!'

'It is, you are right.'

Turning with majesty towards the startled and delighted assembly, the Admiral then said –

'This man you may be interested to know gentlemen was for a good number of years the hall-porter at the Teneriffe Club! He was known there as *Perce*, which was short for Percy.'

Sensation.

The Commander sprang to his feet at this with an alacrity strangely contrasting with his period-descent into the chair – with all the picturesque precautions against the tweaks of the correctest Club-land lumbago. Also as he rose he sent flying several of the more clinging of his listeners, and actually he kicked Monty Mayors slightly upon the mouth – which Monty Mayors had wide open with affected surprise.

'Sir, I don't know who you are!' he bawled in a much less genial fashion. 'But what I do know is that I do not propose, as an officer and a gentleman, to sit here and hear myself insulted!'

Exit at top speed bogus-Commander.

All the excited tongues were now loosened at once. But Commander Perse was a local figure greatly respected for miles round – as a very breezy naval personality. On several occasions the

Commander had been entertained by Osmund and never failed to kill everybody with laughter – he was one of the very best of their exhibits, and no one had ever suggested there was anything wrong with him or detected a flaw. And Lord Osmund did not seek to disguise his resentment with the Admiral – from the start the Admiral had been at best a kill-joy! Then after all suppose it were a mistake! But the flight of the Commander suggested that there was some foundation for the scepticism of the Admiral. Who could this daring impersonator of Old Commanders be – that was the question? But then the Admiral, who would not leave bad alone, or leave a shred of illusion to anybody, remarked that he was not even particularly *old*. Osmund was by now quite positive that he did not care for this Admiral, although he had always been very fond of Admirals in the past.

'All that lumbago was put on' insisted this most depressing of all Admirals. 'He was a hale and hearty middle-aged man when I last saw him in uniform – that of a commissionaire – a few years ago. He put on that lumbago for your benefit gentlemen!'

Monty Mayors rose to his feet very annoyed at the kick in the mouth and after him everyone else who was curled up on the ground got up and gradually everyone became very cross and at last decided to go and stop *Perce* and perhaps have him arrested or to duck him. But they most of them passed on to the party devouring Ponto or Teach instead, who by this time were very docile and exhausted and did not move very much.

But from the focal point by the fire, where the impostor had been discovered, even simulating lumbago, discouragement soon had extended throughout the room: and though Lady Harriet's voice could still be heard vociferating *Ten Picked Men*, the collapse of the Commander had thrown a shadow over the entire proceedings. Lord Osmund became a quite listless figure – he snubbed the Admiral of the Fleet, who eventually left the scene altogether and went downstairs to do a little stiff nautical dancing with any Lady Hamiltons who presented themselves. Lord Phoebus dreamily took up one of his toys – a small crinolined doll that squeaked and fainted – and the Blackshirt and Dan relapsed into an unbreakable silence side by side, the Sib slightly snoring now, her mouth open. Only Harriet still nagged away at Ponto in a corner.

XI The Thresholds

Ratner followed Archie in sluggish step, a foot behind, into the American Bar. They stood inside. The Finn roared –

'I *am not* the worsh for drink! *Who* said I was wursh!'

He was struggling in the corner where it was dark, his eyes shining like a cat's at night, and attempting to remove his waistcoat. Three little whispering men were pinning him against the wall and as often as he drew the waistcoat off a check-shirted shoulder, they drew it on again, expostulating under their breaths. He must *not* undress! – they really could not allow him to undress! – Knut slipped through a door that stood open behind them, and the three little fretful shapes of white-breasted men, out of whose grasp he had popped, went too, in a scandalized scuttle – a trio of face-saving demireps.

With an indifference massively-mental Archie surveyed this paltry event. There were perspectives in time as in Space. And Arch's eyes seemed to cast everything that was present back into diminishing distances. Abstract and empty blocks made up his foregrounds. Life's funny flux only existed as it were at the end of a telescope reversed to make objects insignificant. He shot his Match – it flew for him down a perspective of Chirico.

From the Bar-threshold Archie had watched a short-lived event, upon which the door closed with a bang. He had sped a Match – it was his comment upon all actions engaged in by men that had not that orthodox block-like emptiness. He turned about, he passed through the door and stood upon the threshold beyond it, just within the passage. Ratner turned after him – he followed him through and stood at his side. One looked down the passage to the left, the other looked down the passage to the right. The band manufactured its melodic treacle, thumped in imitation of abrupt machinery – a titanic treacle-can factory. Shock after shock – then more sad sickly sugar.

They moved aside to admit people to the American Bar.

'Have you a light?' asked Archie in a husky undertone.

'Yes' croaked the other one thrusting a damp hand into a slit of his dumpy Harlequin get-up, and gave Archie a book of matches. The first Archie tore off and dispatched at a person dressed as a character from a Sovkino Film. He lighted a cigarette and handed the book of matches back to Ratner.

'I shall go out into the garden,' Archie said not looking at Ratner as he said it, and he did not move. In a moment Ratner turned his head in the opposite direction. Then Margolin stealthily left his side, as a man steps away from a sleeper.

When Ratner had heard him disappear, he looked back. The crowded door of the great saloon was facing him across the passage. He walked over to it and stood for some time upon its threshold.

He seemed asleep, he was rocked by the press of people and their contacts were purely mechanical. There was no friction, no fights, upon this sea-bottom. Nothing stung. No one was eaten. Such was the physical law. Mentally there was another one – sting, eat, fight! Several passing Belles Dames sans Merci remarked a coy eye intercepting their own (and anxious to tell them a Complex) coming out of a small man with a sad fat yellow drooping face. His melancholy fish-eye swam after several female forms a little distance. But he abruptly left his slumbrous mooring upon the threshold and took two steps into the crowd.

'Hallo Jimmie!'

A short depressed bald middle-aged man showed great pleasure at seeing what he called "Jimmie".

'Hallo!' in a bitter velvety bass and smirk to match growled Ratner. This was his normal life. In the presence of this person he began to act, becoming the normal Ratner and he was with friends.

XII Now Jonathan Bell was an Old John Bull

A heavy coyness descended upon Ratner. Always coy, with these old friends – these tried, trusty and well-beloved fools – Ratner's great coyness was at its coyest. Elsewhere this great coyness often languished, when he became a listless sullen Joo enough, without any coyness.

Jonathan Bell was a small capitalist – a small useful class. Sometimes 'For Jonathan Bell' a book would be published, as Americans do. Ratner published sometimes a book 'For Jonathan Bell'. At his own valuation (sex-star of first magnitude

– a Dark Star but *Class A* for Sex) the Rat has shone in the firmament of 'John' beside the Scorpion, as unchallenged as the Ram, ever since Armageddon's bloody night had become an institution – 'Jimmie' a 'poet', a notable practical bookman, a poetical-publisher. Whatever Jim wished 'John' to see, 'John' saw. But tactful Jimjulio slyly swallowed as well, by pretending to, much that John set store by – just sentimental odds and ends – there was reciprocity – in brief these two were friends. Two good friends of long-standing they were – one fool and one knave – as simply as the bold images of an Alphabet, or the Jack of a Poker-pack – but the fool had his slyness, though the knave was no fool.

Bell's wife was there tonight as a picturesque *plein-air* drudge – echo of student-days doubtless when all the London art-girls were John-mad and gypsyish – she was an indistinct Chelsea gypsy. As much as her faded face could greet the bilious grease-spot that swam into her ken (in the person of Julius) she mildly greeted it, and all together they passed on down the room and Ratner (easily master in any such mild man-and-wife combination) – so english, so earliest-bloomered-tandem – took the harmless pair out of doors into the garden, become accessible through the french-windows thrown open, with a view of the bandstand.

'I didn't expect to find you here' says Bell.

'I didn't expect to find myself here!' says Ratner, and he looks simultaneously bitter and coy – much more coyer even than before – as bitter as sour-grapes hung a hundred light-years away up in an old star could make an embittered fox.

And immediately Bell and his respectable art-student *gattin* – both nice nobodies and true – *knew* that – well, *as per usual!* – they well-nigh wagged their fingers as they were expected to, at the shrinking smirking Coy-one – they nearly clicked their tongues and tossed their heads at naughty-naughty – that incorrigible 'Jimmie'! They foreboded, nay they as a matter of routine *foreknew*, that (direct-or-indirectly) something affecting the more skittish of the endocrines, the gonadal glands of internal secretion, was at stake, was on foot – those secretions about which they knew so much from incessant hearsay, from indefatigable analysis – from every imaginable meaty angle, both from above and from beneath – whose doctrinal gushings gave birth, if to nothing else, *always* to a 'Complex'. *Know* them! Indeed they camped in these sluggish ratnerish canals – they had followed the rat-like *libido* in all its cloacal windings!

Johathan Bell was an old John Bull and a foolish John Bull was he! Good honest Jonathan Bell was good honest fool enough, and Ratner loved and respected him for it – Ratner did not respect sharp people or sharp mental sharks, that would be self-respect, which was impossible – and Ratner *loved* no one but fools, and the *respectability* it was of Jonathan Bell that made him loved by Ratner and many others and of course *respected* – for being, without effort, so *respectable* – and in consequence so *loved*. When was a fool not a fool? Ultimately these complements agree and are found to be one.

Good oak-timbered 'John' Bell was 'the rudest man in London' – no one was blunter, more straight-from-the-shoulder – *but he was a born audience for a Complex*. Bluff and muddled did blunt 'John' ever ask himself how it was all those love-sick blondes he heard about pursued 'Jimmie' night and day, with their unwanted attentions? *How was it* the blondes that came 'John's' way did not lie awake at night whispering 'John' to a hot pillow? But 'John' Bell was *modest* – as well as being true-blue he did not insist upon Lothario, where himself was concerned at all. But *one* thing there was that certainly *never* occurred to 'John' Bell and that was that the love-sick blondes he heard about and sometimes was told he had caught sight of in the distance, were really being plastered and treated for the heart or heartlessness with the flattering specifics of 'Jim' in tireless ratnerish pursuit – what time 'Jim' loudly protested to 'John' that it was *awful* and all the blondes in the world were hard upon *his* heels – that he did so wish they'd stop and give him a breather! In confidence, in his coyest droop (confiding as man-to-man to 'John' – and then as man-to-woman to Mrs Bell) 'Jimmie' would tell how *sometimes* he hated it and then *sometimes* again he rather liked it! *Sometimes* (he confessed) he wished he could go away somewhere – where he *would never see a woman again*, for six months! – But Mrs Bell had pointed out in private to Mr Bell that *Jim Rat grew fat!* She had drawn the attention of the masculine eye to that accretion of yellow adipose (especially at the neck) but Bell put on weight himself and grew balder daily.

Although glad to hear that Jim Rat grew fat, 'John' Bell was a man of his ease! – Now 'John' Bell was not fond of change and he feared the truth did 'John' Bell, which he fought tooth and nail wherever met – and this sounded like *truth* pardie!

Now *change* was the last thing that 'John' Bell would brave, and change-of-life in friends spelled change-of-life in self, and 'John' would not have much to do with such suggestions, that came from women, and 'John' was a man of his word.

Now 'Jimmie' wished 'John' to believe. Now 'John' did not wish to be troubled to resist and *not* to believe – ever – in anything. Now 'John' would rather *believe* any one who very much wanted him to believe, than give himself the trouble to *disbelieve* – to be sceptic (oh what energy)! Now 'John' had always inclined *to believe* – let others *value* – leave me, as for me, in peace! *Peace in MY Time Oh Lord!* And there was Peace! And the price paid was always – *belief!*

But to cease to give hospitality to Jimmie's valuation of 'Jimmie,' was not that to turn a deaf ear to sweet self, for 'John' Bell? For 'John' Bell to alter his views of his *friends* – why that would be for 'John' Bell to alter all that he saw in himself! *Other* changes, of changing view-points, were involved in this too – much too drastic for comfort – far too truthful for *peace*. (Your friend is your mirror – take care!)

A change of view is a change of life! Out upon such changes! Out upon such face-abouts! No! *'John' Bell would stick to his friends!* (At 'friends' – a tremolo – loud cheers from all Bell's 'friends'!)

So 'friend' Jimmie (though at all times certainly so unaccountably, even for others uncomfortably, *unhappy*-in-love) knew of *one* ear that would never be closed against a good fruity Complex! And that ear was the ear of Jonathan Bell, Patron of Author and Client of Publisher – *Long Live John Bell!* And the dried up little fig of an ear of Mrs Bell – that too would listen and give-ear to the complex – though that was because Jimjulio was a successful private-presser and abetter of her good honest husband, hearty Jonathan Bell (not quite Bull after all).

So Jonathan Bell, frowning nervously, and Mrs Bell, and last but not least Split-Man, sat together at a tin-table, beneath the lenten trees, waiting for coffee. Professional as the catholic Confessor – the Doctor, or the Kislar Aga – Jimjulio bent his heavy piercing and doctrinal eye upon these two dumb heads of sheep – preparatory to propaganda. He bent his shining eyes upon them before teaching them about himself – about themselves – about a quantity of third parties. What part did the gonadal glands play, amongst animals that went upright, separated into female and male, immersed in complex sentimental transactions that obscured the gonadal glands! (Einstein, if that impresses you, was upon the side of the endocrines.) Answer! *A masterpart!* And he would bring tham *back to the (g)Land* – back to their glands – and see that they never moved far away from their glands (for he travelled in sex-literature, and sex-politics, and SEX in all its many forms was the great hobby and profitable business of his earthly days – for everyone who wanted to get away from his glands for half an hour that he knew – to drink a cup of tea or write a letter – Ratner would put the matter in its right light and no sentimental nonsense. Then the triumph of The Glands (like The Sex) spelled 'Power'. And Adler-like (being a minor Adler) Ratner admitted 'power-complex' as basis of ego. (Sex was really all bluff – *power* the thing). And he would *glandify* everything as far as his personal social puddle was concerned, so that he might rule the waves – so that he could pull the sex strings, he would, that made the figure work – in the way *he* required it to work – not in the way *it* might happen to want to work! No! And the fat impending upon the eye – in a straight line across the eyeball, as straight as the path of the print across this page (the upper lid nothing but a rudiment, lost in the bulging drop-curtain of swarthy suet) gave Ratner such a lowering look (he felt as he got ready) of vulpine craft, as he was grinning – that he anticipated the expression of surprise that came into the face of honest 'John', and he understood that there was something that called for immediate correction. So *instinctively* he turned his head *sideways* – and he opened his left eye as wide as it would go, seeking to impart an appearance of absent-minded candour to the face out of which the sex-wisdom was to rattle and drop.

Some heavy he-jokes and the strong meat of a little *for-men-only* observations, passed between 'Jim' and 'John' – Mrs Bell contributed a rather mouldy slice of a care-worn smile, to be a sport. The lynx-eyed Sex-professor began to touch upon various topics of his choice – he touched upon this that and the other – with a heavily-confidential, retiring and apologetic, patronizing omniscience.

There was a peroxide fellow-publisher in a small way, just gone into business. Had 'John' heard? Yes 'John' knew. Jimjulio told 'John' he had seen the press. Of course he had seen the *Press*. 'John' gathered he had had some hand in selling her an old Press and he had. (Jimjulio had long smelt out the land.) But business was not business. Oh no. Or any business got well hidden under the couple of yards of skirt-material of the peroxide person of the new woman publisher. (Name Paula Kennedy. Married. Separated.) What after all does the Press matter John Bell – or any old Press! If you press Mrs Kennedy, in the right place, the Press is yours in theory John Bell! How did the funds behind the venture come? That is the essential point, my little Johnny! Via the peroxide attractions! How by the same token are the funds to go? They can only be extracted if at all *by pressure of the person* – not by attending to the Press! No – there is no occasion to talk about old iron, when there is *that* short-cut my good honest Jonathan – academic to think of Capital as some, solid non-volatile. 'Capital' is the human heart – heart-blood, the ridiculous brain of average men and average women, *and* last but not least don't forget it 'John' Bell (for all 'John' Bells have unreclaimed, darkly-untutored tracts, where there is still the 'cult' of 'spirits', and where Astaroth would be stoned) last not least gonadal centres my boy, of men and of women – and Jimjulio never talked about old iron or about office-furniture or even such baubles as gold and silver, to give 'Jim' his Joo – but *always* about flesh and blood – fleshily about blood, and about flesh fishily – and the blood was always *hot* blood – if *he* was to be believed. *Kaltes Blut* (similar to his) Joo misliked, so he disregarded. The world of cold-bloods was out of the picture. He was out of the picture – out of the machine – he only recognized those that were in it – the sausage-meat – the bluffed not the bluffers. So.

Well then with Mrs Kennedy a problem to frown and also to laugh over was here – a proper sex-puzzle. Well Ratner frowned, and he laughed too – coquettish, *in spite of* his frowning-self, in a rush of quick sneering rattles. He ogled Mrs Bell – he blushed coyly at the simple husband. The stern and unpalatable facts of economics were transmuted (express for the dull ears of honest 'John' Bell) into coarse and juicy morsels at once – all hot and scent-stunk, fat and dripping, from the pantry of 'Analysis': and oh poor 'John' would not have to have second sight he wouldn't to divine that *here* was material for another fine old mess, perhaps the fruitiest yet – into which a seasoned Lothario or a Restive-Old-Bretonne might well get himself my word even at his time of life – and what a fine old litter of 'Complexes' afterwards!

'Well I don't like fat women' said honest 'John' with a ponderous emphasis, as though a fat woman had just dropped on the top of him and forced out of him the uncompromising confession. Something was expected of him of course 'John' understood, and that he got over like this – once and for all – the great 'fatness' of Mrs Kennedy would excuse 'John' Bell for the rest of the time from licking his bull-dog chops at her unseductive peroxide effigy and he was glad, for he had seen her – there could be no illusion!

'No I know you don't 'John'!' Ratner assented. – 'John's' sex should be waived by special decree – that was settled – all right – a *personal* interest, no more.

'So I couldn't sleep with her!' 'John' stood aside – but let there be no misunderstanding – *with any other woman* (except an exceedingly fat woman) – 'John' Bell's your man!

Ratner croaked and sneered, he was all easy indulgence – he rewarded this super-simple old 'John' Bull with the approval conveyed in his laugh of a patron. But after that he smiled circumspectly – for he did not quite like to hear the words *don't want to sleep* from *any* lips – they were boastful and not in the best of taste!

Then Ratner began to look thoughtful, as befitted what he was about to say.

'I don't like fat women' he then weightily confessed. And a hundred greasy beds – a long (unsatisfactory) perspective – were intended to rush into the ken of the person privileged to hear – deeply impressed. – The *Burden of Fat Women* – Ratner gave himself a somewhat cross exhausted expression – as if but just issued from a twelve-hours' closely-contested event – in which he had been matched (alas overmatched – coyness itself!) with a 'fat woman' – the ringside of course the four walls of the 'fat woman's' sumptuous sleeping apartment – *sumptuous*, for of course the 'fat woman' herself (a motherly soul moved to paroxysms of maternal lust you would have to understand at the sight of old Joo) would have provided The Purse – and it would have to have been a *fat* Purse – that went without saying!

'It's such hard work!' Joo jibed in piteous howling accents, cut short by an unexpected eruption of phlegm. (The damp lenten air of the garden. Too many cigarettes!)

'Yes that's what *I* find!' 'John' Bell agreed in a hearty grumble.

'You have to go on and on!' Joo crossly remarked – the licentious subject announcing itself in his face by an expression as if he had a bitter taste in his mouth of gall and wormwood.

'I know' mumbled 'John' Bell frowning at the ground. 'They're sluggish!'

'It takes them usually half-an-hour —.' Ratner removed the phlegm with a handkerchief.

'Some never get there at all!' shouted 'John' Bell – in full tally-ho cry against the fat women.

Mrs Bell gave the two lads her benediction with a fraction of a dry smile, as she watched the dancers upon the gravel, and upon the sodden lenten grass beyond the gravel.

As the band was very crashy and urgent alas, and as Mrs Bell had exclusively watched the dancers, there was nothing for it, Jim Rat. With the same bitter and bilious facial acidity – which threw into relief the lines that depend from the wing of the nostril, sluggishly Jim Rat rose and Mrs Bell, too, supposed she must. So Mrs Bell and Ratner began to perform beneath the eyes of 'John' Bell who did not dance at all, upon the gravel path, at which 'John' gazed with his nervous frown. So very much in spite-of-himself (coyness intensified – a symbolical action to *dance with a woman*) and in spite of Mrs Bell, Ratner allowed himself to be dragged into graceful exercises – as if engaging in a fox-trot with his grandmother, the arm was slipped with a catch-as-catch-can rudeness around the waist of this faded Jane.

So she had the lovely experience and the ritual terminated that was finished. And Mrs 'John' and her fat split partner were back again beside Jonathan Bell at the table, where the coffee had come.

'This coffee is rotten!' 'John' Bell exclaimed.

'I expect it is' said Joo, tasting it with caution. 'Yes, very bad.'

'It is the worst coffee I've ever tasted' said Mrs Bell.

There was a pause, of gastric disappointment, during which 'John' Bell's bowels rolled grim and short.

'They have done it on the cheap' said Ratner. 'The dinner was very bad.'

'Were you here to dinner?' asked 'John' very impressed. 'Not as a guest.' Ratner was lofty and bitter, rebuking 'John' Bell so snobbish and eager.

'Oh' said 'John' Bell.

'I am a super in that play' Ratner told him. 'It is in the Zagreus' troupe. Have you seen the program? Here it is.'

Something flatteringly *obscure* – subaltern and self-effacing – was insinuated into his statement by Split-man – with a stressing of coyest of modest understatements a 'split' nothing he was – a chorus-person – no pompous principal, a coy underling.

'You dined here?' asked Mrs Bell.

'We had some dinner.'

Ratner returned to Mrs Kennedy with 'John' – that getting up and trotting, part of the demonstration, over – now he trained his eyeball, straight and true, again upon 'John' Bell, and touched 'John's' trigger once or twice to make sure if the powder had not got damp. 'John' Bell's body gave a few ashamed lurches of mirth, it showed it was a devil: Ratner told it a story about the peroxide fellow-publisher that made it jolt about until it coughed. But it continued to cough and toss about. So, as the naked all-bald upper-story was exposed to the night-dew, Mrs Bell looked about to see if a treacherous mist was not creeping up and so better to step inside again for 'John' Bell. But it was not so they stayed.

'I like your dress,' Ratner said to 'John.' 'Who are you?'

'I? – Democracy!'

As he spoke and smiled this introspective 'John' Bell's settled frown increased, with the smile, or diminished – only a laugh dispersed it. He was always nervous. A scoffing croak at Democracy was all Ratner said – he awaited 'John' Bell's further remarks now

'I thought I'd come as the figure of Democracy' 'John' Bell announced, with some scholarly unction at the title of a little-known Masque (indeed a Masque under a political cloud for three centuries) 'out of *Albion and Albanius.*'

Both the Bells, sly scholars (to whom their occasional support of a work of genius or erudition was the meat and drink of mind and not as this friend's private-pressing at all) looked at Ratner – who did not know what *Albion* and the rest was and did not care. He said nothing. He smiled back with superiority at the sly scholars – the funny bloomered-tandem of british middle-age and middleclass.

So 'John' Bell swelled out his chest and very fond of his own voice he rolled over the tin-table at Ratner a bit of *Albion* and the rest.

'But you forget the noblest part,
And Master-piece of all your art –
You told him he was sick at heart.
And when you could not work belief
In Albion of the imagined grief;
Your perjured vouchers, in a breath,
Made oath, that he was sick to death.
And then five hundred quacks of skill
Resolved, 'twas fit he should be ill. –
Now hey for a commonwealth
We merrily drink and sing!
'Tis to the nation's health,
For every man's a king!'

But 'John' Bell was intoxicated by the sound of his own voice and he had not the least idea what this was. A passage had been shown him, he had never stopped to consider what was said – he had found it rolled well. Now he sat back, frowning, replete with the sound of the passage. But Ratner sneered gloomily – that was all John got out of Joo.

'What is that?' asked Ratner with a note of sleepy curiosity.

'That?' said 'John' Bell. '*Albion and Albanius.*'

Again he drew thirty cubic inches of damp atmosphere into his lungs and was then able to give out the following without stopping much. In the kind of senatorial garment, he resembled a seated Roman making a solemn plea.

'Our plots and delusions
Have wrought such confusions,
That the monarch's a slave to the crowd.
A design we fomented –
By hell it was new!
A false plot invented –
To cover a true.
First with promised faith we flattered.
Then jealousies and fears we scattered.
We never valued right or wrong,
But as they served our cause.
Our business was to please the throng,
And court their wild applause.
For this we bribed the lawyer's tongue,
And then destroyed the laws.'

Ratner, his jocose mask stationary, watched from his eye-in-profile. He attempted to detect if 'John' Bell did know what he was saying or not – when it became evident to Ratner that 'John' Bell was not present to what his booming parrot-tongue said at all, then he laughed – at this innocent Democrat – who mouthed such virulent passages against the person of what he impersonated.

'Dryden' said 'John' Bell.

'Is it?' Ratner seemed surprised that should be Dryden. But he knew nothing at all about Dryden. – Ratner saw Margolin look at him as he passed – Margolin was by himself, he was heading for the Saloon.

'I think I must go' said Ratner to the two Bells. 'I think our part of the performance is almost due.'

'Shall we see you afterwards?' asked 'John' Bell surprised. 'Perhaps we can meet.'

'It depends what the time is.'

'Yes it is a little late already.'

A little abruptly perhaps Ratner left them – they thought it was abrupt. Bell thought he'd been taken short. – Julius Ratner followed Archie Margolin into the great dancing saloon.

XIII Captain Blunderbuss and his Man Squib

As Ratner entered the great dancing saloon he found (just in the way the Red Sea was chopped in half by his god Jahveh – to make a dryshod passage for his chosen boys and girls) a wide path bisecting the multitude – into this brilliantly lighted hedge of legs and faces came Split Man – not at all like a Chosen Child but with a sour blink – by no means flashing a Phoenix, but rather darkling a night-hawk – or some jaded falcon, fit for nothing. But he beheld a stately procession bearing down upon him with fatal tread (but still stepping with cattish precision as if the ground had lately been wet or disgustingly dirty) and lo this was even my lords Osmund and Phoebus, followed by a select retinue of great propriety – Children of the Chapel but dressed as men, youthful (but circumspect underlings) or learned (but Star-doctors of Manly Beauty) and these were passing unconcerned through the grinning ranks, in the direction of the garden.

Ratner took his place within the wall of people, he contributed his dark tusky grin to the rest of the mock-respect. Jazzing *God Save the King* the negro band hummed the hymn – guests removed their caps if they had been covered (though behind some half-capping occurred) some stood to attention, in the rear some (a blustering group) rendered the *Red Flag*, in the manner of an anthem.

A footman overtook Lord Osmund, and stuck like a stuffed bird with a wire up its centre, but top-heavy, within a yard of his master, with his megaphone windpipe with the throttle off, let fly at his lordship the title and the name of a newcomer.

'Captain Blunderbuss and His Man Squib!'

Lords Osmund and Phoebus turned excitedly about both together.

'Captain Blunderbuss! Not Captain *Blunderbuss!*'

That sound was too good to be true – they had not invented it.

'Who can it be Osmund – I think I know, it must be – you know!'

'Yes – I think it must be *him!*'

'I'm positive it is.'

'Where are Captain Blunderbuss and His Man Squib!'

The footman (who was a true automaton who never looked back) faced about in startled surprise, and failing to see Captain Blunderbuss and His Man Squib he opened his mouth, remaining in that condition. The guests' heads revolved upon their necks, there was nothing but the backs of their heads from where Ratner stood looking too but the door yawned behind Lord Osmund and was empty – as if having admitted Lord Osmund, no lesser Blunderbuss should ever burst out of its portals for quite a month – it was blank! There was no sign anywhere of Captain Blunderbuss and His Man Squib – no shadow without, suggestive of either master or man.

'He has gone my lord' the footman droned, in hollow adieu, to what he had supposed present. 'Captain Blunderbuss is not there my Lord!'

'No so it seems!' sniffed Lord Osmund.

'He has gone!' Lord Phoebus told Lord Osmund.

'I can see that much Phoebus for myself!' Lord Osmund lispily snapped at that poor pierrot Phoebus.

His elder lordship next shot a look of momentary suspicion at the footman.

'Has Captain Blunderbuss disappeared?' he asked him crossly and sharply to bring him to his senses.

'I do not see him now my lord!'

'No – well I'm sure *I* can't – any more than you can! Don't announce people who are not there for the future!'

'No my lord!'

'Another time you might make sure if there's anybody there!' Lord Phoebus scolded him in aggrieved drawling aside.

'I think you must have dreamed it!' said Lord Osmund as a parting shot and turned away.

'Yes my lord!'

This footman for a Lord Mayor's Coach – with a visage of Mar's Ochre to show off his bleached wig – bursting with crestfallen surprise – stepped stiffly back. Lord Osmund touched his right temple with his finger-tip, to suggest non compos mentis for this faulty mechanical inferior. The party resumed its stately progress then, the feet of Lord Osmund sweeping along, falling upon the floor with regularity, in a ceremonial large-scale strut – for the legs to quiver at each massive displacement, pompously flop-flop, in the period-tights, with the shock of the descending footfall. Scrupulously cadet, Lord Phoebus allowed his brother a few inches advance upon himself, he was a solemn willowy shadow of his senior.

But again Lord Osmund stopped, and his retinue halted behind him with a clock-work accord. Looking above the heads of the crowd, his lordship pointed out to Phoebus, to where three conspiratorial steeple-crowns were distinguishable, of a familiar cut.

'What is that dark caucus!' Lord Osmund exclaimed.

'Those are I believe three unimportant conspirators!' Lord Phoebus informed his senior lordship.

'Conspirators!' and Lord Osmund frowned – a treasonable expression!

'I proceed upon the hypothesis, that so far no one has been able to engage them in intelligible conversation.'

'Is that all you have learnt?'

'I think it is a well-grounded opinion!'

This was pronounced in such a tone that Lord Osmund thought it better not to dispute this point any further, and he passed on: the entire nest of dukes and Walking Gentlemen moved out into the free air, pelted with some confetti and one rotten egg, which struck Eric Mastrodonato and although he did not turn round inflamed his southern blood.

Before the lane was quite filled up the Split Man scuttled down it briskly, looking to right and left. But Margolin had gone to join Blunderbuss. Ratner disappeared through the door into the centre of the house.

XIV The Wicked Giant 'Cockeye'

In the private nursery beneath the tower of Lord Phoebus, the family of Finnian Shaw was assembled in the neighbourhood of the fireplace to tell the stories of Cockeye. Some stories were verbatim gems, some had assumed the dramatic form in the telling. A Cockeye Canon existed by this time. Manner and words both, of the fairy stories the such very adult children told each other of Father, were conventionalized. It was in the expectation of plenty that this seasoned caucus of celebrated poetical 'rebels' sat down to rerelish, perhaps for an untold number of retellings, the freaks of that opulent clown – he who had, as it were, given birth to his own private audience – whereas Osmund had his by adoption.

Upon the settee were the heavy-weights – Osmund, Volpemini, and Sib. Lady Harriet sat by Miss Julia Dyott (all smiles) in two chairs, while Monty Mayors had flung himself with such force upon the ground in front of the fire that he had slightly injured two not very hardy æsthetes, who had been warming themselves upon the rug. Two or three only of the male chorus lay there now as they were frankly afraid of Monty Mayors and another very heavy man who was liable to follow Monty's example. Floor-lyers and rug-fiends were collected in the crevices of the large fireplace and between the massive pieces of furniture however. Lord Phoebus was curled up by the coal-scuttle, the Kate Greenaway doll that had the vapours was bare-back astride his bandaged knee.

'Do you remember Harriet how Cockeye said he wanted to see more *aplomb* in the plumber!'

'Yes – I – do!' in the crashing hiss of her dramatic countertenor boo, Lady Harriet Finnian Shaw replied with her customary energy. 'And how the plumber led Cockeye up the garden too!'

'Yes the *plumber* showed more *aplomb* than Cockeye bargained for I think!'

'I think the plumber *did!*'

At the mention only of 'the plumber', it was a great favourite, the entire upper lip and nose of Lord Phoebus wrinkled up, as if he were about to sneeze – though the crash never came. Nothing but a contented cooing high up in his nose followed – but all the chorus convulsed itself – writhing in the crevices and upon the backs of the heavy furniture, squeaking and baying.

'The Gil-hooter!' impulsively Harold Pope, clasping both hands together tightly, cried out in a rich operatic cri-de-cœur.

'Oh yes dooooo let's hear that – when Cockeye went into the *garden!*'

'The gil-hooter is a perfect story!'

There was a hush of sorts, of high-strung expectation. Lord Osmund waited smiling for a moment as if to remember a tune, though all were so word-perfect that such a pause was a flourish only – he knew the *gil-hooter* by heart certainly.

'What is that *hooting* noise I wonder – there is that bird again!' Lord Osmund said, affecting to pay attention to some sound in the distance, cocking his ear for it.

'Yes whatever can that bird be, that always *hoots* about this time! Can it be an *owl* do you suppose?' Harriet responded with a very puzzled look indeed.

'Yes I wonder if it is an *owl!* There it goes again! Do you hear it? It always *hoots* about this time, out in the garden – I think I will go out and see if I can find it.'

'I think it's rather a pretty sound *don't you!*' bayed up Lord Phoebus.

'Yes – but a little *melancholy* – don't you agree!'

'Yes it *is* rather sad! I wonder if the poor bird has *lost* anything!' asked Harriet.

'It may – who knows! – have lost its *young!*' said Osmund, wise and owlish.

'Oh I do hope it hasn't!'

'I don't think it can be *that* Harriet!'

'Why don't you think it could be *that* Osmund?'

'Because I don't think it would mind losing *its young!*'

'Oh Osmund – the poor bird not mind losing *its young!*'

'I don't see why it should – human beings don't mind losing their *young* at all!'

'No I suppose that is true Osmund – they don't seem to, do they, mind losing *their young* very much!'

'Not at all – as far as I have been able to remark!'.

'No I think you are quite right there Osmund – it can't be its *young* I think!'

'No not its *young!*'

'Could it be the old birds perhaps that the poor bird has lost – it may be very young and have lost the father-bird, don't you think that is possible?'

'Yes it *might* be *that!*'

'I feel positive it's something of the sort! The father-bird is dead – that's it. And so it hoots!'

Interruptions at this point throughout the audience – the smiling actors, of this family scene, sit silent. They coo to themselves, while expressions of delight break out on all hands, applauding the performance.

'And then what does Cockeye say!' Harold Pope exclaimed.

Osmund (in the rôle of Cockeye) 'I'm sure I don't know what all you children mean!'

'No! I don't suppose you do!' the truculent Harriet retorts upon this imaginary Cockeye.

Osmund (as Cockeye). 'Not mind losing its *young!*'

Harriet. 'Yes – it *is* difficult to believe isn't it!'

Osmund (as Cockeye) 'I don't understand how the bird can be supposed not to be sad if it has lost its *young!*'

Harriet (as Harriet) 'No I *can't* make it out at all – not at losing its *young!*'

'You see!' muttered Blackshirt to Dan in whose company Dan had been induced to draw near to the inner circle, in common with a dozen or more outsiders who had remained in the room.

'They of course are "the young", that I suppose you have understood! Young is what they chiefly desire to appear – and that aged counterpart of themselves, Cockeye – he certainly is *old* – in fact very old – that is his function in the fairy-tale. The main point of this *Commedia dell'Arte* lies in this agreeable contrast. They certainly still have a *father* – even if aunts are getting a bit scarce. It's peculiar isn't it? However, it does appear, if you study it carefully, that it is lovely to be "children" when one is middle-aged – though a bore at other times, as I daresay you have found.'

And he gave Dan a polite look, which was lost upon Dan, for Dan could have wished that he would not hiss so loudly, as Harriet twice had turned in their direction as if geese had been surreptitiously introduced into the room, and he was sure that what he was saying was not what he should have said so near to them as this.

'Cockeye' Blackshirt argumentatively burst out low down on the scale, his voice singing *Cock-eye-yer* as the first meaty term in a chain of passionate reasoning, to be breathlessly followed – '*he* – my information is of the best – is nothing but an ancient model of this lot here – probably double as cunning, as is to be expected at twice-forty.'

Blackshirt hoarsely whispered *twice-forty* in Dan's ear, behind his hand.

'But according to the rules of the *child-parent-war-game* Cockeye must be honoured with the prodigious charge of having been at the bottom of the European War. You see that don't you? That does Cockeye far too much honour. That Osmund, or that Cockeye, is quite capable of causing a world-war if he got the chance, that is most probable. But this unimportant old landowner – however waspish and destructive, like his offspring – was certainly not responsible for *that* one. That makes no difference! The highly-emotional requirements of the *child-parent-war-game* have to be satisfied. Of the caucus of supposed decrepit old elders who sent the Young Men of 1914 to their death in the Trenches, Cockeye is *their* Elder. So it is automatic that Cockeye should become for them *the Old Man who made the War*. It is very simple. In 1914 that hussar-captain at the time, Lord Osmund, he was sent to his death in the Trenches (Osmund had the good taste not to stop there long – a fortnight or so I think). Lord Phoebus left Harrow and became a hussar and was marked down at once for the Trenches too (but Lord Phoebus was not at all well so didn't go). All this was Cockeye's doing – according to the rules of the *child-parent-war-game*. This makes the good emotional stuff of honest melodrama, but, as you will remark, it makes *historical* nonsense. It serves to give old Cockeye a diabolical political importance he does not deserve. Whoever or whatever caused the European War, it was not Cockeye that did it, with his bow and arrow – not Cockeye, whoever it was!'

And he shot a dark inquisitorial arrow from his dark welshman's eye at the caparisoned bosom of Harriet. But Harriet was busy playing 'Cockeye' with Phoebus, she was taking the part of the Marchioness.

'You must bear in mind' said Blackshirt quickly 'that it is always *the War* that in fact they are talking about. The child-parent-war-game was manufactured in the War-time. Harriet and Osmund took up the cry – they did not invent it – that it was the *Old Colonels*, in league with the *Old Politicans* (and all the sheltered Elders too old to be soldiers, in the decline of their days who thirsted for their children's blood) who were responsible for the European War. There would be no harm in that if it did not serve to screen the actual villain. It is important, you must agree, that the *true* cause should not be lost sight of. But both the *sex-war*, and the *child-parent-war*, each of them advance with a romantic bitterness their bogus claimants, for the honour of being the arch-villain of the European War. The authentic villain rubs his hands I should think as he looks on – and watches from his ambush these subsidiary *Wars* of our Peace-life, which have come out of the stinking bowels of the big one – and plots, who can doubt it, a bigger! – So these are most maddening old women – who still go on with their stupid stories, of their boring old parent, so like themselves, so sly, so complaining, so boring – who ever so mischievously, and sweetly, they have nicknamed as they have – and they still retail the legend of his wickedness with regard the War-time 'young'. That such very mature persons should find a never-cloying satisfaction in this impulsive nursery-philosophy (borrowed during the World-War from somebody far cleverer than themselves) is depressing, is it not? It is depressing. It is exceedingly depressing.'

Dan could not understand why people were always talking about the War – he was so small at the time in Ireland – for him in school-books it was always mixed up in his mind with the Wars of the Roses, and still was, because of *Roses in Picardy*. That was a song they had sung he knew of war-roses blooming, but the Rebellion had made him totally forget the War and its roses and everything about it until he had come to London really. It was a great War for England he supposed – it must have been.

The typical *gil-hooter* dialogue had been acted – the Finnian Shaw Family Repertory Company looked upon it as a tit-bit. It brought out the 'youngness' well – it turned upon the destruction of tender fledglings. For the benefit of any person there not an absolute intimate it must next be interpreted, by Harriet and by Osmund. That was now done. What had just been heard, that was, you must know, a conversation that had once occurred at Balbriggan – that was what they had just said, when they were speaking. The *gil-hooter* was a *hooting sound*. This sound was produced by Cockeye himself. Yes, by Cockeye. It occurred within the nose of Cockeye. It was a strange hooting sound. A sort of *hooting*. They themselves to start with had been puzzled by it. The children of the Marquis (it was explained) would always affect (when they heard the sound) to believe that it was a noise made by some bird. It was a bird (so they would affect to believe) that was hooting, out in the garden. Cockeye would on some occasions get up from the table (it was only at meals as a rule that they saw Cockeye) – he would go over to the window, and there he would stand peering out, to see if he could detect it, in the branches of some tree – although he himself (he was accustomed to affirm) could not hear its cry.

After the *gil-hooter* (a universal favourite) came Cockeye as a Cornet in the Yeomanry Cavalry or was it The Volunteers – he was then all side-whiskered and legginged – a shako two sizes too large for him. That all came from the old irish butler – he had witnessed Cockeye's earliest exploits, in the Curragh or in Gloucester, he described it with relish – he would tell how Cockeye (provided with flasks of cordial) would drive out in a buggy, he was armed to the teeth with a whole arsenal of bloodthirsty weapons. His best story recounted how at a Volunteer-Review Cockeye's rifle went off just as the Prince Consort had inspected his platoon, which caused an uncommon alarm amongst all those present.

When Lord Osmund had described the explosion of the gun and he had made quite a loud bang to show what happened, Dan fairly laughed outright but Blackshirt seized him by the arm, and said with a very stern expression –

'Come!'

Blushing to the roots of his hair Dan was led away – it was plain Blackshirt considered he had disgraced himself or both of them by laughing like that – he questioned if he would ever let him listen to stories after that as he was unable to control himself.

'We will go to the Library!' when they were outside Blackshirt said.

XV The Library

At the thought of *the Library* Dan was deeply depressed but he supposed he had to go with Blackshirt and read the books.

'I have a map of the house' Blackshirt told him. 'Pierpoint gave it to me, I don't know where he got it.'

The piece of paper Blackshirt took from his pocket was dirty, Dan wondered if Pierpoint was a dirty man: For some reason this appeared extremely probable to him – he was a philosopher was the reason.

Dan stopped, why did they not go down the main stairs? But Blackshirt passed on without paying any attention and they went straight forward briskly into a maze of passages, but at last he opened a door and they went into a large room full of books to the ceiling.

'This is the Library,' said Blackshirt, and he started looking at the books to make himself at home.

All the books were made of leather, and there were big windows just as he had expected. But upon a table was a lot of bright buttercup-coloured books. They were like Mélanie had and they were made of bright paper. Seeing all these buttercup-coloured books seemed to make Blackshirt very cross. He threw one down violently and pushed several as if he wished they had not been put there upon the table – he kept returning, one in particular he went on pushing about. There were other books upon this long table that were much more pretty – in bud-green, sapphire, scarlet or violet.

Turning away from the table, Blackshirt went back to the doorway.

'Heraldry a favourite subject' he said, beginning at the beginning, near the doorway. 'I expect *armes parlantes* of Finnian Shaw number one – canting or punning charges – probably an *oar* and to keep it company *a ship* – or perhaps *a shore*. *Shaw* you see.'

Blackshirt seemed very disgusted and if it upset him so much Dan wished he hadn't after all brought him to see the books it wasn't necessary – but was not that perhaps too missish?

'Treatises upon Gothic' Blackshirt said, moving on. 'Baroque. It is a fixed idea. History, and so *family*. With that, apotheosis of *period*. It is a pure case of the *chronological state of mind* – the Time-craze' said the Blackshirt, pointing his finger at another shelf, peering at the name of each book – was he short-sighted?

'Yes.' Dan followed like a lazy disagreeably overgrown school-miss from shelf to shelf. He played slowly with one of the many bonny-blue-ribbons that dangled dreamily upon the period-frock.

'This is Phoebus's bit. He is the historian. These are the furnishings for his romantic historical treatises.' He rattled his forefinger along the swelling breasts of a column of fine upstanding volumes.

'Finnian Shaw archives.' He tapped a few with his knuckle. 'Cockeye's collection I expect. The literary marquis! Here is the literature of a Crusade. All the Crusading bag of tricks – as if tallow-kings cared for Holy Sepulchres – at most interested in the wax-candles for the chapels or high-altar!'

An expansive sensation at this point entered into Dan for all that this kind Blackshirt was. The entire pedagogic presence of his surly guide was suddenly dear to him – for a word uttered by chance had brought back to Dan the very feeling of the perfect presence of Horace! Oh he would give *anything* now for a good stiff 'broadcast'! He even would have been capable of crying *Long Live Pierpoint!* – for was he not a dark horatian figure?

'We arrive at Osmund, man of letters!' Blackshirt exclaimed, as he drew up in front of a modernist galaxy of parti-coloured book-backs, towards which he waved a hand. Upon the hand there was a small silver ring.

'Verses and plays – novelettes and novels – quite a writer!'

Oh the *Ape!* thought Dan with eagerness as he saw what Osmund did. But alas the days of logs scribbled-in by candlelight were over – he drew back discouraged.

Blackshirt took bodily out of the shelf a thick pack of books. He carried the books intact to the big table. Spine up, he stood them, a huddled pack of masterpieces. He removed his hands – a flanking book fell down, the rest remained upright.

Dan approached, gently inquisitive – gently he wondered what Blackshirt was going to do now with the books – was he going to carry them away and hide them in the garden? But the actions of his blackshirted guide belied this entirely – for he was rolling up his blackshirted sleeves a little. This must betoken some fierce demonstration.

In fact the books had been placed upon the table for dissection. Something of the sort became immediately apparent to Dan. Blackshirt was the great anatomist. Dan saw that. *This was a noted anatomist!* He was about to undertake the description of the situation, structure and economy of the organized discourse of this particular mind as discovered by these books. Or this would perhaps be a lesson in Pathologic Anatomy. Dan was the breathless apprentice. – So much, after his manner, Dan understood. – He knew without any telling, from the light in his eye, that Blackshirt was going to be rude to the books, about that there could be little doubt.

But Blackshirt went straight to the heart of the matter. The cardiac region as it were was attacked then and there, his learned knife in hand. Brutally he opened up the third volume, finically he picked it up out of the pack – he opened it up, his two thumbs in its innards. He planted it plumb on its scarlet back, for it was a bright book. He then planted his index-finger upon it, scornfully in mid-page, and stuck it in till he nail-marked it.

'Lord Osmund Finnian-Shaw suffers from a Thymus surplus!'

Dan saw their stout host in a funny surplice of course at once though he knew there was more behind it.

'The whole family is a clear case of the domination of the Endocrine proper to Infancy! That is called the *Thymus Gland of Internal Secretion.* This gland is supposed to disappear or become inactive in the adult-life. It is the gland provided for the tender-years. In the Finnian-Shaw family this particular Endocrine persists. Into the ripest years, it is ridiculously active. It pumps the humours of childhood into that great body of Osmund. As a family they suffer from an over-dose of Thymus – the child-like Endocrine.'

Dan did not know what to say to this but he felt sorry for the entire family, suffering from some subtle tumour.

'Hence the obsession of that fat Old Maid – that spectacular Aunt Mary! Osmund that is.'

Dan looked down at the book, affected by the pierpointean ritual – the rolling up of the sleeves, the pointing of the finger, the solemn passes. He firmly believed that he should presently see a little Old Maid trip out of the open book and he kept his eyes dreamily fixed upon it, expecting this elfish apparition.

'The obsession of that fat Old Maid!'

Blackshirt wetted his unoccupied thumb, in order to turn a page, and Dan craned his neck to watch – for he thought the little wizened old fairy woman was perhaps hiding under it, and he thought that it was Blackshirt's intention to turn it suddenly up, as one would cant up a seaside rock, beneath which marine animals were secreted. But he turned it right over: and there was nothing there. It was disappointing.

'Old Maidenhood!' he said to Dan; and Dan looked again, but without result. 'The bogey of Women, when Victoria was queen. Or really it is merely *oldness* – for after all he is not a female, technically *a virgin*. So it is Old Age that haunts him – but in the way that that would present itself to an unmarried victorian lady, past the years propitious for wedlock. That is it. *He suffers from the bane of Spinsters*. But it is in a maudlin way – reminiscent of some parsonage in A.D. 1850, in the England of Trollope.'

Then Blackshirt added, looking down at the book.

'He is very sentimental.'

Dan looked down as well – and he experienced an uneasy compassion, for he knew that somebody was terribly unhappy (though not technically a virgin) but he could not discover the cause.

'You have seen the Old Colonels. – Here are the Old Maids. The Old Dowagers.'

Dan was all attention for Blackshirt said *he had seen* Old Colonels and he thought he meant in the books – he expected at any moment to see a procession of tin-soldiers across the page where Blackshirt pointed.

'This is a novel.'

Dan knew that some books were called *novel* and this was one. As Blackshirt did not offer an explanation of what *novel* meant he turned away, and then Blackshirt said –

'Otto Weiniger would tell you that Osmund was eight-tenths female in composition: perhaps that is why in fact he suffers from these sentimental hauntings. He is feminine. He is sentimental.'

Otto-somebody might tell that *to Blackshirt* but whether he would tell it *to Dan* was not so certain, but Blackshirt seemed positive that he would – he looked quite convinced about it.

'Or you may prefer to say that Osmund is simply haunted by the thought – *to grow old!* – in the manner of the average Society Hostess. You need to go no farther than that – Society is his native element.'

The average Society Hostess conveyed little to Dan, but his eyes began positively to start out of his head when Blackshirt began to talk about *ghosts*. He could not help wondering if the Library was haunted – because Libraries were usually haunted.

'Here are the Old Maids – the Old Dowagers!' Blackshirt called his attention again to their presences, but Dan felt rather chilly and wished there was a gas-stove.

'In this book a group of dull old women is made into footballs for his tongue – having kicked all the old hags in the stomach in the last chapter, he kills most of them off. This, properly analysed, is a sort of blood-sacrifice – on paper. The god of whom Osmund is the terrified priest demands it. He feels the god might have *him*, if he should present himself empty handed! So. *Blood-sports* in books. You must get hold of that simple idea. A reflection of the War – to which at the time because of its *bloodiness* the Finnian Shaws so rightly objected! The Trenches amongst the pages of the novels – Trench-warfare in the mud of Satire.'

Blackshirt shut the book with a report like a Trench-mortar. Between finger and thumb, he picked out a second from the pack. He burst it brutally open, pinned it upon the table, scrutinized its title – colophon – index and finis – as if it had been a passport or *carte d'identité*.

'Yes' he said – having fastened his finger upon its dazzling white Dutch Mould-made stomach. 'Here again we have Old Age. This treats of Old Age as well as the other. But *any* book here – examine them! – has that for *leit-motiv*. Would you like to pick one out and try? You take my word for it? You would really find that as far as this is concerned I am to be trusted. This one now is a group of lampoons. They are called *Portraits of*

Fiction. In it cæsarean operations are performed upon a dozen old-gentleman-spinsters – sentimental dilettantes of the type of Osmund, but twenty years more advanced than he in the same depressing path. Here they are on their last legs – with painted lips, eyeglasses, cockroach eyebrows, and bellies full of wind.'

Dan felt terribly sorry for all these old *effetes* – on their last legs, with bellies full of wind, and began to feel a little sorry for Lord Osmund – who did not seem able, try as he would, to get the right shampoo (*shampoon* Blackshirt called it but that was because he had a cold in the head he supposed).

Blackshirt was turning back with expert fingers to the opening pages of the book that was the object of this demonstration. After reading there for a moment, he picked up another book. After that he examined the opening pages of a third book, and after that of a fourth. In each case he referred to the title-pages. Then he put them down. At last there were four books lying together face-upward in a row.

'Yes' said Blackshirt, satisfied with his expert examination. 'These are books published over a space of ten years. The hero in every case is naturally Osmund himself – with an author of this description – since it is nothing but the most trivial personal motives that cause him, as a society-lion, ever to write a book you see. That you may always take for granted. In *this* book' and he pressed his finger on it 'which is a recent one – the hero has become *a very distinguished-looking* man of thirty-five. In *this* one however' and he pressed his finger upon another 'the hero is a very handsome and noble person of twenty-seven. But *this* was written five years earlier than *that!*'

Blackshirt blew his nose with the evacuatory gesture of a man spitting to express his contempt. Then he turned to Dan impressively and placed his hand upon his whistle, which was in his left-breast-pocket.

'I am masculine to a fault!' said he. 'I too find it difficult to understand. At first I was entirely at sea. *But here is the evidence.* You can't get away from that! Everything I have seen tonight confirms Pierpoint's diagnosis – things pan out exactly as he says!'

The Blackshirt was triumphant – it had once more been demonstrated that Pierpoint was infallible.

'As to Cockeye' said Blackshirt with studied contempt 'he is an old bird of the same feather. Here is a nest of middle-aged fledglings. It would be found upon examination that they pout and peck with identical movements – they and Cockeye! Harriet at sixty probably will be sitting in one bath-chair, Cockeye will be sitting in another. She will be shaking her fist at Cockeye, while he ripostes by cutting down her allowance for air-balls and acid-drops. The *age-war* or the *child-parent-war-game* will still be in full swing. She will not have children herself now. On the other hand Cockeye is fond of life. So provided the old wretch of a parent-bird keeps alive there is no reason why Harriet should not represent the younger generation until she dies of apoplexy – she will almost certainly succumb to a violent fit of temper.'

Blackshirt took a few steps in the direction of Dan, and lighted a cigarette, employing a match-box in gun-metal which he drew from the pocket where his whistle lay, at the end of its cord.

'You see this match-box?' he said.

Dan took it from his hand. He examined the match-box with a certain alarm – for anything that had reposed in a pocket of the Blackshirt was not to be trifled with Dan very strongly felt, and he returned it to its owner – with a noticeable haste.

'Do you see this device?' The Blackshirt pointed to a black crest in one corner of it. 'That represents the sentimental mug of an abstract *youth* – he is hellenic and hermaphrodite.'

Dan gazed sadly at the hermaphrodite youth.

'That is the seal, for identification, of the C.B.Y. – Communion of British Youth. I was the secretary of that organization, when Pierpoint discovered me. From that boy-scout religion I was rescued by Pierpoint. – So youth-movements are no novelty to *me!*'

Blackshirt thrust out his chest – at all youth-movements, at the C.B.Y. in particular. With a concrete god (as now he had) he swelled against all abstractions.

'I only tell you that. That is of no importance. But when I was mixed up with the C.B.Y. I had a lot of experience. Aspirants for youth-honours in hundreds passed through my hands. It was my duty every day to drive away middle-aged men, panting with enthusiasm, who wished to enrol. We had the communist rule of 25. I was twenty-two. Every week I drove away dozens of pot-bellies, hundreds of heads of grey-hair, swarms of bald persons – you would not credit the numbers! Birth certificates were useless – they used to alter them to suit their fancy. Indeed, the great difficulty was to get any genuine *youths* to join up. That should have caused no surprise – for what *youth* in his senses wants to go about shouting – "Oh look – I am a youth!" Our director the man behind the scenes – he was an ex-banker, called – he had a scotch name – of fifty bright young summers. – I tell you this to show you that I know what I am talking about.'

Dan thought Blackshirt was reproaching him with a lack of attention or scepticism and he attempted to correct this bad impression at once. He fixed his eyes upon Blackshirt's hands, sometimes upon one, sometimes the other.

'The Finnian Shaw family-group I should describe as a sort of middle-aged *youth-movement*. It is confined to a particular family and their dependants. This they have become in their capacity of "rebels" against authority. The dangers of the War first must have driven them into that attitude. The idea of "youth" supervened – afterwards. It coloured with a desirable advertisement-value their special brand of rich-man's gilded bolshevism. In the fairy-tales they have spun about this theme ever since, Cockeye has always been the wicked Giant who tried to kill them during the big bad naughty World War. You see the idea? Psychologically the habit of mind illustrated by them is not without significance. It is a formidable absurdity. It will bear thinking about a great deal.'

Dan sank back sitting upon the table and he frowned, in his attempt to follow the story of this fairy-tale – about the Wicked Giant 'Cockeye'. But he was unable to do so, because *the War* kept coming into it as usual. That spoilt the story and indeed made it quite meaningless for him.

'Osmund however feels the giant-limbs of Cockeye waxing upon *himself*. Thinks he – "I shall soon be a full-blown Giant now!" The portcullis of the Roaring Forties frowns immediately in front of him. Once in there – thinks Osmund – I shall be of the race of Giants – a Cockeye! And it is impossible to disguise the fact that Harriet is *already* a Giantess! A female Cockeye. She still romps outside the cockeyed Bastille where dwell the sinister communion of Wicked Giants! But the nearer Lord Osmund draws to the Castle of the Giants, the more gloomy he becomes. Imagine a child, as he read in some fairy-book, growing and growing – until he was forced to recognize that he was now a giant like the one in the story! Here beneath my hand are the written records of these people's intense alarm. It is the Thymus gland doing its fell work!'

Blackshirt placed his hand in an insulting caress upon the motley pack of books. He withdrew, between thumb and index as if with forceps, a third volume from the pack.

'This is the last – it is the best. That is speaking simply as a pathologist.'

Blackshirt opened it up, he planted his palm upon its centre and crushed it flat upon the table.

'A longish novel!' he remarked, jaunty and solemn. 'The subject is an ideal illustration – the brilliant diagnosis which I have in my pocket by Pierpoint is confirmed to the letter.'

Dan looked over his shoulder, but to his great disappointment he could see no *illustrations* at all.

'This is the story of a beautiful young flaxen british poet, he goes to America. Of the most noble stock – already, in spite of youth, famous. He decides to take a trip to New York. Although so young he is not very well – the sea-air will do him good. Impulsively he embarks at the last moment – overnight he makes up his mind – within twelve hours he is packed and has been put in a train by his valet. Osmund's heroes always have valets because Osmund has a valet. They all have a *tendency* to corpulence. There is nothing they have, Osmund has not got, or is supposed to have got – *in fact* they possess many things O. is only supposed to have. Daydreams of his mind you see – the naïve personalities of this gilded riff-raff are advertised like a soap or sewing machine. When this young poet then boards the superliner, bound for New York City, he is shown into an inferior D deck stateroom, which he is compelled to occupy with another passenger. It is the height of the season – the liner is full, this is all that the Company is able to offer him. It was by a stroke of luck that this arrangement was possible. A stroke of luck indeed! *Ill-luck* for the poor young poet – for this accident in the sequel is seen to blast the whole of his young life! When first shown into the stateroom he is to occupy, he does not see his fellow-passenger. He dresses hurriedly and is soon enjoying the delights of a floating Ritz, as befits his rank and wealth. It is after midnight when he retires to his sleeping quarters. He is still unaware who the person may be with whom he is to share the cabin. When he enters the cabin, he remarks that the other berth is now occupied. But all he can see is *a long white beard* hanging out of the bed – a *Cockeyed*-affair in fact. The morning come, he gets up and his neighbour gets up too and mumbles *Good Morning* and he says *Good Morning Sir!* – all is quite in order. But as these two face one another the hero of the story feels himself seized with a terrible faintness! For here, locked up with him in this confined space, far out upon the ocean, is a person that he recognizes to be *himself* – no other! – only an Osmund of about seventy-five – a contemporary of Cockeye – with long white beard complete! With this other self he then spends the eight days of the voyage out. His flaxen hair turns quite white as a result of this experience.'

Blackshirt smiled ironically. Lord Osmund's tale was told – Dan felt a little seasick as he was a bad sailor – he wished Blackshirt would tell him more about the *Giants* and *Giantesses* and not so much about the sea.

'Now I have displayed for you, Daniel Boleyn' said the Blackshirt grandly 'the Pierpointean Analysis – that is our procedure. I have revealed the dominant impulse beneath these many painfully personal utterances of Lord Osmund Finnian Shaw, in his rôle of author. I have now shown you the Library. I have shown you the soul of our host. There is no occasion to go through the works of his sister Harriet or his brother Phoebus. They are of a piece. This is a united family! The neurosis in question reaches its maximum development in Osmund. It is least acute in Harriet. That condition is natural in Harriet (an authentic old maid) which is sickly and unnatural in Osmund – *masculine sex* upon his identity card. – That is all.'

Leaving the books lying there – the three he had last dissected, still opened up, side by side upon the table, cut down the centre as though with a knife – Blackshirt turned on his heel and Dan followed him out of the Library with a sense of the greatest relief, congratulating himself upon not having been asked to read all these books – just told a few fairy-stories and then taken away again!

XVI Albino Blushes

As Blackshirt and Dan who could be taken for an eloping couple, came round a dark corner, a door was ajar. The whispering of intriguers and reports of protest, spitting and a slap, sounded behind the door. As they drew abreast, the door bounded open, and rushing out upon them as if from its veritable lair was the Bonassus. Dan gave a faint shriek, naturally, he fell back at the sight of the Bonassus. Blackshirt stood his ground: it was in its shirt only, but still with its red ears on. Dan was not really very alarmed because he knew it was human now but he was startled at its rushing out in this savage manner all the same.

Upon the heels of the Bonassus, streaming after it down the gallery, went three little white-fronted men with high-pitched voices.

'Kanute – Kanute!' they yodelled as they ran.

One of them scolded –

'You mustn't go down there do you hear! Come back at once!'

Another said –

'I shouldn't run so quickly if I were you – the pigeon will escape!'

But they were lost to sight. Turning to the left Dan was relieved to find himself upon the main staircase – he had complete confidence in Blackshirt that was understood but he recognized that Blackshirt was foolhardy, and with nothing but a small map scribbled upon an odd and end of notepaper he had gone into the large unlighted parts of the house single-handed and they might have stepped over the edge of something and never come back, or been involved in a disconcerting cul de sac. Upon his *Street-map of London* Dan marked dark streets with a cross and never entered them, by day or night. – Upon the big staircase, half-way down they stopped – it gave them a prospect of the great dancing saloon and its main ormolu chandelier – it was full of servants now setting chairs in rows and taking in by sections a small stage.

Blackshirt fed his eyes with the prospect, narrowly observing the preparations, for some time – a little black-breasted Napoleon upon the slopes of a gilded Alp. He swelled in a hemispheric fascistic chestiness – about forty cubic inches of tidal air passed into his lung-sacs.

'Did you know that the albino blushed in his eyes?' he asked Dan.

Dan blushed all over his neck and hands, giving the albino points on the spot – giving *Horace* points, on neck and hand.

'Light passing through the iris and pupil of an albino comes out *red* – on account of bloodvessels at the back. That is why their *eyes blush*, at the same time their face blushes.'

Dan's eyes felt very hot, as if they had been filled with Cayenne.

'Because Zagreus is an albino' said Blackshirt 'he blushes with his *eyes* – I once saw Zagreus blush, it was when Pierpoint told him he was too rich.'

Dan observed dark lanugo upon the blackshirted wrists after the cuffs, and upon the hand, as he was adjusting his heavy legionary's whistle, and he wondered if he was quite english or irish.

Blackshirt took up again the unhurried descent of the emblazoned stairway, and they found themselves pell-mell among the personnel, they were struck with the four-square spikes of chairs.

XVII Dan and the Tropical Man

'Will you have a drink?'

Blackshirt having made this remark, he entered the *American Bar* and Dan went too of course. The prospect of refreshment made Dan look up. It was then he saw the Negro! This was a genuine *Tropical Man!* There were even two, but the other was on duty at the other end of the Bar. It was the *Tropical Man* in front of him that he saw.

Gazing at this black bugbear across the Bar, Blackshirt placed one hand upon his hip. The other he placed upon his whistle. He fixed his eye upon the *Tropical Man* before him. Blackshirt was no friend of *The Tropics*. Again Dan remarked the dark lanugo upon his wrists and turned away his head with alarm – some of the hair from the terrifying Black looked as if it had stuck to the wrists of the Blackshirt.

'His skin is only a smoked glass as it were you know.' The Blackshirt nodded at the Negro. 'That is the principle. You need not be afraid of him!'

And he demonstrated to Dan the true attitude, devoid of alarm, to be adopted if you should encounter unexpectedly a truly *Tropical Man*.

But Dan could not be otherwise it was no use talking – he was quite unable to master his consternation at the presence (just across the counter) of this *Tropical Man*. The savage grinned at him – for the creature seemed to recognize the fear he inspired in Dan. Oh why had God made these Tropical Persons – was God too at heart perhaps *unkind?*

'Champagne?' asked Blackshirt.

Champagne it was evidently to be and the Black creature executed their orders with an animal dexterity that, Dan discovered, fascinated at the same time that it repelled. Drinkers kept coming in. The black hands were moving all the time, deft and black.

Dan drank the champagne. But as he swallowed the first sips, an evil spirit would seem to have come to life in him, out of its spurious sparkle. His sufferings had been too intense for it to be safe to give him champagne immediately. As he put it away, in bolder sips – that celebrated drink, to which so often in the past his intellect had been compared by Horace, under happier circumstances – in an abrupt uncomfortable way (it is true) he suddenly felt possessed of a magical strength. He even looked for a second at the *Tropical Man* (that savage so near him as to be unsafe) and the Negro immediately exhibited a row of chalky incisors (which more philosophical savages knock out, to look unlike animals) and filled up Dan's glass again. Dan emptied the glass at one wild toss.

Blackshirt saw this happen in the mirror with a dull surprise.

'Well!' he said. That was all. And then he looked away.

But Dan felt the lumps of depression begin to break up inside his constipated heart. The Black Man refilled the glass. At once Dan took it up and at one toss he dispatched it as he had the first.

'Here!' Blackshirt now considered him attentively. It dawned upon him with a disagreeable suddenness that something was amiss, and that there was some threatened indiscipline or some minor case of something worse.

This situation was one for which the political-secretary possessed no fool-proof rule of thumb whatever. But between the Black bugbear and Dan there was now an alarming rapprochement. Dan even softened his eye to allow it to dwell upon this friend-in-disguise – got up in that black skin that was smoked glass – who had in his keeping the fierce drinks, those that stupefy the oppressed, whatever their pigment.

Dan advanced his glass, to the foot of the Negro's hand. The Negro put the fire-water in it, and Dan dispatched that too. A kaleidoscope of exploded depressions kicked inside in crude can-can. In Dan's melting heart as the sparkle of the liquid-dynamite dropped into the body, rushed round, and upset the brain – the depressions took on a giddy veneer.

But two more glasses followed the second and it was in quick succession – it was a series now.

'What's the big idea!' asked the Blackshirt slowly. And he examined his big girl-charge (this beskirted six-footer, like a folk-dancing impostor) she put away the bad fizz. He could detect nothing (such for instance as a will-to-drink – a streak of depravity – or some brain-wave that had taken the wrong turning). It could after all merely be an ill-directed thirst. He shrugged his shoulders. For never had it occurred to him to ask the correct procedure if your dummy suddenly appeared to make up its mind to inebriate itself, and he regretted now that he had not.

Dan without looking up at either the *Tropical Man* or his own fair classic mask in the glass pushed up his goblet, his eye upon the stoppered magnum. With the unaffected attractiveness of practically all his fellow-Blacks the Bar-tender filled up the glass. All Dan's movements were followed closely by Blackshirt in the looking-glass however. With particular care he noted the reckless throwing back of the head – he watched for signs of *satisfaction* upon the face immediately afterwards. But this was all to no purpose. In his cups this baffling deaf-mute was exactly as he was out of them. What an enigma!

'Well!' Blackshirt said again, and he finished his own drink soberly and thoughtfully.

'Well!' echoed the Black. '*Well – well – Waal!*'

The Blackshirt gave the Negro a severe glance. He did not want any of his Tropical nonsense! – he put his hand aimlessly upon his whistle. But with Dan two months of sorrow broke into a mass of hours – the hours danced inside, falling into a shower of minutes – there was a carnival of black moods – with the movement of unattached black rocks shaken against by a champagne of waters. His brain became simply a torrent. The dark facts shot intact up to the flashing surface – there was *Horace horrid* – a black fact – and *kinder* Horace than he had ever been – but forever, naturally, Horace and nobody else was in the picture. Then a certain pleasant glow made itself felt. At length there was a soft something. A still small voice in Dan said *Whoops!* instead of *Alanna!*

Blackshirt threw himself back upon his stool and simply stared the simpleton out of countenance in the glass. With the faintest smile a sub-rosa one – a *don't tell Blackshirt!* one – his face spoke volumes, of occult mischief, and Dan pushed up the glass. The kind Black hand carried it to the tap. The tap dripped from the last. Filled, back it came, stamped with bogus fizz-foam – up it went – the lips chopped into the cheap foam – Dan dropped it down his throat. The glass went to the counter, in one sweep, it was pushed up for another – the Black hand filled up – the cup foamed – Dan drank – his upturned face came down (perpendicular features that expressed nothing) – he returned the goblet to the Black – the Black to him and vice versa.

'Well!' said the Blackshirt. He scratched his black head. If he had only been *told* now – it was vexatious! Nothing had been said. This had been sprung upon him – there was no word to the effect that the dumb brute *drank*. Blackshirt turned his face round to Dan, and showed him how blank it was, how Dan was dumbfounding, in addition to a deaf-mute, and dum at that, and with lustreless eyes he stared at his strange charge dully. Again he put up his hand to scratch the close-cropped bristles at a loss.

Evidently this dummy's habit was to do this – it was its cunning. It got into a Bar in a dream – once there it intoxicated itself. What action to take in cases of dummies etc., etc.? – he would hand this hard case back to its master. It was not his funeral if the thing went gay all of a sudden – he had not brought it to this party.

A further prompt glass was put away by Dan. The Negro then looked under the counter. He drew out a second magnum, uncorked it with a dull pneumatic bang, filled a glass and placed it beside the first, transferring the stop-cock.

Dan drank the fresh glass. – As he put it down he frankly gave a friendly giggle, and the Tropical Man giggled back. But at this sound Blackshirt jumped. He had had enough of this! Rapidly getting down from his stool, he looked with such solemnity into the face of his charge that Dan bit his lip.

'Yes?' Blackshirt asked.

He peered into the expressionless dummy-countenance – with especial closeness at the lips that had let pass the unmistakable giggle. Nothing was forthcoming from this deceitful dummy-countenance, it persisted in its expression of mild dismay. Just maiden meditation very slightly flushed. He turned to the Tropical Man, who was quite hysterical. Blackshirt sternly pointed to his own glass. He drank and turned again to Dan.

But now the mysterious fool had changed. An anamorphosis produced by blackshirted pressure from without was resulting in a dangerous torpor.

'Come!' he commanded hoarsely. 'The garden.'

But at 'garden' Dan smiled openly. The Blackshirt started back a couple of stage-paces of pure astonishment – taken unawares. Then he approached Dan again, his jaw set, and he forced him roughly off the stool at once. Dan rose, the Blackshirt was on his guard. As Dan was pushed he swayed gracefully. There was a moment during which they both swayed hither and thither, in front of the Bar, beneath the eyes of the *Tropical Man.* Then arm-in-arm with Blackshirt (who grasped his intoxicated dummy firmly under the arm-pits, hoping for the best) Dan moved away, with the step of an automaton – stiff, but still goat-footed.

XVIII Post-Champagne

It was dark, and with the dark came sudden cold – Dan felt the Blackshirt knock against him, he could not keep him off. What an unsteady reeling man! He surmised that the Blackshirt had looked upon the wine when it was red – or perhaps champagned – but Dan was glad for this relieved him of a certain embarrassing sense of something not quite right with himself that he certainly felt as he got into the garden. Just after that the people were dancing in wigs upon the green. They came out of the dark – many powerful lights shone now upon Dan – he put up his hand to his face to banish the lights before it. Outside, Blackshirt went off when it was light. Dan drew nearer and nearer to the cataract. Inside his head the cataract made a loud subterranean sound. But his cavern floated – he carried the roaring sound along with him in his head, up to the waterfall, and as he drew near he saw the giant mouth of the gramophone. He saw the sound coming out – it was unmistakable – here it was deliciously cool and fresh: seizing the sides of the metal crater, he hung his head over the edge and could not help attempting in fun of course to catch some foam upon the sides of his cheeks. But it began turning round. He feared he might fall in – he felt quickly quite sick in the full blast of the cold sound that came out. Then he fell a little unexpectedly down beside the instrument. As he lay there he noticed that his skirt was up over his knees too far for the girl he was thought to be. With a gesture that was convulsive, because it was nothing short of an effort – but with painful frowning out of wounded modesty – he thrust down the obstinate cloying garment that went under him and so was pinned to the ground (and would not run up and down like a roller blind at all as it should) so could not be made to comply easily – but a stooping man had passed a hand beneath him, and two passers-by joined themselves to this man and began passing their hands under him. Soon he was most uncomfortable. He struggled *of course* – what girl would not and he must too – but all together they dragged him up out of the ground. He lay upon the bosom of the first, while the others moved most eccentrically (to left and right) beside them – now there were two men however for one, and a double bosom as it happened – between the cleft-bosom he plunged face-downwards head-on towards the earth – he did not see how he could possibly save himself from falling. The man took a fall too. He had him by the neck.

Blackshirt was furious.

'Didn't I tell you to stop where you sat till I got back!'

Now he was in *Blackshirt's* arms – he smelt of drink he thought – ah these men (he smiled) they're all the same! Been back to the Bar no doubt – that was plain enough – not surprised at that *at all!* He held him much more passionately than the other man – what a passionate nature! or perhaps it was drink.

'Can you walk! Keep still can't you! Can you walk?'

Could he *not* walk. He could – and would – *run!* He ran. Blackshirt overtook him and they got up. But they fell down again. When they were on their feet however they went very rapidly under the trees where it was dark. Blackshirt told him it was all up with him or words to that effect. But he made up his mind to get out of the garden for he knew the Mazes were now open and if they continued to circle about aimlessly and so quickly as they were at present doing, without reason, they could not fail to fall into them. If Blackshirt had a map it might be out-of-date like the one Mélanie gave him of Hyde Park, the first time. So worse than useless. *He* would not answer for what might not happen to *himself*.

'All right – *don't* go that way! Come this!'

Well, he asked nothing better – *that* was the way he *had* wanted to go! He could not follow what Blackshirt was so cross about. But if he only knew how lucky he was to be out with a *girl-in-a-thousand* (Oh Horace! Your words – but *so unkind!*) he would think twice before giving way to such petulance. Now he would steady himself against this big tree – for he was not walking so well as he might it had to be conceded, and his toes were also particularly sore – that was the running he expected, when they fell over. Attempting to pick one up in his hand – grasping his foot with it low down – he knew he was falling. Yes – indeed soon it was so. Bump. Still the same foot up in his hand, he had come down heavily. He was down upon the grass and could not let go.

He thought he would go to sleep now and he slept at once.

But up till then he had been convinced that it was late. As he woke he did not at all know what the time was. Horace was standing not far away with Split-man – for whom he had a fixed and most prejudiced hatred there was no denying it, ever since the kitchen.

'There he is!'

It was the horrid coarse mock-gentleman's voice of the Split-Man. He seemed to be whispering something to Horace, and Horace said 'Yes I know' and Dan thought 'tell him off.'

Dan still had hold of his bad foot. He sat up and his back scraped a tree. He stopped and he felt the tree stop. They sat pressed together. The tree was a heavy tree.

Horace was not looking at him. He was not sorry really. He was looking away into a field. Sweet Horace! Too good to be true! He longed to call *Horace!* quietly but he restrained the impulse easily though he could have attracted his attention by the merest sound.

Dan noticed the limits of the estate – Horace and Split-Man and he were quite near a gate. Horace perhaps would come over to him in a moment, he might enquire after his health. Why health? Horace often did. He wished it had occurred to him to stand up – when he got home he would have some good stiff coffee, for tea was a morning's slop he long had renounced – sugared coffee with strong red toast – maybe a new bald shining egg upon it (slash the yoke – that juice was horrid!). If Horace spoke he would pretend he had sat there (for quite some time). Why not? What was the use of rising? Ladies never rose – it was at Horace's wish that he had become a lady.

But Willie Service appeared in the black field. He was followed by Harry Caldicott, the old devil. Willie Service was in his shirt-sleeves. His white car-cap was reversed – that looked like the yankee A.B.'s gob-cap that way. Horace was in a towering passion.

'Where have you been?' said he.

'What's that to do with you?' said Willie.

Mind your own business! thought Dan on the ground and in the dark he smiled to himself.

'Who said you could leave the premises?' Horace said quite the boss, to his car-slave.

'You didn't!' Willie Service seemed to say – he said something.

Willie Service was very angry. That was because he had been found out. He was so angry he was quite unlike – never seen Willie so!

'What – is this *service* – is this for wages!'

Horace seemed in a *towering* passion – never seen Horace so! – because of what Willie Service had done.

'Ab-loootions!' boomed the *beau*, hurrying.

'If you want to know I've been having a dip in the lake.'

'Well I don't wish you to go to the lake with gentlemen at the party and have dips.'

Willie had been standing on the other side of a sunk fence or *ha-ha* and now he leapt it and Harry Caldicott negotiated it. But Horace left the scene. First he said bitterly, as he was leaving.

'You have got the key of my box.'

'Yes!'

'How can I get at my screens for the big Vanish! Madre di dio!' Horace shook his fist at the deshabille of his domestic, but then suddenly he turned with a two-fisted threat upon the poor old Split-Man (his familiar, bogey-man, money-lender, clown all in one) who jumped – menacing him like a Fantee about to destroy his fetish, because some matter had miscarried.

But Willie Service jumped back over the ha-ha or the sunk fence and was lost to sight in the black field. Horace had gone and now Dan was all alone, and as there was a soft bunt in the earth just upon where he was – where one of the roots had risen to the left, the rest dropping down to compensate – or an ant's nest had been left and caved in or something else productive of great softness – he was comfortable, and he pressed up against the rough back of the tree – there was no front, all being back it is understood in a round tree. He might at this point like Arethusa have vanished into the earth himself, a fair fountain as at Eblis might have gushed up brightly where he sat to ponder before sinking – to mark the spot of the Vanish – to be discovered subsequently by Blackshirt in place of Dan. But he did not go, he sat on tranquil enough, the master of his fate – though his foot, which he still held, was terribly sore indeed and troublesome.

What should he see but a great grinning satyr though staring down at him (as if it were Arethusa there indeed and she been prevented from sinking by some hitch – from hatching her spring – and, sitting on, had been surprised by a violent denizen of the backwoods, horned though human, who looked and looked with the most eager shining eyes). Then the satyr bit its finger as if it had been a stick of toffee. From its mouth welled forth a volume of rich sound.

'Oh Madam – if I am not *de trop!* – if you have sought these sylvan shades – in search of solitude – *then* I intrude!'

Dan could scarce forbear to smile, and yet he had never been in such a fix before – that he would answer for – never had such a trap been set for his innocence and he caught napping.

'Intrude!' shouted the Blackshirt.

Evidently he had been behind the tree.

The Blackshirt blew his whistle.

'*Intrude* – you again, Harry Caldicott!'

The old period-beau took a lethargic sniff of stately snuff.

'My scheme for accompanying your chauffeur' he drawled in the most brazen way – 'up out of the water – where the poor lad all but drowned – it was I that rescued him – rendering first aid – reanimating the corpse I may say – that having proved impracticable – I am strolling here for my health – before returning to the rout.'

'Return to it at once – *Harry* Caldicott!' thundered the Blackshirt sternly at him. 'This is no place for you! It is not healthy – *here* – for *you* – Harry *Cald*-i-cott!'

Dan shuddered at the impact of the Adelphi norwester, but was very proud of his champion he had to confess. This was the *second* time!

'On the contrary!'

'Go – Harry Caldicott! Go – while the going is good!'

'I am *sorry*!' the beau sneered 'very sorry. I see that I *intrude!*'

Shrugging his braided period shoulders the obscene interloper passed on, and was immediately lost to view – taking a prodigious pinch of contumelious snuff to temper his exit.

Where *Blackshirt* went again Dan could not pretend to

determine. But he thought it was in front of the tree. He conjectured that he always went – when he was not there – in front of the tree.

But Blackshirt came round upon the other flank of Dan and kicked him. Dan placed his hand upon the place where he had experienced the blow and slowly rubbed it – looking down, his lips a-quiver for it had been to say the least unkind.

'Get up!' said Blackshirt.

When Dan heard him he thought at first that he would probably be rude, but Blackshirt kicked him again.

'If you're well enough to *get off* you're well enough to *get up!*' he exclaimed.

Well! he would not like to be married to a man like this who was *jealous* into the bargain! He was very strong and without removing himself from the tree Dan climbed up it three or four foot backwards, and now he was taller than Blackshirt, at whom he smiled provokingly.

'Yes you may smile!' Blackshirt retorted. 'He smiles best who smiles last! We know all about the Silent Woman – I suppose you think you're a great guy!'

Evidently Blackshirt thought he was a deep one – and he thought he had been fooled entirely because Dan had not said much. Taking him by the arm very roughly like a little black cop in fact, he shook him off the tree. Kneeing him disgracefully in a most offensive way, he propelled him and Dan staggered off with him and they staggered into the house. All the lights in the garden followed them into the passage like troops of fireflies and the stars of rockets, and quite dazzling at first. The Jack o' the Clock did not speak but it looked volumes and everybody seemed rushing to the lavatory as they passed. The other Bar was crowded with people. The ascent of the stairs was partly on all fours and Blackshirt was brutally cross – they burst into Lord Phoebus's room and Dan fell upon the floor – oh dear, it was a bump!

'Oh now they're getting intoxicated!' he could hear Lord Osmund at once – so he lay *very* still. 'Eustace, you might be more careful and not let them in when they can't *stand!* I do think when they can't *stand* you might see they don't get in!'

The master of the house was clearly annoyed, and Dan pretended to be dead.

'She's slipped' he heard Blackshirt say.

'I can see she's *slipped!*' he could hear Lord Osmund calling back. 'I noticed that she'd *slipped!*'

To him shamming-dead Blackshirt hissed in his ear, as savage as possible –

'Get up or I'll wring your neck!'

Well I must say! thought Dan and it would be quite evident now that he wasn't dead after all. He climbed in a very muscular way up the back of a chair the wrong way round hurting his back on a tin-tack, and when he was up again Blackshirt seized him and stumbling terribly they went over more dead than alive to the window-seat, where Dan left Blackshirt, who swayed about, as black as thunder.

'Sit there!' the Blackshirt said, with great unnecessary blackshirted sternness – as they were up in the quarters of Phœbus again he was pointing at the window-seat, where Dan already was – he was only showing off he knew. He strolled over at once to talk with Lady Harriet – that sparse hair was of a more spidery sparseness, of the old blond poll – the shrew-mouth thinner – eyes closer together, as Harriet saw him arrive. The diadem imposed upon della Francesca's masterpiece was slipped a little drunkenly to one side too, in the violence of the late sport. But Lord Osmund was headachy. His lordship had just taken a triple aspirin – Phoebus had retired to the upper floor of his stucco tower.

Dan, out of an eye that was sleep-weighted, saw the door beyond Lord Osmund open with stealth. But Lord Osmund although so indisposed was very sensitive to the movements of the door. Touch it only and he would look up with passion – however fatigued. As he saw him prick his ear – then turn and shout – Dan could not refrain from smiling to himself. One by one, the Dark Caucus, the 'unimportant conspirators' (who had learnt nothing, and forgotten nothing) came in, and closed the door, like everybody else. As they hugged the wall Dan did not see them after that for a moment, although he knew quite well they were there, but they advanced in indian file – signalling to one another as they made progress.

'I suppose you see what's happening!' Lord Osmund called angrily to Eustace. 'I suppose you're aware what's happened *now* Eustace!'

'Yes I *do*!' said Eustace.

'Oh I'm glad of *that!*'

'I saw them at once!'

'This is too much!' Osmund's throatiest complaint thrilled the assembly.

In the bombastic attitude of a beardless Henry *viii*, legs spread wide apart, with a great effect of burgess overbearingness, he stood and contemplated the intruders. He waited till they were well in, then he commenced to express himself.

'I'm not going to have *that*, anyhow! I know it's narrow-minded – but I do draw the line *somewhere!*'

And Lord Osmund took several threatening steps in the direction of the Mysterious Three and stopped.

Lady Harriet had been very thin-lipped and peak-nosed with the Blackshirt, for the circumstances of his recent entrance had not escaped her – with his intoxicated wife probably, she supposed. Now Frank Brunner who was standing there had explained to Lady Harriet what Lord Osmund's anger meant. This was the first she had heard of the Mysterious Three. But no sooner was she in possession of the facts than her passionate attitude altogether eclipsed that of her brother. The 3 were in fact pursued with the icy gimlets of her gothic eyes. Next her drawling bay made itself heard and she shouted –

'People seem to take this room for a *garderobe* or a place for making assignations!'

'I know!' said Osmund.

'I may be old-fashioned, but I really think they might show a little consideration for their hosts!'

'You ask them to a party, and they invade your private rooms as if the place belonged to them!'

'I know. Without a-by-your-leave!'

'I know! There are notices up everywhere. But they can't read apparently!'

But there was a prolonged gasp from Osmund – and he was joined by Harriet in a loud astonished roar.

'*Well!* – I must say!'

'Naturally! *Now they are going upstairs!*'

'I shouldn't wonder if they were going to look for a place to lie down in!' Harriet screamed in thrilling counter-tenor.

'Nor should I!' Lord Osmund answered in his sneering bay, as he went forward, with his fat man's massive strut. 'They're tired of the party – so they think they will go to bed! It's not a bad idea at all!'

'Exactly! I only hope they find an apple-pie bed!'

'I only hope Phoebus meets them at the top with a rousing welcome!'

'I hope they break their necks – that may be a warning to them next time!'

'I knew this would happen! Eustace has been letting people in all the evening!'

Lord Osmund reached the foot of the stairs. He bellowed up, holding his outspread hands on either side of his mouth.

'Hallo I say! do you mind terribly! I'm terribly sorry to have to trouble you – but this *is* a private house! No! It's *not* a public-house! No! I really am exceedingly sorry! Yes. Come down again do you mind!'

The various people collected in the room had now begun to move over to the foot of the stairs. Harriet screamed from the fireplace –

'Tell them Phoebus is asleep. Say there is a dangerous watch-dog on the stairs!'

'Trespassers will be prosecuted!'

'Yes! There is *a reward* for anybody giving information!'

The crowd drew closer as the three trespassers came out. One by one they came out of the staircase but it was impossible to say what their impression had been of what had occurred or what they proposed to do. There was a great confusion for some moments. Then Osmund burst out of the crowd.

'How stupid of me!' he called to Harriet. 'They are friends of Rupert's!'

He held in his hand a large ticket, upon which the compelling words A COACHFUL were printed.

Harriet was standing in front of Dan's recess and Osmund came up to her with the ticket.

'They can't speak English!' he said.

'Why didn't Rupert tell us they were coming!'

'They are from Budapest. They speak french luckily.'

'Budapest – '

'Yes from the Pester Dewlap or the Pester Lloyd George or something!'

Then Lady Harriet and Lord Osmund moved away, and the crowd began to disperse. Into Dan's recess came the Sib and the old Don doddering together and the Sib looked with a grimace of recognition at Dan. They sat down.

'What were they?' asked the Don.

'Three hungarian reporters.'

'Oh was that all!'

'They have come to London to study Gossip-column technique.'

'What is that?'

'I don't know!'

'Are they Magyars?' Pronounced by the Don *Mod-yor*.

'Something like that. They had note-books full of notes.'

'What was that for?'

'I suppose they are pioneers of Gossip – I suppose there is no Gossip in Budapest!'

'How heavenly – do you suppose so really?'

'That's what they said. They had come here to study "Le Gossipe".'

A *hooting* sound came from the direction of the Finnian Shaw inner circle. Osmund and Harriet, for the benefit of the distinguished would-be Gossip-guests, were doing in french the *gilhooter*.

'Il me semble que c'est un oiseau – qui a perdu ses jeunes!'

'Mais non! cela ne peut pas être un oiseau qui a perdu ses jeunes!'

'Mais si! C'est pour cela qu'il est si triste!'

'Mais qui donc! Soyez raisonable! *Triste* et parce qu'il avait perdu ses *jeunes!*'

The Sib breathed heavily and sweetly, attempting to coo.

'How *sweet* they are!' she burst forth softly, like the power-burst of a desiccated vegetable in the sun.

(*And* it was to be presumed that *Cockeye* would be the first name in the first Gossip-column of the first Budapest Daily first to adopt "Gossip" – *and* that soon perhaps an endemic magyar Cockeye would be discovered!)

Blackshirt had left the room but now he returned accompanied by another Blackshirt, and they both directed their steps marching in time to where Dan was, who was fast asleep. Seizing him very brutally by the shoulders, they raised him from the window-seat. One Blackshirt holding his legs, the other his head, they removed him from the room. There were loud cries of 'ABDUCTION! ABDUCTION!' but that was all.

As he swung between the two hearties, his head rolling upon the bosom of his own particular Blackshirt, Dan smiled a drunken smile at the bold word *Abduction* rolling up from sofas and settees – in his hammocky progress, ever so comfortable, he smiled. If they only knew!

XIX Killed by Kindness

With all the effrontery of which he was master Dan blushing brushed the marks of rough-usage off his person but did not quite venture to look very much at the men with their horrid language, going up and down in a great hurry, who trampled where he was. There was no protection – his girl's dress was worse than none. Their feet caused him great pain, but they were footmen, and Lord Osmund had looked down at him, that was from the stage. He made a peculiar cooing sound in his nose and went back into the Stage.

Dan was behind the stage and he had heard Horace rebuke the Blackshirts. That was for throwing him down. In the stage he could hear Horace shouting.

It was dirty and Dan crouched in against the high metal case for the properties. People came and went for they went up into the stage or round it at the side, usually to the left hand, and there was a door at the back out of which they went too. How silly! They thought he was resting and as he was a girl they took no notice. It was just as if he *were* a girl – he could not forbear to smile behind his hand, which seemed very large and rough.

All the people were the other side of the stage, where the hall was he was in. He could hear more people coming all the time, until there must have been so many that all their voices together were like one person's. It never stopped. All the people came into the hall evidently and that was to see Horace. When they saw Horace they stamped. He knew they had all seen Horace because they called Zag-rooosss. Horace laughed. Dan felt sea-sick. The swaying movement as he was carried made by the Blackshirts was awful, in his stomach, and that was the main difficulty.

A volume of sound of a low orchestra of voices hung like a cloud. From time to time it thundered suddenly. That was when Horace went up into the stage, or before he came out. While he was in there, there were often great laughs outside. Then there was clapping Dan thought would never stop. *That was praise for Horace!* Dan clapped a little, too, himself. But a footman saw him. Then he blushed violently at the footman, but he stopped. He pretended he had been dusting his hands. He felt quite angry with this servant.

When Horace had done something clever he came out of the stage. He drank a glass of water. Then he went back into the stage. A bell rang and everybody stamped their feet. He could hear Horace talking. Then everyone stamped and their voices rose and seemed to burst – it lasted sometimes a minute. He listened, he was really tremendously proud of Horace.

Dan's head was splitting. He was less sea-sick but it was worse. His thoughts all rolled about in his head. Over and over again he said *Killed with Kindness!* He said it – *Killed with Kindness* – and he considered heavily what it meant – to be killed because one was kind – to be killed with *that* seemed so strange a thing really.

Whenever Horace had been standing there waiting to go into his stage with perhaps Split-Man, he had shown him kindness – he did not think once he had been *really rude*. That was all – and it was quite certain.

Before he had never felt his thoughts loose as they were now and they all rolled about like separate objects. He dreaded their collisions and tried to keep his head without moving, but still it moved, and the thoughts grew bigger and after that went down again to their original sizes. So it was all right again really.

What he really wished to think was, if he couldn't remember Horace being rude. Of course one could. But time and place was lacking. Some notorious rudeness of Horace! he knew he was longing to recall such an occasion and could not do so – though he knew quite well it was there all the time – there had been no lack of *Horace rude* – it was *Horace kind* that it should be (one would have thought) difficult to discover. Wanted! A really bad case of Horace's rudeness! But he did at last find a very bad and painful specimen of Horace's rudeness – *Horace at his horridest* it was – and he was immediately his old self. His head ached no more. He closed his eyes. The broad peace of the self-forgetting of the deep smile of the handsome militant drunken-dummy of Blackshirt! At this point it consented to return and be worn on his face – that deep self-forgetting militant dummy-laughter!

After this Horace hurt him several times with kindness. But he minded less. When Horace would go into his stage with a jolly word of kindness – oh he would long to follow! He bit his lip to stop from weeping. He longed for nothing but *continual bad cases of utter rudeness* – without provocation!

When Horace patted the rabbit that he held in a silk-hat he felt sorry for it. A tear came into his eye. After Horace had gone back into the stage with the rabbit he poked one finger between the bars of the pigeon-box. The pigeons naturally saw the finger, they picked their feet up – they were suspicious of the tender groping claw of Man.

Horace was very much praised for what he did to the rabbit. He came back looking pleased Dan thought – he held the rabbit up on his chest and stroked it. When he saw how kind Horace was with the rabbit Dan melted again and melted so much that he gave an obvious sob. He knew he was crying. When Horace asked him if he felt all right so kindly after that, he gave a gulp. Only that was a hiccup, as it turned out, and he laughed outright. Horace laughed too.

'When I stamp!' said Horace giving Archie the end of a string. Horace went back into the stage taking a vase of beautiful flowers that closed up out of his sleeve. Dan could see into the stage because the curtain was open where it was lifted up upon a white cupboard that lay there. There was a great deal of noise. He was watching Margolin. Suddenly the little cad pulled the string. At that there was quite an uproar. Horace came rushing out of the stage and Margolin too. Horace was taking his jacket off. They were fixing something in it. They both went away, but they did not return to the stage. They went out at the left.

Next to the crates for the live-stock, the rabbits and pigeons, stood the skeleton-table – Horace only travelled one table, so he said, and Dan thought that must be right. Upon this stood decanters and glasses for conjuring. There was one scarlet and one sky-blue handkerchief for simple Vanishes – also the celebrated Egg-Bag. A few gasketted paper-bags and other articles to be spirited away were there too. But Dan singled out the decanter upon the left. He reached out an arm and he grasped it, to see how it smelt. Taking the stopper out, he put it to his nose and it stank. Scotch or Irish. He sniffed the hole. He put it to his lips – the whisky which he had recognized did a quick Vanish, but there was not much. He held it upon his knee, slowly he hiccupped with dignity and Margolin put his head through the curtain – he had not seen him go into the stage, but he was behind the curtain.

Dan just nodded his head slowly up and down and smiled at Margolin, and that was all he did – while his rival looked down at him as he lay with the empty decanter in his hand, and after a moment Margolin nodded too. Then he took his hand away from the curtain and it came out again at-the-cock and he sped a Safety Match at the head of Dan and it struck him a light tap upon the right temple. And again as if nodding to himself Dan gave a few pensive smiling assents. And then the head above shot back and the curtain closed.

After that Ratner came out of the stage. He stood looking in a mirror and doing something to his face. Horace came out of the stage. He was talking to Ratner. After some time they went into the stage and a bell rang fast. For a long time he saw nobody. He only heard a great deal of noise. He put his fingers in his ears. Then he closed his eyes and it seemed that he slept quite well, his cheek by the pigeons, who made a soothing sound inside the box.

XX God Always Desires to Manifest Himself

A great mass-roar had gone up – of imprisoned wind trapped in pneumatic animal systems, released by button-pressing – at a signal *to roar*. The curtains shook. The Split-Man had been restored to life, made whole by the bogus magician. Then there was a further roaring, upon which the Split-Man appeared to Dan and he came down the steps towards him.

To be present to a great crowd – a central actor in the dream of all its brains – for a specified moment, had stamped the excited mask of Julius Ratner. Dan hoped he would not come up to him. The face of the Split-Man had that drugged look of stupid power of the *Consul Romanus*, seen by the Opium-eater. Dan shrank from such a cruel look!

At all events one half of a Roman Triumph (the optical side of it split away from the rest) had been his, Jimjulio's – rather than Julius – and the lips of Ratner showed plainly that they had tasted one of the satisfactions of power – *to be seen* – since does not all power that is *real* exact that it shall be *visible* – does not God always desire to manifest himself! But the Rat had offered – as much as a divine rat might, in a spangled temple of Cloacina – his visible self to the regards of all. *To be seen* – it was to be distinctly present to the many retinas of an important horde that was the very life that was flesh and blood – upon *any* terms that this should be granted – that plum of plums, that essential thing! The Rat had tasted that nectarine! His body glowed as if from a massage. He had come down the stepladder flushed in consequence, from a flesh and blood *event* – a *time-truth*, that was something *historical* – unobtrusively he had molested the eye of a considerable gathering with the photograph of his fat split-person – *that* they had been compelled to cinematograph! To be the technical principal, that had not been his Rat's lot. He had been as it were *the victim* – as it were of a peculiar magical street-accident. But masses of eyeballs had opened their lids to *an event* – brains had clicked their indifferent responses. That much-advertised mock-execution – of a perpendicular dismemberment (leaving the pudenda intact upon the left leg) – had not he been half of that pictorial integer, the half that was *victim?* Then afterwards the great surgeon of these claptrap mysteries had made him whole just like a bogus Saviour, with the touch of a stick. It was a description of miracle – upon the historical plane of visible truth. No one had fathomed the trick of the illusionist – Ratner had been that man-cut-in-half for a wager and then stuck together again. But it was *his* body oh yes – of that favourite of his – Julius. And the overpowering coyness – the discreet, the respectful humbleness – the circumspection in all the well-studied movements of the accommodating body – limbs that were raised or dropped, in passive abandon, to suggest an act of love, of which he was the hypnotized *victim* – anxious to remove any bodily obstacle to the aggressor – then afterwards, in coy retreat, hand-in-hand with Horace, that *bald bashfulness* of the yellow grin, of foot-lit suet, fanged with a fierce peep of rabbit-teeth – as, but so deferentially (as convention demanded) Ratner had hung back in the rear of his principal (wishing to walk off to wings, restraining himself to give pleasure to Authority) – with a sly saffron smirk, and bowed so gentlemanly – self-possessed – that was as near as a Rat could get to the great fact of power – to be a victim – some bashful accessory.

XXI The Vanish

Exhibitionism satisfied in this manner upon the housetops – pausing to be seen by the massed citizenry, a coy ogle dropped by Mr Rat – in a bald ratnerish super-ogle – after a humble flourish of his mephisto-mocking rat's-tail – he sat down beside Dan and wondered what the time was. *The sooner we leave now the better* was the idea, the not-so-well-known-as-he-ought-to-be porno-publisher-poet now chopped in half and stuck-up with the stick-fast of wizardry. The cream of the Show. He yawned. The empty-decanter had been replaced by Dan. Merely, from his lustrous eyes of super-velvet, he threw Julius Ratner a bewitching glance of radical vacuity, which broke its dreamy wave upon the dark anfractuous sneer of his fanged friend. But Horace came down the steps and Dan gazed away into that lovely oblivion where the Great Beyond is situated, also the Place Where The Rainbow Ends. Margolin followed Horace carrying a sword.

'Do you feel up to it or not?' Horace asked of him, softly holding his conjurer's baton of ivory, and Dan smiled broadly.

Up to him! For sure Horace! And he got up shortly with good grace, and he stood expectant. Very gently he smiled at Margolin. Was not he a flower of Horace's raising – a rare fungoid bud of his? Was he not now the *moron of Horace*? He very very very much was by way of pitying Margolin – *moron of Horace* – I am Horace's moron – he is Horace's moron – Dan was not sure which, but he pitied *a moron of Horace* from the bottom of his great irish heart he was sure! And he would go up and perform as if nothing had happened at all, a smile on his lips, and those curious in what related to Horace and him would never guess what he had suffered never – they would not be apprised by him, by gesture or by look!

Horace was removing from inside his sleeve a fishing line and a loop of catgut, which he placed upon the table. Margolin picked it up and examined it at once.

'I shall have to Vanish you' said Horace to Dan. 'You know you will have to Vanish.'

Horace seemed not to know how he could do whatever he liked with his moron! *Vanish* – Dan asked nothing better! *Vanish* – but of course! And he put his foot on the ladder and up he went and before he knew where he was he was inside the stage, and Horace was there looking at him. Horace looked at him for a long time.

The other side of the stage-curtain, which was one wall of this room (which was beautifully painted to resemble the Vatican) cut them off from a world of disorder. What an uneasy apartment! It was like a roaring in a wall! All that was people! They were thick behind, it moved continually. He heard a shout out of the rest of the loud talking. It had the musical quality of a verse of poetry but it was spoken in a strange chanting accent. Dan thought that some foreigners might speak in verses as he had spoken latin – he had heard they did he was positive.

SEE, SEE, OUR OWN TRUE PHOEBUS WEARS THE BAYS!

Pretty and peculiar thought he, to call *our own true Phœbus* the more sympathetic of their hosts – that one that had the lovely doll in fact that the fifty-tonner had snatched at.

Still Dan was alone with Horace in the empty chamber. Behind him was the Vatican. Was it the Vatican now – was not that the Vatican? (It was a baroque backcloth – it revealed a vista of bold converging colonnades.) A large white cupboard was all the room contained. And Dan could not but feel uneasy.

Most fixedly Horace regarded him, and Dan could not escape from a terrible sense of impending calamity. For it did not require very much intelligence, to conclude – from all that he saw, and from the rather strange manner of Horace – that eventually it was the intention of Horace to put him into the big white cupboard!

Now – after smiling once or twice, in what in another person would have been a rather deceitful way – Horace led him up to the cupboard. Smiling (for Horace) still more deceitfully (where Horace had got these deceitful ways from *it was not difficult to guess!*) he gave him his hand – he no longer made any disguise of the fact that he intended that he should go into it.

He allowed himself to be assisted up into the cupboard. What else was there to do? And he certainly made no protest when Horace brutally – thrusting him in with both hands – without another word closed and made fast the door of this sinister cabinet. But by this time thoroughly frightened, he pushed up against it, in mute moist-eyed despair, and so violent was the trembling of all his body that he shook the cupboard to its foundations, which were not very solid, and Horace opened the door again.

Ashamed as he was of what he had done, he still could not master his shuddering legs once they had started and the thing continued to rattle.

But Horace told him kindly but sternly to flatten himself and press a button in the roof. He shrank against the inner wall of the cupboard and pressed the button, when a blind flew down at his back. Once more he found himself darkly occulted, but in a still more confined space. Horace told him to press again upon the button and he pressed as he was told. Thereupon he was as before in the centre of the cupboard. Horace was standing there outside and looking in at him. Did he see, Horace asked him, what he was to do, did he think? And he said yes – he flattened himself and touched the button. Then he was once again in the dark. A further press on the hidden button, the blind flew up, and again he stepped out into the centre of the cabinet.

Now Horace made him get out of the cupboard and then get in again. He told him to hide himself and he hid himself. Horace called softly *Come out!* Dan pressed upon the hidden button and he came out. – That was the *Vanish.* He smiled at Horace and Horace was very very kind and he smiled. They went back to the cupboard, Horace whispered to him to hide. *Hide!* he whispered. And Dan hid. *Come out!* said Horace and Dan came out. And Dan liked the game so much he did it again – and as often as he did it Horace whispered *Hide!* and he hid – or *Come out!* and he pressed the button and there he was.

Now they went back out of the stage. They were all together below. Margolin went up into the stage and came back. Then Horace and he went into the stage again. A bell rang and the curtain began going up, noiselessly from the ground into the air, and there beneath it or where it had been he saw in the dark a great collection of faces, and he was before the audience with Horace at his side. He saw Blackshirt at once, he could not help but smile, it seemed so funny Blackshirt being in the crowd, watching what Horace and he did. Horace and he were quite at home and in no hurry to do anything. He stood on the edge of the room and smiled down at Blackshirt, shaking his head a little sadly as he did so. And Horace was playing with a stick which he was making crawl all over him like a snake.

A footman brought in the pigeons and Horace began to play with the pigeons. He hid one in a hat. Another he produced from his mouth and this looked so funny that as it burst out of Horace's lips with its wings Dan laughed outright, he could not help it.

This must have disturbed Horace, for the pigeon struggled and suddenly it flew away, escaping from his hand and outside into the room. There was a wild scream as it flew up. In the greatest alarm Dan gazed out at everybody moving and turning. Quite in the distance he perceived the body of the Bonassus being carried out of the great lighted door, beside the gallery, at the opposite extremity of the place – where he could easily see Lord Osmund and Lord Phoebus, with Lady Harriet and other ladies and gentlemen sitting in the gallery where the band had been.

'He thinks the pigeon escaped from his mouth!' somebody said beneath him and Dan looked down at once. 'It is a Trinity Complex!'

Now Horace began talking to him, and soon (as he had

expected) Horace began leading him towards the cupboard. He did not feel so alarmed seeing that now all those people were there, but he felt a little giddy and he missed his footing as he was getting into the cupboard.

But Horace helped him up with considerable politeness – taking into account that he was a lit-lady – and he got in again, 'When I close the door *hide!*' said Horace. 'And when you hear me say *Come out*, press the button and I will open the door.' And Horace showed all the people the inside of the cupboard, hitting it with his stick, and Dan stood there in the middle of it smiling and then Horace closed the door.

He flattened himself and pressed the button and there he was. Horace opened the door again as he could hear, and there was a great deal of noise as the people expressed their astonishment at not seeing Dan. They had quite expected to see Dan standing there. And Dan smiled to himself. All of them had decidedly been imposed upon! But it was very tight. Horace closed the door again and then he began hitting the cupboard from the outside. That was to show it was empty. (Horace *was* in some ways deceitful!) He had not noticed that his nose had started bleeding but now it bled all down the front of him. He could hear it dripping on the floor. The noise outside increased all of a sudden and Dan could hear the word BLOOD! They were all saying BLOOD. Then Horace said *Come out!* and he gladly pressed the button and went into the middle of the cupboard, wiping the blood from his face. At that moment Horace opened the door and there he stood and he could see now it was light inside the cupboard that he was covered with blood.

Horace held out his hand and he fell rather than walked out of the cupboard. The most horrid loud laughs with a great deal of stamping and rude calling out followed them and Horace led him out of the stage. They went down the steps and he lay down on the floor on his back. He heard Horace say – 'He bled in the cupboard in the middle of the Vanish. The blood came through between the boards.' Both Margolin and Ratner gave the most horrid laughs and then he fell asleep. That ended the Vanish.

XXII The Play

'Do you feel up to it!' Horace said. He gave him a basin and towels and he was to wash his face. Horace rubbed the front of his dress to get the blood stains off and they all went into the stage. The room was different now, except for the picture at the back of the Vatican and he sat down before a large mirror in which he saw all the room. 'I shall come in' said Horace, and he sat looking in the mirror, while the bell rang. The curtain went up again from the floor slowly, and there were all the people in the dark as they were before. Blackshirt was there who seemed nearer and he encountered his eyes at once and he thought he looked very angry now. He probably wished to 'broadcast'. Poor Blackshirt! Dan smiled kindly at him – but Horace came in and said, in a loud and measured voice –

'But be she fair indeed, a pure sanguine complexion, neck soft and plump – body, hands, feet all fair and lovely, an absolute piece: let her head be from Prague, paps out of Austria, belly from France, feet from Rhine, buttocks from Switzerland – after she hath been married a small while and the black ox hath trodden on her toe, she will be so much altered thou wilt not know her!'

Dan did not know which way to look. Lower and lower hung his head, to hide his blushes, at these descriptions. This catalogue of things – those things that were *never mentioned* – shouted out by Horace beside him there, before *everybody* – never could he have imagined anything so bad – and the blush burst a blood-vessel. Steadily Dan began bleeding again down upon his snow-white triangle – the man-tempting flesh-fragment cut out of the horrid frock, and so damp and trickly down inside. But Horace had stopped and there was a fierce outcry.

But out of one eye (hemmed in by a cruel blush) Dan was able to remark a noticeably dark form, and then another, standing and shouting beneath. All the people were turning round. A black arm was held haughtily on high, in the fashion of the fascist salute. A voice of angry authority cried out and Dan recognized at once the tone of that overbearing address that had put to flight the offensive Harry. It was the voice of his blackshirted deliverer, that made itself heard beneath.

'Stop!' it called. 'Stop! Horace Zagreus! I forbid you to proceed any further!'

Full scandal *lazzi* shook the house and Dan gently bled upon his marble chest – red nose-tears of blank dismay. Mr Zagreus had gravely stopped in his declamation. With arms akimbo he awaited the arrival of the interrupter.

'I hold up your performance of this play' the figure that was Blackshirt said 'until I have had a word with you!'

'What is this Starr-Smith!' Dan heard his master ask, in tones that were both stern and mild. And the Blackshirt replied – for he was standing now just at the foot of them, in company with the other Blackshirts –

'Zagreus! I have been forced to do this to bring you to reason!' And he vaulted up and stood a few feet from Dan while his friends remained below. Margolin and Ratner and also one other person, in blue overalls, had come out of the wings, and they all stood together.

'You cannot treat Pierpoint in this way!' the Blackshirt objected.

'I don't understand you Starr-Smith!' Horace was almost but not quite smiling.

'I have explained before you started. But you would not listen.'

'Yes I listened.'

'You listened. But you have gone on with it!'

'Of course I have. I had announced it.'

'What right had you to announce it! It was not yours Zagreus to announce!'

'I have explained to you Starr-Smith.'

'If it rested with Pierpoint he would allow himself to be plundered by anybody. They would pick his brains – and then not pay!'

'That is not fair Starr-Smith!'

'It is my business to see that he isn't!'

'Oh yes!'

'You are playing the same game Zagreus as the people whom he denounces – and whom *you* denounce.'

'I denounce all that he denounces!'

In solemn tones Horace assented.

'That is it! But you are as bad as the rest!'

'No you are quite wrong. I would do nothing to injure our master.'

'Is this not an injury!'

'To me, yes. You have now spoilt my performance! I have learnt my part for nothing!'

'I can't help that Zagreus!'

'Well there it is – you won't let me do the play, so we must ring down.'

'I am afraid so.'

'I will see Pierpoint tomorrow and explain. It doesn't matter.'

'I will explain too!' Starr-Smith cried excitedly and Dan moved in against the wall, still bleeding and he had no handkerchief.

'All right – you see him too Starr-Smith. We'll both see him' Horace laughed good-naturedly.

'Whatever he says, I know I have done right.'

'Starr-Smith!' Horace exclaimed, demonstrative and with a slight gesture of his hand. 'You are the only man in this room that I like!'

As he heard this Dan felt a dagger plunged into his heart and he bled more freely than before at the nose.

'No' said Horace, 'what you feel for our master does you great credit!'

'I am obliged to you for that Zagreus. But fair play is fair play.'

'I have explained to you Starr-Smith in confidence my difficulties and yet you attack me publicly in this way. Is that fair play Starr-Smith?'

'Yes! Yes it is! Tell me why you have not –'

But with a rapid gesture Horace Zagreus stopped him and he turned now to his assistants.

'Ratner – pull down the curtain. Curtain!'

But Ratner did not seem to have heard Horace at all, for he stood there as before and all he did was, holding himself in an attitude of coy restraint, to direct his offensively smothered I-hope-you-don't-see-it (I'm-doing-my-best-to-hide-it) grin of superior-cunning, first at Horace, then at Blackshirt, and so back again. Horace looked at Ratner, awaiting the appropriate response to the stimulus, and a complete silence fell upon the assistants, and all the outcry and disturbance outside the stage broke in violently upon them.

'Take that grin off your face!' Blackshirt shouted suddenly at Ratner.

'What have I done?' Ratner protested archly as if he had been waiting for that. He looked at Horace for an explanation at once.

'I do not answer you!' Blackshirt exclaimed violently.

'No?' said Ratner.

'No!' said Starr-Smith.

'Don't lose your temper Starr-Smith with only *half* a man!' Zagreus was in the best of humour – and said to himself, as a matter of fact, a few lines more of his part, under his breath.

'Half a – kaka!' Blackshirt vociferated, brandishing his arms as if they were clubs. He grew more and more welsh with every word and that celtic light in his eyes had been lighted which nothing but a hard kick upon the especially-inflated portable stomach of a leather football can put out – upon a damp welsh afternoon – and Dan could not help it, he gave a smile.

But Ratner was simply turning tippet and the pogromed animal of another day came out, and the grinning face was frankly used as a bait to the blackshirted ruffian, to draw blood – an auto-blood-letting – he ogled the other inviting a good stiff blow and the Blackshirt felt it being drawn out of him by that hypnotic fish-eye in profile starkly – and he started back as he felt the infernal attraction, sullenly drawing in his horns.

'You aren't violent are you Starr-Smith!' Ratner croaked. And as he heard the exultant provocative croak of his Split-Man, Zagreus turned quickly away, as if giving it up as a bad job, and awaiting the event with his back turned.

Blackshirt stood his ground. For several full seconds he held back but Ratner's eye had the better of the argument. Steadily it milked away at him in puissant glances of seductive insult – drawing that famous *violence* out of him. Slowly it was driven into his little fists – it clenched them up, and it locked in a bull-dog grip his big pugnacious teeth – tightened up his thigh muscles – charged him irresistibly with opposite electricity. It was as good as done. Then Ratner, with perfect judgment, spoke two words.

'*Are you!*' said Ratner.

And it was all over with poor Blackshirt, for he leapt up as he started to move forward – for he had not understood how his body had acquired a peculiar rigor – the shock was considerable.

'I will show you what *violence* is, that I will quickly show you too – you will tell me when you know – I wonder! Take that for your *violent* now – take that too look you – when next – and that now! Ah!'

Dan shrunk back and hid his face. The feet of all the people in the stage began thundering on the boards together it seemed, and everyone's breath came fast and hot. Dan heard horrid blows upon india-rubber that squeaked. There were loud sounds as if sacks of vegetables were being swiftly transferred from one point to another – bangs and bumps that made his heart jump into his throat – stamping, and the rush of blustering projectiles or a sudden football-match. And then suddenly there was a larger thump, and a great peace succeeded the thump – and everybody breathed hard, but that was all. Dreading what his eyes might reveal to him, he lifted them timidly up and he saw that Julius Ratner had quite disappeared from the stage. This was another Vanish he said to himself with candour, and he looked at the cupboard but it stood open, and everybody was looking out of the stage.

'Let him now say I am violent I allow him to. I *am* violent!' the Blackshirt suddenly shouted.

'Oh!' said Horace who had been reading a letter with his back turned.

'Yes! Violent is just what I am!'

Horace walked over to the edge of the stage and looked down. Dan remarked that all the people had come in a great crowd up to the stage, and were bending down examining something underneath.

'It's all right' said Horace very coolly and he went into the wings and the curtain began to move down – he was doing it and Margolin went in after him.

'Look out Starr-Smith!' Horace called.

Blackshirt was leaning out of the stage and talking to the other Blackshirts. He looked up and as he saw the moving curtain he jumped off the edge. The curtain came down to the floor.

It was quite light outside the stage now. Horace went out

on the other side of the curtain and Dan heard him say, while people stopped speaking to hear him –

'You see Ladies and Gentlemen that a difficulty has arisen. A little drama has succeeded to a slight difference of opinion. One of my assistants has been knocked off the stage by a member of the audience, who objected to the manner in which the play was being produced. My assistant, I am glad to say, is not hurt, I think.' (There was a pause – someone was heard to say 'He says he is all right'). 'I have much pleasure in announcing that Mr Starr-Smith has won by a knock-out. Lord Osmund Finnian Shaw has been kind enough to let it be known that he will match Mr Starr-Smith against Dempsey, for a purse of a hundred guineas! In any event, this resourceful member of the audience, in substituting his own melodrama for mine, has proved an excellent entertainer. I suggest that he be offered a hearty vote of thanks. That Ladies and Gentlemen will conclude the performance!'

There was a great deal of noise and they were evidently praising Horace very much and Dan was very glad for this and got up and sat in the open cupboard. Horace came out of the corner of the curtain, and he said to Dan –

'Help me carry that cabinet.'

He pointed to the cupboard, in which Dan sat.

He and Horace took the big cupboard down the steps and Margolin came round from the front of the stage.

'Is Ratner all right?' Horace asked him.

Dan was weak because the cupboard was terribly heavy with the loss of blood and he dropped it. He sat down. Margolin came round and picked it up, and they went on with it.

Margolin seemed full of genius and he smiled and smiled at Horace and he smiled back at him as Dan dropped the cupboard.

'Some ladies are putting butter on his eye!' with great split-tyre-like splutters Archie told Horace, and they laughed at the thought.

Then Ratner came round the corner. He had a handkerchief tied round his head with blood on it, and Dan thought he looked like a pirate. He was smiling, he looked very coy and pleased. He had not seen him since he disappeared.

Horace sat down on the big case and Willie Service was there.

'Did he hurt you?' asked Horace, taking a cigarette out of his case.

'No Horace. – He nearly broke my neck. I cut myself.' Ratner pointed to his head.

'You must go and see Mrs Bosun!' said Horace.

'Must I?'

Ratner croaked and grinned horridly – the coyest stoic ever bred upon a roman receipt for ills of a very unroman complexion – as pleased as Punch when that puppet had bludgeoned a cop or tripped up a turnkey. Margolin himself was in such high spirits and limitless form, that Dan turned away his head, with a pained expression, as if his eyes were not very strong and a light were attempting to dazzle them.

Horace laughed, sitting on the box.

'They say a cat has nine lives!' he said.

Ratner replied with a sepulchral croak of fierce disdainful masochism. He turned away from Horace as if to prevent himself from laughing with bitter exultation, in mock-politeness. Willie Service stood silent, his car-cap canted over his eyes, and he looked at Dan fixedly.

Lord Osmund came round the corner followed by Lord Phoebus. The coyness, of the masochistic stoicism, of Ratner became so marked, that both Horace and Margolin laughed together. Dan smiled wistfully at the floor.

'Are you hurt?' asked Lord Osmund with a commiseration that was more lofty when he ended the remark even than when he had begun it.

The painfully-grinning lips of Ratner, with the discreet peep of rabbit-fangs, dripped with coyness, as he answered –

'Oh no thank you Lord Osmund! I fell on my head!'

(*My head* Lord Osmund – it was my little headie-beddie that had that great fall! – your lordship's own little julian Humpty-Dumpty!)

'I saw you do *that*!' said Lord Osmund however. A much nearer view of the victim did not seem to prejudice Lord Osmund in his favour at all – he seemed to wish to be turning away. 'But I thought you might be *hurt!*'

'It's nothing really!' croaked Ratner bitterly – for he saw

that Lord Osmund took no interest in his version of Humpty-Dumpty and that no amount of blood would wash out the painful fact of his partnership for his lordship.

'I'm so glad!' said Lord Osmund with a slight sniff, looking at Zagreus.

'So am I!' abruptly bayed Lord Phoebus very loudly indeed, his eyes flying away, like a haughty gazelle's – but easily startled – in the other direction.

Lord Osmund and Lord Phoebus passed on and Margolin, Service and Horace, began to pack what had been in the stage, helped by two footmen and a boots.

XXIII Beware of Pickpockets

Two bedrooms had been allotted them but when they reached the hall it was impossible to cross it. The main staircase was besieged by a heavy crowd, which shouted complaints. Hostile cries seemed to be breaking from everyone. Upon the stairs stood Lord Osmund and Lord Phoebus at bay, two footmen and many osmundians were there holding back the crowd and higher up on the stairs the Finnian Shaw family seemed very angry indeed.

'I can't help it if you've lost your fur-coat!' Lord Osmund was shouting at Lady Truncheon, and the two bunters were in tears, while Lady Truncheon had a noisy faction.

'One would have thought in your house Lord Osmund that it was safe to deposit a coat – !'

'What! With people of *this* sort about!'

And Lord Osmund distributed a glance over the shouting people.

'They are your guests aren't they? These are guests you have invited.'

'All these people my guests! I should be sorry to think so! I have not the least idea who they are! I know what they *look* like!'

'Is there no protection!'

'Absolutely none! I would not leave anything worth a penny where they could lay their hands on it! As it is we have lost half our plate! Luckily it all was bought at Woolworths!'

'Then do I understand there is nothing to be done about my coat!'

'Certainly you are to understand that! Can't you read? Haven't you seen the notices *Beware of Pickpockets!*'

'I thought in such a house as this that notice was a joke!'

'No joke at all, I can promise you!' Lord Phoebus bayed down at her.

'It's disgraceful!'

'It is!' Lord Osmund said. 'Very disgraceful!'

'Your attitude is disgraceful!'

'Is it Lady Truncheon?'

'You are a cad!'

'That's as it may be!'

'I shall send for the police!'

Lady Harriet appeared at the top of the stairs and she recognized Lady Truncheon and her eye gleamed.

'Yes that's right send for the police!' Lady Harriet screamed over the heads of her brothers. 'I don't believe she ever had a fur-coat! Telephone for the police at once! She's trying a bit of blackmail, for a change!'

From the doorway beyond, which led into the courtyard, an enraged guest tore his way through a knot of sight-seeing chauffeurs.

'My car has been taken' he bellowed. 'What am I to do!'

'Buy another one!' screamed Harriet.

'Go to the devil!' said Lord Osmund, and he turned and started to ascend his baroque staircase, with a contemptuous waggle of his insolent behind, shrugging his shoulders as he went at Phoebus.

'That's all very well!' shouted another angry person brandishing his hand. 'But how about *my* things! They've taken my attaché case and everything!'

'And what about *mine!* Here is my cloakroom ticket – but the things have gone! What's the use of a *ticket!* It's preposterous!'

Lord Osmund turned at the word *preposterous* and stopped a moment to shout down –

'*I* haven't got your things!'

'I didn't say you had!'

'I should go and take somebody else's!' shouted Harriet.

'You should look after your things! I've seen with my own

eyes a half-dozen pickpockets at work! I nearly lost the buckles off my shoes just now!' Osmund kicked out a gilt-shoed foot.

'A nice party!'

'I agree with you! A *lovely* party!' Lord Osmund again gave the crowd a comprehensive glance.

And all the world of Osmund sneered down upon the plundered guests.

'I'm glad you see that!'

'Don't mention it! – Peters! Peters!'

'My lord!'

'Close that Bar at once. And the other one! Yes – both! Don't serve them with any more drinks! Half of them are drunk. We don't want them here all night, picking each other's pockets!'

As the greatest confusion continued to prevail in the central hall and one man continued to shout about his coat, another his hat, another calling piteously for a car, for an attaché case, and Lady Truncheon sat down on the staircase and wept for her lost sables, and everyone raised contrary cries, some for and some against, and there was a drunken fight proceeding because one woman accused another of having stolen her man – Horace led his company back to the stage, and there they made their exit by the small door to the rear of it.

When Horace shook Dan, with fast-shut eyes Dan clung to his dream which the unkind hand sought to rob him of. It was a sweet dream about Horace. But even in his dream Horace had been horrid. He had disguised himself and he could not make out which was Horace, as there were several persons that might be he and he could not decide which to confide in – in other words to entrust his *genius* to – which he had under his pillow and which turned out to be a *rabbit* – a very pretty little thing and when Horace at last got hold of it he caressed it very much.

As a cape upon his shoulder Horace had an overcoat, and in his hand was an electric torch. Dan got up of course as he soon parted from his dream when the real Horace commanded him to, and he saw a small bottom in the window and it was Margolin leaning out. Ratner sat upon his bed and his eyes were almost completely closed with the unhealthy swellings of his sleep, and scowled out from under the bandage very sluggishly at Dan.

Dan put on the footman's trousers that were there for him and he felt so shy as a man at first and just like a girl, and when Horace spoke to him he blushed.

When Dan was dressed they went out and the others were still dressed as when he last saw them. As they went along the moonlit passages, Horace's torch flashing about like a restless eye, Dan thought he saw the doors moving. Looking back he caught sight of white faces, which had come out of them suddenly to spy.

They went down the state-staircase. Horace crossed the hall to the American Bar. He opened the door, and flashed his torch all over it, not in the bar but at the door. Then he closed it again. After that he approached the double-doors of the Great Saloon and he looked at them in the same way. These he opened up, they were bolted. He flashed his torch – he reminded Dan of a burglar and took a few tools out of his pocket. Margolin held the electric torch and he started to remove the left hand door, it was a big one, standing upon a chair to reach the upper hinges. But the house began to echo with a hoarse whispering and the boards creaked. From almost every shady recess or convenient corner eyes seemed to be watching them at work.

When the door came off, Margolin and Ratner held it up on end. Then Horace seized it, and together they began going with it towards the entrance hall. In a bright haddock-pink dressing-gown Lord Osmund stepped out of a lavatory where he had been hiding. He said to Horace in a low voice as if he did not wish to disturb anybody –

'Must you take it away?'

'It is essential!' Horace replied without stopping.

'I only thought it might not matter!'

'No.'

'Because I would *rather* you left it if it's all the same to you!'

'I do want it however I think.'

'Very well. Only you *will* bring it back!'

Horace did not say he would bring it back and Lord Osmund went away. They were near the front door. Margolin was undoing the bolts. Noticing a flyflot hackencross design in a rug at his feet, Horace drew Ratner's attention to it but Ratner thought it was *nothing Horace*. Horace did not seem satisfied but as the door was now open they passed on with the half of a door.

Dan looked up as every Irishman does when he goes out of doors and he saw a great many gently lighted dove-grey clouds and he knew that the pale white-rose of the new sun that lay in the black spaces underneath was there, sending up its weak preliminary mirage, and the keen wind from the dove-grey cliffs came down and blew in their faces. Ratner coughed. The moon was a neat slice of ice that was upside-down and was a quite brilliant fragment, and Zagreus gave it a glance again, for its own sake this time for that ever-vivid meniscus.

They stopped all together, setting down the door, by the high flank of the barn. Zagreus and Margolin laid down the door between them upon the wet turf. Zagreus took from his pocket a little flute and put it to his lips. Margolin leapt into the centre of the large and panelled door and commenced a dance. Coyly sneering, Ratner as well stepped up upon the door brought out to be a stage and stiffly worked his legs about just as much as was necessary for a puppet, and his performance looked like that.

But Dan wandered on to the door too, and he found himself, with arms outstretched, accompanying the measure, placing the points of his feet first here then there, and beating a sort of time.

As he looked up, Dan saw that the windows of the house were full of people. They were in pyjamas with ruffled hair or their bald heads shone palely in the last rays of the moon and the large lamp swinging in the courtyard.

Willie Service sprang out of the ground and touched his hat. They all fled from the borrowed door as a pistol shot rang out. It was Cockeye's burglar-alarm, which fired a pistol, that was supposed to frighten thieves.

Part 13

THE GENERAL STRIKE

DAN took out his log and he read the pathetic heading THE FIRST APE. That had been his first APE OF GOD! He dispersed a full-blooded scalding tear that stood in his eye and another took its place, of a similar volume, volcanically hot. It thudded upon the log – it scalded the FIRST APE. A third tear rose upon the parapet of the lid. He discharged it – to rid the lid of its weight and to see clear. Others followed. He turned over the page. But he could read no more in that sad historic log. For him the last Ape he was ever to meet had been met with – his log was at last a museum of natural history – there was every variety of ape-like creature, to show like Darwin out of what men came – submen and supermen. For the last time he had seen those potent gestures with which Zagreus or Starr-Smith – great understudies of that invisible magnifico Pierpoint – pointed towards some embodiment of impotence. And he must say goodbye to all that *genius* too, which had been the star and the wild plum – the lode-stone and the baksheesh – the spell and the *solatium*. Amen!

And so he slowly tore that log in pieces. Then after that he tore the letter containing the *Encyclical*, and all those other notes and letters whatsoever, written to him by Horace in good faith, before he had found him out – for he had been found out. His fingers did their sad last work well, and strangled the log and letters. They divided everything – everything in the world – into smaller and smaller pieces – till no sentence at all was intact in all that mass of flattering precept and objurgation. Alas!

Last of all came the last letter, that was the one just now to hand, that bitter epistle. The last kick of that pragmatical pedantry of his cruel task-master was the worst yet. With much convulsive reluctance to take it up he seized it and for a time it lay open upon his knee.

Dear Dan – he read. Dear Dan! (A great tear rushed out and spat upon the page.)

Then he read for the last time how Horace said – 'I am confronted with the necessity of immediately reducing my expenditure.' (And another mighty six-foot person's tear hit the page with a gravitational smack that rang out in the room.) 'I find I am compelled to pay off Willie Service and I fear that I shall no longer be able to defray the very considerable cost of your prolonged apprenticeship. But perhaps after all this is just as well. You may not be so fitted for these severe exercises of the intellect as I had at first believed. (We all make mistakes sometimes.) Recently you have shown a strange and insubordinate spirit which did not hold forth much promise for the future progress of your studies. *Absolute obedience*, you will recall, was the capital condition – the Society of Jesus itself could not exact a more implicit abnegation than is required in such an undertaking as that I proposed to you. Submissive at first, you have become of late so violent and overbearing – so disposed to question the least order or to misunderstand my intentions for you – and have often taken the law into your own unpractised hands, that I confess at times I have felt myself in the midst of some sentimental 'bottom-dog' Revolt, or that I had taken to my bosom a barbarian, instead of one (as I had fondly believed) who had the makings of a disciplined and rational person – destined to be a fine *Frontkämpfer* of the new idea. Finally, your disgraceful drunkenness at the Lenten Party given at the country-house of Lord Osmund Finnian Shaw, upon the occasion of that recent fiasco, opened my eyes, there is no denying. Not content with flinging off a high stage a person half your size and twice your age – unable to take his own part, coming as he does of a celebrated race of financial wizards, essentially unmilitary – feeble in body, who (although I am sure not from lack of will) had never in his life done you any injury – not content with that ruffianly act, by your brutal trampling dance upon your departure you made a gigantic fissure in the door borrowed from Lord Osmund for a little *pas-de-quatre* in the best peasant-tradition of the land where he exercises power – and that august irish gentleman has now (not unnaturally) sent me in the bill! And from Ratner – not unnaturally – I have another bill for medical attendance and subsequent night and day nurses. All was as merry as music – only you were out of key, moody and spoiling for mischief! – No! all things considered it is perhaps as well that we are proceeding no further together. I must confess that, latterly, the patent danger attending your society has caused me at times some misgiving, on the score of my personal safety. As Pierpoint put the matter to me (when we talked it over) – 'to have such a great athletic brute as that around Zagreus,' said he ' – violent at the best of times, by all accounts, but into the bargain an *alcoholic* – consuming, as Starr-Smith tells me, twenty glasses of intoxicant without turning a hair! – That is neither desirable nor, with due regard to safety, wise!' That was Pierpoint's view of the matter. But when one further considers that even the whisky used in my simple Vanishes was not sacred to you, but fair game for your ungovernable thirst – for I had scarcely turned my back when you had dispatched the better part of a pint, of the best Glen Livet – well Dan I think you must agree that it is high time I separated myself from a person who (for all your excellent qualities – in some cases, I have at times believed, amounting almost to *genius*) in such a striking degree betrays that notorious failing of your race. With such intemperate habits even the greatest genius cannot go far. – In conversation with Starr-Smith – who is a keen observer if nothing else – I learnt of your behaviour in the American Bar and elsewhere. According to that witness you never opened your mouth once during the entire period you remained beneath his charge but maintained sullen and insubordinate silence. In your intoxicated condition – so I am informed by him – he experienced the greatest trouble in mastering you – and Starr-Smith is a brave and muscular young man – he has played centre-forward for Llandudno Wells on two occasions, and is I am told an intrepid half-back and fast hockey-crack. Yet he tells me that several times in succession you threw him to the ground – that when he requested you to rise, you attempted to defy him by swarming up a tree (an ape-like proceeding) and then abruptly changing your mind, you fell upon him, seized him about the waist and flung him with such violence to the ground that you caused him to break a rib. (For that I have another bill in my pocket.) Starr-Smith affirms that alternately you would invite him to dance, with an immodest effrontery (seeing how you were dressed at the time) and take him up in your arms and crush him like a polar bear. His report to Pierpoint was (as summarized afterwards for my benefit) that you are one of the most dangerous and treacherous young men it would be possible to find – that you are quite unsuited for such society as your duties with me would naturally take you into. – But I will not say that I endorse all these judgments and many more occurring in this abstract of Starr-Smith's, and delivered by him in conversation. My picture of you would be far less radical. Some bias, too, had I think crept in – for I have, on occasion, known you to be quite docile and even when it suited you, not ungentle. This view I upheld when pressed by Pierpoint upon the matter. I daresay that the fracture to his right rib influenced Starr-Smith to some extent, and perhaps warped his judgment. – All the same you should take this to heart – you should remember what a great ox-like fellow you are you know (you must forgive me, but the fact remains) – it is no joke to have you on one's hands when you are demented with drink. It is excellent to have a giant's strength – *to use it* like a giant is another matter and causes one to be unpopular – you know the english adage I suppose about giants! Remember that the English invented parliamentary democracy. So, just because you have been cast in a titanic mould, like some legendary warrior of Ossian, that is no reason why you should make everyone feel the weight of your legendary right arm. That is to be a *bully*. This term used by the English to describe a giant who insists on behaving like one – refusing to accept the necessary conditions of urbane life within the herd – is very useful as a term. But it is abusive. The *als ob* doctrine of a sportsmanlike *average*, that is the perfect democrat – rather aim at that you follow me! I may still be permitted to advise you. You are not asked to regard yourself as a pigmy: on the other hand it is expected of you to contrive to give the impression of *being no-bigger-than-anybody-else*. Woe to you if you don't! If you do not acquire this simple democratic habit of make-believe, there is no place for you in contemporary life – you may really take this from me. (I have had some!) However, your violence of disposition – that makes it worse, much worse – to put a passionate savagery into being *big*. What I am talking about may only be a part of your gigantic lack-of-tact. You *may* be less violent than you *seem* Dan. But in that case you should remember that if a giant blows his nose that sounds just as if he were positively *roaring*. So, if you seize a person around the waist in play with what to you perhaps seems only a hearty non-committal hug – then to the person so handled it will appear a rape and an assault. He will put you down as *violent* – especially if you break his rib. As to the intemperance – that is no doubt in the blood – that will, I am persuaded remain your greatest social handicap. As a first step toward combating that, I suggest you get hold of some suitable Temperance Tract. (Always avoid Temperance Hotels however – they immediately drive a susceptible person to the bottle.) So farewell. I wish you every success in your new life. But never come to me for a *character* – not after the episode of the *decanter of whisky!*

P.S. – It may be of some interest to you to know (simply for old times' sake) that I have a new *tame devil*, and have told Ratner that I shall not require his services in future. I daresay you were not aware of it, Ratner was of some little use to me in certain financial matters, but I have been enabled entirely to discharge my indebtedness to him and I may add that this is a considerable relief for he was apt of late to interfere. In talking this matter over with Archie Margolin, he agreed with me that Pierpoint's estimate of Ratner was in some ways fallacious, and Pierpoint has now come to be of my opinion. – You know my system. I believe that as *genius* represents all that is high, so there must be something in every person's social life to stand for all that is the reverse of that. (To this factor or representative of all that is material, mean, and ill-favoured in our life I attribute a similar function to that of the *catharsis* of the attic drama.) But *now* I have the sleekest old demon you ever saw! You can read all his thoughts, but as it were upside down. Virtue is *the right way up of everything* – am I not right? As 'A Jew' he is really what Lord Osmund's 'Old Colonels' are – Elizabethan perhaps as they are Regency. Such people scarcely exist any longer outside of books – and newspapers. Starr-Smith told me how you kicked one of the *Colonels*, and after that, so he said, he explained very thoroughly to you just what they were – the *Old Colonels*. Well, *you would certainly kick* my new acquisition! But he would expect it. Whereas Ratner was not quite flesh, fowl, nor good red herring – that is of course his tragedy. My present find – about him there is no nonsense! He is adorably tortuous. When I ask him to meet me at the north end of the Burlington Arcade, I always take up my position at the South – and there he is to the minute – but at the *opposite* point of the compass and the *opposite* hour of the day – for I have found that he somehow works it out that when I say 5 I really mean 2.30 or 10, and of the two he takes that *furthest off* – that is his system. – He was found for me by Archie Margolin – indeed he is a relative of his – he is a maternal uncle. (I am informed by Archie that he belongs to one of the *worst* and *most diabolical* sephardic stocks in all Galicia!) All his instincts are topsy-turvy – where Ratner was merely *split*, this one is inverted and introverted – he does not know what truth means – he has no standards *whatever!* He is not a *bad* man, he is rather good-hearted and in many matters he is to my great surprise *extremely liberal*. (My settlement with Ratner has been at his instigation.) He is not humanly bad therefore, he is – how shall I say? – simply *satanic*. He is worth ten of old Ratner! Ratner was a fake-intellectual. Again he was so disgustingly *gentlemanly* and bourgeois. He was a minor Satan perverted by his little literary vanity, and so really a sort of Ape of God rather than a minor Satan. But this one is a perfect minor Satan of the first water (no pretences whatever of intellect) and he feeds out of my hand. (Oddly enough, he has a great admiration for his nephew. – Margolin is, I think, the greatest genius – always bar one – I have ever met! He seems to understand *everything!* He is also the first Jew I have met who has *genius* – he is another Spinoza! The Jews dislike him, as they did the great Portuguese! It is another proof that with these ancient races they are either better than the average of other races, or else far worse – at all events crazy.)

(*Signed*) HORACE ZAGREUS

The apparition of himself that emerged from these descriptions filled Dan with great fear and stupefaction. Horace was holy writ and his word was physical law, in consequence the facts of the natural world were at fault, in this startling disparity between the Dan he knew and that version of Horace, of a Dan that was man-eating. As a result of this he had the sensations of madness now, for his brains performed somersaults, and he stood quite giddy as if he had recently been champagning again. – Certainly such a self was an apparition – of a dreadful giant – but that simply must be the real and the true. But the Dan of his past experience of himself now – *that* was a gentle spectre which had been cast up to deceive him. A maidenly young man he had been accustomed to see, instead of a blackguard and rib-breaker, it was a fact. So *who* could this ruffian be who was the villain of this awful epistle? *He* was that fellow! It was *Dan* who was that who could doubt? And thereupon he was so frightened of himself and his wild ways, that he jumped when he so much as moved a little brusquely, and expected that he might be the victim from one moment to the next of his own lawless arms and hands.

There was still one matter attributed to him that was the outcome perhaps of a mistake. He could not be sure if he was the man or not. Was it in fact these arms (whose presence at his side was so upsetting) that had indeed hurled the Split-Man off a high stage and down into the body of the throng – subsequent to the Vanish? He thought not. No, he answered quite finally for himself; upon that head – he had experienced nothing of the sort at the time and he would probably have known if he had been doing it. No that was not him but some blunder, in the recital. He began to be particular about the accuracy of the events occurring in this epic, since he had been seen to occupy such an outstanding part. So brooding very quietly over his dark exploits, Horace, he believed he remembered, had not been looking. Horace had been looking away when that happened. – There was a chance therefore if nothing more that he had not thrown Ratner off a high stage, but somebody else had, when no one was looking. Oh what a brute he had been – except for that (if he hadn't)! And he simply blushed his head off at the mere mention in the letter of his beastly drunkenness and standing up quickly he tore up the letter with a brutality to be expected of the brute Horace held up to him in the terrible letter – in order to be obedient! But feeling how beastly brutal he was being, he left off being so savage. The last remaining pieces he tore up apologetically with the greatest restraint – for it was too awful to be such a brute, and he scrutinized the remarkable muscles in his hand – tracking them under the skin and lying in wait for them as if they were hidden fishes, as they rose to the surface disturbing the cuticle. Especially ferocious were those connected with the thumb. He had never suspected before the presence of all these monsters of muscles – only just inside! Thoroughly horror-struck, but determined to go through with it, he bent down and got hold of the leading muscles of his calves, which were well hidden but had great bodies like scottish salmon, and in each thigh there was at least a strapping life-size sturgeon. His body was swarming. It was a plain *brute's* body nothing less. His *height* he preferred not to think about – but he held himself slightly crouched all day not to be too wildly upstanding.

One letter remained upon the table. They were notes from Michael and Mélanie. It said Michael would fetch him at seven o'clock. Now it was not more than one or twelve. With the scowl of a sheer brute in the only looking-glass – from which he moved away in haste – he said it would be impossible to remain with himself until seven – quite out of the question. The people in the streets were bad enough but they were better than him. Willie Service had left him – he probably knew about him. Harry

Caldicott had fetched Willie Service the day before and Willie Service had not returned, he hadn't expected he would.

Before leaving Willie Service had taken Dan's suitcase to pawn, with his one extra posh suit as well to make it worth while. He had given Dan a half-a-crown. More roughly than he had ever put anything in his pocket he pushed Mélanie's letter away anyhow in his trousers – poking it down into his pocket like a brute. Also his *London Street-guide* was violently sequestered. His hat and coat were thrown on and struck down, upon his head and shoulders, without ceremony. That was all he had and he went out.

When he went out he thought the streets were quiet today. Some days previous to that he had noticed a street he went into was quiet. But he had hurried back because two gentlemen in cars seemed to follow him with sunny suggestive smiles and he had turned back without hesitation. He found he could cross the first street quite easily. To be on the safe side he stood upon the curb until there was absolutely nothing in sight. There was no one near him and nothing in the street. Then he crossed. He went into a big street where there was a chocolate omnibus. The omnibus was quite full of policemen. He turned his head away and he blushed a little – the sight of all these darkly-dressed brutes all together, with their peaked helmets, made him hot – he had never that he could recollect seen so many policemen together before and he did not wish to catch their eyes. Another omnibus appeared. He did not like to look at it, but it was very crowded, and he noticed a policeman sitting beside the driver and he looked very stern. He supposed that the driver had done something wrong and he was sorry for the driver at once. Poor driver! – the driver couldn't help being a brute!

A good many motor-cars were coming along the big street and Dan could not help remarking that several gentlemen driving in them alone looked at him, as if they knew him. He was positive he didn't know *them*. One looked a little familiar but he was positive he had never spoken to him. He could not understand this unscrupulous behaviour. Usually people in motor-cars minded their own business and it was only from pedestrians that one had to fear any low familiarity coming from strangers, which one was liable to meet with, and which made walking in

London so unpleasant. Naturally he turned his head away. But several shouted rudely to him. They could not possibly be *gentlemen.* Not gentlemen – only half-sirs and spalpeens conducted themselves in that egregious manner in a public place!

At length a gentleman by himself (or with the deceptive appearance of one) more forward than the rest, actually began to go slower with his machine and came in with it quite near to the edge of the pavement, until he could almost have touched him and the fellow smiled in the most open way, as if he had been acquainted.

'Would you like a lift?'

He heard the gentleman's voice – if it was a gentleman's – but he declined to believe his ears.

'Which way are you going?'

It was an educated gentleman he could tell at once now, and he did not doubt that he was somebody of means. But how he could conduct himself in this manner he could not think – very hurriedly turning Dan showed what he thought of him and stopped to allow him to proceed with his machine. He was facing a large window and he looked into a large shop.

'I will take you anywhere you like!'

Surely this ill-bred assault upon the privacy of a passer-by was unheard of even in London! – the gentleman had come to a stop in his little machine, and was rudely accosting him without on his side the provocation of a glance! He declared this was the summit of ill-manners! – Dan walked sideways a few feet, he was pretending all the time to be engrossed with the purchases, as if he wanted to buy what was there. Unluckily as it turned out, this was the inside of a lady's bedroom, in the shop. There were two ladies undressed. The ladies were nothing but wax and puppets only but they were two terribly lifelike undressed women, and wherever he looked their eyes seemed to be seeking him out to smile at him. All sorts of nether garments for nude ladies were there – some were horridly round and there were splits in them with buttons – he blushed all the way up the backs of his legs. He had a centripetal shame in him, for all this immodesty – though in this case it was wax decoy-ducks, and not actual ladies. For nothing in the world would he be found looking! It would be better he almost felt to confront that person who had halted behind him in his car rather than to go on standing there. But the gentleman had accosted some other passers-by and they had got into the car with him. He could see it going on plainly in the window-glass. There were other gentlemen passing slowly in cars he could see – one or two wore smiles, and one beckoned to a somebody invitingly. He rushed from where he had been standing without looking up.

After this experience Dan hurried into a side street and there he breathed freely at last. He resolved to avoid the central thoroughfares as much as possible. He walked on in this way, seeing big roads with cars or vans in the distance upon either hand. One he crossed at a run. At last he quite lost himself, and then he went on doggedly, suddenly feeling very brutal and scowling at two passers-by who looked him up and down – scowling at their feet.

He thought he would cross the Hyde Park, as he saw it not far off. But when he came up to it, it was closed. With a certain astonishment he remarked that it was full of milkcans, as big as himself. There were tents there too – so he had to go round the Hyde Park and there was a great deal of bustle. He knew there was a great *Arch* – it was called that, the Arch – not far away – he had once taken refuge under it, when there was a rough crowd, and in his Street-map too there was a picture of it. If he walked along these big railings he would come to the *Arch*.

Several times after he had started going along the big railings in the direction of where the *Arch* was, he was compelled to suffer a great deal of annoyance and rudeness from gentlemen, half-sirs, and spalpeens, both in cars and in vans, and also he was sorry to have to say from several well-bred ladies (as he could judge from their voices). Once he was the object of the shameful solicitation of two ladies who were quite elderly ladies, in a large and noiseless machine which crept up behind him. After this he left the high railings dashing across the road as fast as his feet would carry him, narrowly escaping. Without further ado he entered a narrow street. Later he found he was descending a long respectable street named apparently *South Audley* – it was printed on a house. It was a very quiet respectable street. In fact there were shutters in all the windows of the houses – but he knew this was a street where rich well-bred persons had houses – evidently these well-to-do influential persons were abroad at the moment, because it had been somewhat cold and disagreeable.

Two policemen were hiding behind a pillar. He caught sight of them at once, he could see their helmets. He crossed over the road. They came out together from behind the pillar. He did not look at them at all but they followed him a long way. He walked quickly and they could not catch up. He crossed the road three times back and forth. Then he turned to the left and that shook them off he thought. They did not follow. He expected they could not come out of the street as they had the duty of guarding it. He was for the second time beside the Hyde Park. He stopped and looked about him and immediately detected the *Arch* in question, it might have been a stone's throw – it was large and empty and quite by itself – some policemen were hanging their coats upon the railings. Policemen were mounted on horses near the *Arch* and they seemed to want to go into the *Hyde Park*. There was a row of omnibuses in front of the *Arch*, and he could see little vegetable-vans with little seats in them for passengers too.

When he got to a spot where Service had told him they had found malefactor's bones, because it was where murderers had been buried when there were cruel chopping or hanging courts, for more dangerous offenders – traitors and witches – he saw a red bus and he passed it. Some men were standing beside it and laughing in a cruel and repulsive fashion as if they did not wish to laugh at all, at the driver – who had a policeman up with him upon the box. The men who were in check caps were ridiculing the driver for something, and he heard them pass some very horrid remarks but the driver did not answer them, and the policeman did not seem to mind. Someone said it was a picket. He thought the policeman was pretending not to hear the men and pretending that he could not see them, and then that he would suddenly jump off and catch them in the act. But without saying anything the bus started: the men in check-caps were shouting more and more rudely and laughing in a fierce and scornful way, so the driver drove off although some people were still getting in, and Dan thought he was quite right to start, and the policeman went with him, holding on to the box for all he was worth.

If he remained in the very big streets Dan was always accosted by gentlemen who were riding up and down. So he went aside into the very smallest streets, and at last he came to the house of Mélanie which was a great relief.

Mélanie was not there but Michael was there – he seemed quite surprised to see Dan and took him into a room where he had been sitting with a dog. It was Rabs.

'Did you get my letter?' he asked.

Dan showed it to him. The letter from Mélanie was wrapped up in Michael's letter. Dan put them down upon the table.

'Mélanie wired me to-day – she says to take you away from London at once and bring you to Azay-le-Promis. I have got the tickets. – She's afraid of the Strike!'

Michael smiled, and, his shoulders very high and his eyebrows raised, he exhaled very slowly some turkish cigarette-smoke through his nose as usual, tasting the strong smoke as if he had a tongue in his stomach. He held his breath, looking arrogant and dreamy. Then he puffed it out.

'It *is* a very bad strike' Michael said lazily to Dan – they were sitting with Rabs between them. 'It is a General Strike. She told me to tell you that London is not safe. She said it was very unsafe. I was to tell you.'

Michael smiled again. Dan did not smile – he was reflecting that London (except for the shocking under-bred behaviour of many of the motorists) was much safer than it had ever been since he had known it – Mélanie was wrong. Michael gazed at him, smoke still coming out of his nose, weighing him in blue filmy ironical scales, his eyebrows held high up, so that his eyes might delicately measure the object they had focused.

'This General Strike is a great bore,' he said to Dan. 'All I hope is that the boat-train will be running. The trains are being run by volunteers. How did you get here? Did you get a lift?'

By immediately looking at his two feet, Dan indicated that he had walked – but at the question relative to 'a lift' he simply blushed and scorned to reply.

'On foot? There are a lot of people going about in private cars and giving people lifts. They take work-girls up and down from the City.' He smiled, but as Dan seemed very uncomfortable at that topic, he then said: 'The train is supposed to go at nine or ten tonight. Are you ready?'

Dan was ready.

'I have had to hire a car to take us to the station. What a bore this Strike is! There are no papers.'

Dan never saw the newspapers, although he knew the names of most of the principal ones, like the *Daily Express* and *Daily Telegraph*, but he thought this must be something of the same sort as the Rebellion and felt that it was perhaps just as well that Michael was going to take him away with a safe-conduct to Azay-le-Promis, in the South of France. For he felt he could not again stand the sound of all that firing in the streets, if it was a Rebellion.

*

The whole townland of London was up in arms and as silent as the grave and it was reported that in its eastern quarters, in the slum-wards such as Poplar, a Police-inspector and two Specials had been kicked to death and there were more and more violent riots in Hammersmith, where trams had been wrecked and street-rails torn up by the mob, and the Police stoned and injured: while it was confidently stated that in the North crowds had sacked the better quarters, in the big factory-towns, mines were flooded, mills were blazing, and the troops were firing with machine-guns upon the populace. The absence of newspapers fostered every report of disorder.

It was a grand and breathless calm in the rich neighbourhoods and at last peace had fallen (for the first time since the death of the Nineteenth-Century Middleclass Elizabeth, Victoria) upon all that private-thoroughfare where the mansion of the proud Folletts reared its victorian battlements to the May-sky – all was dead and pleasant. But it was a death of life – the throbbing circulation of incessant machines, in thunderous rotation, in the arteries of London was stopped. A Follett footman came out and looked down the street, and the gummy-footed cop in his helmet, who stood by the letter-box of ceiling-wax scarlet, came over to the footman, in strong silent pacing out of the broad road, rolling from side to side, and said nothing, but put up his helmeted half-face quickly and smiled a boyish smile. The footman said –

'Is that right – that they've done in an inspector, down East?'

The young constable rolled about knowingly and silently for some moments, in labour with the gigantic official secrets inside him, and was dumb. Then the young footman thought he knew more than he would say. Slowly the constable replied however, in the accent of his somersetshire hamlet (where *all are king's-men* more or less) –

'If you was to believe all wot you was *told!*'

'Ah!' said the footman.

'All I can say is' and he paused to roll about a little more as if poising himself to lift a monster dumb-bell – 'that *I* ain't 'erd nothin' – 'cept wot you see in the Gazette.'

Then the young footman went back into the house.

The Private Road terminated in a high majestic gate. Now it was locked, as if against a mob. A top-hatted long-coated gate-keeper stood inside it and beside him was a pale cockney police-man. He looked out into the trafficless thoroughfare, as if watching it closely – having, unexpectedly, found it so still. Side by side they stood and watched the occasional vans that passed fitted with cross benches for passengers, and the two and four-seaters of the embattled Motorist-Middleclass, ad-vertising their useful intentions – carrying motorless clerks to wealthy offices. The absence of weighty traffic made the avenue, secluded by a by-law, noiseless and peaceful. The top-hatted gold-laced janitor felt a touch of stronger responsibility to which the constable responded *Oh dear Mabel!* He did not feel respon-sibility. But the gatekeeper inscrutably regarded, from under his top-hat, an infrequent volunteer omnibus – he had nothing in common with the omnibus, for he was a Lord-Mayor's-Show luxury-figure – his super-world had nothing in common with omnibuses.

The top-hatted gatekeeper was royalist and rothschildean, and the cockney constable was communist. But the constable did not expect much from a Soviet of Constables (he had thought it best, that was all, to be on the safe side) so he was fairly roths-childean and royalist, though not so sternly so as the other guardian of the Private Road beside him – who was a sterling *class-A* watch-dog of the Pound Sterling when met with in regal bulk and ten-figure quantity, and a cast-iron King's-man to the core. So the constable who was languidly muscovite and luke-warmly royalist, and his uniform was very heavy, seemed to take an interest in nothing, whereas the top-hatted gate-keeper seemed sternly indifferent to everything.

Two figures greatly disproportionate in size had ascended the avenue, from the farther extremity, where there was another gate. At this moment they handed their hats to a waiting foot-man, and, leaving Archie Margolin to be conducted into the drawing-room, Mr Zagreus stormed the stairs with all his peculiar stair-storming theatrical impetuosity.

Knocking upon the door of Lady Fredigonde's own private apartment, he paused for a moment, his eyes brilliant with a suppressed anticipation of persuasive speech. Then looking up quickly he flung the door wide open. Then he paused again – he perceived Sir James unexpectedly seated there, in his indoor-bathchair. After that, with a triumphant rapid step he entered the room, looking to left and right.

'Sir!' he thundered 'I have brought to see you the most astonishing *genius*. I really believe this time there is no doubt about it! *It is the goods!*'

Mr Zagreus stopped however, for Sir James it would appear was asleep. He turned towards Lady Fredigonde, and she was in her chair facing the sleeping baronet and upon him her eyes were fixed in a static manner that also suggested sleep. In her hand she held, it was remarked at once by Zagreus, a little silver bell and her immaculately-capped head was decorated with the ribbons of the savage tartan of her tribe.

'Shake him Zagreus!' she exclaimed as Zagreus stopped. 'He is only shamming sleep.'

'Do you think so?'

'Yes. Shake him, I tell you.'

'I don't think I will.'

'Today he is very aggravating! The Strike has upset him I think.'

'Oh – *the strike!*'

'I know. But he has a stupid theory that it is the work of the

Clydeside Scotch. My ribbons' she indicated her head 'put him beside himself with rage!'

'He is, I believe, in fact asleep.'

'Not a bit of it! Don't you run away with that idea! You don't know him as well as I do! Give him a good shake!'

Mr Zagreus laughed.

'Sir James might not thank me for waking him.'

'Let sleeping dogs lie!'

'I would not say that.'

'No but I would – with the accent on the *dog!*'

Mr Zagreus looked at Lady Fredigonde with a quick inquisitive brightness, and then back at Sir James – he looked longer at Sir James this time, and then swiftly he approached him, and placed a hand upon his shoulder.

'Won't you wake up sir! I have some news for you!'

But as he allowed his hand to rest after that with more insistence upon the bowed shoulder, Sir James' head rolled over away from him, and he dropped his hand suddenly and stood back.

'I believe Sir James has had a stroke,' Mr Zagreus said.

'Yes – a fit of temper!' Lady Fredigonde replied.

'Shall I call somebody? Where is Bridget?'

'I told her not to return just yet. – As a matter of fact Zagreus, Sir James is *dead*.'

'Dead? Do you think so? I hope not. Then I had better call his man!'

'No do not do that Zagreus. I wish to say something to you before you do that.'

Like a wild horse that had consented to the rules of a circus – always with the air of being destined, at a pistol-shot, to rush away, returning to its savagery – yet civilly inclining its head to the behests of some fantoche at which it never looks, but which it only hears: so Zagreus stood untamed but politely transfixed. In an opposite way to the horse, he fastened unmeaningly-brilliant eyes upon the speaker's lips – but never heard at all, he only saw. And that surprising flourishing figure named Zagreus for convenience, albino tropically-bronzed, triply-armed with pierpointean dialectic, was more than ever at this juncture, as he stood there in suspense, a circus-oddity – with the upturned silver moustaches (of a fierce equestrian magister, a *dompteur* of performing dumb animals) incongruously stuck upon the stoic lips of a Choktaw chief on-show, gaunt and erect in all his fluttering feathers. – So his eyes upon her ladyship's lips, his back to Sir James, he waited before calling the servant.

'I think I had better tell you Zagreus that I believe I have killed Sir James.'

Mr Zagreus said nothing – he might not have understood this language – his eyes at their brightest, impassibly sparkling, he remained intent to spring – at the bell – at her ladyship – out of the window – or else off and away to the miraculous pastures where *genius* wandered – his happy-hunting-grounds after all.

'I arranged that Bridget should steal this bell!'

Fredigonde held up the bell a little, holding it by its tiny clapper.

'When Sir James desired to return to his own apartments, he found he had no bell to summon his man. It was then that I showed it him. But I would not ring it for him.'

She slowly shook her head.

The expression of Zagreus did not change – his face was alight with enthusiasm for genius, and that was all.

'His temper is so violent, that that is what he has done. He has destroyed himself with rage!' Her ladyship succumbed to a fit of subterranean laughter. Then she said –

'For once he was compelled to listen to what I had to say. And he died of rage at what he heard!'

Zagreus turned about and looked at the baronet, and he came to the conclusion that in fact he was dead. Then he looked back with the same absent brightness at the visible morse of the lips of her ladyship, signalling to him.

'Zagreus!' she said. He could see with great force she had uttered his name – and he remarked the imperious flashing of her eyes. 'I *intended* him to die!'

Zagreus smiled with a gesture of deprecation.

'I got possession of this bell with *that* in view!'

Again she held up the bell a few inches.

'Did you get my letter?' Zagreus asked Lady Fredigonde.

'I got your letter Zagreus. You asked for ten thousand

pounds I think. Yes it was ten thousand pounds. *Then* I had not got that sum to dispose of. Not *then*.'

Zagreus raised his eyebrows, as if in polite amazement.

'You said the last time we met that Dick Whittingdon might be circumvented' he said.

'I have circumvented Dick Whittingdon, put your mind at rest!'

Mr Zagreus smiled, with detached elation.

'Dick is no obstacle. I have him on the hip – I have gone into everything.'

'That is excellent.'

'Zagreus. I have a proposal to make to you. Will you hear it?' she said.

The magnificent albino, erect, unearthly, electric with a slight smile at her ladyship, folded his arms rather like the recumbent effigy of a crusader suddenly set up on end, and he watched the lips of destiny, that were so numbed with age.

'What is that?' he asked politely.

'You will think it strange I expect.'

'I will tell you if I do when I hear it.'

'I am an old woman.'

Mr Zagreus simply indulged in the flashing smile that meant nothing, of the superb shavian Methuselah of sixty-odd. He was again steadfast and attentive.

'Can you picture a person of my years as one of the season's brides!' she blandly muttered.

'What kind of bride?' he asked.

'A bride of love!' crashed Fredigonde suddenly in the most uncompromising manner, as if his question had smelt of criticism. 'I love you Horace! I desire to be *your* bride!'

There was then one wild uncanny flash of half-wit understanding, coming into the bronze-embedded blue piratic eyes. The folded arms of the crusader collapsed and fell apart, dropping to his side, as if some superior tension had then been abruptly relaxed. He approached Lady Fredigonde across the floor, as if advancing upon his prey.

'Done!' he exclaimed. 'There is no woman I would sooner marry!'

'Not if they were young and fair!'

'Not if they were positive Helens!' he exclaimed again. 'Of all the women that I know, I would soonest have you for a *bride!*'

The two crippled stumps of her arms went out – the short way that they could, and aspired to rise the necessary inches to circumscribe her splendid groom. A dark spasm visited the corpse-like carcass beneath – strapped into position, in the giant chair which might have been constructed to accommodate a circus-elephant, who had been taught to sit down to table and discuss a two-gallon tankard of ale, in imitation of humanity, as a compliment to the squatting audience. In the head above, clear of this investing corruption, that pushed up into the throat, the child-soul of that sylph – once 'Lady Freddy' of the brightest Gossip, the Chattiest social column, piped in the chirping accents of first-love –

'Horace!'

And Zagreus accommodated his great stature in such a way that the robot-stumps of the extinct hands, of pinkish shrivelled hide, could clip him upon either side, and in a ringing voice he shouted in her face, with a thrilling r-roll –

'Fredigonde!'

Their lips met, and the love-light softened the old discoloured corneous surface of the fredigondean eyeball, once a lacteous blue. Over this conventionally she dropped her lids in token of virgin-rapture. – In the street outside there was a frenzied rattle. *Death the Drummer!* That was his fierce opening castanette! Immediately the mechanistic rattle penetrated to the inmost recesses of these embraces. Her eyes started open with a bang, glaring at the untimely summons, the sorry advent. It was that fatal step she hated. The dove-light changed to the red-rose of battle. There was a drum-tap. Like rain drops, there was a constant tapping, a sharp drip upon the loud parchment. Then came the first soft crash of the attendant cymbal – it was the prelude of the thunder. And in the gutter the crazy instruments at last struck up their sentimental jazzing one-time stutter – gutter-thunder.

Whoddle ah *doo*
Wen *yoo*
Are *far*

Away
An *I*
am *bloo*
Whoddle ah *doo*
Whoddlah DOOOO!

In the great reception-room immediately beneath Archie Margolin, as he heard the first notes of the street-instrumentalists, stiffened, and, with elf-like nigger-bottom-wagging, he traversed the oppressive spaces of this monster apartment – built for victorian 'giants' in their first flower – smiling at himself as he advanced (with his St Vitus puppet-shiver) in the mighty victorian looking-glasses.

CLASSICS OF THE TWENTIETH CENTURY

The Age of Reason Jean-Paul Sartre

The first part of Sartre's classic trilogy, set in the volatile Paris summer of 1938, is itself 'a dynamic, deeply disturbing novel' (Elizabeth Bowen) which tackles some of the major issues of our time.

Three Lives Gertrude Stein

A turning point in American literature, these portraits of three women – thin, worn Anna, patient, gentle Lena and the complicated, intelligent Melanctha – represented in 1909 one of the pioneering examples of modernist writing.

Doctor Faustus Thomas Mann

Perhaps the most convincing description of an artistic genius ever written, this portrait of the composer Leverkuhn is a classic statement of one of Mann's obsessive themes: the discord between genius and sanity.

The New Machiavelli H. G. Wells

This autobiography of a man who has thrown up a glittering political career and marriage to go into exile with the woman he loves also contains an illuminating Introduction by Melvyn Bragg.

The Collected Poems of Stevie Smith

Amused, amusing and deliciously barbed, this volume includes many poems which dwell on death; as a whole, though, as this first complete edition in paperback makes clear, Smith's poetry affirms an irrepressible love of life.

Rhinoceros / The Chairs / The Lesson Eugène Ionesco

Three great plays by the man who was one of the founders of what has come to be known as the Theatre of the Absurd.

CLASSICS OF THE TWENTIETH CENTURY

Gertrude Hermann Hesse

A sensitive young composer, the narrator is drawn to Gertrude through their mutual love of music. Gradually, he is engulfed by an enduring and hopeless passion for her. 'It would be a pity to miss this book – it has such a rare flavour of truth and simplicity' – Stevie Smith in the *Observer*

If It Die André Gide

A masterpiece of French prose, *If It Die* is Gide's record of his childhood, his friendships, his travels, his sexual awakening and, above all, the search for truth which characterizes his whole life and all his writing.

Dark as the Grave wherein my Friend is Laid Malcolm Lowry

A Dantean descent into hell, into the infernal landscape of Mexico, the same Mexico as Lowry's *Under the Volcano*, a country of mental terrors and spiritual chasms.

The Collected Short Stories Katherine Mansfield

'She could discern in a trivial event or an insignificant person some moving revelation or motive or destiny . . . There is an abundance of that tender and delicate art which penetrates the appearances of life to discover the elusive causes of happiness and grief' – W. E. Williams in his Introduction to *The Garden Party and Other Stories*

Sanctuary William Faulkner

Faulkner draws America's Deep South exactly as he saw it: seething with life and corruption; and *Sanctuary* asserts itself as a compulsive and unsparing vision of human nature.

The Expelled and Other Novellas Samuel Beckett

Rich in verbal and situational humour, the four stories in this volume offer the reader a fascinating insight into Beckett's preoccupation with the helpless individual consciousness, a preoccupation which has remained constant throughout Beckett's work.